DOROTHY L. SAYERS

ABOUT THE AUTHOR

British author DOROTHY L. SAYERS (1893-1957) is widely recognized as a master of the detective story genre. Her fourteen novels that feature aristocrat, scholar, and sleuth Lord Peter Wimsey were well received in their first publication, and have become bestselling classics.

Sayers was one of the first women ever to receive a degree from Oxford, in the field of medieval linguistics. Her other works include plays, critical essays on medieval literature, and a translation of Dante's *Divine Comedy*.

DOROTHY L. SAYERS

ON THE CASE WITH LORD PETER WIMSEY

THREE COMPLETE NOVELS

STRONG POISON

HAVE HIS CARCASE

UNNATURAL DEATH

WINGS BOOKS

NEW YORK · AVENEL, NEW JERSEY

This 1991 edition is published by Wings Books
distributed by Random House Value Publishing, Inc.,
40 Engelhard Avenue, Avenel New Jersey 07001,
by arrangement with Harper Collins Publishers.

Random House
New York • Toronto • London • Sydney • Auckland

Designed by Helene Berinsky

Library of Congress Cataloging-in-Publication Data
Sayers, Dorothy L. (Dorothy Leigh), 1893-1957.
   Three complete Lord Peter Wimsey Novels : a new collection / Dorothy L.
Sayers.
      p.   cm.
   Contents: Have his carcase—Strong poison—Unnatural death.
   ISBN 0-517-07243-2
   1. Wimsey, Peter, Lord (Fictitious character) —Fiction. 2. Detective and
mystery stories, English. I. Title. II. Title: 3 Complete Lord Peter Wimsey
novels.
PR6037.A95A6   1992a
823'.912—dc20   91-27242
                                                CIP

12 11 10 9 8 7 6 5 4 3

CONTENTS

WIMSEY, Peter Death Bredon, D.S.O.; *born 1890, 2nd son* of Mortimer Gerald Bredon Wimsey, 15th Duke of Denver, and of Honoria Lucasta, *daughter of* Francis Delagardie of Bellingham Manor, Hants. *Married* 1935, Harriet Deborah Vane, *daughter of* Henry Vane, M.D.; one *son* (Bredon Delagardie Peter) *born* 1936.

Educated: Eton College and Balliol College, (1st class honours), Sch. of Mod. hist. 1912; served with H.M. Forces 1914/18 (Major, Rifle Brigade). *Author of:* "Notes on the Collecting of Incunabula," "The Murderer's Vade-Medum," etc. Recreations: Criminology; bibliophily; music; cricket.

Clubs: Marlborough; Egotists'; Bellona. *Residences:* 110A, Piccadilly, W.; Bredon Hall, Duke's Denver, Norfolk.

Arms: Sable, 3 mice courant, argent; crest, a domestic cat crouched as to spring, proper; motto: As my Whimsy takes me.

BIOGRAPHICAL NOTE
Communicated by Paul Austin Delagardie

I am asked by Miss Sayers to fill up certain lacunae and correct a few trifling errors of fact in her account of my nephew Peter's career. I shall do so with pleasure. To appear publicly in print is every man's ambition, and by acting as a kind of running footman to my nephew's triumph I shall only be showing a modesty suitable to my advanced age.

The Wimsey family is an ancient one—too ancient, if you ask me. The only sensible thing Peter's father ever did was to ally his exhausted stock with the vigorous French-English strain of the Delagardies. Even so, my nephew Gerald (the present Duke of Denver) is nothing but a beef-witted English squire, and my niece Mary was flighty and foolish enough till she married a policeman and settled down. Peter, I am glad to say, takes after his mother and me. True, he is all nerves and nose—but that is better than being all brawn and no brains like his father and brother, or a bundle of emotions like Gerald's boy, Saint-George. He has at least inherited the Delagardie brains, by way of safeguard to the unfortunate Wimsey temperament.

Peter was born in 1890. His mother was being very much worried at the time by her husband's behaviour (Denver was always tiresome, though the big scandal did not break out till the Jubilee year), and her anxieties may have affected the boy. He was a colorless shrimp of a child, very restless and mischievous, and always much too sharp for his age. He had nothing of Gerald's robust beauty, but he developed what I can best call a kind of bodily cleverness, more skill than strength. He had a quick eye for a ball and beautiful hands for a horse. He had the devil's own pluck, too: the intelligent sort of pluck that sees the risk before it takes it. He suffered badly from nightmares as a child. To his father's consternation he grew up with a passion for books and music.

His early school-days were not happy. He was a fastidious child, and I suppose it was natural that his school-fellows should call him "Flimsy" and treat him as a kind of comic turn. And he might, in sheer self-protection, have accepted the position and degenerated into a mere licensed buffoon, if some games-master at Eton had not discovered that he was a brilliant natural cricketer. After that, of course, all his eccentricities were accpeted as wit, and Gerald underwent the salutary shock of seeing his despised younger brother become a bigger personality than himself. By the time he reached the Sixth Form, Peter had contrived to become the fashion—athlete, scholar, *arbiter elegantiarum*—*nec pluribus impar*. Cricket had a great deal to do with it—plenty of Eton men will remember the "Great Flim" and his performance against Harrow—but I take credit to myself for introducing him to a good tailor, showing him the way about Town, and teaching him to distinguish good wine from bad. Denver bothered little about him—he had too many entanglements of his own and in addition was taken up with Gerald, who by this time was making a prize fool of himself at Oxford. As a matter of fact Peter never got on with his father, he was a ruthless young critic of the paternal misdemeanours, and his sympathy for his mother had a destructive effect upon his sense of humour.

Denver, needless to say, was the last person to tolerate his own failings in his offspring. It cost him a good deal of money to extricate Gerald from the Oxford affair, and he was willing enough to turn his other son over to me. Indeed, at the age of seventeen, Peter came to me of his own accord. He was old for his age and exceedingly reasonable, and I treated him as a man of the world. I established him in trustworthy hands in Paris, instructing him to keep his affairs upon a sound business footing and to see that they terminated with goodwill on both sides and generosity on his. He fully justified my confidence. I believe that no woman has ever found cause to complain of Peter's treatment; and two at least of them have since married royalty (rather obscure royalties, I admit, but royalty of a sort). Here again, I insist upon my due share of the credit; however good the material one has to work upon it is ridiculous to leave any young man's social education to chance.

The Peter of this period was really charming, very frank, modest and well-mannered, with a pretty, lively wit. In 1909 he went up with a scholarship to read History at Balliol, and here, I must confess, he became rather intolerable. The world was at his feet, and he began to give himself airs. He acquired affectations, an exaggerated Oxford manner and a monocle, and aired his opinions a good deal, both in and out of the Union, though I will do him the justice to say that he never attempted to patronise his mother or me. He was in his second year when Denver broke his neck out hunting and Gerald succeeded to the title. Gerald showed more sense of responsibility than I had expected in dealing with the estate; his worst mistake was to marry his cousin Helen, a scrawny, over-bred prude, all country from head to heel. She and Peter loathed each other cordially; but he could always take refuge with his mother at the Dower House.

And then, in his last year at Oxford, Peter fell in love with a child of seventeen and instantly forgot everything he had ever been taught. He treated that girl as if she was made of gossamer, and me as a hardened old monster of depravity who had made him unfit to touch her delicate purity. I won't deny that they made an exquisite pair—all white and gold—a prince and princess of moonlight, people said. Moonshine would have been nearer the mark. What Peter was to do in twenty years' time with a wife who had neither brains nor character nobody but his mother and myself ever troubled to ask, and he, of course, was completely besotted. Happily, Barbara's parents decided that she was too young to marry; so Peter went in for his final Schools in the temper of a Sir Eglamore achieving his first dragon; laid his First-Class Honours at his lady's feet like the dragon's head, and settled down to a period of virtuous probation.

Then came the War. Of course the young idiot was mad to get married before he went. But his own honourable scruples made him mere wax in other people's hands. It was pointed out to him that if he came back mutilated it would be very unfair to the girl. He hadn't thought of that, and rushed off in a frenzy of self-abnegation to release her from the engagement. I had no hand in that; I was glad enough of the result, but I couldn't stomach the means.

He did very well in France; he made a good officer and the men liked him. And then, if you please, he came back on leave with his captaincy in '16, to find the girl married—to a hard-bitten rake of a Major Somebody, whom she had nursed in the V.A.D. hospital, and whose motto with women was catch 'em quick and treat 'em rough. It was pretty brutal; for the girl hadn't had the nerve to tell Peter beforehand. They got married in a hurry when they heard he was coming home, and all he got on landing was a letter, announcing the *fait accompli* and reminding him that he had set her free himself.

I will say for Peter that he came straight to me and admitted that he had been a fool. "All right," said I, "you've had your lesson. Don't go and make a fool of yourself in the other direction." So he went back to his job with (I am sure) the fixed intention of getting killed; but all he got was his majority and his D.S.O. for some recklessly good intelligence work behind the German front. In 1918 he was blown up and buried in a shell-hole near Caudry, and that left him with a bad nervous breakdown, lasting, on and off, for two years. After that, he set himself up in a flat in Piccadilly, with the man Bunter (who had been his sergeant and was, and is, devoted to him), and started out to put himself together again.

I don't mind saying that I was prepared for almost anything. He had lost all his beautiful frankness, he shut everybody out of his confidence, including his mother and me, adopted an impenetrable frivolity of manner and a dilettante pose, and became, in fact, the complete comedian. He was wealthy and could do as he chose, and it gave me a certain amount of sardonic entertainment to watch the efforts of post-war feminine London to capture him. "It can't," said one solicitous matron, "be good for poor Peter to live like a hermit." "Madam," said I, "if he did, it wouldn't be." No; from that point of view he gave me no anxiety. But I could not but think it dangerous that a man of his ability should have no job to occupy his mind, and I told him so.

In 1921 came the business of the Attenbury Emeralds. That affair has never been written up, but it made a good deal of noise, even at that noisiest of periods. The trial of the thief was a series of red-hot sensations, and the biggest sensation of the bunch was when Lord Peter Wimsey walked into the witness-box as chief witness for the prosecution.

That was notoriety with a vengeance. Actually, to an experienced intelligence officer, I don't suppose the investigation had offered any great difficulties; but a "noble sleuth" was something new in thrills. Gerald was furious; personally, I didn't mind what Peter did, provided he did something. I thought he seemed happier for the work, and I liked the Scotland Yard man he had picked up during the run of the case. Charles Parker is a quiet, sensible, well-bred fellow, and has been a good friend and brother-in-law to Peter. He has the valuable quality of being fond of people without wanting to turn them inside out.

The only trouble about Peter's new hobby was that it had to be more than a hobby, if it was to be any hobby for a gentlemen. You cannot get murderers hanged for your private entertainment. Peter's intellect pulled him one way and his nerves another, till I began to be afraid they would pull him to pieces. At the end of every case we had the old nightmares and shell-shock over again. And then Gerald, of all people—Gerald, the crashing great booby, in the middle of his fulminations against Peter's degrading and notorious police activities, must needs get himself indicted on a murder charge and stand his trial in the House of Lords, amid a blaze of publicity which made all Peter's efforts in that direction look like damp squibs.

Peter pulled his brother out of that mess, and, to my relief, was human enough to get drunk on the strength of it. He now admits that his "hobby" is his legitimate work for society, and has developed sufficient interest in public affairs to undertake small diplomatic jobs from time to time under the Foreign Office. Of late he has become a little more ready to show his feelings, and a little less terrified of having any to show.

His latest eccentricity has been to fall in love with that girl whom he cleared of the charge of poisoning her lover. She refused to marry him, as any woman of character would. Gratitude and a humiliating inferiority complex are no foundation for matrimony; the position was false from the start. Peter had the sense, this time, to take my advice. "My boy," said I, "what was wrong for you twenty years back is right now. It's not the innocent young things that need gentle handling—it's the ones that have been frightened and hurt. Begin again from the beginning—I warn you that you will need all the self-discipline you have ever learnt."

Well, he has tried. I don't think I have ever seen such patience. The girl has brains and character and honesty; but he has got to teach her how to take, which is far more difficult than learning to give. I think they will find one another, if they can keep their passions from running ahead of their wills. He does realise, I know, that in this case there can be no consent but free consent.

Peter is forty-five now, it is really time he was settled. As you will see, I have been one of the important formative influences in his career, and on the whole, I feel he does me credit. He is a true Delagardie, with little of the Wimseys about him except (I must be fair) that underlying sense of social responsibility which prevents the English landed gentry from being a total loss, spiritually speaking. Detective or no detective, he is a scholar and a gentleman; it will amuse me to see what sort of shot he makes at being a husband and father. I am getting an old man, and have no son of my own (that I know of); I should be glad to see Peter happy. But as his mother says, "Peter has always had everything except the things he really wanted," and I suppose he is luckier than most.

PAUL AUSTIN DELAGARDIE

STRONG POISON

"Where gat ye your dinner, Lord Rendal, my son?
Where gat ye your dinner, my handsome young man?"
"—O I dined with my sweetheart, Mother, make my bed
  soon,
For I'm sick to the heart and I fain wad lie down."

"Oh that was strong poison, Lord Rendal, my son,
O that was strong poison, my handsome young man,"
"—O yes, I am poisoned, Mother, make my bed soon,
For I'm sick to the heart, and I fain wad lie down."

Old Ballad

1

There were crimson roses on the bench; they looked like splashes of blood.

The judge was an old man; so old, he seemed to have outlived time and change and death. His parrot-face and parrot-voice were dry, like his old, heavily-veined hands. His scarlet robe clashed harshly with the crimson of the roses. He had sat for three days in the stuffy court, but he showed no sign of fatigue.

He did not look at the prisoner as he gathered his notes into a neat sheaf and turned to address the jury, but the prisoner looked at him. Her eyes, like dark smudges under the heavy square brows, seemed equally without fear and without hope. They waited.

"Members of the jury—"

The patient old eyes seemed to sum them up and take stock of their united intelligence. Three respectable tradesmen—a tall, argumentative one, a stout, embarrassed one with a drooping moustache, and an unhappy one with a bad cold; a director of a large company anxious not to waste valuable time; a publican, incongruously cheerful; two youngish men of the artisan class; a nondescript, elderly man, of educated appearance, who might have been anything; an artist with a red beard disguising a weak chin; three women—an elderly spinster, a stout capable woman who kept a sweet-shop, and a harassed wife and mother whose thoughts seemed to be continually straying to her abandoned hearth.

"Members of the jury—you have listened with great patience and attention to the evidence in this very distressing case, and it is now my duty to sum up the facts and arguments which have been put before you by the learned Attorney-General and by the learned Counsel for the Defence, and to put them in order as clearly as possible, so as to help you in forming your decision.

"But first of all, perhaps I ought to say a few words with regard to that decision itself. You know, I am sure, that it is a great principle of English law that every accused person is held to be innocent unless and until he is proved otherwise. It is not necessary for him, or her, to prove innocence; it is, in the modern slang phrase, 'up to' the Crown to prove guilt, and unless you are quite satisfied that the Crown has done this beyond all reasonable doubt, it is your duty to return a verdict of 'Not Guilty.' That does not necessarily mean that the prisoner has established her innocence by proof; it simply means that the Crown has failed to produce in your minds an undoubted conviction of her guilt."

Salcombe Hardy, lifting his drowned-violet eyes for a moment from his reporter's note-book, scribbled two words on a slip of paper and pushed them over to Waffles Newton. "Judge hostile." Waffles nodded. They were old hounds on this blood-trail.

The judge creaked on.

"You may perhaps wish to hear from me exactly what is meant by those words 'reasonable doubt.' They mean, just so much doubt as you might have in every-day life about an ordinary matter of business. This is a case of murder, and it might be natural for you to think that, in such a case, the words mean more than this. But that is not so. They do not mean that you must cast about for fantastical solutions of what seems to you plain and simple. They do not mean those nightmare doubts which sometimes torment us at four o'clock in the morning when we have not slept very well. They only mean that the proof must be such as you would accept about a plain matter of buying and selling, or some such commonplace transaction. You must not strain your belief in favour of the prisoner any more, of course, than you must accept proof of her guilt without the most careful scrutiny.

"Having said just these few words, so that you may not feel too much over-whelmed by the heavy responsibility laid upon you by your duty to the State, I will now begin at the beginning and try to place the story that we have heard, as clearly as possible before you.

"The case for the Crown is that the prisoner, Harriet Vane, murdered Philip Boyes by poisoning him with arsenic. I need not detain you by going through the proofs offered by Sir James Lubbock and the other doctors who have given evidence as to the cause of death. The Crown says he died of arsenical poison-ing, and the defence do not dispute it. The evidence is, therefore, that the death was due to arsenic, and you must accept that as a fact. The only question that remains for you is whether, in fact, that arsenic was deliberately administered by the prisoner with intent to murder.

"The deceased, Philip Boyes, was, as you have heard, a writer. He was thirty-six years old, and he had published five novels and a large number of essays and articles. All these literary works were of what is sometimes called an 'advanced' type. They preached doctrines which may seem to some of us immoral or seditious, such as atheism, and anarchy, and what is known as free love. His private life appears to have been conducted, for some time at least, in accor-dance with these doctrines.

"At any rate, at some time in the year 1927, he became acquainted with Harriet Vane. They met in some of those artistic and literary circles where 'advanced' topics are discussed, and after a time they became very friendly. The prisoner is also a novelist by profession, and it is very important to remember that she is a writer of so-called 'mystery' or 'detective' stories, such as deal with various ingenious methods of committing murder and other crimes.

"You have heard the prisoner in the witness-box, and you have heard the various people who came forward to give evidence as to her character. You have been told that she is a young woman of great ability, brought up on strictly religious principles, who, through no fault of her own was left, at the age of twenty-three, to make her own way in the world. Since that time—and she is now twenty-nine years old—she has worked industriously to keep herself, and it is very much to her credit that she has, by her own exertions, made herself independent in a legitimate way, owing nothing to anybody and accepting help from no one.

"She has told us herself, with great candour, how she became deeply attached to Philip Boyes, and how, for a considerable time, she held out against his persuasions to live with him in an irregular manner. There was, in fact, no reason at all why he should not have married her honourably; but apparently he represented himself as being conscientiously opposed to any formal marriage. You have the evidence of Sylvia Marriott and Eiluned Price that the prisoner was made very unhappy by this attitude which he chose to take up, and you have heard also that he was a very handsome and attractive man, whom any woman might have found it difficult to resist.

"At any rate, in March of 1928, the prisoner, worn out, as she tells us, by his unceasing importunities, gave in, and consented to live on terms of intimacy with him, outside the bonds of marriage.

"Now you may feel, and quite properly, that this was a very wrong thing to do. You may, after making all allowances for this young woman's unprotected position, still feel that she was a person of unstable moral character. You will not be led away by the false glamour which certain writers contrive to throw about 'free love,' into thinking that this was anything but an ordinary, vulgar act of misbehavior. Sir Impey Biggs, very rightly using all his great eloquence on behalf of his client, has painted this action of Harriet Vane's in very rosy colours; he has spoken of unselfish sacrifice and self-immolation, and has reminded you that, in such a situation, the woman always has to pay more heavily than the man. You will not, I am sure, pay too much attention to this. You know quite well the difference between right and wrong in such matters, and you may think that, if Harriet Vane had not become to a certain extent corrupted by the unwholesome influences among which she lived, she would have shown a truer heroism by dismissing Philip Boyes from her society.

"But, on the other hand, you must be careful not to attach the wrong kind of importance to this lapse. It is one thing for a man or woman to live an immoral life, and quite another thing to commit murder. You may perhaps think that one step into the path of wrongdoing makes the next one easier, but you must not give too much weight to that consideration. You are entitled to take it into account, but you must not be too much prejudiced."

The judge paused for a moment, and Freddy Arbuthnot jerked an elbow into the ribs of Lord Peter Wimsey, who appeared to be a prey to gloom.

"I should jolly well hope not. Damn it, if every little game led to murder, they'd be hanging half of us for doin' in the other half."

"And which half would *you* be in?" enquired his lordship, fixing him for a moment with a cold eye and then returning his glance to the dock.

"Victim," said the Hon. Freddy, "victim. Me for the corpse in the library."

"Philip Boyes and the prisoner lived together in this fashion," went on the judge, "for nearly a year. Various friends have testified that they appeared to live on terms of the greatest mutual affection. Miss Price said that, although Harriet Vane obviously felt her unfortunate position very acutely—cutting herself off from her family friends and refusing to thrust herself into company where her social outlawry might cause embarrassment and so on—yet she was extremely loyal to her lover and expressed herself proud and happy to be his companion.

"Nevertheless, in February 1929 there was a quarrel, and the couple separated. It is not denied that the quarrel took place. Mr. and Mrs. Dyer, who occupy the flat immediately above Philip Boyes', say that they heard loud talking in angry voices, the man swearing and the woman crying, and that the next day, Harriet Vane packed up all her things and left the house for good. The curious feature in the case, and one which you must consider very carefully, is the reason assigned for the quarrel. As to this, the only evidence we have is the prisoner's own. According to Miss Marriott, with whom Harriet Vane took refuge after the separation, the prisoner steadily refused to give any information on the subject, saying only that she had been painfully deceived by Boyes and never wished to hear his name spoken again.

"Now it might be supposed from this that Boyes had given the prisoner cause for grievance against him, by unfaithfulness, or unkindness, or simply by a continued refusal to regularise the situation in the eyes of the world. But the prisoner absolutely denies this. According to her statement—and on this point her evidence is confirmed by a letter which Philip Boyes wrote to his father—Boyes did at length offer her legal marriage, and this was the cause of the quarrel. You may think this a very remarkable statement to make, but that is the prisoner's evidence on oath.

"It would be natural for you to think that this proposal of marriage takes away any suggestion that the prisoner had a cause of grievance against Boyes. Anyone would say that, under such circumstances, she could have no motive for wishing to murder this young man, but rather the contrary. Still, there is the fact of the quarrel, and the prisoner herself states that this honourable, though belated, proposal was unwelcome to her. She does not say—as she might very reasonably say, and as her counsel has most forcefully and impressively said for her, that this marriage-offer completely does away with any pretext for enmity on her part towards Philip Boyes. Sir Impey Biggs says so, but that is not what the prisoner says. She says—and you must try to put yourselves in her place and understand her point of view if you can—that she was angry with Boyes because, after persuading her against her will to adopt his principles of conduct, he then renounced those principles and so, as she says, 'made a fool of her.'

"Well, that is for you to consider: whether the offer which was in fact made could reasonably be construed into a motive for murder. I must impress upon you that no other motive has been suggested in evidence."

At this point the elderly spinster on the jury was seen to be making a note—a vigorous note, to judge from the action of her pencil on the paper. Lord Peter Wimsey shook his head slowly two or three times and muttered something under his breath.

"After this," said the judge, "nothing particular seems to have happened to these two people for three months or so, except that Harriet Vane left Miss Marriott's house and took a small flat of her own in Doughty Street, while Philip Boyes, on the contrary, finding his solitary life depressing, accepted the invitation of his cousin, Mr. Norman Urquhart, to stay at the latter's house in Woburn Square. Although living in the same quarter of London, Boyes and the accused do not seem to have met very often after the separation. Once or twice there was an accidental encounter at the house of a friend. The dates of these occasions cannot be ascertained with any certainty—they were informal parties—but there is some evidence that there was a meeting towards the end of March, another in the second week in April, and a third some time in May. These times are worth noting, though, as the exact day is left doubtful, you must not attach too much importance to them.

"However, we now come to a date of the very greatest importance. On April 10th, a young woman, who has been identified as Harriet Vane, entered the chemist's shop kept by Mr. Brown in Southampton Row, and purchased two ounces of commercial arsenic, saying that she needed it to destroy rats. She signed the poison-book in the name of Mary Slater, and the handwriting has been identified as that of the prisoner. Moreover, the prisoner herself admits having made this purchase, for certain reasons of her own. For this reason it is comparatively unimportant—but you may think it worth noting—that the housekeeper of the flats where Harriet Vane lives has come here and told you that there are no rats on the premises, and never have been in the whole time of her residence there.

"On May 5th, we have another purchase of arsenic. The prisoner, as she herself states, this time procured a tin of arsenical weed-killer, of the same brand that was mentioned in the Kidwelly poisoning case. This time she gave the name of Edith Waters. There is no garden attached to the flats where she lives, nor could there be any conceivable use for weed-killer on the premises.

"On various occasions also, during the period from the middle of March to the beginning of May, the prisoner purchased other poisons, including prussic acid (ostensibly for photographic purposes) and strychnine. There was also an attempt to obtain aconitine, which was not successful. A different shop was approached and different name given in each case. The arsenic is the only poison which directly concerns this case, but these other purchases are of some importance, as throwing light on the prisoner's activities at this time.

"The prisoner has given an explanation of these purchases which you must consider for what it is worth. She says that she was engaged at that time in writing a novel about poisoning, and that she bought the drugs in order to prove by experiment how easy it was for an ordinary person to get hold of deadly poisons. In proof of this, her publisher, Mr. Trufoot, has produced the manu-script of the book. You have had it in your hands, and you will be given it again, if you like, when I have finished my summing-up, to look at in your own room. Passages were read out to you, showing that the subject of the book was murder by arsenic, and there is a description in it of a young woman going to a chemist's shop and buying a considerable quantity of this deadly substance. And I must mention here what I should have mentioned before, namely, that the arsenic purchased from Mr. Brown was the ordinary commercial arsenic, which is col-oured with charcoal or indigo, as the law requires, in order that it may not be mistaken for sugar or any other innocent substance."

Salcombe Hardy groaned: "How long, O Lord, how long shall we have to listen to all this tripe about commercial arsenic? Murderers learn it now at their mother's knee."

"I particularly want you to remember those dates—I will give them to you again—the 10th. April and the 5th. May." (The Jury wrote them down. Lord Peter Wimsey murmured: "They all wrote down on their slates, 'She doesn't believe there's an atom of meaning in it.'" The Hon. Freddy said "What? What?" and the judge turned over another page of his notes.)

"About this time, Philip Boyes began to suffer from renewed attacks of a gastric trouble to which he had been subject from time to time during his life. You have read the evidence of Dr. Green, who attended him for something of the sort during his University career. That is some time ago; but there is also Dr. Weare, who, in 1925 prescribed for a similar attack. Not grave illnesses, but painful and exhausting, with sickness and so on, and aching in the limbs. Plenty of people have such troubles from time to time. Still, there is a coincidence of dates here which may be significant. We get these attacks—noted in Dr. Weare's case-book—one on the 31st. of March, one on the 15th. of April and one on the 12th. of May. Three sets of coincidences—as you may perhaps think them to be—Harriet Vane and Philip Boyes meet 'towards the end of March,' and he has an attack of gastritis on March 31st; on 10th. April Harriet Vane purchases two ounces of arsenic—they meet again 'in the second week in April,' and on April 15th, he has another attack; on 5th. May, there is the purchase of weed-killer—'some time in May' there is another meeting, and on the 12th. May he is taken ill for the third time. You may think that is rather curious, but you must not forget that the Crown has failed to prove any purchase of arsenic before the meeting in March. You must bear that in mind when considering this point.

"After the third attack—the one in May—the doctor advises Boyes to go away for a change, and he selects the northwest corner of Wales. He goes to Harlech, and spends a very pleasant time there and is much better. But he has a friend to accompany him, Mr. Ryland Vaughan, whom you have seen, and this friend says that 'Philip was not happy.' In fact, Mr. Vaughan formed the opinion that he was fretting after Harriet Vane. His bodily health improved, but he grew mentally depressed. And so on June 16th, we find him writing a letter to Miss Vane. Now that is an important letter, so I will read it to you once more:

'Dear Harriet,

Life is an utter mess-up. I can't stick it out here any longer. I've decided to cut adrift and take a trip out West. But before I go, I want to see you once again and find out if it isn't possible to put things straight again. You must do as you like, of course, but I still cannot understand the attitude you take up. If I can't make you see the thing in the right perspective this time I'll chuck it for good. I shall be in town on the 20th. Let me have a line to say when I can come round.

Yours,
P.'

"Now that, as you have realised, is a most ambiguous letter. Sir Impey Biggs, with arguments of great weight, has suggested that by the expressions 'cut adrift and take a trip out West,' 'I can't stick it out here,' and 'chuck it for good,' the writer was expressing his intention to make away with himself if he could not effect a reconciliation with the accused. He points out that 'to go west' is a well-known metaphor for dying, and that, of course, may be convincing to you. But Mr. Urquhart, when examined on the subject by the Attorney-General, said that he supposed the letter to refer to a project which he himself had suggested to the deceased, of taking a voyage across the Atlantic to Barbados, by way of change of scene. And the learned Attorney-General makes this other point that when the writer says, 'I can't stick it out *here* any longer,' he means, here in Britain, or perhaps merely 'here at Harlech,' and that if the phrase had reference to suicide it would read simply, 'I can't stick it out any longer.'

"No doubt you have formed your own opinion on this point. It is important to note that the deceased asks for an appointment on the 20th. The reply to this letter is before us; it reads:

'Dear Phil,

You can come round at 9:30 on the 20th. if you like, but you certainly will not make me change my mind.'

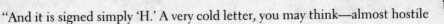
"And it is signed simply 'H.' A very cold letter, you may think—almost hostile in tone. And yet the appointment is made for 9:30.

"I shall not have to keep your attention very much longer, but I do ask for it at this point, specially—though you have been attending most patiently and industriously all the time—because we now come to the actual day of the death itself."

The old man clasped his hands one over the other upon the sheaf of notes and leaned a little forward. He had it all in his head, though he had known nothing of it until the last three days. He had not reached the time to babble of green fields and childhood ways; he still had firm hold of the present; he held it pinned down flat under his wrinkled fingers with their grey, chalky nails.

"Philip Boyes and Mr. Vaughan came back to town together on the evening of the 19th, and there would seem to be no doubt at all that Boyes was then in the best of health. Boyes spent the night with Mr. Vaughan, and they breakfasted together in the usual way upon bacon and eggs, toast, marmalade and coffee. At 11 o'clock Boyes had a Guinness, observing that, according to the advertisements it was 'Good for you.' At 1 o'clock he ate a hearty lunch at his club, and in the afternoon he played several sets at tennis with Mr. Vaughan and some other friends. During the game the remark was made by one of the players that Harlech had done Boyes good, and he replied that he was feeling fitter than he had done for many months.

"At half-past seven he went round to have dinner with his cousin, Mr. Norman Urquhart. Nothing at all unusual in his manner or appearance was noticed, either by Mr. Urquhart or by the maid who waited at table. Dinner was served at 8 o'clock exactly, and I think it would be a good thing if you were to write down that time (if you have not already done so) and also the list of things eaten and drunk.

"The two cousins dined alone together, and first, by way of cocktail, each had a glass of sherry. The wine was a fine Oleroso of 1847, and the maid decanted it from a fresh bottle and poured it into the glasses as they sat in the library. Mr. Urquhart retains the dignified old-fashioned custom of having the maid in attendance throughout the meal, so that we have here the advantage of two witnesses during this part of the evening. You saw the maid, Hannah Westlock, in the box, and I think you will say she gave the impression of being a sensible and observant witness.

"Well, there was the sherry. Then came a cup of cold bouillon, served by Hannah Westlock from the tureen on the sideboard. It was very strong, good soup, set to a clear jelly. Both men had some, and, after dinner, the bouillon was finished by the cook and Miss Westlock in the kitchen.

"After the soup came a piece of turbot with sauce. The portions were again carved at the sideboard, the sauceboat was handed to each in turn, and the dish was then sent out to be finished in the kitchen.

"Then came a *poulet en casserole*—that is, chicken cut up and stewed slowly with vegetables in a fireproof cooking utensil. Both men had some of this, and the maids finished the dish.

"The final course was a sweet omelette, which was made at the table in a chafing-dish by Philip Boyes himself. Both Mr. Urquhart and his cousin were very particular about eating an omelette the moment it came from the pan— and a very good rule it is, and I advise you all to treat omelettes in the same way and never to allow them to stand, or they will get tough. Four eggs were brought to the table in their shells, and Mr. Urquhart broke them one by one into a bowl, adding sugar from a sifter. Then he handed the bowl to Mr. Boyes, saying: 'You're the real dab at omelettes, Philip—I'll leave this to you.' Philip Boyes then beat the eggs and sugar together, cooked the omelette in the chafing-dish, filled it with hot jam, which was brought in by Hannah Westlock, and then himself divided it into two portions, giving one to Mr. Urquhart and taking the remainder himself.

"I have been a little careful to remind you of all these things, to show that we have good proof that every dish served at dinner was partaken of by two people at least, and in most cases by four. The omelette—the only dish which did not go out to the kitchen—was prepared by Philip Boyes himself and shared by his cousin. Neither Mr. Urquhart, Miss Westlock nor the cook, Mrs. Pettican, felt any ill-effects from this meal.

"I should mention also that there was one article of diet which was partaken of by Philip Boyes alone, and that was a bottle of Burgundy. It was a fine old Corton, and was brought to the table, in its original bottle. Mr. Urquhart drew the cork and then handed the bottle intact to Philip Boyes, saying that he himself would not take any—he had been advised not to drink at mealtimes. Philip Boyes drank two glassfuls and the remainder of the bottle was fortunately preserved. As you have already heard, the wine was later analysed and found to be quite harmless.

"This brings us to 9 o'clock. After dinner, coffee is offered, but Boyes excuses himself on the ground that he does not care for Turkish coffee, and moreover will probably be given coffee by Harriet Vane. At 9:15 Boyes leaves Mr. Urquhart's house in Woburn Square, and is driven in a taxi to the house where Miss Vane has her flat, No. 100 Doughty Street—a distance of about half a mile. We have it from Harriet Vane herself, from Mrs. Bright, a resident on the ground floor flat, and from Police Constable D.1234 who was passing along the street at the time, that he was standing on the doorstep, ringing the prisoner's bell, at 25 minutes past 9. She was on the look-out for him and let him in immediately.

"Now, as the interview was naturally a private one, we have no account of it to go upon but that of the prisoner. She has told us that as soon as he came in, she offered him 'a cup of coffee which was standing ready upon the gas-ring.' Now, when the learned Attorney-General heard the prisoner say that, he immediately asked what the coffee was standing ready in. The prisoner, apparently not quite understanding the purport of the question, replied 'in the fender, to keep hot.' When the question was repeated more clearly, she explained that the coffee was made in a saucepan, and that it was this which was placed upon the gas-ring in the fender. The Attorney-General then drew the prisoner's attention to her previous statement made to the police, in which this expression appeared: 'I had a cup of coffee ready for him on his arrival.' You will see at once the importance of this. If the cups of coffee were prepared and poured out separately before the arrival of the deceased, there was every opportunity to place poison in one of the cups beforehand and offer the prepared cup to Philip Boyes; but if the coffee was poured out from the saucepan in the deceased's presence, the opportunity would be rather less, though of course the thing might easily be done while Boyes' attention was momentarily distracted. The prisoner explained that in her statement she used the phrase 'a cup of coffee' merely as denoting 'a certain quantity of coffee.' You yourselves will be able to judge whether that is a usual and natural form of expression. The deceased is said by her to have taken no milk or sugar in his coffee, and you have the testimony of Mr. Urquhart and Mr. Vaughan that it was his usual habit to drink his after-dinner coffee black and unsweetened.

"According to the prisoner's evidence, the interview was not a satisfactory one. Reproaches were uttered on both sides, and at 10 o'clock or thereabouts, the deceased expressed his intention of leaving her. She says that he appeared uneasy and remarked that he was not feeling well, adding that her behaviour had greatly upset him.

"At 10 minutes past 10—and I want you to note these times very carefully, the taxi-driver Burke, who was standing on the rank in Guilford Street, was approached by Philip Boyes and told to take him to Woburn Square. He says that Boyes spoke in a hurried and abrupt tone, like that of a person in distress of mind or body. When the taxi stopped before Mr. Urquhart's house, Boyes did not get out, and Burke opened the door to see what was the matter. He found the deceased huddled in a corner with his hand pressed over his stomach and his face pale and covered with perspiration. He asked him whether he was ill, and the deceased replied: 'Yes, rotten.' Burke helped him out and rang the bell, supporting him with one arm as they stood on the doorstep. Hannah Westlock opened the door. Philip Boyes seemed hardly able to walk; his body was bent almost double, and he sank groaning into a hallchair and asked for brandy. She brought him a stiff brandy-and-soda from the dining-room, and after drinking this, Boyes recovered sufficiently to take money from his pocket and pay for the taxi.

"As he still seemed very ill, Hannah Westlock summoned Mr. Urquhart from the library. He said to Boyes, 'Hullo, old man—what's the matter with you?' Boyes replied, 'God knows! I feel awful. It can't have been the chicken.' Mr. Urquhart said he hoped not, he hadn't noticed anything wrong with it, and Boyes answered, No, he supposed it was one of his usual attacks, but he'd never felt anything like this before. He was taken upstairs to bed, and Dr. Grainger was summoned by telephone, as being the nearest physician available.

"Before the doctor's arrival, the patient vomited violently, and thereafter continued to vomit persistently. Dr. Grainger diagnosed the trouble as acute gastritis. There was a high temperature and rapid pulse, and the patient's abdomen was acutely painful to pressure, but the doctor found nothing indicative of any trouble in the nature of appendicitis or peritonitis. He therefore went back to his surgery, and made up a soothing medicine to control the vomiting—a mixture of bicarbonate of potash, tincture of oranges, and chloroform—no other drugs.

"Next day the vomiting still persisted, and Dr. Weare was called in to consult with Dr. Grainger, as he was well acquainted with the patient's constitution."

Here the judge paused and glanced at the clock.

"Time is getting on, and as the medical evidence has still to be passed in review, I will adjourn the Court now for lunch."

"He would," said the Hon. Freddy, "just at the beastliest moment when everybody's appetite is thoroughly taken away. Come on, Wimsey, let's go and fold a chop into the system, shall we?—Hullo!"

Wimsey had pushed past without heeding him, and was making his way down into the body of the court, where Sir Impey Biggs stood conferring with his juniors.

"Seems to be in a bit of a stew," said Mr. Arbuthnot, meditatively. "Gone to put an alternative theory of some kind, I expect. Wonder why I came to this bally show. Tedious, don't you know, and the girl's not even pretty. Don't think I'll come back after grub."

He struggled out, and found himself face to face with the Dowager Duchess of Denver.

"Come and have lunch, Duchess," said Freddy, hopefully. He liked the Dowager.

"I'm waiting for Peter, thanks, Freddy. Such an interesting case and interesting people, too, don't you think, though what the jury make of it I don't know, with faces like hams most of them, except the artist, who wouldn't have any features at all if it wasn't for that dreadful tie and his beard, looking like Christ, only not really Christ but one of those Italian ones in a pink frock and blue top thing. Isn't that Peter's Miss Climpson on the jury, how does she get there, I wonder?"

"He's put her into a house somewhere round about, I fancy," said Freddy, "with a typewriting office to look after and live over the shop and run those comic charity stunts of his. Funny old soul, isn't she? Stepped out of a magazine of the 'nineties. But she seems to suit his work all right and all that."

"Yes—such a good thing too, answering all those shady advertisements and then getting the people shown up and so courageous too, some of them the horridest oily people, and murderers I shouldn't wonder with automatic thing-ummies and life-preservers in every pocket, and very likely a gas-oven full of bones like Landru, so clever, wasn't he? And really *such* women—born murder-ees as somebody says—quite pig-faced but not of course deserving it and possibly the photographs don't do them justice, poor things."

The Duchess was even more rambling than usual, thought Freddy, and as she spoke her eyes wandered to her son with a kind of anxiety unusual in her.

"Top-hole to see old Wimsey back, isn't it?" he said, with simple kindliness. "Wonderful how keen he is on this sort of thing, don't you know. Rampages off the minute he gets home like the jolly old war-horse sniffing the T.N.T. Regularly up to the eyes in it."

"Well, it's one of Chief-Inspector Parker's cases, and they're such great friends, you know, quite like David and Beersheba—or do I mean Daniel?"

Wimsey joined them at this complicated moment, and tucked his mother's arm affectionately in his own.

"Frightfully sorry to keep you waiting, Mater, but I had to say a word to Biggy. He's having a rotten time, and that old Jeffreys of a judge looks as though he was getting measured for a black cap. I'm going home to burn my books. Dangerous to know too much about poisons, don't you think? Be thou as chaste as ice, as pure as snow, thou shalt not escape the old Bailey."

"The young woman doesn't seem to have tried that recipe, does she?" remarked Freddy.

"You ought to be on the jury," retorted Wimsey, with unusual acidity, "I bet that's what they're all saying at this moment. I'm convinced that that foreman is a teetotaller—I saw ginger-beer going into the jury-room, and I only hope it explodes and blows his inside through the top of his skull."

"All right, all right," returned Mr. Arbuthnot, soothingly, "what you want is a drink."

2

The scramble for places subsided; the jury returned; the prisoner reappeared in the dock suddenly, like a jack-in-the-box; the judge resumed his seat. Some petals had split from the roses. The old voice took up its tale where it had left off.

"Members of the jury—there is no need, I think, for me to recall the course of Philip Boyes' illness in great detail. The nurse was called in on June 21st, and during that day the doctors visited the patient three times. His condition grew steadily worse. There was persistent vomiting and diarrhoea, and he could not keep any food or medicine down at all. On the day after, the 22nd, he was worse still—in great pain, the pulse growing weaker, and the skin about the mouth getting dry and peeling off. The doctors gave him every attention, but could do nothing for him. His father was summoned, and when he arrived he found his son conscious, but unable to lift himself. He was able to speak, however, and in the presence of his father and Nurse Williams he made the remark, 'I'm going out, Dad, and I'm glad to be through with it. Harriet'll be rid of me now—I didn't know she hated me quite so much.' Now that was a very remarkable speech, and we have heard two very different interpretations put upon it. It is for you to say whether, in your opinion, he meant: 'She hated me enough to poison me,' or whether he meant, 'When I realised she hated me so much, I decided I did not want to live any longer'—or whether, perhaps, he meant neither of these things. When people are very ill, they sometimes get fantastic ideas, and sometimes they wander in their minds; perhaps you may feel that it is not profitable to take too much for granted. Still, those words are part of the evidence, and you are entitled to take them into account.

"During the night he became gradually weaker and lost consciousness, and at 3 o'clock in the morning he died, without ever regaining it. That was on the 23rd. of June.

"Now, up to this time, no suspicion of any kind had been aroused. Both Dr. Grainger and Dr. Weare formed the opinion that the cause of death was acute gastritis, and we need not blame them for coming to this conclusion, because it was quite consistent both with the symptoms of the illness and with the past history of the patient. A death-certificate was given in the usual way, and the funeral took place on the 28th.

"Well, then something happened which frequently does happen in cases of this kind, and that is that somebody begins to talk. It was Nurse Williams who talked in this particular case, and while you will probably think that this was a very wrong and a very indiscreet thing for a nurse to do, yet, as it turns out, it was a good thing that she did. Of course, she ought to have told Dr. Weare or Dr. Grainger of her suspicions at the time, but she did not do this, and we may at least feel glad to know that, in the doctors' opinions, even if she had done so, and if they had discovered that the illness was caused by arsenic, they would not have been able to do anything more to save the life of this unfortunate man. At any rate, what happened was that Nurse Williams was sent, during the last week of June, to nurse another patient of Dr. Weare's, who happened to belong to the same literary set in Bloomsbury as Philip Boyes and Harriet Vane, and while she was there, she spoke about Philip Boyes, and said that, in her opinion, the illness looked very much like poisoning, and she even mentioned the word arsenic. Well, you know how a thing like that gets about. One person tells another and it is discussed at tea parties, or what are known, I believe, as cocktail parties, and very soon a story gets spread about, and people mention names and take sides. Miss Marriott and Miss Price were told about it, and it also got to the ears of Mr. Vaughan. Now Mr. Vaughan had been greatly distressed and surprised by Philip Boyes' death, especially as he had been with him in Wales, and knew how much he had improved in health while on his holiday, and he also felt very strongly that Harriet Vane had behaved badly about the love-affair. Mr. Vaughan felt that some action ought to be taken about the matter, and went to Mr. Urquhart and put the story before him. Now Mr. Urquhart is a solicitor, and is therefore inclined to take a cautious view of rumours and suspicions, and he warned Mr. Vaughan that it was not wise to go about making accusations against people, for fear of an action for libel. At the same time, he naturally felt uneasy that such a thing should be said about a relation who had died in his house. He took the course—the very sensible course—of consulting Dr. Weare and suggesting that, if he was quite certain that the illness was due to gastritis and nothing else, he should take steps to rebuke Nurse Williams and put an end to the talk. Dr. Weare was naturally very much surprised and upset to hear what was being said, but, since the suggestion had been made, he could not deny that—taking the symptoms only into account—there was just the bare possibility of something of the sort, because, as you have already heard in the medical evidence, the symptoms of arsenical poisoning and of acute gastritis are really indistinguishable.

"When this was communicated to Mr. Vaughan, he was confirmed in his suspicions, and wrote to the elder Mr. Boyes suggesting an enquiry. Mr. Boyes was naturally very much shocked, and said at once that the matter should be taken up. He had known of the liaison with Harriet Vane, and had noticed that she did not come to enquire after Philip Boyes, nor attend the funeral, and this had struck him as heartless behavior. In the end, the police were communicated with and an exhumation order obtained.

"You have heard the result of the analysis made by Sir James Lubbock and Mr. Stephen Fordyce. There was a great deal of discussion about methods of analysis and the way that arsenic behaves in the body and so on, but I think we need not trouble too much about those fine details. The chief points in the evidence seemed to me to be these, which you may note down if you care to do so.

"The analysts took certain organs of the body—the stomach, intestines, kidneys, liver and so on, and analyzed portions of these and found that they all contained arsenic. They were able to weight the quantity of arsenic found in these various portions, and they calculated from that the quantity of arsenic present in the whole body. Then they had to allow so much for the amount of arsenic eliminated from the body by the vomiting and diarrhoea and also through the kidneys, because the kidneys play a very large part in the elimination of this particular poison. After making allowance for all these things, they formed the opinion that a large and fatal dose of arsenic—four or five grains, perhaps, had been taken about three days before the death.

"I do not know whether you quite followed all the technical arguments about this. I will try to tell you the chief points as I understood them. The nature of arsenic is to pass through the body very quickly, especially if it is taken with food or immediately following a meal, because the arsenic irritates the lining of the internal organs and speeds up the process of elimination. The action would be quicker if the arsenic were taken in liquid than if it were taken in the form of a powder. Where arsenic was taken with, or immediately on top of a meal, nearly the whole of it would be evacuated within twenty-four hours after the onset of the illness. So you see that, although the actual quantities found in the body may seem to you and me very small indeed, the mere fact that they were found there at all, after three days of persistent vomiting and diarrhoea and so on, points to a large dose having been taken at some time.

"Now there was a great deal of discussion about the time at which the symptoms first set in. It is suggested by the defence that Philip Boyes may have taken the arsenic himself at some time between leaving Harriet Vane's flat and hailing the taxi in Guilford Street; and they bring forward books which show that in many cases the onset of symptoms takes place in a very short time after taking the arsenic—a quarter of an hour, I think, was the shortest time mentioned where the arsenic was taken in liquid form. Now the prisoner's statement —and we have no other—is that Philip Boyes left her at 10 o'clock, and at ten minutes past he was in Guilford Street. He was then looking ill. It would not take many minutes to drive to Woburn Square at that hour of night, and by the time he got there, he was already in acute pain, and hardly able to stand. Now Guilford Street is a very short way from Doughty Street—perhaps three minutes' walk—and you must ask yourselves, if the prisoner's statement is correct, what he did with those ten minutes. Did he occupy himself in going to some quiet spot and taking a dose of arsenic, which he must in that case have brought with him in anticipation of an unfavourable interview with the prisoner? And I may remind you here, that the defence have brought no evidence to show that Philip Boyes ever bought any arsenic, or had access to any arsenic. That is not to say he could not have obtained it—the purchases made by Harriet Vane show that the law about the sale of poisons is not always as effective as one would like it to be—but the fact remains that the defence have not been able to show that the deceased ever had arsenic in his possession. And while we are on this subject, I will mention that, curiously enough, the analysts could find no traces of the charcoal, or indigo, with which commercial arsenic is supposed to be mixed. Whether it was bought by the prisoner or by the deceased himself, you would expect to find traces of the colouring matter. But you may think it likely that all such traces would be removed from the body by the vomiting and purging which took place.

"As regards the suggestion of suicide, you will have to ask yourselves about those ten minutes—whether Boyes was taking a dose of arsenic, or whether, as is also possible, he felt unwell and sat down somewhere to recover himself, or whether, perhaps, he was merely roaming about in the vague way we sometimes do when we are feeling upset and unhappy. Or you may think that the prisoner was mistaken, or not speaking the truth, about the time he left the flat.

"You have also the prisoner's statement that Boyes mentioned, before he left her, that he was feeling unwell. If you think this had anything to do with the arsenic, it of course disposes of the suggestion that he took poison after leaving the flat.

"Then, when one looks into it, one finds that this question about the onset of symptoms is left very vague. Various doctors came here and told you about their own experiences and the cases quoted by medical authorities in books, and you will have noticed that there is no certainty at all about the time when the symptoms may be expected to appear. Sometimes it is a quarter of an hour or half an hour, sometimes two hours, sometimes as much as five or six, and, I believe, in one case as much as seven hours after taking the poison."

Here the Attorney-General rose respectfully and said: "In that case, me lud, I think I am right in saying that the poison was taken on an empty stomach."

"Thank you, I am much obliged to you for the reminder. That was a case in which the poison was taken on an empty stomach. I only mention these cases to show that we are dealing with a very uncertain phenomenon, and that is why I was particular to remind you of all the occasions on which Philip Boyes took food during the day—the 20th of June, since there is always the possibility that you may have to take them into consideration."

"A beast, but a just beast," murmured Lord Peter Wimsey.

"I have purposely left out of consideration until now another point which arose out of the analysis, and that is the presence of arsenic in the hair. The deceased had curly hair, which he wore rather long; the front portion, when straightened out, measured about six or seven inches in places. Now, in this hair, arsenic was found, at the end closest to the head. It did not extend to the tips of the longest hair, but it was found near the roots, and Sir James Lubbock says that the quantity was greater than could be accounted for in any natural way. Occasionally, quite normal people are found to have minute traces of arsenic in the hair and skin and so on, but not to the amount found here. That is Sir James' opinion.

"Now you have been told—and the medical witnesses all agree in this—that if a person takes arsenic, a certain proportion of it will be deposited in the skin, nails and hair. It will be deposited in the root of the hair, and as the hair grows, the arsenic will be carried along with the growth of the hair, so that you get a rough idea, from seeing the position of the arsenic in the hair, how long the administration has been going on. There was a good deal of discussion about this, but I think there was a fairly general agreement that, if you took a dose of arsenic, you might expect to find traces of it in the hair, close to the scalp, after about ten weeks. Hair grows at the rate of about six inches in a year, and the arsenic will grow out with it till it reaches the far end and is cut off. I am sure that the ladies on the jury will understand this very well, because I believe that the same thing occurs in the case of what is termed a 'permanent wave.' The wave is made in a certain portion of the hair, and after a time it grows out, and the hair near the scalp comes up straight and has to be waved again. You can tell by the position of the wave, how long ago the waving was done. In the same way, if a finger-nail is bruised, the discolouration will gradually grow up the nail until it reaches the point where you can cut it off with the scissors.

"Now it has been said that the presence of arsenic in and about the roots of Philip Boyes' hair indicates that he must have taken arsenic three months at least before his death. You will consider what importance is to be attached to this in view of the prisoner's purchases of arsenic in April and May, and of the deceased's attacks of sickness in March, April and May. The quarrel with the prisoner took place in February; he was ill in March and he died in June. There are five months between the quarrel and the death, and four months between the first illness and the death, and you may think that there is some significance in these dates.

"We now come to the enquiries made by the police. When suspicion was aroused, detectives investigated Harriet Vane's movements and subsequently went to her flat to take a statement from her. When they told her that Boyes was found to have died of arsenic poisoning, she appeared very much surprised, and said, 'Arsenic? What an extraordinary thing!' And then, she laughed, and said, 'Why, I am writing a book all about arsenic poisoning.' They asked her about the purchases of arsenic and other poisons which she had made and she admitted them quite readily in court. They asked what she had done with the poisons, and she replied that she had burnt them because they were dangerous things to have about. The flat was searched, but no poisons of any kind were found, except such things as aspirin and a few ordinary medicines of that kind. She absolutely denied having administered arsenic or any kind of poison to Philip Boyes. She was asked whether the arsenic could possibly have got into the coffee by accident and replied that that was quite impossible, as she had destroyed all the poisons before the end of May."

Here Sir Impey Biggs interposed and begged with submission to suggest that his lordship should remind the jury of the evidence given by Mr. Challoner.

"Certainly, Sir Impey, I am obliged to you. You remember that Mr. Challoner is Harriet Vane's literary agent. He came here to tell us that he had discussed with her as long ago as last December the subject of her forthcoming book, and she then told him that it was to be about poisons, and very probably about arsenic. So you may think it is a point in the prisoner's favour that this intention of studying the purchase and administration of arsenic was already in her mind some time before the quarrel with Philip Boyes took place. She evidently gave considerable thought to the subject, for there were a number of books on her shelves dealing with forensic medicine and toxicology, and also the reports of several famous poison trials, including the Madeleine Smith case, the Seddon case and the Armstrong case—all of which were cases of arsenical poisoning.

"Well, I think that is the case as it is presented to you. This woman is charged with having murdered her former lover by arsenic. He undoubtedly did take arsenic, and if you are satisfied that she gave it to him with intent to injure or kill him, and that he died of it, then it is your duty to find her guilty of murder.

"Sir Impey Biggs, in his able and eloquent speech, has put it to you that she had very little motive for such a murder, but I am bound to tell you that murders are very often committed for what seem to be most inadequate motives —if, indeed, any motive can be called adequate for such a crime. Especially where the parties are husband and wife, or have lived together as husband and wife, there are likely to be passionate feelings which may tend to crimes of violence in persons with inadequate moral standards and of unbalanced mind.

"The prisoner had the means—the arsenic—she had the expert knowledge, and she had the opportunity to administer it. The defence say that this is not enough. They say the Crown must go further and prove that the poison could not have been taken in any other way—by accident, or with suicidal intent. This is for you to judge. If you feel that there is any reasonable doubt that the prisoner gave the poison to Philip Boyes deliberately, you must bring her in Not Guilty of murder. You are not bound to decide how it was given, if it was not given by her. Consider the circumstances of the case as a whole, and say what conclusion you have come to."

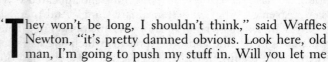"They won't be long, I shouldn't think," said Waffles Newton, "it's pretty damned obvious. Look here, old man, I'm going to push my stuff in. Will you let me know what happens?"

"Sure," said Salcombe Hardy, "if you don't mind dropping mine in at our place as you go. You couldn't send me a drink by 'phone, could you? My mouth's like the bottom of a parrot's cage." He looked at his watch. "We shall miss the 6:30 edition, I'm afraid, unless they hurry up. The old man is careful but he's damned slow."

"They can't in decency not make a pretence of consulting about it," said Newton. "I give them twenty minutes. They'll want a smoke. So do I. I'll be back at ten to, in case."

He wriggled his way out. Cuthbert Logan, who reported for a morning paper, and was a man of more leisure, settled down to write up a word-picture of the trial. He was a phlegmatic and sober person and could write as comfortably in court as anywhere else. He liked to be on the spot when things happened, and to note down glances, tones of voice, colour effects and so forth. His copy was always entertaining, and sometimes even distinguished.

Freddy Arbuthnot, who had not, after all, gone home after lunch, thought it was time to do so now. He fidgeted, and Wimsey frowned at him. The Dowager Duchess made her way along the benches and squeezed in next to Lord Peter. Sir Impey Biggs, having watched over his client's interests to the last, disappeared, chatting cheerfully to the Attorney-General, and followed by the smaller legal fry. The dock was deserted. On the bench the red roses stood solitary, their petals dropping.

Chief-Inspector Parker, disengaging himself from a group of friends, came slowly up through the crowd and greeted the Dowager. "And what do you think of it, Peter?" he added, turning to Wimsey, "rather neatly got up, eh?"

"Charles," said Wimsey, "you ought not to be allowed out without me. You've made a mistake, old man."

"Made a mistake?"

"She didn't do it."

"Oh, come!"

"She did not do it. It's very convincing and water-tight, but it's all wrong."

"You don't really think that."

"I do."

Parker looked distressed. He had confidence in Wimsey's judgment, and, in spite of his own interior certainty, he felt shaken.

"My dear man, where's the flaw in it?"

"There isn't one. It's damnably knife-proof. There's nothing wrong about it at all, except that the girl's innocent."

"You're turning into a common or garden psychologist," said Parker, with an uneasy laugh, "isn't he, Duchess?"

"I wish I had known that girl," replied the Dowager, in her usual indirect manner, "so interesting and a really remarkable face, though perhaps not strictly good-looking, and all the more interesting for that, because good-looking people are so often cows. I have been reading one of her books, really quite good and so well-written, and I didn't guess the murderer till page 200, rather clever, because I usually do it about page 15. So very curious to write books about crimes and then be accused of a crime one's self, some people might say it was a judgment. I wonder whether, if she didn't do it, she has spotted the murderer herself? I don't suppose detective writers detect much in real life, do they, except Edgar Wallace of course, who always seems to be everywhere and dear Conan Doyle and the black man what was his name and of course the Slater person, such a scandal, though now I come to think of it that was in Scotland where they have such very odd laws about everything particularly getting married. Well, I suppose we shall soon know now, not the truth, necessarily, but what the jury have made of it."

"Yes; they are being rather longer than I expected. But, I say, Wimsey, I wish you'd tell me—"

"Too late, too late, you cannot enter now. I have locked my heart in a silver box and pinned it wi' a golden pin. Nobody's opinion matters now, except the jury's. I expect Miss Climpson is telling 'em all about it. When once she starts she doesn't stop for an hour or two."

"Well, they've been half-an-hour now," said Parker.

"Still waiting?" said Salcombe Hardy, returning to the presstable.

"Yes—so this is what you call twenty minutes! Three-quarters of an hour, I make it."

"They've been out an hour-and-a-half," said a girl to her fiancé, just behind Wimsey. "What can they be discussing?"

"Perhaps they don't think she did it after all."

"What nonsense! Of course she did it. You could see it by her face. Hard, that's what I call it, and she never once cried or anything."

"Oh, I dunno," said the young man.

"You don't mean to say you admired her, Frank?"

"Oh, well, I dunno. But she didn't look to me like a murderess."

"And how do you know what a murderess looks like? Have you ever met one?"

"Well, I've seen them at Madame Tussaud's."

"Oh, wax-works. Everybody looks like a murderer in a wax-works."

"Well, p'raps they do. Have a choc."

"Two hours and a quarter," said Waffles Newton, impatiently. "They must have gone to sleep. Have to be a special edition. What happens if they are all night about it?"

"We sit here all night, that's all."

"Well, it's my turn for a drink. Let me know, will you?"

"Right-ho!"

"I've been talking to one of the ushers," said the Man Who Knows the Ropes, importantly, to a friend. "The judge has just sent round to the jury to ask if he can help them in any way."

"Has he? And what did they say?"

"I don't know."

"They've been out three hours and a half now," whispered the girl behind Wimsey. "I'm getting fearfully hungry."

"Are you, darling? Shall we go?"

"No—I want to hear the verdict. We've waited so long now, we may as well stop on."

"Well, I'll go out and get some sandwiches."

"Oh, that would be nice. But don't be long, because I'm sure I shall get hysterics when I hear the sentence."

"I'll be as quick as ever I can. Be glad you're not the jury—they're not allowed anything at all."

"What, nothing to eat or drink?"

"Not a thing. I don't think they're supposed to have light or fire either."

"Poor things! But it's central-heated, isn't it?"

"It's hot enough here, anyway. I'll be glad of a breath of fresh air."

Five hours.

"There's a terrific crowd in the street," said the Man Who Knows the Ropes, returning from a reconnaissance. "Some people started booing the prisoner and a bunch of men attacked them, and one fellow has been carried off in an ambulance."

"Really, how amusing! Look! There's Mr. Urquhart; he's come back. I'm so sorry for him, aren't you? It must be horrid having somebody die in your house."

"He's talking to the Attorney-General. They've all had a proper dinner, of course."

"The Attorney-General isn't as handsome as Sir Impey Biggs. Is it true he keeps canaries?"

"The Attorney-General?"

"No, Sir Impey."

"Yes, quite true. He takes prizes with them."

"What a funny idea!"

"Bear up, Freddy," said Lord Peter Wimsey. "I perceive movements. They are coming, my own, my sweet, were it never so airy a tread."

The court rose to its feet. The judge took his seat. The prisoner, very white in the electricity, re-appeared in the dock. The door leading to the jury-room opened.

"Look at their faces," said the fiancée, "they say if it's going to be Guilty they never look at the prisoner. Oh, Archie, hold my hand!"

The Clerk of Assizes addressed the jury in tones in which formality struggled with reproach.

"Members of the jury, have you all agreed upon your verdict?"

The foreman rose with an injured and irritable countenance.

"I am sorry to say that we find it impossible to come to an agreement."

A prolonged gasp and murmur went round the court. The judge leaned forward, very courteous and not in the least fatigued.

"Do you think that with a little more time you may be able to reach an agreement?"

"I'm afraid not, my lord." The foreman glanced savagely at one corner of the jury-box, where the elderly spinster sat with her head bowed and her hands tightly clasped. "I see no prospect at all of our ever agreeing."

"Can I assist you in any way?"

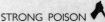
"No, thank you, my lord. We quite understand the evidence, but we cannot agree about it."

"That is unfortunate. I think perhaps you had better try again, and then, if you are still unable to come to a decision, you must come back and tell me. In the meantime, if my knowledge of the law can be of any assistance to you, it is, of course, quite at your disposal."

The jury stumbled sullenly away. The judge trailed his scarlet robes out of the back of the bench. The murmur of conversation rose and swelled into a loud rumble.

"By jove," said Freddy Arbuthnot, "I believe it's your Miss Climpson that's holdin' the jolly old show up, Wimsey. Did you see how the foreman glared at her?"

"Good egg," said Wimsey, "oh, excellent, excellent egg! She has a fearfully tough conscience—she may stick it out yet."

"I believe you've been corrupting the jury, Wimsey. Did you signal to her or something?"

"I didn't," said Wimsey. "Believe me or believe me not, I refrained from so much as a lifted eyebrow."

"And he himself has said it," muttered Freddy, "and it's greatly to his credit. But it's damned hard on people who want their dinners."

Six hours. Six hours and a half.

"At last!"

As the jury filed back for the second time, they showed signs of wear and tear. The harassed woman had been crying and was still choking into her handkerchief. The man with the bad cold looked nearly dead. The artist's hair was rumpled into an untidy bush. The company director and the foreman looked as though they would have liked to strangle somebody, and the elderly spinster had her eyes shut and her lips moving as though she were praying.

"Members of the jury, are you agreed upon your verdict?"

"No; we are quite sure that it is impossible for us ever to agree."

"You are quite sure?" said the judge. "I do not wish to hurry you in any way. I am quite prepared to wait here as long as ever you like."

The snarl of the company director was audible even in the gallery. The foreman controlled himself, and replied in a voice ragged with temper and exhaustion.

"We shall never agree, my lord—not if we were to stay here till Doomsday."

"That is very unfortunate," said the judge, "but in that case, of course, there is nothing for it but to discharge you and order a fresh trial. I feel sure that you have all done your best and that you have brought all the resources of your intelligence and conscience to bear on this matter to which you have listened with so much patient and zealous attention. You are discharged, and you are entitled to be excused from all further jury service for the next twelve years."

Almost before the further formalities were completed, and while the judge's robes still flared in the dark little doorway, Wimsey had scrambled down into the well of the court. He caught the defending counsel by the gown.

"Biggy—well done! You've got another chance. Let me in on this and we'll put it off."

"You think so, Wimsey? I don't mind confessing that we've done better than I ever expected."

"We'll do better still next time. I say, Biggy, swear me in as a clerk or something. I want to interview her."

"Who, my client?"

"Yes, I've got a hunch about this case. We've got to get her off, and I know it can be done."

"Well, come and see me tomorrow. I must go and speak to her now. I'll be in my chambers at ten. Good-night."

Wimsey darted off and rushed round to the side-door, from which the jury were emerging. Last of them all, her hat askew and her mackintosh dragged awkwardly round her shoulders, came the elderly spinster. Wimsey dashed up to her and seized her hand.

"Miss Climpson!"

"Oh, Lord Peter. Oh, dear! What a dreadful day it has been. Do you know, it was me that caused the trouble, mostly, though two of them most bravely backed me up, and oh, Lord Peter, I hope I haven't done wrong, but I couldn't, no I *couldn't* in conscience say she had done it when I was sure she hadn't, could I? Oh, dear, oh, dear!"

"You're absolutely right. She didn't do it, and thank God you stood up to them and gave her another chance. I'm going to prove she didn't do it. And I'm going to take you out to dinner, and—I say, Miss Climpson!"

"Yes?"

"I hope you won't mind, because I haven't shaved since this morning, but I'm going to take you round the next quiet corner and kiss you."

4

The following day was a Sunday, but Sir Impey Biggs cancelled an engagement to play golf (with the less regret as it was pouring cats and dogs), and held an extraordinary council of war.

"Well, now, Wimsey," said the advocate, "what is your idea about this? May I introduce Mr. Crofts of Crofts & Cooper, solicitors for the defence."

"My idea is that Miss Vane didn't do it," said Wimsey. "I dare say that's an idea which has already occurred to you, but with the weight of my great mind behind it, no doubt it strikes the imagination more forcibly."

Mr. Crofts, not being quite clear whether this was funny or fatuous, smiled deferentially.

"Quite so," said Sir Impey, "but I should be interested to know how many of the jury saw it in that light."

"Well, I can tell you that, at least, because I know one of them. One woman and half a woman and about three-quarters of a man."

"Meaning precisely?"

"Well, the woman I know stuck out for it that Miss Vane wasn't that sort of person. They bullied her a good deal, of course, because she couldn't lay a finger on any real weakness in the chain of evidence, but she said the prisoner's demeanour was part of the evidence and that she was entitled to take that into consideration. Fortunately, she is a tough, thin, elderly woman with a sound digestion and a militant High-Church conscience of remarkable staying-power, and her wind is excellent. She let 'em all gallop themselves dead, and then said she still didn't believe it and wasn't going to say she did."

"Very useful," said Sir Impey. "A person who can believe all the articles of the Christian faith is not going to boggle over a trifle of adverse evidence. But we can never hope for a whole jury-box full of ecclesiastical diehards. How about the other woman and the man?"

"Well, the woman was rather unexpected. She was the stout, prosperous party who keeps a sweet-shop. She said she didn't think the case was proved, and that it was perfectly possible that Boyes had taken the stuff himself, or that his cousin had given it to him. She was influenced, rather oddly, by the fact that she had attended one or two arsenic trials, and had not been satisfied by the verdict in some other cases—notably the Seddon trial. She has no opinion of men in general (she has buried her third) and she disbelieves all expert evidence on principle. She said that, personally, she thought Miss Vane might have done it, but she wouldn't really hang a dog on medical evidence. At first she was ready to vote with the majority, but she took a dislike to the foreman, who tried to bear her down by his male authority, and eventually she said she was going to back up my friend Miss Climpson."

Sir Impey laughed.

"Very interesting. I wish we always got this inside information about juries. We sweat like hell to prepare evidence, and then one person makes up her mind on what isn't really evidence at all, and another supports her on the ground that evidence can't be relied on. How about the man?"

"The man was the artist, and the only person who really understood the kind of life these people were leading. He believed your client's version of the quarrel, and said that, if the girl really felt like that about the man, the last thing she would want to do would be to kill him. She'd rather stand back and watch him ache, like the man with the hollow tooth in the comic song. He was also able to believe the whole story about purchasing the poisons, which to the others, of course, seemed extremely feeble. He also said that Boyes, from what he had heard, was a conceited prig, and that anybody who disposed of him was doing a public service. He had had the misfortune to read some of his books, and considered the man an excrescence and a public nuisance. Actually he thought it more than likely that he had committed suicide, and if anybody was prepared to take that point of view he was ready to second it. He also alarmed the jury by saying that he was accustomed to late hours and a stale atmosphere, and had not the slightest objection to sitting up all night. Miss Climpson also said that, in a righteous cause, a little personal discomfort was a trifle, and added that her religion had trained her to fasting. At that point, the third woman had hysterics and another man, who had an important deal to put through next day, lost his temper, so, to prevent bodily violence, the foreman said he thought they had better agree to disagree. So that's how it was."

"Well, they've given us another chance," said Mr. Crofts, "so it's all to the good. It can't come on now till the next sessions, which gives us about a month, and we'll probably get Bancroft next time, who's not such a severe judge as Crossley. The thing is, can we do anything to improve the look of our case?"

"I'm going to have a strenuous go at it," said Wimsey. "There must *be* evidence somewhere, you know. I know you've all worked like beavers, but I'm going to work like a king beaver. And I've got one big advantage over the rest of you."

"More brains?" suggested Sir Impey, grinning.

"No—I should hate to suggest that, Biggy. But I do believe in Miss Vane's innocence."

"Damn it, Wimsey, didn't my eloquent speeches convince you that I was a whole-hearted believer?"

"Of course they did. I nearly shed tears. Here's old Biggy, I said to myself, going to retire from the Bar and cut his throat if this verdict goes against him, because he won't believe in British justice any more. No—it's your triumph at having secured a disagreement that gives you away, old horse. More than you expected. You said so. By the way, if it's not a rude question, who's paying you, Biggy?"

"Crofts and Cooper," said Sir Impey, slyly.

"They're in the thing for their health, I take it?"

"No, Lord Peter. As a matter of fact, the costs in this case are being borne by Miss Vane's publishers and by a—well, a certain newspaper, which is running her new book as a serial. They expect a scoop as the result of all this. But frankly, I don't quite know what they'll say to the expense of a fresh trial. I'm expecting to hear from them this morning."

"The vultures," said Wimsey. "Well, they'd better carry on, but tell 'em I'll see they're guaranteed. Don't bring my name in, though."

"This is very generous—"

"Not at all. I wouldn't lose the fun of all this for the world. Sort of case I fairly wallow in. But in return you must do something for me. I want to see Miss Vane. You must get me passed in as part of your outfit, so that I can hear her version of the story in reasonable privacy. Get me?"

"I expect that can be done," said Sir Impey. "In the meantime you have nothing to suggest?"

"Haven't had time yet. But I'll fish out something, don't you worry. I've already started to undermine the confidence of the police. Chief-Inspector Parker has gone home to twine willow-wreaths for his own tomb-stone."

"You'll be careful," said Sir Impey. "Anything we can discover will come in much more effectively if the prosecution don't know of it beforehand."

"I'll walk as on egg-shells. But if I find the real murderer (if any), you won't object to my having him or her arrested, I take it?"

"No; I won't object to that. The police may. Well, gentlemen, if there's nothing further at the moment, we'd better adjourn the meeting. You'll get Lord Peter the facilities he wants, Mr. Crofts?"

Mr. Crofts exerted himself with energy, and on the following morning, Lord Peter presented himself at the gates of Holloway Gaol, with his credentials.

"Oh, yes, my lord. You are to be treated on the same footing as the prisoner's solicitor. Yes, we have had a separate communication from the police and that will be quite all right, my lord. The warder will take you down, and explain the regulations to you."

Wimsey was conducted through a number of bare corridors to a small room with a glass door. There was a long deal table in it and a couple of repellent chairs, one at either end of the table.

"Here you are, my lord. You sit at one end and the prisoner at the other, and you must be careful not to move from your seats, nor to pass any object over the table. I shall be outside and see you through the glass, my lord, but I shan't be able to overhear nothing. If you will take a seat, they'll bring the prisoner in, my lord."

Wimsey sat down and waited, a prey to curious sensations. Presently there was a noise of footsteps, and the prisoner was brought in, attended by a female wardress. She took the chair opposite to Wimsey, the wardress withdrew and the door was shut. Wimsey, who had risen, cleared his throat.

"Good afternoon, Miss Vane," he said, unimpressively.

The prisoner looked at him.

"Please sit down," she said, in the curious, deep voice which had attracted him in Court. "You are Lord Peter Wimsey, I believe, and have come from Mr. Crofts."

"Yes," said Wimsey. Her steady gaze was unnerving him. "Yes, I—er—I heard the case and all that, and—er—I thought there might be something I could do, don't you know.".

"That was very good of you," said the prisoner.

"Not at all, not at all, dash it! I mean to say, I rather enjoy investigating things, if you know what I mean."

"I know. Being a writer of detective stories, I have naturally studied your career with interest."

She smiled suddenly at him and his heart turned to water.

"Well, that's rather a good thing in a way, because you'll understand that I'm not really such an ass as I'm looking at present."

That made her laugh.

"You're not looking an ass—at least, not more so than any gentleman should under the circumstances. The background doesn't altogether suit your style, but you are a very refreshing sight. And I'm really very grateful to you, though I'm afraid I'm rather a hopeless case."

"Don't say that. It can't be hopeless, unless you actually did it, and I know you didn't."

"Well, I didn't, as a matter of fact. But I feel it's like one book I wrote, in which I invented such a perfectly watertight crime that I couldn't devise any way for any detective to prove it, and had to fall back on the murderer's confession."

"If necessary, we'll do the same. You don't happen to know who the murderer is, I suppose?"

"I don't think there is one. I really believe Philip took the stuff himself. He was rather a defeatist sort of person, you know."

"I suppose he took your separation pretty hard?"

"Well, I daresay it was partly that. But I think it was more that he didn't feel he was sufficiently appreciated. He was apt to think that people were in league to spoil his chances."

"And were they?"

"No, I don't think so. But I do think he offended a great many people. He was rather apt to demand things as a right—and that annoys people, you know."

"Yes, I see. Did he get on all right with his cousin?"

"Oh, yes; though of course he always said it was no more than Mr. Urquhart's duty to look after him. Mr. Urquhart is fairly well off, as he has quite a big professional connection, but Philip really had no claim on him, as it wasn't family money or anything. His idea was that great artists deserved to be boarded and lodged at the expense of the ordinary man."

Wimsey was fairly well acquainted with this variety of the artistic temperament. He was struck, however, by the tone of the reply, which was tinged, he thought, with bitterness and even some contempt. He put his next question with some hesitation.

"Forgive my asking, but—you were very fond of Philip Boyes?"

"I must have been, mustn't I—under the circumstances?"

"Not necessarily," said Wimsey, boldly, "you might have been sorry for him—or bewitched by him—or even badgered to death by him."

"All those things."

Wimsey considered for a moment.

"Were you friends?"

"No." The word broke out with a kind of repressed savagery that startled him. "Philip wasn't the sort of man to make a friend of a woman. He wanted devotion. I gave him that. I did, you know. But I couldn't stand being made a fool of. I couldn't stand being put on probation, like an office-boy, to see if I was good enough to be condescended to. I quite thought he was honest when he said he didn't believe in marriage—and then it turned out that it was a test, to see whether my devotion was abject enough. Well, it wasn't. I didn't like having matrimony offered as a bad-conduct prize."

"I don't blame you," said Wimsey.

"Don't you?"

"No. It sounds to me as if the fellow was a prig—not to say a bit of a cad. Like that horrid man who pretended to be a landscape-painter and then embarrassed the unfortunate young woman with the burden of an honour unto which she was not born. I've no doubt he made himself perfectly intolerable about it, with his ancient oaks and family plate, and the curtseying tenantry and all the rest of it."

Harriet Vane laughed once more.

"Yes—it's ridiculous—but humiliating too. Well, there it is. I thought Philip had made both himself and me ridiculous, and the minute I saw that—well, the whole thing simply shut down—flop!"

She sketched a gesture of finality.

"I quite see that," said Wimsey. "Such a Victorian attitude, too, for a man with advanced ideas. He for God only, she for God in him, and so on. Well, I'm glad you feel like that about it."

"Are you? It's not going to be exactly helpful in the present crisis."

"No; I was looking beyond that. What I mean to say is, when all this is over, I want to marry you, if you can put up with me and all that."

Harriet Vane, who had been smiling at him, frowned, and an indefinable expression of distaste came into her eyes.

"Oh, are you another of them? That makes forty-seven."

"Forty-seven what?" asked Wimsey, much taken aback.

"Proposals. They come in by every post. I suppose there are a lot of imbeciles who want to marry anybody who's at all notorious."

"Oh," said Wimsey. "Dear me, that makes it very awkward. As a matter of fact, you know, I don't need any notoriety. I can get into the papers off my own bat. It's no treat to me. Perhaps I'd better not mention it again."

His voice sounded hurt, and the girl eyed him rather remorsefully.

"I'm sorry—but one gets rather a bruised sort of feeling in my position. There have been so many beastlinesses."

"I know," said Lord Peter. "It was stupid of me—"

"No, I think it was stupid of me. But why—?"

"Why? Oh, well—I thought you'd be rather an attractive person to marry. That's all. I mean, I sort of took a fancy to you. I can't tell you why. There's no rule about it, you know."

"I see. Well, it's very nice of you."

"I wish you wouldn't sound as if you thought it was rather funny. I know I've got a silly face, but I can't help that. As a matter of fact, I'd like somebody I could talk sensibly to, who would make life interesting. And I could give you a lot of plots for your books, if that's any inducement."

"But you wouldn't want a wife who wrote books, would you?"

"But I should; it would be great fun. So much more interesting than the ordinary kind that is only keen on clothes and people. Though of course, clothes and people are all right too, in moderation. I don't mean to say I object to clothes."

"And how about the old oaks and the family plate?"

"Oh, you wouldn't be bothered with them. My brother does all that. I collect first editions and incunabulae, which is a little tedious of me, but you wouldn't need to bother with them either unless you liked."

"I don't mean that. What would your family think about it?"

"Oh, my mother's the only one that counts, and she likes you very much from what she's seen of you."

"So you had me inspected?"

"No—dash it all, I seem to be saying all the wrong things today. I was absolutely stunned that first day in court, and I rushed off to my mater, who's an absolute dear, and the kind of person who really understands things, and I said, 'Look here! here's the absolutely one and only woman, and she's being put through a simply ghastly awful business and for God's sake come and hold my hand!' You simply don't know how foul it was."

"That does sound rather rotten. I'm sorry I was brutal. But, by the way, you're bearing in mind, aren't you, that I've had a lover?"

"Oh, yes. So have I, if it comes to that. In fact, several. It's the sort of thing that might happen to anybody. I can produce quite good testimonials. I'm told I make love rather nicely—only I'm at a disadvantage at the moment. One can't be very convincing at the other end of a table with a bloke looking in at the door."

"I will take your word for it. But, however entrancing it is to wander unchecked through a garden of bright images, are we not enticing your mind from another subject of almost equal importance? It seems probable—"

"And if you can quote *Kai Lung*, we should certainly get on together."

"It seems very probable that I shall not survive to make the experiment."

"Don't be so damned discouraging," said Wimsey. "I have already carefully explained to you that this time *I* am investigating this business. Anybody would think you had no confidence in me."

"People have been wrongly condemned before now."

"Exactly; simply because I wasn't there."

"I never thought of that."

"Think of it now. You will find it very beautiful and inspiring. It might even help to distinguish me from the other forty-six, if you should happen to mislay my features, or anything. Oh, by the way—I don't positively repel you or anything like that, do I? Because, if I do, I'll take my name off the waiting-list at once."

"No," said Harriet Vane, kindly and a little sadly. "No, you don't repel me."

"I don't remind you of white slugs or make you go gooseflesh all over?"

"Certainly not."

"I'm glad of that. Any minor alterations, like parting the old mane, or growing a tooth-brush, or cashiering the eyeglass, you know, I should be happy to undertake, if it suited your ideas."

"Don't," said Miss Vane, "please don't alter yourself in any particular."

"You really mean that?" Wimsey flushed a little. "I hope it doesn't mean that nothing I could do would make me even passable. I'll come in a different set of garments each time, so as to give you a good all-round idea of the subject. Bunter—my man, you know—will see to that. He has excellent taste in ties, and socks, and things like that. Well, I suppose I ought to be going. You—er—you'll think it over, won't you, if you have a minute to spare. There's no hurry. Only don't hesitate to say if you think you couldn't stick it at any price. I'm not trying to blackmail you into matrimony, you know. I mean, I should investigate this for the fun of the thing, whatever happened, don't you see."

"It's very good of you—"

"No, no, not at all. It's my hobby. Not proposing to people, I don't mean, but investigating things. Well, cheer-frightfully-ho and all that. And I'll call again, if I may."

"I will give the footman orders to admit you," said the prisoner, gravely; "you will always find me at home."

Wimsey walked down the dingy street with a feeling of being almost light-headed.

"I do believe I'll pull it off—she's sore, of course—no wonder, after that rotten brute—but she doesn't feel repelled—one couldn't cope with being repulsive—her skin is like honey—she ought to wear deep red—and old garnets—and lots of rings, rather old-fashioned ones—I could work to make it up to her—she's got a sense of humour too—brains—one wouldn't be dull—one would wake up, and there'd be a whole day for jolly things to happen in—and then one would come home and go to bed—that would be jolly, too—and while she was writing, I could go out and mess round, so we shouldn't either of us be dull—I wonder if Bunter was right about this suit—it's a little dark, I always think, but the line is good—"

He paused before a shop window to get a surreptitious view of his own reflection. A large coloured window-bill caught his eye

GREAT SPECIAL OFFER
ONE MONTH ONLY

"Oh, God!" he said softly, sobered at once. "One month—four weeks—thirty-one days. There isn't much time. And I don't know where to begin."

5

"**W**ell now," said Wimsey, "why do people kill people?"
He was sitting in Miss Katharine Climpson's
private office. The establishment was ostensibly a
typing bureau, and indeed there were three efficient female typists who did very
excellent work for authors and men of science from time to time. Apparently the
business was a large and flourishing one, for work frequently had to be refused
on the ground that the staff was working at full pressure. But on other floors of
the building there were other activities. All the employees were women—mostly
elderly, but a few still young and attractive—and if the private register in the
steel safe had been consulted, it would have been seen that all these women
were of the class unkindly known as "superfluous." There were spinsters with
small fixed incomes, or no income at all; widows without family; women deserted by peripatetic husbands and living on a restricted alimony, who, previous
to their engagement by Miss Climpson, had had no resources but bridge and
boardinghouse gossip. There were retired and disappointed school-teachers; out-
of-work actresses; courageous people who had failed with hatshops and tea-
parlours; and even a few Bright Young Things, for whom the cocktail-party and
the night-club had grown boring. These women seemed to spend most of their
time in answering advertisements. Unmarried gentlemen who desired to meet
ladies possessed of competences, with a view to matrimony; sprightly sex-
agenarians, who wanted housekeepers for remote country districts; ingenious
gentlemen with financial schemes on the look-out for capital; literary gentlemen, anxious for female collaborators; plausible gentlemen about to engage
talent for productions in the provinces; benevolent gentlemen, who could tell
people how to make money in their spare time—gentlemen such as these were
very liable to receive applications from members of Miss Climpson's staff. It
may have been coincidence that these gentlemen so very often had the misfortune to appear shortly afterwards before the magistrate on charges of fraud,
blackmail or attempted procuration, but it is a fact that Miss Climpson's office
boasted a private telephone-line to Scotland Yard, and that few of her ladies
were quite so unprotected as they appeared. It is also a fact that the money
which paid for the rent and upkeep of the premises might, by zealous enquirers,
have been traced to Lord Peter Wimsey's banking account. His lordship was
somewhat reticent about this venture of his, but occasionally, when closeted
with Chief-Inspector Parker or other intimate friends, referred to it as "My
Cattery."

Miss Climpson poured out a cup of tea before replying. She wore a quantity of
little bangles on her spare, lace-covered wrists, and they chinked aggressively
with every movement.

"I really don't know," she said, apparently taking the problem as a psychological one, "it is so *dangerous*, as well as so terribly *wicked*, one wonders that

anybody has the *effrontery* to undertake it. And very often they gain so *little* by it."

"That's what I mean," said Wimsey, "what do they set out to gain? Of course, some people seem to do it for the fun of the thing, like that German female, what's her name, who enjoyed seeing people die."

"Such a *strange* taste," said Miss Climpson. "No sugar, I think?—You know, dear Lord Peter, it has been my melancholy duty to attend *many* death-beds, and though a number of them—such as my dear father's—were *most* Christian and beautiful, I could not call them *fun*. People have very different ideas of fun, of course, and personally I have never greatly cared for George Robey, though Charlie Chaplin always makes me laugh—still, you know, there are *disagreeable details* attending *any* death-bed which one would think could hardly be to anybody's taste, however depraved."

"I quite agree with you," said Wimsey. "But it must be fun, in one sense, to feel that you can control the issues of life and death, don't you know."

"That is an *infringement* upon the prerogative of the Creator," said Miss Climpson.

"But rather jolly to know yourself divine, so to speak. Up above the world so high, like a tea-tray in the sky. I admit the fascination. But for practical purposes that theory is the devil—I beg your pardon, Miss Climpson, respect for sacred personages—I mean, it's unsatisfactory, because it would suit one person just as well as another. If I've got to find a homicidal maniac, I may as well cut my throat at once."

"Don't say *that*," pleaded Miss Climpson, "even in jest. Your work here—so good, so valuable—would be worth living for in spite of the *saddest* personal disappointments. And I have known jokes of that kind turn out very badly, in the most surprising ways. There was a young man we used to know, who was given to talking in a sadly *random* way—a long time ago, dear Lord Peter, while you were still in the nursery, but young men were wild, even then, whatever they say now about the 'eighties—and he said one day to my poor, dear Mother, 'Mrs. Climpson, if I don't make a good bag today, I shall shoot myself' (for he was very fond of sport), and he went out with his gun and as he was getting over a stile, he caught the trigger in the hedge and the gun went off and blew his head to pieces. I was quite a girl, and it upset me *dreadfully*, because he was a very handsome young man, with whiskers which we all admired very much, though today they would be smiled at, and they were burnt *right off* him with the explosion, and a shocking hole in the side of his head, so they said, for of course I was not allowed to see him."

"Poor chap," said his lordship. "Well, let's dismiss homicidal mania from our minds for the moment. What else do people kill people for?"

"There is—passion," said Miss Climpson, with a slight initial hesitation at the word, "for I should not like to call it *love*, when it is so unregulated."

"That is the explanation put forward by the prosecution," said Wimsey. "I don't accept it."

"Certainly not. But—it might be possible, might it not, that there was some other unfortunate young woman who was attached to this Mr. Boyes, and felt vindictively towards him?"

"Yes, or a man who was jealous. But the time is the difficulty. You've got to have some plausible pretext for giving a bloke arsenic. You can't just catch him standing on a doorstep, and say, 'Here, have a drink of this,' can you?"

"But there were ten minutes unaccounted for," said Miss Climpson, shrewdly. "Might he not have entered some public-house for refreshment, and there met an enemy?"

"By jove, that's a possibility." Wimsey made a note, and shook his head dubiously. "But it's rather a coincidence. Unless there was a previous appointment to meet there. Still, it's worth looking into. At any rate, it's obvious that Mr. Urquhart's house and Miss Vane's flat were not the only conceivable places where Boyes might have eaten or drunk between seven and 10:10 that evening. Very well: under the head 'Passion' we find (1) Miss Vane (ruled out ex hypothesi), (2) jealous lover, (3) ditto rival. Place, Public-house (query). Now we go on to the next motive, and that's Money. A very good motive for murdering anybody who has any, but a poor one in Boyes' case. Still, let us say, Money. I can think of three sub-headings for that: (1) Robbery from the person (very improbable); (2) insurance; (3) inheritance."

"What a clear mind you have," said Miss Climpson.

"When I die you will find 'Efficiency' written on my heart. I don't know what money Boyes had on him, but I shouldn't think it was much. Urquhart and Vaughan might know; still, it's not very important, because arsenic isn't a sensible drug to use on anyone you want to rob. It takes a long time, comparatively, to begin business, and it doesn't make the victim helpless enough. Unless we suppose the taxi-driver drugged and robbed him, there was no one who could possibly profit by such a silly crime."

Miss Climpson agreed, and buttered a second teacake.

"Then, insurance. Now we come to the region of the possible. Was Boyes insured? It doesn't seem to have occurred to anybody to find out. Probably he wasn't. Literary blokes have very little forethought, and are careless about trifles like premiums. But one ought to know. Who might have an insurable interest? His father, his cousin (possibly), other relations (if any), his children (if any) and —I suppose—Miss Vane, if he took out the policy while he was living with her. Also, anybody who may have lent him money on the strength of such insurance. Plenty of possibilities there. I'm feeling better already, Miss Climpson, fitter and brighter in every way. Either I'm getting a line on the thing, or else it's your tea. That's a good, stout-looking pot. Has it got any more in it?"

"Yes, indeed," said Miss Climpson, eagerly. "My dear father used to say I was a great hand at getting the *utmost* out of a tea-pot. The secret is to *fill* up as you *go* and never empty the pot completely."

"Inheritance," pursued Lord Peter. "Had he anything to leave? Not much, I shouldn't think. I'd better hop round and see his publisher. Or had he lately come into anything? His father or cousin would know. The father is a parson— 'slashing trade, that,' as the naughty bully says to the new boy in one of Dean Farrar's books. He has a thread-bare look. I shouldn't think there was much money in the family. Still, you never know. Somebody might have left Boyes a fortune for his *beaux yeux* or out of admiration for his books. If so, to whom did Boyes leave it? Query: did he make a will? But surely the defence must have thought of these things. I am getting depressed again."

"Have a sandwich," said Miss Climpson.

"Thank you," said Wimsey, "or some hay. There is nothing like it when you are feeling faint, as the White King truly remarked. Well, that more or less disposes of the money motive. There remains Blackmail."

Miss Climpson, whose professional connection with the Cattery had taught her something about blackmail, assented with a sigh.

"Who was this fellow Boyes?" enquired Wimsey rhetorically. "I know nothing about him. He may have been a blackguard of the deepest dye. He may have known unmentionable things about all his friends. Why not? Or he may have been writing a book to show somebody up, so that he had to be suppressed at all costs. Dash it all, his cousin's a solicitor. Suppose he has been embezzling Trust deeds or something, and Boyes was threatening to split on him? He'd been living in Urquhart's house, and had every opportunity for finding out. Urquhart drops some arsenic into his soup, and—Ah! there's the snag. He puts arsenic into the soup and eats it himself. That's awkward. I'm afraid Hannah Westlock's evidence rather knocks that on the head. We shall have to fall back on the mysterious stranger in the pub."

He considered a little, and then said:

"And there's suicide, of course, which is what I'm really rather inclined to believe in. Arsenic is tomfool stuff to commit suicide with, but it has been done. There was the duc de Praslin, for instance—if his *was* suicide. Only, where's the bottle?"

"The bottle?"

"Well, he must have carried it in something. It might be in a paper, if he took the powdered form, though that would be awkward. Did anybody look for a bottle or paper?"

"Where would they look for it?" asked Miss Climpson.

"That's the rub. If it wasn't on him, it would be anywhere round about Doughty Street, and it's going to be a job looking for a bottle or paper that was chucked away six months ago. I do loathe suicides—they're so difficult to prove. Oh, well, faint heart never won so much as a scrap of paper. Now look here, Miss Climpson. We've got about a month to work this out in. The Michaelmas Term ends on the 21st; this is the 15th. They can't very well bring it up before then, and the Hilary term starts on January 12th. They'll probably take it early, unless we can show reason for delay. Four weeks to get fresh evidence. Will you reserve the best efforts of yourself and the staff? I don't know yet what I shall want, but I shall probably want something done."

"Of course I will, Lord Peter. You know that it is only *too* great a pleasure to do *anything* for you—even if the whole office were not your own property, which it *is*. Only let me know, at *any* minute of the night or day, and I will do my *very* best to help you."

Wimsey thanked her, made a few enquiries about the work of the bureau and departed. He hailed a taxi and was immediately driven to Scotland Yard.

Chief Detective-Inspector Parker was, as usual, delighted to see Lord Peter, but there was a worried expression on his plain though pleasant face as he greeted his visitor.

"What is it, Peter? The Vane case again?"

"Yes. You've come a mucker over this, old man, you really have."

"Well, I don't know. It looked pretty straight-forward to us."

"Charles, acushla, distrust the straight-forward case, the man who looks you straight in the eyes, and the tip straight from the horse's mouth. Only the most guileful deceiver can afford to be so aggressively straight. Even the path of light is curved—or so they tell us. For God's sake, old man, do what you can to put the thing right before next assizes. If you don't, I'll never forgive you. Damn it, you don't *want* to hang the wrong person, do you?—especially a woman and all that."

"Have a fag," said Parker. "You're looking quite wild about the eyes. What have you been doing with yourself? I'm sorry if we've got the wrong pig by the ear, but it's the defence's business to point out where we're wrong, and I can't say they put up a very convincing show."

"No, confound them. Biggy did his best, but that fool and beast Crofts gave him no materials at all. Blast his ugly eyes! I know the brute thinks she did it. I hope he will fry in hell and be served up with cayenne pepper on a red-hot dish!"

"What eloquence!" said Parker, unimpressed. "Anybody would think you'd gone goopy over the girl."

"That's a damned friendly way to talk," said Wimsey, bitterly. "When you went off the deep end about my sister, I may have been unsympathetic—I daresay I was—but I swear I didn't dance on your tenderest feelings and call your manly devotion 'going goopy over a girl.' I don't know where you pick up such expressions, as the clergyman's wife said to the parrot. 'Goopy,' indeed! I never heard anything so vulgar!"

"Good lord," exclaimed Parker, "you don't seriously say—"

"Oh, no!" retorted Wimsey, bitterly. "I'm not expected to be serious. A buffoon, that's what I am. I now know exactly what Jack Point feels like. I used to think the 'Yeomen' sentimental tosh, but it is all too true. Would you like to see me dance in motley?"

"I'm sorry," said Parker, taking his cue rather from the tone than the words. "If it's like that, I'm damned sorry, old man. But what can I do?"

"Now you're talking. Look here—the most likely thing is that this unsavoury blighter Boyes committed suicide. The unspeakable defence haven't been able to trace any arsenic to his possession—but then they probably couldn't trace a herd of black cattle over a snow-bound field in broad noonday with a microscope. I want your people to take it up."

"Boyes—query arsenic," said Parker, making a note on a pad. "Anything else?"

"Yes. Find out if Boyes visited any pub, in the neighbourhood of Doughty Street between say, 9:50 and 10:10 on the night of Jan. 20th—if he met anybody, and what he took to drink."

"It shall be done. Boyes—query pub." Parker made another note. "Yes?"

"Thirdly, if any bottle or paper that might have contained arsenic was picked up in that district."

"Oh, indeed? And would you like me to trace the 'bus ticket dropped by Mrs. Brown outside Selfridge's in the last Christmas rush? No use making it too easy."

"A bottle is more likely than a paper," went on Wimsey, ignoring him, "because I think the arsenic must have been taken in liquid form to work so quickly."

Parker made no further protest, but noted down "Boyes—Doughty Street— query bottle," and paused expectantly.

"Yes?"

"That's all for the moment. By the way, I should try the garden in Mecklenburgh Square. A thing might lie quite a long time under those bushes."

"Very well. I'll do my best. And if you find out anything which really proves that we've been on the wrong tack, you'll let us know, won't you? We don't want to make large and ignominious public mistakes."

"Well—I've just earnestly promised the defence that I'll do no such thing. But if I spot the criminal, I'll let you arrest him."

"Thanks for small mercies. Well, good luck! Funny for you and me to be on opposite sides, isn't it?"

"Very," said Wimsey. "I'm sorry about it, but it's your own fault."

"You shouldn't have been out of England. By the way—"

"Yes?"

"You realise that probably all our young friend did during those missing ten minutes was to stand about in Theobalds Road or somewhere, looking for a stray taxi."

"Oh, shut up!" said Wimsey, crossly, and went out.

6

The next day dawned bright and fair, and Wimsey felt a certain exhilaration as he purred down to Tweedling Parva. "Mrs. Merdle" the car, so called because, like that celebrated lady, she was averse to "row," was sparking merrily on all twelve cylinders, and there was a touch of frost in the air. These things conduce to high spirits.

Wimsey reached his destination about 10 o'clock, and was directed to the vicarage, one of those large, rambling and unnecessary structures which swallow the incumbent's income during his life and land his survivors with a heavy bill for dilapidations as soon as he is dead.

The Rev. Arthur Boyes was at home, and would be happy to see Lord Peter Wimsey.

The clergyman was a tall, faded man, with lines of worry deeply engraved upon his face, and mild blue eyes a little bewildered by the disappointing difficulty of things in general. His black coat was old, and hung in depressed folds from his stooping, narrow shoulders. He gave Wimsey a thin hand and begged him to be seated.

Lord Peter found it a little difficult to explain his errand. His name evidently aroused no associations in the mind of this gentle and unworldly parson. He decided not to mention his hobby of criminal investigation, but to represent himself, with equal truth, as a friend of the prisoner's. That might be painful, but it would be at least intelligible. Accordingly, he began, with some hesitation:

"I'm fearfully sorry to trouble you, especially as it's all so very distressin' and all that, but it's about the death of your son, and the trial and so on. Please don't think I'm wanting to make an interfering nuisance of myself, but I'm deeply interested—personally interested. You see, I know Miss Vane—I—in fact I like

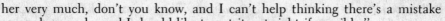
her very much, don't you know, and I can't help thinking there's a mistake somewhere and—and I should like to get it put right if possible."

"Oh—oh, yes!" said Mr. Boyes. He carefully polished a pair of pince-nez and balanced them on his nose, where they sat crookedly. He peered at Wimsey and seemed not to dislike what he saw, for he went on:

"Poor misguided girl! I assure you, I have no vindictive feelings—that is to say, nobody would be more happy than myself to know that she was innocent of this dreadful thing. Indeed, Lord Peter, even if she were guilty, it would give me great pain to see her suffer the penalty. Whatever we do, we cannot bring back the dead to life, and one would infinitely prefer to leave all vengeance in the hand of Him to whom it belongs. Certainly, nothing could be more terrible than to take the life of an innocent person. It would haunt me to the end of my days if I thought there were the least likelihood of it. And I confess that, when I saw Miss Vane in court, I had grievous doubts whether the police had done rightly in accusing her."

"Thank you," said Wimsey, "It is very kind of you to say that. It makes the job much easier. Excuse me, you say, 'when you saw her in court.' You hadn't met her previously?"

"No. I knew, of course, that my unhappy son had formed an illicit connection with a young woman, but—I could not bring myself to see her—and indeed, I believe that she, with very proper feeling, refused to allow Philip to bring her into contact with any of his relations. Lord Peter, you are a younger man than I am, you belong to my son's generation, and you will perhaps understand that—though he was not bad, not depraved, I will never think that—yet somehow there was not that full confidence between us which there should be between father and son. No doubt I was much to blame. If only his mother had lived—"

"My dear sir," mumbled Wimsey, "I perfectly understand. It often happens. In fact, it's continually happening. The post-war generation and so on. Lots of people go off the rails a bit—no real harm in 'em at all. Just can't see eye to eye with the older people. It generally wears off in time. Nobody really to blame. Wild oats and, er, all that sort of thing."

"I could not approve," said Mr. Boyes, sadly, "of ideas so opposed to religion and morality—perhaps I spoke my mind too openly. If I had sympathised more—"

"It can't be done," said Wimsey. "People have to work it out for themselves. And, when they write books and so on, and get into that set of people, they tend to express themselves rather noisily, if you see what I mean."

"Maybe, maybe. But I reproach myself. Still, this does not help you at all. Forgive me. If there is any mistake and the jury were evidently not satisfied, we must use all our endeavours to put it right. How can I assist?"

"Well, first of all," said Wimsey, "and I'm afraid this is rather a hateful question, did your son ever say anything, or write anything to you which might lead you to think that he—was tired of his life or anything of that kind? I'm sorry."

"No, no—not at all. I was, of course, asked the same question by the police and by the counsel for the defence. I can truly say that such an idea never occurred to me. There was nothing at all to suggest it."

"Not even when he parted company with Miss Vane?"

"Not even then. In fact, I gathered that he was rather more angry than despondent. I must say that it was a surprise to me to hear that, after all that had passed between them, she was unwilling to marry him. I still fail to comprehend it. Her refusal must have come as a great shock to him. He wrote so cheerfully to me about it beforehand. Perhaps you remember the letter?" He fumbled in an untidy drawer. "I have it here, if you would like to look at it."

"If you would just read the passage, sir," suggested Wimsey.

"Yes, oh certainly. Let me see. Yes. 'Your morality will be pleased to hear, Dad, that I have determined to regularise the situation, as the good people say.' He had a careless way of speaking and writing sometimes, poor boy, which doesn't do justice to his good heart. Dear me. Yes. 'My young woman is a good little soul, and I have made up my mind to do the thing properly. She really deserves it, and I hope that when everything is made respectable, you will extend your paternal recognition to her. I won't ask you to officiate—as you know, the registrar's office is more in my line, and though she was brought up in the odour of sanctity, like myself, I don't think she will insist on the Voice that Breathed o'er Eden. I will let you know when it's to be, so that you can come and give us your blessing (quâ father if not quâ parson) if you should feel so disposed.' You see, Lord Peter, he quite meant to do the right thing, and I was touched that he should wish for my presence."

"Quite so," said Lord Peter, and thought, "If only that young man were alive, how dearly I should love to kick his bottom for him."

"Well, then there is another letter, saying that the marriage had fallen through. Here it is. 'Dear Dad—sorry, but I'm afraid your congratulations must be returned with thanks. The wedding is off, and the bride has run away. There's no need to go into the story. Harriet has succeeded in making a fool of herself and me, so there's no more to be said.' Then later I heard that he had not been feeling well—but all that you know already."

"Did he suggest any reason for these illnesses of his?"

"Oh, no—we took it for granted that it was a recurrence of the old gastric trouble. He was never a very robust lad. He wrote in very hopeful mood from Harlech, saying that he was much better, and mentioning his plan of a voyage to Barbados."

"He did?"

"Yes. I thought it would do him a great deal of good, and take his mind off other things. He spoke of it only as a vague project, not as though anything were settled."

"Did he say anything more about Miss Vane?"

"He never mentioned her name to me again until he lay dying."

"Yes—and what did you think of what he said then?"

"I don't know what to think. We had no idea of any poisoning then, naturally, and I fancied it must refer to the quarrel between them that had caused the separation."

"I see. Well now, Mr. Boyes. Supposing it was not self-destruction—"

"I really do not think it could have been."

"Now is there anybody else at all who could have an interest in his death?"

"Who could there be?"

"No—no other woman, for instance?"

"I never heard of any. And I think I should have done. He was not secretive about these things, Lord Peter. He was remarkably open and straightforward."

"Yes," commented Wimsey internally, "like to swagger about it, I suppose.

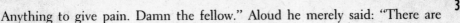
Anything to give pain. Damn the fellow." Aloud he merely said: "There are other possibilities. Did he, for instance, make a will?"

"He did. Not that he had much to leave, poor boy. His books were very cleverly written—he had a fine intellect, Lord Peter—but they did not bring him in any great sums of money. I helped him with a little allowance, and he managed on that and on what he made from his articles in the periodicals."

"He left his copyrights to somebody, though, I take it?"

"Yes. He wished to leave them to me, but I was obliged to tell him that I could not accept the bequest. You see, I did not approve of his opinions, and I should not have thought it right to profit by them. No; he left them to his friend Mr. Vaughan."

"Oh!—may I ask when this will was made?"

"It is dated at the period of his visit to Wales. I believe that before that he had made one leaving everything to Miss Vane."

"Indeed!" said Wimsey. "I suppose she knew about it." His mind reviewed a number of contradictory possibilities, and he added: "But it would not amount to an important sum, in any case?"

"Oh, no. If my son made £50 a year by his books, that was the utmost. Though they tell me," added the old gentleman with a sad smile, "that, after this, his new book will do better."

"Very likely," said Wimsey. "Provided you get into the papers, the delightful reading public don't mind what it's for. Still—Well, that's that. I gather he would have no private money to leave?"

"Nothing whatever. There has never been any money in our family, Lord Peter, nor yet in my wife's. We're quite the proverbial Church mice." He smiled faintly at this little clerical jest. "Except, I suppose, for Cremorna Garden."

"For—I beg your pardon?"

"My wife's aunt, the notorious Cremorna Garden of the 'sixties."

"Good lord, yes—the actress?"

"Yes. But she, of course, was never, never mentioned. One did not enquire into the way she got her money. No worse than others, I dare say—but in those days we were very easily shocked. We have seen and heard nothing of her for well over fifty years. I believe she is quite childish now."

"By jove! I'd no idea she was still alive!"

"Yes, I believe she is, though she must be well over ninety. Certainly Philip never had any money from her."

"Well, that rules money out. Was your son's life insured, by any chance?"

"Not that I ever heard of. We found no policy among his papers, and so far as I know, nobody has made any claim."

"He left no debts?"

"Only trifling ones—tradesmen's accounts and so on. Perhaps fifty pounds' worth altogether."

"Thank you so much," said Wimsey, rising, "that has cleared the ground a good deal."

"I am afraid it has not got you much farther."

"It tells me where not to look, at any rate," said Wimsey, "and that all saves time, you know. It's frightfully decent of you to be bothered with me."

"Not at all. Ask me anything you want to know. Nobody would be more glad than myself to see that unfortunate young woman cleared."

Wimsey again thanked him and took his leave. He was a mile up the road before a regretful thought overtook him. He turned Mrs. Merdle's bonnet round, skimmed back to the church, stuffed a handful of treasury notes with some difficulty into the mouth of a box labelled "Church expenses," and resumed his way to town.

As he manoeuvred the car through the City, a thought struck him, and instead of heading for Piccadilly, where he lived, he turned off into a street south of the Strand, in which was situated the establishment of Messrs. Grimsby & Cole, who published the works of Mr. Philip Boyes. After a little delay, he was shown into Mr. Cole's office.

Mr. Cole was a stout and cheerful person, and was much interested to hear that the notorious Lord Peter Wimsey was concerning himself with the affairs of the equally notorious Mr. Boyes. Wimsey represented that, as a collector of First Editions, he would be glad to secure copies of all Philip Boyes' works. Mr. Cole regretted extremely that he could not help him, and, under the influence of an expensive cigar, became quite confidential.

"Without wishing to seem callous, my dear Lord Peter," he said, throwing himself back in his chair, and creasing his three chins into six or seven as he did so, "between you and me, Mr. Boyes could not have done better for himself than to go and get murdered like this. Every copy was sold out a week after the result of the exhumation became known, two large editions of his last book were disposed of before the trial came on—at the original price of 7/6, and the libraries clamoured so for the early volumes that we had to reprint the lot. Unfortunately we had not kept the type standing, and the printers had to work night and day, but we did it. We are rushing the three-and-sixpennies through the binders' now, and the shilling edition is arranged for. Positively, I don't think you could get a First Edition in London for love or money. We have nothing here but our own file copies, but we are putting out a special memorial edition, with portraits, on hand-made paper, limited and numbered, at a guinea. Not the same thing of course, but—"

Wimsey begged to put his name down for a set at a guinea a-piece, adding:

"Sad and all that, don't you know, that the author can't benefit by it, what?"

"Deeply distressing," agreed Mr. Cole, compressing his fat cheeks by two longitudinal folds from the nostril to the mouth. "And sadder still that there can be no more work to come from him. A very talented young man, Lord Peter. We shall always feel a melancholy pride, Mr. Grimsby and myself, in knowing that we recognised his quality, before there was any likelihood of financial remuneration. A *succès d'estime*, that was all, until this very grievous occurrence. But when the work is good, it is not our habit to boggle about monetary returns."

"Ah, well!" said Wimsey, "it sometimes pays to cast your bread upon the waters. Quite religious, isn't it—you know, the bit about 'plenteously bringing out good works may of thee be plenteously rewarded.' Twenty-fifth after Trinity."

"Quite," said Mr. Cole, with a certain lack of enthusiasm, possibly because he was imperfectly acquainted with the book of Common Prayer, or possibly because he detected a hint of mockery in the other's tone. "Well, I have very much enjoyed this chat. I am sorry I can do nothing for you about First Editions."

Wimsey begged him not to mention it, and with a cordial farewell ran hastily down the stairs.

His next visit was to the office of Mr. Challoner, Harriet Vane's agent.

Challoner was an abrupt, dark, militant-looking little man, with untidy hair and thick spectacles.

"Boom?" said he, when Wimsey had introduced himself and mentioned his interest in Miss Vane. "Yes, of course there is a boom. Rather disgusting, really, but one can't help that. We have to do our best for our client, whatever the circumstances. Miss Vane's books have always sold reasonably well—round about the three or four thousand mark in this country—but of course this business has stimulated things enormously. The last book has gone to three new editions, and the new one has sold seven thousand before publication."

"Financially, all to the good, eh?"

"Oh, yes—but frankly I don't know whether these artificial sales do very much good to an author's reputation in the long run. Up like a rocket, down like the stick, you know. When Miss Vane is released—"

"I am glad you say 'when.'"

"I am not allowing myself to contemplate any other possibility. But *when* that happens, public interest will be liable to die down very quickly. I am, of course, securing the most advantageous contracts I possibly can at the moment, to cover the next three or four books, but I can only really control the advances. The actual receipts will depend on the sales, and that is where I foresee a slump. I am, however, doing well with serial rights, which are important from the point of view of immediate returns."

"On the whole, as a business man, you are not altogether glad that this has happened?"

"Taking the long view, I am not. Personally, I need not say that I am extremely grieved, and feel quite positive that there is some mistake."

"That's my idea," said Wimsey.

"From what I know of your lordship, I may say your interest and assistance are the best stroke of luck Miss Vane could have had."

"Oh, thanks—thanks very much. I say—this arsenic book—you couldn't let me have a squint at it, I suppose?"

"Certainly, if it would help you." He touched a bell. "Miss Warburton, bring me a set of galleys of 'Death in the Pot.' Trufoot's are pushing publication as fast as possible. The book was still unfinished when the arrest took place. With rare energy and courage, Miss Vane has put the finishing touches and corrected the proofs herself. Of course, everything had to go through the hands of the prison authorities. However, we were anxious to conceal nothing. She certainly knows all about arsenic, poor girl. These are complete, are they, Miss Warburton? Here you are. Is there anything else?"

"Only one thing. What do you think of Messrs. Grimsby & Cole?"

"I never contemplate them," said Mr. Challoner. "Not thinking of doing anything with them, are you, Lord Peter?"

"Well, I don't know that I am—seriously."

"If you do, read your contract carefully. I won't say, bring it to us—"

"If ever I do publish with Grimsby & Cole," said Lord Peter, "I'll promise to do it through you."

7

Lord Peter Wimsey almost bounced into Holloway Prison next morning. Harriet Vane greeted him with a kind of rueful smile.

"So you've reappeared?"

"Good lord, yes! Surely you expected me to. I fancied I'd left that impression. I say—I've thought of a good plot for a detective story."

"Really?"

"Top-hole. You know, the sort people bring out and say, 'I've often thought of doing it myself, if I could only find time to sit down and write it.' I gather that sitting down is all that is necessary for producing masterpieces. Just a moment, though. I must get through my business first. Let me see—" He made believe to consult a notebook. "Ah, yes? Do you happen to know whether Philip Boyes made a will?"

"I believe he did, when we were living together."

"In whose favour?"

"Oh, in mine. Not that he had much to leave, poor man. It was chiefly that he wanted a literary executor."

"Are you, in point of fact, his executrix now?"

"Good heavens! I never thought of that. I took it for granted he would have altered it when we parted. I think he must have, or I should have heard about it when he died, shouldn't I?"

She looked candidly at him, and Wimsey felt a little uncomfortable.

"You didn't *know* he had altered it, then? Before he died, I mean?"

"I never thought a word more about it, as a matter of fact. If I had thought—of course I should have assumed it. Why?"

"Nothing," said Wimsey. "Only I'm rather glad the will wasn't brought up at the thingummy bob."

"Meaning the trial? You needn't be so delicate about mentioning it. You mean, if I had thought I was still his heir, I might have murdered him for his money. But it didn't amount to a hill of beans, you know. I was making four times as much as he was."

"Oh, yes. It was only this silly plot I'd got in my mind. But it *is* rather silly, now I come to think of it."

"Tell me."

"Well, you see—" Wimsey choked a little, and then rattled his idea out with an exaggerated lightness.

"Well—it's about a girl (or a man would do, but we'll call it a girl) who writes novels—crime stories, in fact. And she has a—a friend who also writes. Neither of them best-sellers, you see, but just ordinary novelists."

"Yes? That's a kind of thing that might happen."

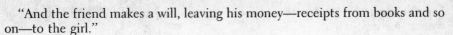
"And the friend makes a will, leaving his money—receipts from books and so on—to the girl."

"I see."

"And the girl—who has got rather fed up with him, you know, thinks of a grand scoop, that will make both of them best-sellers."

"Oh, yes?"

"Yes. She polishes him off by the same method she has used in her latest crime-thriller."

"A daring stroke," said Miss Vane, with grave approval.

"Yes. And of course, his books immediately become best-sellers. And she grabs the pool."

"That's really ingenious. An entirely new motive for murder—the thing I've been looking for for years. But don't you think it would be a little dangerous? She might even be suspected of the murder."

"Then *her* books would become best-sellers, too."

"How true that is! But possibly she wouldn't live to enjoy the profits."

"That, of course," said Wimsey, "is the snag."

"Because, unless she were suspected and arrested and tried, the scoop would only half come off."

"There you are," said Wimsey. "But, as an experienced mystery-monger, couldn't you think of a way round that?"

"I daresay. She might prove an ingenious alibi, for instance. Or, if she were very wicked, manage to push the blame on somebody else. Or lead people to suppose that her friend had made away with himself."

"Too vague," said Wimsey. "How would she do that?"

"I can't say, off-hand. I'll give it careful thought and let you know. Or—here's an idea!"

"Yes?"

"She is a person with a monomania—no, no—not a homicidal one. That's dull, and not really fair to the reader. But there is somebody she wishes to benefit—somebody, say a father, mother, sister, lover or cause, that badly needs money. She makes a will in his, her or its favour, and lets herself be hanged for the crime, knowing that the beloved object will then come in for the money. How's that?"

"Great!" cried Wimsey, carried away. "Only—wait a minute. They wouldn't give her the friend's money, would they? You're not allowed to profit by a crime."

"Oh, hang! That's true. It would only be her own money, then. She could make that over by a deed of gift. Yes—look! If she did that immediately after the murder—a deed of gift of everything she possessed—that would include every-thing she came into under the friend's will. It would then all go direct to the beloved object, and I don't believe the law could stop it!"

She faced him with dancing eyes.

"See here," said Wimsey. "You're not safe. You're too clever by half. But I say, it's a good plot, isn't it?"

"It's a winner! Shall we write it?"

"By jove, let's!"

"Only, you know, I'm afraid we shan't get the chance."

"You're not to say that. Of course we're going to write it. Damn it, what am I here for? Even if I could be reconciled to losing you, I couldn't lose the chance of writing my best-seller!"

"But what you've done so far is to provide me with a very convincing motive for murder. I don't know that that's going to help us a great lot."

"What I've done," said Wimsey, "is to prove that that was not the motive, anyway."

"Why?"

"You wouldn't have told me if it had been. You would have gently led me away from the subject. And besides—"

"Well?"

"Well, I've seen Mr. Cole of Grimsby & Cole, and I know who is going to get the major part of Philip Boyes' profits. And I don't somehow fancy that he is the beloved object."

"No?" said Miss Vane, "and why not? Don't you know that I passionately dote on every chin on his face?"

"If it's chins you admire," said Wimsey, "I will try to grow some, though it will be rather hard work. Anyway, keep smiling—it suits you."

"It's all very well, though," he thought to himself, when the gates had closed behind him. "Bright back-chat cheers the patient, but gets us no forrarder. How about this fellow Urquhart? He looked all right in court, but you never can tell. I think I'd better pop round and see him."

He presented himself accordingly in Woburn Square, but was disappointed. Mr. Urquhart had been called away to a sick relative. It was not Hannah Westlock who answered the door, but a stout elderly woman, whom Wimsey supposed to be the cook. He would have liked to question her, but felt that Mr. Urquhart would hardly receive him well if he discovered that his servants had been pumped behind his back. He therefore contented himself with enquiring how long Mr. Urquhart was likely to be away.

"I couldn't rightly say, sir. I understand it depends how the sick lady gets on. If she gets over it, he'll be back at once, for I know he is very busy just now. If she should pass away, he would be engaged some time, with settling up the estate."

"I see," said Wimsey. "It's a bit awkward, because I wanted to speak to him rather urgently. You couldn't give me his address, by any chance?"

"Well, sir, I don't rightly know if Mr. Urquhart would wish it. If it's a matter of business, sir, they could give you information at his office in Bedford Row."

"Thanks very much," said Wimsey, noting down the number. "I'll call there. Possibly they'd be able to do what I want without bothering him."

"Yes, sir. Who should I say called?"

Wimsey handed over his card, writing at the top, "In re R. v. Vane," and added:

"But there is a chance he may be back quite soon?"

"Oh, yes, sir. Last time he wasn't away more than a couple of days, and a merciful providence I am sure that was, with poor Mr. Boyes dying in that dreadful manner."

"Yes, indeed," said Wimsey, delighted to find the subject introducing itself of its own accord. "That must have been a shocking upset for you all."

"Well there," said the cook, "I don't hardly like to think of it, even now. A gentleman dying in the house like that, and poisoned too, when one's had the cooking of his dinner—it do seem to bring it home to one, like."

"It wasn't the dinner that was at fault, anyway," said Wimsey, genially.

"Oh, dear, no, sir—we proved that most careful. Not that any accident could happen in my kitchen—I should like to see it! But people do say such things if they get half a chance. Still, there wasn't a thing ate but master and Hannah and I had some of it, and very thankful I was for that, I needn't tell you."

"You must be; I am sure." Wimsey was framing a further enquiry, when the violent ringing of the area bell interrupted them.

"There's that butcher," said the cook, "you'll excuse me, sir. The parlour-maid's in bed with the influenza, and I'm single-handed this morning. I'll tell Mr. Urquhart you called."

She shut the door, and Wimsey departed for Bedford Row, where he was received by an elderly clerk, who made no difficulty about supplying Mr. Urquhart's address.

"Here it is, my lord. Care of Mrs. Wrayburn, Applefold, Windle, Westmorland. But I shouldn't think he would be very long away. In the meantime, could we do anything for you?"

"No, thanks. I rather wanted to see him personally, don't you know. As a matter of fact, it's about that very sad death of his cousin, Mr. Philip Boyes."

"Indeed, my lord? Shocking affair, that. Mr. Urquhart was greatly upset, with it happening in his own house. A very fine young man, was Mr. Boyes. He and Mr. Urquhart were great friends, and he took it greatly to heart. Were you present at the trial, my lord?"

"Yes. What did you think of the verdict?"

The clerk pursed up his lips.

"I don't mind saying I was surprised. It seemed to me a very clear case. But juries are very unreliable, especially nowadays, with women on them. We see a good deal of the fair sex in this profession," said the clerk, with a sly smile, "and very few of them are remarkable for possessing the legal mind."

"How true that is," said Wimsey. "If it wasn't for them, though, there'd be much less litigation, so it's all good for business."

"Ha, ha! Very good, my lord. Well, we have to take things as they come, but in my opinion—I'm an old-fashioned man—the ladies were most adorable when they adorned and inspired and did not take an active part in affairs. Here's our young lady clerk—I don't say she wasn't a good worker—but a whim comes over her and away she goes to get married, leaving me in the lurch, just when Mr. Urquhart is away. Now, with a young man, marriage steadies him, and makes him stick closer to his job, but with a young woman, it's the other way about. It's right she should get married, but it's inconvenient, and in a solicitor's office one can't get temporary assistance very well. Some of the work is confidential, of course, and in any case, an atmosphere of permanence is desirable."

Wimsey sympathised with the head-clerk's grievance, and bade him an affable good-morning. There is a telephone box in Bedford Row, and he darted into it and immediately rang up Miss Climpson.

"Lord Peter Wimsey speaking—oh, hullo, Miss Climpson! How is everything? All bright and beautiful? Good!—Yes, now listen. There's a vacancy for a confidential female clerk at Mr. Norman Urquhart's, the solicitor's in Bedford Row—Have you got anybody?—Oh, good!—Yes, send them all along—I particularly want to get someone in there—Oh, no! no special enquiry—just to pick up any gossip about the Vane business—Yes, pick out the steadiest-looking, not too much face-powder, and see that their skirts are the regulation four inches below the knee—the head-clerk's in charge, and the last girl left to be married, so he's feeling anti-sex-appeal. Right ho! Get her in and I'll give her her instructions. Bless you, may your shadow never grow bulkier!"

8

"**B**unter!"

"My lord?"

Wimsey tapped with his fingers a letter he had just received.

"Do you feel at your brightest and most truly fascinating? Does a livelier iris, winter weather notwithstanding, shine upon the burnished Bunter? Have you got that sort of conquering feeling? The Don Juan touch, so to speak?"

Bunter, balancing the breakfast tray on his fingers, coughed deprecatingly.

"You have a good, upstanding, impressive figure, if I may say so," pursued Wimsey, "a bold and roving eye when off duty, a ready tongue, Bunter—and, I am persuaded, you have a way with you. What more should any cook or house-parlour-maid want?"

"I am always happy," replied Bunter, "to exert myself to the best of my capacity in your lordship's service."

"I am aware of it," admitted his lordship. "Again and again I say to myself, Wimsey, this cannot last. One of these days this worthy man will cast off the yoke of servitude and settle down in a pub, or something, but nothing happens. Still, morning by morning, my coffee is brought, my bath is prepared, my razor laid out, my ties and socks sorted and my bacon and eggs brought to me in a lordly dish. No matter. This time I demand a more perilous devotion—perilous for us both, my Bunter, for if you were to be carried away, a helpless martyr to matrimony, who then would bring my coffee, prepare my bath, lay out my razor and perform all those other sacrificial rites? And yet—"

"Who is the party, my lord?"

"There are two of them, Bunter, two ladies lived in a bower, Binnorie, O Binnorie! The parlourmaid you have seen. Her name is Hannah Westlock. A woman in her thirties, I fancy and not ill-favored. The other, the cook—I cannot lisp the tender syllables of her name, for I do not know it, but doubtless it is Gertrude, Cecily, Magdalen, Margaret, Rosalys or some other sweet symphonious sound—a fine woman, Bunter, on the mature side, perhaps, but none the worse for that."

"Certainly not, my lord. If I may say so, the woman of ripe years and queenly figure is frequently more susceptible to delicate attentions than the giddy and thoughtless young beauty."

"True. Let us suppose, Bunter, that you were to be the bearer of a courteous missive to one Mr. Norman Urquhart of Woburn Square. Could you, in the short space of time at your disposal, insinuate yourself, snakelike, as it were, into the bosom of the household?"

"If you desire it, my lord, I will endeavour to insinuate myself to your lordship's satisfaction."

"Noble fellow. In case of an action for breach, or any consequence of that description, the charges will, of course, be borne by the management."

"I am obliged to your lordship. When would your lordship wish me to commence?"

"As soon as I have written a note to Mr. Urquhart. I will ring."

"Very good, my lord."

Wimsey moved over to the writing-desk. After a few moments he looked up, a little peevishly.

"Bunter, I have a sensation of being hovered over. I do not like it. It is unusual and it unnerves me. I implore you not to hover. Is the proposition distasteful, or do you want me to get a new hat? What is troubling your conscience?"

"I beg your lordship's pardon. It had occurred to my mind to ask your lordship, with every respect——"

"Oh, God, Bunter—don't break it gently. I can't bear it. Stab and end the creature—to the heft! What is it?"

"I wished to ask you, my lord, whether your lordship thought of making any changes in your establishment?"

Wimsey laid down his pen and stared at the man.

"Changes, Bunter? When I have just so eloquently expressed to you my undying attachment to the loved routine of coffee, bath, razor, socks, eggs and bacon and the old, familiar faces? You're not giving me warning, are you?"

"No, indeed, my lord. I should be very sorry to leave your lordship's service. But I had thought it possible that, if your lordship was about to contract new ties——"

"I *knew* it was something in the haberdashery line! By all means, Bunter, if you think it necessary. Had you any particular pattern in mind?"

"Your lordship misunderstands me. I referred to domestic ties, my lord. Sometimes, when a gentleman reorganizes his household on a matrimonial basis, the lady may prefer to have a voice in the selection of the gentleman's personal attendant, in which case——"

"Bunter!" said Wimsey, considerably startled, "may I ask where you have contracted these ideas?"

"I ventured to draw an inference, my lord."

"This comes of training people to be detectives. Have I been nourishing a sleuth-hound on my own hearth-stone? May I ask if you have gone so far as to give a name to the lady?"

"Yes, my lord."

There was a pause.

"Well?" said Wimsey, in a rather subdued tone, "what about it, Bunter?"

"A very agreeable lady, if I may say so, my lord."

"It strikes you that way, does it? The circumstances are unusual, of course."

"Yes, my lord. I might perhaps make so bold as to call them romantic."

"You may make so bold as to call them damnable, Bunter."

"Yes, my lord," said Bunter, in a tone of sympathy.

"You won't desert the ship, Bunter?"

"Not on any account, my lord."

"Then don't come frightening me again. My nerves are not what they were. Here is the note. Take it round and do your best."

"Very good, my lord."

"Oh, and Bunter."

"My lord?"

"It seems that I am being obvious. I have no wish to be anything of the kind. If you see me being obvious, will you drop me a hint?"

"Certainly, my lord."

Bunter faded gently out, and Wimsey stepped anxiously to the mirror.

"I can't see anything," he said to himself. "No lily on my cheek with anguish moist and fever-dew. I suppose, though, it's hopeless to try and deceive Bunter. Never mind. Business must come first. I've stopped one, two, three, four earths. What next? How about this fellow Vaughan?"

When Wimsey had any researches to do in Bohemia, it was his custom to enlist the help of Miss Marjorie Phelps. She made figurines in porcelain for a living, and was therefore usually to be found either in her studio or in some one else's studio. A telephone-call at 10 a.m. would probably catch her scrambling eggs over her own gas-stove. It was true that there had been passages, about the time of the Bellona Club affair,* between her and Lord Peter which made it a little embarrassing and unkind to bring her in on the subject of Harriet Vane, but with so little time in which to pick and choose his tools, Wimsey was past worrying about gentlemanly scruples. He put the call through and was relieved to hear an answering "Hullo!"

"Hullo, Marjorie! This is Peter Wimsey. How goes it?"

"Oh, fine, thanks. Glad to hear your melodious voice again. What can I do for the Lord High Investigator?"

"Do you know one Vaughan, who is mixed up in the Philip Boyes murder mystery?"

"Oh, Peter! Are you on to that? How gorgeous! Which side are you taking?"

"For the defence."

"Hurray!"

"Why this pomp of jubilee?"

"Well, it's much more exciting and difficult, isn't it?"

"I'm afraid it is. Do you know Miss Vane, by the way?"

"Yes and no. I've seen her with the Boyes-Vaughan crowd."

"Like her?"

"So-so."

"Like him? Boyes, I mean?"

"Never stirred a heart-beat."

"I said, did you like him?"

"One didn't. One either fell for him or not. He wasn't the merry bright-eyed pal of the period, you know."

"Oh! What's Vaughan?"

"Hanger-on."

"Oh?"

---

* See *The Unpleasantness at the Bellona Club*

"House-dog. Nothing must interfere with the expansion of my friend the genius. That sort."

"Oh!"

"Don't keep saying, 'Oh!' Do you want to meet the man Vaughan?"

"If it's not too much trouble."

"Well, turn up to-night with a taxi and we'll go the rounds. We're certain to drop across him somewhere. Also the rival gang, if you want them—Harriet Vane's supporters."

"Those girls who gave evidence?"

"Yes. You'll like Eiluned Price, I think. She scorns everything in trousers, but she's a good friend at a pinch."

"I'll come, Marjorie. Will you dine with me?"

"Peter, I'd adore to, but I don't think I will. I've got an awful lot to do."

"Right-ho! I'll roll round about nine, then."

Accordingly, at 9 o'clock, Wimsey found himself in a taxi with Marjorie Phelps, headed for a round of the studios.

"I've been doing some intensive telephoning," said Marjorie, "and I think we shall find him at the Kropotkys'. They are pro-Boyes, Bolshevik and musical, and their drinks are bad, but their Russian tea is safe. Does the taxi wait?"

"Yes; it sounds as if we might want to beat a retreat."

"Well, it's nice to be rich. It's down the court here, on the right, over the Petrovitchs' stable. Better let me grope first."

They stumbled up a narrow and encumbered stair, at the top of which a fine confused noise of a piano, strings and the clashing of kitchen utensils announced that some sort of entertainment was in progress.

Marjorie hammered loudly on a door, and, without waiting for an answer, flung it open. Wimsey, entering on her heels, was struck in the face, as by an open hand, by a thick muffling wave of heat, sound, smoke and the smell of frying.

It was a very small room, dimly lit by a single electric bulb, smothered in a lantern of painted glass, and it was packed to suffocation with people, whose silk legs, bare arms and pallid faces loomed at him like glow-worms out of the obscurity. Coiling wreaths of tobacco-smoke swam slowly to and fro in the midst. In one corner an anthracite stove, glowing red and mephitical, vied with a roaring gas-oven in another corner to raise the atmosphere to roasting-pitch. On the stove stood a vast and steaming kettle; on a side-table stood a vast and steaming samovar; over the gas, a dim figure stood turning sausages in a pan with a fork, while an assistant attended to something in the oven, which Wimsey, whose nose was selective, identified among the other fragrant elements in this compound atmosphere, and identified rightly, as kippers. At the piano, which stood just inside the door, a young man with bushy red hair was playing something of a Czecho-Slovakian flavour, to a violin obligato by an extremely loose-jointed person of indeterminate sex in a Fair-Isle jumper. Nobody looked round at their entrance. Marjorie picked her way over the scattered limbs on the floor and, selecting a lean young woman in red, bawled into her ear. The young woman nodded and beckoned to Wimsey. He negotiated a passage and was introduced to the lean woman by the simple formula: "Here's Peter—this is Nina Kropotky."

"So pleased," shouted Madame Kropotky through the clamour. "Sit by me. Vanya will get you something to drink. It is beautiful, yes? That is Stanislas—

such a genius—his new work on the Piccadilly Tube Station—great, n'est-ce-pas? Five days he was continually travelling upon the escalator to absorb the tone-values."

"Colossal!" yelled Wimsey.

"So—you think? Ah! You can appreciate! You understand it is really for the big orchestra. On the piano it is nothing. It needs the brass, the effects, the timpani-b'rrrrrrr! So! But one seizes the form, the outline! Ah! it finishes! Superb! Magnificent!"

The enormous clatter ceased. The pianist mopped his face and glared haggardly round. The violinist put down its instrument and stood up, revealing itself, by its legs, to be female. The room exploded into conversation. Madame Kropotky leapt over her seated guests and embraced the perspiring Stanislas on both cheeks. The frying-pan was lifted from the stove in a fusillade of spitting fat, a shriek went up for 'Vanya' and presently a cadaverous face was pushed down to Wimsey's, and a deep guttural voice barked at him: "What will you drink?" while simultaneously a plate of kippers came hovering perilously over his shoulder.

"Thanks," said Wimsey, "I have just dined—just *dined*," he roared despairingly, "full up, complet!"

Marjorie came to the rescue with a shriller voice and more determined refusal.

"Take those dreadful things away, Vanya. They make me sick. Give us some tea, tea!"

"Tea!" echoed the cadaverous man, "they want tea! What do you think of Stanislas' tone-poem? Strong, modern, eh? The soul of rebellion in the crowd—the clash, the revolt at the heart of the machinery. It gives the bourgeois something to think of, oh, yes!"

"Bah!" said a voice in Wimsey's ear, as the cadaverous man turned away, "it is nothing. Bourgeois music. Programme music. Pretty!—You should hear Vrilovitch's 'Ecstasy on the letter Z.' That is pure vibration with no antiquated pattern in it. Stanislas—he thinks much of himself, but it is old as the hills—you can sense the resolution at the back of all his discords. Mere harmony in camouflage. Nothing in it. But he takes them all in because he has red hair and reveals his bony structure."

The speaker certainly did not err along these lines, for he was as bald and round as a billiard-ball. Wimsey replied soothingly:

"Well, what can you do with the wretched and antiquated instruments of our orchestra? A diatonic scale, bah! Thirteen miserable, bourgeois semi-tones, pooh! To express the infinite complexity of modern emotion, you need a scale of thirty-two notes to the octave."

"But why cling to the octave?" said the fat man. "Till you can cast away the octave and its sentimental associations, you walk in fetters of convention."

"That's the spirit!" said Wimsey. "I would dispense with all definite notes. After all, the cat does not need them for his midnight melodies, powerful and expressive as they are. The love-hunger of the stallion takes no account of octave or interval in giving forth the cry of passion. It is only man, trammelled by a stultifying convention—Oh, hullo, Marjorie, sorry—what is it?"

"Come and talk to Ryland Vaughan," said Marjorie. "I have told him you are a tremendous admirer of Philip Boyes' books. Have you read them?"

"Some of them. But I think I'm getting light-headed."

"You'll feel worse in an hour or so. So you'd better come now." She steered him to a remote spot near the gas-oven, where an extremely elongated man was sitting curled up on a floor cushion, eating caviare out of a jar with a pickle-fork. He greeted Wimsey with a sort of lugubrious enthusiasm.

"Hell of a place," he said, "hell of a business altogether. This stove's too hot. Have a drink. What the devil else can one do? I come here, because Philip used to come here. Habit, you know. I hate it, but there's nowhere else to go."

"You knew him very well, of course," said Wimsey, seating himself in a waste-paper basket, and wishing he was wearing a bathing-suit.

"I was his only real friend," said Ryland Vaughan, mournfully. "All the rest only cared to pick his brains. Apes! parrots! all the bloody lot of them."

"I've read his books and thought them very fine," said Wimsey, with some sincerity. "But he seemed to me an unhappy soul."

"Nobody understood him," said Vaughan. "They called him difficult—who wouldn't be difficult with so much to fight against? They sucked the blood out of him, and his damned thieves of publishers took every blasted coin they could lay their hands on. And then that bitch of a woman poisoned him. My God, what a life!"

"Yes, but what made her do it—if she did do it?"

"Oh, she did it all right. Sheer, beastly spite and jealousy, that's all there was to it. Just because she couldn't write anything but tripe herself. Harriet Vane's got the bug all these damned women have got—fancy they can do things. They hate a man and they hate his work. You'd think it would have been enough for her to help and look after a genius like Phil, wouldn't you? Why, damn it, he used to ask her advice about his work, her advice, good lord!"

"Did he take it?"

"Take it? She wouldn't give it. Told him she never gave opinions on other authors' work. *Other* authors! The impudence of it! Of course she was out of things among us all, but why couldn't she realise the difference between her mind and his? Of course it was hopeless from the start for Philip to get entangled with that kind of woman. Genius must be served, not argued with. I warned him at the time, but he was infatuated. And then, to want to marry her—"

"Why did he?" asked Wimsey.

"Remains of parsonical upbringing, I suppose. It was really pitiful. Besides, I think that fellow Urquhart did a lot of mischief. Sleek family lawyer—d'you know him?"

"No."

"He got hold of him—put up to it by the family, I imagine. I saw the influence creeping over Phil long before the real trouble began. Perhaps it's a good thing he's dead. It would have been ghastly to watch him turn conventional and settle down."

"When did this cousin start getting hold of him, then?"

"Oh—about two years ago—a little more, perhaps. Asked him to dinner and that sort of thing. The minute I saw him I knew he was out to ruin Philip, body and soul. What he wanted—what Phil wanted, I mean—was freedom and room to turn about in, but what with the woman and the cousin and the father in the background—oh, well! It's no use crying about it now. His work is left, and that's the best part of him. He's left me that to look after, at least. Harriet Vane didn't get her finger in that pie, after all."

"I'm sure it's absolutely safe in your hands," said Wimsey.

"But when one thinks what there might have been," said Vaughan, turning his blood-shot eyes miserably on Lord Peter, "it's enough to make one cut one's throat, isn't it?"

Wimsey expressed agreement.

"By the way," he said, "you were with him all that last day, till he went to his cousin's. You don't think he had anything on him in the way of—poison or anything? I don't want to seem unkind—but he was unhappy—it would be rotten to think that he—"

"No," said Vaughan, "no. That I'll swear he never did. He would have told me —he trusted me in those last days. I shared all his thoughts. He was miserably hurt by that damned woman, but he wouldn't have gone without telling me or saying good-bye. And besides—he wouldn't have chosen that way. Why should he? I could have given him—"

He checked himself, and glanced at Wimsey, but, seeing nothing in his face beyond sympathetic attention, went on:

"I remember talking to him about drugs. Hyoscine—veronal—all that sort of thing. He said, 'If ever I want to go out, Ryland, you'll show me the way.' And I would have—if he'd really wanted it. But arsenic! Philip, who loved beauty so much—do you think he would have chosen arsenic?—the suburban poisoner's outfit? That's absolutely impossible."

"It's not an agreeable sort of thing to take, certainly," said Wimsey.

"Look here," said Vaughan, hoarsely and impressively—he had been putting a constant succession of brandies on top of the caviare, and was beginning to lose his reserve—"Look here! See this!" He pulled a small bottle from his breastpocket. "That's waiting, till I've finished editing Phil's books. It's a comfort to have it there to look at, you know. Peaceful. Go out through the ivory gate—that's classical—they brought me up on the classics. These people would laugh at a fellow, but you needn't tell them I said it—funny, the way it sticks— 'tendebantque manus ripae ulterioris amore, ulterioris amore'—what's that bit about the souls thronging thick as leaves in Vallombrosa—no, that's Milton— 'amorioris ultore—ultoriore—damn it—poor Phil!"

Here Mr. Vaughan burst into tears and patted the little bottle.

Wimsey, whose head and ears were thumping as though he were sitting in an engine-room, got up softly and withdrew. Somebody had begun a Hungarian song and the stove was white-hot. He made signals of distress to Marjorie, who was sitting in a corner with a group of men. One of them appeared to be reading his own poems with his mouth nearly in her ear, and another was sketching something on the back of an envelope, to the accompaniment of yelps of merriment from the rest. The noise they made disconcerted the singer, who stopped in the middle of a bar, and cried angrily:

"Ach! this noise! these interruptions! they are intolerable! I lose myself! Stop! I begin all over again, from the beginning."

Marjorie sprang up, apologising.

"I'm a brute—I'm not keeping your menagerie in order, Nina—we're being perfect nuisances. Forgive me, Marya, I'm in a bad temper. I'd better pick up Peter and toddle away. Come and sing to me another day, darling, when I'm feeling better and there is more room for my feelings to expand. Good-night, Nina—we've enjoyed it frightfully and, Boris, that poem's the best thing you've done, only I couldn't hear it properly. Peter, tell them what a rotten mood I'm in to-night and take me home."

"That's right," said Wimsey, "nervy, you know—bad effect on the manners and so on."

"Manners," said a bearded gentleman suddenly and loudly, "are for the bourgeois."

"Quite right," said Wimsey. "Beastly bad form, and gives you repressions in the what-not. Come on, Marjorie, or we shall all be getting polite."

"I begin again," said the singer, "from the beginning."

"Whew!" said Wimsey, on the staircase.

"Yes, I know. I think I'm a perfect martyr to put up with it. Anyway, you've seen Vaughan. Nice dopey specimen, isn't he?"

"Yes, but I don't think he murdered Philip Boyes, do you? I had to see him to make sure. Where do we go next?"

"We'll try Joey Trimbles'. That's the stronghold of the opposition show."

Joey Trimbles occupied a studio over a mews. Here there was the same crowd, the same smoke, more kippers, still more drinks and still more heat and conversation. In addition there was a blaze of electric light, a gramophone, five dogs and a strong smell of oil-paints. Sylvia Marriott was expected. Wimsey found himself involved in a discussion of free love, D. H. Lawrence, the prurience of prudery and the immoral significance of long skirts. In time, however, he was rescued by the arrival of a masculine-looking middle-aged woman with a sinister smile and a pack of cards, who proceeded to tell everybody's fortune. The company gathered around her, and at the same time a girl came in and announced that Sylvia had sprained her ankle and couldn't come. Everybody said warmly, "Oh, how sickening, poor dear!" and forgot the subject immediately.

"We'll scoot off," said Marjorie. "Never mind about saying good-bye. Nobody marks you. It's good luck about Sylvia, because she'll be at home and can't escape us. I sometimes wish they'd all sprain their ankles. And yet, you know, nearly all those people are doing very good work. Even the Kropotky crowd. I used to enjoy this kind of thing myself, once."

"We're getting old, you and I," said Wimsey. "Sorry, that's rude. But do you know, I'm getting on for forty, Marjorie."

"You wear well. But you are looking a bit fagged tonight, Peter dear. What's the matter?"

"Nothing at all but middle-age."

"You'll be settling down if you're not careful."

"Oh, I've been settled for years."

"With Bunter and the books. I envy you sometimes, Peter."

Wimsey said nothing. Marjorie looked at him almost in alarm, and tucked her arm in his.

"Peter—do please be happy. I mean, you've always been the comfortable sort of person that nothing could touch. Don't alter, will you?"

That was the second time Wimsey had been asked not to alter himself; the first time, the request had exalted him; this time, it terrified him. As the taxi lurched along the rainy Embankment, he felt for the first time the dull and angry helplessness which is the first warning stroke of the triumph of mutability. Like the poisoned Athulf in Fool's Tragedy, he could have cried, "Oh, I am changing, changing, fearfully changing." Whether his present enterprise failed or succeeded, things would never be the same again. It was not that his heart would be broken by a disastrous love—he had outlived the luxurious agonies of youthful blood, and in this very freedom from illusion he recognized the loss of something. From now on, every hour of light-heartedness would be, not a prerogative but an achievement—one more axe or case-bottle or fowling-piece, rescued, Crusoe-fashion, from a sinking ship.

For the first time, too, he doubted his own power to carry through what he had undertaken. His personal feelings had been involved before this in his investigations, but they had never before clouded his mind. He was fumbling— grasping uncertainly here and there at fugitive and mocking possibilities. He asked questions at random, doubtful of his object, and the shortness of the time, which would once have stimulated, now frightened and confused him.

"I'm sorry, Marjorie," he said, rousing himself, "I'm afraid I'm being damned dull. Oxygen-starvation, probably. D'you mind if we have the window down a bit? That's better. Give me good food and a little air to breathe and I will caper, goatlike, to a dishonourable old age. People will point me out, as I creep, bald and yellow and supported by discreet corsetry, into the night-clubs of my great-grandchildren, and they'll say, 'Look, darling! that's the wicked Lord Peter, celebrated for never having spoken a reasonable word for the last ninety-six years. He was the only aristocrat who escaped the guillotine in the revolution of 1960. We keep him as a pet for the children.' And I shall wag my head and display my up-to-date dentures and say, 'Ah, ha! They don't have the fun we used to have in my young days, the poor, well-regulated creatures!' "

"There won't be any night-clubs then for you to creep into, if they're as disciplined as all that."

"Oh, yes—nature will have her revenge. They will slink away from the Government Communal Games to play solitaire in catacombs over a bowl of unster-ilised skim milk. Is this the place?"

"Yes; I hope there's someone to let us in at the bottom, if Sylvia's bust her leg. Yes—I hear footsteps. Oh, it's you, Eiluned; how's Sylvia?"

"Pretty all right, only swelled up—the ankle, that is. Coming up?"

"Is she visible?"

"Yes, perfectly respectable."

"Good, because I'm bringing Lord Peter Wimsey up, too."

"Oh," said the girl. "How do you do? You detect things, don't you? Have you come for the body or anything?"

"Lord Peter's looking into Harriet Vane's business for her."

"Is he? That's good. Glad somebody's doing something about it." She was a short, stout girl with a pugnacious nose and a twinkle. "What do you say it was? I say he did it himself. He was the self-pitying sort, you know. Hullo, Syl—here's Marjorie, with a bloke who's going to get Harriet out of jug."

"Produce him instantly!" was the reply from within. The door opened upon a small bed-sitting room, furnished with the severest simplicity, and inhabited by a pale spectacled young woman in a Morris chair, her bandaged foot stretched out upon a packing-case.

"I can't get up, because, as Jenny Wren said, my back's bad and my leg's queer. Who's the champion, Marjorie?"

Wimsey was introduced, and Eiluned Price immediately inquired, rather truculently:

"Can he drink coffee, Marjorie? Or does he require masculine refreshment?"

"He's perfectly godly, righteous and sober, and drinks anything but cocoa and fizzy lemonade."

"Oh! I only asked because some of your male belongings need stimulating, and we haven't got the wherewithal, and the pub's just closing."

She stumped over to a cupboard, and Sylvia said:

"Don't mind Eiluned; she likes to treat 'em rough. Tell me, Lord Peter, have you found any clues or anything?"

"I don't know," said Wimsey. "I've put a few ferrets down a few holes. I hope something may come up the other end."

"Have you seen the cousin yet—the Urquhart creature?"

"Got an appointment with him for tomorrow. Why?"

"Sylvia's theory is that he did it," said Eiluned.

"That's interesting. Why?"

"Female intuition," said Eiluned, bluntly. "She doesn't like the way he does his hair."

"I only said he was too sleek to be true," protested Sylvia. "And who else could it have been? I'm sure it wasn't Ryland Vaughan; he's an obnoxious ass, but he is genuinely heartbroken about it all."

Eiluned sniffed scornfully, and departed to fill a kettle at a tap on the landing.

"And whatever Eiluned thinks, I can't believe Phil Boyes did it himself."

"Why not?" asked Wimsey.

"He talked such a lot," said Sylvia. "And he really had too high an opinion of himself. I don't think he would have wilfully deprived the world of the privilege of reading his books."

"He would," said Eiluned. "He'd do it out of spite, to make the grown-ups sorry. No, thanks," as Wimsey advanced to carry the kettle, "I'm quite capable of carrying six pints of water."

"Crushed again!" said Wimsey.

"Eiluned disapproves of conventional courtesies between the sexes," said Marjorie.

"Very well," replied Wimsey, amiably. "I will adopt an attitude of passive decoration. Have you any idea, Miss Marriott, why this over-sleek solicitor should wish to make away with his cousin?"

"Not the faintest. I merely proceed on the old Sherlock Holmes basis, that when you have eliminated the impossible, then whatever remains, however improbable, must be true."

"Dupin said that before Sherlock. I grant the conclusion, but in this case I question the premises. No sugar, thank you."

"I thought all men liked to make their coffee into syrup."

"Yes, but then I am very unusual. Haven't you noticed it?"

"I haven't had much time to observe you, but I'll count the coffee as a point in your favour."

"Thanks frightfully. I say—can you people tell me just what was Miss Vane's reaction to the murder?"

"Well—" Sylvia considered a moment. "When he died—she was upset, of course—"

"She was startled," said Miss Price, "but it's my opinion she was thankful to be rid of him. And no wonder. Selfish beast! He'd made use of her and nagged her to death for a year and insulted her at the end. And he was one of your greedy sort that wouldn't let go. She *was* glad, Sylvia—what's the good of denying it?"

"Yes, perhaps. It was a relief to know he was finished with. But she didn't know then that he'd been murdered."

"No. The murder spoilt it a bit—if it was a murder, which I don't believe. Philip Boyes was always determined to be a victim, and it was very irritating of him to succeed in the end. I believe that's what he did it for."

"People do do that kind of thing," said Wimsey, thoughtfully. "But it's difficult to prove. I mean, a jury is much more inclined to believe in some tangible sort of reason, like money. But I can't find any money in this case."

Eiluned laughed.

"No, there never was much money, except what Harriet made. The ridiculous public didn't appreciate Phil Boyes. He couldn't forgive her that, you know."

"Didn't it come in useful?"

"Of course, but he resented it all the same. She ought to have been ministering to his work, not making money for them both with her own independent trash. But that's men all over."

"You haven't much opinion of us, what?"

"I've known too many borrowers," said Eiluned Price, "and too many that wanted their hands held. All the same, the women are just as bad, or they wouldn't put up with it. Thank Heaven, I've never borrowed and never lent—except to women, and they pay back."

"People who work hard usually do pay back, I fancy," said Wimsey, "—except geniuses."

"Women geniuses don't get coddled," said Miss Price, grimly, "so they learn not to expect it."

"We're getting rather off the subject, aren't we?" said Marjorie.

"No," replied Wimsey, "I'm getting a certain amount of light on the central figures in the problem—what journalists like to call the protagonists." His mouth gave a wry little twist. "One gets a lot of illumination in that fierce light that beats upon a scaffold."

"Don't say that," pleaded Sylvia.

A telephone rang somewhere outside, and Eiluned Price went out to answer it.

"Eiluned's anti-man," said Sylvia, "but she's a very reliable person."

Wimsey nodded.

"But she's wrong about Phil—she couldn't stick him, naturally, and she's apt to think—"

"It's for you, Lord Peter," said Eiluned, returning. "Fly at once—all is known. You're wanted by Scotland Yard."

Wimsey hastened out.

"That you, Peter? I've been scouring London for you. We've found the pub."

"Never!"

"Fact. And we're on the track of a packet of white powder."

"Good God!"

"Can you run down first thing tomorrow? We may have it for you."

"I will skip like a ram and hop like a high hill. We'll beat you yet, Mr. Bleeding Chief-Inspector Parker."

"I hope you will," said Parker, amiably, and rang off.

Wimsey pranced back into the room.

"Miss Price's price has gone to odds on," he announced. "It's suicide, fifty to one and no takers. I am going to grin like a dog and run about the city."

"I'm sorry I can't join you," said Sylvia Marriott, "but I'm glad if I'm wrong."

"I'm glad I'm right," said Eiluned Price, stolidly.

"And you are right and I am right and everything is quite all right," said Wimsey.

Marjorie Phelps looked at him and said nothing. She suddenly felt as though something inside her had been put through a wringer.

9

By what ingratiating means Mr. Bunter had contrived to turn the delivery of a note into the acceptance of an invitation to tea was best known to himself. At half-past four on the day which ended so cheerfully for Lord Peter, he was seated in the kitchen of Mr. Urquhart's house, toasting crumpets. He had been trained to a great pitch of dexterity in the preparation of crumpets, and if he was somewhat lavish in the matter of butter, that hurt nobody except Mr. Urquhart. It was natural that the conversation should turn to the subject of murder. Nothing goes so well with a hot fire and buttered crumpets as a wet day without and a good dose of comfortable horrors within. The heavier the lashing of the rain and the ghastlier the details, the better the flavour seems to be. On the present occasion, all the ingredients of an enjoyable party were present in full force.

" 'Orrible white, he looked, when he came in," said Mrs. Pettican the cook. "I see him when they sent for me to bring up the 'ot bottles. Three of them, they 'ad, one to his feet and one to his back and the big rubber one to 'is stummick. White and shiverin', he was, and that dreadful sick, you never would believe. And he groaned pitiful."

"Green, he looked to me, Cook," said Hannah Westlock, "or you might perhaps call it a greenish-yellow. I thought it was jaundice a-coming on—more like them attacks he had in the Spring."

"He was a bad colour then," agreed Mrs. Pettican, "but nothink like to what he was that last time. And the pains and cramps in his legs were agonising. That struck Nurse Williams very forcible—a nice young woman she was, and not stuck-up like some as I could name. 'Mrs. Pettican,' she said to me, which I call it better manners than callin' you Cook as they mostly do, as though they paid your wages for the right of callin' you out of your name—'Mrs. Pettican,' said she, 'never did I see anythink to equal them cramps except in one other case that was the dead spit of this one,' she said 'and you mark my words, Mrs. Pettican, them cramps ain't there for nothin'. Ah! little did I understand her meanin' at the time."

"That's a regular feature of these arsenical cases, or so his lordship tells me," replied Bunter. "A very distressing symptom. Had he ever had anything of the sort before?"

"Not what you could call cramps," said Hannah, "though I remember when he was ill in the Spring he complained of getting the fidgets in the hands and feet. Something like pins-and-needles, by what I understood him to say. It was a worrit to him, because he was finishing one of his articles in a hurry, and what with that and his eyes being so bad, the writing was a trial to him, poor thing."

"From what the gentleman for the prosecution said, talking it out with Sir James Lubbock," said Mr. Bunter, "I gathered that those pins-and-needles, and bad eyes and so on, were a sign he'd been given arsenic regularly, if I may so phrase it."

"A dreadful wicked woman she must 'a' been," said Mrs. Pettican, "—'ev another crumpet, do, Mr. Bunter—a-torturin' of the poor soul that long-winded way. Bashin' on the 'ed or the 'asty use of a carvin' knife when roused I can understand, but the 'orrors of slow poisonin' is the work of a fiend in 'uman form, in my opinion."

"Fiend is the only word, Mrs. Pettican," agreed the visitor.

"And the wickedness of it," said Hannah, "quite apart from the causing of a painful death to a fellow-being. Why, it's only the mercy of Providence we weren't all brought under suspicion."

"Yes, indeed," said Mrs. Pettican. "Why, when master told us about them diggin' poor Mr. Boyes up and findin' him full of that there nasty arsenic, it give me sech a turn, I felt as if the room was a-goin' round like the gallopin' 'orses at the roundabouts. 'Oh, sir!' I ses, 'what, in our 'ouse!' That's what I ses, and he ses, 'Mrs. Pettican,' he ses, 'I sincerely hope not.' "

Mrs. Pettican, having imparted this Macbeth-like flavour to the story, was pleased with it, and added:

"Yes, that's what I said to 'im. 'In our 'ouse,' I said, and I'm sure I never slep' a wink for three nights afterwards, what with the police and the fright and one thing and another."

"But of course you had no difficulty in proving that it hadn't happened in this house?" suggested Bunter. "Miss Westlock gave her evidence so beautifully at the trial, I'm sure she made it clear as clear could be to judge and jury. The judge congratulated you, Miss Westlock, and I'm sure he didn't say nearly enough—so plainly and well as you spoke up before the whole court."

"Well, I never was one to be shy," confessed Hannah, "and then, what with going through it all so careful with the master and then with the police, I knew what the questions would be and was prepared, as you might say."

"I wonder you could speak so exactly to every little detail, all that time ago," said Bunter, with admiration.

"Well, you see, Mr. Bunter, the very morning after Mr. Boyes was took ill, master comes down to us and he says, sitting in that chair ever so friendly, just as you might be yourself, 'I'm afraid Mr. Boyes is very ill,' he says, 'He thinks he must have ate something as disagreed with him,' he says, 'and perhaps as it might be the chicken. So I want you and Cook,' he says, 'to run through with me everything we had for dinner last night to see if we can think what it could have been.' 'Well, sir,' I said, 'I don't see that Mr. Boyes could have ate anything unwholesome here, for Cook and me had just the same, put aside yourself, sir, and it was all as sweet and good as it could be,' I said."

"And I said the same," said the Cook. "Sech a plain, simple dinner as it was, too—no oysters nor mussels nor anything of that sort, as it's well known shell-fish is poison to some people's stummicks, but a good stren'thenin' drop o' soup, and a bit of nice fish and a casseroled chicken with turnips and carrots done in the gravy, and a omelette, wot could be lighter and better? Not but there's people as can't relish eggs in any form, my own mother was just the same, give her so much as a cake what had bin made with a egg in it and she'd be that sick and come out all over spots like nettle-rash, you'd be surprised. But Mr. Boyes was a great gentleman for eggs, and omelettes was his particular favourite."

"Yes, he made the omelette himself that very night, didn't he?"

"He did," said Hannah, "and well I remember it, for Mr. Urquhart asked particular after the eggs, was they new-laid, and I reminded him they was some he had brought in himself that afternoon from that shop on the corner of Lamb's Conduit Street where they always have them fresh from the farm, and I reminded him that one of them was a little cracked and he'd said, 'We'll use that in the omelette tonight, Hannah,' and I brought out a clean bowl from the kitchen and put them straight in—the cracked one and three more besides, and never touched them again till I brought them to table. 'And what's more, sir,' I said, 'there's the other eight still here out of the dozen, and you can see for yourself they're as good and fresh as they can be.' Didn't I, Cook?"

"Yes, Hannah. And as for the chicken, that was a little beauty. It was that young and tender, I says to Hannah at the time as it seemed a shame to casserole it, for it would 'ave roasted beautiful. But Mr. Urquhart is very partial to a casseroled chicken; he says as there's more flavour to 'em that way, and I dunno but what he's right."

"If done with a good beef stock," pronounced Mr. Bunter, judicially, "the vegetables well packed in layers, on a foundation of bacon, not too fat, and the whole well seasoned with salt, pepper and paprika, there are few dishes to beat a casseroled chicken. For my own part I would recommend a soupçon of garlic, but I am aware that such is not agreeable to all tastes."

"I can't abear the smell or sight of the stuff," said Mrs. Pettican, frankly, "but as for the rest I'm with you, always allowing that the giblets is added to the stock, and I would personally favour mushrooms when in season, but not them tinned or bottled sorts as looks pretty but has no more taste to 'em than boot-buttons if so much. But the secret is in the cooking, as you know well, Mr. Bunter, the lid being kep' well sealed down to 'old the flavour and the cookin' bein' slow to make the juices perambulate through *and* through each other as you might say. I'm not denyin' as sech is very 'ighly enjoyable, and so Hannah and me found it, though fond of a good roast fowl also, when well-basted with a good rich stuffing to rejuice the dryness. But as to roasting it, Mr. Urquhart wouldn't hear of it, and bein' as it's him that pays the bills, he has the right to give his orders."

"Well," said Bunter, "it's certain if there had been anything unwholesome about the casserole, you and Miss Westlock could scarcely have escaped it."

"No, indeed," said Hannah, "for I won't conceal that, being blessed with hearty appetites, we finished it every bit, except a little piece I gave to the cat. Mr. Urquhart asked to see the remains of it next day and seemed quite put out to find it was all gone and the dish washed up—as though any washing-up was ever left over-night in *this* kitchen."

"I couldn't abear myself if I had to begin the day with dirty dishes," said Mrs. Pettican. "There was a drop of the soup left—not much, jest a wee drain, and Mr. Urquhart took that up to show to the doctor, and he tasted it and said it was very good, so Nurse Williams told us, though she didn't have none of it herself."

"And as for the burgundy," said Hannah Westlock, "which was the only thing

Mr. Boyes had to himself, like, Mr. Urquhart told me to cork it up tight and keep it. And just as well we did, because, of course, the police asked to see it when the time came."

"It was very far-seeing of Mr. Urquhart to take such precautions," said Bunter, "when there wasn't any thought at the time but that the poor man died naturally."

"That's what Nurse Williams said," replied Hannah, "but we put it down to him being a solicitor and knowing what ought to be done in a case of sudden death. Very particular he was, too—got me to put a bit of sticking-plaster over the mouth of the bottle and write my initials on it, so that it shouldn't be opened accidental. Nurse Williams always said he expected an inquest, but Dr. Weare being there to speak to Mr. Boyes having had these kind of bilious attacks all his life, of course there was no question raised about giving the certificate."

"Of course not," said Bunter, "but it's very fortunate as it turns out that Mr. Urquhart should have understood his duty so well. Many's the case his lordship has seen in which an innocent man has been brought near to the gallows for lack of a simple little precaution like that."

"And when I think how near Mr. Urquhart was to being away from 'ome at the time," said Mrs. Pettican, "the thought fair gives me palpitations. Called away, he was, to that tiresome old woman what's always a-dying and never dies. Why, he's there now—Mrs. Wrayburn, up in Windle. Rich as Sneezes, she is, by all accounts, and no good to nobody, for she's gone quite childish, so they say. A wicked old woman she was, too, in 'er day, and 'er other relations wouldn't 'ave nothink to do with 'er, only Mr. Urquhart, and I don't suppose 'e wouldn't, neither, only 'es her solicitor and it's his duty so to do."

"Duty does not always lie in pleasant places," commented Mr. Bunter, "as you and I well know, Mrs. Pettican."

"Them that are rich," said Hannah Westlock, "find no difficulty about getting their duties performed for them. Which I will make bold to say, Mrs. Wrayburn would not have done if she had been poor, great-aunt or no great-aunt, knowing Mr. Urquhart."

"Ah!" said Bunter.

"I pass no comments," said Miss Westlock, "but you and me, Mr. Bunter, know how the world goes."

"I suppose Mr. Urquhart stands to gain something when the old woman does peg out," suggested Bunter.

"That's as may be; he's not a talker," said Hannah, "but it stands to reason he wouldn't be always giving up his time and tearing off to Westmorland for nothing. Though I wouldn't care myself to put my hand to money that's wickedly come by. It would not bring a blessing with it, Mr. Bunter."

"It's easy talking, my girl, when you ain't likely to be put in the way of temptation," said Mrs. Pettican. "There's many great families in the Kingdom what never would a bin 'eard of if somebody 'adn't bin a little easier in their ways than what we've bin brought up to. There's skelintons in a many cupboards if the truth was known."

"Ah!" said Bunter, "I believe you. I've seen diamond necklaces and fur coats that should have been labelled Wages of Sin if deeds done in the dark were to be proclaimed upon the house tops, Mrs. Pettican. And there are families that hold their heads high that wouldn't ever have existed but for some king or other taking his amusements on the wrong side of the blanket as the old saying goes."

"They say as some that was high up wasn't too high to take notice of old Mrs. Wrayburn in her young days," said Hannah, darkly. "Queen Victoria wouldn't never allow her to act before the Royal Family—she knew too much about her goings-on."

"An actress, was she?"

"And a very beautiful one, they say, though I can't rightly recollect what her stage name was," mused Mrs. Pettican. "It was a queer one, I know—'Yde Park, or somethink of that. This Wrayburn as she married, 'e was nobody—jest to kiver up the scandal that's what she married 'im for. Two children she 'ad—but 'ose I would not take it upon me to say—and they both died in the cholera, which no doubt it was a judgment."

"That's not what Mr. Boyes called it," said Hannah, with a self-righteous sniff. "The devil took care of his own, that was his way of putting it."

"Ah! he talked careless," said Mrs. Pettican, "and no wonder, seeing the folks he lived with. But he'd a sobered down in time if he'd bin spared. A very pleasant way he 'ad with 'im when 'e liked. Come in here, he would, and chat upon one thing and another, very amusing-like."

"You're too soft with the gentlemen, Mrs. Pettican," said Hannah. "Anyone as has taking ways and poor health is ewelambs to you."

"So Mr. Boyes knew all about Mrs. Wrayburn?"

"Oh, yes—it was all in the family, you see, and no doubt Mr. Urquhart would a told him more than he'd say to us. Which train did Mr. Urquhart say he was a-comin' by, Hannah?"

"He said dinner for half-past seven. That'll be the six-thirty, I should think."

Mrs. Pettican glanced at the clock and Bunter, taking this as a hint, rose and made his farewells.

"And I 'opes as you'll come again, Mr. Bunter," said the Cook, graciously. "The master makes no objections to respectable gentlemen visitors at tea-time. Wednesday is my 'arf-day."

"Mine is Friday," added Hannah, "and every other Sunday. If you should be Evangelical, Mr. Bunter, the Rev. Crawford in Judd Street is a beautiful preacher. But maybe you'll be going out of town for Christmas."

Mr. Bunter replied that that season would undoubtedly be spent at Duke's Denver, and departed in a shining halo of vicarious splendour.

10

"Here you are, Peter," said Chief-Inspector Parker, "and here is the lady you are anxious to meet. Mrs. Bulfinch, allow me to introduce Lord Peter Wimsey."

"Pleased, I am sure," said Mrs. Bulfinch. She giggled, and dabbed her large, blonde face with powder.

"Mrs. Bulfinch, before her union with Mr. Bulfinch, was the life and soul of the saloon bar at the Nine Rings in Grays Inn Road," said Mr. Parker, "and well-known to all for her charm and wit."

"Go on," said Mrs. Bulfinch, "you're a one, aren't you? Don't you pay no attention to him, your lordship. You know what these police fellows are."

"Sad dogs," said Wimsey, shaking his head. "But I don't need his testimonials, I can trust my own eyes and ears, Mrs. Bulfinch, and I can only say that, if I had had the happiness to make your acquaintance before it was too late, it would have been my life-time's ambition to wipe Mr. Bulfinch's eye."

"You're every bit as bad as he is," said Mrs. Bulfinch, highly gratified, "and what Bulfinch would say to you I *don't* know. Quite upset, he was, when the officer came round to ask me to pop along to the Yard. 'I don't like it, Gracie,' he says, 'we've always bin respectable in this house and no trouble with disorderlies nor drinks after hours, and once you get among them fellows you don't know the things you may be asked.' 'Don't be so soft,' I tells him, 'the boys all know me and they haven't got nothing against me, and if it's just to tell them about the gentleman that left the packet behind him at the Rings, I haven't no objection to tell them, having nothing to reproach myself with. What'd they think,' I said, 'if I refused to go? Ten to one they'd think there was something funny about it.' 'Well,' he says, 'I'm coming with you.' 'Oh, are you?' I says, 'and how about the new barman you was going to engage this morning? For,' I said, 'serve in the jug and bottle I will not, never having been accustomed to it, so you can do as you like.' So I came away and left him to it. Mind you, I like him for it. I ain't saying nothing against Bulfinch, but police or no police, I reckon I know how to take care of myself."

"Quite so," said Parker, patiently. "Mr. Bulfinch need feel no alarm. All we want you to do is to tell us, to the best of your recollection, about that young man you spoke of and help us to find the white-paper packet. You may be able to save an innocent person from being convicted, and I am sure your husband could not object to that."

"Poor thing!" said Mrs. Bulfinch, 'I'm sure when I read the account of the trial I said to Bulfinch—"

"Just a moment. If you wouldn't mind beginning at the beginning, Mrs. Bulfinch, Lord Peter would understand better what you have to tell us."

"Why, of course. Well, my lord, before I was married I was barmaid at the Nine Rings, as the Chief-Inspector says. Miss Montague I was then—it's a better name than Bulfinch, and I was almost sorry to say good-bye to it, but there! a girl has to make a lot of sacrifices when she marries and one more or less is nothing to signify. I never worked there but in the saloon bar, for I wouldn't undertake the four-ale business, it not being a refined neighbourhood, though there's a lot of very nice legal gentlemen drops in of an evening on the saloon side. Well, as I was saying, I was working there up to my marriage, which was last August Bank Holiday, and I remember one evening a gentleman coming in—"

"Could you remember the date, do you think?"

"Not within a day or so I couldn't, for I wouldn't wish to swear to a fib, but it wasn't far off the longest day, for I remember making that same remark to the gentleman for something to say, you know."

"That's near enough," said Parker. "Round about June 20th, or 21st, or something like that?"

"That's right, as near as I can speak to it. And as to the time of night, that I *can* tell you—knowing how keen you 'tecs always are on the hands of the clock."

Mrs. Bulfinch giggled again and looked archly round for applause. "There was a gentleman sitting there—I didn't know him, he was a stranger to the district—and he asked what was our closing hour and I told him 11 o'clock, and he said, 'Thank God! I thought I was going to be turned out at 10:30,' and I looked at the clock and said, 'Oh, you're all right, anyhow, sir; we always keep that clock a quarter of an hour fast.' The clock said twenty past, so I know it must have been five past ten really. So we got talking a bit about these prohibitionists and the way they had been trying it on again to get our licensing-hour altered to half-past ten, only we had a good friend on the Bench in Mr. Judkins, and while we was discussing it, I remember so well, the door was pushed open hurried-like and a young gentleman comes in, almost falls in, I might say, and he calls, 'Give me a double brandy, quick.' Well, I didn't like to serve him all at once, he looked so white and queer, I thought he'd had one or two over the eight already, and the boss was most particular about that sort of thing. Still, he spoke all right—quite clear and not repeating himself nor nothing, and his eyes, though they did look a bit funny, weren't fixed-like, if you understand me. We get to size folks up pretty well in our business, you know. He sort of held on to the bar, all scrunched up together and bent double, and he says, 'Make it a stiff one, there's a good girl, I'm feeling awful bad.' The gentleman I'd been talking to, he says to him, 'Hold up,' he says, 'what's the matter?' and the gentleman says, 'I'm going to be ill.' And he puts his hands across his waistcoat like so!"

Mrs. Bulfinch clasped her waist and rolled her big blue eyes dramatically.

"Well, then I see he wasn't drunk, so I mixed him a double Martell with just a splash of soda and he gulps it down, and says, 'That's better.' And the other gentleman puts his arm round him and helps him to a seat. There was a good many other people in the bar, but they didn't notice much, being full of the racing news. Presently the gentleman asks me for a glass of water, and I fetched it to him, and he says: 'Sorry if I frightened you, but I've just had a bad shock, and it must have gone to my inside. I'm subject to gastric trouble,' he says, 'and any worry or shock always affects my stomach. However,' he says, 'perhaps this will stop it.' And he takes out a white paper packet with some powder in it, and drops it into the glass of water and stirs it up with a fountain-pen and drinks it off."

"Did it fizz or anything?" asked Wimsey.

"No; it was just a plain powder, and it took a bit of a time to mix. He drank it off and said, 'That settles it,' or 'That'll settle it,' or something of that sort. And then he says. 'Thanks very much. I'm better now and I'd better get home in case it takes me again.' And he raised his hat—he was quite the gentleman—and off he goes."

"How much powder do you think he put in?"

"Oh, a good dollop. He didn't measure it or anything, just shot it in out of the packet. Near a dessert spoonful it might have been."

"And what happened to the packet?" prompted Parker.

"Ah, there you are." Mrs. Bulfinch took a glance at Wimsey's face and seemed pleased with the effect she was producing.

"We'd just got the last customer out—about five past eleven, that would be, and George was locking the door, when I see something white on the seat. Somebody's handkerchief I thought it was, but when I picked it up, I see it was the paper packet. So I said to George, 'Hullo! the gentleman's left his medicine behind him.' So George asked what gentleman, and I told him, and he said,

'What is it?' and I looked, but the label had been torn off. It was just one of them chemist's packets, you know, with the ends turned up and a label stuck across, but there wasn't a bit of the label left."

"You couldn't even see whether it had been printed in black or in red?"

"Well now." Mrs. Bulfinch considered. "Well, no, I couldn't say that. Now you mention it, I do seem to recollect that there was something red about the packet, somewhere, but I can't clearly call it to mind. I wouldn't swear. I know there wasn't any name or printing of any kind, because I looked to see what it was."

"You didn't try tasting it, I suppose?"

"Not me. It might have been poison or something. I tell you, he was a funny-looking customer." (Parker and Wimsey exchanged glances.)

"Was that what you thought at the time?" enquired Wimsey, "or did it only occur to you later on—after you'd read about the case, you know?"

"I thought it at the time, of course," retorted Mrs. Bulfinch, snappishly. "Aren't I telling you that's why I didn't taste it? I said so to George at the time, what's more. Besides, if it wasn't poison, it might be 'snow' or something. 'Best not touch it,' that's what I said to George, and he said 'Chuck it in the fire.' But I wouldn't have that. The gentleman might have come back for it. So I stuck it up on the shelf behind the bar, where they keep the spirits, and never thought of it again from that day to yesterday, when your policeman came round about it."

"It's been looked for there," said Parker, "but they can't seem to find it anywhere."

"Well, I don't know about that. I put it there and I left the Rings in August, so what's gone with it I can't say. Daresay they threw it away when they were cleaning. Wait a bit, though—I'm wrong when I say I never thought about it again. I did just wonder about it when I read the report of the trial in the *News of the World*, and I said to George, 'I wouldn't be surprised if that was the gentleman who came into the Rings one night and seemed so poorly—just fancy!' I said—just like that. And George said, 'Now don't you get fancies, Gracie my girl; you don't want to get mixed up in a police case.' George has always held his head high, you see."

"It's a pity you didn't come forward with this story," said Parker, severely.

"Well, how was I to know it was important? The taxi-driver had seen him a few minutes afterwards and he was ill then, so the powder couldn't have had anything to do with it, if it was him, which I couldn't swear to. And anyhow, I didn't see about it till the trial was all over and finished with."

"There will be a new trial, though," said Parker, "and you may have to give evidence at that."

"You know where to find me," said Mrs. Bulfinch, with spirit. "I shan't run away."

"We're very much obliged to you for coming now," added Wimsey, pleasantly.

"Don't mention it," said the lady. "Is that all you want, Mr. Chief-Inspector?"

"That's all at present. If we find the packet, we may ask you to identify it. And, by the way, it's advisable not to discuss these matters with your friends, Mrs. Bulfinch. Sometimes ladies get talking, and one thing leads to another, and in the end they remember incidents that never took place at all. You understand."

"I never was one for talking," said Mrs. Bulfinch, offended. "And it's my opinion, when it comes to putting two-and-two together to make five of 'em, the ladies aren't in it with the gentlemen."

"I may pass this on to the solicitors for the defence, I suppose?" said Wimsey, when the witness had departed.

"Of course," said Parker, "that's why I asked you to come and hear it—for what it's worth. Meanwhile, we shall of course have a good hunt for the packet."

"Yes," said Wimsey, thoughtfully, "yes—you will have to do that—naturally."

Mr. Crofts did not look best pleased when this story was handed on to him.

"I warned you, Lord Peter," he said, "what might come of showing our hand to the police. Now they've got hold of this incident, they will have every opportunity to turn it to their own advantage. Why didn't you leave it to us to make the investigation?"

"Damn it," said Wimsey angrily, "it was left to you for about three months and you did absolutely nothing. The police dug it up in three days. Time's important in this case, you know."

"Very likely, but don't you see that the police won't rest now till they've found this precious packet?"

"Well?"

"Well, and suppose it isn't arsenic at all? If you'd left it in our hands, we could have sprung the thing on them at the last moment, when it was too late to make enquiries, and then we should have knocked the bottom out of the prosecution. Give the jury Mrs. Bulfinch's story as it stands and they'd have to admit there was some evidence that the deceased poisoned himself. But now, of course, the police will find or fake something and show that the powder was perfectly harmless."

"And supposing they find it and it *is* arsenic?"

"In *that* case, of course," said Mr. Crofts, "we shall get an acquittal. But do you believe in that possibility, my lord?"

"It's perfectly evident that *you* don't," said Wimsey, hotly. "In fact, you think your client's guilty. Well, I don't."

Mr. Crofts shrugged his shoulders.

"In our client's interests," he said, "we are bound to look at the unfavourable side of all evidence, so as to anticipate the points that are likely to be made by the prosecution. I repeat, my lord, that you have acted indiscreetly."

"Look here," said Wimsey, "I'm not out for a verdict of 'Not Proven.' As far as Miss Vane's honour and happiness are concerned, she might as well be found guilty as acquitted on a mere element of doubt. I want to see her absolutely cleared and the blame fixed in the right quarter. I don't want any shadow of doubt about it."

"Highly desirable, my lord," agreed the solicitor, "but you will allow me to remind you that it is not merely a question of honour or happiness, but of saving Miss Vane's neck from the gallows."

"And I say," said Wimsey, "that it would be better for her to be hanged outright than to live and have everybody think her a murderess who got off by a fluke."

"Indeed?" said Mr. Crofts. "I fear that is not an attitude that the defence can very well adopt. May I ask if it is adopted by Miss Vane herself?"

"I shouldn't be surprised if it was," said Wimsey. "But she's innocent, and I'll make you damn well believe it before I've done."

"Excellent, excellent," said Mr. Crofts, suavely, "nobody will be more delighted than myself. But I repeat that, in my humble opinion, your lordship will be wiser not to betray too many confidences to Chief-Inspector Parker."

Wimsey was still simmering inwardly from this encounter when he entered Mr. Urquhart's office in Bedford Row. The head-clerk remembered him and greeted him with the deference due to an exalted and expected visitor. He begged his lordship to take a seat for a moment, and vanished into an inner office.

A woman typist, with a strong, ugly, rather masculine face, looked up from her machine as the door closed, and nodded abruptly to Lord Peter. Wimsey recognized her as one of the "Cattery," and put a commendatory mental note against Miss Climpson's name for quick and efficient organisation. No words passed, however, and in a few moments the head-clerk returned and begged Lord Peter to step inside.

Norman Urquhart rose from his desk and held out a friendly hand of greeting. Wimsey had seen him at the trial, and noted his neat dress, thick, smooth dark hair and general appearance of brisk and business-like respectability. Seeing him now more closely, he noticed that he was rather older than he had appeared at a distance. He put him down as being somewhere about the middle forties. His skin was pale and curiously clear, except for a number of little freckles, like sun-spots, rather unexpected at that time of the year, and in a man whose appearance conveyed no other suggestion of an out-door life. The eyes, dark and shrewd, looked a little tired, and were blistered about the orbits, as though anxiety were not unknown to them.

The solicitor welcomed his guest in a high, pleasant voice and asked what he could do for him.

Wimsey explained that he was interested in the Vane poisoning trial, and that he had the authority of Messrs. Crofts & Cooper to come and bother Mr. Urquhart with questions, adding, as usual, that he was afraid he was being a nuisance.

"Not at all, Lord Peter, not at all. I'm only too delighted to help you in any way, though really I'm afraid you have heard all I know. Naturally, I was very much taken aback by the result of the autopsy, and rather relieved, I must admit, to find that no suspicion was likely to be thrown on me, under the rather peculiar circumstances."

"Frightfully tryin' for you," agreed Wimsey. "But you seem to have taken the most admirable precautions at the time."

"Well, you know, I suppose we lawyers get into a habit of taking precautions. Not that I had any idea of poison at the time—or, needless to say, I should have insisted on an enquiry then and there. What was in my mind was more in the nature of some kind of food-poisoning; not botulism, the symptoms were all wrong for that, but some contamination from cooking utensils or from some bacillus in the food itself. I am glad it turned out not to be that, though the reality was infinitely worse in one way. I suppose, really, in all cases of sudden and unaccountable illness, an analysis of the secretions ought to be made as a routine part of the business, but Dr. Weare appeared perfectly satisfied, and I trusted entirely to his judgment."

"Obviously," said Wimsey. "One doesn't naturally jump to the idea that people are bein' murdered—though I dare say it happens more often than one is apt to suppose."

"It probably does, and if I'd ever had the handling of a criminal case, the suspicion might have occurred to me, but my work is almost entirely conveyancing and that sort of business—and probate and divorce and so on."

"Talkin' of probate," said Wimsey, carelessly, "had Mr. Boyes any sort of financial expectations?"

"None at all that I know of. His father is by no means well off—the usual country parson with a small stipend and a huge Vicarage and tumble-down Church. In fact, the whole family belongs to the unfortunate professional middle-class—over-taxed and with very little financial stamina. I shouldn't think there were more than a few hundred pounds to come to Philip Boyes, even if he had outlived the lot of them."

"I had an idea there was a rich aunt somewhere."

"Oh, no—unless you're thinking of old Cremorna Garden. She's a great-aunt, on the mother's side. But she hasn't had anything to do with them for very many years."

At this moment Lord Peter had one of those bursts of illumination which come suddenly when two unrelated facts make contact in the mind. In the excitement of hearing Parker's news about the white paper packet, he had paid insufficient attention to Bunter's account of the tea-party with Hannah Westlock and Mrs. Pettican, but now he remembered something about an actress, with a name like ''Yde Park or something of that.' The readjustment made itself so smoothly and mechanically in his mind that his next question followed almost without a pause.

"Isn't that Mrs. Wrayburn of Windle in Westmorland?"

"Yes," said Mr. Urquhart. "I've just been up to see her, as a matter of fact. Of course, yes, you wrote to me there. She's been quite childish, poor old lady, for the last five years or so. A wretched life—dragging on like that, a misery to herself and everybody else. It always seems to me a cruel thing that one may not put these poor old people out of the way, as one would a favourite animal—but the law will not let us be so merciful."

"Yes, we'd be hauled over the coals by the N.S.P.C.A. if we let a cat linger on in misery," said Wimsey. "Silly, isn't it? But it's all of a piece with the people who write to the papers about keepin' dogs in draughty kennels and don't give a hoot—or a penny—to stop landlords allowin' a family of thirteen to sleep in an undrained cellar with no glass in the windows and no windows to put it in. It really makes me quite cross, sometimes, though I'm a peaceful sort of idiot as a rule. Poor old Cremorna Garden—she might be gettin' on now, though. Surely she can't last much longer."

"As a matter of fact, we all thought she'd gone the other day: Her heart is giving out—she's over ninety, poor soul, amazing vitality in some of these ancient ladies."

"I suppose you're about her only living relation now."

"I suppose I am, except for an uncle of mine in Australia." Mr. Urquhart accepted the fact of the relationship without enquiring how Wimsey came to know about it. "Not that my being there can do her any good. But I'm her man of business, too, so it's just as well I should be on the spot when anything happens."

"Oh, quite, quite. And being her man of business, of course you know how she has left her money."

"Well, yes, of course. Though I don't quite see, if you'll forgive my saying so, what that has to do with the present problem."

"Why, don't you see," said Wimsey, "it just occurred to me that Philip Boyes might have got himself into some kind of financial mess-up—it happens to the best of men—and have, well, taken the short way out of it. But, if he had any expectations from Mrs. Wrayburn, and the old girl, I mean, the poor old lady, was so near shuffling off this mortal thingummy, why, then, don't you know, he would have waited, or raised the wind on the strength of a post-obit or something or the other. You get my meaning, what?"

"Oh, I see—you are trying to make out a case for suicide. Well, I agree with you that it's the most hopeful defense for Miss Vane's friends to put up, and as far as that goes, I can support you. Inasmuch, that is, as Mrs. Wrayburn did not leave Philip anything. Nor, so far as I know, had he the smallest reason to suppose she would do so."

"You're positive of that?"

"Quite. As a matter of fact," Mr. Urquhart hesitated, "well, I may as well tell you that he asked me about it one day, and I was obliged to tell him that he hadn't the least chance of getting anything from her."

"Oh—he did actually ask?"

"Well, yes, he did."

"That's rather a point, isn't it? How long ago would that be?"

"Oh—about eighteen months ago, I fancy. I couldn't be sure."

"And as Mrs. Wrayburn is now childish, I suppose he couldn't entertain any hope that she would ever alter the will?"

"Not the slightest."

"No, I see. Well, I think we might make something of that. Great disappointment, of course—one would make out that he had counted a good deal upon it. Is it much, by the way?"

"Pretty fair—about seventy or eighty thousand."

"Very sickening, to think of all that good stuff going west and not getting a look-in one's self. By the way, how about you? Don't you get anything? I beg your pardon, fearfully inquisitive and all that, but I mean to say, considering you've been looking after her for years and are her only available relation so to speak, it would be a trifle thick, what?"

The solicitor frowned, and Wimsey apologised.

"I know, I know—I've been fearfully impudent. It's a failing of mine. And anyhow, it'll all be in the papers when the old lady does pop off, so I don't know why I should be so anxious to pump you. Wash it out—I'm sorry."

"There's no real reason why you shouldn't know," said Mr. Urquhart, slowly, "though one's professional instinct is to avoid disclosing one's clients' affairs. As a matter of fact, I am the legatee myself."

"Oh?" said Wimsey, in a disappointed voice. "But in that case—that rather weakens the story, doesn't it? I mean to say, your cousin might very well have felt, in that case, that he could look to you for—that is—of course I don't know what your ideas might have been—"

Mr. Urquhart shook his head.

"I see what you are driving at, and it is a very natural thought. But actually, such a disposal of the money would have been directly contrary to the expressed wish of the testatrix. Even if I could legally have made it over, I should have been morally bound not to do so, and I had to make that clear to Philip. I might, of course, have assisted him with casual gifts of money from time to time, but, to tell the truth, I should hardly have cared to do so. In my opinion, the only hope of salvation for Philip would have been to make his way by his own work. He was a little inclined—though I don't like speaking ill of the dead—to—to rely too much on other people."

"Ah, quite. No doubt that was Mrs. Wrayburn's idea also?"

"Not exactly. No. It went rather deeper than that. She considered that she had been badly treated by her family. In short, well, as we have gone so far, I don't mind giving you her *ipsissima verba*."

He rang a bell on his desk.

"I haven't got the will itself here, but I have the draft. Oh, Miss Murchison, would you kindly bring me in the deed-box labelled 'Wrayburn'? Mr. Pond will show it to you. It isn't heavy."

The lady from the "Cattery" departed silently in quest of the box.

"This is all rather irregular, Lord Peter," went on Mr. Urquhart, "but there are times when too much discretion is as bad as too little, and I should like you to see exactly why I was forced to take up this rather uncompromising attitude towards my cousin. Ah, thank you, Miss Murchison."

He opened the deed-box with a key attached to a bunch which he took from his trousers' pocket, and turned over a quantity of papers. Wimsey watched him with the expression of a rather foolish terrier who expects a tit-bit.

"Dear, dear," ejaculated the solicitor, "it doesn't seem to be—oh! of course, how forgetful of me. I'm so sorry, it's in my safe at home. I got it out for reference last June, when the previous alarm occurred about Mrs. Wrayburn's illness, and in the confusion which followed on my cousin's death I quite forgot to bring it back. However, the gist of it was—"

"Never mind," said Wimsey, "there's no hurry. If I called at your house tomorrow, perhaps I could see it then."

"By all means, if you think it important. I do apologise for my carelessness. In the meantime, is there anything else I can tell you about the matter?"

Wimsey asked a few questions, covering the ground already traversed by Bunter in his investigations, and took his departure. Miss Murchison was again at work in the outer office. She did not look up as he passed.

"Curious," mused Wimsey, as he pattered along Bedford Row, "everybody is so remarkably helpful about this case. They cheerfully answer questions which one has no right to ask and burst into explanations in the most unnecessary manner. None of them seem to have anything to conceal. It's quite astonishing. Perhaps the fellow really did commit suicide. I hope he did. I wish I could question *him*. I'd put him through it, blast him. I've got about fifteen different analyses of his character already—all different. . . . It's very ungentlemanly to commit suicide without leaving a note to say you've done it—gets people into trouble. When I blow my brains out—"

He stopped.

"I hope I shan't want to," he said. "I hope I shan't need to want to. Mother wouldn't like it, and it's messy. But I'm beginning to dislike this job of getting people hanged. It's damnable for their friends. . . . I won't think about hang-ing. It's unnerving."

11

Wimsey presented himself at Mr. Urquhart's house at 9 o'clock the next morning, and found that gentleman at breakfast.

"I thought I might catch you before you went down to the office," said his lordship, apologetically. "Thanks awfully, I've had my morning nosebag. No, really, thanks—I never drink before eleven. Bad for the inside."

"Well, I've found the draft for you," said Mr. Urquhart pleasantly. "You can cast your eye over it while I drink my coffee, if you'll excuse my going on. It exposes the family skeleton a little, but it's all ancient history now."

He fetched a sheet of typescript from a side-table and handed it to Wimsey, who noticed, mechanically, that it had been typed on a Woodstock machine, with a chipped lower case p, and an A slightly out of alignment.

"I'd better make quite clear the family connection of the Boyes's and the Urquharts's," he went on, returning to the breakfast-table, "so that you will understand the will. The common ancestor is old John Hubbard, a highly respectable banker at the beginning of the last century. He lived in Nottingham, and the bank, as usual in those days, was a private, family concern. He had three daughters, Jane, Mary and Rosanna. He educated them well, and they ought to have been heiresses in a mild way, but the old boy made the usual mistakes, speculated unwisely, allowed his clients too much rope—the old story. The bank broke, and the daughters were left penniless. The eldest, Jane, married a man called Henry Brown. He was a schoolmaster and very poor and quite repellently moral. They had one daughter, Julia, who eventually married a curate, the Rev. Arthur Boyes, and was the mother of Philip Boyes. The second daughter, Mary, did rather better financially, though socially she married beneath her. She accepted the hand of one Josiah Urquhart, who was engaged in the lace-trade. This was a blow to the old people, but Josiah came originally of a fairly decent family, and was a most worthy person, so they made the best of it. Mary had a son, Charles Urquhart, who contrived to break away from the degrading associations of trade. He entered a solicitor's office, and did well, and finally became a partner in the firm. He was my father, and I am his successor in the legal business.

"The third daughter, Rosanna, was made of different stuff. She was very beautiful, a remarkably fine singer, a graceful dancer and altogether a particularly attractive and spoilt young person. To the horror of the parents she ran away and went on the stage. They erased her name from the family Bible. She determined to justify their worst suspicions. She became the spoilt darling of fashionable London. Under her stage name of Cremorna Garden, she went from one disreputable triumph to another. And, mind you, she had brains—nothing of the Nell Gwyn business about her. She was the take-it-and-keep-it sort. She took everything—money, jewels, apartments, meublés, horses, carriages, all the rest of it, and turned it into good consolidated funds. She was never prodigal of anything except her person, which she considered to be a sufficient return for all favours, and I daresay it was. I never saw her till she was an old woman, but before she had the stroke which destroyed her brain and body, she still kept the remains of remarkable beauty. She was a shrewd old woman in her way, and grasping. She had those tight little hands, plump and narrow, that give nothing away—except for cash down. You know the sort.

"Well, the long and the short of it was that the eldest sister, Jane—the one who married the schoolmaster—would have nothing to do with the family black sheep. She and her husband wrapped themselves up in their virtue and shuddered when they saw the disgraceful name of Cremorna Garden billed outside the Olympic or the Adelphi. They returned her letters unopened and forbade her the house, and the climax was reached when Henry Brown tried to have her turned out of the Church on the occasion of his wife's funeral.

"My grand-parents were less strait-laced. They didn't call on her and didn't invite her, but they occasionally took a box for her performances and they sent her a card for their son's wedding, and were polite in a distant kind of way. In consequence, she kept up a civil acquaintance with my father, and eventually put her business into his hands. He took the view that property was property, however acquired, and said that if a lawyer refused to handle dirty money he would have to show half his clients the door.

"The old lady never forgot or forgave anything. The very mention of the Brown-Boyes connection made her foam at the mouth. Hence, when she came to make her will, she put in the paragraph you have before you now. I pointed out to her that Philip Boyes had had nothing to do with the persecution, as, indeed, neither had Arthur Boyes, but the old sore rankled still, and she wouldn't hear a word in his favour. So I drew up the will as she wanted it; if I hadn't, somebody else would have done so, you know."

Wimsey nodded, and gave his attention to the will, which was dated eight years previously. It appointed Norman Urquhart as sole executor, and, after a few legacies to servants and to theatrical charities, it ran as follows:—

"All the rest of my property whatsoever and wheresoever situated I give to my great nephew Norman Urquhart of Bedford Row Solicitor for his lifetime and at his death to be equally divided among his legitimate issue but if the said Norman Urquhart should decease without legitimate issue the said property to pass to (here followed the names of the charities previously specified). And I make this disposition of my property in token of gratitude for the consideration shown to me by my said great-nephew Norman Urquhart and his father the late Charles Urquhart throughout their lives and to ensure that no part of my property shall come into the hands of my great-nephew Philip Boyes or his descendants. And to this end and to mark my sense of the inhuman treatment meted out to me by the family of the said Philip Boyes I enjoin upon the said Norman Urquhart as my dying wish that he neither give, lend or convey to the said Philip Boyes any part of the income derived from the said property enjoyed by him the said Norman Urquhart during his lifetime nor employ the same to assist the said Philip Boyes in any manner whatsoever."

"H'm!" said Wimsey, "that's pretty clear, and pretty vindictive."

"Yes, it is—but what are you to do with old ladies who won't listen to reason? She looked pretty sharply to see that I had got the wording fierce enough before she would put her name to it."

"It must have depressed Philip Boyes all right," said Wimsey. "Thank you—I'm glad I've seen that; it makes the suicide theory a good deal more probable."

In theory it might do so, but the theory did not square as well as Wimsey could have wished with what he had heard about the character of Philip Boyes. Personally, he was inclined to put more faith in the idea that the final interview with Harriet had been the deciding factor in the suicide. But this, too, was not quite satisfactory. He could not believe that Philip had felt that particular kind of affection for Harriet Vane. Perhaps, though, it was merely that he did not want to think well of the man. His emotions, he feared, clouded his judgment a little.

He went back home and read the proofs of Harriet's novel. Undoubtedly she could write well, but undoubtedly she knew only too much about the administration of arsenic. Moreover, the book was about two artists who lived in Bloomsbury and led an ideal existence, full of love and laughter and poverty, till somebody unkindly poisoned the young man and left the young woman inconsolable and passionately resolved to avenge him. Wimsey ground his teeth and went down to Halloway Gaol, where he very nearly made a jealous exhibition of himself. Fortunately, his sense of humour came to the rescue when he had cross-examined his client to the verge of exhaustion and tears.

"I'm sorry," he said; "the fact is, I'm most damnably jealous of this fellow Boyes. I oughtn't to be, but I am."

"That's just it," said Harriet, "and you always would be."

"And if I was, I shouldn't be fit to live with. Is that it?"

"You would be very unhappy. Quite apart from all the other drawbacks."

"But look here," said Wimsey, "if you married me I shouldn't be jealous, because then I should know that you really liked me and all that."

"You think you wouldn't be. But you would."

"Should I? Oh, surely not. Why should I? It's just the same as if I married a widow. Are all second husbands jealous?"

"I don't know. But it's not quite the same. You'd never really trust me, and we should be wretched."

"But damn it all," said Wimsey, "if you would once say you cared a bit about me it would be all right. I should believe that. It's because you won't say it that I imagine all sort of things."

"You would go on imagining things in spite of yourself. You couldn't give me a square deal. No man ever does."

"Never?"

"Well, hardly ever."

"That would be rotten," said Wimsey, seriously. "Of course, if I turned out to be that sort of idiot, things would be pretty hopeless. I know what you mean. I knew a bloke once who got that jealous bug. If his wife wasn't always hanging around his neck, he said it showed he meant nothing to her, and if she did express her affection he called her a hypocrite. It got quite impossible, and she ran away with somebody she didn't care twopence for, and he went about saying that he had been right about her all along. But everybody else said it was his own silly fault. It's all very complicated. The advantage seems to be with the person who gets jealous first. Perhaps you could manage to be jealous of me. I wish you would, because it would prove that you took a bit of interest in me. Shall I give you some details of my hideous past?"

"Please don't."

"Why not?"

"I don't want to know about all the other people."

"Don't you, by jove? I think that's rather hopeful. I mean, if you just felt like a mother to me, you would be anxious to be helpful and understanding. I loathe being helped and understood. And, after all, there was nothing in any of them— except Barbara, of course."

"Who was Barbara?" asked Harriet, quickly.

"Oh, a girl. I owe her quite a lot, really," replied Wimsey, musingly. "When she married the other fellow, I took up sleuthing as a cure for wounded feelings and it's really been great fun, take it all in all. Dear me, yes—I was very much bowled over that time. I even took a special course in logic for her sake."

"Good gracious!"

"For the pleasure of repeating 'Barbara celarent darii ferio baralipton.' There was kind of mysterious romantic lilt about the thing which was somehow expressive of passion. Many a moonlight night have I murmured it to the nightingales which haunt the gardens of St. Johns—though, of course, I was a Balliol man myself, but the buildings are adjacent."

"If anybody ever marries you, it will be for the pleasure of hearing you talk piffle," said Harriet, severely.

"A humiliating reason, but better than no reason at all."

"I used to piffle rather well myself," said Harriet, with tears in her eyes, "but it's got knocked out of me. You know—I was really meant to be a cheerful person —all this gloom and suspicion isn't the real me. But I've lost my nerve, some-how."

"No wonder, poor kid. But you'll get over it. Just keep on smiling, and leave it to Uncle Peter."

When Wimsey got home, he found a note awaiting him.

Dear Lord Peter,

As you saw, I got the job. Miss Climpson sent six of us, all with different stories and testimonials, of course, and Mr. Pond (the head-clerk) engaged me, subject to Mr. Urquhart's approval.

I've only been here a couple of days, so there isn't very much I can tell you about my employer, personally, except that he has a sweet tooth and keeps secret stores of chocolate cream and Turkish delight in his desk, which he surreptitiously munches while he is dictating. He seems pleasant enough.

But there's just one thing. I fancy it would be interesting to investigate his financial activities. I've done a good bit one way and another with stockbroking, you know, and yesterday in his absence I took a call for him which I wasn't meant to hear. It wouldn't have told the ordinary person anything, but it did me, because I knew something about the man at the other end. Find out if Mr. U. had been doing anything with the Megatherium Trust before their big crash.

Further reports when anything turns up.

Yours sincerely.
Joan Murchison.

"Megatherium Trust?" said Wimsey. "That's a nice thing for a respectable solicitor to get mixed up with. I'll ask Freddy Arbuthnot. He's an ass about everything except stocks and shares, but he does understand them, for some ungodly reason."

He read the letter again, mechanically noting that it was typed on a Woodstock machine, with a chipped lower case p, and a capital A that was out of alignment.

Suddenly he woke up and read it a third time, noticing by no means mechanically, the chipped p and the irregular capital A.

Then he sat down, wrote a line on a sheet of paper, folded it, addressed it to Miss Murchison and sent Bunter out to post it.

For the first time, in this annoying case, he felt the vague stirring of the waters as a living idea emerged slowly and darkly from the innermost deeps of his mind.

12

Wimsey was accustomed to say, when he was an old man and more talkative even than usual, that the recollection of that Christmas at Duke's Denver had haunted him in nightmares, every night regularly, for the following twenty years. But it is possible that he remembered it with advantages. There is no doubt that it tried his temper severely. It began inauspiciously at the tea-table, when Mrs. "Freak" Dimsworthy fluted out in her high, overriding voice: "And is it true, Lord Peter dear, that you are defending that frightful poisoning woman?" The question acted like the drawing of a champagne cork. The whole party's bottled-up curiosity about the Vane case creamed over in one windy gust of stinging froth.

"I've no doubt she did it, and I don't blame her," said Captain Tommy Bates, "perfectly foul blighter. Has his photograph on the dust-cover of his books, you know, that's the sort of squit he was. Wonderful, the rotters these highbrow females will fall for. The whole lot of 'em ought to be poisoned like rats. Look at the harm they do to the country."

"But he was a very fine writer," protested Mrs. Featherstone, a lady in her thirties, whose violently compressed figure suggested that she was engaged in a perpetual struggle to compute her weight in terms of the first syllables of her name rather than the last. "His books are positively Gallic in their audacity and restraint. Audacity is not rare—but that perfect concision of style is a gift which—"

"Oh, if you like dirt," interrupted the Captain, rather rudely.

"I wouldn't call it that," said Mrs. Featherstone. "He is frank, of course, and that is what people in this country will not forgive. It is part of our national hypocrisy. But the beauty of the writing puts it all on a higher plane."

"Well, I wouldn't have the muck in the house," said the Captain, firmly. "I caught Hilda with it, and I said, 'Now you send that book straight back to the library.' I don't often interfere, but one must draw the line somewhere."

"How did you know what it was like?" asked Wimsey, innocently.

"Why, James Douglas' article in the *Express* was good enough for me," said Captain Bates. "The paragraphs he quoted were filthy, positively filthy."

"Well, it's a good thing we've all read them," said Wimsey. "Forewarned is forearmed."

"We owe a great debt of gratitude to the press," said the Dowager Duchess, "so kind of them to pick out all the plums for us and save the trouble of reading the books, don't you think, and such a joy for the poor dear people who can't afford seven-and-sixpence, or even a library subscription, I suppose, though I'm sure that works out cheaply enough if one is a quick reader. Not that the cheap ones will take those books for I asked my maid, such a superior girl and so keen on improving her mind, which is more than I can say for most of my friends, but no doubt it is all due to free education for the people and I suspect her in my heart of voting labour though I never ask because I don't think it's fair, and besides, if I did, I couldn't very well take any notice of it, could I?"

"Still, I don't suppose the young woman murdered him on that account," said her daughter-in-law. "From all accounts she was just as bad as he was."

"Oh, come," said Wimsey, "you can't think that, Helen. Damn it, she writes detective stories and in detective stories virtue is always triumphant. They're the purest literature we have."

"The devil is always ready to quote scripture when it pays him to do so," said the younger Duchess, "and they say the wretched woman's sales are going up by leaps and bounds."

"It's my belief," said Mr. Harringay, "that the whole thing is a publicity stunt gone wrong." He was a large, jovial man, extremely rich and connected with the City. "You never know what these advertising fellows are up to."

"Well, it looks like a case of hanging the goose that lays the golden eggs this time," said Captain Bates, with a loud laugh. "Unless Wimsey means to pull off one of his conjuring tricks."

"I hope he does," said Miss Titterton. "I adore detective stories. I'd commute the sentence to penal servitude on condition that she turned out a new story every six months. It would be much more useful than picking oakum or sewing mail-bags for the post-office to mislay."

"Aren't you being a bit previous?" suggested Wimsey, mildly. "She's not convicted yet."

"But she will be next time. You can't fight facts, Peter."

"Of course not," said Captain Bates. "The police know what they're about. They don't put people into the dock if there isn't something pretty shady about 'em."

Now this was a fearful brick, for it was not so many years since the Duke of Denver had himself stood his trial on a mistaken charge of murder. There was a ghastly silence, broken by the Duchess, who said icily: "Really, Captain Bates!"

"What? eh? Oh, of course, I mean to say, I know mistakes do happen sometimes, but that's a very different thing. I mean to say, this woman, with no morals at all, that is, I mean—"

"Have a drink, Tommy," said Lord Peter, kindly. "You aren't quite up to your usual standard of tact today."

"No, but do tell us, Lord Peter," cried Mrs. Dimsworthy, "what the creature is *like*. Have you talked to her? I thought she had rather a nice voice, though she's as plain as a pancake."

"Nice voice, Freakie? Oh, no," said Mrs. Featherstone. "I should have called it rather sinister. It absolutely thrilled me, I got shudders all the way down my spine. A genuine *frisson*. And I think she would be quite attractive, with those queer, smudgy eyes, if she were properly dressed. A sort of *femme fatale*, you know. Does she try to hypnotise you, Peter?"

"I saw in the papers," said Miss Titterton, "that she had had hundreds of offers of marriage."

"Out of one noose into the other," said Harringay, with his noisy laugh.

"I don't think I should care to marry a murderess," said Miss Titterton, "especially one that's been trained on detective stories. One would be always wondering whether there was anything funny about the taste of the coffee."

"Oh, these people are all mad," said Mrs. Dimsworthy. "They have a morbid longing for notoriety. It's like the lunatics who make spurious confessions and give themselves up for crimes they haven't committed."

"A murderess might make quite a good wife," said Harringay. "There was Madeleine Smith, you know—she used arsenic too, by the way—she married somebody and lived happily to a respectable old age."

"But did her husband live to a respectable old age?" demanded Miss Titterton. "That's more to the point, isn't it?"

"Once a poisoner, always a poisoner, *I* believe," said Mrs. Featherstone. "It's a passion that grows upon you—like drink or drugs."

"It's the intoxicating sensation of power," said Mrs. Dimsworthy. "But, Lord Peter, *do* tell us—"

"Peter!" said his mother, "I do wish you'd go an see what's happened to Gerald. Tell him his tea is getting cold. I think he's in the stables talking to Freddy about thrush or cracked heels or something, so tiresome the way horses are always getting something the matter with them. You haven't trained Gerald properly, Helen, he used to be quite punctual as a boy. Peter was always the tiresome one, but he's becoming almost human in his old age. It's that wonderful man of his who keeps him in order, really a remarkable character and so intelligent, quite one of the old sort, you know, a perfect autocrat, and such manners too. He would be worth thousands to an American millionaire, most impressive, I wonder Peter isn't afraid he'll give warning one of these days, but I really believe he is positively attached to him. Bunter attached to Peter, I mean, though the other way on would be true too, I'm sure Peter pays more attention to his opinion than he does to mine."

Wimsey had escaped, and was by now on his way to the stables. He met Gerald, Duke of Denver, returning, with Freddy Arbuthnot in tow. The former received the Dowager's message with a grin.

"Got to turn up, I suppose," he said. "I wish nobody had ever invented tea. Ruins your nerves and spoils your appetite for dinner."

"Beastly sloppy stuff," agreed the Hon. Freddy. "I say, Peter, I've been wanting to get hold of you."

"Same here," said Wimsey, promptly. "I'm feelin' rather exhausted with conversation. Let's wander through the billiard-room and build our constitutions up before we face the barrage."

"Today's great thought," said Freddy, enthusiastically. He pattered happily after Wimsey into the billiard-room, and flung himself down in a large chair. "Great bore, Christmas, isn't it? All the people one hates most gathered together in the name of goodwill and all that."

"Bring a couple of whiskies," said Wimsey to the footman. "And, James, if anybody asks for Mr. Arbuthnot or me, you rather think we have gone out. Well, Freddy, here's luck! Has anything transpired, as the journalists say?"

"I've been sleuthing like stink on the tracks of your man," said Mr. Arbuthnot. "Really, don't you know, I shall soon be qualified to set up in your line of business. Our financial column, edited by Uncle Buthie—that sort of thing. Friend Urquhart has been very careful, though. Bound to be—respectable family lawyer and all that. But I saw a man yesterday who knows a fellow who had it from a chappie that said Urquhart had been dipping himself a bit recklessly off the deep end."

"Are you sure, Freddy?"

"Well, not to say sure. But this man, you see, owes me one, so to speak, for having warned him off the Megatherium before the band began to play, and he thinks, if he can get hold of the chappie that knows, not the fellow that told him, you understand, but the other one, that he might be able to get something out of him, don't you see, especially if I was able to put this other chappie in the way of something or the other, what?"

"And no doubt you have secrets to sell."

"Oh, well, I daresay I could make it worth this other chappie's while, because I've got an idea, through this other fellow that my bloke knows, that the chappie is rather up against it, as you might say, through being caught short on some Airways stock, and if I was to put him in touch with Goldberg, don't you see, it might get him out of a hole and so on. And Goldberg will be all right, because, don't you see, he's a cousin of old Levy's, who was murdered, you know, and all these Jews stick together like leeches and as a matter of fact, I think it's very fine of them."

"But what has old Levy got to do with it?" asked Wimsey, his mind running over the incidents in that half-forgotten murder-episode.

"Well, as a matter of fact," said the Hon. Freddy, a little nervously, "I've—er—done the trick as you might say. Rachel Levy is—er, in fact—going to become Mrs. Freddy and all that sort of thing."

"The devil she is," said Wimsey, ringing the bell. "Tremendous congratters and all that. It's been a long time working up, hasn't it?"

"Why, yes," said Freddy. "yes, it has. You see, the trouble was that I was a Christian—at least, I was christened and all that, though I pointed out I wasn't at all a good one, except, of course, that one keeps up the family pew and turns out on Christmas Day and so on. Only it seems they didn't mind that so much as my bein' a Gentile. Well that, of course, is past prayin' for. And then there was the difficulty about the kids—if any. But I explained that I didn't mind what they counted them as—and I don't, you know, because, as I was saying, it would be all to the little beggars' advantage to be in with the Levy and Goldberg crowd, especially if the boys were to turn out anything in the financial way. And then I rather got round Lady Levy by sayin' I had served nearly seven years for Rachel—that was rather smart, don't you think?"

"Two more whiskies, James," said Lord Peter. "It was brilliant, Freddy. How did you come to think of it?"

"In church," said Freddy, "at Diana Rigby's wedding. The bride was fifty minutes late and I had to do something, and somebody had left a Bible in the pew. I saw that—I say, old Laban was a bit of a tough, wasn't he?—and I said to myself, 'I'll work that off the next time I call,' and so I did, and the old lady was uncommonly touched by it."

"And the long and the short of it is, you're fixed up," said Wimsey. "Well, cheerio, here's to it. Am I best man, Freddy, or do you bring it off at the Synagogue?"

"Well, yes—it is to be at the Synagogue—I had to agree to that," said Freddy, "but I believe some sort of bridegroom's friend comes into it. You'll stand by me, old bean, won't you? You keep your hat on, don't forget."

"I'll bear it in mind," said Wimsey, "and Bunter will explain the procedure to me. He's bound to know. He knows everything. But look here, Freddy, you won't forget about this little enquiry, will you?"

"I won't, old chap—upon my word I won't. I'll let you know the very second I hear anything. But I really think you may count on there being something in it."

Wimsey found some consolation in this. At any rate, he so far pulled himself together as to be the life and soul of the rather restrained revels at Duke's Denver. The Duchess Helen, indeed, observed rather acidly to the Duke that Peter was surely getting too old to play the buffoon, and that it would be better if he took things seriously and settled down.

"Oh, I dunno," said the Duke, "Peter's a weird fish—you never know what he's thinkin' about. He pulled me out of the soup once and I'm not going to interfere with him. You leave him alone, Helen."

Lady Mary Wimsey, who had arrived late on Christmas Eve, took another view of the matter. She marched into her younger brother's bedroom at 2 o'clock on the morning of Boxing Day. There had been dinner and dancing and charades of the most exhausting kind. Wimsey was sitting thoughtfully over by the fire in his dressing-gown.

"I say, old Peter," said Lady Mary, "you're being a bit fevered, aren't you? Anything up?"

"Too much plum-pudding," said Wimsey, "and too much county. I'm a martyr, that's what I am—burning in brandy to make a family holiday."

"Yes, it's ghastly, isn't it? But how's life? I haven't seen you for an age. You've been away such a long time."

"Yes—and you seem very much taken up with this house-decorating job you're running."

"One must do something. I get rather sick of being aimless, you know."

"Yes. I say, Mary, do you ever see anything of old Parker these days?"

Lady Mary stared into the fire.

"I've had dinner with him once or twice, when I was in town."

"Have you? He's a very decent sort. Reliable, homespun—that sort of thing. Not amusing, exactly."

"A little solid."

"As you say—a little solid." Wimsey lit a cigarette. "I should hate anything upsettin' to happen to Parker. He'd take it hard. I mean to say, it wouldn't be fair to muck about with his feelin's and so on."

Mary laughed.

"Worried, Peter?"

"N-no. But I'd rather like him to have fair play."

"Well, Peter—I can't very well say yes or no till he asks me, can I?"

"Can't you?"

"Well, not to him. It would upset his ideas of decorum, don't you think?"

"I suppose it would. But it would probably upset them just as much if he did ask you. He would feel that the mere idea of hearing a butler announce 'Chief-Detective-Inspector and Lady Mary Parker' would have something shocking about it."

"It's stalemate, then, isn't it?"

"You could stop dining with him."

"I could do that, of course."

"And the mere fact that you don't—I see. Would it be any good if I demanded to know his intentions in the true Victorian manner?"

"Why this sudden thirst for getting your family off your hands, old man? Peter—nobody's being horrible to you, are they?"

"No, no. I'm just feeling rather like a benevolent uncle, that's all. Old age creeping on. That passion for being useful which attacks the best of us when we're getting past our prime."

"Like me with the house-decorating. I designed these pajamas, by the way. Don't you think they're rather entertaining? But I expect Chief-Inspector Parker prefers the old-fashioned night-gown, like Dr. Spooner or whoever it was."

"That would be a wrench," said Wimsey.

"Never mind. I'll be brave and devoted. Here and now I cast off my pajamas for ever!"

"No, no," said Wimsey, "not here and now. Respect a brother's feelings. Very well. I am to tell my friend Charles Parker, that if he will abandon his natural modesty and propose, you will abandon your pajamas and say yes."

"It will be a great shock for Helen, Peter."

"Blast Helen. I daresay it won't be the worst shock she'll get."

"Peter, you're plotting something devilish. All right. If you want me to administer the first shock and let her down by degrees—I'll do it."

"Right-ho!" said Wimsey, casually.

Lady Mary twisted one arm about his neck and bestowed on him one of her rare sisterly caresses.

"You're a decent old idiot," she said, "and you look played-out. Go to bed."

"Go to blazes," said Lord Peter, amiably.

13

Miss Murchison felt a touch of excitement in her well-regulated heart, as she rang the bell of Lord Peter's flat. It was not caused by the consideration of his title or his wealth or his bachelorhood, for Miss Murchison had been a business woman all her life, and was accustomed to visiting bachelors of all descriptions without giving a second thought to the matter. But his note had been rather exciting.

Miss Murchison was thirty-eight, and plain. She had worked in the same financier's office for twelve years. They had been good years on the whole, and it was not until the last two that she had even begun to realise that the brilliant financier who juggled with so many spectacular undertakings was juggling for his life under circumstances of increasing difficulty. As the pace grew faster, he added egg after egg to those which were already spinning in the air. There is a limit to the number of eggs which can be spun by human hands. One day an egg slipped and smashed—then another—then a whole omelette of eggs. The juggler fled from the stage and escaped abroad, his chief assistant blew out his brains, the audience booed, the curtain came down, and Miss Murchison, at 37, was out of a job.

She had put an advertisement in the papers and had answered many others. Most people appeared to want their secretaries young and cheap. It was discouraging.

Then her own advertisement had brought an answer from a Miss Climpson, who kept a typing bureau.

It was not what she wanted, but she went. And she found that it was not quite a typing bureau after all, but something more interesting.

Lord Peter Wimsey, mysteriously at the back of it all, had been abroad when Miss Murchison entered the "Cattery," and she had never seen him till a few weeks ago. This would be the first time she had actually spoken to him. An odd-looking person, she thought, but people said he had brains. Anyhow—

The door was opened by Bunter, who seemed to expect her and showed her at once into a sitting-room lined with bookshelves. There were some fine prints on the walls, an Aubusson carpet, a grand piano, a vast Chesterfield and a number of deep and cosy chairs, upholstered in brown leather. The curtains were drawn, a wood-fire blazed on the hearth, and before it stood a table, with a silver tea-service whose lovely lines were delightful to the eye.

As she entered, her employer uncoiled himself from the depths of an arm-chair, put down a black-letter folio which he had been studying and greeted her in the cool, husky and rather languid tones which she had already heard in Mr. Urquhart's office.

"Frightfully good of you to come round, Miss Murchison. Beastly day, isn't it? I'm sure you want your tea. Can you eat crumpets? Or would you prefer something more up-to-date?"

"Thanks," said Miss Murchison, as Bunter hovered obsequiously at her elbow, "I like crumpets very much."

"Oh, good! Well, Bunter, we'll struggle with the teapot ourselves. Give Miss Murchison another cushion and then you can toddle off. Back at work, I suppose? How's our Mr. Urquhart?"

"He's all right." Miss Murchison had never been a chatty girl. "There's one thing I wanted to tell you—"

"Plenty of time," said Wimsey. "Don't spoil your tea." He waited on her with a kind of anxious courtesy which pleased her. She expressed admiration of the big bronze chrysanthemums heaped here and there about the room.

"Oh! I'm glad you like them. My friends say they give a feminine touch to the place, but Bunter sees to it, as a matter of fact. They make a splash of colour and all that, don't you think?"

"The books look masculine enough."

"Oh, yes—they're my hobby, you know. Books—and crime, of course. But crime's not very decorative, is it? I don't care about collecting hangmen's ropes and murderers' overcoats. What are you to do with 'em? Is the tea all right? I ought to have asked you to pour out, but it always seems to me rather unfair to invite a person and then make her do all the work. What do you do when you're not working, by the way? Do you keep a secret passion for anything?"

"I go to concerts," said Miss Murchison. "And when there isn't a concert I put something on the gramophone."

"Musician?"

"No—never could afford to learn properly. I ought to have been, I daresay. But there was more money in being a secretary."

"I suppose so."

"Unless one is absolutely first-class, and I should never have been that. And third-class musicians are a nuisance."

"They have a rotten time, too," said Wimsey. "I hate to see them in cinemas, poor beasts, playing the most ghastly tripe, sandwiched in with snacks of Mendelssohn and torn-off gobbets of the 'Unfinished.' Have a sandwich. Do you like Bach? or only the Moderns?"

He wriggled on to the piano stool.

"I'll leave it to you," said Miss Murchison, rather surprised.

"I feel rather like the Italian Concerto this evening. It's better on the harpsichord, but I haven't got one here. I find Bach good for the brain. Steadying influence and all that."

He played the Concerto through, and then, after a few seconds' pause went on to one of the "Forty-eight." He played well, and gave a curious impression of controlled power, which, in a man so slight and so fantastical in manner, was unexpected and even a little disquieting. When he had finished, he said, still sitting at the piano:

"Did you make the enquiry about the typewriter?"

"Yes; it was bought new three years ago."

"Good. I gather, by the way, that you are probably right about Urquhart's connection with the Megatherium Trust. That was a very helpful observation of yours. Consider yourself highly commended."

"Thank you."

"Anything fresh?"

"No—except that the evening after you called at Mr. Urquhart's office, he stayed on a long time after we had gone, typing something."

Wimsey sketched an arpeggio with his right hand and demanded:

"How do you know how long he stayed and what he was doing if you had all gone?"

"You said you wanted to know of anything, however small, that was in the least unusual. I thought it might be unusual for him to stay on by himself, so I walked up and down Princeton Street and round Red Lion Square till half past seven. Then I saw him put the light out and go home. Next morning I noticed that some papers I had left just inside my typewriter cover had been disturbed. So I concluded that he had been typing."

"Perhaps the charwoman disturbed them?"

"Not she. She never disturbs the dust, let alone the cover."

Wimsey nodded.

"You have the makings of a first-class sleuth, Miss Murchison. Very well. In that case, our little job will have to be undertaken. Now, look here—you quite understand that I'm going to ask you to do something illegal?"

"Yes, I understand."

"And you don't mind?"

"No. I imagine that if I'm taken up you will pay any necessary costs."

"Certainly."

"And if I go to prison?"

"I don't think it will come to that. There's a slight risk, I admit—that is, if I'm wrong about what I think is happening—that you might be brought up for attempted theft or for being in possession of safebreaking tools, but that is the most that could happen."

"Oh! well, it's all in the game, I suppose."

"You mean that?"

"Yes."

"Splendid. Well—you know that deed-box you brought in to Mr. Urquhart's room the day I was there?"

"Yes, the one marked Wrayburn."

"Where is it kept? In the outer office, where you could get hold of it?"

"Oh, yes—on a shelf with a lot of others."

"Good. Would it be possible for you to get left alone in the office any day for, say, half an hour?"

"Well—at lunch-time I'm supposed to go out at half-past twelve and come back at half-past one. Mr. Pond goes out then, but Mr. Urquhart sometimes comes back. I couldn't be certain that he wouldn't pop out on me. And it would look funny if I wanted to stay on after four-thirty, I expect. Unless I pretended I had made a mistake and wanted to stay and put it right. I could do that. I might come extra early in the morning when the charwoman is there—or would it matter her seeing me?"

"It wouldn't matter very much," said Wimsey, thoughtfully. "She'd probably think you had legitimate business with the box. I'll leave it to you to choose the time."

"But what am I to do? Steal the box?"

"Not quite. Do you know how to pick a lock?"

"Not in the least, I'm afraid."

"I often wonder what we go to school for," said Wimsey. "We never seem to learn anything really useful. I can pick quite a pretty lock myself, but, as we haven't much time and as you'll need some rather intensive training, I think I'd better take you to an expert. Should you mind putting your coat on and coming round with me to see a friend?"

"Not at all. I should be delighted."

"He lives in the Whitechapel Road, but he's a very pleasant fellow, if you can overlook his religious opinions. Personally, I find them rather refreshing. Bunter! Get us a taxi, will you?"

On the way to the East End, Wimsey insisted upon talking music—rather to Miss Murchison's disquietude; she began to think there was something a little sinister in this pointed refusal to discuss the object of their journey.

"By the way," she ventured, interrupting something Wimsey was saying about fugal form, "this person we are going to see—has he a name?"

"Now you mention it, I believe he has, but he's never called by it. It's Rumm."

"Not very, perhaps, if he—er—gives lessons in lockpicking."

"I mean, his name's Rumm."

"Oh; what is it then?"

"Dash it! I mean, Rumm is his name."

"Oh! I beg your pardon."

"But he doesn't care to use it, now that he is a total abstainer."

"Then what does one call him?"

"I call him Bill," said Wimsey, as the taxi drew up at the entrance to a narrow court, "but when he was at the head of his profession, they called him 'Blindfold Bill.' He was a very great man in his time."

Paying off the taxi-man (who had obviously taken them for welfare-workers till he saw the size of his tip, and now did not know what to make of them), Wimsey steered his companion down the dirty alleyway. At the far end was a small house, from whose lighted windows poured forth the loud strains of a chorus of voices, supported by a harmonium and other instruments.

"Oh, dear!" said Wimsey, "we've struck a meeting. It can't be helped. Here goes."

Pausing until the strains of "Glory, glory, glory," had been succeeded by a sound as of fervent prayer, he hammered lustily at the door. Presently a small girl put her head out and, seeing Lord Peter, uttered a shrill cry of delight.

"Hullo, Esmeralda Hyacinth," said Wimsey. "Is Dad in?"

"Yes, sir, please, sir, they'll be so pleased, will you step in and oh, please?"

"Well?"

"Please, sir, will you sing 'Nazareth'?"

"No, I will not sing 'Nazareth' on any account, Esmeralda; I'm surprised at you."

"Daddy says 'Nazareth' isn't worldly, and you do sing it so beautiful," said Esmeralda, her mouth drooping.

Wimsey hid his face in his hands.

"This comes of having done a foolish thing once," he said. "One never lives it down. I won't promise, Esmeralda, but we'll see. But I want to talk business with Dad when the meeting's over."

The child nodded; at the same moment, the praying voice within the room ceased, amid ejaculations of "Alleluia!" and Esmeralda, profiting by this momentary pause, pushed open the door and said loudly:

"Here's Mr. Peter and a lady."

The room was small, very hot and very full of people. In one corner was the harmonium, with the musicians grouped about it. In the middle, standing by a round table covered with a red cloth, was a stout, square man, with a face like a bulldog. He had a book in his hand, and appeared to be about to announce a hymn, but, seeing Wimsey and Miss Murchison, he came forward, stretching out a large and hearty hand.

"Welcome one and welcome all!" he said. "Brethren, 'ere is a dear brother and sister in the Lord as is come out of the 'aunts of the rich and the riotous living of the Westend to join with us in singing the Songs of Zion. Let us sing and give praise. Alleluia! We know that many shall come from the East *and* from the West and sit down at the Lord's feast, while many that thinks theirselves chosen shall be cast into outer darkness. Therefore let us not say, because this man wears a shiny eyeglass, that he is not a chosen vessel, or because this woman wears a di'mond necklace and rides in her Rolls-Royce, she will not therefore wear a white robe and a gold crown in the New Jerusalem, nor because these people travels in the Blue Train to the Rivereera, therefore they shall not be seen a-castin' down their golden crowns by the River of the Water of Life. We 'ears that there talk sometimes in 'Yde Park o' Sundays, but it's bad and foolish and leads to strife and envyings and not to charity. All we like sheep 'ave gone astray and well I may say so, 'avin' been a black and wicked sinner myself till this 'ere gentleman, for such 'e truly is, laid 'is 'and upon me as I was a-bustin' of 'is safe and was the instrument under God of turnin' me from the broad way that leadeth to destruction. Oh, brethren, what a 'appy day that was for me, alleluia! What a shower of blessings come to me by the grace of the Lord! Let us unite now in thanksgiving for 'eaven's mercies in Number One 'Undred and Two. (Esmeralda, give our dear friends a 'ymn-book.)"

"I'm sorry," said Wimsey to Miss Murchison. "Can you bear it? I fancy this is the final outbreak."

The harmonium, harp, sackbut, psaltery, dulcimer and all kinds of music burst out with a blare which nearly burst the ear-drum, the assembly lifted its combined voices, and Miss Murchison, to her amazement, found herself joining —at first self-consciously and then with a fine fervour in that stirring chant—

"Sweeping through the gates,
Sweeping through the gates of the New Jerusalem,
Washed in the Blood of the Lamb."

Wimsey, who appeared to find it all very good fun, carolled away happily, without the slightest embarrassment; whether because he was accustomed to the exercise, or merely because he was one of those imperturbably self-satisfied people who cannot conceive of themselves as being out of place in any surroundings, Miss Murchison was unable to determine.

To her relief, the religious exercise came to an end with the hymn, and the company took their leave, with many hand-shakings all around. The musicians emptied the condensed moisture from their wind-instruments politely into the fireplace and the lady who played the harmonium drew the cover over the keys and came forward to welcome the guests. She was introduced simply as Bella and Miss Murchison concluded, rightly, that she was the wife of Mr. Bill Rumm and the mother of Esmeralda.

"Well, now," said Bill, "it's dry work preachin' and singin'—you'll take a cup of tea or coffee, now, won't you?"

Wimsey explained that they had just had tea, but begged that the family might proceed with their own meal.

"It ain't 'ardly supper-time yet," said Mrs. Rumm. 'P'raps if you was to do your business with the lady and gentleman, Bill, they might feel inclined to take a bite with us later. It's trotters," she added, hopefully.

"Trotters want a lot of beating," said Wimsey, "and since our business may take a little time we'll accept with pleasure—if you're sure we're not putting you out."

"Not at all," said Mrs. Rumm, heartily. "Eight beautiful trotters they is, and with a bit of cheese they'll go round easy. Come along,—'Meraldy, your Dad's got business."

"Mr. Peter's going to sing," said the child, fixing reproachful eyes on Wimsey.

"Now don't you worrit his lordship," rebuked Mrs. Rumm. "I declare I'm ashamed of you."

"I'll sing after supper, Esmeralda," said Wimsey. "Hop along now like a good girl or I'll make faces at you. Bill, I've brought you a new pupil."

"Always 'appy to serve you, sir, knowing as it's the Lord's work. Glory be."

"Thank you," said Wimsey, modestly. "It's a simple matter, Bill, but as the young lady is inexperienced with locks and so on, I've brought her along to be coached. You see, Miss Murchison, before Bill here saw the light—"

"Praise God!" put in Bill.

"He was the most accomplished burglar and safe-breaker in the three kingdoms. He doesn't mind my telling you this, because he's taken his medicine and finished with it all and is now a very honest and excellent locksmith of the ordinary kind."

"Thanks be to Him that giveth the victory!"

"But from time to time, when I need a little help in a righteous cause, Bill gives me the benefit of his great experience."

"And oh! what 'appiness it is, miss, to turn them talents which I so wickedly abused to the service of the Lord. His 'oly Name be blessed that bringeth good out of evil."

"That's right," said Wimsey, with a nod. "Now, Bill, I've got my eye on a solicitor's deed-box, which may or may not contain something which will help me to get an innocent person out of trouble. This young lady can get access to the box, Bill, if you can show her the way inside it."

"If?" grunted Bill, with sovereign contempt. " 'Course I can! Deed-box, that's nuffin'. That ain't no field for a man's skill. Robbin' the kids' money-box, that's what it is with they trumpery little locks. There ain't a deed-box in this 'ere city wot I couldn't open blindfold in boxing-gloves with a stick of boiled macaroni."

"I know, Bill; but it isn't you that's got to do it. Can you teach the lady how to work it?"

"Sure I can. What kinder lock is it, lidy?"

"I don't know," said Miss Murchison. "An ordinary lock, I think. I mean, it has the usual sort of key—not a Bramah, or anything of that kind. Mr.—that is, the solicitor has one set of keys and Mr. Pond has another—just plain keys with barrels and wards."

"Ho!" said Bill, "then 'arf an hour will teach you all you want, miss." He went to a cupboard and brought out half a dozen lock-plates and a bunch of curious, thin wire hooks, strung on a ring like keys.

"Are those pick locks?" asked Miss Murchison, curiously.

"That's what they are, miss. Ingines of Satan!" He shook his head as he lovingly fingered the bright steel. "Many's the time sech keys as these 'ave let pore sinners in by the back gate into 'ell."

"This time," said Wimsey, "they'll let a poor innocent out of prison into the sunshine—if any, in this beastly climate."

"Praise Him for His manifold mercies! Well, miss, the fust thing is to understand the construction of a lock. Now jest you look 'ere."

He picked up one of the locks and showed how, by holding up the spring, the catch could be thrust back.

"There ain't no need of all them fancy wards, you see, miss. The barrel and the spring—that's all there is to it. Jest you try."

Miss Murchison accordingly tried, and forced several locks with an ease that astonished her.

"Well now, miss, the difficulty is, you see, that when the lock's in place, you can't use your eyes, but you 'as your 'earin' and you 'as the feelin' in your fingers, giv' you by Providence (praise His Name!) for that purpose. Now what you 'as to do, miss, is to shet your eyes and see with your fingers, like, w'en you've got your spring 'ooked back sufficient ter let the catch go past."

"I'm afraid I'm very clumsy," said Miss Murchison, at the fifth or sixth attempt.

"Now don't you fret, miss. Jest take it easy and you'll find the right way of it come to you all of a sudden, like. Jest feel when it seems to go sweet and use your 'ands independent. Would you like to 'ave a little go at a Combination while you're 'ere, sir? I've got a beauty 'ere. Giv' to me it was by Sam, you know 'oo I mean. Many's the time I've tried to show 'im the error of 'is ways. 'No, Bill,' 'e ses, 'I ain't got no use for religion,' 'e ses, pore lost sheep, 'but I ain't got no quarrel with you, Bill, ses 'e, 'and I'd like for ter give you this 'ere little sooveneer.' "

"Bill, Bill," said Wimsey, shaking a reproachful finger, "I'm afraid this wasn't honestly come by."

"Well, sir, if I knowed the owner I'd 'and it over to 'im with the greatest of pleasure. It's quite good, you see. Sam put the soup in at the 'inges and it blowed the 'ole front clean off, lock and all. It's small, but it's a real beauty—new pattern to me, that is. But I mastered it," said Bill, with unregenerate pride, "in an hour or two."

"It'd have to be a good bit of work to beat you, Bill"; Wimsey set the lock up before him, and began to manipulate the knob, his fingers moving with micrometer delicacy and his ear bent to catch the fall of the tumblers.

"Lord!" said Bill—this time with no religious intention—"wot a cracksman you'd a-made, if you'd a-given your mind to it—which the Lord in His mercy forbid you should!"

"Too much work in that life for me, Bill," said Wimsey. "Dash it! I lost it that time."

He turned the knob back and started over again.

By the time the trotters arrived, Miss Murchison had acquired considerable facility with the more usual types of lock and a greatly enhanced respect for burglary as a profession.

"And don't you let yourself be 'urried, miss," was Bill's final injunction, "else you'll leave scratches on the lock and do yourself no credit. Lovely bit of work, that, ain't it, Lord Peter, sir?"

"Beyond me, I'm afraid," said Wimsey, with a laugh.

"Practice," said Bill, "that's all it is. If you'd a-started early enough you'd a-been a beautiful workman." He sighed. "There ain't many of 'em now-adays—glory be!—that can do a real artistic job. It fair goes to my 'eart to see a elegant bit o' stuff like that blowed all to bits with gelignite. Wot's gelignite? Any fool can 'andle it as doesn't mind makin' a blinkin' great row. Brutal, I calls it."

"Now, don't you get 'ankerin' back after them things, Bill," said Mrs. Rumm, reprovingly. "Come along, do, now and eat yer supper. Ef anybody's goin' ter do sech a wicked thing as breakin' safes, wot do it matter whether it's done artistic or inartistic?"

"Ain't that jest like a woman?—beggin' your pardon, miss."

"Well, you know it's true," said Mrs. Rumm.

"I know those trotters look very artistic," said Wimsey, "and that's quite enough for me."

The trotters having been eaten, and "Nazareth" duly sung, to the great admiration of the Rumm family, the evening closed pleasantly with the performance of a hymn, and Miss Murchison found herself walking up the

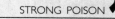
Whitechapel Road, with a bunch of picklocks in her pocket and some surprising items of knowledge in her mind.

"You make some very amusing acquaintances, Lord Peter."

"Yes—rather a jape, isn't it? But Blindfold Bill is one of the best. I found him on my premises one night and struck up a sort of an alliance with him. Took lessons from him and all that. He was a bit shy at first, but he got converted by another friend of mine—it's a long story—and the long and short of it was, he got hold of this locksmith business, and is doing very well at it. Do you feel quite competent about locks now?"

"I think so. What am I to look for when I get the box open?"

"Well," said Wimsey, "the point is this. Mr. Urquhart showed me what purported to be the draft of a will made five years ago by Mrs. Wrayburn. I've written down the gist of it on a bit of paper for you. Here it is. Now the snag about it is that that draft was typed on a machine which, as you tell me, was bought new from the makers only three years ago."

"Do you mean that's what he was typing that evening he stayed late at the office?"

"It looks like it. Now, why? If he had the original draft, why not show me that? Actually, there was no need for him to show it to me at all, unless it was to mislead me about something. Then, though he said he had the thing at home, and must have known he had it there, he pretended to search for it in Mrs. Wrayburn's box. Again, why? To make me think that it was already in existence when I called. The conclusion I drew is that, if there is a will, it's not along the lines of the one he showed me."

"It looks rather like that, certainly."

"What I want you to look for is the real will—either the original or the copy ought to be there. Don't take it away, but try to memorise the chief points in it, especially the names of the chief legatee or legatees and of the residuary legatee. Remember that the residuary legatee gets everything which falls in by a legatee's dying before the testatrix. I specially want to know whether anything was left to Philip Boyes or if any mention of the Boyes family is made in the will. Failing a will, there might be some other interesting document, such as a secret trust, instructing the executor to dispose of the money in some special way. In short, I want particulars of any document which may seem to be of interest. Don't waste too much time making notes. Carry the provisions in your head if you can and note them down privately when you get away from the office. And be sure you don't leave those skeleton keys about for people to find."

Miss Murchison promised to observe these instructions, and, a taxi coming up at that moment, Wimsey put her into it and sped her to her destination.

14

Mr. Norman Urquhart glanced at the clock, which stood at 4:15, and called through the open door:

"Are those affidavits nearly ready, Miss Murchison?"

"I am just on the last page, Mr. Urquhart."

"Bring them in as soon as you've finished. They ought to go round to Hanson's tonight."

"Yes, Mr. Urquhart."

Miss Murchison galloped noisily over the keys, slamming the shift-lever over with unnecessary violence, and causing Mr. Pond once more to regret the intrusion of female clerks. She completed her page, ornamented the foot of it with a rattling row of fancy lines and dots, threw over the release, spun the roller, twitching the foolscap sheets from under it in vicious haste, flung the carbons into the basket, shuffled the copies into order, slapped them vigorously on all four edges to bring them into symmetry, and bounced with them into the inner office.

"I haven't had time to read them through," she announced.

"Very well," said Mr. Urquhart.

Miss Murchison retired, shutting the door after her. She gathered her belongings together, took out a hand-mirror and unashamedly powdered her rather large nose, stuffed a handful of odds-and-ends into a bulging hand-bag, pushed some papers under her typewriter cover ready for the next day, jerked her hat from the peg and crammed it on her head, tucking wisps of hair underneath it with vigorous and impatient fingers.

Mr. Urquhart's bell rang—twice.

"Oh, bother!" said Miss Murchison, with heightened colour.

She snatched the hat off again, and answered the summons.

"Miss Murchison," said Mr. Urquhart, with an expression of considerable annoyance, "do you know that you have left out a whole paragraph on the first page of this?"

Miss Murchison flushed still more deeply.

"Oh, have I? I'm very sorry."

Mr. Urquhart held up a document resembling in bulk that famous one of which it was said that there was not truth enough in the world to fill so long an affidavit.

"It is very annoying," he said. "It is the longest and most important of the three, and is urgently required first thing tomorrow morning."

"I can't think how I could have made such a silly mistake," muttered Miss Murchison. "I will stay on this evening and retype it."

"I'm afraid you will have to. It is unfortunate, as I shall not be able to look it through myself, but there is nothing else to be done. Please check it carefully this time, and see that Hanson's have it before ten o'clock tomorrow."

"Yes, Mr. Urquhart. I will be extremely careful. I am very sorry indeed. I will make sure that it is quite correct and take it round myself."

"Very well, that will do," said Mr. Urquhart. "Don't let it happen again."

Miss Murchison picked up the papers and came out, looking flustered. She dragged the cover off the typewriter with sound and fury, jerked out the desk-drawers till they slammed against the drawer-stops, shook the top-sheet, carbons and flimsies together as a terrier shakes a rat, and attacked the machine tempestuously.

Mr. Pond, who had just locked his desk, and was winding a silk scarf about his throat, looked at her in mild astonishment.

"Have you some more typing to do tonight, Miss Murchison?"

"Got to do the whole bally thing again," said Miss Murchison. "Left out a paragraph on page one—it would be page one, of course—and he wants the tripe round at Hanson's by 10 o'clock."

Mr. Pond groaned slightly and shook his head.

"Those machines make you careless," he reproved her. "In the old days, clerks thought twice about making foolish mistakes, when it meant copying the whole document out again by hand."

"Glad I didn't live then," said Miss Murchison, shortly. "One might as well have been a galley-slave."

"And we didn't knock off at half-past four, either," said Mr. Pond. "We *worked* in those days."

"You may have worked longer," said Miss Murchison, "but you didn't get through as much in the time."

"We worked accurately and neatly," said Mr. Pond, with emphasis, as Miss Murchison irritably disentangled two keys which had jammed together under her hasty touch.

Mr. Urquhart's door opened and the retort on the typist's lips was silenced. He said good-night and went out. Mr. Pond followed him.

"I suppose you will have finished before the cleaner goes, Miss Murchison," he said. "If not, please remember to extinguish the light and to hand the key to Mrs. Hodges in the basement."

"Yes, Mr. Pond. Good-night."

"Good-night."

His steps pattered through the entrance, sounded again loudly as he passed the window, and died away in the direction of Brownlow Street. Miss Murchison continued typing till she calculated that he was safely on the tube at Chancery Lane. Then she rose, with a quick glance round her and approached a higher tier of shelves, stacked with black deed-boxes, each of which bore the name of a client in bold white letters.

WRAYBURN was there, all right, but had mysteriously shifted its place. This in itself was unaccountable. She clearly remembered having replaced it, just before Christmas, on top of the pile MORTIMER—SCROGGINS—LORD COOTE—DOLBY BROS. AND WINGFIELD; and here it was, on the day after Boxing Day, at the bottom of a pile, heaped over and kept down by BODGERS—SIR J. PENKRIDGE—FLATSBY & COATEN —TRUBODY LTD. and UNIVERSAL BONE TRUST. Somebody had been spring-cleaning, apparently, over the holidays, and Miss Murchison thought it improbable that it was Mrs. Hodges.

It was tiresome, because all the shelves were full, and it would be necessary to lift down all the boxes and stand them somewhere before she could get out WRAYBURN. And Mrs. Hodges would be in soon, and though Mrs. Hodges didn't really matter, it might look odd . . .

Miss Murchison pulled the chair from her desk (for the shelf was rather high) and, standing on it, lifted down UNIVERSAL BONE TRUST. It was heavyish, and the chair (which was of the revolving kind, and not the modern type with one spindly leg and a stiffly sprung back, which butts you in the lower spine and keeps you up to your job) wobbled unsteadily as she carefully lowered the box and balanced it on the narrow top of the cupboard. She reached up again and took down TRUBODY LTD., and placed it on BONE TRUST. She reached up for the third time and seized FLATSBY & COATEN. As she stooped with it a step sounded in the doorway and an astonished voice said behind her:

"Are you looking for something, Miss Murchison?"

Miss Murchison started so violently that the treacherous chair swung through a quarter-turn, nearly shooting her into Mr. Pond's arms. She came down awkwardly, still clasping the black deed-box.

"How you startled me, Mr. Pond! I thought you had gone."

"So I had," said Mr. Pond, "but when I got to the Underground I found I had left a little parcel behind me. So tiresome—I had to come back for it. Have you seen it any where? A little round jar, done in brown paper."

Miss Murchison set FLATSBY & COATEN on the seat of the chair and gazed about her.

"It doesn't seem to be in my desk," said Mr. Pond. "Dear, dear, I shall be so late. And I can't go without it, because it's wanted for dinner—in fact, it's a little jar of caviare. We have guests tonight. Now, where can I have put it?"

"Perhaps you put it down when you washed your hands," suggested Miss Murchison, helpful.

"Well now, perhaps I did." Mr. Pond fussed out and she heard the door of the little lavabo in the passage open with a loud creak. It suddenly occurred to her that she had left her handbag open on her desk. Suppose the skeleton keys were visible. She darted towards the bag, just as Mr. Pond returned in triumph.

"Much obliged to you for your suggestion, Miss Murchison. It was there all the time. Mrs. Pond would have been so much upset. Well, good-night again." He turned towards the door. "Oh, by the way, were you looking for something?"

"I was looking for a mouse," replied Miss Murchison with a nervous giggle. "I was just sitting working when I saw it run along the top of the cupboard and—er —up the wall behind those boxes."

"Dirty little beasts," said Mr. Pond. "The place is overrun with them. I have often said we ought to have a cat here. No hope of catching it now, though. You're not afraid of mice apparently?"

"No," said Miss Murchison, holding her eyes, by a strenuous physical effort, on Mr. Pond's face. If the skeleton keys were—as it seemed to her they must be —indecently exposing their spidery anatomy on her desk, it would be madness to look in that direction. "No—in your days I suppose all women were afraid of mice."

"Yes, they were," admitted Mr. Pond, "but then, of course, their garments were longer."

"Rotten for them," said Miss Murchison.

"They were very graceful in appearance," said Mr. Pond. "Allow me to assist you in replacing those boxes."

"You will miss your train," said Miss Murchison.

"I have missed it already," replied Mr. Pond, glancing at his watch. "I shall have to take the 5:30." He politely picked up FLATSBY & COATEN and climbed perilously with it in his hands to the unsteady seat of the rotatory chair.

"It's extremely kind of you," said Miss Murchison, watching him as he restored it to its place.

"Not at all. If you would kindly hand me up the others—"

Miss Murchison handed him TRUBODY LTD., and UNIVERSAL BONE TRUST.

"There!" said Mr. Pond, completing the pile and dusting his hands. "Now let us hope the mouse has gone for good. I will speak to Mrs. Hodges about procuring a suitable kitten."

"That would be a very good idea," said Miss Murchison. "Good-night, Mr. Pond."

"Good-night, Miss Murchison."

His footsteps pattered down the passage, sounded again more loudly beneath the window and for the second time died away in the direction of Brownlow Street.

"Whew!" said Miss Murchison. She darted to her desk. Her fears had deceived her. The bag was shut and the keys invisible.

She pulled her chair back to its place and sat down as a clash of brooms and pails outside announced the arrival of Mrs. Hodges.

"Ho!" said Mrs. Hodges, arrested on the threshold at sight of the lady clerk industriously typing away, "beg your pardon, miss, but I didn't know as how anybody was here."

"Sorry, Mrs. Hodges, I've got a little bit of work to finish. But you carry on. Don't mind me."

"That's all right, miss," said Mrs. Hodges, "I can do Mr. Partridge's office fust."

"Well, if it's all the same to you," said Miss Murchison. "I've just got to type a few pages and—er—make a précis—notes—you know, of some documents for Mr. Urquhart."

Mrs. Hodges nodded and vanished again. Presently a loud bumping noise overhead proclaimed her presence in Mr. Partridge's office.

Miss Murchison waited no longer. She dragged her chair to the shelves again, took down swiftly, one after the other, BONE TRUST, TRUBODY LTD., FLATSBY & COATEN, SIR J. PENKRIDGE and BODGERS. Her heart beat heavily as at last she seized WRAYBURN and carried it across to her desk.

She opened her bag and shook out its contents. The bunch of picklocks clattered upon the desk, mixed up with a handkerchief, a powder compact and a pocket-comb. The thin and shining steel barrels seemed to burn her fingers.

As she picked the bunch over, looking for the most suitable implement, there came a loud rap at the window.

She wheeled round, terrified. There was nothing there. Thrusting the picklocks into the pocket of her sports-coat, she tiptoed across and looked out. In the lamplight she observed three small boys engaged in climbing the iron railings which guard the sacred areas of Bedford Row. The foremost child saw her and gesticulated, pointing downwards. Miss Murchison waved her hand and cried, "Be off with you!"

The child shouted something unintelligible and pointed again. Putting two and two together, Miss Murchison deduced from the rap at the window, the gesture and the cry, that a valuable ball had fallen into the area. She shook her head with severity and returned to her task.

But the incident had reminded her that the window had no blinds and that, under the glare of the electric light, her movements were as visible to anybody in the street as though she stood on a lighted stage. There was no reason to suppose that Mr. Urquhart or Mr. Pond was about, but her uneasy conscience vexed her. Moreover, if a policeman should pass by, would he not be able to recognise picklocks a hundred yards away? She peered out again. Was it her agitated fancy, or was that a sturdy form in dark blue emerging from Hand Court?

Miss Murchison fled in alarm and, snatching up the deedbox, carried it bodily into Mr. Urquhart's private office.

Here, at least, she could not be overlooked. If anybody came in—even Mrs. Hodges—her presence might cause surprise but she would hear them coming and be warned in advance.

Her hands were cold and shaking, and she was not in the best condition to profit by Blindfold Bill's instructions. She drew a few deep breaths. She had been told not to hurry herself. Very well, then, she would not.

She chose a key with care and slipped it into the lock. For years, as it seemed to her, she scratched about aimlessly, till at length she felt the spring press against the hooked end. Pushing and lifting steadily with one hand, she introduced her second key. She felt the lever move—in another moment there was a sharp click and the lock was open.

There were not a great many papers in the box. The first document was a long list of securities, endorsed "Securities deposited with Lloyd's Bank." Then came the copies of some title-deeds, of which the originals were similarly deposited. Then came a folder filled with correspondence. Some of this consisted of letters from Mrs. Wrayburn herself, the latest letter being dated five years previously. In addition there were letters from tenants, bankers and stockbrokers; with copies of the replies written from the office and signed by Norman Urquhart.

Miss Murchison hastened impatiently through all this. There was no sign of a will or copy of a will—not even of the dubious draft that the solicitor had shown to Wimsey. Two papers only now remained at the bottom of the box. Miss Murchison picked up the first. It was a Power of Attorney, dated January 1925, giving Norman Urquhart full powers to act for Mrs. Wrayburn. The second was thicker and tied neatly with red tape. Miss Murchison slipped this off and unfolded the document.

It was a Deed of Trust, making over the whole of Mrs. Wrayburn's property to Norman Urquhart, in trust for herself, and providing that he should pay into her current account, for the estate, a certain fixed annual sum for personal expenses. The deed was dated July 1920 and attached to it was a letter, which Miss Murchison hastily read through:

Appleford, Windle.
15th May, 1920

My dear Norman,

Thank you very much, my dear boy, for your birthday letter and the pretty scarf. It is good of you to remember your old aunt so faithfully.

It has occurred to me that, now that I am over eighty years old, it is time that I put my business into your hands entirely. You and your father have managed very well for me all these years, and you have, of course, always very properly consulted me before taking any step with regard to investments. But I am getting such a *very old woman now* that I am quite out of touch with the modern world, and I cannot pretend that my opinions are of any real value. I am a *tired* old woman, too, and though you always explain everything *most clearly*, I find the *writing of letters a gêne* and a burden to me at my advanced age.

So I have determined to put my property in Trust with you for my lifetime, so that you may have full power to handle everything according to your own discretion, without having to consult me every time. And also, though I am strong and healthy yet, I am glad to say, and have my wits quite about me, still, that happy state of things might alter at any time. I might become paralysed or feeble in my head, or want to make some foolish use of my money, as silly old women have done before now.

So will you draw up a deed of this kind and bring it to me and I will sign it. And at the same time I will give you instructions about my will.

Your affec. Great-Aunt,
Rosanna Wrayburn.

"Hurray!" said Miss Murchison. "There *was* a will, then! And this Trust—that's probably important, too."

She read the letter again, skimmed through the clauses of the Trust, taking particular notice that Norman Urquhart was named as sole Trustee, and finally made a mental note of some of the larger and more important items in the list of securities. Then she replaced the documents in their original order, relocked the box—which yielded to treatment like an angel—carried it out, replaced it, piled the other boxes above it, and was back at her machine, just as Mrs. Hodges re-entered the office.

"Just finished, Mrs. Hodges," she called out cheerfully.

"I wondered if yer would be," said Mrs. Hodges, "I didn't hear the typewriter a-going."

"I was making notes by hand," said Miss Murchison. She crumpled together the spoiled front page of the affidavit and threw it into the waste-paper basket together with the re-type which she had begun. From her desk-drawer she produced a correctly typed first page, provided before-hand for the purpose, added it to the bundle of script, put the top copy and the required sets of flimsies into an envelope, sealed it, addressed it to Messrs. Hanson & Hanson, put on her hat and coat and went out, bidding a pleasant farewell to Mrs. Hodges at the door.

A short walk brought her to Messrs. Hansons' office, where she delivered the affidavit through the letter-box. Then, with a brisk step and humming to herself, she made for the 'bus-stop at the junction of Theobald's Road and Cray's Inn Road.

"I think I deserve a little supper in Soho," said Miss Murchison.

She was humming again as she walked from Cambridge Circus into Frith Street. "What *is* this beastly tune?" she asked herself abruptly. A little consideration reminded her that it was "Sweeping through the gates . . ."

"Bless me!" said Miss Murchison. "Going dotty, that's what I am."

15

Lord Peter congratulated Miss Murchison and gave her a rather special lunch at Rules, where there is a particularly fine old Cognac for those that appreciate such things. Indeed, Miss Murchison was a little late in returning to Mr. Urquhart's office, and in her haste omitted to hand back the skeleton keys. But when the wine is good and the company agreeable one cannot always think of everything.

Wimsey himself, by a great act of self-control, had returned to his own flat to think, instead of bolting away to Halloway Gaol. Although it was a work of charity and necessity to keep up the spirits of the prisoner (it was in this way that he excused his almost daily visits) he could not disguise from himself that it would be even more useful and charitable to get her innocence proved. So far, he had not made much real progress.

The suicide theory had been looking very hopeful when Norman Urquhart had produced the draft of the will; but his belief in that draft had now been thoroughly undermined. There was still a faint hope of retrieving the packet of white powder from the Nine Rings, but as the days passed remorselessly on, the hope diminished almost to vanishing-point. It irked him to be taking no action in the matter—he wanted to rush to the Gray's Inn Road, to cross-question, bully, bribe, ransack every person and place in and about the Rings but he knew that the police could do this better than he could.

Why had Norman Urquhart tried to mislead him about the will? He could so easily have refused all information. There must be some mystery about it. But if Urquhart were not, in fact, the legatee, he was playing rather a dangerous game. If the old lady died, and the will was proved, the facts would probably be published—and she might die any day.

How easy it would be, he thought, regretfully, to hasten Mrs. Wrayburn's death a trifle. She was ninety-three and very frail. An over-dose of something—a shake—a slight shock, even—it did not do to think after that fashion. He wondered idly who lived with the old woman and looked after her. . . .

It was the 30th. of December, and he still had no plan. The stately volumes on his shelves, rank after rank of Saint, historian, poet, philosopher, mocked his impotence. All that wisdom and all that beauty, and they could not show him how to save the woman he imperiously wanted from a sordid death by hanging.

And he had thought himself rather clever at that kind of thing. The enormous and complicated imbecility of things was all round him like a trap. He ground his teeth and raged helplessly, striding about the suave, wealthy, futile room. The great Venetian mirror over the fireplace showed him his own head and shoulders. He saw a fair, foolish face, with straw-coloured hair sleeked back; a monocle clinging incongruously under a ludicrously twitching brow; a chin shaved to perfection, hairless, epicene; a rather high collar, faultlessly starched, a tie elegantly knotted and matching in colour the handkerchief which peeped coyly from the breast-pocket of an expensive Savile-Row-tailored suit. He snatched up a heavy bronze from the mantelpiece—a beautiful thing, even as he snatched it, his fingers caressed the patina—and the impulse seized him to smash the mirror and smash the face—to break out into great animal howls and gestures.

Silly! One could not do that. The inherited inhibitions of twenty civilised centuries tied one hand and foot in bonds of ridicule. What if he did smash the mirror? Nothing would happen. Bunter would come in, unmoved and unsurprised, would sweep up the debris in a dust-pan, would prescribe a hot bath and massage. And next day a new mirror would be ordered, because people would come in and ask questions, and civilly regret the accidental damage to the old one. And Harriet Vane would still be hanged, just the same.

Wimsey pulled himself together, called for his hat and coat, and went away in a taxi to call on Miss Climpson.

"I have a job," he said to her, more abruptly than was his wont, "which I should like you to undertake yourself. I can't trust anybody else."

"How *kind* of you to put it like that," said Miss Climpson.

"The trouble is, I can't in the least tell you how to set about it. It all depends on what you find when you get there. I want you to go to Windle in Westmorland and get hold of an imbecile and paralysed old lady called Mrs. Wrayburn, who lives at a house called Appleford. I don't know who looks after her, or how you are to get into the house. But you've got to find out where her will is kept, and, if possible, see it."

"Dear me!" said Miss Climpson.

"You see," said Wimsey, "unless we can give some very good reason for delay, they're bound to take the Vane case almost first thing next sessions. If I could persuade the lawyers for the defence that there is the least chance of securing fresh evidence, they could apply for a postponement. But at present I have nothing that could be called evidence—only the vaguest possible hunch."

"I see," said Miss Climpson. "Well, none of us can do more than our best, and it is very necessary to have Faith. That moves mountains, we are told."

"Then for Heaven's sake lay in a good stock of it," said Wimsey, gloomily, "because as far as I can see, this job is like shifting the Himalayas and the Alps, with a spot of frosty Caucasus and a touch of the Rockies thrown in."

"You may count on me to do my poor best," replied Miss Climpson, "and I will ask the dear vicar to say a Mass of special intention for one engaged in a difficult undertaking. When would you like me to start?"

"At once," said Wimsey. "I think you had better go just as your ordinary self, and put up at the local hotel—no—a boarding-house, there will be more opportunities for gossip. I don't know much about Windle, except that there is a bootfactory there and rather a good view, but it's not a large place, and I should think everybody would know about Mrs. Wrayburn. She is very rich, and was notorious in her time. The person you'll have to cotton on to is the female—there must be one of some sort—who nurses and waits on Mrs. Wrayburn and is, generally speaking, about her path and about her bed and all that. When you find out her special weakness, drive a wedge into it like one o'clock. Oh! by the way—it's quite possible the will isn't there at all, but in the hands of a solicitor-fellow called Norman Urquhart who hangs out in Bedford Row. If so all you can do is to get the pump to work and find out anything—anything at all—to his disadvantage. He's Mrs. Wrayburn's great-nephew, and goes to see her sometimes."

Miss Climpson made a note of these instructions.

"And now I'll tootle off and leave you to it," said Wimsey. "Draw on the firm for any money you want. And if you need any special outfit, send me a wire."

On leaving Miss Climpson, Lord Peter Wimsey again found himself a prey to Weltschmerz and self-pity. But it now took the form of a gentle, pervading melancholy. Convinced of his own futility, he determined to do what little good lay in his power before retiring to a monastery or to the frozen wastes of the Antarctic. He taxied purposefully round to Scotland Yard, and asked for Chief-Inspector Parker.

Parker was in his office, reading a report which had just come in. He greeted Wimsey with an expression which seemed more embarrassed than delighted.

"Have you come about that packet of powder?"

"Not this time," said Wimsey. "I don't suppose you'll ever hear anything more of that. No. It's—rather a more—er—delicate matter. It's about my sister."

Parker started and pushed the report to one side.

"About Lady Mary?"

"Er—yes. I understand she's been going about with you—er—dining—and all that sort of thing, what?"

"Lady Mary has honoured me—on one or two occasions—with her company," said Parker. "I did not think—I did not know—that is I understood—"

"Ah! but *did* you understand, that's the point?" said Wimsey, solemnly. "You see, Mary's a very nice-minded sort of girl, though I say it, and—"

"I assure you," said Parker, "that there is no need to tell me that. Do you suppose that I should misinterpret her kindness? It is the custom now-a-days for women of the highest character to dine unchaperoned with their friends, and Lady Mary has—"

"I'm not suggesting a chaperon," said Wimsey, "Mary wouldn't stick it for one thing, and I think it's all bosh, anyhow. Still, bein' her brother, and all that—it's Gerald's job really, of course, but Mary and he don't altogether hit it off, you know, and she wouldn't be likely to burble any secrets into his ear, especially as it would all be handed on to Helen—what was I going to say? Oh, yes—as Mary's brother, you know, I suppose it's my so to speak duty to push round and drop the helpful word here and there."

Parker jabbed the blotting-paper thoughtfully.

"Don't do that," said Wimsey, "it's bad for your pen. Take a pencil."

"I suppose," said Parker, "I ought not to have presumed—"

"What did you presume, old thing?" said Wimsey, his head cocked, sparrow-fashion.

"Nothing to which anybody could object," said Parker, hotly. "What are you thinking of, Wimsey? I quite see that it is unsuitable, from your point of view, that Lady Mary Wimsey should dine in public restaurants with a policeman, but if you imagine I have ever said a word to her that could not be said with the greatest propriety—"

"—in the presence of her mother, you wrong the purest and sweetest woman that ever lived, and insult your friend," interrupted Peter, snatching the words from his mouth and rattling them to a glib conclusion. "What a perfect Victorian you are, Charles. I should like to keep you in a glass case. Of course you haven't said a word. What I want to know is, why?"

Parker stared at him.

"For the last five years or so," said Wimsey, "you have been looking like a demented sheep at my sister, and starting like a rabbit whenever her name is mentioned. What do you mean by it? It is not ornamental. It is not exhilarating. You unnerve the poor girl. You give me a poor idea of your guts, if you will pardon the expression. A man doesn't like to see a man go all wobbly about his sister—at least, not with such a prolonged wobble. It's unsightly. It's irritating. Why not slap the manly thorax and say, 'Peter my dear old mangel-wurzel, I have decided to dig myself into the old family trench and be a brother to you'? What's stopping you? Is it Gerald? He's an ass, I know, but he's not a bad old stick, really. Is it Helen? She's a bit of a wart, but you needn't see much of her. Is it me? Because, if so, I'm thinking of becoming a hermit—there was a Peter the Hermit, wasn't there?—So I shouldn't be in your way. Cough up the difficulty, old thing, and we will have it removed in a plain van. Now, then!"

"Do you—are you asking me—?"

"I'm asking you your intentions, damn it!" said Wimsey, "and if that's not Victorian enough, I don't know what is. I quite understand your having given Mary time to recover from the unfortunate affair with Cathcart and the Goyles fellow, but, dash it all, my dear man, one can overdo the delicacy business. You can't expect a girl to stand on and off for ever, can you? Are you waiting for Leap Year, or what?"

"Look here, Peter, don't be a damned fool. How can I ask your sister to marry me?"

"*How* you do it is your affair. You might say: 'What about a spot of matrimony, old dear?' That's up-to-date, and plain and unmistakable. Or you could go down on one knee and say, 'Will you honour me with your hand and heart?' which is pretty and old-fashioned and has the merit of originality in these times. Or you could write, or wire, or telephone. But I leave that to your own individual fancy."

"You're not serious."

"Oh, God! Shall I ever live down this disastrous reputation for tom-foolery? You're making Mary damned unhappy, Charles, and I wish you'd marry her and have done with it."

"Making her unhappy?" said Parker, almost in a shout, "me—her—unhappy?"

Wimsey tapped his forehead significantly.

"Wood—solid wood! But the last blow seems to have penetrated. Yes, you—her—unhappy—do you get it now?"

"Peter—if I really thought that—"

"Now don't go off the deep end," said Wimsey, "it's wasted on me. Keep it for Mary. I've done my brotherly duty and there's an end of it. Calm yourself. Return to your reports—"

"Oh, lord, yes," said Parker. "Before we go any farther, I've got a report for you."

"You have? Why didn't you say so at first."

"You wouldn't let me."

"Well, what is it?"

"We've found the packet."

"What?"

"We've found the packet."

"Actually found it?"

"Yes. One of the barmen—"

"Never mind the barmen. You're sure it's the right packet?"

"Oh, yes; we've identified it."

"Get on. Have you analysed it?"

"Yes, we've analysed it."

"Well, what is it?"

Parker looked at him with the eyes of one who breaks bad news, and said, reluctantly:

"Bicarbonate of soda."

16

Mr. Crofts, excusably enough, said, "I told you so"; Sir Impey Biggs observed curtly, "Very unfortunate."

To chronicle Lord Peter Wimsey's daily life during the ensuing week would be neither kind nor edifying. An enforced inactivity will produce irritable symptoms in the best of men. Nor did the imbecile happiness of Chief-Inspector Parker and Lady Mary Wimsey tend to soothe him, accompanied as it was by tedious demonstrations of affection for himself. Like the man in Max Beerbohm's story, Wimsey "hated to be touching." He was only moderately cheered by hearing from the industrious Freddy Arbuthnot that Mr. Norman Urquhart was found to be more or less deeply involved in the disasters of the Megatherium Trust.

Miss Kitty Climpson, on the other hand, was living in what she herself liked to call a "whirl of activity." A letter, written the second day after her arrival in Windle, furnishes us with a wealth of particulars.

Hillside View,
Windle, Westmorland.
1st Jan. 1930.

My dear Lord Peter,

I feel sure you will be anxious to hear, at the *earliest possible* moment *how* things are *going,* and though I have only been here *one* day, I really think I have *not* done so *badly,* all things considered!

My train got in quite late on Monday night, after a *most dreary* journey, with a *lugubrious* wait at *Preston*, though thanks to your kindness in insisting that I should travel *First-class*, I was not really at all tired! Nobody can realise what a *great* difference these extra comforts make, especially when one is *getting on* in years, and after the *uncomfortable* travelling which I had to endure in my days of poverty, I feel that I am living in almost *sinful* luxury! The carriage was *well* heated—indeed, *too much so* and I should have liked the window down, but that there was a *very fat* business man, *muffled* to the eyes in *coats* and *woolly waistcoats* who *strongly* objected to fresh air! Men are such HOT-HOUSE PLANTS nowadays, are they not, quite unlike my dear father, who would never permit a *fire* in the house *before* November the 1st, or *after* March 31st even though the thermometer was at *freezing-point!*

I had *no* difficulty in getting a comfortable room at the Station Hotel, *late* as it was. In the *old* days, an *unmarried woman arriving alone at midnight* with a *suitcase* would hardly have been considered *respectable*—what a wonderful difference one finds today! I am *grateful* to have lived to see such changes, because whatever old-fashioned people may say about the greater *decorum* and *modesty* of women in Queen Victoria's time, those who can remember the old conditions know how *difficult* and *humiliating* they were!

Yesterday morning, of course, my *first* object was to find a *suitable boarding-house*, in accordance with your instructions, and I was *fortunate* enough to hit upon this house at the *second* attempt. It is very well run and *refined*, and there are three *elderly ladies* who are *permanent* boarders here, and are *well up* in all the GOSSIP of the town, so that nothing could be more *advantageous* for our purpose!!

As soon as I had engaged my room, I went out for a little *voyage of discovery*. I found a very helpful *policeman* in the High Street, and asked him where to find Mrs. Wrayburn's house. He knew it quite well, and told me to take the *omnibus* and it would be a penny ride to the "Fisherman's Arms" and then about 5 minutes' walk. I followed his directions, and the 'bus took me right into the country to a *cross-roads* with the "Fisherman's Arms" at the corner. The conductor was most polite and helpful and showed me the way, so I had *no difficulty* in finding the house.

It is a *beautiful old place*, standing in its own grounds—quite a *big* house built in the *eighteenth century*, with an *italian* porch and a lovely green lawn with a cedar-tree and formal flower-beds, and in summer must be really a *garden of Eden*. I looked at it from the road for a little time—I did not think this would be at all *peculiar* behaviour, if anybody saw me, because *anybody* might be interested in such a fine old place. Most of the *blinds* were down, as though the greater part of the house were *uninhabited*, and I could not see any *gardener* or anybody about—I suppose there is not very much to be done in the garden this time of the year. One of the *chimneys* was smoking, however, so there were *some* signs of life about the place.

I took a little *walk* down the road and then turned back and passed the house again, and this time I saw a servant just passing round the corner of the house, but of course she was *too far off* for me to speak to. So I took the omnibus back again and had lunch at Hillside View, so as to make acquaintance with my fellow-boarders.

Naturally I did not want to seem *too eager* all at once, so I said nothing about Mrs. Wrayburn's house *at first*, but just talked *generally* about Windle.

I had some difficulty in parrying the *questions* of the good ladies, who *wondered* very much *why* a stranger had come to Windle at this time of year, but without telling many actual *untruths* I think I left them with the *impression* that I had come into a little fortune (!) and was visiting the Lake District to find a suitable spot in which to settle next *summer!* I talked about *sketching*— as girls we were *all* brought up to dabble a little in water-colours, so that I was able to display quite sufficient *technical knowledge to satisfy them!*

That gave me quite a *good* opportunity to ask about the *house!!* Such a *beautiful* old place, I said, and did anybody live there? (Of *course* I did not blurt this out *all at once*—I waited till they had told me of the many *quaint spots* in the district that would interest an artist!) Mrs. Pegler, a very *stout,* PUSSY old lady, with a LONG TONGUE (!) was able to tell me *all* about it. My dear Lord Peter, what I do *not* know now about the *abandoned wickedness* of Mrs. Wrayburn's early life is really NOT WORTH KNOWING!! But what was *more to the point* is that she told me the *name* of Mrs. Wrayburn's *nurse-companion.* She is a MISS BOOTH, a retired nurse, about *sixty* years old, and she lives *all alone* in the house with Mrs. Wrayburn, except for the *servants,* and a *housekeeper.* When I heard that Mrs. Wrayburn was so *old,* and *paralysed* and *frail,* I said was it not very *dangerous* that Miss Booth should be the only attendant, but Mrs. Pegler said the housekeeper was a *most trustworthy* woman who had been with Mrs. Wrayburn for many years, and was *quite* capable of looking after her any time when Miss Booth was out. So it appears that Miss Booth does go out sometimes! Nobody in this house seems to *know* her *personally,* but they say she is often to be seen in the town in *nurse's uniform.* I managed to extract quite a good description of her, so if I should happen to meet her, I daresay I shall be *smart* enough to *recognise* her!

That is really *all* I have been able to discover in *one* day. I hope you will not be *too* disappointed, but I was obliged to listen to a terrible amount of *local history* of one kind and another, and of course I could not FORCE the conversation round to Mrs. Wrayburn in any suspicious way.

I will let you know as *soon* as I get the *least bit* more information.

> Most sincerely yours,
> Katharine Alexandra Climpson.

Miss Climpson finished her letter in the privacy of her bedroom, and secured it carefully in her capacious handbag before going downstairs. A long experience of boarding-house life warned her that to display openly an envelope addressed even to a minor member of the nobility would be to court a quite unnecessary curiosity. True, it would establish her status, but at that moment Miss Climpson hardly wished to move in the limelight. She crept quietly out at the hall door, and turned her steps towards the centre of the town.

On the previous day, she had marked down one principal tea-shop, two rising and competitive tea-shops, one slightly passé and declining tea-shop, a Lyons and four obscure and, on the whole, negligible tea-shops which combined the service of refreshments with a trade in sweets. It was now half-past ten. In the next hour and a half she could, with a little exertion, pass in review all that part of the Windle population which indulged in morning coffee.

She posted her letter and then debated with herself where to begin. On the whole, she inclined to leave the Lyons for another day. It was an ordinary plain Lyons, without orchestra or soda-fountain. She thought that its clientele would be chiefly housewives and clerks. Of the other four, the most likely was, perhaps, the "Central." It was fairly large, well-lighted and cheerful and strains of music issued from its doors. Nurses usually like the large, well-lighted and melodious. But the "Central" had one drawback. Anyone coming from the direction of Mrs. Wrayburn's house would have to pass all the others to get to it. This fact unfitted it for an observation post. From this point of view, the advantage lay with "Ye Cosye Corner," which commanded the 'bus-stop. Accordingly, Miss Climpson decided to start her campaign from that spot. She selected a table in the window, ordered a cup of coffee and a plate of digestive biscuits and entered upon her vigil.

After half an hour, during which no woman in nurse's costume had been sighted, she ordered another cup of coffee and some pastries. A number of people—mostly women—dropped in, but none of them could by any possibility be identified with Miss Booth. At half-past eleven, Miss Climpson felt to stay any longer would be conspicuous and might annoy the management. She paid her bill and departed.

The "Central" had rather more people in it than "Ye Cosye Corner," and was in some ways an improvement, having comfortable wicker chairs instead of fumed oak settles, and brisk waitresses instead of languid semi-gentle-women in art-linen. Miss Climpson ordered another cup of coffee and a roll and butter. There was no window-table vacant, but she found one close to the orchestra from which she could survey the whole room. A fluttering dark-blue veil at the door made her heart beat, but it proved to belong to a lusty young person with two youngsters and a perambulator, and hope withdrew once more. By twelve o'clock, Miss Climpson decided that she had drawn blank at the "Central."

Her last visit was to the "Oriental"—an establishment singularly ill-adapted for espionage. It consisted of three very small rooms of irregular shape, dimly lit by forty-watt bulbs in Japanese shades, and further shrouded by bead curtains and draperies. Miss Climpson, in her inquisitive way, wandered into all its nooks and corners, disturbing several courting couples, before returning to a table near the door and sitting down to consume her fourth cup of coffee. Half-past twelve came, but no Miss Booth. "She can't come now," thought Miss Climpson, "she will have to get back and give her patient lunch."

She returned to Hillside View with but little appetite for the joint of roast mutton.

At half-past three she sallied out again, to indulge in an orgy of teas. This time she included the Lyons and the fourth tea-shop, beginning at the far end of the town and working her way back to the 'bus-stop. It was while she was struggling with her fifth meal, in the window of "Ye Cosye Corner," that a hurrying figure on the pavement caught her eye. The winter evening had closed in, and the street-lights were not very brilliant, but she distinctly saw a stoutish middle-aged nurse in a black veil and grey cloak pass along on the nearer pavement. By craning her neck, she could see her make a brisk spurt, scramble on the 'bus at the corner and disappear in the direction of the "Fisherman's Arms."

"How vexatious!" said Miss Climpson, as the vehicle disappeared. "I must have just missed her somewhere. Or perhaps she was having tea in a private house. Well, I'm afraid this is a blank day. And I do feel so *full* of tea!"

It was fortunate that Miss Climpson had been blest by Heaven with a sound digestion, for the next morning saw a repetition of the performance. It was possible, of course, that Miss Booth only went out two or three times a week, or that she only went out in the afternoon, but Miss Climpson was taking no chances. She had at least achieved the certainty that the 'bus-stop was the place to watch. This time she took up her post at "Ye Cosye Corner" at 11 o'clock and waited till twelve. Nothing happened and she went home.

In the afternoon she was there again at three. By this time the waitress had got to know her, and betrayed a certain amused and tolerant interest in her comings and goings. Miss Climpson explained that she liked so much to watch the people pass, and spoke a few words in praise of the café and its service. She admired a quaint old inn on the opposite side of the street, and said she thought of making a sketch of it.

"Oh, yes," said the girl, "there's a many artists come here for that."

This gave Miss Climpson a bright idea, and the next morning she brought a pencil and sketch-book with her.

By the extraordinary perversity of things in general, she had no sooner ordered her coffee, opened the sketch-book and started to outline the gables of the inn, than a 'bus drew up, and out of it stepped the stout nurse in the black and grey uniform. She did not enter "Ye Cosye Corner," but marched on at a brisk pace down the opposite side of the street, her veil flapping like a flag.

Miss Climpson uttered a sharp exclamation of annoyance, which drew the waitress's attention.

"How provoking!" said Miss Climpson. "I have left my rubber behind. I must just run out and buy one."

She dropped the sketch-book on the table and made for the door.

"I'll cover your coffee up for you, miss," said the girl, helpfully. "Mr. Bulteel's, down near the 'Bear,' is the best stationer's."

"Thank you, thank you," said Miss Climpson, and darted out.

The black veil was still flapping in the distance. Miss Climpson pursued breathlessly, keeping to the near side of the road. The veil dived into a chemist's shop. Miss Climpson crossed the road a little behind it and stared into a window full of baby-linen. The veil came out, fluttered undecidedly on the pavement, turned, passed Miss Climpson and went into a bootshop.

"If it's shoe-laces, it'll be quick," thought Miss Climpson, "but if it's trying-on it may be all morning." She walked slowly past the door. By good luck a customer was just coming out, and, peering past him, Miss Climpson just caught a glimpse of the black veil vanishing into the back premises. She pushed the door boldly open. There was a counter for sundries in the front of the shop, and the doorway through which the nurse had vanished was labelled "Ladies' Department."

While buying a pair of brown silk laces, Miss Climpson debated with herself. Should she follow and seize this opportunity? Trying on shoes is usually a lengthy business. The subject is marooned for long periods in a chair, while the assistant climbs ladders and collects piles of cardboard boxes. It is also comparatively easy to enter into conversation with a person who is trying on shoes. But there is a snag in it. To give colour to your presence in the Fitting department, you must yourself try on shoes. What happens? The assistant first disables you by snatching off your right-hand shoe, and then disappears. And supposing, meanwhile, your quarry completes her purchase and walks out? Are you to follow, hopping madly on one foot? Are you to arouse suspicion by hurriedly replacing your own footgear and rushing out with laces flying and an unconvincing murmur about a forgotten engagement? Still worse, suppose you are in an

amphibious condition, wearing one shoe of your own and one of the establishment's? What impression will you make by suddenly bolting with goods to
which you are not entitled? Will not the pursuer very quickly become the
pursued?

Having weighed this problem in her mind, Miss Climpson paid for her shoe-
laces and retired. She had already bilked a tea-shop, and one misdemeanour in a
morning was about as much as she could hope to get away with.

The male detective, particularly when dressed as a workman, an errand-boy or
a telegraph-messenger, is favourably placed for "shadowing." He can loaf without attracting attention. The female detective must not loaf. On the other
hand, she can stare into shop-windows for ever. Miss Climpson selected a hatshop. She examined all the hats in both windows attentively, coming back to
gaze in a purposeful manner at an extremely elegant model with an eye-veil and
a pair of excrescences like rabbits'-ears. Just at the moment when any observer
might have thought that she had at last made up her mind to go in and ask the
price, the nurse came out of the boot-shop. Miss Climpson shook her head
regretfully at the rabbits'-ears, darted back to the other window, looked,
hovered, hesitated—and tore herself away.

The nurse was now about thirty yards ahead, moving well, with the air of a
horse that sights his stable. She crossed the street again, looked into a window
piled with coloured wools, thought better of it, passed on, and turned in at the
door of the Oriental Café.

Miss Climpson was in the position of one who, after prolonged pursuit, has
clapped a tumbler over a moth. For the moment the creature is safe and the
pursuer takes breath. The problem now is to extract the moth without damage.

It is easy, of course, to follow a person into a café and sit down at her table, if
there is room there. But she may not welcome you. She may feel it perverse in
you to thrust yourself upon her when other tables are standing empty. It is
better to offer some excuse, such as restoring a dropped handkerchief or drawing
attention to an open handbag. If the person will not provide you with an excuse,
the next best thing is to manufacture one.

The stationer's shop was only a few doors off. Miss Climpson went in and
purchased an indiarubber, three picture postcards, a BB pencil and a calendar,
and waited while they were made up into a parcel. Then she slowly made her
way across the street and turned into the "Oriental."

In the first room she found two women and a small boy occupying one recess,
an aged gentleman drinking milk in another, and a couple of girls consuming
coffee and cakes in a third.

"Excuse me," said Miss Climpson to the two women, "but does this parcel
belong to you? I picked it up just outside the door."

The elder woman, who had evidently been shopping, hastily passed in review
a quantity of miscellaneous packages, pinching each one by way of refreshing
her memory as to the contents.

"I don't think it's mine, but really I can't say for certain. Let me see. That's
eggs and that's bacon and—what's this, Gertie? Is that the mouse-trap? No, wait
a minute, that's cough-mixture, that is—and that's Aunt Edith's cork soles, and
that's Nugget—no, bloater paste, this here's the Nugget—why, bless my soul, I
believe I *have* been and gone and dropped the mousetrap—but that don't look
like it to me."

"No, Mother," said the younger woman, "don't you remember, they were sending round the mouse-trap with the bath."

"Of course, so they were. Well, that accounts for that. The mouse-trap and the two frying-pans, they was all to go with the bath, and that's all except the soap, which you've got, Gertie. No, thank you very much, all the same, but it isn't ours; somebody else must have dropped it."

The old gentleman repudiated it firmly but politely, and the two girls merely giggled at it. Miss Climpson passed on. Two young women with their attendant young men duly thanked her in the second room, but said the parcel was not theirs.

Miss Climpson passed into the third room. In one corner was a rather talkative party of people with an Airedale, and at the back, in the most obscure and retired of all the Oriental nooks and corners, sat the nurse, reading a book.

The talkative party had nothing to say to the parcel, and Miss Climpson, with her heart beating fast, bore down upon the nurse.

"Excuse me," she said, smiling graciously, "but I think this little parcel must be yours. I picked it up just in the doorway and I've asked all the other people in the café."

The nurse looked up. She was a grey-haired, elderly woman, with those curious large blue eyes which disconcert the beholder by their intense gaze, and are usually an index of some emotional instability. She smiled at Miss Climpson and said pleasantly:

"No, no, it isn't mine. So kind of you. But I have all my parcels here."

She vaguely indicated the cushioned seat which ran round three sides of the alcove, and Miss Climpson, accepting the gesture as an invitation, promptly sat down.

"How very odd," said Miss Climpson, "I made sure someone must have dropped it coming in here. I wonder what I had better do with it." She pinched it gently. "I shouldn't think it was valuable, but one never knows. I suppose I ought to take it to the police-station."

"You could hand it to the cashier," suggested the nurse, "in case the owner came back here to claim it."

"Well now, so I could," cried Miss Climpson. "How clever of you to think of it. Of course, yes, that would be the best way. You must think me very foolish, but the idea never occurred to me. I'm not a very practical person, I'm afraid, but I do so admire the people who are. I should never do to take up *your* profession, should I? Any little emergency leaves me *quite* bewildered."

The nurse smiled again.

"It is largely a question of training," she said. "And of *self*-training, too, of course. All these little weaknesses can be cured by placing the mind under a Higher Control—don't you believe that?"

Her eyes rested hypnotically upon Miss Climpson's.

"I suppose that is true."

"It is such a mistake," pursued the nurse, closing her book and laying it down on the table, "to imagine that anything in the mental sphere is large or small. Our least thoughts and actions are equally directed by the higher centres of spiritual power, if we can bring ourselves to believe it."

A waitress arrived to take Miss Climpson's order.

"Oh, dear! I seem to have intruded myself upon your table . . ."

"Oh, don't get up," said the nurse.

"Are you sure? Really? because I don't want to interrupt you—"

"Not at all. I live a very solitary life, and I am always glad to find a friend to talk to."

"How nice of you. I'll have scones and butter, please, and a pot of tea. This is such a nice little café, don't you think?—so quiet and peaceful. If only those people wouldn't make such a noise with that dog of theirs. I don't like those great big animals, and I think they're quite dangerous, don't you?"

The reply was lost on Miss Climpson, for she had suddenly seen the title of the book on the table, and the Devil, or a Ministering Angel (she was not quite sure which), was, so to speak, handing her a fullblown temptation on a silver salver. The book was published by the Spiritualist Press and was called *"Can the Dead Speak?"*

In a single moment of illumination, Miss Climpson saw her plan complete and perfect in every detail. It involved a course of deception from which her conscience shrank appalled, but it was certain. She wrestled with the demon. Even in a righteous cause, could anything so wicked be justified?

She breathed what she thought was a prayer for guidance, but the only answer was a small whisper in her ear, "Oh, jolly good work, Miss Climpson!" and the voice was the voice of Peter Wimsey.

"Pardon me," said Miss Climpson, "but I see you are a student of spiritualism. How interesting that is!"

If there was one subject in the world about which Miss Climpson might claim to know something, it was Spiritualism. It is a flower which flourishes bravely in a boardinghouse atmosphere. Time and again, Miss Climpson had listened while the apparatus of planes and controls, correspondences and veridical communications, astral bodies, auras and ectoplastic materialisations was displayed before her protesting intelligence. That to the Church it was a forbidden subject she knew well enough, but she had been paid companion to so many old ladies and had been forced so many times to bow down in the House of Rimmon.

And then there had been the quaint little man from the Psychical Research Society. He had stayed a fortnight in the same private hotel with her at Bournemouth. He was skilled in the investigation of haunted houses and the detection of poltergeists. He had rather liked Miss Climpson, and she had passed several interesting evenings hearing about the tricks of mediums. Under his guidance she had learnt to turn tables and produce explosive cracking noises; she knew how to examine a pair of sealed slates for the marks of the wedges which let the chalk go in on a long black wire to write spirit-passages. She had seen the ingenious rubber gloves which leave the impression of spirit hands in a bucket of paraffin-wax, and which, when deflated, can be drawn delicately from the hardened wax through a hold narrower than a child's wrist. She even knew theoretically, though she had never tried it, how to hold her hands to be tied behind her back so as to force that first deceptive knot which makes all subsequent knots useless, and how to flit about the room banging tambourines in the twilight in spite of having been tied up in a black cabinet with both fists filled with flour. Miss Climpson had wondered greatly at the folly and wickedness of mankind.

The nurse went on talking, and Miss Climpson answered mechanically.

"She's only a beginner," said Miss Climpson to herself. "She's reading a textbook. . . . And she is quite uncritical. . . . Surely she knows that that woman was exposed long ago. . . . People like her shouldn't be allowed out alone— they're living incitements to fraud. . . . I don't know this Mrs. Craig she is talking about, but I should say she was as twisty as a corkscrew. . . . I must avoid Mrs. Craig, she probably knows too much . . . if the poor deluded creature will swallow that, she'll swallow anything."

"It does seem *most* wonderful, doesn't it?" said Miss Climpson, aloud. "But isn't it a wee bit *dangerous?* I've been told I'm sensitive myself, but I have never dared to *try*. Is it *wise* to open one's mind to these supernatural influences?"

"It's not dangerous if you know the right way," said the nurse. "One must learn to build up a shell of pure thoughts about the soul, so that no evil influences can enter it. I have had the most marvellous talks with the dear ones who have passed over. . . ."

Miss Climpson refilled the tea-pot and sent the waitress for a plate of sugary cakes.

". . . unfortunately I am not mediumistic myself—not yet, that is. I can't get anything when I'm alone. Mrs. Craig says that it will come by practice and concentration. Last night I was trying with the Ouija board, but it would only write spirals."

"Your conscious mind is too active, I expect," said Miss Climpson.

"Yes, I daresay that is it. Mrs. Craig says that I am wonderfully sympathetic. We get the most wonderful results when we sit together. Unfortunately she is abroad just now."

Miss Climpson's heart gave a great leap, so that she nearly spilled her tea.

"You yourself are a medium, then?" went on the nurse.

"I have been told so," said Miss Climpson, guardedly.

"I wonder," said the nurse, "whether if we sat together—"

She looked hungrily at Miss Climpson.

"I don't really like—"

"Oh, do! You are such a sympathetic person. I'm sure we should get good results. And the spirits are so pathetically anxious to communicate. Of course, I wouldn't like to try unless I was sure of the person. There are so many fraudulent mediums about"—("So you do know that much!" thought Miss Climpson)—"but with somebody like yourself one is absolutely safe. You would find it made such a difference in your life. I used to be so unhappy over all the pain and misery in the world—we see so much of it, you know—till I realised the certainty of survival and how all our trials are merely sent to fit us for life on a higher plane."

"Well," said Miss Climpson, slowly, "I'm willing just to try. But I can't say I really *believe* in it, you know."

"You would—you would."

"Of course, I've seen one or two strange things happen—things that couldn't be tricks, because I knew the people—and which I couldn't explain—"

"Come up and see me this evening, now do!" said the nurse, persuasively. "We'll just have one quiet sitting and then we shall see whether you really are a medium. I've no doubt you are."

"Very well," said Miss Climpson. "What is your name, by the way?"

"Caroline Booth—Miss Caroline Booth. I'm nurse to an old, paralysed lady in the big house along the Kendal Road."

"Thank goodness for that, anyway," thought Miss Climpson. Aloud she said:

"And my name is Climpson; I think I've got a card somewhere. No—I've left it behind. But I'm staying at Hillside View. How do I get to you?"

Miss Booth mentioned the address and the time of the 'bus, and added an invitation to supper, which was accepted. Miss Climpson went home and wrote a hurried note:

> My dear Lord Peter—
>
> I am sure you have been *wondering* what has *happened* to me. But at *last* I have NEWS! I have STORMED THE CITADEL!!! I am going to the *house tonight* and you may expect GREAT THINGS!!!
>
> In *haste,*
Yours very sincerely,
Katharine A. Climpson.

Miss Climpson went out into the town again after lunch. First, being an honest woman, she retrieved her sketch-book from "Ye Cosye Corner" and paid her bill, explaining that she had run across a friend that morning and been detained. She then visited a number of shops. Eventually she selected a small metal soap-box which suited her requirements. Its sides were slightly convex, and when closed and pinched slightly, it sprang back with a hearty cracking noise. This, with a little contrivance and some powerful sticking-plaster, she fixed to a strong elastic garter. When clasped about Miss Climpson's bony knee and squeezed sharply against the other knee, the box emitted a series of cracks so satisfying as to convince the most sceptical. Miss Climpson, seated before the looking-glass, indulged in an hour's practice before tea, till the crack could be produced with the minimum of physical jerk.

Another purchase was a length of stiff black-bound wire, such as is used for making hat-brims. Used double, neatly bent to a double angle and strapped to the wrist, this contrivance was sufficient to rock a light table. The weight of a heavy table would be too much for it, she feared, but she had had no time to order blacksmith's work. She could try, anyway. She hunted out a black velvet rest-gown with long, wide sleeves, and satisfied herself that the wires could be sufficiently hidden.

At six o'clock, she put on this garment, fastened the soapbox to her leg—turning the box outward, lest untimely cracks should startle her fellow-travellers, muffled herself in a heavy rain-cloak of Inverness cut, took hat and umbrella and started on her way to steal Mrs. Wrayburn's will.

17

Supper was over. It had been served in a beautiful old panelled room with an Adam ceiling and fireplace, and the food had been good. Miss Climpson felt braced and ready.

"We'll sit in my own room, shall we?" said Miss Booth. "It's the only really comfortable place. Most of this house is shut up, of course. If you'll excuse me, dear, I will just run up and give Mrs. Wrayburn her supper and make her comfortable, poor thing, and then we can begin. I shan't be more than half an hour or so."

"She's quite helpless, I suppose?"

"Yes, quite."

"Can she speak?"

"Not to say speak. She mumbles sometimes, but one can't make anything of it. It's sad, isn't it, and her so rich. It will be a happy day for her when she passes over."

"Poor soul!" said Miss Climpson.

Her hostess led her into a small, gaily-furnished sitting-room and left her there among the cretonne covers and the ornaments. Miss Climpson ran her eyes rapidly over the books, which were mostly novels, with the exception of some standard works on Spiritualism, and then turned her attention to the mantelpiece. It was crowded with photographs, as the mantelpieces of nurses usually are. Conspicuous among hospital groups and portraits inscribed "From your grateful patient," was a cabinet photograph of a gentleman in the dress and moustache of the 'nineties, standing beside a bicycle, apparently upon a stone balcony in mid-air with a distant view over a rocky gorge. The frame was silver, heavy and ornate.

"Too young for a father," said Miss Climpson, as she turned it over and pulled back the catch of the frame, "either sweetheart or favourite brother. H'm! 'My dearest Lucy from her ever-loving Harry.' Not a brother, I fancy. Photographer's address, Coventry. Cycle trade, possibly. Now what happened to Harry? Not matrimony, obviously. Death, or infidelity. First-class frame and central position; bunch of hot-house narcissus in a vase—I think Harry has passed over. What next? Family group? Yes. Names conveniently beneath. Dearest Lucy in a fringe, Papa and Mamma, Tom and Gertrude. Tom and Gertrude are older, but they may be still alive. Papa is a parson. Largeish house—country rectory, perhaps. Photographer's address, Maidstone. Wait a minute. Here's Papa in another group, with a dozen small boys. Schoolmaster, or takes private pupils. Two boys have straw hats with zig-zag ribbons—school, probably, then. What's that silver cup? Thos. Booth and three other names—Pembroke College Fours 1883. Not an expensive college. Wonder whether Papa objected to Harry on account of the cycle-manufacturing connection? That book over there looks like a school prize. It is. Maidstone Ladies' College—for distinction in English Literature. Just so. Is she coming back?—No, false alarm. Young man in khaki, 'Your loving nephew, G. Booth'—ah! Tom's son, I take it. Did he survive, I wonder? Yes—she is coming this time."

When the door opened, Miss Climpson was sitting by the fire, deeply engaged in *Raymond*.

"So sorry to keep you waiting," said Miss Booth, "but the poor old dear is rather restless this evening. She'll do now for a couple of hours, but I shall have to go up again later. Shall we begin at once? I'm *so* eager to try."

Miss Climpson readily agreed.

"We usually use this table," said Miss Booth, bringing forward a small, round table of bamboo, with a shelf between its legs. Miss Climpson thought she had never seen a piece of furniture more excellently adapted for the faking of phenomena, and heartily approved of Mrs. Craig's choice.

"Do we sit in the light?" she inquired.

"Not in full light," said Miss Booth. "Mrs. Craig explained to me that the blue rays of daylight or electricity are too hard for the spirits. They shatter the vibrations, you see. So we usually put out the light and sit in the firelight, which is quite bright enough for taking notes. Will you write down, or shall I?"

"Oh, I think you had better do it as you're more accustomed to it," said Miss Climpson.

"Very well." Miss Booth fetched a pencil and a pad of paper and switched off the light.

"Now we just sit down and place our thumbs and finger-tips lightly on the table, near the edge. It's better to make a circle, of course, but one can't do that with two people. And just at first, I think it's better not to talk—till a rapport is established, you know. Which side will you sit?"

"Oh, this will do for me," said Miss Climpson.

"You don't mind the fire on your back?"

Miss Climpson most certainly did not.

"Well, that's a good arrangement, because it helps to screen the rays from the table."

"That's what I thought," said Miss Climpson, truthfully.

They placed thumbs and finger-tips on the table and waited.

Ten minutes passed.

"Did you feel any movement?" whispered Miss Booth.

"No."

"It sometimes takes a little time."

Silence.

"Ah! I thought I felt something then."

"I've got a feeling like pins and needles in my fingers."

"So have I. We shall get something soon."

A pause.

"Would you like to rest a little?"

"My wrists ache rather."

"They do till you get used to it. It's the power coming through them."

Miss Climpson lifted her fingers and rubbed each wrist gently. The thin black hooks came quietly down to the edge of the black velvet sleeve.

"I feel sure there is power all about us. I can feel a cold thrill on my spine."

"Let's go on," said Miss Climpson. "I'm quite rested now."

Silence.

"I feel," whispered Miss Climpson, "as though something was gripping the back of my neck."

"Don't move."

"And my arms have gone dead from the elbow."

"Hush! so have mine."

Miss Climpson might have added that she had a pain in her deltoids, if she had known the name for them. This is not an uncommon result of sitting with the thumbs and fingers on a table without support for the wrist.

"I'm tingling from head to foot," said Miss Booth.

At this moment the table gave a violent lurch. Miss Climpson had over-estimated the force necessary to move bamboo furniture.

"Ah!"

After a slight pause for recuperation, the table began to move again, but more gently, till it was rocking with a regular see-saw motion. Miss Climpson found that by gently elevating one rather large foot, she could take practically all the weight off her wrist-hooks. This was fortunate, as she was doubtful whether their constitution would stand the strain.

"Shall we speak to it?" asked Miss Climpson.

"Wait a moment," said Miss Booth. "It wants to go sideways."

Miss Climpson was surprised by this statement, which seemed to argue a high degree of imagination, but she obligingly imparted a slight gyratory movement to the table.

"Shall we stand up?" suggested Miss Booth.

This was disconcerting, for it is not easy to work a vibrating table while stooping and standing on one leg. Miss Climpson decided to fall into a trance. She dropped her head on her chest and uttered a slight moan. At the same time she pulled back her hands, releasing the hooks, and the table continued to revolve jerkily, spinning beneath their fingers.

A coal fell from the fire with a crash, sending up a bright jet of flame. Miss Climpson started, and the table ceased spinning and came down with a little thud.

"Oh, dear!" exclaimed Miss Booth. "The light has dispersed the vibrations. Are you all right, dear?"

"Yes, yes," said Miss Climpson, vaguely. "Did anything happen?"

"The power was tremendous," said Miss Booth. "I've never felt it so strong."

"I think I must have fallen asleep," said Miss Climpson.

"You were entranced," said Miss Booth. "The control was taking possession. Are you very tired, or can you go on?"

"I feel quite all right," said Miss Climpson, "only a little drowsy."

"You're a wonderfully strong medium," said Miss Booth.

Miss Climpson, surreptitiously flexing her ankle, was inclined to agree.

"We'll put a screen before the fire this time," said Miss Booth. "That's better. Now!"

The hands were replaced on the table, which began to rock again almost immediately.

"We won't lose any more time," said Miss Booth. She cleared her throat slightly, and addressed the table.

"Is there a spirit here?"

Crack!

The table ceased moving.

"Will you give me one knock for 'Yes' and two for 'No'?"

Crack!

The advantage of this method of interrogation is that it obliges the enquirer to put leading questions.

"Are you the spirit of one who has passed over?"

"Yes."

"Are you Fedora?"

"No."

"Are you one of the spirits who have visited me before?"

"No."

"Are you friendly to us?"

"Yes."

"Are you pleased to see us?"

"Yes. Yes. Yes."

"Are you happy?"

"Yes."

"Are you here to ask anything for yourself?"

"No."

"Are you anxious to help us personally?"

"No."

"Are you speaking on behalf of another spirit?"

"Yes."

"Does he want to speak to my friend?"

"No."

"To me, then?"

"Yes. Yes. Yes. Yes." (The table rocked violently.)

"Is it the spirit of a woman?"

"No."

"A man?"

"Yes."

A little gasp.

"Is it the spirit I have been trying to communicate with?"

"Yes."

A pause and a tilting of the table.

"Will you speak to us by means of the alphabet? One knock for A, two for B, and so on?"

("Belated caution," thought Miss Climpson.)

"Crack!"

"What is your name?"

Eight taps, and a long indrawn breath.

One tap—

"H—A—"

A long succession of taps.

"Was that an R? You go too fast."

"Crack!"

"H—A—R—is that right?"

"Yes."

"Is it Harry?"

"Yes, yes, yes."

"Oh, Harry! At last! How are you? Are you happy?"

"Yes—no—lonely."

"It wasn't my fault, Harry."

"Yes. Weak."

"Ah, but I had my duty to think of. Remember who came between us."

"Yes. F—A—T—H—E—"

"No, no, Harry! It was mo—"

"—A—D!" concluded the table, triumphantly.

"How can you speak so unkindly?"

"Love comes first."

"I know that now. But I was only a girl. Won't you forgive me now?"

"All forgiven. Mother forgiven too."

"I'm so glad. What do you do where you are, Harry?"

"Wait. Help. Atone."

"Have you any special message for me?"

"Go to the Coventry!" (Here the table became agitated.)

This message seemed to overwhelm the seeker.

"Oh, it really is you, Harry! You haven't forgotten the dear old joke. Tell me—"

The table showed great signs of excitement at this point and poured out a volley of unintelligible letters.

"What do you want?"

"G—G—G—"

"It must be somebody else interrupting," said Miss Booth. "Who is that, please?"

"G—E—O—R—G—E" (very rapidly).

"George? I don't know any George, except Tom's boy. Has anything happened to him, I wonder."

"Ha! ha! ha! not George Booth, George Washington."

"George Washington?"

"Ha! ha!" (The table became convulsively agitated, so much so that the medium seemed hardly able to hold it. Miss Booth, who had been noting down the conversation, now put her hands back on the table, which stopped capering and began to rock.)

"Who is here now?"

"Pongo."

"Who is Pongo?"

"Your control."

"Who was that talking just now?"

"Bad spirit. Gone now."

"Is Harry still there?"

"Gone."

"Does anybody else want to speak?"

"Helen."

"Helen who?"

"Don't you remember? Maidstone."

"Maidstone? Oh, do you mean Ellen Pate?"

"Yes, Pate."

"Fancy that! Good-evening, Ellen. How nice to hear from you."

"Remember row."

"Do you mean the big row in the dormitory?"

"Kate bad girl."

"No, I don't remember Kate, except Kate Hurley. You don't mean her, do you?"

"Naughty Kate. Lights out."

"Oh, I *know* what she's trying to say. The cakes after lights were out."

"That's right."

"You still spell badly, Ellen."

"Miss—Miss—"

"Mississippi? Haven't you learnt it yet?"

"Funny."

"Are there many of our class where you are?"

"Alice and Mabel. Send love."

"How sweet of them. Give them my love too."

"Yes. All love. Flowers. Sunshine."

"What do you—"

"P," said the table, impatiently.

"Is that Pongo again?"

"Yes. Tired."

"Do you want us to stop?"

"Yes. Another time."

"Very well, good-night."

"Good-night."

The medium leaned back in her chair with an air of exhaustion which was perfectly justified. It is very tiring to rap out letters of the alphabet, and she was afraid the soap-box was slipping.

Miss Booth turned on the light.

"That was wonderful!" said Miss Booth.

"Did you get the answers you wanted?"

"Yes, indeed. Didn't you hear them?"

"I didn't follow it all," said Miss Climpson.

"It is a little difficult, counting, till you're used to it. You must be dreadfully tired. We'll stop now and make some tea. Next time perhaps we could use the Ouija. It doesn't take nearly so long to get the answers with that."

Miss Climpson considered this. Certainly it would be less wearisome, but she was not sure of being able to manipulate it.

Miss Booth put the kettle on the fire and glanced at the clock.

"Dear me! it's nearly eleven. How the time has flown! I must run up and see to my old dear. Would you like to read through the questions and answers? I don't suppose I shall be many minutes."

Satisfactory, so far, thought Miss Climpson. Confidence was well established. In a few days' time, she would be able to work her plan. But she had nearly tripped up over George. And it was stupid to have said 'Helen.' Nellie would have done for either—there was a Nellie in every school forty-five years ago. But after all, it didn't much matter what you said—the other person was sure to help you out of it. How desperately her legs and arms were aching. Wearily she wondered if she had missed the last bus.

"I'm afraid you have," said Miss Booth, when the question was put to her on her return. "But we'll ring up a taxi. At my expense, of course, dear. I insist, as you were so good in coming all this way, entirely to please me. Don't you think the communications are too marvellous? Harry would never come before—poor Harry! I'm afraid I was very unkind to him. He married, but you see he has never forgotten me. He lived at Coventry and we used to have a joke about it—that's what he meant by saying that. I wonder which Alice and Mabel that was. There was an Alice Gibbons and an Alice Roach—both such nice girls; I think Mabel must be Mabel Herridge. She married and went out to India years and years ago. I can't remember her married name and I've never heard from her since, but she must have passed to the other side. Pongo is a new control. We must ask him who he is. Mrs. Craig's control is Fedora—she was a slave-girl at the court of Poppaea."

"Really!" said Miss Climpson.

"She told us her story one night. So romantic. She was thrown to the lions because she was a Christian and refused to have anything to do with Nero."

"How very interesting."

"Yes, isn't it? But she doesn't speak very good English, and it's sometimes rather hard to understand her. And she sometimes lets the tiresome ones in. Pongo was very quick at getting rid of George Washington. You will come again, won't you? Tomorrow night?"

"Certainly, if you like."

"Yes, please do. And next time you must ask for a message for yourself."

"I will indeed," said Miss Climpson. "It has all been *such* a revelation—quite *wonderful*. I never *dreamed* that I had such a gift."

And that was true, also.

18

It was, of course, useless for Miss Climpson to try to conceal from the boarding-house ladies where she had been and what she had been doing. Her return at midnight in a taxi had already aroused the liveliest curiosity, and she told the truth to avoid being accused of worse dissipations.

"My dear Miss Climpson," said Mrs. Pegler, "you will not, I trust, think me interfering, but I must caution you against having anything to do with Mrs. Craig or her friends. I have no doubt Miss Booth is an excellent woman, but I do not like the company she keeps. Nor do I approve of spiritualism. It is a prying into matters which we are not intended to know about, and may lead to very undesirable results. If you were a married woman, I could explain myself more clearly, but you may take it from me that these indulgences may have serious effects upon the character in more ways than one."

"Oh, Mrs. Pegler," said Miss Etheredge, "I don't think you should say that. One of the most beautiful characters I know—a woman whom it is a privilege to call one's friend—is a spiritualist, and she is a real saint in her life and influence."

"Very likely, Miss Etheredge," replied Mrs. Pegler, drawing her stout figure to its most impressive uprightness, "but that is not the point. I do not say that a spiritualist *may* not live a good life, but I *do* say that the majority of them are most unsatisfactory people, and far from truthful."

"I have happened to meet with a number of so-called mediums in the course of my life," agreed Miss Tweall, acidly, "and all of them, without *any* exception, were people I would not have trusted any further than I could see them—if as far."

"That is very true of a great many of them," said Miss Climpson, "and I am sure *nobody* could have better opportunities of judging than *myself*. But I think and hope that some of them are at least *sincere* if *mistaken* in their claims. What do *you* think, Mrs. Liffey?" she added, turning to the proprietress of the establishment.

"We-ll," said Mrs. Liffey—obliged, in her official capacity, to agree as far as possible with all parties. "I must say, from what I have read, and that is not a great deal, for I have little time for reading—still, I think there is a certain amount of evidence to show that, in certain cases and under strictly safeguarded conditions, there is possibly some foundation of truth beneath the spiritualists' claims. Not that I should care to have anything to do with it personally; as Mrs. Pegler says, I do not as a rule care very much for the sort of people who go in for it, though doubtless there are many exceptions. I think perhaps that the subject should be left to properly qualified investigators."

"There I agree with you," said Mrs. Pegler. "No words can express the disgust I feel at the intrusion of women like this Mrs. Craig into realms that should be sacred to us all. Imagine, Miss Climpson, that that woman—whom I do not know and have no intention of knowing—actually had the impertinence once to write to me and say that she had received a message at one of her séances, as she calls them, purporting to come from my dear husband. I cannot tell you what I felt. To have the General's name actually brought up, in public, in connection with such wicked nonsense! And of course it was the purest invention, for the General was the *last* man to have anything to do with goings-on. 'Pernicious poppy-cock,' he used to call it in his bluff military way. And when it came to telling me, his widow, that he had come to Mrs. Craig's house and played the accordion and asked for special prayers to deliver him from a place of punishment, I could only look on it as a calculated insult. The General was a regular Churchgoer and entirely opposed to prayers for the dead or anything popish; and as to being in any undesirable place, he was the best of men, even if he was a little abrupt at times. As for accordions, I hope, wherever he is, he has something better to do with his time."

"A most shameful business," said Miss Tweall.

"Who is this Mrs. Craig?" asked Miss Climpson.

"She is said to be a doctor's widow," said Mrs. Liffey.

"It's my opinion," said Mrs. Tweall, "that she is no better than she should be."

"A woman of her age," said Mrs. Pegler, "with henna'd hair and earrings a foot long—"

"And going about in those extraordinary clothes," said Miss Tweall.

"And having such very odd people to stay with her," said Mrs. Pegler. "You remember that black man, Mrs. Liffey, who wore a green turban and used to say his prayers in the front garden, till the police interfered."

"What I should like to know," said Miss Tweall, "is, where she gets her money from."

"If you ask me, my dear, the woman's on the make. Heaven knows what she persuades people to do in these spiritualistic meetings."

"But what brought her to Windle?" asked Miss Climpson. "I should have thought London, or some big town, would have been a better place for her if she is the kind of person you describe."

"I shouldn't be surprised if she was in hiding," said Miss Tweall, darkly. "There is such a thing as making a place too hot to hold you."

"Without altogether subscribing to your wholesale condemnation," said Miss Climpson, "I must agree that psychical research can be *very dangerous indeed* in the *wrong hands*, and from what Miss Booth tells me, I do doubt very *much* whether Mrs. Craig is a suitable guide for the inexperienced. Indeed, I quite felt it my *duty* to put Miss Booth on her guard, and that is what I am endeavouring to do. But, as you know, one may merely, so to speak, put the person's back up.

The first step is to gain her *confidence*, and then, little by little, one may be able to induce a more wholesome frame of mind."

"That's *so* true," said Miss Etheredge, eagerly, her pale blue eyes lighting with something that was almost animation. "I very nearly fell under the influence of a dreadful, fraudulent person myself, till my dear friend showed me a better way."

"Maybe," said Mrs. Pegler, "but in my opinion the whole thing is best left alone."

Undeterred by this excellent advice, Miss Climpson kept her appointment. After a spirited exhibition of table-rocking, Pongo consented to communicate by means of the Ouija board, though at first he was rather awkward with it. He attributed this, however, to the fact that he had never learned to write while on earth. Asked who he was, he explained that he was an Italian acrobat of the Renaissance period, and that his full name was Pongocelli. He had lived a sadly irregular life, but had redeemed himself by heroically refusing to abandon a sick child during the time of the Great Plague in Florence. He had caught the plague and died of it, and was now working out the period of probation for his sins by serving as guide and interpreter to other spirits. It was a touching story, and Miss Climpson was rather proud of it.

George Washington was rather intrusive, and the séance also suffered from a number of mysterious interruptions from what Pongo described as a "jealous influence." Nevertheless, "Harry" reappeared and delivered some consolatory messages, and there were further communications from Mabel Herridge, who gave a vivid description of her life in India. On the whole, and taking the difficulties into account, a successful evening.

On Sunday there was no séance, owing to the revolt of the medium's conscience. Miss Climpson felt that she could not, really could not, bring herself to do it. She went to church instead, and listened to the Christmas message with a distracted mind.

On Monday, however, the two enquirers again took their seats about the bamboo table, and the following is the report of the séance, as noted down by Miss Booth.

7:30 p.m.

On this occasion proceedings were begun at once with the Ouija board; after a few minutes, a loud succession of raps announced the presence of a control.

Question: Good-evening. Who is that?

Answer: Pongo here. Good evening! Heaven bless you.

Q. We are very glad to have you with us, Pongo.

A. Good—very good. Here we are again!

Q. Is that you, Harry?

A. Yes, only to give my love. Such a crowd.

Q. The more the better. We are glad to meet all our friends. What can we do for you?

A. Attend. Obey the spirits.

Q. We will do all we can, if you will tell us what to do.

A. Boil your heads!

Q. Go away, George, we don't want you.

A. Get off the line, silly.

Q. Pongo, can't you send him away?

(Here the pencil drew the sketch of an ugly face.)

Q. Is that your portrait?

A. That's me. G. W. Ha, ha!

(The pencil zig-zagged violently and drove the board right over the edge of the table. When it was replaced it started to write in the hand we associate with Pongo.)

A. I have sent him away. Very noisy tonight. F. jealous and sends him to disturb us. Never mind. Pongo more powerful.

Q. Who do you say is jealous?

A. Never mind. Bad person. Maladetta.

Q. Is Harry still there?

A. No. Other business. There is a spirit here who wishes your help.

Q. Who is it?

A. Very hard. Wait.

(The pencil made a series of wide loops.)

Q. What letter is that?

A. Silly! don't be impatient. There is difficulty. I will try again.

(The pencil scribbled for a few minutes and then wrote a large C.)

Q. We have got the letter C. Is that right?

A. C-C-C

Q. We have got C.

A. C-R-E

(Here there was another violent interruption.)

A. (in Pongo's writing) She is trying, but there is much opposition. Think helpful thoughts.

Q. Would you like us to sing a hymn?

A. (Pongo again, very angry) Stupid! Be quiet! (Here the writing changed again) M-O-

Q. Is that part of the same word?

A. R-N-A.

Q. Do you mean Cremorna?

A. (in the new writing) Cremorna, Cremorna. Through! Glad, glad, glad!

At this point, Miss Booth turned to Miss Climpson and said in a puzzled voice:

"This is very strange. Cremorna was Mrs. Wrayburn's stage name. I do hope —surely she can't have passed away suddenly. She was perfectly comfortable when I left her. Had I better go and see?"

"Perhaps it's another Cremorna?" suggested Miss Climpson.

"But it's such an unusual name."

"Why not ask who it is?"

Q. Cremorna—what is your second name?

A. (The pencil writing very fast) Rosegarden—easier now.

Q. I don't understand you.

A. Rose—Rose—Rose—Silly!

Q. Oh!—(My dear, she's mixing up the two names)—Do you mean Cremorna Garden?

A. Yes.

Q. Rosanna Wrayburn?

A. Yes.

Q. Have you passed over?

A. Not yet. In exile.

Q. Are you still in the body?

A. Neither in the body nor out of the body. Waiting. (Pongo interposing) When what you call the mind is departed, the spirit waits in exile for the Great Change. Why can't you understand? Make haste. Great difficulties.

Q. We are so sorry. Are you in trouble about something?

A. Great trouble.

Q. I hope it isn't anything in Dr. Brown's treatment, or mine—

A. (Pongo) Do not be so foolish. (Cremorna) My will.

Q. Do you want to alter your will?

A. No.

Miss Climpson. That is fortunate, because I don't think it would be legal. What do you want us to do about it, dear Mrs. Wrayburn?

A. Send it to Norman.

Q. To Mr. Norman Urquhart?

A. Yes. He knows.

Q. He knows what is to be done with it?

A. He wants it.

Q. Very well. Can you tell where to find it?

A. I have forgotten. Search.

Q. Is it in the house?

A. I tell you I have forgotten. Deep waters. No safety. Failing, failing . . . (Here the writing became very faint and irregular.)

Q. Try to remember.

A. In the B—B—B—(a confusion and the pencil staggering wildly)—No good. (Suddenly, in a different hand and very vigorously) Get off the line, get off the line, get off the line.

Q. Who is that?

A. (Pongo) She has gone. The bad influence back. Ha, ha! Get off ! Finished now. (The pencil ran right out of the medium's control, and on being replaced on the table, refused to answer any further questions.)

"How dreadfully vexatious!" exclaimed Miss Booth.

"I suppose you have no idea where the will is?"

"Not the least. 'In the B—' she said. Now, what could that be?"

"In the Bank, perhaps," suggested Miss Climpson.

"It might be. If so, of course, Mr. Urquhart would be the only person who could get it out."

"Then why hasn't he? She said he wanted it."

"Of course. Then it must be somewhere in the house. What could B stand for?"

"Box, Bag, Bureau—?"

"Bed? It might be almost anything."

"What a pity she couldn't finish the message. Shall we try again? Or shall we look in all the likely places?"

"Let's look first, and then, if we can't find it, we can try again."

"That's a good idea. There are some keys in one of the bureau drawers that belong to her boxes and things."

"Why not try them?" said Miss Climpson, boldly.

"We will. You'll come and help, won't you?"

"If you think it advisable. I'm a stranger, you know."

"The message came to you as much as to me. I'd rather you came with me. You might be able to suggest places."

Miss Climpson made no further ado, and they went upstairs. It was a queer business—practically robbing a helpless woman in the interests of someone she had never seen. Queer. But the motive must be a good one, if it was Lord Peter's.

At the top of the beautiful staircase with its ample curve was a long, wide corridor, the walls hung thickly from floor to ceiling with portraits, sketches, framed autograph letters, programmes, and all the reminiscent bric-à-brac of the greenroom.

"All her life is here and in these two rooms," said the nurse. "If this collection was to be sold, it would fetch a lot of money. I suppose it will be some day."

"Whom does the money go to, do you know?"

"Well, I've always thought it would be to Mr. Norman Urquhart—he's a relation of hers, about the only one, I believe. But I've never been told anything about it."

She pushed open a tall door, graceful with curved panels and classical architrave, and turned on the light.

It was a stately great room, with three tall windows and a ceiling gracefully moulded with garlands of flowers and flambeaux. The purity of its lines was, however, defaced and insulted by a hideous rose-trellised wall-paper, and heavy plush curtains of a hot crimson with thick gold fringes and ropes, like the drop-curtain of a Victorian playhouse. Every foot of space was crammed thick with furniture—buhl tables incongruously jostling mahogany chiffoniers; whatnot tables strewn with ornaments cuddling the bases of heavy German marbles and bronzes; lacquer screens, Sheraton bureaux, Chinese vases, alabaster lamps, chairs, ottomans of every shape, colour and period, clustered thick as plants wrestling for existence in a tropical jungle. It was the room of a woman without taste or moderation, who refused nothing and surrendered nothing, to whom the fact of possession had become the one steadfast reality in a world of loss and change.

"It may be in here or in the bedroom," said Miss Booth. "I'll get her keys."

She opened a door on the right. Miss Climpson, endlessly inquisitive, tip-toed in after her.

The bedroom was even more of a nightmare than the sitting-room. A small electric reading-lamp burned dimly by the bed, huge and gilded, with hangings of rose brocade cascading in long folds from a tester supported by fat golden cupids. Outside the narrow circle of light loomed monstrous wardrobes, more cabinets, tall chests of drawers. The dressing-table, frilled and flounced, held a wide, three-fold mirror, and a monstrous cheval-glass in the centre of the room darkly reflected the towering and shadowy outlines of the furniture.

Miss Booth opened the middle door of the largest wardrobe. It swung back with a creak, letting out a great gush of frangipani. Nothing, evidently, had been altered in this room since silence and paralysis had struck the owner down.

Miss Climpson stepped softly up to the bed. Instinct made her move cautiously as a cat, though it was evident that nothing would ever startle or surprise its occupant.

An old, old face, so tiny in the vast expanse of sheet and pillow that it might have been a doll, stared up at her with unblinking, unseeing eyes. It was covered with fine surface-wrinkles, like a hand sodden with soapy water, but all the great lines carved by experience had been smoothed out and crumpled. It reminded Miss Climpson of a child's pink balloon, from which nearly all the air has leaked away. The escaping breath puffed through the lax lips in little blowing, snorting sounds and added to the resemblance. From under the frilled night-cap straggled a few lank wisps of whitened hair.

"Funny, isn't it," said Miss Booth, "to think that with her lying like that, her spirit can communicate with us."

Miss Climpson was overcome by a sense of sacrilege. It was only by a great effort that she prevented herself from confessing the truth. She had pulled the garter with the soap-box above her knee for safety, and the elastic was cutting painfully into the muscles of her leg—a kind of reminder of her iniquities.

But Miss Booth had already turned away, and was pulling open the drawers of one of the bureaux.

Two hours passed, and they were still searching. The letter B. opened up a particularly wide field of search. Miss Climpson had chosen it on that account, and her foresight was rewarded. By a little ingenuity, that useful letter could be twisted to fit practically any hiding-place in the house. The things that were neither bureaux, beds, bags, boxes, baskets nor bibelot-tables could usually be described as big, black, brown or buhl or, at a pinch, as being bedroom or boudoir furniture, and since every shelf, drawer and pigeon-hole in every object was crammed full of newspaper-cuttings, letters and assorted souvenirs, the searchers soon found their heads, legs and backs aching with effort.

"I'd no idea," said Miss Booth, "that there could be so many possible places."

Miss Climpson, sitting on the floor, with her back hair uncoiling itself and her decent black petticoats tucked up nearly to the soap-box, agreed wearily.

"It's dreadfully exhausting, isn't it?" said Miss Booth. "Wouldn't you like to stop? I can go on searching tomorrow by myself. It's a shame to tire you out in this way."

Miss Climpson turned this over in her mind. If the will were found in her absence and sent to Norman Urquhart, would Miss Murchison be able to get hold of it before it was again hidden away or destroyed? She wondered.

Hidden away, not destroyed. The mere fact that the will had been sent to him by Miss Booth would prevent the solicitor from making away with it, for there would be a witness to its existence. But he might successfully conceal it for a considerable time—and time was of the essence of the adventure.

"Oh, I'm not a scrap tired," she said brightly, sitting up on her heels and restoring her coiffure to something more like its usual neatness. She had a black note-book in her hand, taken from a drawer in one of the Japanese cabinets, and was turning its pages mechanically. A line of figures caught her eye: 12, 18, 4, 0, 9, 3, 15, and she wondered vaguely what they referred to.

"We've looked through everything here," said Miss Booth. "I don't believe we've missed anything—unless, of course, there is a secret drawer somewhere."

"Could it be in a book, do you think?"

"A book! Why, of course it might. How silly of us not to think of that! In detective stories, wills are always hidden in books."

"More often than in real life," thought Miss Climpson, but she got up and dusted herself and said cheerfully:

"So they are. Are there many books in the house?"

"Thousands," said Miss Booth. "Downstairs in the library."

"I shouldn't have expected Mrs. Wrayburn to be a great reader, somehow."

"Oh, I don't think she was. The books were bought with the house, so Mr. Urquhart told me. They're nearly all old ones, you know—big things bound in leather. Dreadfully dull. I've never found a thing to read there. But they're just the sort of books to hide wills in."

They emerged into the corridor.

"By the way," said Miss Climpson, "won't the servants think it funny of us to be wandering about the place so late?"

"They all sleep in the other wing. Besides, they know that I sometimes have visitors. Mrs. Craig has often been here as late as this when we have had interesting sittings. There's a spare bedroom where I can put people up when I want to."

Miss Climpson made no more objections, and they went downstairs and along the hall into the library. It was big, and books filled the walls and bays in serried ranks—a heart-breaking sight.

"Of course," said Miss Booth, "if the communication hadn't insisted on something beginning with B—"

"Well?"

"Well—I should have expected any papers to be in the safe down here."

Miss Climpson groaned in spirit. The obvious place, naturally! If only her misplaced ingenuity—well! one must make the best of it.

"Why not look?" she suggested. "The letter B. may have been referring to something quite different. Or it may have been an interruption from George Washington. It would be quite like him to use words beginning with a B, don't you think?"

"But if it was in the safe, Mr. Urquhart would know about it."

Miss Climpson began to feel that she had let her invention play about too freely.

"It wouldn't do any harm to make sure," she suggested.

"But I don't know the combination," said Miss Booth. "Mr. Urquhart does, of course. We could write and ask him."

An inspiration came to Miss Climpson.

"I believe I know it," she exclaimed. "There was a row of seven figures in that black note-book I was looking at just now, and it passed through my mind that they must be a memorandum of something."

"Black Book!" cried Miss Booth. "Why, there you are! How could we have been so silly! Of course, Mrs. Wrayburn was trying to tell us where to find the combination!"

Miss Climpson again blessed the all-round utility of the letter B.

"I'll run up and fetch it," she cried.

When she came down again, Miss Booth was standing before a section of the bookshelves, which had swung out from the wall, disclosing the green door of a built-in safe. With trembling hands, Miss Climpson touched the milled knob and turned it.

The first attempt was unsuccessful, owing to the fact that the note did not make it clear which way the knob should be turned first, but at the second attempt the pointer swung over on the seventh figure with a satisfying click.

Miss Booth seized the handle, and the heavy door moved and stood open.

A bundle of papers lay inside. On the top, staring them in the face, was a long, sealed envelope. Miss Climpson pounced upon it.

"Will of Rosanna Wrayburn
5 June 1920."

"Well, isn't that marvellous?" cried Miss Booth. On the whole, Miss Climpson agreed with her.

19

Miss Climpson stayed the night in the spare bedroom. "The best thing," she said, "will be for you to write a little letter to Mr. Urquhart, explaining about the séance, and saying that you thought it best and safest to send the will on to him."

"He will be very much surprised," said Miss Booth. "I wonder what he will say. Lawyers don't believe in spirit communications as a rule. And he'll think it rather funny that we should have managed to open the safe."

"Well, but the spirit led us directly to the combination, didn't it? He could hardly expect you to ignore a message like that, could he? The proof of your good faith is that you are sending the will straight to him. And it would be as well, don't you think, if you asked him to come up and check the other contents of the safe and have the combination altered."

"Wouldn't it be better if I kept the will and asked him to come for it?"

"But perhaps he requires it urgently?"

"Then why hasn't he been to fetch it?"

Miss Climpson noted with some irritation that, where spiritualistic messages were not concerned, Miss Booth showed signs of developing an independent judgment.

"Perhaps he doesn't know yet that he wants it. Perhaps the spirits foresaw an urgent need that will only arise tomorrow."

"Oh, yes, that's quite likely. If only people would avail themselves more fully of the marvellous guidance given to them, so much might be foreseen and provided for! Well, I think you are right. We will find a big envelope to fit it, and I will write a letter and we will send it by the first post tomorrow."

"It had better be registered," said Miss Climpson. "If you will entrust it to me, I will take it down to the post office first thing."

"Will you? That will be a great relief to my mind. Well now, I'm sure you're as tired as I am, so I'll put on a kettle for the hot-water bottles and we'll turn in. Will you make yourself comfy in my sitting-room? I've only got to put the sheets on your bed. What? No, indeed, I can do it in a moment; *please* don't bother. I'm so used to making beds."

"Then I'll see to the kettles," said Miss Climpson. "I simply *must* make myself useful."

"Very well. It won't take long. The water is quite hot in the kitchen boiler."

Left alone in the kitchen, with a kettle bumping and singing on its way to boiling-point, Miss Climpson wasted no time. She tip-toed quickly out again and stood with ear cocked at the foot of the stairs, listening to the nurse's footsteps as they pattered into the distance. Then she slipped into the little sitting-room, took up the will in its sealed envelope, and a long thin paper-knife which she had already marked down as a useful weapon, and hastened back to the kitchen.

It is astonishing how long a kettle which seems to be on the verge of boiling will take before the looked-for jet of steady steam emerges from its spout. Delusive little puffs and deceptive pauses in the song tantalise the watcher interminably. It seemed to Miss Climpson that there would have been time to make twenty beds before the kettle boiled that evening. But even a watched pot cannot absorb heat for ever. After what appeared to be an hour, but was actually about seven minutes, Miss Climpson, guilty and furtive, was holding the flap of the envelope before the scalding steam.

"I mustn't hurry," said Miss Climpson, "oh, blessed saints, I mustn't hurry, or I shall tear it."

She slipped the paper-knife under the flap; it lifted; it opened cleanly, just as Miss Booth's step resounded in the passage.

Miss Climpson adroitly dropped the paper-knife behind the stove and thrust the envelope, with the flap doubled back to prevent it from re-sticking itself, behind a dish-cover on the wall.

"The water's ready!" she cried blithely. "Where are the bottles?"

It is a tribute to her nerve that she filled them with a steady hand. Miss Booth thanked her, and departed upstairs, a bottle in each hand.

Miss Climpson pulled the will from its hiding-place, drew it from its envelope and glanced swiftly through it.

It was not a long document, and in spite of the legal phraseology, its purport was easily gathered. Within three minutes she had replaced it, moistened the gum and stuck the flap down again. She put it in her petticoat-pocket—for her garments were of a useful and old-fashioned kind—and went to hunt in the pantry. When Miss Booth returned, she was making tea peacefully.

"I thought it would refresh us after our labours," she remarked.

"A very good idea," said Miss Booth; "in fact, I was just going to suggest it."

Miss Climpson carried the tea-pot to the sitting-room, leaving Miss Booth to follow with the cups, milk and sugar on a tray. With the tea-pot on the hob and the will once more lying innocently on the table, she smiled and breathed deeply. Her mission was accomplished.

Letter from Miss Climpson to Lord Peter Wimsey.
Tuesday, Jan. 7, 1930.

My dear Lord Peter,

As my *telegram* this morning will have informed you, I have SUCCEEDED!! Though what excuse I can find in my *conscience* for the *methods* I have used, I *don't* KNOW! but I believe the Church takes into account the necessity of *deception* in certain *professions*, such as that of a *police-detective* or a SPY in time of WARFARE, and I *trust* that my *subterfuges* may be allowed to come under that *category*. However, you will not want to hear about my *religious scruples*! So I will hasten to let you know *what* I have DISCOVERED!!

In my last letter I explained the *plan* I had in mind, so you will know what to do about the *Will itself*, which was duly *despatched* by *Registered Post* this morning under cover to *Mr. Norman Urquhart*. How surprised he will be to get it!!! Miss Booth wrote an excellent *covering letter*, which I *saw* before it went, which explains the circumstances and *mentions* NO NAMES!! I have wired to Miss Murchison to *expect* the package, and I hope that when it comes she will contrive to be *present* at the opening, so as to constitute *yet another* WITNESS to its existence. In any case, I should not think he would *venture* to *tamper* with it. Perhaps Miss Murchison may be able to INVESTIGATE it in detail, which I had not *time* to do (it was all *most* adventurous! and I am looking forward to *telling* you ALL ABOUT IT when I come back), but in case she is *not* able to do so, I will give you the *rough outline*.

The property consists of *real estate* (the house and grounds) and a *personalty* (am I not *good* at legal terms??) which I am not able to calculate *exactly*. But the gist of it all is this:—

The *real estate* is left to *Philip Boyes*, absolutely.

Fifty thousand pounds is left to *Philip Boyes* also, in *cash*.

The remainder (is not this called the residue?) is left to NORMAN URQUHART, who is appointed sole executor.

There are a few *small legacies* to Stage Charities, of which I did not manage to memorise any *particulars*.

There is a special paragraph, explaining that the greater part of the property is left to *Philip Boyes* in token that the testatrix FORGIVES the ill-treatment meted out to her by *his family*, for which he was *not responsible*.

The date of the Will is 5 June 1920, and the *witnesses* are *Eva Gubbins*, housekeeper, and *John Briggs*, gardener.

I hope, dear Lord Peter, that this information will be enough for your purpose. I had hoped that even *after* Miss Booth had enclosed the Will in a *covering envelope* I might be able to take it out and *peruse* it at leisure, but unfortunately she *sealed* it for greater security with Mrs. Wrayburn's *private seal*, which I had not sufficient *dexterity* to *remove and replace*, though I understand it is possible to *do so* with a *hot knife*.

You will *understand* that I cannot leave Windle *just yet*—it would look so odd to do so immediately after this occurrence. Besides, I am hoping, in a further series of "sittings," to *warn* Miss Booth against Mrs. Craig and her "control" Fedora, as I am *quite sure* that this person is *quite* as great a *charlatan* as I AM!!!—and without my *altruistic* motives!! So you will not be surprised if I am away from Town for, say, *another week!* I am a little worried about the *extra expense* of this, but if you do not think it *justified* for the sake of safety, *let me know*—and I will alter my arrangements accordingly.

Wishing you *all success*, dear Lord Peter,

Most sincerely yours,
Katharine A. Climpson.

P.S. I managed to do the "job" *very nearly* within the stipulated week, you see. I am *so sorry* it was not *quite* finished yesterday, but I was so *terrified* of *spoiling* the WHOLE THING by *rushing* it!!

"Bunter," said Lord Peter, looking up from this letter, "I *knew* there was something fishy about that will."

"Yes, my lord."

"There is something about wills which brings out the worst side of human nature. People who under ordinary circumstances are perfectly upright and amiable, go as curly as corkscrews and foam at the mouth, whenever they hear the words 'I devise and bequeath.' That reminds me, a spot of champagne in a silver tankard is no bad thing to celebrate on. Get up a bottle of the Pommery and tell Chief-Inspector Parker I should be glad of a word with him. And bring me those notes of Mr. Arbuthnot's. And oh, Bunter!"

"My lord?"

"Get Mr. Crofts on the 'phone and give him my compliments, and say I have found the criminal and the motive and hope presently to produce proof of the way the crime was done, if he will see that the case is put off for a week or so."

"Very good, my lord."

"All the same, Bunter, I really don't know how it *was* done."

"That will undoubtedly suggest itself before long, my lord."

"Oh, yes," said Wimsey, airily. "Of course. Of course. I'm not worrying about a trifle like that."

20

"**T**ch! t'ch!" said Mr. Pond, clicking his tongue against his denture.

Miss Murchison looked up from her typewriter.

"Is anything the matter, Mr. Pond?"

"No, nothing," said the head-clerk, testily. "A foolish letter from a foolish member of your sex, Miss Murchison."

"That's nothing new."

Mr. Pond frowned, conceiving the tone of his subordinate's voice to be impertinent. He picked up the letter and its enclosure and took them into the inner office.

Miss Murchison nipped swiftly across to his desk and glanced at the registered envelope which lay upon it, open. The post-mark was "Windle."

"That's luck," said Miss Murchison, to herself. "Mr. Pond is a better witness than I should be. I'm glad he opened it."

She regained her place. In a few minutes Mr. Pond emerged, smiling slightly.

Five minutes later, Miss Murchison, who had been frowning over her short-hand note-book, rose up and came over to him.

"Can you read short-hand, Mr. Pond?"

"No," said the head-clerk. "In my day it was not considered necessary."

"I can't make out this outline," said Miss Murchison. "It looks like 'give consent to,' but it may be only 'give consideration to'—there's a difference, isn't there?"

"There certainly is," said Mr. Pond drily.

"P'raps I'd better not risk it," said Miss Murchison. "It's got to go off this morning. I'd better ask him."

Mr. Pond snorted—not for the first time—over the carelessness of the female typist.

Miss Murchison walked briskly across the room and opened the inner door without knocking—an informality which left Mr. Pond groaning again.

Mr. Urquhart was standing up with his back to the door, doing something or other at the mantelpiece. He turned round sharply, with an exclamation of annoyance.

"I have told you before, Miss Murchison, that I like you to knock before entering."

"I am very sorry; I forgot."

"Don't let it happen again. What is it?"

He did not return to his desk, but stood leaning against the mantelshelf. His sleek head, outlined against the panelling, was a little thrown back, as though—Miss Murchison thought—he were protecting or defying somebody.

"I could not quite make out my shorthand note of your letter to Tewke & Peabody," said Miss Murchison, "and I thought it better to come and ask you."

"I wish," said Mr. Urquhart, fixing a stern eye upon her, "that you would take your notes clearly at the time. If I am going too fast for you, you should tell me so. It would save trouble in the end—wouldn't it?"

Miss Murchison was reminded of a little set of rules which Lord Peter Wimsey—half in jest and half in earnest—had once prepared for the guidance of "The Cattery." Of Rule Seven, in particular, which ran: "Always distrust the man who looks you straight in the eyes. He wants to prevent you from seeing something. Look for it."

She shifted her eyes under her employer's gaze.

"I'm very sorry, Mr. Urquhart. I won't let it occur again," she muttered. There was a curious dark line at the edge of the panelling just behind the solicitor's head, as though the panel did not quite fit its frame. She had never noticed it before.

"Well, now, what is the trouble?"

Miss Murchison asked her question, got her answer and retired. As she went, she cast a glance over the desk. The will was not there.

She went back and finished her letters. When she took them in to be signed, she seized the opportunity to look at the panelling again. There was no dark line to be seen.

Miss Murchison left the office promptly at half-past four. She had a feeling that it would be unwise to linger about the premises. She walked briskly away through Hand Court, turned to the right along Holborn, dived to the right again through Featherstone Buildings, made a detour through Red Lion Street and debouched into Red Lion Square. Within five minutes she was at her old walk round the square, and up Princeton Street. Presently, from a safe distance, she saw Mr. Pond come out, thin, stiff and stooping, and walk down Bedford Row towards Chancery Lane Station. Before very long, Mr. Urquhart followed. He stood a moment on the threshold, glancing to left and right, then came straight across the street towards her. For a moment she thought he had seen her, and she dived hurriedly behind a van that was standing at the kerb. Under its shelter, she withdrew to the corner of the street, where there is a butcher's shop, and scanned a windowful of New Zealand lamb and chilled beef. Mr. Urquhart came nearer. His steps grew louder—then paused. Miss Murchison glued her eyes on a round of meat marked 4½ lb. ¾ d. A voice said: "Good evening, Miss Murchison. Choosing your supper-chop?"

"Oh! Good evening, Mr. Urquhart. Yes—I was just wishing that Providence had seen fit to provide more joints suitable for single people."

"Yes—one gets tired of beef and mutton."

"And pork is apt to be indigestible."

"Just so. Well, you should cease to be single, Miss Murchison."

Miss Murchison giggled.

"But this is so sudden, Mr. Urquhart."

Mr. Urquhart flushed under his curious freckled skin.

"Good-night," he said abruptly, and with extreme coldness.

Miss Murchison laughed to herself as he strode off.

"Thought that would settle him. It's a great mistake to be familiar with your subordinates. They take advantage of you."

She watched him out of sight on the far side of the Square, then returned along Princeton Street, crossed Bedford Row and re-entered the office building. The charwoman was just coming downstairs.

"Well, Mrs. Hodges, it's me again! Do you mind letting me in? I've lost a pattern of silk. I think I must have left it in my desk, or dropped it on the floor. Have you come across it?"

"No, miss, I ain't done your office yet."

"Then I'll have a hunt round for it. I want to get up to Bourne's before half-past six. It's such a nuisance."

"Yes, miss, and such a crowd always with the buses and things. Here you are, miss."

She opened the door, and Miss Murchison darted in.

"Shall I 'elp you look for it, miss?"

"No, thank you, Mrs. Hodges, please don't bother. I don't expect it's far off."

Mrs. Hodges took up a pail and went to fill it at a tap in the back yard. As soon as her heavy steps had ascended again to the first floor, Miss Murchison made for the inner office.

"I must and will see what's behind this panelling."

The houses in Bedford Row are Hogarthian in type, tall, symmetrical, with the glamour of better days upon them. The panels in Mr. Urquhart's room, though defaced by many coats of paint, were handsomely designed, and over the mantelpiece ran a festoon of flowers and fruit, rather florid for the period, with a ribbon and basket in the center. If the panel was controlled by a concealed spring, the boss that moved it was probably to be found among this decorative work. Pulling a chair to the fireplace, Miss Murchison ran her fingers quickly over the festoon, pushing and pressing with both hands, while keeping her ear cocked for intruders.

This kind of investigation is easy for experts, but Miss Murchison's knowledge of secret hiding places was only culled from sensational literature; she could not find the trick of the thing. After nearly a quarter of an hour, she began to despair.

Thump—thump—thump—Mrs. Hodges was coming downstairs.

Miss Murchison sprang away from the panelling so hastily that the chair slipped, and she had to thrust hard at the wall to save herself. She jumped down, restored the chair to its place, glanced up—and saw the panel standing wide open.

At first she thought it was a miracle, but soon realised that in slipping she had thrust sideways at the frame of the panel. A small square of woodwork had slipped away sideways, and exposed an inner panel with a keyhole in the middle.

She heard Mrs. Hodges in the outer room, but she was too excited to bother about what Mrs. Hodges might be thinking. She pushed a heavy chair across the door, so that nobody could enter without noise and difficulty. In a moment Blindfold Bill's keys were in her hand—how fortunate that she had not returned them! How fortunate, too, that Mr. Urquhart had relied on the secrecy of the panel, and had not thought it worth while to fit his cache with a patent lock!

A few moment's quick work with the keys, and the lock turned. She pulled the little door open.

Inside was a bundle of papers. Miss Murchison ran them over—at first quickly —then again, with a puzzled face. Receipts for securities—Share certificates— Megatherium Trust—surely the names of those investments were familiar— where had she . . . ?

Suddenly Miss Murchison sat down, feeling quite faint, the bundle of papers in her hand.

She realised now what had happened to Mrs. Wrayburn's money, which Norman Urquhart had been handling under that confiding Deed of Trust, and why the matter of the will was so important. Her head whirled. She picked up a sheet of paper from the desk and began jotting down in hurried shorthand the particulars of the various transactions of which these documents were the evidence.

Somebody bumped at the door.

"Are you in here, miss?"

"Just a moment, Mrs. Hodges. I think I must have dropped it on the floor in here."

She gave the big chair a sharp push, effectually closing the door.

She must hurry. Anyway she had got down enough to convince Lord Peter that Mr. Urquhart's affairs needed looking into. She put the papers back into the cupboard, in the exact place from which she had taken them. The will was there, too, she noticed, laid on one side by itself. She peered in. There was something else, tucked away at the back. She thrust her hand in and pulled the mysterious object out. It was a white paper packet, labelled with the name of a foreign chemist. The end had been opened and tucked in again. She pulled the paper apart, and saw that the packet contained about two ounces of a fine white powder.

Next to hidden treasure and mysterious documents, nothing is more full of sensational suggestion than a packet of anonymous white powder. Miss Murchison caught up another sheet of clean paper, tipped a thimbleful of the powder into it, replaced the packet at the back of the cupboard and re-locked the door with the skeleton key. With trembling fingers she pushed the panel back into place, taking care to shut it completely, so as to show no betraying dark line.

She rolled the chair away from the door and cried out gaily:

"I've got it, Mrs. Hodges!"

"There, now!" said Mrs. Hodges, appearing in the doorway.

"Just fancy!" said Miss Murchison. "I was looking through my patterns when Mr. Urquhart rang, and this one must have stuck to my frock and dropped on the floor in here."

She held up a small piece of silk triumphantly. She had torn it from the lining of her bag in the course of the afternoon—a proof, if any were needed, of her devotion to her work, for the bag was a good one.

"Dearie me," said Mrs. Hodges. "What a good thing you found it, wasn't it, miss?"

"I nearly didn't," said Miss Murchison, "it was right in this dark corner. Well, I must fly to get there before the shop shuts. Good-night, Mrs. Hodges."

But long before the accommodating Messrs. Bourne & Hollingsworth had closed their doors, Miss Murchison was ringing the second floor bell at IICa, Piccadilly.

She found a council in progress. There was the Hon. Freddy Arbuthnot, looking amiable, Chief-Inspector Parker, looking worried, Lord Peter, looking somnolent, and Bunter, who having introduced her, retired to a position on the fringe of the assembly and hovered there looking correct.

"Have you brought us news, Miss Murchison? If so, you have come at the exact right moment to find the eagles gathered together. Mr. Arbuthnot, Chief-Inspector Parker, Miss Murchison. Now let's all sit down and be happy together. Have you had tea? or will you absorb a spot of something?"

Miss Murchison declined refreshment.

"H'm!" said Wimsey. "The patient refuses food. Her eyes glitter wildly. The expression is anxious. The lips are parted. The fingers fumble with clasp of the bag. The symptoms point to an acute attack of communicativeness. Tell us the worst, Miss Murchison."

Miss Murchison needed no urging. She told her adventures, and had the pleasure of holding her audience enthralled from the first word to the last. When she finally produced the screw of paper containing the white powder, the sentiments of the company expressed themselves in a round of applause, in which Bunter joined discreetly.

"Are you convinced, Charles?" asked Wimsey.

"I admit that I am heavily shaken," said Parker. "Of course, the powder must be analysed—"

"It shall, embodied caution," said Wimsey. "Bunter, make ready the rack and thumbscrew. Bunter has been taking lessons in Marsh's test, and performs it to admiration. You know all about it too, Charles, don't you?"

"Enough for a rough test."

"Carry on then, my children. In the meanwhile, let us sum up our feelings."

Bunter went out and Parker, who had been making entries in a note-book, cleared his throat.

"Well," he said, "the matter stands, I take it, like this. You say that Miss Vane is innocent, and you undertake to prove this by bringing a convincing accusation against Norman Urquhart. So far, your evidence against him is almost entirely concerned with motive, bolstered up by proofs of intent to mislead enquiry. You say that your investigations have brought the case against Urquhart to a point at which the police can, and ought to, take it up, and I am inclined to agree with you. I warn you, however, that you still have to establish evidence as to means and opportunity."

"I know that. Tell us a new one."

"All right, as long as you know it. Very well. Now Philip Boyes and Norman Urquhart are the only surviving relations of Mrs. Wrayburn, or Cremorna Garden, who is rich, and has money to leave. A number of years ago, Mrs. Wrayburn put all her affairs into the hands of Urquhart's father, the only member of the family with whom she remained on friendly terms. On his father's death, Norman Urquhart took over those affairs himself, and in 1920, Mrs. Wrayburn executed a Deed of Trust, giving him sole authority to handle her property. She also made a will, dividing her property unequally between her two great-nephews. Philip Boyes got all the real estate and £50,000, while Norman Urquhart took whatever was left and was also sole executor. Norman Urquhart when questioned about this Will, deliberately told you an untruth, saying that the bulk of the money was left to him, and even went so far as to produce a document purporting to be a draft of such a will. The pretended date of this draft is subsequent to that of the Will discovered by Miss Climpson, but there is no doubt that the draft itself was drawn out by Urquhart, certainly within the last three years and probably within the last few days. Moreover, the fact that the actual Will, though lying in a place accessible to Urquhart, was not destroyed by him, suggests that it was not, in fact, superseded by any subsequent testamentary disposition. By the way, Wimsey, why didn't he simply take the will and destroy it? As the sole surviving heir, he would then inherit without dispute."

"Perhaps it didn't occur to him. Or there might even be other relatives surviving. How about that uncle in Australia?"

"True. At any rate he didn't destroy it. In 1925, Mrs. Wrayburn became completely paralysed and imbecile, so that there was no possibility of her ever enquiring into the disposition of her estate or making another will.

"About this time, as we know from Mr. Arbuthnot, Urquhart took the dangerous step of plunging into speculation. He made mistakes, lost money, plunged more deeply to recover himself, and was involved to a large extent in the great crash of Megatherium Trust, Ltd. He certainly lost far more than he could possibly afford, and we now find, from Miss Murchison's discoveries—of which I must say that I should hate to have to take official notice—that he had been consistently abusing his position as Trustee and employing Mrs. Wrayburn's money for his private speculations. He deposited her holdings as security for large loans, and embarked the money thus raised in the Megatherium and other wild-cat schemes.

"As long as Mrs. Wrayburn lived, he was fairly safe, for he only had to pay to her the sums necessary to keep up her house and establishment. In fact, all the household bills and so on were settled by him as her man of affairs under Power of Attorney, all salaries were paid by him, and so long as he did this, it was nobody's business to ask what he had done with the capital. But as soon as Mrs. Wrayburn died, he would have to account to the other heir, Philip Boyes, for the capital which he had misappropriated.

"Now in 1929, just about the time that Philip Boyes quarrelled with Miss Vane, Mrs. Wrayburn had a serious attack of illness and very nearly died. The danger passed, but might recur at any moment. Almost immediately afterwards we find him becoming friendly with Philip Boyes and inviting him to stay at his house. While living with Urquhart, Boyes has three attacks of illness, attributed by his doctor to gastritis, but equally consistent with arsenical poisoning. In June 1929, Philip Boyes goes away to Wales and his health improves.

"While Philip Boyes is absent, Mrs. Wrayburn has another alarming attack, and Urquhart hastens up to Windle, possibly with the idea of destroying the will in case the worst happens. It does not happen, and he comes back to London, just in time to receive Boyes on his return from Wales. That night, Boyes is taken ill with symptoms similar to those of the previous spring, but much more violent. After three days he dies.

"Urquhart is now perfectly safe. As residuary legatee, he will receive, at Mrs. Wrayburn's death, all the money bequeathed to Philip Boyes. That is, he will not get it, because he has already taken it and lost it, but he will no longer be called upon to produce it and his fraudulent dealings will not be exposed.

"So far, the evidence as to motive is extremely cogent, and far more convincing than the evidence against Miss Vane.

"But here is your snag, Wimsey. When and how was the poison administered? We know that Miss Vane possessed arsenic and that she could easily have given it to him without witnesses. But Urquhart's only opportunity was at the dinner he shared with Boyes, and if anything in this case is certain, it is that the poison was not administered at that dinner. Everything which Boyes ate or drank was equally eaten and drunk by Urquhart and the servants, with the single exception of the burgundy, which was preserved and analysed and found to be harmless."

"I know," said Wimsey, "but that is what is so suspicious. Did you ever hear of a meal hedged round with such precautions? It's not natural, Charles. There's the sherry, poured out by the maid from the original bottle, the soup, fish and casseroled chicken—so impossible to poison in one portion without poisoning the whole—the omelette, so ostentatiously prepared at the table by the hands of the victim—the wine, sealed up and marked—the remnants consumed in the kitchen—you would think the man had gone out of his way to construct a suspicion-proof meal. The wine is the final touch which makes the thing incredible. Do you tell me that at that earliest moment when everybody supposes the illness to be a natural one, and when the affectionate cousin ought to be overwhelmed with anxiety for the sick man, it is natural or believable that an innocent person's mind should fly to accusations of poisoning? If he was innocent himself, then he suspected something. If he did suspect, why didn't he tell the doctor and have the patient's secretions and so on analysed? Why should he ever have thought of protecting himself against accusation when no accusation had been made, unless he knew that an accusation would be well-founded? And then there's the business about the nurse."

"Exactly. The nurse did have her suspicions."

"If he knew about them, he ought to have taken steps to refute them in the proper way. But I don't think he did know about them. I was referring to what you told us today. The police have got in touch with the nurse again, Miss Williams, and she tells them that Norman Urquhart took special pains never to be left alone with the patient, and never to give him any food or medicine, even when she herself was present. Doesn't that argue a bad conscience?"

"You won't find any lawyer or jury to believe it, Peter."

"Yes, but look here, doesn't it strike you as funny? Listen to this, Miss Murchison. One day the nurse was doing something or the other in the room, and she had got the medicine there on the mantelpiece. Something was said about it, and Boyes remarked, 'Oh, don't bother, Nurse. Norman can give me my dope.' Does Norman say, 'Right-ho, old man!' as you or I would? No! He says: 'No, I'll leave it to Nurse—I might make a mess of it.' Pretty feeble, what?"

"Lots of people are nervous about looking after invalids," said Miss Murchison.

"Yes, but most people can pour stuff out of a bottle into a glass. Boyes wasn't *in extremis*—he was speaking quite rationally and all that. I say the man was deliberately protecting himself."

"Possibly," said Parker, "but after all, old man, when *did* he administer the poison?"

"Probably not at the dinner at all," said Miss Murchison. "As you say, the precautions seem rather obvious. They may have been intended to make people concentrate on the dinner and forget other possibilities. Did he have a whisky when he arrived or before he went out or anything?"

"Alas, he did not. Bunter has been cultivating Hannah Westlock almost to breach of promise point, and she says that she opened the door to Boyes on his arrival, that he went straight upstairs to his room, that Urquhart was out at the time and only came in a quarter of an hour before dinner-time, and that the two men met for the first time over the famous glass of sherry in the library. The folding-doors between the library and dining-room were open and Hannah was buzzing round the whole time laying the table, and she is sure that Boyes had the sherry and nothing but the sherry."

"Not so much as a digestive tablet?"

"Nothing."

"How about after dinner?"

"When they had finished the omelette, Urquhart said something about coffee. Boyes looked at his watch and said, 'No time, old chap, I've got to be getting along to Doughty Street.' Urquhart said he would ring up a taxi, and went out to do so. Boyes folded up his napkin, got up and went into the hall. Hannah followed and helped him on with his coat. The taxi arrived. Boyes got in and off he went without seeing Urquhart again."

"It seems to me," said Miss Murchison, "That Hannah is an exceedingly important witness for Mr. Urquhart's defence. You don't think—I hardly like to suggest it—but you don't think that Bunter is allowing his feelings to overcome his judgment?"

"He says," replied Lord Peter, "that he believes Hannah to be a sincerely religious woman. He has sat beside her in chapel and shared her hymn-book."

"But that may be the merest hypocrisy," said Miss Murchison, rather warmly, for she was militantly rationalist. "I don't trust these unctuous people."

"I didn't offer that as a proof of Hannah's virtue," said Wimsey, "but of Bunter's unsusceptibility."

"But he looks like a deacon himself."

"You've never seen Bunter off duty," said Lord Peter, darkly. "I have, and I can assure you that a hymn-book would be about as softening to his heart as neat whisky to an Anglo-Indian liver. No; if Bunter says Hannah is honest, then she *is* honest."

"Then that definitely cuts out the drinks and the dinner," said Miss Murchison, unconvinced, but willing to be open-minded. "How about the water-bottle in the bedroom?"

"The devil!" cried Wimsey. "That's one up to you, Miss Murchison. We didn't think of that. The water-bottle—yes—a perfectly fruity idea. You recollect, Charles, that in the Bravo case, it was suggested that a disgruntled servant had put tartar emetic in the water-bottle. Oh, Bunter—here you are! Next time you hold Hannah's hand, will you ask her whether Mr. Boyes drank any water from his bedroom water-bottle before dinner?"

"Pardon me, my lord, the possibility had already presented itself to my mind."

"It had?"

"Yes, my lord."

"Do you never overlook anything, Bunter?"

"I endeavour to give satisfaction, my lord."

"Well then, don't talk like Jeeves. It irritates me. What about the water-bottle?"

"I was about to observe, my lord, when this lady arrived, that I had elicited a somewhat peculiar circumstance relating to the water-bottle."

"Now we're getting somewhere," said Parker, flattening out a new page of his note-book.

"I would not go so far as to say that, sir. Hannah informed me that she showed Mr. Boyes into his bedroom on his arrival and withdrew, as it was her place to do. She had scarcely reached the head of the staircase, when Mr. Boyes put his head out of the door and recalled her. He then asked her to fill his water-bottle. She was considerably astonished at this request, since she had a perfect recollection of having previously filled it when she put the room in order."

"Could he have emptied it himself?" asked Parker, eagerly.

"Not into his interior, sir—there had not been time. Nor had the drinking-glass been utilised. Moreover, the bottle was not merely empty, but dry inside. Hannah apologised for the neglect, and immediately rinsed out the bottle and filled it from the tap."

"Curious," said Parker. "But it's quite likely she never filled it at all."

"Pardon me, sir. Hannah was so much surprised by the episode that she mentioned it to Mrs. Pettican, the cook, who said that she distinctly recollected seeing her fill the bottle that morning."

"Well, then," said Parker, "Urquhart or somebody must have emptied it and dried it out. Now, why? What would one naturally do if one found one's water-bottle empty?"

"Ring the bell," said Wimsey, promptly.

"Or shout for help," added Parker.

"Or," said Miss Murchison, "if one wasn't accustomed to being waited on, one might use the water from the bedroom jug."

"Ah! . . . of course Boyes was used to a more or less Bohemian life."

"But surely," said Wimsey, "that's idiotically roundabout. It would be much simpler just to poison the water in the bottle. Why direct attention to the thing by making it more difficult? Besides, you couldn't count on the victim's using the jug-water—and, as a matter of fact, he didn't."

"And he *was* poisoned," said Miss Murchison, "so the poison wasn't either in the jug or the bottle."

"No—I'm afraid there's nothing to be got out of the jug and bottle department. Hollow, hollow, hollow all delight, Tennyson."

"All the same," said Parker, "that incident convinces me. It's too complete, somehow. Wimsey's right; it's not natural for a defence to be so perfect."

"My God," said Wimsey, "we have convinced Charles Parker. Nothing more is needed. He is more adamantine than any jury."

"Yes," said Parker, modestly, "but I'm more logical, I think. And I'm not being flustered by the Attorney-General. I should feel happier with a little evidence of a more objective kind."

"You would. You want some real arsenic. Well, Bunter, what about it?"

"The apparatus is quite ready, my lord."

"Very good. Let us go and see if we can give Mr. Parker what he wants. Lead and we follow."

In a small apartment usually devoted to Bunter's photographic work, and furnished with a sink, a bench and a bunsen burner, stood the apparatus necessary for making a Marsh's test of arsenic. The distilled water was already bubbling gently in the flask, and Bunter lifted the little glass tube which lay across the flame of the burner.

"You will perceive, my lord," he observed, "that the apparatus is free from contamination."

"I see nothing at all," said Freddy.

"That, as Sherlock Holmes would say, is what you may expect to see when there is nothing there," said Wimsey, kindly. "Charles, you will pass the water and the flask and the tube, old Uncle Tom Cobley and all as being arsenic-free."

"I will."

"Wilt thou love, cherish and keep her, in sickness or in health—sorry! turned over two pages at once. Where's that powder? Miss Murchison, you identify this sealed envelope as being the one you brought from the office, complete with mysterious white powder from Mr. Urquhart's secret hoard?"

"I do."

"Kiss the Book. Thank you. Now then—"

"Wait a sec," said Parker, "you haven't tested the envelope separately."

"That's true. There's always a snag somewhere. I suppose, Miss Murchison, you haven't such a thing as another office envelope about you?"

Miss Murchison blushed, and fumbled in her handbag.

"Well—there's a little note I scribbled this afternoon to a friend—"

"*In* your employer's time, *on* your employer's paper," said Wimsey. "Oh, how right Diogenes was when he took his lantern to look for an honest typist! Never mind. Let's have it. Who wills the end, wills the means."

Miss Murchison extracted the envelope and freed it from the enclosure. Bunter, receiving it respectfully on a developing dish, cut it into small pieces which he dropped into the flask. The water bubbled brightly, but the little tubes still remained stainless from end to end.

"Does something begin to happen soon?" enquired Mr. Arbuthnot. "Because I feel this show's a bit lackin' in pep, what?"

"If you don't sit still I shall take you out," retorted Wimsey. "Carry on, Bunter. We'll pass the envelope."

Bunter accordingly opened the second envelope, and delicately dropped the white powder into the wide mouth of the flask. All five heads bent eagerly over the apparatus. And presently, definitely, magically, a thin silver stain began to form in the tube where the flame impinged upon it. Second by second it spread and darkened to a deep brownish-black ring with a shining metallic centre.

"Oh, lovely, lovely," said Parker, with professional delight.

"Your lamp's smoking or something," said Freddy.

"Is that arsenic?" breathed Miss Murchison, gently.

"I hope so," said Wimsey, gently detaching the tube and holding it up to the light. "It's either arsenic or antimony."

"Allow me, my lord. The addition of a small quantity of solute chlorinated lime should decide the question beyond reach of cavil."

He performed this further test amid an anxious silence. The stain dissolved out and vanished under the bleaching solution.

"Then it is arsenic," said Parker.

"Oh, yes," said Wimsey, nonchalantly, "of course it is arsenic. Didn't I tell you?" His voice wavered a little with suppressed triumph.

"Is that all?" inquired Freddy, disappointed.

"Isn't it enough?" said Miss Murchison.

"Not quite," said Parker, "but it's a long way towards it. It proves that Urquhart has arsenic in his possession, and by making an official enquiry in France, we can probably find out whether this packet was already in his possession last June. I notice, by the way, that it is ordinary white arsenious acid, without any mixture of charcoal or indigo, which agrees with what was found at the post-mortem. That's satisfactory, but it would be even more satisfactory if we could provide an opportunity for Urquhart to have administered it. So far, all we have done is to demonstrate clearly that he couldn't have given it to Boyes either before, during or after dinner, during the period required for the symptoms to develop. I agree that an impossibility so bolstered up by testimony is suspicious in itself, but, to convince a jury, I should prefer something better than a *credo quia impossibile.*"

"Riddle-me-right, and riddle-me-ree," said Wimsey, imperturbably. "We've overlooked something, that's all. Probably something quite obvious. Give me the statutory dressing-gown and ounce of shag, and I will undertake to dispose of this little difficulty for you in a brace of shakes. In the meantime, you will no doubt take steps to secure, in an official and laborious manner, the evidence which our kind friends here have already so ably gathered in by unconventional methods, and will stand by to arrest the right man when the time comes?"

"I will," said Parker, "gladly. Apart from all personal considerations, I'd far rather see that oily-haired fellow in the dock than any woman, and if the Force has made a mistake, the sooner it's put right the better for all concerned."

Wimsey sat late that night in the black-and-primrose library, with the tall folios looking down at him. They represented the world's accumulated hoard of mellow wisdom and poetical beauty, to say nothing of thousands of pounds in cash. But all these counsellors sat mute upon their shelves. Strewn on tables and chairs lay the bright scarlet volumes of the Notable British Trials—Palmer, Pritchard, Maybrick, Seddon, Armstrong, Madeleine Smith—the great practitioners in arsenic—huddled together with the chief authorities on Forensic Medicine and Toxicology.

The theatre-going crowds surged home in saloon and taxi, the lights shone over the empty width of Piccadilly, the heavy night-lorries rumbled slow and seldom over the black tarmac, the long night waned and the reluctant winter dawn struggled wanly over the tiled roofs of London. Bunter, silent and anxious, sat in his kitchen, brewing coffee on the stove and reading the same page of the "British Journal of Photography" over and over again.

At half-past eight the library bell rang.

"My lord?"

"My bath, Bunter."

"Very good, my lord."

"And some coffee."

"Immediately, my lord."

"And put back all the books except these."

"Yes, my lord."

"I know now how it was done."

"Indeed, my lord? Permit me to offer my respectful congratulations."

"I've still got to prove it."

"A secondary consideration, my lord."

Wimsey yawned. When Bunter returned a minute or two later with the coffee, he was asleep.

Bunter put the books quietly away, and looked with some curiosity at the chosen few left open on the table. They were: "The Trial of Florence Maybrick"; Dixon Mann's "Forensic Medicine and Toxicology"; a book with a German title which Bunter could not read; and A. E. Houseman's "A Shropshire Lad."

Bunter studied these for a few moments, and then slapped his thigh softly.

"Why, of course!" he said under his breath, "why, what a mutton-headed set of chumps we've all been!" He touched his master lightly on the shoulder,

"Your coffee, my lord."

21

"**T**hen you won't marry me?" said Lord Peter.

The prisoner shook her head.

"No. It wouldn't be fair to you. And besides—"

"Well?"

"I'm frightened of it. One couldn't get away. I'll live with you, if you like, but I won't marry you."

Her tone was so unutterably dreary that Wimsey could feel no enthusiasm for this handsome offer.

"But that sort of thing doesn't always work," he expostulated. "Dash it all, you ought to know—forgive my alluding to it and all that—but it's frightfully inconvenient, and one has just as many rows as if one was married."

"I know that. But you could cut loose any time you wanted to."

"But I shouldn't want to."

"Oh, yes, you would. You've got a family and traditions, you know. Caesar's wife and that sort of thing."

"Blast Caesar's wife! And as for the family traditions—they're on my side, for what they're worth. Anything a Wimsey does is right and heaven help the person who gets in the way. We've even got a damned old family motto about it—'I hold by my Whimsy'—quite right too. I can't say that when I look in the glass I exactly suggest to myself the original Gerald de Wimsey, who bucked about on a cart horse at the Siege of Acre, but I do jolly well intend to do what I like about marrying. Who's to stop me? They can't eat me. They can't even cut me, if it comes to that. Joke, unintentional, officers, for the use of."

Harriet laughed.

"No, I suppose they can't cut you. You wouldn't have to slink abroad with your impossible wife and live at obscure continental watering-places like people in Victorian novels."

"Certainly not."

"People would forget I'd had a lover?"

"My dear child, they're forgetting that kind of thing every day. They're experts at it."

"And was supposed to have murdered him?"

"And were triumphantly acquitted of having murdered him, however greatly provoked."

"Well, I won't marry you. If people can forget all that, they can forget we're not married."

"Oh, yes, *they* could. I couldn't, that's all. We don't seem to be progressing very fast with this conversation. I take it the general idea of living with me does not hopelessly repel you?"

"But this is also preposterous," protested the girl. "How can I say what I should or shouldn't do if I were free and certain of—surviving?"

"Why not? I can imagine what I should do even in the most unlikely circumstances, whereas this really is a dead cert, straight from the stables."

"I can't," said Harriet, beginning to wilt. "Do please stop asking me. I don't know. I can't think. I can't see beyond the—beyond the—beyond the next few weeks. I only want to get out of this and be left alone."

"All right," said Wimsey, "I won't worry you. Not fair. Abusing my privilege and so on. You can't say 'Pig' and sweep out, under the circs., so I won't offend again. As a matter of fact I'll sweep out myself, having an appointment—with a manicurist. Nice little girl, but a trifle refained in her vowels. Cheerio!"

The manicurist, who had been discovered by the help of Chief-Inspector Parker and his sleuths, was a kitten-faced child with an inviting manner and a shrewd eye. She made no bones about accepting her client's invitation to dine, and showed no surprise when he confidentially murmured that he had a little proposition to put before her. She put her plump elbows on the table, cocked her head at a coy angle, and prepared to sell her honour dear.

As the proposition unfolded itself, her manner underwent an alteration that was almost comical. Her eyes lost their round innocence, her very hair seemed to grow less fluffy, and her eyebrows puckered in genuine astonishment.

"Why, of course I could," she said finally, "but whatever do you want them for? Seems funny to me."

"Call it just a joke," said Wimsey.

"No." Her mouth hardened. "I wouldn't like it. It doesn't make sense, if you see what I mean. What I mean, it sounds a queer sort of joke and that kind of thing might get a girl into trouble. I say, it's not one of those, what do they call 'em?—there was a bit about it in Madame Crystal's column last week, in *Susie's Snippets*—spells, you know, witchcraft—the occult, that sort of thing? I wouldn't like it if it was to do any harm to anybody."

"I'm not going to make a waxen image, if that's what you mean. Look here, are you the sort of girl who can keep a secret?"

"Oh, I don't talk. I never was one to let my tongue wag around. I'm not like ordinary girls."

"No, I thought you weren't. That's why I asked you to come out with me. Well, listen, and I'll tell you."

He leaned forward and talked. The little painted face upturned to his grew so absorbed and so excited that a bosom friend, dining at a table some way off, grew quite peevish with envy, being sure that darling Mabel was being offered a flat in Paris, a Daimler car and a thousand-pound necklace, and quarrelled fatally with her own escort in consequence.

"So you see," said Wimsey, "it means a lot to me."

Darling Mabel gave an ecstatic sigh.

"Is that all true? You're not making it up? It's better than any of the talkies."

"Yes, but you mustn't say one word. You're the only person I've told. You won't give me away to him?"

"Him? He's a stingy pig. Catch me giving him anything. I'm on. I'll do it for you. It'll be a bit difficult, cause I'll have to use the scissors, which we don't do as a rule. But I'll manage. You trust me. They won't be big ones, you know. He comes in pretty often, but I'll give you all I get. And I'll fix Fred. He always has Fred. Fred'll do it if I ask him. What'll I do with them when I get them?"

Wimsey drew an envelope from his pocket.

"Sealed up inside this," he said, impressively, "there are two little pill-boxes. You mustn't take them out till you get the specimens, because they've been carefully prepared so as to be absolutely chemically clean, if you see what I mean. When you're ready, open the envelope, take out the pill-boxes, put the parings into one and the hair into the other, shut them up at once, put them into a clean envelope and post them to this address. Get that?"

"Yes." She stretched out an eager hand.

"Good girl. And not a word."

"Not—one—word!" She made a gesture of exaggerated caution.

"When's your birthday?"

"Oh, I don't have one. I never grow up."

"Right; then I can send you an unbirthday present any day in the year. You'd look nice in mink, I think."

"Mink, I think," she mocked him. "Quite a poet, aren't you?"

"You inspire me," said Wimsey, politely.

22

"**I** have come round," said Mr. Urquhart, "in answer to your letter. I am greatly interested to hear that you have some fresh information about my unfortunate cousin's death. Of course I shall be delighted to give you any assistance I can."

"Thank you," said Wimsey. "Do sit down. You have dined, of course? But you will have a cup of coffee. You prefer the Turkish variety, I fancy. My man brews it rather well."

Mr. Urquhart accepted the offer, and complimented Bunter on having achieved the right method of concocting that curiously syrupy brew, so offensive to the average Occidental.

Bunter thanked him gravely for his good opinion, and proffered a box of that equally nauseating mess called Turkish Delight, which not only gluts the palate and glues the teeth, but also smothers the consumer in a floury cloud of white sugar. Mr. Urquhart immediately plugged his mouth with a large lump of it, murmuring indistinctly that it was the genuine Eastern variety. Wimsey, with an austere smile, took a few sips of strong black coffee without sugar or milk, and poured himself out a glass of old brandy. Bunter retired, and Lord Peter, laying a notebook open upon his knee, glanced at the clock and began his narrative.

He recapitulated the circumstances of Philip Boyes' life and death at some length. Mr. Urquhart, yawning surreptitiously, ate, drank and listened.

Wimsey, still with his eye on the clock, then embarked upon the story of Mrs. Wrayburn's will.

Mr. Urquhart, considerably astonished, set his coffee-cup aside, wiped his sticky fingers upon his handkerchief, and stared.

Presently he said:

"May I ask how you have obtained this very remarkable information?"

Wimsey waved his hand.

"The police," he said, "wonderful thing, police organisation. Surprisin' what they find out when they put their minds to it. You're not denying any of it, I presume?"

"I am listening," said Mr. Urquhart, grimly. "When you have finished this extraordinary statement, I may perhaps discover exactly what it is I have to deny."

"Oh, yes," said Wimsey, "I'll try to make that clear. I'm not a lawyer, of course, but I'm tryin' to be as lucid as I can."

He droned remorselessly on, and the hands of the clock went round.

"So far as I make it out," he said, when he had reviewed the whole question of motive, "it was very much to your interest to get rid of Mr. Philip Boyes. And indeed the fellow was, in my opinion, a pimple and a wart, and in your place I should have felt much the same about him."

"And is this the whole of your fantastic accusation?" enquired the solicitor.

"By no means. I am now coming to the point. Slow but sure is the motto of yours faithfully. I notice that I have taken up seventy minutes of your valuable time, but believe me, the hour has not been unprofitably spent."

"Allowing that all this preposterous story were true, which I most emphatically deny," observed Mr. Urquhart, "I should be greatly interested to know how you imagine that I administered the arsenic. Have you worked out something ingenious for that? Or am I supposed to have suborned my cook and parlourmaid to be my accomplices? A little rash of me, don't you think, and affording remarkable opportunities for blackmail?"

"So rash," said Wimsey, "that it is quite out of the question for a man so full of forethought as yourself. The sealing-up of that bottle of burgundy, for example, argues a mind alive to possibilities—unusually so. In fact, the episode attracted my attention from the start."

"Indeed?"

"You ask me how and when you administered the poison. It was not before dinner, I think. The thoughtfulness shown in emptying the bedroom water-bottle—oh, no! that point was not missed—the care displayed in meeting your cousin before a witness and never being left alone with him—I think that rules out the period before dinner."

"I should think it might."

"The sherry," pursued Wimsey, thoughtfully. "It was a new bottle, freshly decanted. The disappearance of the remains might be commented on. I fancy we can absolve the sherry."

Mr. Urquhart bowed ironically.

"The soup—it was shared by the cook and parlourmaid and they survived. I am inclined to pass the soup, and the same thing applies to the fish. It would be easy to poison a portion of fish, but it would involve the co-operation of Hannah Westlock, and that conflicts with my theory. A theory is a sacred thing to me, Mr. Urquhart—almost a what d'you call it—a dogma."

"An unsafe attitude of mind," remarked the lawyer, "but in the circumstances I will not quarrel with it."

"Besides," said Wimsey, "if the poison had been given in the soup or the fish, it might have started to work before Philip—I may call him so, I hope?—had left the house. We come to the casserole. Mrs. Pettican and Hannah Westlock can give the casserole a clean bill of health, I fancy. And by the way, from the description it must have been most delicious. I speak as a man with some considerable experience in gastronomic matters, Mr. Urquhart."

"I am well aware of it," said Mr. Urquhart, politely.

"And now there remains only the omelette. A most admirable thing when well made and eaten—that is so important—eaten immediately. A charming idea to have the eggs and sugar brought to the table and prepared and cooked on the spot. By the way, I take it there was no omelette left over for the kitchen? No, no! One does not let a good thing like that go out half-eaten. Much better that the good cook should make a fine, fresh omelette for herself and her colleague. Nobody but yourself and Philip partook of the omelette, I am sure."

"Quite so," said Mr. Urquhart, "I need not trouble to deny it. But you will bear in mind that I did partake of it, without ill-effects. And moreover, that my cousin made it himself."

"So he did. Four eggs, if I remember rightly, with sugar and jam from what I may call the common stock. No—there would be nothing wrong with the sugar or the jam. Er—I believe I am right in saying that one of the eggs was cracked when it came to the table?"

"Possibly. I do not really remember."

"No? Well, you are not on oath. But Hannah Westlock remembers that when you brought the eggs in—you purchased them yourself, you know, Mr. Urquhart —you mentioned that one was cracked and particularly desired that it should be used for the omelette. In fact, you yourself laid it in the bowl for that purpose."

"What about it?" asked Mr. Urquhart, perhaps a trifle less easily than before.

"It is not very difficult to introduce powdered arsenic into a cracked egg," said Wimsey. "I have made the experiment myself with a small glass tube. Perhaps a small funnel would be even easier. Arsenic is a fairly heavy substance—7 or 8 grains will go into a tea-spoon. It collects at one end of the egg, and any traces on the exterior of the shell can be readily wiped off. Liquid arsenic could be poured in still more easily, of course, but for a particular reason I made my experiment with the ordinary white powder. It is fairly soluble."

Mr. Urquhart had taken a cigar from his case, and was making rather a business of lighting it.

"Do you suggest," he enquired, "that in the whisking together of four eggs, one particular poisoned egg was somehow kept miraculously separated from the rest and deposited with its load of arsenic at one end of the omelette only? Or that my cousin deliberately helped himself to the poisoned end and left the rest to me?"

"Not at all, not at all," said Wimsey. "I suggest merely that the arsenic was in the omelette and came there by way of the egg."

Mr. Urquhart threw his match into the fireplace.

"There seem to be some flaws in your theory, as well as in the egg."

"I haven't finished the theory yet. My next bit of it is built up from very trifling indications. Let me enumerate them. Your disinclination to drink at dinner, your complexion, a few nail-pairings, a snipping or so from your very well-kept hair—I put these together, add a packet of white arsenic from the secret cupboard in your office, rub the hands a little—so—and produce—hemp, Mr. Urquhart, hemp."

He sketched the shape of a noose lightly in the air.

"I don't understand you," said the solicitor, hoarsely.

"Oh *you* know," said Wimsey. "Hemp—what they make ropes of. Great stuff, hemp. Yes, well, about this arsenic. As you know, it's not good for people in a general way, but there are some people—those tiresome peasants in Styria one hears so much about—who are supposed to eat it for fun. It improves their wind, so they say, and clears their complexions and makes their hair sleek, and they give it to their horses for the same reason; bar the complexion, that is, because a horse hasn't much complexion, but you know what I mean. Then there was that horrid man Maybrick—he used to take it, or so they say. Anyhow, it's well known that some people do take and manage to put away large dollops after a bit of practice—enough to kill any ordinary person. But you know all this."

"This is the first time I've heard of such a thing."

"Where *do* you expect to go to? Never mind. We'll pretend this is all new to you. Well, some fellow—I've forgotten his name,* but it's all in Dixon Mann— wondered how the dodge was worked, and he got going on some dogs and things and he dosed 'em and killed a lot of 'em I daresay, and in the end he found that whereas liquid arsenic was dealt with by the kidneys and was uncommonly bad for the system, solid arsenic could be given day by day, a little bigger dose each time, so that in time the doings—what an old lady I knew in Norfolk called 'the tubes'—got used to it and could push it along without taking any notice of it, so to speak. I read a book somewhere which said it was all done by leucocytes— those jolly little white corpuscles, don't you know—which sort of got round the stuff and bustled it along so that it couldn't do any harm. At all events, the point is that if you go on taking solid arsenic for a good long time—say a year or so— you establish a what-not, an immunity, and can take six or seven grains at a time without so much as a touch of indijaggers."

"Very interesting," said Mr. Urquhart.

"Apparently these beastly Styrian peasants do it that way, and they're very

* Valetta.

careful not to drink for two hours or thereabouts after taking it, for fear it should all get washed into the kidneys and turn poisonous on 'em. I'm not bein' very technical, I'm afraid, but that's the gist of it. Well, it occurred to me, don't you see, old horse, that if you'd had the bright idea to immunise yourself first, you could easily have shared a jolly old arsenical omelette with a friend. It would kill him and it wouldn't hurt you."

"I see."

The solicitor licked his lips.

"Well, as I say, you have a nice clear complexion—except that I notice the arsenic has pigmented the skin here and there (it does sometimes), and you've got the sleek hair and so on, and I noticed you were careful not to drink at dinner, and I said to myself, 'Peter, my bright lad, what about it?' And when they found a packet of white arsenic in your cupboard—never mind how for the moment!—I said, 'Hullo, hullo, how long has this been going on?' Your handy foreign chemist has told the police two years—is that right? About the time of the Megatherium crash that would be, wouldn't it? All right, don't tell me if you don't want to. Then we got hold of some bits of your hair and nails, and lo and behold, they were bungfull of arsenic. And we said, 'What-ho!' So that's why I asked you to come along and have a chat with me. I thought you might like to offer some sort of suggestion, don't you know."

"I can only suggest," said Urquhart, with a ghastly face but a strictly professional manner, "that you should be careful before you communicate this ludicrous theory to anybody. What you and the police—whom, frankly, I believe to be capable of anything—have been planting on my premises I do not know, but to give out that I am addicted to drug-taking habits is slander and criminal. It is quite true that I have for some time been taking a medicine which contains slight traces of arsenic—Dr. Grainger can furnish the prescription—and that may very likely have left a deposit in my skin and hair, but further than that, there is no foundation for this monstrous accusation."

"None?"

"None."

"Then how is it," asked Wimsey, coolly, but with something menacing in his rigidly controlled voice, "how is it that you have this evening consumed, without apparent effect, a dose of arsenic sufficient to kill two or three ordinary people? That disgusting sweetmeat on which you have been gorging yourself in, I may say, a manner wholly unsuited to your age and position, is smothered in white arsenic. You ate it, God forgive you, an hour and a half ago. If arsenic can harm you, you should have been rolling about in agonies for the last hour."

"You devil!"

"Couldn't you try to get up a few symptoms?" said Wimsey, sarcastically. "Shall I bring you a basin? Or fetch the doctor? Does your throat burn? Is your inside convulsed with agony? It is rather late in the day, but with a little goodwill you could surely produce *some* display of feeling, even now."

"You are lying. You wouldn't dare to do such a thing! It would be murder."

"Not in this case, I fancy. But I am willing to wait and see."

Urquhart stared at him. Wimsey got out of his chair in a single swift movement and stood over him.

"I wouldn't use violence if I were you. Let the poisoner stick to his bottle. Besides, I am armed. Pardon the melodrama. Are you going to be sick or not?"

"You're mad."

"Don't say that. Come, man—pull yourself together. Have a shot at it. Shall I show you the bathroom?"

"I'm ill."

"Of course; but your tone is not convincing. Through the door, along the passage, and third on the left."

The lawyer stumbled out. Wimsey returned to the library and rang the bell.

"I think, Bunter, Mr. Parker may require some assistance in the bathroom."

"Very good, my lord."

Bunter departed and Wimsey waited. Presently there were sounds of a scuffle in the distance. A group appeared at the door. Urquhart, very white, his hair and clothes disordered, flanked by Parker and Bunter, who held him firmly by the arms.

"Was he sick?" asked Wimsey, with interest.

"No, he wasn't," said Parker, grimly, snapping the handcuffs on his prey. "He cursed you fluently for five minutes, then tried to get out of the window, saw it was a three-story drop, charged in through the dressing-room door and ran straight into me. Now don't struggle, my lad, you'll only hurt yourself."

"And he still doesn't know whether he's poisoned or not?"

"He doesn't seem to think he is. At any rate, he made no effort about it. His one idea was to hop it."

"That's feeble," said Wimsey, "if I wanted people to think I'd been poisoned I'd put up a better show than that."

"Stop talking, for God's sake," said the prisoner. "You've got me, by a vile, damnable trick. Isn't that enough? You can shut up about it."

"Oh," said Parker, "we've got you, have we? Well, I warned you not to talk, and if you *will* do it, it's not my fault. By the way, Peter, I don't suppose you did actually poison him, did you? It doesn't seem to have hurt him, but it'll affect the doctor's report."

"No, I didn't, as a matter of fact," said Wimsey. "I only wanted to see how he'd react to the suggestion. Well, cheerio! I can leave it to you now."

"We'll look after him," said Parker. "But you might let Bunter ring up a taxi."

When the prisoner and his escort had departed, Wimsey turned thoughtfully to Bunter, glass in hand.

"*Mithridates he died old,* says the poet. But I doubt it, Bunter. In this case I very much doubt it."

23

There were golden chrysanthemums on the judge's bench; they looked like burning banners.

The prisoner, too, had a look in her eyes that was a challenge to the crowded court, as the clerk read the indictment. The judge, a plump, elderly man with an eighteenth-century face, looked expectantly at the Attorney-General.

"My lord—I am instructed that the Crown offers no evidence against this prisoner."

The gasp that went round the room sounded like the rustle of trees in a rising wind.

"Do I understand that the charge against the prisoner is withdrawn?"

"Those are my instructions, my lord."

"In that case," said the judge, impassively, turning to the jury, "there is nothing left for you but to return a verdict of 'Not Guilty.' Usher, keep those people quiet in the gallery."

"One moment, my lord." Sir Impey Biggs rose up, large and majestic.

"On my client's behalf—on Miss Vane's behalf, my lord, I beg your lordship's indulgence for a few words. A charge has been brought against her, my lord, the very awful charge of murder, and I should like it to be made clear, my lord, that my client leaves this court without a stain upon her character. As I am informed, my lord, this is not a case of the charge being withdrawn in default of evidence. I understand, my lord, that further information has come to the police which definitely proves the entire innocence of my client. I also understand, my lord, that a further arrest has been made and that an inquiry will follow, my lord, in due course. My lord, this lady must go forth into the world acquitted, not only at this bar, but at the bar of public opinion. Any ambiguity would be intolerable, and I am sure, my lord, that I have the support of the learned Attorney-General for what I say."

"By all means," said the Attorney. "I am instructed to say, my lord, that in withdrawing the charge against the prisoner, the Crown proceeds from complete conviction of her absolute innocence."

"I am very glad to hear it," said the judge. "Prisoner at the bar, the Crown, by unreservedly withdrawing this dreadful charge against you, has demonstrated your innocence in the clearest possible way. After this, nobody will be able to suppose that the slightest imputation rests upon you, and I most heartily congratulate you on this very satisfactory ending to your ordeal. Now, please—I sympathise very much with the people who are cheering, but this is not a theatre or a football match, and if they are not quiet, they will have to be put out. Members of the jury, do you find the Prisoner Guilty or Not Guilty?"

"Not Guilty, my lord."

"Very good. The prisoner is discharged without a stain upon her character. Next case."

So ended, sensational to the last, one of the most sensational murder trials of the century.

Harriet Vane, a free woman, found Eiluned Price and Sylvia Marriott waiting for her as she descended the stairs.

"Darling!" said Sylvia.

"Three loud cheers!" said Eiluned.

Harriet greeted them a little vaguely.

"Where is Lord Peter Wimsey?" she enquired. "I must thank him."

"You won't," said Eiluned, bluntly. "I saw him drive off the moment the verdict was given."

"Oh!" said Miss Vane.

"He'll come and see you," said Sylvia.

"No, he won't," said Eiluned.

"Why not?" said Sylvia.

"Too decent," said Eiluned.

"I'm afraid you're right," said Harriet.

"I like that young man," said Eiluned. "You needn't grin. I do like him. He's not going to do the King Cophetua stunt, and I take off my hat to him. If you want him, you'll have to send for him."

"I won't do that," said Harriet.

"Oh, yes, you will," said Sylvia. "I was right about who did the murder, and I'm going to be right about this."

Lord Peter Wimsey went down to Duke's Denver that same evening. He found the family in a state of perturbation, all except the Dowager, who sat placidly making a rug in the midst of the uproar.

"Look here, Peter," said the Duke, "you're the only person with any influence over Mary. You've got to do something. She wants to marry your policeman friend."

"I know," said Wimsey. "Why shouldn't she?"

"It's ridiculous," said the Duke.

"Not at all," said Lord Peter. "Charles is one of the best."

"Very likely," said the Duke, "but Mary can't marry a policeman."

"Now, look here," said Wimsey, tucking his sister's arm in his, "you leave Polly alone. Charles made a bit of a mistake at the beginning of this murder case, but he doesn't make many, and one of these days he'll be a big man, with a title, I shouldn't wonder, and everything handsome about him. If you want to have a row with somebody, have it with me."

"My God!" said the Duke, "you're not going to marry a policewoman?"

"Not quite," said Wimsey. "I intend to marry the prisoner."

"What?" said the Duke. "Good lord, what, what?"

"If she'll have me," said Lord Peter Wimsey.

HAVE HIS
CARCASE

NOTES

In *The Five Red Herrings*, the plot was invented to fit a real locality; in this book, the locality has been invented to fit the plot. Both places and people are entirely imaginary.

All the quotations at the chapter heads have been taken from T. L. Beddoes.

My grateful acknowledgements are due to Mr. John Rhode, who gave me generous help with all the hard bits.

DOROTHY L. SAYERS

CONTENTS

1

THE EVIDENCE OF
THE CORPSE

The track was slippery with spouting blood.
—Rodolph

THURSDAY, 18 JUNE

The best remedy for a bruised heart is not, as so many people seem to think, repose upon a manly bosom. Much more efficacious are honest work, physical activity, and the sudden acquisition of wealth. After being acquitted of murdering her lover, and, indeed, in consequence of that acquittal, Harriet Vane found all three specifics abundantly at her disposal; and although Lord Peter Wimsey, with a touching faith in tradition, persisted day in and day out in presenting the bosom for her approval, she showed no inclination to recline upon it.

Work she had in abundance. To be tried for murder is a fairly good advertisement for a writer of detective fiction. Harriet Vane thrillers were booming. She had signed up sensational contracts in both continents, and found herself, consequently, a very much richer woman than she had ever dreamed of becoming. In the interval between finishing *Murder by Degrees* and embarking on *The Fountain-Pen Mystery*, she had started off on a solitary walking-tour: plenty of exercise, no responsibilities and no letters forwarded. The time was June, the weather, perfect; and if she now and again gave a thought to Lord Peter Wimsey diligently ringing up an empty flat, it did not trouble her, or cause her to alter her steady course along the southwest coast of England.

On the morning of the 18th June, she set out from Lesston Hoe with the intention of walking along the coast to Wilvercombe, sixteen miles away. Not that she particularly looked forward to Wilvercombe, with its seasonal population of old ladies and invalids and its subdued attempts at the gay life, seeming somehow themselves all a little invalid and old-ladyish. But the town made a convenient objective, and one could always choose some more rural spot for a night's lodging. The coast-road ran pleasantly at the top of a low range of cliffs, from which she could look down upon the long yellow stretch of the beach, broken here and there by scattered rocks, which rose successively, glistening in the sunlight, from the reluctant and withdrawing tide.

Overhead, the sky arched up to an immense dome of blue, just fretted here and there with faint white clouds, very high and filmy. The wind blew from the west, very softly, though the weather-wise might have detected in it a tendency to freshen. The road, narrow and in poor repair, was almost deserted, all the heavy traffic passing by the wider arterial road which ran importantly inland from town to town, despising the windings of the coast with its few scattered

153

hamlets. Here and there a drover passed her with his dog, man and beast alike indifferent and preoccupied; here and there a couple of horses out at grass lifted shy and foolish eyes to look after her; here and there a herd of cows, rasping their jawbones upon a stone wall, greeted her with heavy snufflings. From time to time the white sail of a fishing-boat broke the seaward horizon. Except for an occasional tradesman's van, or a dilapidated Morris, and the intermittent appearance of white smoke from a distant railway-engine, the landscape was as rural and solitary as it might have been two hundred years before.

Harriet walked sturdily onwards, the light pack upon her shoulders interfering little with her progress. She was twenty-eight years old, dark, slight, with a skin naturally a little sallow, but now tanned to an agreeable biscuit-colour by sun and wind. Persons of this fortunate complexion are not troubled by midges and sunburn, and Harriet, though not too old to care for her personal appearance, was old enough to prefer convenience to outward display. Consequently, her luggage was not burdened by skin-creams, insect-lotion, silk frocks, portable electric irons or other impedimenta beloved of the "Hikers' Column." She was dressed sensibly in a short skirt and thin sweater and carried, in addition to a change of linen and an extra provision of footwear, little else beyond a pocket edition of *Tristram Shandy*, a vest-pocket camera, a small first-aid outfit and a sandwich lunch.

It was about a quarter to one when the matter of the lunch began to loom up importantly in Harriet's mind. She had come about eight miles on her way to Wilvercombe, having taken things easily and made a detour to inspect certain Roman remains declared by the guide-book to be "of considerable interest." She began to feel both weary and hungry, and looked about her for a suitable lunching-place.

The tide was nearly out now, and the wet beach shimmered golden and silvery in the lazy noonlight. It would be pleasant, she thought, to go down to the shore —possibly even to bathe, though she did not feel too certain about that, having a wholesome dread of unknown shores and eccentric currents. Still, there was no harm in going to see. She stepped over the low wall which bounded the road on the seaward side and set about looking for a way down. A short scramble among rocks tufted with scabious and seapink brought her easily down to the beach. She found herself in a small cove, comfortably screened from the wind by an outstanding mass of cliff, and with a few convenient boulders against which to sit. She selected the cosiest spot, drew out her lunch and *Tristram Shandy*, and settled down.

There is no more powerful lure to slumber than hot sunshine on a sea-beach after lunch; nor is the pace of *Tristram Shandy* so swift as to keep the faculties working at high pressure. Harriet found the book escaping from her fingers. Twice she caught it back with a jerk; the third time it eluded her altogether. Her head dropped over at an unbecoming angle. She dozed off.

She was awakened suddenly by what seemed to be a shout or cry almost in her ear. As she sat up, blinking, a gull swooped close over her head, squawking and hovering over a stray fragment of sandwich. She shook herself reprovingly and glanced at her wrist-watch. It was two o'clock. Realising with satisfaction that she could not have slept very long, she scrambled to her feet, and shook her crumbs from her lap. Even now, she did not feel very energetic, and there was plenty of time to make Wilvercombe before evening. She glanced out to sea, where a long belt of shingle and a narrow strip of virgin and shining sand stretched down to the edge of the water.

There is something about virgin sand which arouses all the worst instincts of the detective-story writer. One feels an irresistible impulse to go and make footprints all over it. The excuse which the professional mind makes to itself is that the sand affords a grand opportunity for observation and experiment. Harriet was no stranger to this impulse. She determined to walk out across that tempting strip of sand. She gathered her various belongings together and started off across the loose shingle, observing, as she had often observed before, that footsteps left no distinguishable traces in the arid region above high-water mark.

Soon, a little belt of broken shells and half-dry seaweed showed that the tide-mark had been reached.

"I wonder," said Harriet to herself, "whether I ought to be able to deduce something or other about the state of the tides. Let me see. When the tide is at neaps, it doesn't rise or fall so far as when it is at springs. Therefore, if that is the case, there ought to be two seaweedy marks—one quite dry and farther in, showing the highest point of spring tides, and one damper and farther down, showing to-day's best effort." She glanced backwards and forwards. "No; this is the only tide-mark. I deduce, therefore, that I have arrived somewhere about the top of springs, if that's the proper phrase. Perfectly simple, my dear Watson. Below tide-mark, I begin to make definite footprints. There are no others anywhere, so that I must be the only person who has patronised this beach since last high tide, which would be about—ah! yes, there's the difficulty. I know there should be about twelve hours between one high tide and the next, but I haven't the foggiest notion whether the sea is coming in or going out. Still, I do know it was going out most of the time as I came along, and it looks a long way off now. If I say that nobody has been here for the last five hours I shan't be far out. I'm making very pretty footprints now, and the sand is, naturally, getting wetter. I'll see how it looks when I run."

She capered a few paces accordingly, noticing the greater depth of the toe-prints and the little spurt of sand thrown out at each step. This outburst of energy brought her round the point of the cliff and into a much larger bay, the only striking feature of which was a good-sized rock, standing down at the sea's edge, on the other side of the point. It was roughly triangular in shape, standing about ten feet out of the water, and seemed to be crowned with a curious lump of black seaweed.

A solitary rock is always attractive. All right-minded people feel an overwhelming desire to scale and sit upon it. Harriet made for it without any mental argument, trying to draw a few deductions as she went.

"Is that rock covered at high tide? Yes, of course, or it wouldn't have seaweed on top. Besides, the slope of the shore proves it. I wish I was better at distances and angles, but I should say it would be covered pretty deep. How odd that it should have seaweed only in that lump at the top. You'd expect it at the foot, but the sides seem quite bare, nearly down to the water. I suppose it *is* seaweed. It's very peculiar. It looks almost more like a man lying down; is it possible for seaweed to be so very—well, so very localized?"

She gazed at the rock with a faint stirring of curiosity, and went on talking aloud to herself, as was her rather irritating habit.

"I'm dashed if it isn't a man lying down. What a silly place to choose. He must feel like a bannock on a hot griddle. I could understand it if he was a sun-bathing fan, but he seems to have got all his clothes on. A dark suit at that. He's very quiet. He's probably fallen asleep. If the tide comes in at all fast, he'll be cut off, like the people in the silly magazine stories. Well, I'm not going to rescue him. He'll have to take his socks off and paddle, that's all. There's plenty of time yet."

She hesitated whether to go on down to the rock. She did not want to wake the sleeper and be beguiled into conversation. Not but what he would prove to be some perfectly harmless tripper. But he would certainly be somebody quite uninteresting. She went on, however, meditating, and drawing a few more deductions by way of practice.

"He must be a tripper. Local inhabitants don't take their siestas on rocks. They retire indoors and shut all the windows. And he can't be a fisherman or anything of that kind; they don't waste time snoozing. Only the black-coated brigade does that. Let's call him a tradesman or a bank-clerk. But then they usually take their holidays complete with family. This is a solitary sort of fowl. A schoolmaster? No. Schoolmasters don't get off the lead till the end of July. How about a college undergraduate? It's only *just* the end of term. A gentleman of no particular occupation, apparently. Possibly a walking tourist like myself—but the costume doesn't look right." She had come nearer now and could see the sleeper's dark blue suit quite plainly. "Well, I can't place him, but no doubt Dr. Thorndyke would do so at once. Oh, of course! How stupid! He must be a literary bloke of some kind. They moon about and don't let their families bother them."

She was within a few yards of the rock now, gazing up at the sleeper. He lay uncomfortably bunched up on the extreme seaward edge of the rock, his knees drawn high and showing his pale mauve socks. The head, tucked closely down between the shoulders, was invisible.

"What a way to sleep," said Harriet. "More like a cat than a human being. It's not natural. His head must be almost hanging over the edge. It's enough to give him apoplexy. Now, if I had any luck, he'd be a corpse, and I should report him and get my name in the papers. That would be something like publicity. 'Well-known Woman Detective-Writer Finds Mystery Corpse on Lonely Shore.' But these things never happen to authors. It's always some placid labourer or night-watchman who finds corpses. . . ."

The rock lay tilted like a gigantic wedge of cake, its base standing steeply up to seaward, its surface sloping gently back to where its apex entered the sand. Harriet climbed up over its smooth, dry surface till she stood almost directly over the man. He did not move at all. Something impelled her to address him.

"Oy!" she said, protestingly.

There was neither movement nor reply.

"I'd just as soon he didn't wake up," thought Harriet. "I can't imagine what I'm shouting for. *Oy!*"

"Perhaps he's in a fit or a faint," she said to herself. "Or he's got sunstroke. That's quite likely. It's very hot." She looked up, blinking, at the brazen sky, then stooped and laid one hand on the surface of the rock. It almost burnt her. She shouted again, and then, bending over the man, seized his shoulder.

"Are you all right?"

The man said nothing and she pulled upon the shoulder. It shifted slightly—a dead weight. She bent over and gently lifted the man's head.

Harriet's luck was in.

It *was* a corpse. Not the sort of corpse there could be any doubt about, either. Mr. Samuel Weare of Lyons Inn, whose "throat they cut from ear to ear," could not have been more indubitably a corpse. Indeed, if the head did not come off in Harriet's hands, it was only because the spine was intact, for the larynx and all the great vessels of the neck had been severed "to the hause-bone," and a frightful stream, bright red and glistening, was running over the surface of the rock and dripping into a little hollow below.

Harriet put the head down again and felt suddenly sick. She had written often enough about this kind of corpse, but meeting the thing in the flesh was quite different. She had not realised how butcherly the severed vessels would look, and she had not reckoned with the horrid halitus of blood, which steamed to her nostrils under the blazing sun. Her hands were red and wet. She looked down at her dress. That had escaped, thank goodness. Mechanically, she stepped down again from the rock and went round to the edge of the sea. There she washed her fingers over and over again, drying them with ridiculous care upon her handkerchief. She did not like the look of the red trickle that dripped down the face of the rock into the clear water. Retreating, she sat down rather hastily on some loose boulders.

"A dead body," said Harriet, aloud to the sun and the seagulls. "A dead body. How—how appropriate!" She laughed.

"The great thing," Harriet found herself saying, after a pause, "the great thing is to keep cool. Keep your head, my girl. What would Lord Peter Wimsey do in such a case? Or, of course, Robert Templeton?"

Robert Templeton was the hero who diligently detected between the covers of her own books. She dismissed the image of Lord Peter Wimsey from her mind, and concentrated on that of Robert Templeton. The latter was a gentleman of extraordinary scientific skill, combined with almost fabulous muscular development. He had arms like an orang-outang and an ugly but attractive face. She conjured up this phantom before her in the suit of rather loud plus-fours with which she was accustomed to invest him, and took counsel with him in spirit.

Robert Templeton, she felt, would at once ask himself, "Is it Murder or Suicide?" He would immediately, she supposed, dismiss the idea of accident. Accidents of that sort do not happen. Robert Templeton would carefully examine the body, and pronounce—

Quite so; Robert Templeton would examine the body. He was, indeed, notorious for the sang-froid with which he examined bodies of the most repulsive description. Bodies reduced to boneless jelly by falling from aeroplanes; bodies charred into "unrecognisable lumps" by fire; bodies run over by heavy vehicles, and needing to be scraped from the road with shovels—Robert Templeton was accustomed to examine them all, without turning a hair. Harriet felt that she had never fully appreciated the superb nonchalance of her literary offspring.

Of course, any ordinary person, who was not a Robert Templeton, would leave the body alone and run for the police. But there were no police. There was not a man, woman or child within sight; only a small fishing-boat, standing out to sea some distance away. Harriet waved wildly in its direction, but its occupants either did not see her or supposed that she was merely doing some kind of reducing exercise. Probably their own sail cut off their view of the shore, for they were tacking up into the wind, with the vessel lying well over. Harriet shouted, but her voice was lost amid the crying of the gulls.

As she stood, hopelessly calling, she felt a wet touch on her foot. The tide had undoubtedly turned, and was coming in fast. Quite suddenly, this fact registered itself in her mind and seemed to clear her brain completely.

She was, as she reckoned, at least eight miles from Wilvercombe, which was the nearest town. There might be a few scattered houses on the road, but they would probably belong to fishermen, and ten to one she would find nobody at home but women and children, who would be useless in the emergency. By the time she had hunted up the men and brought them down to the shore, the sea would very likely have covered the body. Whether this was suicide or murder, it was exceedingly necessary that the body should be examined, before everything was soaked with water or washed away. She pulled herself sharply together and walked firmly up to the body.

It was that of a young man, dressed in a neat suit of dark blue serge, with rather over-elegant, narrow-soled brown shoes, mauve socks and a tie which had also been mauve before it had been horridly stained red. The hat, a grey soft felt, had fallen off—no, had been taken off and laid down upon the rock. She picked it up and looked inside, but saw nothing but the maker's name. She recognised it as that of a well-known, but not in the best sense, famous, firm of hatters.

The head which it had adorned was covered with a thick and slightly too-long crop of dark, curly hair, carefully trimmed and smelling of brilliantine. The complexion was, she thought, naturally rather white and showed no signs of sunburn. The eyes, fixed open in a disagreeable stare, were blue. The mouth had fallen open, showing two rows of carefully-tended and very white teeth. There were no gaps in the rows, but she noticed that one of the thirteen-year-old molars had been crowned. She tried to guess the exact age of the man. It was difficult, because he wore—very unexpectedly—a short, dark beard, trimmed to a neat point. This made him look older, besides giving him a somewhat foreign appearance, but it seemed to her that he was a very young man, nevertheless. Something immature about the lines of the nose and face suggested that he was not much more than twenty years old.

From the face she passed on to the hands, and here she was again surprised Robert Templeton or no Robert Templeton, she had taken for granted that this elegantly-dressed youth had come to his incongruous and solitary spot to commit suicide. That being so, it was surely odd that he should be wearing gloves. He had lain doubled up with his arms beneath him, and the gloves were very much stained. Harriet began to draw off one of them, but was overcome by the old feeling of distaste. She saw that they were loose chamois gloves of good quality, suitable to the rest of the costume.

Suicide—with gloves on? Why had she been so certain that it was suicide? She felt sure she had a reason.

Well, of course. If it was not suicide, where had the murderer gone? She knew he had not come along the beach from the direction of Lesston Hoe, for she remembered that bare and shining strip of sand. There was her own solitary line of footprints leading across from the shingle. In the Wilvercombe direction, the sand was again bare except for a single track of footmarks—presumably those of the corpse.

The man, then, had come down to the beach, and he had come alone. Unless his murderer had come by sea, he had been alone when he died. How long had he been dead? The tide had only turned recently, and there were no keelmarks on the sand. No one, surely, would have climbed the seaward face of the rock.

How long was it since there had been a sufficient depth of water to bring a boat within easy reach of the body?

Harriet wished she knew more about times and tides. If Robert Templeton had happened, in the course of his brilliant career, to investigate a sea-mystery, she would, of course, have had to look up information on this point. But she had always avoided sea-and-shore problems, just precisely on account of the labour involved. No doubt the perfect archetypal Robert Templeton knew all about it, but the knowledge was locked up within his shadowy and ideal brain. Well, how long had the man been dead, in any case?

This was a thing Robert Templeton would have known, too, for he had been through a course of medical studies among other things and, moreover, never went out without a clinical thermometer and other suitable apparatus for testing the freshness or otherwise of bodies. But Harriet had no thermometer, nor, if she had had one, would she have known how to use it for the purpose. Robert Templeton was accustomed to say, airily, "Judging by the amount of rigor and the temperature of the body, I should put the time of death at such-and-such," without going into fiddling details about the degrees Fahrenheit registered by the instrument. As for rigor, there certainly was not a trace of it present— naturally; since rigor (Harriet did know this bit) does not usually set in till from four to ten hours after death. The blue suit and brown shoes showed no signs of having been wet by sea-water; the hat was still lying on the rock. But four hours earlier, the water must have been over the rock and over the footprints. The tragedy must be more recent than that. She put her hand on the body. It seemed quite warm. But anything would be warm on such a scorching day. The back and top of the head were almost as hot as the surface of the rock. The under surface, being in shadow, felt cooler, but no cooler than her own hands which she had dipped in the sea-water.

Yes—but there was one criterion she *could* apply. The weapon. No weapon, no suicide—that was a law of the Medes and Persians. There was nothing in the hands—no signs of that obliging "death-grip" which so frequently preserves evidence for the benefit of detectives. The man had slumped forward—one arm between his body and the rock, the other, the right, hanging over the rock-edge just beneath his face. It was directly below this hand that the stream of blood ran down so uninvitingly, streaking the water. If the weapon was anywhere it would be here. Taking off her shoes and stockings, and turning her sleeve up to the elbow, Harriet groped cautiously in the water, which was about eighteen inches deep at the base of the rock. She stepped warily, for fear of treading on a knife-edge, and it was as well that she did, for presently her hand encountered something hard and sharp. At the cost of a slight cut on her finger, she drew up an open cut-throat razor, already partially buried in the sand.

The weapon was there, then; suicide seemed to be the solution after all. Harriet stood with the razor in her hand, wondering whether she was leaving finger-prints on the wet surface. The suicide, of course, would have left none, since he was wearing gloves. But once again, why that precaution? It is reasonable to wear gloves to commit a murder, but not to commit suicide. Harriet dismissed this problem for future consideration, and wrapped her handkerchief round the razor.

The tide was coming in inexorably. What else could she do? Ought she to search any pockets? She had not the strength of Robert Templeton to haul the body above highwater mark. That was really a business for the police, when the body was removed, but it was just possible that there might be papers, which the water would render illegible. She gingerly felt the jacket pockets, but the dead man had obviously attached too much importance to the set of his clothes to carry very much in them. She found only a silk handkerchief with a laundry-mark, and a thin gold cigarette-case in the right-hand pocket; the other was empty. The outside breast-pocket held a mauve silk handkerchief, obviously intended for display rather than for use; the hip-pocket was empty. She could not get at the trouser-pockets without lifting the corpse, which, for many reasons, she did not want to do. The inner breast-pocket, of course, was the one for papers, but Harriet felt a deep repugnance to handling the inner breast-pocket. It appeared to have received the full gush of blood from the throat. Harriet excused herself by thinking that any papers in *that* pocket would be illegible already. A cowardly excuse, possibly—but there it was. She could not bring herself to touch it.

She secured the handkerchief and cigarette-case and once more looked around her. Sea and sand were as deserted as ever. The sun still shone brightly, but a mass of cloud was beginning to pile up on the seaward horizon. The wind, too, had hauled round to the south-west and was strengthening every moment. It looked as though the beauty of the day would not last.

She still had to look at the dead man's footprints, before the advancing water obliterated them. Then, suddenly, she remembered that she had a camera. It was a small one, but it did include a focusing adjustment for objects up to six feet from the lens. She extracted the camera from her pack, and took three snapshots of the rock and the body from different viewpoints. The dead man's head lay still as it had fallen when she moved it—canted over a little sideways, so that it was just possible to secure a photograph of the features. She expended a film on this, racking the camera out to the six-foot mark. She had now four films left in the camera. On one, she took a general view of the coast with the body in the foreground, stepping a little way back from the rock for the purpose. On the second, she took a closer view of the line of footprints, stretching from the rock across the sand in the direction of Wilvercombe. On the third, she made a close-up of one of the footprints, holding the camera, set to six feet, at arm's-length above her head and pointing the lens directly downwards to the best of her judgment.

She looked at her watch. All this had taken her about twenty minutes from the time that she first saw the body. She thought she had better, while she was about it, spare time to make sure that the footprints belonged to the body. She removed one shoe from the foot of the corpse, noticing as she did so that, though the sole bore traces of sand, there were no stains of sea-water upon the leather of the uppers. Inserting the shoe into one of the footprints, she observed that they corresponded perfectly. She did not care for the job of replacing the shoe, and therefore took it with her, pausing as she regained the shingle, to take a view of the rock from the landward side.

The day was certainly clouding over and the wind getting up. Looking out beyond the rock, she saw a line of little swirls and eddies, which broke from time to time into angry-looking spurts of foam, as though breaking about the tops of hidden rocks. The waves everywhere were showing feathers of foam, and dull yellow streaks reflected the gathering cloudmasses further out to sea. The fishing-boat was almost out of sight, making for Wilvercombe.

Not quite sure whether she had done the right thing or the wrong, Harriet gathered up her belongings, including the shoe, hat, razor, cigarette-case and handkerchief, and started to scramble up the face of the cliff. It was then just after half-past two.

2

THE EVIDENCE OF THE ROAD

None sit in doors,
Except the babe, and his forgotten grandsire,
And such as, out of life, each side to lie
Against the shutter of the grave or womb.
—The Second Brother

THURSDAY, 18 JUNE

The road, when Harriet reached it, seemed as solitary as before. She turned in the direction of Wilvercombe and strode along at a good, steady pace. Her instinct was to run, but she knew that she would gain nothing by pumping herself out. After about a mile, she was delighted by the sight of a fellow-traveller; a girl of about seventeen, driving a couple of cows. She stopped the girl and asked her way to the nearest house.

The girl stared at her. Harriet repeated her request.

The reply came in so strong a west-country accent that Harriet could make little of it, but at length she gathered that "Will Coffin's, over to Brennerton," was the nearest habitation, and that it could be reached by following a winding lane on the right.

"How far is it?" asked Harriet.

The girl opined that it was a good piece, but declined to commit herself in yards or miles.

"Well, I'll try there," said Harriet. "And if you meet anybody on the road, will you tell them there's a dead man on the beach about a mile back and that the police ought to be told."

The girl stared dumbly.

Harriet repeated the message, adding, "Do you understand?"

"Yes, miss," said the girl, in the voice which makes it quite clear that the hearer understands nothing.

As Harriet hurried away up the lane, she saw the girl still staring after her.

Will Coffin's proved to be a small farmhouse. It took Harriet twenty minutes to reach it, and when she did reach it, it appeared to be deserted. She knocked at the door without result; pushed it open and shouted, still without result; then she went round to the back.

When she had again shouted several times, a woman in an apron emerged from an outbuilding and stood gazing at her.

"Are any of the men about?" asked Harriet.

The woman replied that they were all up to the seven-acre field, getting the hay in.

Harriet explained that there was a dead man lying on the shore and that the police ought to be informed.

"That do be terrible, surely," said the woman. "Will it be Joe Smith? He was out with his boat this morning and the rocks be very dangerous thereabouts. The Grinders, we call them."

"No," said Harriet; "it isn't a fisherman—it looks like somebody from the town. And he isn't drowned. He's cut his throat."

"Cut his throat?" said the woman, with relish. "Well, now, what a terrible thing, to be sure."

"I want to let the police know," said Harriet, "before the tide comes in and covers the body."

"The police?" the woman considered this. "Oh, yes," she said, after mature thought. "The police did ought to be told about it."

Harriet asked if one of the men could be found and sent with a message. The woman shook her head. They were getting in the hay and the weather did look to be changing. She doubted if anybody could be spared.

"You're not on the telephone, I suppose?" asked Harriet.

They were not on the telephone, but Mr. Carey at the Red Farm, he was on the telephone. To get to the Red Farm, the woman added, under interrogation, you would have to go back to the road and take the next turning, and then it was about a mile or maybe two.

Was there a car Harriet could borrow?

The woman was sorry, but there was no car. At least, there was one, but her daughter had gone over to Heathbury market and wouldn't be back till late.

"Then I must try and get to the Red Farm," said Harriet, rather wearily. "If you *do* see anybody who could take a message, would you tell them that there's a dead man on the shore near the Grinders, and that the police ought to be informed."

"Oh, I'll tell them sure enough," said the woman, brightly. "It's a very terrible thing, isn't it? The police did ought to know about it. You're looking very tired, miss; would you like a cup of tea?"

Harriet refused the tea, and said she ought to be getting on. As she passed through the gate, the woman called her back. Harriet turned hopefully.

"Was it you that found him, miss?"

"Yes, I found him."

"Lying there dead?"

"Yes."

"With his throat cut?"

"Yes."

"Dear, dear," said the woman. " 'Tis a terrible thing, to be sure."

Back on the main road, Harriet hesitated. She had lost a good deal of time on this expedition. Would it be better to turn aside again in search of the Red Farm, or to keep to the main road where there was more chance of meeting a passer-by? While still undecided, she arrived at the turn. An aged man was hoeing turnips in a field close by. She hailed him.

"Is this the way to the Red Farm?"

He paid no attention, but went on hoeing turnips.

"He must be deaf," muttered Harriet, hailing him again. He continued to hoe turnips. She was looking about for the gate into the field when the aged man paused to straighten his back and spit on his hands, and in so doing brought her into his line of vision.

Harriet beckoned to him, and he hobbled slowly up to the wall, supporting himself on the hoe as he went.

"Is this the way to the Red Farm?" She pointed up the lane.

"No," said the old man, "he ain't at home."

"Has he got a telephone?" asked Harriet.

"Not till to-night," replied the ancient. "He's over to Heathbury market."

"A telephone," repeated Harriet, "has he got a telephone?"

"Oh, ay," said the old man, "you'll find her somewhere about." While Harriet was wondering whether the pronoun was the one usually applied in that county to telephones, he dashed her hopes by adding: "Her leg's bad again."

"How far is it to the farm?" shouted Harriet, desperately.

"I shouldn't wonder if 'twas," said the old man, resting on the hoe, and lifting up his hat to admit the breeze to his head, "I tell'd her o'Saturday night she hadn't no call to do it."

Harriet, leaning far over the wall, advanced her mouth to within an inch of his ear.

"How *far* is it?" she bawled.

"There ain't no need to shout," said the old man. "I bain't deaf. Eighty-two come Michaelmas, and all my faculties, thank God."

"How far—" began Harriet.

"I'm tellin 'ee, amn't I? Mile and a half by the lane, but if you was to take the short cut through the field where the old bull is—"

A car came suddenly down the road at considerable speed and vanished into the distance.

"Oh, bother!" muttered Harriet. "I might have stopped that if I hadn't wasted my time on this old idiot."

"You're quite right, miss," agreed Old Father William, catching the last word with the usual perversity of the deaf. "Madmen, I calls 'em. There ain't no sense in racketing along at that pace. My niece's young man—"

The glimpse of the car was a deciding factor in Harriet's mind. Far better to stick to the road. If once she began losing herself in by-ways on the chance of finding an elusive farm and a hypothetical telephone, she might wander about till dinner-time. She started off again, cutting Father William's story off abruptly in the middle, and did another dusty half-mile without further encounter.

It was odd, she thought. During the morning she had seen several people and quite a number (comparatively) of tradesmen's vans. What had happened to them all? Robert Templeton (or possibly even Lord Peter Wimsey, who had been brought up in the country) would have promptly enough found the answer to the riddle. It was market-day at Heathbury, and early-closing day at Wilvercombe and Lesston Hoe—the two phenomena being, indeed, interrelated so as to permit the inhabitants of the two watering-places to attend the important function at the market-town. Therefore there were no more tradesmen's deliveries along the coast-road. And therefore all the local traffic to Heathbury was already well away inland. Such of the aborigines as remained were at work in the hayfields. She did, indeed, discover a man and a youth at work with a two-horse haycutter, but they stared aghast at her suggestion that they should leave their work and their horses to look for the police. The farmer himself was (naturally) at Heathbury market. Harriet, rather hopelessly, left a message with them and trudged on.

Presently there came slogging into view a figure which appeared rather more hopeful; a man clad in shorts and carrying a pack on his back—a hiker, like herself. She hailed him imperiously.

"I say, can you tell me where I can get hold of somebody with a car or a telephone? It's frightfully important."

The man, a weedy, sandy-haired person with a bulging brow and thick spectacles, gazed at her with courteous incompetence.

"I'm afraid I can't tell you. You see, I'm a stranger here myself."

"Well, could you—?" began Harriet, and paused. After all, what could he do? He was in exactly the same boat as herself. With a foolish relic of Victorianism she had somehow imagined that a man would display superior energy and resourcefulness, but, after all, he was only a human being, with the usual outfit of legs and brains.

"You see," she explained, "there's a dead man on the beach over there." She pointed vaguely behind her.

"No, really?" exclaimed the young man. "I say, that's a bit thick, isn't it? Er— friend of yours?"

"Certainly not," retorted Harriet. "I don't know him from Adam. But the police ought to know about it."

"The police? Oh, yes, of course, the police. Well, you'll find them in Wilvercombe, you know. There's a police-station there."

"I know," said Harriet, "but the body's right down near low-water mark, and if I can't get somebody along pretty quick the tide may wash him away. In fact, it's probably done so already. Good lord! It's almost four o'clock."

"The tide? Oh, yes. Yes, I suppose it would. If"—he brightened up with a new thought—"if it's coming in. But it might be going out, you know, mightn't it?"

"It might, but it isn't," said Harriet, grimly. "It's been coming in since two o'clock. Haven't you noticed?"

"Well, no, I can't say I have. I'm shortsighted. And I don't know much about it. I live in London, you see. I'm afraid I can't quite see what I can do about it. There don't seem to be any police about here, do there?"

He gazed round about, as though he expected to sight a constable on point-duty in the middle-distance.

"Have you passed any cottages lately?" asked Harriet.

"Cottages? Oh, yes—yes, I believe I did see some cottages a little way back. Oh, yes, I'm sure I did. You'll find somebody there."

"I'll try there, then. And if you meet anybody would you mind telling them about it. A man on the beach—with his throat cut."

"His throat?"

"Yes. Near some rocks they call the Grinders."

"Who cut his throat?"

"How should I know? I should think he probably did it himself."

"Yes—oh, naturally. Yes. Otherwise it would be murder, wouldn't it?"

"Well, it *may* be murder, of course."

The hiker clutched his staff nervously.

"Oh! I shouldn't think so, should you?"

"You never know," said Harriet, exasperated. "If I were you, I'd be getting along quickly. The murderer may be somewhere about, you know."

"Good heavens!" said the young man from London. "But that would be awfully dangerous."

"Wouldn't it? Well, I'll be pushing on. Don't forget, will you? A man with his throat cut near the Grinders."

"The Grinders. Oh, yes. I'll remember. But, I say?"

"Yes?"

"Don't you think I'd better come along with you? To protect you, you know, and that sort of thing?"

Harriet laughed. She felt convinced that the young man was not keen on passing the Grinders.

"As you like," she said indifferently, walking on.

"I could show you the cottages," suggested the young man.

"Very well," said Harriet. "Come along. We'll have to be as quick as we can."

A quarter of an hour's walk brought them to the cottages—two low thatched buildings standing on the right-hand side of the road. In front of them a high hedge had been planted, screening them from the sea-gales and, incidentally, helping to cut off all view of the shore. Opposite them, on the other side of the road, a narrow walled lane twisted down to the sea's edge. From Harriet's point of view the cottages were a disappointment. They were inhabited by an aged crone, two youngish women and some small children, but the men were all out fishing. They were late back to-day but were expected on the evening tide. Harriet's story was listened to with flattering interest and enthusiasm, and the wives promised to tell their husbands about it when they came in. They also offered refreshment which, this time, Harriet accepted. She felt pretty sure that the body would by now be covered by the tide and that half an hour could make no real difference. Excitement had made her weary. She drank the tea and was thankful.

The companions then resumed their walk, the gentleman from London, whose name was Perkins, complaining of a blistered heel. Harriet ignored him. Surely something would soon come along.

The only thing that came was a fast saloon car, which overtook them about half a mile further on. The proud chauffeur, seeing two dusty trampers signalling, as it appeared to him, for a lift, put his stern foot down on the accelerator and drove on.

"The beastly road-hog!" said Mr. Perkins, pausing to caress his blistered heel.

"Saloons with chauffeurs are never any good," said Harriet. "What we want is a lorry, or a seven-year-old Ford. Oh, look! What's that?"

"That" was a pair of gates across the road and a little cottage standing beside it.

"A level-crossing, by all that's lucky!" Harriet's sinking courage revived. "There *must* be somebody here."

There was. There were, in fact, two people—a cripple and a small girl. Harriet eagerly asked where she could get hold of a car or a telephone.

"You'll find that all right in the village, miss," said the cripple. "Leastways, it ain't what you'd call a village, exactly, but Mr. Hearn that keeps the grocery, he's got a telephone. This here's Darley Halt, and Darley is about ten minutes' walk. You'll find somebody there all right, miss, for certain. Excuse me a minute, miss. Liz! the gates!"

The child ran out to open the gates to let through a small boy leading an immense cart-horse.

"Is there a train coming through?" asked Harriet, idly, as the gates were pushed across the road again.

"Not for half an hour, miss. We keeps the gates shut most times. There ain't a deal of traffic along this road, and they keeps the cattle from straying on to the line. There's a good many trains in the day. It's the main line from Wilvercombe to Heathbury. Of course, the expresses don't stop here, only the locals, and they only stops twice a day, except market days."

"No, I see." Harriet wondered why she was asking about the trains, and then suddenly realised that, with her professional interest in time-tables, she was instinctively checking up the ways and means of approaching the Grinders. Train, car, boat—how had the dead man got there?

"What time—?"

No, it didn't matter. The police could check that up. She thanked the gate-keeper, pushed her way through the side-wickets and strode on, with Mr. Perkins limping after her.

The road still ran beside the coast, but the cliffs here gradually sloped down almost to sea-level. They saw a clump of trees and a hedge and a little lane, curving away past the ruins of an abandoned cottage to a wide space of green on which stood a tent, close by the sandy beach, with smoke going up from a campers' fire beside it. As they passed the head of this lane a man emerged from it, carrying a petrol-tin. He wore a pair of old flannel slacks, and a khaki shirt with sleeves rolled up to the elbow. His soft hat was pulled down rather low over his eyes, which were further protected by a pair of dark spectacles.

Harriet stopped him and asked if they were anywhere near the village.

"A few minutes farther on," he replied, briefly, but civilly enough.

"I want to telephone," went on Harriet. "I'm told I can do so at the grocer's. Is that right?"

"Oh, yes. Just across on the other side of the green. You can't mistake it. It's the only shop there is."

"Thank you. Oh, by the way—I suppose there isn't a policeman in the village?"

The man halted as he was about to turn away and stared at her, shading his eyes from the sun's glare. She noticed a snake tattooed in red and blue upon his forearm, and wondered whether he might perhaps have been a sailor.

"No, there's no policeman living in Darley. We share a constable with the next village, I believe—he floats round on a bicycle occasionally. Anything wrong?"

"There's been an accident along the coast," said Harriet. "I've found a dead man."

"Good lord! Well, you'd better telephone through to Wilvercombe."

"Yes, I will, thanks. Come along, Mr. Perkins. Oh! he's gone on."

Harriet caught up to her companion, rather annoyed by his patent eagerness to dissociate himself from her and her errand.

"There's no need to stop and speak to everybody," complained Mr. Perkins, peevishly. "I don't like the look of that fellow, and we're quite near the place now. I came through here this morning, you know."

"I only wanted to ask if there was a policeman," explained Harriet, peaceably. She did not want to argue with Mr. Perkins. She had other things to think of.

Cottages had begun to appear, small, sturdy buildings, surrounded by little patches of gay garden. The road turned suddenly inland, and she observed with joy telegraph poles, more houses and at length a little green, with a smithy at one corner and children playing cricket on the grass. In the centre of the green stood an ancient elm, with a seat round it and an ancient man basking in the sunshine; and on the opposite side was a shop, with "Geo. Hearn: Grocer," displayed on a sign above it.

"Thank goodness!" said Harriet.

She almost ran across the little green and into the village shop, which was festooned with boots and frying-pans, and appeared to sell everything from acid drops to corduroy trousers.

A bald-headed man advanced helpfully from behind a pyramid of canned goods.

"Can I use your telephone, please?"

"Certainly, miss; what number?"

"I want the Wilvercombe police-station."

"The police-station?" The grocer looked puzzled—almost shocked. "I'll have to look up the number for you," he said, hesitatingly. "Will you step into the parlour, miss—and sir?"

"Thank you," said Mr. Perkins. "But really—I mean—it's the lady's business really. I mean to say—if there's any sort of hotel hereabouts, I think I'd better—that is to say—er—good-evening."

He melted unobtrusively out of the shop. Harriet, who had already forgotten his existence, followed the grocer into the back room and watched him with impatience as he put on his spectacles and struggled with the telephone directory.

3

THE EVIDENCE OF THE HOTEL

Little and grisly, or bony and big,
White, and clattering, grassy and yellow;
The partners are waiting, so strike up a jig,
Dance and be merry, for Death's a droll fellow.

. . . .
Where's Death and his sweetheart? We want
to begin.
                                      —Death's Jest-Book

THURSDAY, 18 JUNE

It was a quarter-past five when the grocer announced that Harriet's call was through. Allowing for stoppages and for going out of her way to the Brennerton Farm, she had covered rather more than four miles of the distance between the Grinders and

Wilvercombe in very nearly three hours. True, she had actually walked six miles or more, but she felt that a shocking amount of time had been wasted. Well, she had done her best, but fate had been against her.

"Hullo!" she said, wearily.

"Hullo!" said an official voice.

"Is that the Wilvercombe police?"

"Speaking. Who are you?"

"I'm speaking from Mr. Hearn's shop at Darley. I want to tell you that this afternoon at about two o'clock I found the dead body of a man lying on the beach near the Grinders.

"Oh!" said the voice. "One moment, please. Yes. The dead body of a man at the Grinders. Yes?"

"He'd got his throat cut," said Harriet.

"Throat cut," said the official voice. "Yes?"

"I also found a razor," said Harriet.

"A razor?" The voice seemed rather pleased, she thought, by this detail. "Who is it speaking?" it went on.

"My name is Vane, Miss Harriet Vane. I am on a walking-tour, and happened to find him. Can you send someone out to fetch me, or shall I—?"

"Just a moment. Name of Vane—V-A-N-E—yes. Found at two o'clock, you say. You're a bit late letting us know, aren't you?"

Harriet explained that she had had difficulty in getting through to them.

"I see," said the voice. "All right, miss, we'll be sending a car along. You just stay where you are till we come. You'll have to go along with us and show us the body."

"I'm afraid there won't be any body by now," said Harriet. "You see, it was down quite close to the sea, on that big rock, you know, and the tide—"

"We'll see to that, miss," replied the voice, confidently, as though the Nautical Almanack might be expected to conform to police regulations. "The car'll be along in about ten minutes or so."

The receiver clicked and was silent. Harriet replaced her end of the instrument and stood for a few minutes, hesitating. Then she took the receiver off again.

"Give me Ludgate 6000—quick as ever you can. Urgent press call. I must have it within five minutes."

The operator began to make objections.

"Listen—that's the number of the *Morning Star*. It's a priority call."

"Well," said the operator, dubiously, "I'll see what I can do."

Harriet waited.

Three minutes passed—four—five—six. Then the bell rang. Harriet snatched the receiver down.

"*Morning Star.*"

"Give me the news-room—quick."

Buzz—click.

"*Morning Star* news-editor."

Harriet gathered herself together to cram her story into the fewest and most telling words.

"I am speaking from Darley near Wilvercombe. The dead body of a man was found at two o'clock this afternoon—all right. Ready?—on the coast this afternoon with his throat cut from ear to ear. The discovery was made by Miss

Harriet Vane, the well-known detective novelist. . . . Yes, that's right—the Harriet Vane who was tried for murder two years ago. . . . Yes. . . . The dead man appears to be about twenty years of age—blue eyes—short dark beard—dressed in a dark-blue lounge suit with brown shoes and chamois-leather gloves. . . . A razor was found near the body. . . . Probably suicide. . . . Oh, yes, it *might* be murder; or call it mysterious circumstances. . . . Yes. . . . Miss Vane, who is on a walking-tour, gathering material for her forthcoming book, *The Fountain-Pen Mystery*, was obliged to walk for several miles before getting help. . . . No, the police haven't seen the body yet. . . . it's probably under water by now, but I suppose they'll get it at low tide. . . . I'll ring you later. . . . Yes. . . . What?. . . . Oh, this *is* Miss Vane speaking. . . . Yes. . . . No, I'm giving you this exclusively. . . . Well, I suppose it will be all over the place presently, but I'm giving you *my* story exclusively . . . provided, of course, you give me a good show. . . . Yes, of course. . . . Oh! well, I suppose I shall be staying in Wilvercombe. . . . I don't know; I'll ring you up when I know where I'm staying. . . . Right. . . . right. . . . Goodbye."

As she rang off, she heard a car draw up to the door, and emerged through the little shop to encounter a large man in a grey suit, who began immediately: "I am Inspector Umpelty. What's all this about?"

"Oh, Inspector! I'm so glad to see you. I began to think I never *should* get hold of anybody with any common-sense about them. I've had a trunk-call, Mr. Hearn. I don't know what it costs, but here's a ten-bob note. I'll call for the change another time. I've told my friends I shall be stuck in Wilvercombe for a few days, Inspector. I suppose that's right, isn't it?"

This was disingenuous, but novelists and police-inspectors do not always see eye to eye as regards publicity.

"That's right, miss. Have to ask you to stay on a bit while we look into this. Better jump into the car and we'll run out to where you say you saw this body. This gentleman is Dr. Fenchurch. This is Sergeant Saunders."

Harriet acknowledged the introduction.

"Why *I've* been brought along I *don't* know," said the police-surgeon in an aggrieved voice. "If this man was down near low-water mark at two o'clock, we shan't see much of him to-night. Tide's more than half-full now, and a strong wind blowing."

"That's the devil of it," agreed the Inspector.

"I know," said Harriet, mournfully, "but really I did my best." She recounted the details of her odyssey, mentioning everything she had done at the rock and producing the shoe, the cigarette-case, the hat, the handkerchief and the razor.

"Well, there," said the Inspector, "you seem to have done a pretty tidy job, miss. Anybody'd think you'd made a study of it. Taking photographs and all. Not but what," he added, sternly, "if you'd started sooner you'd have been here before."

"I didn't waste much time," pleaded Harriet, "and I thought, supposing the body got washed away, or anything, it would be better to have *some* record of it."

"That's very true, miss, and I shouldn't wonder but what you did the right thing. Looks like a big wind rising, and that'll hold the tide up."

"Due south-west it is," put in the policeman who was driving the car. "That there rock will be a-wash next low tide if it goes on like this, and with the sea running it'll be a bit of a job to get out there."

"Yes," said the Inspector. "The current sets very strong round the bay, and you can't get a boat in past the Grinders—not without you want her bottom stove in."

Indeed, when they arrived at "Murder Bay," as Harriet had mentally christened it, there were no signs of the rock, still less of the body. The sea was half-way up the sand, rolling in heavily. The little line of breakers that had shown the hidden tops of the Grinders reef had disappeared. The wind was freshening still more, and the sun gleamed in spasms of brilliance between thickening banks of cloud.

"That's the place, miss, is it?" asked the Inspector.

"Oh, yes, that's the place," replied Harriet, confidently.

The Inspector shook his head.

"There's seventeen feet of water over that rock by now," he said. "Tide'll be full in another hour. Can't do anything about it now. Have to wait for low tide. That'll be two ack emma, or thereabouts. Have to see if there's any chance of getting out to it then, but if you ask me, it's working up for roughish weather. There's the chance, of course, that the body may get washed off and come ashore somewhere. I'll run you up to Brennerton, Saunders; try and get some of the men there to keep a look-out up and down the shore, and I'll cut along back to Wilvercombe and see what I can arrange about getting a boat out. You'll have to come along with me, miss, and make a statement."

"By all means," said Harriet, rather faintly.

The Inspector turned round and took a look at her.

"I expect you're feeling a bit upset, miss," he said, kindly, "and no wonder. It's not a pleasant thing for a young lady to have to deal with. It's a miracle to me, the way you handled it. Why, most young ladies would have run away, let alone taking away all these boots and things."

"Well, you see," explained Harriet, "I know what ought to be done. I write detective stories, you know," she added, feeling as she spoke that this must appear to the Inspector an idle and foolish occupation.

"There now," said the Inspector. "It isn't often, I daresay, you get a chance of putting your own stories into practice, as you might say. What did you say your name was, miss? Not that I read those sort of books much, except it might be Edgar Wallace now and again, but I'll have to know your name, of course, in any case."

Harriet gave her name and her London address. The Inspector seemed to come to attention rather suddenly.

"I fancy I've heard that name before," he remarked.

"Yes," said Harriet, a little grimly; "I expect you have. I am—" she laughed rather uncomfortably—"I'm the notorious Harriet Vane, who was tried for poisoning Philip Boyes two years ago."

"Ah, just so!" replied the Inspector. "Yes. They got the fellow who did it, too, didn't they? Arsenic case. Yes, of course. There was some very pretty medical evidence at the trial, if I remember rightly. Smart piece of work. Lord Peter Wimsey had something to do with it, didn't he?"

"Quite a lot," said Harriet.

"He seems to be a clever gentleman," observed the Inspector. "One's always hearing of him doing something or other."

"Yes," agreed Harriet; "he's—full of activities."

"You'll know him very well, I expect?" pursued the Inspector, filled with what Harriet felt to be unnecessary curiosity.

"Oh, yes, quite well. Yes, of course." It struck her that this sounded ungracious, seeing that Wimsey had undoubtedly saved her from a very disagreeable position, if not from an ignominious death, and she went on, hastily and stiltedly, "I have a great deal to thank him for."

"Naturally," replied the Inspector. "Not but what" (loyally) "Scotland Yard would probably have got the right man in the end. Still" (here local patriotism seemed to take the upper hand), "they haven't the advantages in some ways that we have. They can't know all the people in London same as we know everybody hereabouts. Stands to reason they couldn't. Now, in a case like this one here, ten to one we shall be able to find all about the young man in a turn of the hand, as you might say."

"He may be a visitor," said Harriet.

"Very likely," said the Inspector, "but I expect there'll be somebody that knows about him, all the same. This is where you get off, Saunders. Raise all the help you can, and get Mr. Coffin to run you over to Wilvercombe when you're through. Now then, miss. What did you say this young chap was like?"

Harriet again described the corpse.

"Beard, eh?" said the Inspector. "Sounds like a foreigner, doesn't it? I can't just place him for the moment, but there's not much doubt he'll be pretty easily traced. Now, here we are at the police-station, miss. If you'll just step in here a minute, the Superintendent would like to see you."

Harriet accordingly stepped in and told her story once again, this time in minute detail, to Superintendent Glaisher, who received it with flattering interest. She handed over the various things taken from the body and her roll of film, and was then questioned exhaustively as to how she had spent the day, both before and after finding the body.

"By the way," said the Superintendent, "this young fellow you met on the road—what's become of him?"

Harriet stared about her as though she expected to find Mr. Perkins still at her elbow.

"I haven't the slightest idea. I'd forgotten all about him. He must have gone off while I was ringing you up."

"Odd," said Glaisher, making a note to inquire after Mr. Perkins.

"But he can't possibly know anything about it," said Harriet. "He was fearfully surprised—and frightened. That's why he came back with me."

"We'll have to check up on him, though, as a matter of routine," said the Superintendent. Harriet was about to protest that this was a waste of time, when she suddenly realised that in all probability it was her own story that was due to be "checked up on." She was silent, and the Superintendent went on:

"Well, now, Miss Vane. I'm afraid we shall have to ask you to stay within reach for a few days. What were you thinking of doing?"

"Oh, I quite understand that. I suppose I'd better put up somewhere in Wilvercombe. You needn't be afraid of *my* running away. I want to be in on this thing."

The policeman looked a little disapproving. Everybody is, of course, only too delighted to take the limelight in a gruesome tragedy, but a lady ought, surely, to pretend the contrary. Inspector Umpelty, however, merely replied with the modest suggestion that Clegg's Temperance Hostel was generally reckoned to be as cheap and comfortable as you could require.

Harriet laughed, remembering suddenly that a novelist owes a duty to her newspaper reporters. "Miss Harriet Vane, when interviewed by our correspondent at Clegg's Temperance Hostel—" That would never do.

"I don't care for Temperance Hostels," she said, firmly. "What's the best hotel in the town?"

"The Resplendent is the largest," said Glaisher.

"Then you will find me at the Resplendent," said Harriet, picking up her dusty knapsack and preparing for action.

"Inspector Umpelty will run you down there in the car," said the Superintendent, with a little nod to Umpelty.

"Very good of him," answered Harriet, amused.

Within a very few minutes the car deposited her at one of those monster seaside palaces which look as though they had been designed by a German manufacturer of children's cardboard toys. Its glass porch was crowded with hothouse plants and the lofty dome of its reception-hall was supported on gilt pilasters rising out of an ocean of blue plush. Harriet tramped heedlessly through its spacious splendours and demanded a large single bedroom with private bath, on the first floor, and overlooking the sea.

"Ai'm afraid," said the receptionist, casting a languid glance of disfavour at Harriet's knapsack and shoes, "that all our rooms are engaged."

"Surely not," said Harriet, "so early in the season. Just ask the manager to come and speak to me for a moment." She sat down with a determined air in the nearest well-stuffed armchair and, hailing a waiter, demanded a cocktail.

"Will you join me, Inspector?"

The Inspector thanked her, but explained that a certain discretion was due to his position.

"Another time, then," said Harriet, smiling, and dropping a pound-note on the waiter's tray, with a somewhat ostentatious display of a well-filled note-case.

Inspector Umpelty grinned faintly as he saw the receptionist beckon to the waiter. Then he moved gently across to the desk and spoke a few words. Presently the assistant-receptionist approached Harriet with a deprecating smile.

"We find, Madam, that we can efter all accommodate you. An American gentleman has informed us thet he is vacating his room on the first floor. It overlooks the Esplanade. Ai think you will find it quaite satisfactory."

"Has it a private bath?" demanded Harriet, without enthusiasm.

"Oh, yes, madam. And a balcony."

"All right," said Harriet. "What number? Twenty-three. It has a telephone, I suppose? Well, Inspector, you'll know where to find me, won't you?"

She grinned a friendly grin at him.

"Yes, miss," said Inspector Umpelty, grinning also. He had his private cause for amusement. If Harriet's note-case had ensured her reception at the Resplendent, it was his own private whisper of "friend of Lord Peter Wimsey" that had produced the view over the sea, the bath and the balcony. It was just as well that Harriet did not know this. It would have annoyed her.

Curiously enough, however, the image of Lord Peter kept intruding upon her mind while she was telephoning her address to the Morning Star, and even while she was working her way through the Resplendent's expensive and admirable dinner. If the relations between them had not been what they were, it would have been only fair to ring him up and tell him about the corpse with the cut throat. But under the circumstances, the action might be misinterpreted. And, in any case, the thing was probably only the dullest kind of suicide, not worth bringing to his attention. Not nearly so complicated and interesting a problem, for instance, as the central situation in *The Fountain-Pen Mystery*. In that absorbing mystery, the villain was at the moment engaged in committing a crime in Edinburgh, while constructing an ingenious alibi involving a steam-yacht, a wireless time-signal, five clocks and the change from summer to winter time. (Apparently the cut-throat gentleman had come from the Wilvercombe direction. By road? by train? Had he walked from Darley Halt? If not, who had brought him?) Really, she must try and concentrate on this alibi. The town-clock was the great difficulty. How could that be altered. And altered it must be, for the whole alibi depended on its being heard to strike midnight at the appropriate moment. Could the man who looked after it be made into an accomplice? Who did look after town-hall clocks? (Why gloves? And had she left her own finger-prints on the razor?) Was it, after all, going to be necessary to go to Edinburgh? Perhaps there was no town-hall and no clock. A church-clock would do, of course. But church-clocks and bodies in belfries had been rather overdone lately. (It was odd about Mr. Perkins. If the solution was murder after all, could not the murderer have walked through the water to some point? Perhaps she ought to have followed the shore and not the coast-road. Too late now, in any case.) And she had not properly worked out the speed of the steam-yacht. One ought to know about these things. Lord Peter would know, of course; he must have sailed in plenty of steam-yachts. It must be nice to be *really* rich. Anybody who married Lord Peter would be rich, of course. And he was amusing. Nobody could say he would be dull to live with. But the trouble was that you never knew what anybody was like to live with except by living with them. It wasn't worth it. Not even to know all about steam-yachts. A novelist couldn't possibly marry all the people from whom she wanted specialised information. Harriet pleased herself over the coffee with sketching out the career of an American detective-novelist who contracted a fresh marriage for each new book. For a book about poisons, she would marry an analytical chemist; for a book about somebody's will, a solicitor; for a book about strangling, a—a hangman, of course. There might be something in it. A spoof book, of course. And the villainess might do away with each husband by the method described in the book she was working on at the time. Too obvious? Well, perhaps.

She got up from the table and made her way into a kind of large lounge, where the middle space was cleared for dancing. A select orchestra occupied a platform at one end, and small tables were arranged all around the sides of the room, where visitors could drink coffee or liqueurs and watch the dancing. While she took her place and gave her order, the floor was occupied by a pair of obviously professional dancers, giving an exhibition waltz. The man was tall and fair, with sleek hair plastered closely to his head, and a queer, unhealthy face with a wide, melancholy mouth. The girl, in an exaggerated gown of petunia satin with an enormous bustle and a train, exhibited a mask of Victorian coyness as she revolved languidly in her partner's arms to the strains of the "Blue Danube." "*Autres temps, autres moeurs*," thought Harriet. She looked about the room. Long skirts and costumes of the 'seventies were in evidence—and even ostrich feathers and fans. Even the coyness had its imitators. But it was so obviously an imitation. The slender-seeming waists were made so, not by savage tight-lacing, but by sheer expensive dressmaking. Tomorrow, on the tennis-court, the short, loose tunic-frock would reveal them as the waists of muscular young women of the day, despising all bonds. And the sidelong glances, the downcast eyes, the mock-modesty—masks, only. If this was the "return to womanliness" hailed by the fashion-correspondents, it was to a quite different kind of womanliness—set on a basis of economic independence. Were men really stupid enough to believe that the good old days of submissive womanhood could be brought back by milliners' fashions? "Hardly," thought Harriet, "when they know perfectly well that one has only to remove the train and the bustle, get into a short skirt and walk off, with a job to do and money in one's pocket. Oh, well, it's a game, and presumably they all know the rules."

The dancers twirled to a standstill with the conclusion of the waltz. The instrumentalists tweaked a string and tightened a peg here and there and re-arranged their music, under cover of perfunctory applause. Then the male dancer selected a partner from one of the nearer tables, while the petunia-clad girl obeyed a summons from a stout manufacturer in tweeds on the other side of the room. Another girl, a blonde in pale blue, rose from her solitary table near the platform and led out an elderly man. Other visitors rose, accompanied by their own partners, and took the floor to the strains of another waltz. Harriet beckoned to the waiter and asked for more coffee.

Men, she thought, like the illusion that woman is dependent on their appro-bation and favour for her whole interest in life. But do they like the reality? Not, thought Harriet, bitterly, when one is past one's first youth. The girl over there, exercising S.A. on a group of rather possessive-looking males, will turn into a predatory hag like the woman at the next table, if she doesn't find something to occupy her mind, always supposing that she has a mind. Then the men will say she puts the wind up them.

The "predatory hag" was a lean woman, pathetically made-up, dressed in an exaggeration of the fashion which it would have been difficult for a girl of nineteen to carry off successfully. She had caught Harriet's attention earlier by her look of radiant, almost bridal exaltation. She was alone, but seemed to be expecting somebody, for her gaze roamed incessantly about the room, concen-trating itself chiefly on the professionals' table near the platform. Now she appeared to be getting anxious. Her ringed hands twitched nervously, and she lighted one cigarette after another, only to stub it out, half-smoked, snatch at the mirror in her handbag, readjust her make-up, fidget, and then begin the whole process again with another cigarette.

"Waiting for her gigolo," diagnosed Harriet, with a kind of pitiful disgust. "The frog-mouthed gentleman, I suppose. He seems to have better fish to fry."

The waiter brought the coffee, and the woman at the next table caught him on his way back.

"Is Mr. Alexis not here to-night?"

"No, madam." The waiter looked a little nervous. "No. He is unavoidably absent."

"Is he ill?"

"I do not think so, madam. The manager has just said he will not be coming."

"Did he send no message?"

"I could not say, madam." The waiter was fidgeting with his feet. "Mr. Antoine will no doubt be happy. . . ."

"No, never mind. I am accustomed to Mr. Alexis. His step suits me. It does not matter."

"No, madam, thank you, madam."

The waiter escaped. Harriet saw him exchange a word and a shrug with the head waiter. Lips and eyebrows were eloquent. Harriet felt annoyed. Did one come to this, then, if one did not marry? Making a public scorn of one's self before the waiters? She glanced again at the woman, who was rising to leave the lounge. She wore a wedding-ring. Marriage did not save one, apparently. Single, married, widowed, divorced, one came to the same end. She shivered a little, and suddenly felt fed-up with the lounge and the dance-floor. She finished her coffee and retired to the smaller lounge, where three stout women were engaged in an interminable conversation about illnesses, children and servants. "Poor Muriel—*quite* an invalid since the birth of her last baby. . . . I spoke quite firmly, I said, 'Now you quite understand, if you leave before your month you will be liable to me for the money.' . . . Twelve guineas a week, and the surgeon's fee was a hundred guineas. . . . Beautiful boys, both of them, but with Ronnie at Eton and Wilfred at Oxford. . . . They oughtn't to *let* boys run up these bills . . . my dear, *pounds* thinner, I hardly knew her, but I wouldn't care to . . . some kind of electric heat treatment, too marvellous . . . and what with rates and taxes and all this terrible unemployment. . . . You can't argue with nervous dyspepsia, but it makes things very difficult . . . left me high and dry with the house full of people, these girls have *no* gratitude."

"And these," thought Harriet, "are the happy ones, I suppose. Well, dash it! How about that town-clock?"

4

THE EVIDENCE OF THE RAZOR

Well, thou art
A useful tool sometimes, thy tooth works quickly,
And if thou gnawest a secret from the heart
Thou tellest it not again.
—Death's Jest-Book

FRIDAY, 19 JUNE

In spite of the horrors she had witnessed, which ought to have driven all sleep away from the eyelids of any self-respecting female, Harriet slept profoundly in her first-floor bedroom (with bathroom, balcony and view over Esplanade) and came down to breakfast with a hearty appetite.

She secured a copy of the *Morning Star*, and was deep in the perusal of her own interview (with photograph) on the front page, when a familiar voice addressed her:

"Good morning, Sherlock. Where is the dressing-gown? How many pipes of shag have you consumed? The hypodermic is on the dressing-room table."

"How in the world," demanded Harriet, "did *you* get here?"

"Car," said Lord Peter, briefly. "Have they produced the body?"

"Who told you about the body?"

"I nosed it from afar. Where the carcase is, there shall the eagles be gathered together. May I join you over the bacon-and-eggs?"

"By all means," said Harriet. "Where did you come from?"

"From London—like a bird that hears the call of its mate."

"I didn't—" began Harriet.

"I didn't mean you. I meant the corpse. But still, talking of mates, will you marry me?"

"Certainly not."

"I thought not, but I felt I might as well ask the question. Did you say they had found the body?"

"Not that I know of."

"I don't expect they will, then, for a bit. There's a regular sou'wester blowing great guns. Tiresome for them. Can't have an inquest without a body. You must produce the body, as it says in the Have-His-Carcase Act."

"No, but really," protested Harriet, "how did you hear about it?"

"Salcombe Hardy rang me up from the *Morning Star*. Said 'my Miss Vane' had found a corpse, and did I know anything about it. I said I knew nothing about it and that Miss Vane was unhappily not mine—yet. So I buzzed off, and here I am. I brought Sally Hardy down with me. I expect that's what he really rang me up for. Smart old bird, Sally—always on the spot."

"He told you where to find me, I suppose."

"Yes—he seemed to know all about it. I was rather hurt. Fancy having to ask the *Morning Star* where the pole-star of one's own heaven has gone to. Hardy seemed to know all about it. How do these things get into the papers?"

"I rang them up myself," replied Harriet. "First-class publicity, you know, and all that."

"So it is," agreed Wimsey, helping himself lavishly to butter. "Rang 'em up, did you, with all the gory details?"

"Naturally; that was the first thing I thought of."

"You're a woman of business. But does it not, pardon me, indicate a certain coarsening of the fibres?"

"Obviously," said Harriet. "My fibres at this moment resemble coconut matting."

"Without even 'Welcome' written across them. But, look here, beloved, bearing in mind that I'm a corpse-fan, don't you think you might, as man to man, have let me in on the ground-floor?"

"If you put it that way," admitted Harriet, rather ashamed of herself, "I certainly might. But I thought—"

"Women *will* let the personal element crop in," said Wimsey, acutely. "Well, all I can say is, you owe it to me to make up for it now. All the details, please."

"I'm tired of giving details," grumbled Harriet, perversely.

"You'll be tireder before the police and the newspaper lads have finished with you. I have been staving off Salcombe Hardy with the greatest difficulty. He is in the lounge. The *Banner* and the *Clarion* are in the smoking-room. They had a fast car. The *Courier* is coming by train (it's a nice, respectable, old-fashioned paper), and the *Thunderer* and the *Comet* are hanging about outside the bar, hoping you may be persuaded to offer them something. The three people arguing with the commissionaire are, I fancy, local men. The photographic contingent have gone down en masse, packed in a single Morris, to record the place where the body was found, which, as the tide is well up, they will not see. Tell me all, here and now, and I will organise your publicity for you."

"Very well," said Harriet. "I tell thee all, I can no more."

She pushed her plate aside and took up a clean knife.

"This," she said, "is the coast-road from Lesston Hoe to Wilvercombe. The shore bends about like this—" She took up the pepper-pot.

"Try salt," suggested Wimsey. "Less irritatin' to the nasal tissues."

"Thank you. This line of salt is the beach. And this piece of bread is a rock at low-water level."

Wimsey twitched his chair closer to the table.

"And this salt-spoon," he said, with childlike enjoyment, "can be the body."

He made no comment while Harriet told her story, only interrupting once or twice with a question about times and distances. He sat drooping above the sketch-map she was laying out among the breakfast-things, his eyes invisible, his long nose seeming to twitch like a rabbit's with concentration. When she had finished, he sat silent for a moment and then said:

"Let's get this clear. You got to the place where you had lunch—when, exactly?"

"Just one o'clock. I looked at my watch."

"As you came along the cliffs, you could see the whole shore, including the rock where you found the body."

"Yes; I suppose I could."

"Was anybody on the rock then?"

"I really don't know. I don't even specially remember noticing the rock. I was thinking about my grub, you see, and I was really looking about at the side of the road for a suitable spot to scramble down the cliff. My eyes weren't focused for distance."

"I see. That's rather a pity, in a way."

"Yes, it is; but I can tell you one thing. I'm quite sure there was nothing *moving* on the shore. I did give one glance round just before I decided to climb down. I distinctly remember thinking that the beach seemed absolutely and gloriously deserted—a perfect spot for a picnic. I hate picnicking in a crowd."

"And a single person on a lonely beach would be a crowd?"

"For picnicking purposes, yes. You know what people are. The minute they see anyone having a peaceful feed they gather in from the four points of the compass and sit down beside one, and the place is like the Corner House in the rush hour."

"So they do. That must be the symbolism of the Miss Muffet legend."

"I'm positive there wasn't a living soul walking or standing or sitting anywhere within eyeshot. But as to the body's being already on the rock, I wouldn't swear one way or the other. It was a goodish way out, you know, and when I saw it from the beach I took the body for seaweed just at first. I shouldn't make a mental note of seaweed."

"Good. Then at one o'clock the beach was deserted, except possibly for the body, which may have been there making a noise like seaweed. Then you got down the side of the cliff. Was the rock visible from where you had lunch?"

"No, not at all. There is a sort of little bay there—well, scarcely that. The cliff juts out a bit, and I was sitting close up against the foot of the rocks, so as to have something to lean against. I had my lunch—it took about half an hour altogether."

"You heard nothing then? No footsteps or anything? No car?"

"Not a thing."

"And then?"

"Then I'm afraid I dozed off."

"What could be more natural? For how long?"

"About half an hour. When I woke I looked at my watch again."

"What woke you?"

"A sea-gull squawking round after bits of my sandwich."

"That makes it two o'clock."

"Yes."

"Just a minute. When I arrived here this morning it was a bit early for calling on one's lady friends, so I toddled down to the beach and made friends with one of the fishermen. He happened to mention that it was low tide off the Grinders yesterday afternoon at 1.15. Therefore when you arrived, the tide was practically out. When you woke, it had turned and had been coming in for about forty-five minutes. The foot of your rock—which, by the way, is locally named The Devil's Flat-Iron—is only uncovered for about half an hour between tide and tide, and that only at the top of springs, if you understand that expression."

"I understand perfectly, but I don't see what that has to do with it."

"Well, this—that if anybody had come walking along the edge of the water to the rock, he could have got there without leaving any footprints."

"But he did leave footprints. Oh, I see. You're thinking of a possible murderer."

"I should prefer it to be murder, naturally. Shouldn't you?"

"Yes, of course. Well, that's a fact. A murderer might have walked along from either direction, if he did it that way. If he came from Lesston Hoe he must have arrived after me, because I could see the shore as I walked along, and there was no one walking there then. But he could have come at any time from the Wilvercombe side."

"No, he couldn't," said Wimsey. "He wasn't there, you said, at one o'clock."

"He might have been standing on the seaward side of the Flat-Iron."

"So he might. Now, how about the corpse? We can tell pretty closely when *he* came."

"How?"

"You said there were no wet stains on his shoes. Therefore he went dry-shod to the rock. We only have to find out exactly when the sand on the landward side of the rock is uncovered."

"Of course. How stupid of me. Well, we can easily find that out. Where had I got to?"

"You had been awakened by the cry of a sea-gull."

"Yes. Well, then, I walked round the point of the cliff and out to the rock, and there he was."

"And at that moment there was nobody within sight?"

"Not a single soul, except a man in a boat."

"Yes—the boat. Now, supposing the boat had come in when the tide was out, and the occupant had walked or waded up to the rock—"

"That's possible, of course. The boat was some way out."

"It all seems to depend on when the corpse got there. We must find that out."

"You're determined it should be murder."

"Well, suicide seems so dull. And why go all that way to commit suicide?"

"Why not? Much tidier than doing it in your bedroom or anywhere like that. Aren't we beginning at the wrong end? If we knew who the man was, we might find he had left an explanatory note behind him to say why he was going to do it. I daresay the police know all about it by now."

"Possibly," said Wimsey in a dissatisfied tone.

"What's worrying you?"

"Two things. The gloves. Why should anybody cut his throat in gloves?"

"I know. That bothered me too. Perhaps he had some sort of skin disease and was accustomed to wearing gloves for everything. I ought to have looked. I did start to take the gloves off, but they were—messy."

"Um! I see you still retain a few female frailties. The second point that troubles me is the weapon. Why should a gentleman with a beard sport a cut-throat razor?"

"Bought for the purpose."

"Yes; after all, why not? My dear Harriet, I think you are right. The man cut his throat, and that's all there is to it. I am disappointed."

"It is disappointing, but it can't be helped. Hallo! here's my friend the Inspector."

It was indeed Inspector Umpelty who was threading his way between the tables. He was in mufti—a large, comfortable-looking tweed-clad figure. He greeted Harriet pleasantly.

"I thought you might like to see how your snaps have turned out, Miss Vane. And we've identified the man."

"No? Have you? Good work. This is Inspector Umpelty—Lord Peter Wimsey."

The Inspector appeared gratified by the introduction.

"You're early on the job, my lord. But I don't know that you'll find anything very mysterious about this case. Just a plain suicide, I fancy."

"We had regretfully come to that conclusion," admitted Wimsey.

"Though why he should have done it, I don't know. But you never can tell with these foreigners, can you?"

"I thought he looked rather foreign," said Harriet.

"Yes. He's a Russian, or something of that. Paul Alexis Goldschmidt, his name is; known as Paul Alexis. Comes from this very hotel, as a matter of fact. One of the professional dancing-partners in the lounge here—you know the sort. They don't seem to know much about him. Turned up here just over a year ago and asked for a job. Seemed to be a good dancer and all that and they had a vacancy, so they took him on. Age twenty-two or thereabouts. Unmarried. Lived in rooms. Nothing known against him."

"Papers in order?"

"Naturalised British subject. Said to have escaped from Russia at the Revolution. He must have been a kid of about nine, but we haven't found out yet who had charge of him. He was alone when he turned up here, and his landlady doesn't ever seem to have heard of anybody belonging to him. But we'll soon find out when we go through his stuff."

"He didn't leave any letter for the coroner, or anything?"

"We've found nothing so far. And as regards the coroner, that's a bit of a bother, that is. I don't know how long it'll be, miss, before you're wanted. You see, we can't find the body."

"You don't mean to tell me," said Wimsey, "that the evil-eyed doctor and the mysterious Chinaman have already conveyed it to the lone house on the moor?"

"You will have your fun, my lord, I see. No—it's a bit simpler than that. You see, the current sets northwards round the bay there, and with this sou'wester blowing, the body will have been washed off the Flat-Iron. It'll either come ashore somewhere off Sandy Point, or it'll have got carried out and caught up in the Grinders. If that's where it is, we'll have to wait till the wind goes down. You can't take a boat in there with this sea running, and you can't dive off the rocks —even supposing you knew whereabouts to dive. It's a nuisance, but it can't be helped."

"H'm," said Wimsey. "Just as well you took those photographs, Sherlock, or we'd have no proof that there ever had been a body."

"Coroner can't sit on a photograph, though," said the Inspector, gloomily. "Howsomever, it looks like a plain suicide, so it doesn't matter such a lot. Still, it's annoying. We like to get these things tidied up as we go along."

"Naturally," said Wimsey. "Well, I'm sure if anybody can tidy up, you can, Inspector. You impress me as being a man with an essentially tidy mind. I will engage to prophesy, Sherlock, that before lunch-time Inspector Umpelty will have sorted out the dead man's papers, got the entire story from the hotel-manager, identified the place where the razor was bought and explained the mysterious presence of the gloves."

The Inspector laughed.

"I don't think there's much to be got out of the manager, my lord, and as for the razor, that's neither here nor there."

"But the gloves?"

"Well, my lord, I expect the only person that could tell us about that is the poor blighter himself, and he's dead. But as regards the papers, you're dead right. I'm going along there now." He paused, doubtfully, and looked from Harriet to Wimsey and back again.

"No," said Wimsey. "Set your mind at rest. We are not going to ask to come with you. I know that the amateur detective has a habit of embarrassing the police in the execution of their duty. We are going out to view the town like a perfect little lady and gentleman. There's only one thing I *should* like to have a look at, if it isn't troubling you too much—and that's the razor."

The Inspector was very willing that Lord Peter should see the razor. "And if you like to comerlongerme," he added kindly, "you'll dodge all these reporters."

"Not me!" said Harriet. "I've got to see them and tell them all about my new book. A razor is only a razor, but good advance publicity means sales. You two run along; I'll follow you down."

She strolled away in search of the reporters. The Inspector grinned uneasily.

"No flies on that young lady," he observed. "But can she be trusted to hold her tongue?"

"Oh, she won't chuck away a good plot," said Wimsey, lightly. "Come and have a drink."

"Too soon after breakfast," objected the Inspector.

"Or a smoke," suggested Wimsey.

The Inspector declined.

"Or a nice sit-down in the lounge," said Wimsey, sitting down.

"Excuse me," said Inspector Umpelty, "I must be getting along. I'll tell them at the Station about you wanting to look at the razor. . . . Fair tied to that young woman's apron-strings," he reflected, as he shouldered his bulky way through the revolving doors. "The poor mutt!"

Harriet, escaping half an hour later from Salcombe Hardy and his colleagues, found Wimsey faithfully in attendance.

"I've got rid of the Inspector," observed that gentleman, cheerfully. "Get your hat on and we'll go."

Their simultaneous exit from the Resplendent was observed and recorded by the photographic contingent, who had just returned from the shore. Between an avenue of clicking shutters, they descended the marble steps, and climbed into Wimsey's Daimler.

"I feel," said Harriet, maliciously, "as if we had just been married at St. George's, Hanover Square."

"No, you don't," retorted Wimsey. "If we had, you would be trembling like a fluttered partridge. Being married to me is a tremendous experience—you've no idea. We'll be all right at the police-station, provided the Super doesn't turn sticky on us."

Superintendent Glaisher was conveniently engaged, and Sergeant Saunders was deputed to show them the razor.

"Has it been examined for finger-prints?" asked Wimsey.

"Yes, my lord."

"Any result?"

"I couldn't exactly say, my lord, but I believe not."

"Well, anyway, one is allowed to handle it." Wimsey turned it over in his fingers, inspecting it carefully, first with the naked eye and secondly with a watchmaker's lens. Beyond a very slight crack on the ivory handle, it showed no very striking peculiarities.

"If there's any blood left on it, it will be hanging about the joint," he observed. "But the sea seems to have done its work pretty thoroughly."

"You aren't suggesting," said Harriet, "that the weapon isn't really the weapon after all?"

"I should like to," said Wimsey. "The weapon never is the weapon, is it?"

"Of course not; and the corpse is never the corpse. The body is, obviously, not that of Paul Alexis—"

"But of the Prime Minister of Ruritania—"

"It did not die of a cut throat—"

"But of an obscure poison, known only to the Bushmen of Central Australia—"

"And the throat was cut after death—"

"By a middle-aged man of short temper and careless habits, with a stiff beard and expensive tastes—"

"Recently returned from China," finished up Harriet, triumphantly.

The sergeant, who had gaped in astonishment at the beginning of this exchange, now burst into a hearty guffaw.

"That's very good," he said, indulgently. "Comic, ain't it, the stuff these writer-fellows put into their books? Would your lordship like to see the other exhibits?"

Wimsey replied gravely that he should, very much, and the hat, cigarette-case, shoe and handkerchief were produced.

"H'm," said Wimsey. "Hat fair to middling, but not exclusive. Cranial capacity on the small side. Brilliantine, ordinary stinking variety. Physical condition pretty fair—"

"The man was a dancer."

"I thought we agreed he was a Prime Minister. Hair, dark, curly and rather on the long side. Last year's hat, re-blocked, with new ribbon. Shape, a little more emphatic than is quite necessary. Deduction: not wealthy, but keen on his personal appearance. Do we conclude that the hat belongs to the corpse?"

"Yes, I think so. The brilliantine corresponds all right."

"Cigarette-case—this is different. Fifteen-carat gold, plain and fairly new, with monogram P.A. and containing six de Reszkes. The case is pukka, all right. Probably a gift from some wealthy female admirer."

"Or, of course, the cigarette-case appropriate to a Prime Minister."

"As you say. Handkerchief—silk, but not from Burlington Arcade. Colour beastly. Laundry-mark—"

"Laundry-mark's all right," put in the policeman. "Wilvercombe Sanitary Steam Laundry; mark O.K. for this fellow Alexis."

"Suspicious circumstance," said Harriet, shaking her head. "I've got three handkerchiefs in my pack with not only the laundry-marks but the initials of total strangers."

"It's the Prime Minister, all right," agreed Wimsey, with a doleful nod. "Prime Ministers, especially Ruritanian ones, are notoriously careless about their laundry. Now the shoe. Oh, yes. Nearly new. Thin sole. Foul colour and worse shape. Hand-made, so that the horrid appearance is due to malice aforethought. Not the shoe of a man who does much walking. Made, I observe, in Wilvercombe."

"That's O.K. too," put in the sergeant. "We've seen the man. He made that shoe for Mr. Alexis all right. Knows him well."

"And you took this actually off the foot of the corpse? These are deep waters, Watson. Another man's handkerchief is nothing, but a Prime Minister in another fellow's shoes—"

"You will have your joke, my lord," said the sergeant, with another hoot of laughter.

"I never joke," said Wimsey. He brought the lens to bear on the sole of the shoe. "Slight traces of salt water here, but none on the uppers. Inference: he walked over the sand when it was very wet, but did not actually wade through salt water. Two or three scratches on the toe-cap, probably got when clambering up the rock. Well, thanks awfully, sergeant. You are quite at liberty to inform Inspector Umpelty of all the valuable deductions we have drawn. Have a drink."

"Thank you very much, my lord."

Wimsey said nothing more till they were in the car again.

"I'm sorry," he then announced, as they threaded their way through the side-streets, "to renounce our little programme of viewing the town. I should have enjoyed that simple pleasure. But unless I start at once, I shan't get to town and back tonight."

Harriet, who had been preparing to say that she had work to do and could not waste time rubber-necking round Wilvercombe with Lord Peter, experienced an unreasonable feeling of having been cheated.

"To town?" she repeated.

"It will not have escaped your notice," said Wimsey, skimming with horrible dexterity between a bath-chair and a butcher's van, "that the matter of the razor requires investigation."

"Of course—a visit to the Ruritanian Legation is indicated."

"H'm—well; I don't know that I shall get any further than Jermyn Street."

"In search of the middle-aged man of careless habits?"

"Yes, ultimately."

"He really exists, then?"

"Well, I wouldn't swear to his exact age."

"Or his habits?"

"No, they might be the habits of his valet."

"Or his stiff beard and short temper?"

"Well, I think one may be reasonably certain about the beard."

"I give in," said Harriet meekly. "Please explain."

Wimsey drew up the car at the entrance to the Hotel Resplendent, and looked at his watch.

"I can give you ten minutes," he remarked, in an aloof tone. "Let us take a seat in the lounge and order some refreshment. It is a little early, to be sure, but I always drive more mellowly on a pint of beer. Good. Now, as to the razor. You will have observed that it is an instrument of excellent and expensive quality by a first-class maker, and that, in addition to the name of the manufacturer, it is engraved on the reverse side with the mystic word 'Endicott.' "

"Yes; what is Endicott?"

"Endicott is, or was, one of the most exclusive hairdressers in the West End. So fearfully exclusive and grand that he won't even call himself a hairdresser in the snobbish modern way, but prefers to be known by the old-world epithet of 'barber.' He will, or would, hardly condescend to shave anybody who has not been in Debrett for the last three hundred years. Other people, however rich or titled, have the misfortune to find his chairs always occupied and his basins engaged. His shop has the rarefied atmosphere of one of the more aristocratic mid-Victorian clubs. It is said of Endicott's that a certain peer, who made his money during the War by cornering bootlaces or buttons or something, was once accidentally admitted to one of the sacred chairs by a new assistant who had been most unfortunately taken on with insufficient West-end experience during the temporary war-time shortage of barbers. After ten minutes in that dreadful atmosphere, his hair froze, his limbs became perfectly petrified, and he had to be removed to the Crystal Palace and placed among the antediluvian monsters."

"Well?"

"Well! Consider first of all the anomaly of the man who buys his razor from Endicott's and yet wears the regrettable shoes and mass-production millinery found on the corpse. Mind you," added Wimsey, "it is not a question of expense, exactly. The shoes are hand-made—which merely proves that a dancer has to take care of his feet. But *could* a man who is shaved by Endicott possibly order—deliberately *order*—shoes of that colour and shape? A thing imagination boggles at."

"I'm afraid," admitted Harriet, "that I have never managed to learn all the subtle rules and regulations about male clothing. That's why I made Robert Templeton one of those untidy dressers."

"Robert Templeton's clothes have always pained me," confessed Wimsey. "The one blot on your otherwise fascinating tales. But to leave that distressing subject and come back to the razor. That razor has seen a good deal of hard wear. It has been re-ground a considerable number of times, as you can tell by the edge. Now, a really first-class razor like that needs very little in the way of grinding and setting, provided it is mercifully used and kept carefully stropped. Therefore, either the man who used it was very clumsy and careless about using the strop, or his beard was abnormally stiff, or both—probably both. I visualise him as one of those men who are heavy-handed with tools—you know the kind. Their fountain pens always make blots and their watches get over-wound. They neglect to strop their razors until the strop gets hard and dry, and then they strop them ferociously and jag the edge of the blade. Then they lose their tempers and curse the razor and send it away to be ground and set. The new edge only lasts them for a few weeks and then back the razor goes again, accompanied by a rude message."

"I see. Well, I didn't know all that. But why did you say the man was middle-aged?"

"That was rather guess-work. But I suggest that a young man who had so much difficulty with his razor would be more likely to change over to a safety and use a new blade every few days. But a man of middle-age would not be so likely to change his habits. In any case, I'm sure that razor has had more than three years' hard wear. And if the dead man is only twenty-two now, and has a full beard, then I don't see how he could very well have worn the blade down to that extent, with any amount of grinding and setting. We must find out from the hotel manager here whether he was already wearing the beard when he came a year ago. That would narrow the time down still further. But the first thing to do is to trace old Endicott and find out from him whether it was possible for one of his razors to have been sold later than 1925."

"Why 1925?"

"Because that was the date at which old Endicott sold his premises and retired with varicose veins and a small fortune."

"And who kept on the business?"

"Nobody. The shop is now a place where you buy the most recherché kind of hams and potted meats. There were no sons to carry on—the only young Endicott was killed in the Salient, poor chap. Old Endicott said he wouldn't sell his name to anybody. And anyhow, Endicott's without an Endicott wouldn't be Endicott's. So that was that."

"But he might have sold the stock?"

"That's what I want to find out. I'll have to be off now. I'll try and be back to-night, so don't worry."

"I'm not worrying," retorted Harriet, indignantly. "I'm perfectly happy."

"Splendid. Oh! While I'm about it, shall I see about getting a marriage-licence?"

"Don't trouble, thank you."

"Very well; I just thought I'd ask. I say, while I'm away, how would it be if you put in some good work with the other professional dancers here? You might get hold of some gossip about Paul Alexis."

"There's something in that. But I'll have to get a decent frock if there is such a thing in Wilvercombe."

"Well, get a wine-coloured one, then. I've always wanted to see you in wine-colour. It suits people with honey-coloured skin. (What an ugly word 'skin' is.)

'Blossoms of the honey-sweet and honey-coloured menuphar'—I always have a quotation for everything—it saves original thinking."

"Blast the man!" said Harriet, left abruptly alone in the blue-plush lounge. Then she suddenly ran out down the steps and leapt upon the Daimler's running-board.

"Port or sherry?" she demanded.

"What?" said Wimsey, taken aback.

"The frock—port or sherry?"

"Claret," said Wimsey. "Château Margaux 1893 or thereabouts. I'm not particular to a year or two."

He raised his hat and slipped in the clutch. As Harriet turned back, a voice, faintly familiar, accosted her:

"Miss—er—Miss Vane? Might I speak to you for a moment?"

It was the "predatory hag" whom she had seen the evening before in the dance-lounge of the Resplendent.

5

THE EVIDENCE OF THE BETROTHED

He said, dear mother, I should be his countess;
To-day he'd come to fetch me, but with day
I've laid my expectation in its grave.
—The Brides' Tragedy

FRIDAY, 19 JUNE

Harriet had almost forgotten the woman's existence, but now the whole of the little episode came back to her, and she wondered how she could have been so stupid. The nervous waiting; the vague, enraptured look, changing gradually to peevish impatience; the inquiry for Mr. Alexis; the hasty and chagrined departure from the room. Glancing at the woman's face now, she saw it so old, so ravaged with grief and fear, that a kind of awkward delicacy made her avert her eyes and answer rather brusquely:

"Yes, certainly. Come up to my room."

"It is very good of you," said the woman. She paused a moment and then added, as they walked across to the lift:

"My name is Weldon—Mrs. Weldon. I've been staying here some time. Mr. Greely—the manager, that is—knows me very well."

"That's all right," said Harriet. She realised that Mrs. Weldon was trying to explain that she was not a confidence-trickster or a hotel-crook or a white-slave agent, and was herself trying to make it clear that she did not suppose Mrs. Weldon to be any of these things. She felt shy and this made her speak gruffly. She saw a "scene" looming ahead, and she was not one of those women who enjoy "scenes." She led the way in a glum silence to Number 23, and begged her visitor to sit down.

"It's about," said Mrs. Weldon, sinking into an armchair and clasping her lean hands over her expensive handbag—"it's about—Mr. Alexis. The chamber-maid told me a horrible story—I went to the manager—he couldn't tell me anything —I saw you with the police—and all those reporters were talking—they pointed you out—oh, Miss Vane, *please* tell me what has happened."

Harriet cleared her throat and began searching her pockets instinctively for cigarettes.

"I'm awfully sorry," she began. "I'm afraid something rather beastly has happened. You see—I happened to be down on the shore yesterday afternoon, and I found a man lying there—dead. And from what they say, I'm dreadfully afraid it was Mr. Alexis."

No use beating about the bush. This forlorn creature with the dyed hair and haggard, painted face would have to know the truth. She struck a match and kept her eye on the flame.

"That's what I heard. Was it, do you know, was it a heart-attack?"

"Afraid not. No. They—seemed to think he"—(what was the gentlest form of words?)—"did it himself." (At any rate that avoided the word "suicide.")

"Oh, he couldn't have! he couldn't have! Indeed, Miss Vane, there must be a mistake. He must have had an accident."

Harriet shook her head.

"But you don't know—how could you?—how impossible it all is. But people shouldn't say such cruel things. He was so perfectly happy—he *couldn't* have done anything like that. Why, he—" Mrs. Weldon stopped, searching Harriet's face with her famished eyes. "I heard them saying something about a razor— Miss Vane! What killed him?"

There was no kindly words for this—not even a long, scientific, Latin name.

"His throat was cut, Mrs. Weldon."

(Brutal Saxon monosyllables.)

"Oh!" Mrs. Weldon seemed to shrink into a mere set of eyes and bones. "Yes —they said—they said—I couldn't hear properly—I didn't like to ask—and they all seemed so pleased about it."

"I know," said Harriet. "You see—these newspaper men—it's what they live by. They don't mean anything. It's bread-and-butter to them. They can't help it. And they couldn't possibly know that it meant anything to you."

"No—but it does. But you—*you* don't want to make it out worse than it is. I can trust *you*."

"You can trust me," said Harriet slowly, "but really and truly it could not have been an accident. I don't want to give you the details, but believe me, there's no possibility of accident."

"Then it can't be Mr. Alexis. Where is he? Can I see him?"

Harriet explained that the body had not been recovered.

"Then it must be somebody else! How do they know it is Paul?"

Harriet reluctantly mentioned the photograph, knowing what the next request would be.

"Show me the photograph."

"It isn't very pleasant to look at."

"Show me the photograph. *I* couldn't be deceived about it."

Better, perhaps, to set all doubt at rest. Harriet slowly produced the print. Mrs. Weldon snatched it from her hand.

"Oh, God! Oh, God! . . ."

Harriet rang the bell and, stepping out into the corridor, caught the waiter and asked for a stiff whisky-and-soda. When it came, she took it in herself and made Mrs. Weldon drink it. Then she fetched a clean handkerchief and waited for the storm to subside. She sat on the arm of the chair and patted Mrs. Weldon rather helplessly on the shoulder. Mercifully, the crisis took the form of violent sobbing and not of hysterics. She felt an increased respect for Mrs. Weldon. When the sobs had subsided a little, and the groping fingers began to fumble with the handbag, Harriet pushed the handkerchief into them.

"Thank you, my dear," said Mrs. Weldon, meekly. She began to wipe her eyes, daubing the linen with red and black streaks from her make-up. Then she blew her nose and sat up.

"I'm sorry," she began, forlornly.

"That's all right," said Harriet, again. "I'm afraid you've had rather a shock. Perhaps you'd like to bathe your eyes a bit. It'll make you feel better, don't you think?"

She supplied a sponge and towel. Mrs. Weldon removed the grotesque traces of her grief and made her appearance from within the folds of the towel as a sallow-faced woman of between fifty and sixty, infinitely more dignified in her natural complexion. She made an instinctive movement towards her handbag, and then abandoned it.

"I look awful," she said, with a dreary little laugh, "but—what's it matter, now?"

"I shouldn't mind about it," said Harriet. "You look quite nice. Really and truly. Come and sit down. Have a cigarette. And let me give you a phenacetin or something. I expect you've got a bit of a headache."

"Thank you. You're very kind. I won't be stupid again. I'm giving you a lot of trouble."

"Not a bit. I only wish I could help you."

"You can. If you only would. I'm sure you're clever. You look clever. I'm not clever. I do wish I was. I think I should have been happier if I'd been clever. It must be nice to *do* things. I've so often thought that if I could have painted pictures or ridden a motor-cycle or something, I should have got more out of life."

Harriet agreed, gravely, that it was perhaps a good thing to have an occupation of some sort.

"But of course," said Mrs. Weldon, "I was never brought up to that. I have lived for my emotions. I can't help it. I suppose I am made that way. Of course, my married life was a tragedy. But that's all over now. And my son—you might not think I was old enough to have a grownup son, my dear, but I was married scandalously young—my son has been a sad disappointment to me. He has no heart—and that does seem strange, seeing that I am really all heart myself. I am *devoted* to my son, dear Miss Vane, but young people are so unsympathetic. If only he had been kinder to me, I could have lived *in* and *for* him. Everybody always said what a wonderful mother I was. But it's terribly lonely when one's own child deserts one, and one can't be blamed for snatching a little happiness, can one?"

"I know that," said Harriet. "I've tried snatching. It didn't work, though."

"Didn't it?"

"No. We quarrelled, and then—well, he died and they thought I'd murdered him. I didn't, as a matter of fact. Somebody else did; but it was all very disagreeable."

"You poor thing. But, of course, you are clever. You *do* things. That must make it easier. But what am I to do? I don't even know how to set about clearing up all this terrible business about Paul. But you are clever and you will help me—won't you?"

"Suppose you tell me just exactly what you want done."

"Yes, of course. I'm so stupid—I can't even explain things properly. But you see, Miss Vane, I *know*, I know absolutely, that poor Paul couldn't have—done anything rash. He couldn't. He was so utterly happy with me, and looking forward to it all."

"To what?" asked Harriet.

"Why, to our marriage," said Mrs. Weldon, as though the matter was self-evident.

"Oh, I see. I'm so sorry. I didn't realise you were going to be married. When?"

"In a fortnight's time. As soon as I could be ready for it. We were so happy—like children—"

Tears gathered again in Mrs. Weldon's eyes.

"I will tell you all about it. I came here last January. I had been very ill and the doctor said I needed a mild climate, and I was so tired of the Riviera. I thought I'd try Wilvercombe just for a change. I came here. It really is a very nice hotel, you know, and I'd been here once before with Lady Hartlepool—but she died last year, you know. The very first night I was here, Paul came over and asked me to dance. We seemed to be drawn together. From the moment our eyes met, we knew we had found one another. He was lonely, too. We danced together every night. We went for long drives together and he told me all about his sad life. We were both exiles in our own way."

"Oh, yes—he came from Russia."

"Yes, as a tiny boy. Poor little soul. He was really a prince, you know—but he never liked to say too much about that. Just a hint here and there. He felt it very much, being reduced to being a professional dancer. I told him—when we got to know one another better—that he was a prince in my heart now, and he said that that was better to him than an Imperial crown, poor boy. He loved me terribly. He quite frightened me sometimes. Russians are so passionate, you know."

"Of course, of course," said Harriet. "You didn't have any misunderstanding or anything that might have led him—?"

"Oh, *no!* We were too marvellously at one together. We danced together that last night, and he whispered to me that there was a *great* and wonderful change coming into his life. He was all eagerness and excitement. He used to get terribly excited over the least little thing, of course—but this was a real, big excitement and happiness. He danced so wonderfully that night. He told me it was because his heart was so full of joy that he felt as if he was dancing on air. He said: 'I may have to go away to-morrow—but I can't tell you yet where or why.' I didn't ask him anything more, because that would have spoilt it, but naturally I knew what he meant. He had been getting the licence, and we should be married in a fortnight after that."

"Where were you going to be married?"

"In London. In church, of course, because I think a registrar's office is *so* depressing. Don't you? Of course he'd have to go and stay in the parish—that was what he meant by going away. We didn't want anybody here to know our secret beforehand, because there might have been unkind talk. You see, I'm a little bit older than he was, and people say such horrid things. I was a little worried about it myself, but Paul always said, 'It is the heart that counts, Little Flower'—he called me that, because my name is Flora—such a dreadful name, I can't think how my poor dear parents came to choose it—'It is the heart that counts, and your heart is just seventeen.' It was beautiful of him, but quite true. I felt seventeen when I was with him."

Harriet murmured something inaudible. This conversation was dreadful to her. It was nauseating, pitiful, artificial yet horribly real; grotesquely comic and worse than tragic. She wanted to stop it at all costs, and she wanted at all costs to go on and disentangle the few threads of fact from the gaudy tangle of absurdity.

"He had never loved anybody till he met me," went on Mrs. Weldon. "There is something so fresh and sacred in a young man's first love. One feels—well, almost reverent. He was jealous of my former marriage, but I told him he need not be. I was such a child when I married John Weldon, *far* too young to realise what love meant. I was utterly unawakened till I met Paul. There had been other men, I don't say there hadn't, who wanted to marry me (I was left a widow very early), but they meant nothing to me—nothing at all. 'The heart of a girl with the experience of a woman'—that was Paul's lovely way of putting it. And it was true, my dear, indeed it was."

"I'm sure it was," said Harriet, trying to put conviction into her tone.

"Paul—he was so handsome and so graceful—if you could have seen him as he was! And he was very modest and not the least bit spoilt, though *all* the women ran after him. He was afraid to speak to me for a long time—to tell me how he felt about me, I mean. As a matter of fact, I had to take the first step, or he never would have dared to speak, though it was quite obvious how he felt. In fact, though we got engaged in February, he suggested putting the wedding off till June. He felt—so sweet and thoughtful of him—that we ought to wait and try to overcome my son's opposition. Of course, Paul's position made him very sensitive. You see, I'm rather well off, and of course, he hadn't a penny, poor boy, and he always refused to take any presents from me before we were married. He'd had to make his own way all alone, because those horrible Bolsheviks didn't leave him anything."

"Who looked after him when he first came to England?"

"The woman who brought him over. He called her 'old Natasha,' and said she was a peasant-woman and absolutely devoted to him. But she died very soon, and then a Jewish tailor and his family were kind to him. They adopted him and made him a British subject, and gave him their own name of Goldschmidt. After that, their business failed somehow, and they were terribly poor. Paul had to run errands and sell newspapers. Then they tried emigrating to New York, but that was still worse. Then they died, and Paul had to look after himself. Paul didn't like to say very much about that part of his life. It was all so terrible to him—like a bad dream."

"I suppose he went to school somewhere."

"Oh, yes—he went to the ordinary State school with all the poor little East-side children. But he hated it. They used to laugh at him because he was delicate. They were rough with him and once he got knocked down in the playground and was ill for a long time. And he was terribly lonely."

"What did he do when he left school?"

"He got work at a night-club, washing up glasses. He says the girls there were kind to him, but of course, he never talked much about that time. He was sensitive, you see. He thought people would look down on him if they knew he had done that kind of work."

"I suppose that was where he learnt to dance," said Harriet, thoughtfully.

"Oh, yes—he was a marvellous dancer. It was in his blood, you know. When he was old enough, he got work as a professional partner and did very well, though of course it wasn't the kind of life he wanted."

"He managed to make quite a good living at it," said Harriet, thoughtfully, thinking of the too-smart clothes and the hand-made shoes.

"Yes; he worked very hard. But he never was strong, and he told me that he wouldn't be able to keep on much longer with the dancing. He had some trouble in one of his knees—arthritis or something, and he was afraid it would get worse and cripple him. Isn't it all terribly pathetic? Paul was so romantic, you know, and he wrote beautiful poetry. He loved everything that was beautiful."

"What brought him to Wilvercombe?"

"Oh, he came back to England when he was seventeen, and got work in London. But the place went bankrupt, or got shut up by the police, or something, and he came here for a little holiday on what he had saved. Then he found they wanted a dancer here and he took the job temporarily, and he was so brilliant that the management kept him on."

"I see." Harriet reflected that it was going to be too difficult to trace these movements of Alexis through the Ghetto of New York and the mushroom clubs of the West End.

"Yes—Paul used to say it was the hand of Destiny that brought him and me here together. It does seem strange, doesn't it? We both just happened to come —by accident—just as though we were fated to meet. And now—"

The tears ran down Mrs. Weldon's cheeks, and she gazed up helplessly at Harriet.

"We were both so sad and lonely; and we were going to be happy together."

"It's frightfully sad," said Harriet, inadequately. "I suppose Mr. Alexis was rather temperamental."

"If you mean," said Mrs. Weldon, "that he did this awful thing himself—no, never! I know he didn't. He was temperamental, of course, but he was radiantly happy with me. I'll never believe he just went away like that, without even saying good-bye to me. It isn't possible, Miss Vane. You've got to *prove* that it wasn't possible. You're so clever, I know you can do it. That's why I wanted so see you and tell you about Paul."

"You realise," said Harriet, slowly, "that if he didn't do it himself, somebody else must have done it."

"Why not?" cried Mrs. Weldon, eagerly. "Somebody must have envied our happiness. Paul was so handsome and romantic—there must have been people who were jealous of us. Or it may have been the Bolsheviks. Those horrible men would do anything, and I was only reading in the paper yesterday that England was simply swarming with them. They say all this business about passports isn't a bit of good to keep them out. I call it absolutely wicked, the way we let them come over here and plot against everybody's safety and this Government simply encourages them. They've killed Paul, and I shouldn't wonder if they started throwing bombs at the King and Queen next. It ought to be stopped, or we shall have a revolution. Why, they even distribute their disgusting pamphlets to the Navy."

"Well," said Harriet, "we must wait and see what they find out. I'm afraid you may have to tell the police about some of this. It won't be very pleasant for you, I'm afraid, but they'll want to know everything they can."

"I'm sure I don't mind what I have to go through," said Mrs. Weldon, wiping her eyes resolutely, "if only I can help to clear Paul's memory. Thank you *very* much, Miss Vane. I'm afraid I've taken up your time. You've been very kind."

"Not at all," said Harriet. "We'll do our best."

She escorted her visitor to the door, and then returned to an armchair and a thoughtful cigarette. Was the imminent prospect of matrimony with Mrs. Weldon a sufficient motive for suicide? She was inclined to think not. One can always take flight from these things. But with temperamental people, of course, you never can tell.

6

THE EVIDENCE OF THE FIRST BARBER

Old, benevolent man.
—The Second Brother

"FRIDAY, 19 JUNE—Afternoon and evening
Can you tell me," inquired Lord Peter, "what has become of old Mr. Endicott these days?"

The manager of the ham-shop, who liked to attend personally to distinguished customers, arrested his skewer in the very act of thrusting it into the interior of a ham.

"Oh, yes, my lord. He has a house at Ealing. He occasionally looks in here for a jar of our Gentleman's Special Pickle. A very remarkable old gentleman, Mr. Endicott."

"Yes, indeed. I hadn't seen him about lately. I was afraid perhaps something had happened to him."

"Oh, dear no, my lord. He keeps his health wonderfully. He has taken up golf at seventy-six and collects papier-mâché articles. Nothing like an interest in life, he says, to keep you hearty."

"Very true," replied Wimsey. "I must run out and see him some time. What is his address?"

The manager gave the information, and then, returning to the matter in hand, plunged the skewer into the ham close to the bone, twirled it expertly and, withdrawing it, presented it politely by the handle. Wimsey sniffed it gravely, said "Ah!" with appropriate relish, and pronounced a solemn benediction upon the ham.

"Thank you, my lord. I think you will find it very tasty. Shall I send it?"

"I will take it with me."

The manager waved forward an attendant, who swathed the article impressively in various layers of grease-proof paper, white paper and brown paper, corded it up with best-quality string, worked the free end of the string into an ingenious handle and stood, dandling the parcel, like a nurse with a swaddled princeling.

"My car is outside," said Wimsey. The assistant beamed gratification. A little ritual procession streamed out into Jermyn Street, comprising: The Assistant, carrying the ham; Lord Peter, drawing on his driving-gloves; the Manager, murmuring a ceremonial formula; the Second Assistant, opening the door and emerging from behind it to bow upon the threshold; and eventually the car glided away amid the reverent murmurings of a congregation of persons gathered in the street to admire its stream-lining and dispute about the number of its cylinders.

Mr. Endicott's house at Ealing was easily found. The owner was at home, and the presentation of the ham and reciprocal offer of a glass of old sherry proceeded with the cheerful dignity suitable to an exchange of gifts among equal, but friendly potentates. Lord Peter inspected the collection of papier-mâché trays, conversed agreeably about golf-handicaps and then, without unseemly haste, opened up the subject of his inquiry.

"I've just come across one of your razors, Endicott, in rather peculiar circumstances. I wonder if you could tell me anything about it?"

Mr. Endicott, with a gracious smile upon his rosy countenance, poured out another glass of the sherry and said he would be happy to assist if he could.

Wimsey described the make and appearance of the razor, and asked if it would be possible to trace the buyer.

"Ah!" said Mr. Endicott. "With an ivory handle, you say. Well, now, it's rather fortunate it should be one of that lot, because we only had the three dozen of them, most of our customers preferring black handles. Yes; I can tell you a bit about them. That particular razor came in during the War—1916, I think it was. It wasn't too easy to get a first-class blade just then, but these were very good. Still, the white handle was against them, and I remember we were glad when we were able to send off a dozen of them to an old customer in Bombay. Captain Francis Egerton, that was. He asked us to send some out for himself and friends. That would be in 1920."

"Bombay? That's a bit far off. But you never know. How about the rest?"

Mr. Endicott, who seemed to have a memory like an Encyclopaedia, plunged his thoughts into the past and said:

"Well, there was Commander Mellon; he had two of them. But it wouldn't be him, because his ship was blown up and sank with all hands and his kit went down with him. In 1917, that would be. A very gallant gentleman, was the Commander, and of good family. One of the Dorset Mellons. The Duke of Wetherby: he had one, and he was telling me the other day that he still had it; it wouldn't be him. And Mr. Pritchard: he had a remarkable experience with his; his personal man went off his head and attacked him with his own razor, but fortunately Mr. Pritchard was able to overpower him. They brought him in guilty of attempted murder but insane, and the razor was an exhibit at the trial. I know Mr. Pritchard came in afterwards and bought a new razor, a black one, because the other had struck the back of a chair during the struggle and had a piece chipped out of the edge, and he said he was going to keep it as a memento of the narrowest shave of his life. That was very good, I thought. Mr. Pritchard was always a very amusing gentleman. Colonel Grimes: he had one, but he had to abandon all his kit in the Retreat over the Marne—I couldn't say what happened to that one. He liked that razor and came back for another one similar, and he has it yet. That makes six out of the second dozen. What happened to the others?—Oh, I know! There was a very funny story about one of them. Young Mr. Ratcliffe—the Hon. Henry Ratcliffe—he came in one day in a great state. 'Endicott,' he said, 'just you look at my razor!' 'Bless me, sir,' I said, 'it looks as if somebody had been sawing wood with it.' 'That's a very near guess, Endicott,' he said. 'My sister-in-law and some of that bright crowd of hers in her studio got the idea that they'd have some private theatricals and used my best razor to cut out the scenery with.' My goodness, he was wild about it! Of course the blade was ruined for ever; he had a different one after that, a very fine French razor which we were trying out at the time. Then, ah, yes! There was poor Lord Blackfriars. A sad business that was. He married one of those film stars, and she ran through his money and went off with a dago—you'll remember that, my lord. Blew his brains out, poor gentleman. He left his pair of razors to his personal man, who wouldn't part with them on any account. Major Hartley had two and so did Colonel Belfridge. They've left Town and gone to live in the country. I could give you their addresses. Sir John Westlock—well, now, I couldn't say for certain about him. There was some sort of trouble and he went abroad, at the time of the Megatherium Scandal. Early in the 'twenties, wasn't it? My memory isn't what it was. He had a pair of razors. Very fond of a good blade, he was, and looked after it very carefully. Mr. Alec Baring—that was sad, too. They said it was in the family, but I always thought that flying crash had something to do with it. I suppose they wouldn't let him have razors where he is now. He only had one of that set, as a replacement for one he left in a hotel. How many does that make? Sixteen altogether, not counting the dozen that went to Bombay. Well, that's nearly the lot, because I gave a round half-dozen to my late head-assistant when we broke up the business. He has an establishment of his own in Eastbourne, and is doing very well there, I'm told. Twenty-two. Now, what about the last pair?"

Mr. Endicott scratched his head with a pained look.

"Sometimes I think I'm beginning to fail a bit," he said, "though my handicap is getting shorter and my wind's as good as ever it was. Now, who *did* have that pair of razors? Well, there! Could it have been Sir William Jones? No, it couldn't. Or the Marquis of—? No. Stop a minute. That was the pair Sir Harry Ringwood bought for his son—young Mr. Ringwood up at Magdalen College. I knew I hadn't seen them about. He had them in 1925, and the young gentleman went out to British East Africa under the Colonial Office when he left the University. There! I knew I should get it in time. That's the lot, my lord."

"Endicott," said Lord Peter, "I think you're marvellous. You're the youngest man of your age I ever struck, and I should like to meet your wine-merchant."

Mr. Endicott, gratified, pushed the decanter across the table and mentioned the name of the vendor.

"A lot of these people we can dismiss at once," said Lord Peter. "Colonel

Grimes is a problem—goodness knows what happened to the kit he left in France, but I expect somebody out there got hold of it. The razor may have returned to this country. He's a possibility. Major Hartley and Colonel Belfridge will have to be traced. I shouldn't think it would be Sir John Westlock. If he was a careful sort of blighter, he probably took his razors with him and cherished them. We'll have to inquire about poor Baring. His razor may have been sold or given away. And we might just ask about young Ringwood, though we can probably count him out. Then there's your head-assistant. Would he be likely to have sold any of them, do you think?"

"Well, no, my lord; I shouldn't think he would. He told me that he should keep them for his own use and for use on his own premises. He liked having the old name on them, you see. But for sale to his customers, he would have his razors marked with his own name. That has a certain value, you see, my lord. It's only if you're in a good way of business and can order in razors in three-dozen lots that you get your own name put on them. He started off very well with a new three dozen Kropp blades, for he told me all about it, and, things being equal, those are what he would supply his customers with."

"Quite. Any likelihood of his selling the others second-hand?"

"That," said Mr. Endicott, "I could not say. There isn't a great deal of business done in second-hand razors, without it's one of these tramp-hairdress-ers now and again."

"What's a tramp-hairdresser?"

"Well, my lord, they're hairdressers out of a job, and they go about from place to place looking to be taken on as extra hands when there's a press of work. We didn't see much of them in *our* place, of course. They're not first-class men as a rule, and I wouldn't have taken it upon me to engage any but a first-class man for *my* gentlemen. But in a place like Eastbourne, where there's a big seasonal custom, you would have them round pretty frequently. It might be worth while asking my late assistant. Plumer, his name is, in Belvedere Road. If you like, I will send him a line."

"Don't bother; I'll run down and see him. Just one other thing. Was any of the customers you've mentioned a clumsy-handed fellow who took a lot out of his razor and was always sending it back to be re-set?"

Mr. Endicott chuckled.

"Ah! now you're talking," he said. "Colonel Belfridge—oh, dear! oh, dear! He was a terribly hard man on his razors—is still, for all I know. Time and again he'd say to me, 'Pon my word, Endicott, I don't know what you *do* to my razors. They don't keep their edge a week. Steel isn't what it was before the War.' But it wasn't the steel, or the War either. He was always the same. I think he took the edge off with the strop, instead of putting it on; I do indeed. He didn't keep a man, you know. The Colonel belongs to one of our best families, but not a wealthy man, by any means. A very fine soldier, I believe."

"One of the old school, eh?" said Wimsey. "Good-hearted but peppery. I know. Where did you say he was living now?"

"Stamford," replied Mr. Endicott, promptly. "He sent me a card last Christ-mas. Very kind of him, I thought it, to remember me. But my old customers are very thoughtful in those ways. They know I value their kind remembrance. Well, my lord, I am exceedingly pleased to have seen you," he added, as Wimsey rose and took up his hat, "and I'm sure I hope I may have been of some assistance to you. You keep very fit, I hope. You're looking well."

"I'm getting old," said Lord Peter. "My hair is turning grey over the temples."
Mr. Endicott emitted a concerned cluck.

"But that's nothing," he hastened to assure his visitor. "Many ladies think it looks more distinguished that way. Not getting thin on the top, I hope and trust."

"Not that I know of. Take a look at it."

Mr. Endicott pushed the straw-coloured thatch apart and peered earnestly at the roots.

"No sign of it," he pronounced, confidently. "Never saw a healthier scalp. At the same time, my lord, if you *should* notice any slight weakening or falling-off, let me know. I should be proud to advise you. I've still got the recipe for Endicott's Special Tonic, and though I say so myself, I've never found anything to beat it."

Wimsey laughed, and promised to call on Mr. Endicott for help at the first symptom of trouble. The old barber saw him to the door, clasping his hand affectionately and begging him to come again. Mrs. Endicott would be so sorry to have missed him.

Seated behind the steering-wheel, Wimsey debated the three courses open to him. He could go to Eastbourne; he could go to Stamford; he could return to Wilvercombe. A natural inclination pointed to Wilvercombe. It was, surely, only justifiable to return at once to the scene of the crime, if it was a crime. The fact that Harriet was also there was a purely accidental complication. On the other hand, his obvious duty was to clear up this razor business as quickly as possible. Musing, he drove to his own flat in Piccadilly, where he found his man, Bunter, mounting photographs in a large album.

To Bunter he laid bare his problem, requesting his advice. Bunter, revolving the matter in his mind, took a little time for consideration and then delivered himself respectfully of his opinion.

"In your lordship's place, my lord, I fancy I should be inclined to go to Stamford. For a variety of reasons."

"You would, would you?"

"Yes, my lord."

"Well, perhaps you are right, Bunter."

"Yes, thank you, my lord. Would your lordship wish me to accompany you?"

"No," said Wimsey. "You can go down to Eastbourne."

"Very good, my lord."

"To-morrow morning. I shall stay the night in Town. You might send off a telegram for me—no, on second thoughts, I'll send it myself."

Telegram from Lord Peter Wimsey to Miss Harriet Vane:

FOLLOWING RAZOR CLUE TO STAMFORD REFUSE RESEMBLE THRILLER HERO WHO HANGS ROUND HEROINE TO NEGLECT OF DUTY BUT WILL YOU MARRY ME—PETER

Telegram from Miss Harriet Vane to Lord Peter Wimsey:

GOOD HUNTING CERTAINLY NOT SOME DEVELOPMENTS HERE—VANE

7

THE EVIDENCE OF THE GIGOLOS

A worthless life, A life ridiculous.
—Death's Jest-Book

FRIDAY, 19 JUNE—Evening

Miss Harriet Vane, in a claret-coloured frock, swayed round the dance-lounge of the Hotel Resplendent in the arms of Mr. Antoine, the fair-haired gigolo.

"I'm afraid I am not a very good dancer," she remarked, apologetically.

Mr. Antoine clasped her a very little more firmly in his competent professional arm, and replied:

"You dance very correctly, mademoiselle. It is only the *entrain* that is a little lacking. It is possible that you are awaiting the perfect partner. When the heart dances with the feet, then it will be *à merveille.*" He met her eyes with a delicately calculated expression of encouragement.

"Is that the kind of thing you have to say to all these old ladies?" asked Harriet, smiling.

Antoine opened his eyes a trifle and then, mocking back to her mockery, said:

"I am afraid so. That is part of our job, you know."

"It must be very tedious."

Antoine contrived to shrug his exquisite shoulders without in any way affecting the lithe grace of his motion.

"*Que voulez-vous?* All work has its tedious moments, which are repaid by those that are more agreeable. One may say truthfully to mademoiselle what might in another case be a mere politeness."

"Don't bother about me," said Harriet. "There's something else I want to talk about. I wanted to ask you about Mr. Alexis."

"*Ce pauvre Alexis!* It was mademoiselle who found him, I understand?"

"Yes. I just wondered what sort of person he was, and why he should have—done away with himself like that."

"Ah! that is what we are all wondering. It is, no doubt, the Russian temperament."

"I had heard"—Harriet felt that she must tread cautiously here—"that he was engaged to be married."

"Oh, yes—to the English lady. That was understood."

"Was he happy about it?"

"Mademoiselle, Alexis was poor and the English lady is very rich. It was advantageous to him to marry her. At first, no doubt, it might offer a little *désagrément,* but afterwards—you understand, mademoiselle, these matters arrange themselves."

"You don't think that he suddenly felt he couldn't face it, and took this way out?"

"That is difficult to say, but—no, I do not think so. He had, after all, only to go away. He was a very good dancer and very popular. He would easily have found another situation, provided his health would permit him to continue."

"I wondered whether there was any other attachment to make things more difficult."

"From what he said to us, mademoiselle, I know of nothing which could not easily have been arranged."

"Women liked him, I suppose?" demanded Harriet, bluntly.

Antoine's smile was a sufficient answer.

"There wasn't any disappointment of any kind?"

"I did not hear of any. But of course, one does not tell one's friends everything."

"Of course not. I don't mean to be inquisitive, but it all seems to me rather odd."

The music stopped.

"What is the arrangement?" asked Harriet. "Do we go on or have you other engagements?"

"There is no reason why we should not continue for the next dance. After that, unless mademoiselle wishes to make a special arrangement with the management, I am expected to attend to my other patrons."

"No," said Harriet, "I don't want to upset things. Is there any reason why you and the two young ladies should not have a little supper with me later on?"

"None at all. It is very kind; very amiable. Leave it to me, mademoiselle. I will arrange it all. It is natural that mademoiselle should take an interest."

"Yes, but I don't want the manager to think that I'm interrogating his staff behind his back."

"*N'ayez pas peur, je m'en charge.* I will ask you to dance again in a little time, and then I will tell you what I have contrived."

He handed her back to her table with a smile, and she saw him gather up a vast and billowy lady in a tightly fitting gown and move smoothly away with her, the eternal semisensuous smile fixed upon his lips as though it was painted there.

About six dances later, the smile reappeared beside her, and Antoine, guiding her steps through a waltz, informed her that if, at 11.30, when the dancing was over, she would be good enough to seek out a small restaurant a few streets away, he, with Doris and Charis, would be there to meet her. It was only a small restaurant, but very good, and the proprietor knew them very well; moreover, Antoine himself lodged in the little hotel attached to the restaurant and would give himself the pleasure of offering mademoiselle a glass of wine. They would be private there, and could speak quite freely. Harriet assented, with the proviso that she should pay for the supper, and accordingly, shortly before midnight, found herself seated on a red-plush settee beneath a row of gilded mirrors, over a pleasant little supper of the Continental sort.

Doris the blonde and Charis the brunette were only too delighted to discuss the affairs of the late Mr. Alexis. Doris appeared to be the official confidante; she could give inside information about her late partner's affairs of the heart. He had had a girl—oh, yes; but some weeks earlier this connection had come to an end rather mysteriously. It was nothing to do with Mrs. Weldon. *That* matter had been, in Mr. Micawber's phrase, already "provided for." No; it was apparently a breaking-off by mutual consent, and nobody seemed to have been much upset by it. Certainly not Alexis, who, though expressing a great deal of conventional regret, had seemed to be rather pleased about it, as though he had brought off a smart piece of business. And since then, the young lady in question had been seen going about with another man, who was supposed to be a friend of Alexis.

"And if you ask me," said Doris, in a voice whose fundamental cockney was overlaid by a veneer of intense refinement, "Alexis pushed her off on to this chap on purpose, to get her out of the way of his other little plans."

"What other little plans?"

"I'm sure I don't know. But he had something up his sleeve these last few weeks. Very grand he was about it; I'm sure one was almost afraid to speak to his high-mightiness. 'You'll see,' he said, 'just you wait a little bit.' 'Well, I'm sure,' I said, 'I have no wish to intrude. You can keep your secrets,' I said, 'for I don't want to know them.' It's my belief he was up to some game or other. Whatever it was, he was like a dog with two tails about it."

Mrs. Weldon too, thought Harriet, had said the same thing. Alexis was going to have some news for her—though Mrs. Weldon had put her own interpretation on the remark. Harriet put out another feeler of inquiry.

"Marriage-licence?" said Charis. "Oh, no! he wouldn't be putting up any flags about that. He couldn't very well *like* the idea of marrying that dreadful old woman. Well, it serves her right now. She's got left. I think that sort of thing is disgusting."

"I am sorry for her," said Antoine.

"Oh, you are always sorry for people. I do think it's beastly. I think these horrible fat men are beastly, too, always pawing a girl about. If Greely wasn't a decent sort, I'd chuck the whole thing, but I will say he does see to it that they behave themselves. But an old *woman*—" Charis, superb in her vigorous youth, expressed contempt by voice and gesture.

"I suppose," suggested Harriet, "that Alexis wanted to feel safe and settled financially. I mean, a dancer can't go on dancing all his life, can he? Particularly if he isn't very strong."

She spoke with hesitation, but to her relief Antoine immediately and emphatically agreed with her.

"You are right. While we are young and gay it is all very good. But presently the head grows bald, the legs grow stiff, and—finish! The manager says, 'It is all very well, you are a good dancer, but my clients prefer a young man, *hein?* Then good-bye the first-class establishment. We go, what you call, down the hill. I tell you, it is a great temptation when somebody comes and says, 'Look! You have only to marry me and I will make you rich and comfortable for life.' And what is it? Only to tell lies to one's wife every night instead of to twenty or thirty silly old ladies. Both are done for money—where is the difference?"

"Yes, I suppose we shall all come to it," said Charis, with a grimace. "Only, from the way Alexis talked, you'd think he'd have wanted a little more poetry about it. All that rubbish about his noble birth and fallen fortunes—like something out of these stories he was so potty about. Quite a hero of romance, according to him. Always wanted to take the spotlight, did Mr. Paul Alexis.

You'd think he did the floor a favour by dancing on it. And then the fairy prince comes down to marrying an old woman for her money."

"Oh, he wasn't so bad," protested Doris. "You oughtn't to talk that way, dear. It's not so easy for we dancers, the way everybody treats us like dirt. Though they're willing enough to take advantage of you if you give them half a chance. Why shouldn't Alexis, or any of us, get a bit of our own back? Anyhow, he's dead, poor boy, and you oughtn't to run him down."

"Ah, *voilà!*" said Antoine. "He is dead. Why is he dead? One does not cut one's throat *pour s'amuser.*"

"That's another thing," said Charis, "that I can't quite make out. The minute I heard about it, I said to myself, 'That's not like Alexis.' He hadn't the nerve to do a thing like that. Why, he was terrified of pricking his little finger. You needn't frown, dear, Alexis was a regular namby-pamby, and if he was dead ten times over it wouldn't make any difference. You used to laugh at him yourself. 'I cannot climb that step-ladder, I am afraid to fall.' 'I do not like to go to the dentist, he might pull my teeth out.' 'Do not shake me when I am cutting the bread, I might cut my fingers.' 'Really, Mr. Alexis,' I used to say to him, 'anybody would think you were made of glass.' "

"I know what mademoiselle is thinking," said Antoine, his melancholy mouth curling. "She thinks: '*Voilà!* that is the gigolo. He is not a man, he is a doll stuffed with sawdust.' He is bought, he is sold, and sometimes there is an unpleasantness. Then the English husband, he say, 'Well, what can you expect? This fellow, he is a nasty piece of work. He lives on foolish women and he does not play the cricket.' Sometimes it is not very nice, but one must live. *Que voulez-vous? Ce n'est pas rigolo que d'être gigolo.*"

Harriet blushed.

"I wasn't thinking that," she said.

"But you were, mademoiselle, and it is very natural."

"Antoine doesn't play cricket," put in Doris, kindly, "but he plays tennis and swims very well."

"It is not me that is in question," said Antoine. "And truly, I cannot understand this business of throat-cutting. It is not reasonable. Why did Alexis go all that distance away? He never walked; he found the walking fatigued him. If he had decided to suicide himself, he would have done it at home."

"And he'd have taken some sleeping-stuff," said Doris, nodding her golden head. "I know that, because he showed it to me once, when he was in one of his blue fits. 'That is my way out of the bad world,' he said, and he talked a lot of poetry. I told him not to be silly—and of course, in half an hour he had got over it. He was like that. But cutting his throat with a razor—no!"

"That's awfully interesting," said Harriet. "By the way," she went on, remembering her conversation with Wimsey, "did he have anything the matter with his skin? I mean, did he always have to wear gloves, or anything of that sort?"

"Oh, no," said Antoine. "The gigolo must not have things the matter with his skin. That would not do at all. Alexis had very elegant hands. He was vain of them."

"He said his skin was sensitive, and that's why he didn't shave," put in Doris.

"Ah, yes! I can tell you about that." Antoine took up his cue. "When he came here about a year ago he asked for a job. Mr. Greely he says to me, 'See him dance.' Because, you see, mademoiselle, the other dancer had just left us, all of a sudden, *comme ça*—without the proper notice. I see him dance and I say to Mr.

Greely, 'That is very good.' The manager say, 'Very well, I take you on trial a little time, but I must not have the beard. The ladies will not like it. It is unheard of, a gigolo with a beard.' Alexis say, 'But if I shave the beard I come out all over buttons.' "

"Pimples," suggested Harriet.

"Yes, pardon, pimples. Well, the gigolo with the pimples, that is unheard of also, you understand. 'Well,' say the manager, 'you can come a little time with the beard till we are suited, but if you want to stay, you remove the beard.' Very well, Alexis come and dance, and the ladies are delighted. The beard is so distinguished, so romantic, so unusual. They come a very long distance express to dance with the beard. Mr. Greely say, 'It is good. I was mistaken. You stay and the beard stay too. My God! What will these ladies want next? The long whiskers, perhaps? Antoine,' he say to me, 'you grow the long whiskers and maybe you get off still better.' But me, no! God has not given me the hair to make whiskers."

"Did Alexis have a razor at all?"

"How should I know? If he knew that the shaving made the pimples, he must have tried to shave, *n'est-ce pas?* But as to the razor, I cannot tell. Do you know, Doris?"

"Me? I like that. Alexis never was my fancy-man. But I'll ask Leila Garland. She ought to know."

"*Sa maîtresse,*" explained Antoine. "Yes, ask her, Doris. Because evidently that is of a considerable importance. I had not thought of that, *mon dieu!*"

"You've told me a lot of interesting things," said Harriet. "I'm very much obliged to you. And I'd be still more obliged if you didn't mention that I'd been asking you, because, what with the newspaper reporters and so on—"

"Oh!" said Antoine. "Listen, mademoiselle, you must not think that because we are the dolls that are bought and sold we have neither eyes nor ears. This gentleman that arrived this morning—do you think we do not know who he is? This Lord Peter, so celebrated, he does not come here for nothing, *hein?* It is not for nothing he talks to you and asks questions. He is not interested because a foreign dancer has cut his throat in a tantrum. No. But, equally, we know how to be discreet. *Ma foi,* if we did not, we should not keep our jobs, you understand. We tell you what we know, and the lady who writes the *romanspoliciers* and the lord who is *connaisseur* in mysteries, they make the investigations. But we say nothing. It is our business to say nothing. That is understood."

"That's right," said Charis. "We won't let on. Not that there's a great deal to tell anybody. We've had the police asking questions, of course, but they never believe anything one says. I'm sure they all think it's something to do with Leila. These policemen always think that if anything happens to a fellow, there must be a girl at the bottom of it."

"But that," said Antoine, "is a compliment."

8

THE EVIDENCE OF THE SECOND BARBER

Send him back again,
An unmasked braggart to his bankrupt den
—*Letter from Göttingen*

SATURDAY, 20 JUNE
SUNDAY, 21 JUNE

"Wimsey, sleek with breakfast, sunshine and sentiment, strolled peacefully upon the close-clipped lawn of the George at Stamford, pausing now and again to inhale the scent of a crimson rose, or to marvel at the age and extent of the wistaria, trailing its lacy tendrils along the grey stone wall. He had covenanted with himself to interview Colonel Belfridge at eleven o'clock. By that time, both of them would have digested their breakfasts and be ready for a small, companionable spot of something. He had a pleasurable interior certainty that he was on the track of a nice, difficult, meaty problem, investigated under agreeable conditions. He lit up a well-seasoned pipe. Life felt good to him.

At ten minutes past eleven, life felt slightly less good. Colonel Belfridge, who looked as though he had been designed by H. M. Bateman in a moment of more than ordinary inspiration, was extremely indignant. It seemed to him that it was an ungentlemanly action to go and interrogate a man's barber, hr'rm, about a man's personal belongings, and he resented the insinuation that a man could possibly be mixed up, hr'rm, in the decease of a damned dago, hr'rm, in an adjectival four-by-three watering-place like Wilvercombe. Wimsey ought to be ashamed, hr'rm, woof! of interfering in what was properly the business of the police, dammit, sir! If the police didn't know their own damned business, what did we pay rates and taxes for, tell me that, sir!

Wimsey apologised for worrying Colonel Belfridge, and protested that a man must take up some sort of hobby.

The Colonel intimated that golf, or hr'rm, breeding spaniels would be a more seemly amusement for a gentleman.

Wimsey said that, having engaged in a spot of intelligence work during the War, he had acquired a kind of a taste for that kind of thing.

The Colonel pounced on this remark immediately, turned Wimsey's war-record inside out, discovered a number of military experiences common to both of them, and presently found himself walking with his visitor down the pansy-edged path of his little garden to display a litter of puppies.

"My dear boy," said Colonel Belfridge, "I shall only be too happy to help you in any way I can. You're not in a hurry, are you? Stay to lunch, and we can talk it over afterwards. Mabel!"—in a stentorian shout.

A middle-aged woman appeared in the back doorway and waddled hastily down the path towards them.

"Gentleman for lunch!" bawled the Colonel. "And decant a bottle of the '04. Carefully now, dammit! I wonder, now," he added, turning to Wimsey, "if you recollect a fellow called Stokes."

It was with very great difficulty that Wimsey detached the Colonel's mind from the events of the Great War and led it back to the subject of razors. Once his attention was captured, however, Colonel Belfridge proved to be a good and reliable witness.

He remembered the pair of razors perfectly. Had a lot of trouble with those razors, hr'rm, woof! Razors were not what they had been in his young days. Nothing was, sir, dammit! Steel wouldn't stand up to the work. What with these damned foreigners and mass-production, our industries were going to the dogs. He remembered, during the Boer War—

Wimsey, after a quarter of an hour, mentioned the subject of razors.

"Ha! yes," said the Colonel, smoothing his vast white moustache down and up at the ends with a vast, curving gesture. 'Ha, hr'rm, yes! The razors, of course. Now, what do you want to know about them?"

"Have you still got them, sir?"

"No, sir, I have not. I got rid of them, sir. A poor lot they were, too. I told Endicott I was surprised at his stocking such inferior stuff. Wanted re-setting every other week. But it's the same story with all of 'em. Can't get a decent blade anywhere nowadays. And we shan't, sir, we shan't, unless we get a strong Conservative Government—I say, a *strong* government, sir, that will have the guts to protect the iron and steel industry. But will they do it? No, damme, sir—they're afraid of losing their miserable votes. Flapper votes! How can you expect a pack of women to understand the importance of iron and steel? Tell me that, ha, hr'rm!"

Wimsey asked what he had done with the razors.

"Gave 'em to the gardener," said the Colonel. "Very decent man. Comes in twice a week. Wife and family. War pensioner with a game leg. Helps with the dogs. Quite a good man. Name of Summers."

"When was that, sir?"

"What? Oh! when did I give 'em to him, you mean. Let me see, now, let me see. That was after Diana had whelped—near thing that—nearly lost her that time, poor bitch. She died two years ago—killed—run over by a damned motorcyclist. Best bitch I ever had. I had him up in court for it—made him pay. Careless young devil. No consideration for anybody. And now they've abolished the speed-limit—"

Wimsey reminded the Colonel that they were talking about razors.

After further consideration, the Colonel narrowed down the period to the year 1926. He was sure about it, because of the spaniel's illness, which had given Summers considerable trouble. He had made the man a present of money, and had added the razors, having just purchased a new pair for himself. Owing to the illness of the mother, only one puppy out of the litter had been successfully reared, and that was Stamford Royal, who had proved a very good dog. A reference to the stud-book clinched the date conclusively.

Wimsey thanked the Colonel, and asked whether he could interview Summers.

By all means. It was not one of Summers' days, but he lived in a little cottage near the bridge. Wimsey could go and see him and mention the Colonel's name. Should the Colonel walk down with Wimsey?

Lord Peter was grateful, but begged the Colonel would not take the trouble. (He felt, indeed, that Summers might be more communicative in Colonel Belfridge's absence.) With some trouble, he disengaged himself from the old soldier's offers of hospitality, and purred away through the picturesque streets of Stamford to the cottage by the bridge.

Summers was an easy man to question—alert, prompt and exact. It was very kind of Colonel Belfridge to give him the razors. He himself could not make use of them, preferring the safety instrument, but of course he had not told the Colonel that, not wishing to hurt his feelings. He had given the razors to his sister's husband, who kept a hairdressing establishment in Seahampton.

Seahampton! Less than 50 miles from Wilvercombe! Had Wimsey struck it lucky with his very first shot? He was turning away, when it occurred to him to ask whether there was any special mark by which either of the razors might be recognized.

Yes, there was. One of them had been accidentally dropped on the stone floor of the cottage and there was a slight, a very slight crack across the ivory. You wouldn't hardly notice it without you looked closely. The other razor was, so far as Summers knew, quite perfect.

Wimsey thanked his informant and rewarded him suitably. He returned to the car and set his course southward. He had always thought Stamford a beautiful town and now, with its grey stone houses and oriel windows bathed in the mellow afternoon sunshine, it seemed to him the loveliest jewel in the English crown.

He slept that night in Seahampton, and on the Sunday morning set forth in search of Summers' brother-in-law, whose name was Merryweather—a name of happy omen. The shop turned out to be a small one, in the neighbourhood of the docks. Mr. Merryweather lived above his premises, and was delighted to give Wimsey information about the razors.

He had had them in 1927, and they were good razors, though they had been badly treated and were considerably worn when they came into his hands. He had one of them still, and it was doing good service. Perhaps his lordship would like to look at it. Here it was.

Wimsey, with a beating heart, turned it over in his hands. It was the exact duplicate of the razor that Harriet had found on the shore. He examined it carefully, but found no crack in the ivory. But what, he asked, almost afraid to put the question for fear of disappointment, what had become of the fellow to it?

"Now that, my lord," said Mr. Merryweather, "I unfortunately cannot show you. Had I known it would be wanted, I certainly would never have parted with it. I sold that razor, my lord, only a few weeks ago, to one of these tramping fellows that came here looking for a job. I had no work for him here, and to tell you the truth, my lord, I wouldn't have given it to him if I had. You'd be surprised, the number of these men who come round, and half of them are no more skilled hairdressers than my tom-cat. Just out for what they can pick up, that's what they are. We generally give them a few razors to set, just to see what they're made of, and the way they set about it, you can tell, nine times out of ten, that they've never set a razor in their lives. Well, this one was like that, and I told him he could push off. Then he asked me if I could sell him a second-hand razor, so I sold him this one to get rid of him. He paid for it and away he went, and that's the last I saw of him."

"What was he like?"

"Oh, a little rat of a fellow. Sandy-haired and too smooth in his manners by half. Not so tall as your lordship, he wasn't, and if I remember rightly he was a bit—not deformed, but what I might call crooked. He might have had one shoulder a trifle higher than the other. Nothing very noticeable, but he gave me that impression. No, he wasn't lame or anything of that kind. Quite spry, he seemed, and quick in his movements. He had rather pale eyes, with sandy eyelashes—an ugly little devil, if you'll excuse me. Very well-kept hands—one notices that, because, of course, when a man asks for a job in this kind of establishment, that's one of the first things one looks for. Dirty or bitten nails, for instance, are what one couldn't stand for for a moment. Let me see, now. Oh, yes—he spoke very well. Spoke like a gentleman, very refined and quiet. That's a thing one notices, too. Not that it's of any great account in a neighbourhood like this. Our customers are sometimes a roughish lot. But one can't help taking notice, you see, when one's been used to it. Besides, it gives one an idea what kind of place a man has been used to."

"Did this man say anything about where he had been employed previously?"

"Not that I remember. My impression of him was that he'd been out of employment for a goodish time, and wasn't too keen on giving details. He said he was on his own. There's plenty of them do that—want you to believe they had their own place in Bond Street and only lost their money through unexampled misfortunes. You know the sort, I expect, my lord. But I didn't pay a lot of attention to the man, not liking the look of him."

"I suppose he gave a name."

"I suppose he did, come to think of it, but I'm dashed if I know now what it was. Henry! What did that sneaking little red-haired fellow that came here the other day say his name was? The man that bought that razor off me?"

Henry, a youth with a crest like a cockatoo, who apparently lodged with his employer, laid aside the Sunday paper which he had been unsuccessfully pretending to read.

"Well, now," he said, "I don't remember, Mr. Merryweather. Some ordinary name. Was it Brown, now? I think it was Brown."

"No, it wasn't," said Mr. Merryweather, suddenly enlightened. "It was Bright, that's what it was. Because don't you remember me saying he didn't act up to his name when it came to setting razors?"

"That's right," said Henry. "Of course. Bright. What's the matter with him? Been getting into trouble?"

"I shouldn't wonder if he had," said Wimsey.

"Police?" suggested Henry, with a sparkling countenance.

"Now, Henry," said Mr. Merryweather. "Does his lordship here look as if he was the police? I'm surprised at you. You'll never make your way in this profession if you don't know better than that."

Henry blushed.

"I'm not the police," said Wimsey, "but I shouldn't be surprised if the police did want to get hold of Mr. Bright one of these days. But don't you say anything about that. Only, if you should happen to see Mr. Bright again, at any time, you might let me know. I'm staying at Wilvercombe at the moment—at the Bellevue—but in case I'm not there, this address will always find me."

He proffered a card, thanked Mr. Merryweather and Henry, and withdrew, triumphant. He felt that he had made progress. Surely there could not be two white Endicott razors, bearing the same evidence of misuse and the same little crack in the ivory. Surely he had tracked the right one, and if so——

Well, then he had only to find Mr. Bright. A tramp-barber with sandy hair and a crooked shoulder ought not to be so very difficult to find. But there was always the disagreeable possibility that Mr. Bright had been a barber for that one performance only. In which case, his name was almost certainly not Bright.

He thought for a moment, then went into a telephone call-box and rang up the Wilvercombe police.

Superintendent Glaisher answered him. He was interested to hear that Wimsey had traced the early history of the razor. He had not personally observed the crack in the ivory, but if his lordship would hold the line for a moment. . . . Hullo! was Wimsey there? . . . Yes, his lordship was quite right. There was a crack. Almost indistinguishable, but it was there. Certainly it was an odd coincidence. It really looked as though it might bear investigation.

Wimsey spoke again.

Yes, by all means. The Seahampton police should be asked to trace Bright. No doubt it would turn out that Alexis had got the razor off Bright, but it was funny that he couldn't have bought one in Wilvercombe if he wanted one. About three weeks ago, was it? Very good. He would see what could be done. He would also find out whether Alexis had been to Seahampton within that period or whether, alternatively, Bright had been seen in Wilvercombe. He was obliged to Lord Peter for the trouble he had taken in the matter, and if his lordship thought of coming back to Wilvercombe, there had been recent developments which might interest him. It was now pretty certain that it was a case of suicide. Still, one had to go into these matters pretty carefully. Had the body been found? No. The body had not come ashore, and the wind was still holding the tide up and making it impossible to undertake any operations off the Grinders.

9

THE EVIDENCE OF
THE FLAT-IRON

Come, tell me now,
How sits this ring?
—*The Brides' Tragedy*

SUNDAY, 21 JUNE

Harriet Vane and Lord Peter Wimsey sat side by side on the beach, looking out towards the Devil's Flat-Iron. The fresh salt wind blew strongly in from the sea, ruffling Harriet's dark hair. The weather was fine, but the sunshine came only in brilliant bursts, as the driven clouds rolled tumultuously across the bellowing vault of the sky. Over the Grinders, the sea broke in furious patches of white. It was about three o'clock in the afternoon, and the tide was at its lowest, but even so, the Flat-Iron was hardly uncovered, and the Atlantic waves, roaring in, made a heavy breach against its foot. A basket of food lay between the pair, not yet unpacked. Wimsey was drawing plans in the damp sand.

"The thing we want to get," he said, "is the time of the death. The police are quite clear about how Alexis came here, and there doesn't seem to be any doubt in the matter, which is a blessing. There's a train from Wilvercombe that stops at Darley Halt on Thursdays at 10.15, to take people in to Heathbury market. Alexis travelled by that train and got out at the Halt. I think it must have been Alexis all right. He was pretty conspicuous with his black beard and his natty gent's outfitting. I think we can take that bit as proved. The guard on the train remembered him, and so did three or four of his fellow-travellers. What's more, his landlady says he left his rooms in time to catch the train, and the booking-clerk remembers him at Wilvercombe. *And*, dear Harriet, there is a first return-ticket from Wilvercombe to the Halt that was never given up and never accounted for."

"A return-ticket?" asked Harriet.

"A return-ticket. And that, as you so acutely remark, Sherlock, seems to knock the suicide theory on the head. I said as much to the Super, and what was his reply? That suicides, let alone foreign suicides, were that inconsistent there was no accounting for them."

"So they may be, in real life," observed Harriet, thoughtfully. "One wouldn't make an intending suicide take a return-ticket in a book, but real people are different. It might have been a slip, or just habit—or he may not have quite made up his mind to the suicide business."

"I thought my friend Chief Inspector Parker was the most cautious beggar on the face of the earth, but you beat him. You can knock out habit. I refuse to believe that our dainty Alexis made a habit of travelling to the Halt in order to walk four and a half miles to weep by the sad sea waves. However, we'll just note the return half of the ticket as something that needs explainin'. Very good. Well, now, there was nobody else got off at the Halt, though quite a bunch of people got in, so we don't know what happened to Alexis; but if we allow that we could walk at the moderate rate of three miles an hour, he can't have got to the Flat-Iron later than, say, 11.45."

"Stop a minute. How about the tide? When was low water on Thursday?"

"At 1.15. I've been into all that. At 11.45 there would be about five feet of water at the foot of the Flat-Iron, but the rock is ten feet high, and rises gradually from the landward side. At 11.45, or very shortly after, our friend could have walked out dry-shod to the rock and sat upon it.

"Good. We know he did go out dry-shod, so that all fits in nicely. What next?"

"Well, what? Whether he cuts his own throat or somebody cut it for him, when did he die? It's an awful pity we've lost the body. Even if it turns up now, it won't tell us a thing. It wasn't stiff, of course, when you saw it, and you say you can't tell if it was cold."

"If," said Harriet, "there had been a block of ice on that rock at that time, you could have boiled eggs on it."

"Tiresome, tiresome. Wait a minute. The blood. How about that? Did you notice whether it was in thick red clots, or whether it was a sort of jelly of white serum, with the red part at the bottom, or anything?"

Harriet shook her head.

"It wasn't. It was liquid."

"It was what?"

"Liquid. When I put my hand into it, it was quite wet."

"Great Scott! Half a sec. Where was the blood? Splashed all over the place, I suppose."

"Not exactly. There was a big pool of it underneath the body—just as though he had leaned over and cut his throat into a basin. It had collected in a sort of hollow in the rock."

"Oh, I see. That explains it. I expect the hollow was full of sea-water left by the tide, and what looked like blood was a mixture of blood and water. I began to think—"

"But listen! It was quite liquid everywhere. It dripped out of his neck. And when I lifted his head up and disturbed the body, it dripped some more. Horrid!"

"But, my darling girl—"

"Yes, and listen again! When I tried to take his glove off, the leather wasn't stiff—it was soft and wet. His hand had been lying right under his throat."

"Good lord! But—"

"That was the left hand. The right hand was hanging over the side of the rock and I couldn't get at it without clambering over him, which I didn't fancy, somehow. Otherwise, I should have tried that. I was wondering, you see, why the gloves?"

"Yes, yes, I know. But we know there was nothing wrong with his hands. That doesn't matter now. It's the blood—do you realise that, if the blood was still liquid, he *can* only have been dead a few minutes?"

"Oh!" Harriet paused in consternation. "What a fool I am! I *ought* to have known that. And I thought I was deducing things so nicely! He couldn't have been bleeding slowly to death for some time, I suppose?"

"With his throat cut to the neck-bone? Dear child, pull yourself together. Look here. Blood clots very quickly—more quickly, of course, on a cold surface. In the ordinary way it will clot almost instantaneously on exposure to the air. I daresay it might take a little longer on a hot surface like the rock you describe so graphically. But it couldn't take more than a few minutes. Say ten, to give it an outside limit."

"Ten minutes. Oh, Peter!"

"Yes?"

"That noise that woke me up. I thought it was a sea-gull. They sound so human. But suppose it was—"

"It must have been. When was that?"

"Two o'clock. I looked at my watch. And I shouldn't think it took me more than ten minutes to reach the rock. But—I say!"

"Well?"

"How about your murder-theory? That's done it in absolutely. If Alexis was murdered at two o'clock, and I was there ten minutes after—*what became of the murderer?*"

Wimsey sat up as suddenly as though he had been stung.

"Oh, *hell!*" he exclaimed. "Harriet; dear, sweet, beautiful Harriet, say you were mistaken. We *can't* be wrong about the murder. I've staked my reputation with Inspector Umpelty that it couldn't have been suicide. I shall have to leave the country. I shall never hold my head up again. I shall have to go and shoot tigers in fever-haunted jungles, and die, babbling of murder between my swollen and blackened lips. Say that the blood was clotted. Or say there were footprints you overlooked. Or that there was a boat within hail. Say something."

"There *was* a boat, but not within hail; because I hailed it."

"Thank God there was a boat! Perhaps I may leave my bones in Old England yet. What do you mean, not within hail because you hailed it? If the murderer was in the boat, naturally he wouldn't have put back if it had hailed sweet potatoes. I wish you wouldn't give me such shocks. My nerves are not what they were."

"I don't know much about boats, but this one looked to me a pretty good way out. The wind was blowing inshore, you know."

"It doesn't matter. So long as there was a good stiff wind, and he could sail close enough to it, he might have made quite a good way in ten minutes. What sort of boat was it?"

Here Harriet's knowledge failed her. She had put it down as a fishing-boat— not because she could scientifically distinguish a fishing-boat from a 5-metre yacht, but because one naturally, when visiting the seaside, puts down all boats as fishing-boats until otherwise instructed. She thought it had a pointed sort of sail—or sails—she couldn't be sure. She was sure it was not, for example, a fully rigged four-masted schooner, but otherwise one sailing-boat was to her exactly like any other; as it is to most town-bred persons, especially to literary young women.

"Never mind," said Wimsey. "We'll be able to trace it all right. All boats must come to shore somewhere, thank goodness. And they're all well known to people along the coast. I only wanted to know what sort of draught the boat was likely to have. You see, if the boat couldn't come right in to the rock, the fellow would have had to row himself in, or swim for it, and that would delay him a good bit. And he'd have to have somebody standing on and off with the boat while he did it, unless he stopped to take in sail, and all that. I mean, you can't just stop a sailing boat and step out of it like a motorcar, leaving it on its own all ready to start. You'd get into difficulties. But that makes no odds. Why shouldn't the murderer have an accomplice? It has frequently happened before. We'd better assume that there were at least two men in a small boat with a very light draught. Then they could bring her close in, and one of the men would bring her round to the wind, while the other waded or rowed alone, did the murder and got back, so that they could make off again without wasting a moment. You see, they've got to do the murder, get back to the boat and clear out to where you saw them within the ten minutes between the cry you heard and the time of your arrival. So we can't allow a lot of time for pulling the boat to shore and making fast and pushing off again and setting sail and all that. Hence I suggest the accomplice."

"But how about the Grinders?" asked Harriet, rather diffidently. "I thought it was very dangerous to bring boats close to shore at that point."

"Blow it! So it is. Well, they must have been very skillful sailors. Or else have come ashore rather further along the bay. But *that* would mean further to row or wade, as the case may be. Bother it! I wish we could allow them rather more time."

"You don't think—" began Harriet. A very unpleasant idea had just struck her. "You don't think the murderer could have been there, quite close, all the time, swimming under water, or something?"

"He'd have had to come up to breathe."

"Yes, but I might not have noticed him. There were lots of times when I wasn't looking at the sea at all. He would have heard me coming, and he might have ducked down close under the rock and waited there till I came down to look for the razor. Then he might have dived and swum away while my back was turned. I don't know if it's possible, and I hope it isn't, because I should hate to think he was there all the time—watching me!"

"It's a nasty thought," said Wimsey. "I rather hope he was there, though. It would give him a beast of a shock to see you hopping round taking photographs and things. I wonder if there is any cleft in the Flat-Iron where he might have hidden himself. Curse the rock! Why can't it come out and show itself like a man? I say, I'm going down to have a look at it. Turn your modest eyes seawards till I have climbed into a bathingsuit, and I'll go down and explore."

Not content with this programme, unsuited to a person of her active temperament, Harriet removed, not only her glance, but her person, to the shelter of a handy rock, and emerged, bathing-suited, in time to catch Wimsey as he ran down over the sand.

"And he strips better than I should have expected," she admitted candidly to herself. "Better shoulders than I realised, and, thank Heaven, calves to his legs." Wimsey, who was rather proud of his figure, would hardly have been flattered could he have heard this modified rapture, but for the moment he was happily unconcerned about himself. He entered the sea near the Flat-Iron with caution, not knowing what bumps and boulders he might encounter, swam a few strokes to encourage himself, and then popped his head out to remark that the water was beastly cold and that it would do Harriet good to come in.

Harriet came in, and agreed that the water was cold and the wind icy. Agreed on this point, they returned to the Flat-Iron, and felt their way carefully round it. Presently Wimsey, who had been doing some under-water investigation on the Wilvercombe side of the rock, came out, spluttering, and asked if Harriet had come down on that side or on the other to hunt for the razor.

"On the other," said Harriet. "It was like this. I was up on top of the rock with the body, like this." She climbed out, walked up to the top of the rock, and stood shivering in the wind. "I looked round on both sides of me like this."

"You didn't look down in this direction, by any chance?" inquired Wimsey's head, standing up sleek as a seal's out of the water.

"No, I don't think so. Then, after I'd fussed about with the corpse a bit, I got down this way. I sat on something just about here and took my shoes and stockings off and tucked my things up. Then I came round in this direction and groped about under the rock. There was about eighteen inches of water then. There are about five feet now, I should think."

"Can you—?" began Wimsey. A wave slapped suddenly over his head and extinguished him. Harriet laughed.

"Can you see me?" he went on, blowing the water out of his nostrils.

"I can't. But I heard you. It was very amusing."

"Well, restrain your sense of humour. You can't see me."

"No. There's a bulge in the rock. Where, exactly, are you, by the way?"

"Standing in a nice little niche, like a saint over a cathedral door. It's just about the size of a coffin. Six feet high or thereabouts, with a pretty little roof and room to squeeze in rather tightly sideways, if you're not what the Leopard called 'too vulgar big.' Come round and try it for yourself."

"What a sweet little spot," said Harriet, scrambling round and taking Wimsey's place in the niche. "Beautifully screened from all sides, except from the sea. Even at quite low tide one couldn't be seen, unless, of course, somebody happened to come round and stand just opposite the opening. I certainly didn't do that. How horrible! The man must have been in here all the time."

"Yes, I think it's more plausible than the boat idea."

"Bright!" said Harriet.

"I'm so glad you think so."

"I didn't mean that—and it was my idea in the first place. I meant Bright, the man who bought the razor. Didn't the hairdresser person say he was a small man —smaller than you, anyway?"

"So he did. One up to you. I wish we could get hold of Bright. I wonder—Oh, I say! I've found something!"

"Oh, what?"

"It's a ring—the sort of thing you tie boats up to, driven right into the rock. It's under water and I can't see it properly, but it's about five feet off the ground and it feels smooth and new, not corroded. Does that help with our boat-theory at all, I wonder?"

"Well," said Harriet, looking round at the lonely sea and shore, "there doesn't seem to be much reason why anyone should habitually tie a boat up here."

"There doesn't. In that case the murderer, if there was one—"

"We're taking him for granted, aren't we?"

"Yes. He may have put this here for his own private use. Either he tied a boat up, or he—"

"Or he didn't."

"I was going to say, used it for something else, but I'm dashed if I know what."

"Well, that's fearfully helpful. I say, I'm getting cold. Let's swim about a bit, and then get dressed and discuss it."

Whether it was the swim or the subsequent race over the sands to get warm that stimulated Harriet's brain is not certain, but when they were again sitting by the lunch-basket, she found herself full of ideas.

"Look here! If you were a murderer, and you saw an interfering woman pottering about among the evidence and then going off in search of help, what would you do?"

"Leg it in the opposite direction."

"I wonder. Would you? Wouldn't you like to keep an eye on her? Or possibly even do away with her? You know, it would have been fearfully easy for Bright— if we may call him so for the moment—to slaughter me then and there?"

"But why should he? Of course he wouldn't. He was trying to make the murder look like suicide. In fact, you were a very valuable witness for him. You'd seen the body and you could prove that there really was a body, in case of its subsequently getting lost. And you could prove that there actually was a weapon there and that therefore suicide was more likely than not. And you could swear to the absence of footprints—another point in favour of suicide. No, my dear girl, the murderer would cherish you as the apple of his eye."

"You're right; he would. Always supposing he wanted the body found. Of course there are lots of reasons why he should want it found. If he inherited under a will, for instance, and had to prove the death."

"I don't fancy friend Alexis will have left much in his will. In fact, I'm pretty sure he didn't. And there might be other reasons for wanting to tell the world he was dead."

"Then you think that when I'd gone, the murderer just trotted off home to Lesston Hoe? He can't have gone the other way, unless he deliberately kept behind me. Do you think he did that? He may have followed me up to see what I was going to do about it."

"He might. You can't say he didn't. Especially as you left the main road quite soon after, to go up to the farm."

"Suppose he missed me there and went on ahead of me along the road to Wilvercombe. Would it be possible to find out if he had passed over the level-crossing at the Halt, for instance? Or—I say! Suppose he'd gone along the main road and then turned back again, so as to pretend he'd come from Wilvercombe?"

"Then you'd have met him."

"Well, suppose I did?"

"But—oh! lord, yes—Mr. What's-his-name from London! By Jove!"

"Perkins. Yes. I wonder. Could anybody be genuinely as foolish as Perkins appeared? He was a rat of a man, too, quite small, and he *was* sandy-haired."

"He was short-sighted, didn't you say, and wore glasses. Merryweather didn't say anything about Bright's wearing them."

"It may have been a disguise. They may have been quite plain glass—I didn't examine them, à la Dr. Thorndyke, to see whether they reflected a candle-flame upside-down or right way up. And, you know, I do think it's awfully funny the way Mr. Perkins simply evaporated when we got to the village shop. He was keen enough to come with me before, and then, just as I'd got into touch with civilisation, he went and vanished. It does look queer. If it was Bright, he might just have hung round to get some idea of what I was going to say to the police, and then removed himself before the inquiry. Good lord! Fancy me, meekly trotting along for a mile and a half hand in hand with a murderer!"

"Juicy," said Wimsey, "very juicy! We'll have to look more carefully into Mr. Perkins. (Can that name be real? It seems almost too suitable.) You know where he went?"

"No."

"He hired a car in the village and got himself driven to Wilvercombe railway station. He is thought to have taken a train to somewhere, but the place was full of hikers and trampers and trippers that day, and so far they haven't traced him further. They'll have to try again. This thing is getting to look almost too neat. Let's see how it goes. First of all, Alexis arrives by the 10.15 at the Halt and proceeds, on foot or otherwise, to the Flat-Iron. Why, by the way?"

"To keep an appointment with Perkins, presumably. Alexis wasn't the sort to take a long country walk for the intoxicating pleasure of sitting on a rock."

"True, O Queen. Live for ever. He went to keep an appointment with Perkins at two o'clock."

"Earlier, surely; or why arrive by the 10.15?"

"That's easy. The 10.15 is the only train that stops there during the morning."

"Then why not go by car?"

"Yes, indeed. Why not? I imagine it was because he had no car of his own and didn't want anybody to know where he was going."

"Then why didn't he hire a car and drive it himself?"

"Couldn't drive a car. Or his credit was bad in Wilvercombe. Or—no!"

"What?"

"I was going to say: because he didn't intend to come back. But that won't work, because of the return-ticket. Unless he took the ticket absentmindedly, he *did* mean to come back. Or perhaps he just wasn't certain about it. He might take a return-ticket on the off-chance—it would only be a matter of a few pence one way or the other. But he couldn't very well just take a hired car and leave it there."

"N-no. Well, he could, if he wasn't particular about other people's property. But I can think of another reason for it. He'd have to leave the car on top of the cliff where it could be seen. Perhaps he didn't want people to know that anybody was down on the Flat-Iron at all."

"That won't do. Two people having a chat on the Flat-Iron would be conspicuous objects from the cliff, car or no car."

"Yes, but unless you went down close to them, you wouldn't know who they were; whereas you can always check up on a car by the number-plates."

"That's a fact—but it seems to me rather a thin explanation, all the same. Still, let it stand. For some reason Alexis thought he would attract less attention if he went by train. In that case, I suppose he walked along the road—he wouldn't want to invite inquiry by taking a lift from anybody."

"Certainly not. Only why in the world he should have picked on such an exposed place for the appointment—"

"You think they ought to have had their chat behind a rock, or under some trees, or in a disused shed or a chalk quarry or something like that?"

"Wouldn't it seem more natural?"

"No. Not if you didn't want to be overheard. If you ever need to talk secrets, be sure you avoid the blasted oak, the privet hedge and the old summer-house in the Italian garden—all the places where people can stealthily creep up under cover with their ears flapping. You choose the middle of a nice open field, or the centre of a lake—or a rock like the Flat-Iron, where you can have half-an-hour's notice of anyone's arrival. And that reminds me, in one of your books—"

"Bother my books! I quite see what you mean. Well, then, some time or the other, Bright arrives to keep his appointment. How? And when?"

"By walking through the edge of the water, from any point you like to suggest. As for the time, I can only suggest that it was while you, my child, were snoozing over *Tristram Shandy*; and I fancy he must have come from the Wilvercombe side, otherwise he would have seen you. He'd hardly have taken the risk of committing a murder if he knew positively that somebody was lying within a few yards of him."

"I think it was pretty careless of him not to take a look round the rocks in any case."

"True; but apparently he didn't do it. He commits the murder, anyhow, and the time of that is fixed at two o'clock. So he must have reached the Flat-Iron between 1.30 and 2—or possibly between one o'clock and two o'clock—because, if you were lunching and reading in your cosy corner, you probably wouldn't have seen or heard him come. It couldn't be earlier than 1 p.m., because you looked along the shore then and were positive that there wasn't a living soul visible from the cliffs."

"Quite right."

"Good. He commits the murder. Poor old Alexis lets out a yell when he sees the razor, and you wake up. Did you shout then, or anything?"

"No."

"Or burst into song?"

"No."

"Or run about with little ripples of girlish laughter?"

"No. At least, I ran about a few minutes later, but I wasn't making a loud noise."

"I wonder why the murderer didn't start off home again at once. If he had, you'd have seen him. Let me see. Ah, I was forgetting the papers! He had to get the papers!"

"What papers?"

"Well, I won't swear it was papers. It may have been the Rajah's diamond or something. He wanted something off the body, of course. And just as he was stooping over his victim, he heard you skipping about among the shingle. Sound carries a long way by the water. The baffled villain pauses, and then, as the sounds come nearer, he hurries down to the seaward side of the Flat-Iron and hides there."

"With all his clothes on?"

"I'd forgotten that. He'd be a bit damp-looking when he came out, wouldn't he? No. Without his clothes on. He left his clothes at wherever it was he started to walk along the shore. He probably put on a bathing-dress, so that if anybody saw him he would just be a harmless sun-bather paddling about in the surf."

"Did he put the razor in the pocket of his regulation suit?"

"No; he had it in his hand, or slung round his neck. Don't ask silly questions. He'd wait in his little niche until you'd gone; then he'd hurry back along the shore—"

"Not in the direction of Wilvercombe."

"Blow! Obviously, you'd have seen him. But not if he kept close to the cliff. He wouldn't have to bother so much about footprints when the tide was coming in. He could manage that all right. Then he'd come up the cliff at the point where he originally got down, follow the main road towards Wilvercombe, turn back at some point or other, and meet you on the way back. How's that?"

"It's very neat."

"The more I look at it, the more I like it. I adore the thought of Bright's being Perkins. I say, though, how about this lop-sided, hunch-backed business. Was Perkins upright as a willow-wand, or how?"

"Not by any means. But I shouldn't have called him actually crooked. More sloppy and round-shouldered. He had a rucksack on his back, and he was walking a bit lame, because he said he had a blister on his foot."

"That would be a good way of disguising any one-sidedness in his appearance. You're always apt to hunch up a bit on the lame side. Bright-Perkins is our man. We ought to get the police on to this right away, only I do so want my lunch. What time is it? *Four* o'clock. I'll slip along in the car and telephone to Glaisher, and then come back. Why should we give up our picnic for any number of murderers?"

10

THE EVIDENCE OF THE POLICE-INSPECTOR

My life upon 't some miser,
Who in the secret hour creeps to his hoard,
And, kneeling at the altar of his love,
Worships that yellow devil, gold.
—*The Brides' Tragedy*

MONDAY, 22 JUNE

"**Y**ou may say what you like, my lord," said Inspector Umpelty, "and I don't mind admitting that the Super is a bit inclined to your way of thinking, but it was suicide for all that, and if I was a sporting man, I wouldn't mind having a bit on it. There's no harm done by tracing this fellow Bright, because, if the identification of the razor is correct, that's who this Alexis must have bought it from, but there's no doubt in my mind that when the poor chap left his lodgings on Thursday, he never meant to come back. You've only got to look at the place. Everything tidied away, bills all paid up, papers burnt in the grate—you might say he'd regular said good-bye and kissed his hand to everything."

"Did he take his latch-key with him?" asked Wimsey.

"Yes, he did. But that's nothing. A man keeps his key in his pocket and he mightn't think to put it out. But he left pretty well everything else in order. You'd be surprised. Not so much as an envelope, there wasn't. Must have had a regular old bonfire there. Not a photograph, not a line that would tell you anything about who he was or where he came from. Clean sweep of the lot."

"No hope of recovering anything from the ashes?"

"Not a thing. Naturally, Mrs. Lefranc—that's the landlady—had had the grate cleaned out on the Thursday morning, but she told me that everything had been broken down into black flinders and dust. And there was a rare old lot of it. I know, because she showed it me in the dust-bin. There certainly was nothing there you could have made out with a microscope. As you know, my lord, generally these folk aren't thorough—they leave a few bits half-burnt, maybe, but this chap had gone the right way about it and no mistake. He must have torn everything into small scraps first, and burnt it on a hot fire and beaten it into atoms with the poker. 'Well,' I said to Mrs. Lefranc, 'this is a nice set-out, this is!' And so it was, too."

"Any books or anything with writing in the fly-leaves?"

"Just a few novels, with 'Paul Alexis' inside, and some with nothing at all, and one or two paper-backed books written in Chinese."

"Chinese?"

"Well, it looked like it. Russian, maybe. Not in proper letters, anyhow. You can see them any time you like, but I don't expect you'll get much out of them. One or two history books there was, mostly about Russia and that. But no writing of any kind."

"Any money?"

"No."

"Had he a banking account?"

"Yes; he had a small account with Lloyds. Matter of a little over three hundred pounds. But he drew the whole lot out three weeks ago."

"Did he? Whatever for? It wouldn't cost him all that to buy a razor."

"No, but I said he'd been settling his debts."

"Three hundred pounds worth of them?"

"I don't say that. Fact is we can't trace more than twenty pounds odd. But he may have owed money in lots of places. As he's burnt all his papers, you see, it's a bit difficult to tell. We shall make inquiries, naturally. But I shouldn't be surprised if those three hundred pounds had gone to some girl or other. There's that Leila Garland—a hard-boiled little piece if ever there was one. *She* could tell a lot if she liked, I daresay, but we aren't allowed to ask anybody any questions these days. If they say they won't answer, they won't and there's an end of it. You can't force 'em."

"Leila Garland—that's the girl he used to go with?"

"That's it, my lord, and from what I can make out she turn d Mister Alexis down good and hard. Terrible cut up he was about it, too, according to her. She's got another fellow now—sort of friend of Alexis, but a cut above him, as far as I can make out. Sort of dago fellow; leads the orchestra down at the Winter Gardens, and makes a pretty good thing out of it, I fancy. You know the sort, all la-di-dah and snake-skin shoes. Nothing wrong with him, though, as far as that goes. He was quite frank about it, and so was the girl. Alexis introduced them, and presently the young woman got the idea that she could do better with the dago than with Alexis. She says Alexis was getting very close with his money, and didn't seem to have his mind as much on Miss Leila as he might have. Possibly he had his eye on somebody else all the time and that was where the money went. Anyhow, Leila makes up her mind to give him the push and takes up with the dago, Luis da Soto, instead. Of course there was a scene, and Alexis threatens to make away with himself—"

"Did he say anything about throat-cutting?"

"Well, no, he didn't. Said he'd take poison. But what's the odds? He said he'd make away with himself and he's done it, and here we are."

"Did you, by any chance, find any poison—you know, sleepy stuff or anything of that sort—in his room?"

"Not a thing," said the Inspector, triumphantly.

"H'm."

"But Inspector," put in Harriet, who had been listening to this conversation in becoming silence, "if you think Alexis had another girl in tow, why should he commit suicide when Leila Garland turned him down?"

"I couldn't say, I'm sure, miss. Maybe the other one turned him down as well."

"And left him a low, lorn crittur, with all the world contrairy with him," said Wimsey.

"Yes, and then there was this Mrs. Weldon. We found out about her through these other girls. Wouldn't you say a prospect like that was enough to make any young fellow cut his throat?"

"He could have gone away," said Harriet.

"And suppose he owed her money and she turned crusty and threatened to put him in court? What about that?"

"Perhaps the three hundred pounds—" began Wimsey.

"Oh, no, *no!*" cried Harriet indignantly. "You mustn't think that. It's absolutely ridiculous. Why, the poor woman was infatuated with him. He could have turned her round his little finger. She'd have given him anything he wanted. Besides, she told me he wouldn't take her money."

"Ah! But supposing he'd have given her the go-by, miss. She might have cut up rough about that."

"*She* would have been the one to kill herself then," said Harriet, firmly. "She wouldn't have harmed him for the world, poor soul. Put him in court? Nonsense!"

"Now you know very well, miss," said Inspector Umpelty, "that it says in the Bible that the infernal regions, begging your pardon, knows no fury like a woman scorned. I've always remembered that from my school-days, and I find it gives a very useful line to follow in our way of business. If this Mrs. Weldon—"

"Rubbish!" said Harriet. "She'd never have done anything of the sort. I *know* she wouldn't."

"Ah!" Inspector Umpelty winked in a friendly manner at Wimsey. "When the ladies get to knowing things by this feminine intuition and all that, there's no arguing with it. But what I say is, let's suppose it, just for the moment."

"I won't suppose it," retorted Harriet.

"We seem to have reached a no-thoroughfare," remarked Wimsey. "Let's leave that for the time being, Inspector. You can come and suppose it in the bar, quietly, later on. Though I don't think it very likely myself. It's our turn to suppose something. Suppose a fishing-boat had wanted to come in at the Flat-Iron just about low tide on Thursday—could she do it?"

"Easy, my lord. Some of these boats don't draw more than a foot of water. You could bring her in beautifully, provided you kept clear of the Grinders, and remembered to reckon with the current."

"A stranger might get into difficulties, perhaps."

"He might, but not if he was a good seaman and could read a chart. He could bring a small boat up within a dozen feet of the Flat-Iron any day, unless the wind was setting with the current across the bay, when he might get driven on to the rocks if he wasn't careful."

"I see. That makes it all very interesting. We are supposing a murder, you see, Inspector, and we've thought out two ways of doing it. We'd be glad to have your opinion."

Inspector Umpelty listened with an indulgent smile to the rival theories of the Man in the Fishing-boat and the Man in the Niche, and then said:

"Well, miss, all I can say is, I'd like to read some of those books of yours. It's wonderful, the way you work it all in. But about that boat. That's queer, that is. We've been trying to get a line on that, because whoever was in it must have seen something. Most of the fishing-boats were out off Shelly Point, but there's a few of them I haven't checked up on, and of course, it might be some of the visitors from Wilvercombe or Lesston Hoe. We're always warning these amateurs to keep away from the Grinders, but do they? No. You'd think some of them was out for a day's suicide, the way they go on. But I've got an idea who it was, all the same."

"How about these cottages along the coast, where I went to try and get help?" asked Harriet. "Surely they must have seen the boat? I thought those sort of people knew every boat in the place by sight."

"That's just it," replied the Inspector. "We've asked them and they're all struck blind and dumb, seemingly. That's why I say I think I could put a name to the boat. But we'll find a way to make them come across with it, never fear. They're a surly lot, those Pollocks and Moggeridges, and up to no good, in my opinion. They're not popular with the other fishers, and when you find a whole family boycotted by the rest of them, there's usually something at the back of it."

"At any rate," said Wimsey, "I think we've got the actual time of the death pretty well fixed by now. That ought to help."

"Yes," admitted Inspector Umpelty, "if what you and the lady tell me is correct, that does seem to settle it. Not but what I'd like a doctor's opinion on it, no offence to you. But I think you're right, all the same. It's a great pity you happened to fall asleep when you did, miss." He looked reproachfully at Harriet.

"But wasn't it lucky I was there at all?"

The Inspector agreed that it was.

"And taking this question of the time as settled," he went on, "we've got some information to hand now that may clear matters up a bit. At least, from all I can see, it just goes to show that this murder-stuff is clean impossible, as I've said it was all along. But if we prove that, then we're all right, aren't we?"

The conference was taking place in the Inspector's cosy little villa in the suburbs of the town. Rising, Mr. Umpelty went to a cupboard and extracted a large sheaf of official reports.

"You see, my lord, we haven't been idle, even though suicide looks more probable than anything else on the face of things. We had to take all the possibilities into account, and we've gone over the district with, as you might say, a magnifying glass."

After an inspection of the reports, Wimsey was obliged to admit that this boast seemed justified. Chance had helped the police very considerably. An application had recently been made by the local authorities to the County Council to have the coast-road between Lesston Hoe and Wilvercombe put into better repair. The County Council, conscious that times were bad and that money was tight, had courteously replied that it did not think there was sufficient traffic along the said coast-road to justify the proposed expenditure. As a result of these negotiations, persons had been appointed (at a modest wage) by the County Council to take a census of the vehicular traffic passing along the said road, and one of these watchers had been stationed, during the whole of Thursday, 18 June, at the junction formed by the coast-road and the high road from Lesston Hoe to Heathbury. At the other end of the twelve miles or so which interested the detectives was Darley Halt, where, as Harriet had already discovered for herself, the gates were always shut unless particularly summoned to be opened for a passing vehicle. On either side of the railway gates was a wicket for foot passengers, but this was of the kind that does not admit anything so large even as a push-cycle. It was clear, therefore, that unless the hypothetical murderer had come on foot, he must have been seen at one end or other of the road, or else have come from some intermediate farm. During the past four days, the police had carefully investigated the bona fides of every traveller over this section of the road. Every car, motorcycle, push-cycle, van, lorry, wagon and beast had been laboriously checked up and accounted for. Nothing had been unearthed to suggest suspicion of any kind. Indeed, all the persons using the road were local inhabitants, well known to all the police officers, and each one of them had been able to give an exact account of his or her movements during the day. This was not so surprising as it may appear, since nearly all of them were either tradesmen, accomplishing a given round in a given time, or farmers with business on their land or in the adjacent towns, who had witnesses to prove their departure and arrival. The only persons whose times could not very well be checked were those who loitered attendance upon cows and sheep in transit; but, apart from the extreme improbability of these rustics having gone out of their way to cut a gentleman's throat with an Endicott razor, Inspector Umpelty was quite ready to vouch personally for all of them.

"In fact, my lord," he said, "you may take it from me that all these people we have checked up are all right. You can put them right out of your mind. The only possibility left now for your murderer is that he came by sea, or else on foot along the shore from either Wilvercombe or Lesston Hoe, and, as this young lady says, Wilvercombe is the more probable direction of the two, because anybody coming from Lesston Hoe would have seen her and put his crime off to a more convenient season, as Shakespeare says."

"Very well," said Wimsey. "All right. We'll admit that. The murderer didn't take any sort of wheeled conveyance for any part of the journey. Still, that leaves a lot of possibilities open. We'll wash out the Lesston Hoe side altogether and only take the Wilvercombe direction. We now have at least three suggestions. One: the murderer walked by the road from Wilvercombe or Darley, came down on to the beach at some point out of view from the Flat-Iron, and thence proceeded by the shore. Two: he came from one of those two cottages where the fishermen live (Pollock and Moggeridge, I think you said the names were). You don't mean to say you'll answer personally for those men, do you, Inspector?"

"No, I don't—only they weren't there," retorted the Inspector, with spirit. "Moggeridge and his two sons were over in Wilvercombe, buying some stuff there—I've got witnesses to that. Old Pollock was out in his boat, because

Freddy Baines saw him, and his eldest boy was probably with him. We're going to pull those two in, and that's why I said the murderer might have come by sea. The only other Pollock is a boy of about fourteen, and you can't suppose it was him that did it, nor yet any of the women and children."

"I see. Well then. Three: the murderer walked the whole way along the coast from Darley or Wilvercombe. By the way, didn't you say there was somebody camping out along there, just beyond Darley Halt."

"Yes," said Harriet, "a square-built sort of man, who spoke—well, not quite like a countryman—like a gentleman of the country sort."

"If anybody had passed that way, he might have seen him."

"So he might," replied the Inspector, "but unfortunately we haven't laid hands on that particular gentleman, though we've got inquiries out after him. He packed up and departed early on Friday morning, taking his belongings in a Morgan. He'd been camping at the bottom of Hinks's Lane since Tuesday, and gave the name of Martin."

"Is that so? And he disappeared immediately after the crime. Isn't that a trifle suspicious?"

"Not a bit." Inspector Umpelty was quite triumphant. "He was having his lunch at the Three Feathers in Darley at one o'clock and he didn't leave till 1.30. If you'll tell me how a man could walk four and a half miles in half-an-hour, I'll get a warrant made out for Mr. Martin's arrest."

"Your trick, Inspector. Well—let's see. Murder at two o'clock—four and a half miles to go. That means that the murderer can't have passed through Darley later than 12.50 at the very outside. That's allowing him to do four miles an hour, and since he would have to do at least part of the distance along the sand it's probably an over-estimate. On the other hand, he wouldn't be likely to do less than three miles an hour. That gives 12.30 as his earliest time—unless, of course, he sat and talked to Alexis for some time before he cut his throat."

"That's just it, my lord. It's all so vague. In any case, Mr. Martin isn't much good to us, because he spent Thursday morning in Wilvercombe—or so he mentioned to the landlord of the Feathers."

"What a pity! He might have been a valuable witness. I suppose you'll go on looking for him, though it doesn't seem as if he'd be very much good to us. Did anybody notice the number of his Morgan?"

"Yes; it belongs to a London garage, where they hire out cars to be driven by the hirer. Mr. Martin came in there last Thursday week, paid his deposit in cash and returned the 'bus on Sunday night. He said he had given up his house and had no fixed address, but gave a reference to a Cambridge banker. His driving-licence was made out in the name of Martin all right. There was no trouble about the insurance, because the garage uses a form of policy that covers all their cars irrespective of who is driving them."

"But wasn't there an address on the driving-licence?"

"Yes; but that was the address of the house he'd given up, so they took no notice of that."

"Do garage-owners usually ask to see people's driving-licences?"

"I don't know that they do. Apparently this fellow showed it to them without being asked."

"Curious. You'd almost think he was going out of his way to forestall criticism. How about the bank?"

"That's all right. Mr. Haviland Martin has been a depositor there for five years. Introduced by another client. No irregularity."

"I suppose they didn't mention the name of his referee nor the amount of his deposit."

"Well, no. Banks don't care about giving away information. You see, we've absolutely nothing against this fellow Martin."

"Exactly. All the same, I'd rather like to have a chat with him. There are points about him which seem to me suggestive, as Sherlock Holmes would say. What do *you* think, my dear Robert Templeton?"

"I think," replied Harriet, promptly, "that if I had been inventing a way for a murderer to reach an appointed spot and leave it again, complete with bag and baggage and without leaving more trail than was absolutely unavoidable, I should have made him act very much as Mr. Martin has acted. He would open an account under a false name at a bank, give the bank's address to the garage-proprietor as sole reference, hire a car and pay cash and probably close the account again in the near future."

"As you say. Still, the dismal fact remains that Mr. Martin obviously did not do the murder, always supposing that the Feathers' clock can be relied on. A little further investigation is indicated, I fancy. Five years seems a longish time to premeditate a crime. You might, perhaps, keep an eye on that bank—only don't make a row about it, or you may frighten the bird away."

"That's so, my lord. All the same, I'd feel more enthusiastic, I don't mind saying, if I had any sort of proof that there really was a murder committed. Just at present it's a bit thin, you'll allow."

"So it is; but there are quite a lot of small things that point that way. Taken separately, they aren't important, but taken together, they have a funny look. There's the razor, and the gloves, and the return-ticket, and the good spirits Alexis was in on the day before his death. And now there's this funny story of the mysterious gentleman who arrived at Darley in time to take a front seat for the crime, and then cleared off with such remarkable precautions to obscure his name and address."

Inspector Umpelty's reply was cut short by the ringing of his telephone. He listened for a moment to its mysterious cluckings, said "I'll be along at once, sir," and rang off.

"Something else funny seems to have turned up," he said. "You'll excuse me if I rush off; I'm wanted down at the Station."

11

THE EVIDENCE OF THE FISHERMAN

There's a fellow
With twisting root-like hair up to his eyes,
And they are streaked with red and starting out
Under their bristling brows; his crooked tusks
Part, like a hungry wolf's, his cursing mouth;
His head is frontless, and a swinish mane
Grows o'er his shoulders: brown and warty hands,
Like roots, with pointed nails—He is the man.

—Fragment

MONDAY, 22 JUNE

Wimsey had not very long to wait before hearing the latest development. He had returned to the Bellevue for lunch, and was having a preliminary refresher in the bar, when he felt a smart tap on his shoulder.

"Lord, Inspector! How you startled me! All right, it's a fair cop. What's it for this time?"

"I just dropped along to tell you the latest, my lord. I thought you'd like to hear it. It's given us something to think about, I don't mind telling you."

"Has it? You look quite agitated. I expect you're out of practice. It is exhausting when you're not used to it. Have one?"

"Thank you, my lord. I don't mind if I do. Now, look here—you remember about our young friend's banking account and the three hundred pounds?"

"Sure thing."

"Well"—the Inspector dropped his voice to a hoarse whisper—"we've found out what he did with it."

Wimsey registered expectation, but this was not enough. Inspector Umpelty evidently felt that he had got hold of a really choice morsel, and was not going to let it go without full dramatic honours.

"I'll buy it, Inspector. *What* did he do with it?"

"Guess, my lord. You can have three guesses, and I bet you anything you like you don't hit on it. Not in twenty guesses."

"Then I mustn't waste your valuable time. Go on. Have a heart. Don't keep me in such ghastly suspense. What *did* he do with it?"

"He went," said the Inspector, lusciously, "and turned it into gold."

"Into WHAT?"

"Three hundred golden sovereigns—that's what he turned it into. Three hundred round, golden jimmy o' goblins."

Wimsey stared blankly at him.

"Three hundred—oh, look here, Inspector, a shock like this is more than frail flesh and blood can stand. There isn't so much gold in the country. I haven't seen more than ten gold sovereigns together since I fought at my grandpapa's side at the Battle of Waterloo. Gold! How did he get it? How did he wangle it? They don't hand it out to you at the banks nowadays. Did he rob the Mint?"

"No, he didn't. He changed notes for it quite honestly. But it's a queer tale for all that. I'll tell you how it was, and how we come to know of it. You may remember that there was a photograph of Alexis published in the newspapers last week?"

"Yes, enlarged from that hotel group they took at the Gala Night last Christmas. I saw it."

"That's right. Only one we could find; Alexis didn't leave anything about. Well, yesterday we had a quaint old bird calling at the Station—Gladstone sort of collar, whiskery bits, four-in-hand tie, cotton gloves, square-crowned bowler, big green gamp—all complete. Said he lived up Princemoor way. He pulls a newspaper out of his pocket and points to the photograph. 'I hear you want information about this poor young man,' he pipes up. 'Yes, we do,' says the Super, 'you know anything about it, Dad?' 'Nothing at all about his death,' says the old boy, 'but I had a very curious little transaction with him three weeks ago,' he says, 'and I thought you perhaps ought to know about it,' he says. 'Quite right, Dad,' says the Super. 'Go ahead.' So he went ahead and told us all about it.

"It seems it was like this. You may remember seeing a while ago—not more than a month or so back—a bit in the papers about a queer old girl who lived all alone in a house in Seahampton with no companion except about a hundred cats. A Miss Ann Bennett—but the name don't matter. Well, one day the usual thing happens. Blinds left down, no smoke from kitchen chimney, milk not taken in, cats yowling fit to break your heart. Constable goes in with a ladder and finds the old lady dead in her bed. Inquest verdict is 'death from natural causes,' which means old age and semi-starvation with neglected pneumonia on top of it. And of course plenty of money in the house, including four hundred gold sovereigns in the mattress. It's always happening."

Wimsey nodded.

"Yes. Well, then, the long-lost next-of-kin turns up and who should it be but this old chap from Princemoor, Abel Bennett. There's a will found, leaving everything to him, and begging him to look after the poor pussies. He's the executor, and he steps in and takes charge. Very good. On the day after the inquest, along comes our young friend Paul Alexis—name correctly given and person identified by the photograph. He tells old Bennett a rambling kind of story about wanting gold sovereigns for some purpose or other. Something about wanting to buy a diamond from a foreign rajah who didn't understand bank-notes—some bosh of that kind."

"He got that out of a book, I expect," said Wimsey. "I've seen something like it somewhere."

"Very likely. Old Bennett, who seems to have had more wits than his sister, didn't swallow the tale altogether, because, as he said, the young fellow didn't look to him like a person who would be buying diamonds off rajahs, but after all it's not criminal to want gold, and it was none of his business what it was wanted for. He put up a few objections, and Alexis offered him three hundred pounds in Bank of England notes, plus a twenty-pound bonus, in exchange for three hundred sovereigns. Old Abel wasn't averse to a buckshee twenty quid and was willing to hand over, on condition he might have the notes vetted for him at a

Seahampton bank. Alexis was agreeable and pulled out the notes then and there. To cut a long story short, they went to the Seahampton branch of the London & Westminster and got the O.K. on the notes, after which Bennett handed over the gold and Alexis took it away in a leather handbag. And that's all there is to it. But we've checked up the dates with the bank-people, and it's quite clear that Alexis drew his money out here for the purpose of changing it into gold as soon as ever he saw the account of Ann Bennett's death in the papers. But why he wanted it or what he did with it, I can't tell you, no more than the Man in the Moon."

"Well," said Wimsey, "I always knew there were one or two oddities about this case, but I don't mind admitting that this beats me. Why on earth should anybody want to clutter himself up with all that gold? I suppose we can dismiss the story of the Rajah's Diamond. A £300 diamond is nothing very out of the way, and if you wanted one you could buy it in Bond Street, without paying in gold or dragging in Indian potentates."

"That's a fact. Besides, where are you going to find a rajah who doesn't understand Bank of England notes? These niggers aren't savages, not by any means. Why, lots of them have been to Oxford."

Wimsey made suitable acknowledgment of this tribute to his own university.

"The only explanation that suggests itself to me," he said, "is that Alexis was contemplating a flitting to some place where Bank of England notes wouldn't pass current. But I hardly know where that could be at this time of day. Central Asia?"

"It may not be that, my lord. From the way he burnt everything before he left, it looks as though he didn't mean to leave any trace of where he was going. Now, you can't very well lose a Bank of England note. The numbers are bound to turn up somewhere or other, if you wait long enough. Currency notes are safe, but it is quite possible that you might have difficulty in exchanging them in foreign parts, once you were off the beaten track. It's my opinion Alexis meant to get away, and he took the gold because it was the only form of money that will pass everywhere and tell no tale. He probably wouldn't be asked about it at the Customs, and if he was, they would be very unlikely to search him."

"True. I think you're right, Inspector. But, I say, you realise this knocks the suicide theory on the head all right?"

"It's beginning to look like it, my lord," admitted Mr. Umpelty, handsomely. "Unless, of course, the stuff was paid out to some party in this country. For instance, suppose Alexis was being blackmailed by someone who wanted to skip. That party might be wanting gold for the very reasons we've been talking about, and he might get Alexis to do the job of getting it for him, so that he shouldn't appear in it himself. Alexis pays up, and then goes off the deep end and cuts his throat."

"You're very ingenious," said Wimsey. "But I still believe I'm right, though if it is a case of murder, it's been so neatly worked out that there doesn't seem to be much of a loophole in it. Unless it's the razor. Look here, Inspector, I've got an idea about the razor, if you'll let me carry it out. Our one hope is to tempt the murderer, if there is one, into making a mistake by trying to be too clever."

He pushed the glasses aside and whispered into the Inspector's ear.

"There's something in that," said Inspector Umpelty. "I don't see why it shouldn't be tried. It may clinch the matter straight off, one way or another.

You'd better ask the Super, but if he's got no objection, I'd say, go ahead. Why not come round and put it to him straight away?"

On arriving at the police-station, Wimsey and the Inspector found the Super-intendent engaged with a crabbed old gentleman in a fisherman's jersey and boots, who appeared to be suffering under a sense of grievance.

"Can't a man take 'is own boat out when he likes and where he likes? Sea's free to all, ain't it?"

"Of course it is, Pollock. But if you were up to no mischief, why take that tone about it? You aren't denying you were there at the time, are you? Freddy Baines swears he saw you."

"Them Baineses!" grumbled Mr. Pollock. "A nasty, peerin', pryin' lot. What's it got to do with them where I was?"

"Well, you admit it anyhow. What time did you get to the Flat-Iron?"

"Per'aps Freddy Baines can tell you that, too. 'E zeems to be bloody free with his information."

"Never mind that. What time do *you* say it was?"

"That ain't no business of yours. Perlice 'ere, perlice there—there ain't no freedom in this blasted country. 'Ave I or 'ave I not the right to go where I like? Answer me that."

"Look here, Pollock. All we want from you is some information. If you've got nothing to hide, why not answer a plain question?"

"Well, what is the question? Were I off the Flat-Iron on Thursday? Yes I were. Wot about it?"

"You came along from your own place, I suppose?"

"Well, I did, if you want to know. Where's the 'arm in that?"

"None whatever. What time did you set out?"

"About one o'clock. Maybe more; maybe less. Round about the slack."

"And you got to the Flat-Iron about two."

"Well, and where's the 'arm in that?"

"Did you see anybody on the shore at any time?"

"Yus, I did."

"You did?"

"Yus. I've got eyes in me 'ed, 'aven't I?"

"Yes. And you may as well have a civil tongue in your head. Where did you see this person?"

"On the shore by the Vlat-Iron—round about two o'clock."

"Were you close enough in to see who it was?"

"No, I weren't. Not to come into your bleedin' court and swear to a pimple, I wasn't; and you can put that in your pipe, Mr. Cocky Superintendent, and smoke it."

"Well, what did you see?"

"I zee a vule of a woman, caperin' about on the beach, goin' on as if she was loony. She runs a bit an' stops a bit, an' pokes in the sand and then runs on a bit. That's what I zee."

"I must tell Miss Vane that," said Wimsey to the Inspector. "It will appeal to her sense of humour."

"Oh, you saw a woman, did you? Did you see what she did after that?"

"She runs up to the Vlat-Iron an' starts messin' about there."

"Was there anybody else on the Flat-Iron?"

"There was a chap lyin' down. At least, it looked so."

"And then?"

"Then she starts a-yowlin' an' wavin' her arms."

"Well?"

"Well, what? I didn't take no notice. I never takes no notice of vemayles."

"Now, Pollock, did you see anybody else at all on the shore that morning?"

"Not a zoul."

"Were you within sight of shore all the time?"

"Yes, I were."

"And you saw nobody except this woman and the man lying down?"

"Ain't I tellin' you? I zee nobody."

"About this man on the Flat-Iron? Was he lying down when you first saw him?"

"Soon as I come in zight of un, I zee un."

"When was that?"

" 'Ow can I tell to a minute? Might be a quarter to two, might be ten minutes to. I wasn't takin' perticklers for the perlice. I were attendin' to my own business, same as I wish other folks would."

"What business?"

"Zailin' the bloody boat. That's my business."

"At any rate, you saw the man some time before you saw the woman, and he was then lying on the rock. Was he dead, do you think, when you first saw him?"

" 'Ow wur I to know if'e wur dead or alive? 'E didn't kiss 'is 'and to me. And if'e 'ad, I shouldn't a' seen un, d'ye zee? I wur too far out."

"But you said you were within sight of shore the whole time."

"Zo I wur. But shore's a big thing. A man couldn't very well miss it. But that's not to zay I could zee every vule on it playin' at kiss-me-'and."

"I see. Were you right out on the Grinders, then?"

"Wot's it matter where I wur? I weren't speckylatin' about corpses, nor yet what vemayles was after with their young men. I've got zummat more to do than zit about watchin' bathin' parties."

"What had you to do?"

"That's my business."

"Well, whatever your business was, it was out in the deep water off the Grinders?"

Mr. Pollock was obstinately silent.

"Was anybody with you in the boat?"

"No, there weren't."

"Then what was that grandson of yours doing?"

"Oh, him? He was with me. I thought you meant was there somebody else, that didn't ought to have been there."

"What do you mean by that?"

"Nothing, only perlicemen is a pack of vules, mostly."

"Where is your grandson?"

"Over to Cork. Went last Zatterday, he did."

"Cork, eh? Smuggling goods into Ireland?"

Mr. Pollock spat profusely.

" 'Course not. Business. My business."

"Your business seems to be rather mysterious, Pollock. You'd better be careful.

We'll want to see that young man when he gets back. Anyway, you say that when the young lady saw you, you had come in, and were putting out again."

"Why not?"

"What did you come in for?"

"That's my business, ain't it?"

The Superintendent gave it up.

"At any rate, are you in a position to say whether you saw anybody walking along the shore between your cottage and the Flat-Iron?"

"Yes, I am. I zee nobody. Not up to quarter to two, anyway. After that, I couldn't swear one way nor t'other, 'avin' my own business to mind, like I zaid."

"Did you see any other boat in the neighbourhood?"

"No, I didn't."

"Very well. If your memory should improve in the next few days, you'd better let us know."

Mr. Pollock muttered something uncomplimentary, and removed himself.

"Not an agreeable old gentleman," said Wimsey.

"An old scoundrel," said Superintendent Glaisher. "And the worst of it is, you can't believe a word he says. I'd like to know what he was really up to."

"Murdering Paul Alexis, perhaps?" suggested the Inspector.

"Or conveying the murderer to the scene of the crime for a consideration," added Wimsey. "That's more likely, really. What motive should he have for murdering Alexis?"

"There's the three hundred pounds, my lord. We mustn't forget that. I know I said it was suicide, and I still think so, but we've got a much better motive for murder than we had before."

"Always supposing Pollock knew about the three hundred pounds. But how should he?"

"See here," said the Superintendent. "Suppose Alexis was wanting to leave England."

"That's what I say," interjected Umpelty.

"And suppose he had hired Pollock to meet him somewhere off-shore with his boat and take him across to a yacht or something. And suppose, in paying Pollock, he'd happened to show him the rest of the money. Couldn't Pollock have put him ashore and cut his throat for him and made away with the gold?"

"But why?" objected Umpelty. "Why put him ashore? Wouldn't it have been easier to cut his throat aboard the boat and drop the body into the sea?"

"No, it wouldn't," said Wimsey, eagerly. "Ever seen 'em stick a pig, Inspector? Ever reckoned how much blood there was to the job? If Pollock had cut Alexis' throat on board, it would take a devil of a lot of swabbing to get the boat properly clean again."

"That's quite true," said the Superintendent. "But in any case, how about Pollock's clothes? I'm afraid we haven't got evidence enough to get a warrant and search his place for bloodstains."

"You could wash 'em off oil-skins pretty easily, too," remarked Wimsey.

The two policemen acquiesced gloomily.

"And if you stood behind your man and cut his throat that way, you'd stand a reasonable chance of not getting so very heavily splashed. It's my belief the man was killed in the place where he was found, murder or no murder. And if you don't mind, Superintendent, I've got a little suggestion which might work and tell us definitely whether it really was murder or suicide."

He again outlined the suggestion, and the Superintendent nodded.

"I see no objection whatever, my lord. Something might quite well come of it. In fact," said Mr. Glaisher, "something of the same kind had passed through my own mind, as you might say. But I don't mind it's appearing to come from your lordship. Not at all."

Wimsey grinned and went in search of Salcombe Hardy, the *Morning Star* reporter, whom he found, as he expected, taking refreshment in the hotel bar. Most of the pressmen had withdrawn by this time, but Hardy, with a touching faith in Lord Peter, had clung to his post.

"Though you're treating me damn badly, old man," he said, raising his mournful violet eyes to Wimsey's grey ones, "I *know* you must have something up your sleeve, or you wouldn't be hanging round the scene of the crime like this. Unless it's the girl. For God's sake, Wimsey, say it isn't the girl. You wouldn't play such a shabby trick on a poor, hardworking journalist. Or, look here! If there's nothing else doing, give me a story about the girl. Anything'll do, so long as it's a story. 'Romantic Engagement of Peer's Son'—that'd be better than nothing. But I must have a story."

"Pull yourself together, Sally," said his lordship, "and keep your inky paws off my private affairs. Come right away out of this haunt of vice and sit down quietly in a corner of the lounge and I'll give you a nice, pretty story all to yourself."

"That's right," said Mr. Hardy, in a burst of emotion. "That's what I expected from a dear old friend. Never let down a pal, even if he's only a poor bloody journalist. Noblesse oblige. That's what I said to those other blighters. 'I'm sticking to old Peter,' I said, 'Peter's the man for my money. He won't see a hardworking man lose a job for want of a good news story.' But these new men— they've no push, no guts. Fleet Street's going to the dogs, curse it. There's nobody left now of the old gang except me. I know where the news is, and I know how to get it. I said to myself, You hang on to old Peter, I said, and one of these days he'll give you a story."

"Splendid fellow!" said Wimsey. "May we ne'er lack a friend or a story to give him. Are you reasonably sober, Sally?"

"Sober?" exclaimed the journalist indignantly. "J'ever know a pressman who wasn't sober when somebody had a story to give him? I may not be a blasted pussyfoot, but my legs are always steady enough to go after a story, and what more could anybody want?"

Wimsey pushed his friend gently into position before a table in the lounge.

"Here you are, then," he said. "You take this stuff down and see that it gets a good show in your beastly rag. You can put in trimmings to suit yourself."

Hardy glanced up sharply.

"Oh!" said he. "Ulterior motive, eh? Not all pure friendship. Patriotism is not enough. Oh, well! as long as it's exclusive and news, the motive is imma—imma —damn the word—immaterial."

"Quite," said Wimsey. "Now then, take this down. 'The mystery surrounding the horrible tragedy at the Flat-Iron deepens steadily with every effort made to solve it. Far from being a simple case of suicide, as at first seemed probable, the horrible death—' "

"All right," interjected Hardy. "I can do that part on my head. What I want is the story."

"Yes; but work up the mystery part of it. Go on, now: 'Lord Peter Wimsey, the celebrated amateur of crime-detection, interviewed by our special correspondent in his pleasant sitting-room at the Hotel Bellevue—' "

"Is the sitting-room important?"

"The address is. I want them to know where to find me."

"Right you are. Go ahead."

"—'at the Hotel Bellevue, Wilvercombe, said that while the police still held strongly to the suicide theory, he himself was by no means satisfied. The point that particularly troubled him was that, whereas the deceased wore a full beard and had never been known to shave, the crime was committed—' "

"Crime?"

"Suicide is a crime."

"So it is. Well?"

"—'committed with an ordinary cut-throat razor, which shows signs of considerable previous hard wear.' Rub that in well, Sally. 'The history of this razor has been traced up to a point—' "

"Who traced it?"

"I did."

"Can I say that?"

"If you like."

"That makes it better. 'Lord Peter Wimsey explained, with his characteristically modest smile, that he had himself been at pains to trace the previous history of the razor, a search which led him—. Where did it lead you, Wimsey?"

"I don't want to tell 'em that. Say that the search covered many hundred miles."

"All right. I can make that sound very important. Anything else?"

"Yes. This is the important bit. Get 'em to put it in black lettering—you know."

"Not my business. Sub-editor. But I'll try. Carry on. 'Leaning over the table and emphasising the point with an eloquent gesture of his artistic hands, Lord Peter said—' "

" 'The trail,' " dictated Wimsey, " 'breaks off at the crucial point. *How did the razor get into the hands of Paul Alexis? If once I could be satisfied of that, the* answer might at once set at rest all my doubt. *If Paul Alexis can be proved to have bought the razor, I shall consider the suicide theory to have been proved up to the hilt. But until that missing link in the chain of evidence is reconstructed, I shall hold that Paul Alexis was foully and brutally murdered,* and I shall spare no efforts to bring the murderer to the judgment he has so richly deserved.' How's that, Sally?"

"Not too bad. I can work that up into something. I shall add, of course, that you, knowing the enormous circulation of the *Morning Star*, are relying on the wide publicity it will give to this statement to etcetera, etcetera. I might even get them to offer a reward."

"Why not? Anyway, pitch it to 'em hot and strong, Sally."

"I will—for better, for worse, for richer, for poorer. Between you and me, *would* you be satisfied that it was suicide if the reward was claimed?"

"I don't know," said Wimsey. "Probably not. In fact, I am never satisfied."

12

THE EVIDENCE OF
THE BRIDE'S SON

How I despise
All such mere men of muscle!
—*Death's Jest-Book*

MONDAY, 22 JUNE

Wimsey looked at his watch. It was half-past one, and he had had no lunch. He remedied the omission, took the car and drove out to Darley. He had to wait for a few moments while the gates were opened at the Halt, and took the opportunity to check up on the police inquiry. He found that the lame gate-keeper knew the mysterious Mr. Martin by sight—had, in fact, met him one evening in the bar of the Feathers. A pleasant gentleman, with a hearty way with him. Suffered from some trouble with his eyes, which obliged him to wear dark glasses, but a very nice gentleman for all that. The gate-keeper was quite positive that Mr. Martin had not passed through the railway-gates at any time on Thursday—not in any car or cart or on a cycle, that was to say. As for passing on foot, he couldn't swear to it, and you couldn't expect it of him.

Here, however, a new witness suddenly came forward. The gate-keeper's little daughter, Rosie, "just going on for five, and a wonderful quick girl for her age," as her father proudly remarked, was emphatic that "the nasty man with the black glasses" had not been seen at the railway-gates during the critical period on the Thursday. Rosie knew him and disliked him, for she had seen him in the village the day before and his horrid black glasses had frightened her. She and a small friend had been "playing Bluebeard" at the railway-gates on Thursday. She knew it was Thursday, because it was market day, when the 10.15 stopped there. She had been Sister Anne on her tower, and had called out to her companion when she saw anybody coming along the road. They had played there from after dinner (12.30 according to the gate-keeper) till nearly teatime (four o'clock). She was absolutely sure the nasty man had not come through the railway-wickets. If he had, she would have run away.

This seemed to dispose of the last lingering possibility that the mysterious Mr. Martin might have left the Feathers rather earlier than he was supposed to have done, walked to the crossing and been picked up by a car on the other side. Wimsey thanked Rosie with grave courtesy, gave her six-pence and drove on.

His next port of call was, of course, the Feathers. The landlord, Mr. Lundy, was ready enough with his information. What he had told the inspector was quite right. He had first seen Mr. Martin on Tuesday—the 16th, that would be. He had arrived about six o'clock and left his Morgan parked on the village green while he came in and took a glass of mild and bitter and asked the way to Mr.

Goodrich's house. Who was Mr. Goodrich? Why, Mr. Goodrich was the gentleman that owned the land down by Hinks's Lane, where Mr. Martin had been camping. All the land thereabouts belonged to Mr. Goodrich.

"I want to be clear about this," said Wimsey. "Did Mr. Martin come here from the direction of Hinks's Lane, or which way did he come?"

"No, sir; he drove in along the Heathbury Road and left his car on the green, same as I said."

"Did he come straight in here?"

"Straight as a swaller to its nest," replied Mr. Lundy, picturesquely. "We was open, you see, sir."

"And did he ask anybody about where he could camp? Or did he ask at once for Mr. Goodrich?"

"He didn't ask no questions at all, sir, only that: Where was Mr. Goodrich's house?"

"He knew Mr. Goodrich's name, then?"

"Seemingly he did, sir."

"Did he say why he wanted to see Mr. Goodrich?"

"No, sir. Just asked the way and drank up his beer and off in the car again."

"I understand he had lunch here last Thursday?"

"That's right, sir. Came in a big open car with a lady. She set him down here and drove off again, and he came in and set down to lunch." He thought it would be about one o'clock, but the girl could tell better than he could.

The girl knew all about it. Yes, as she had already told Inspector Umpelty, Mr. Martin had come in about ten minutes to one. He mentioned to her that he had been to Wilvercombe, and thought he would make a change by lunching at the inn. His car, it seemed, had got something the matter with it, and a passing car had picked him up and taken him to Wilvercombe and back. Yes, he had lunched heartily: roast leg of mutton and potatoes and boiled cabbage and a rhubarb pie to follow.

Wimsey shuddered at the thought of roast mutton and cabbage on a red-hot June day, and asked when Mr. Martin had left the inn.

"It would be half-past one, sir, by the right time. Our clocks are all ten minutes fast, same as the clock in the bar, that's set by the wireless every day. I couldn't say but what Mr. Martin might have stopped in the bar on his way out, but half-past one was when he paid me for his lunch. I couldn't be mistaken about that, sir, because it was my day off and my young man was taking me over to Heathbury on his motorcycle, and I was watching the clock, as you might say, to see how soon I'd get my work finished with. There wasn't nobody come in after Mr. Martin, so I was able to clear away and get dressed and very pleased I was about it."

This was clear enough. Mr. Martin had certainly not left the Three Feathers earlier than 1.30. Undoubtedly he was not the murderer of Paul Alexis. Nevertheless, having begun his investigation, Wimsey determined to carry it through to the bitter end. Alibis, he reminded himself, were made to be broken. He would suppose that, by means of a magic carpet or other device, Mr. Martin had been miraculously wafted from Darley to the Flat-Iron between 1.30 and two o'clock. In that case, did he come back that afternoon, and if so, when? and how?

There were not a great many houses in Darley, and a door-to-door inquiry, though laborious, seemed to be a fairly safe and certain method of answering

these questions. He pulled up his socks and set to work. He had no difficulty in
getting the villagers to talk. The death of Paul Alexis was a local event of an
importance that almost swamped last Saturday's cricket match, and the revolutionary proposal to turn the disused Quaker meeting-house into a cinema; while
the arrival of the Wilvercombe police to make inquiries about the movements of
Mr. Martin had raised the excitement to fever pitch. Darley felt strongly that, if
this kind of thing was going to happen, it might get into the papers again.
Darley had actually been in the papers that year already, when Mr. Gubbins, the
vicar's warden, had drawn a consolation prize in the Grand National sweep. The
sporting half of Darley had been delighted, but envious; the pious half had been
quite unable to understand why the vicar had not immediately dismissed Mr.
Gubbins from his privilege of handing round the plate and sitting on the
Church Council, and thought that Mr. Gubbins's action in devoting a tithe of
his winnings to the Restoration Fund merely piled hypocrisy on the head of
debauchery. But now, with the hope that they might be found to have enter-
tained an angel of darkness unawares, they foresaw all manner of publicity.
Wimsey discovered several people who thought Mr. Martin's manner odd and
had not liked his face and who said so, at considerable length. It was, however,
only after nearly two hours' patient research that he discovered somebody who
had actually seen Mr. Martin on Thursday afternoon. This was, of course, the
most obvious person in the village—namely the proprietor of the little tin
bungalow that did duty for a garage, and the only reason why Wimsey did not
get this information a great deal sooner was that the said proprietor—one Mr.
Polwhistle—had gone out when he first called upon him, to tackle the internals
of a sick petrol-gas engine at a neighbouring farm, leaving behind him only a
young woman to attend to the pump.

Mr. Polwhistle, when he returned in company of a youthful mechanic, was
most discouragingly informative. Mr. Martin?—oh, yes. He (Mr. Polwhistle) had
seen him on Thursday afternoon all right. Mr. Martin had come in—just upon
three o'clock, weren't it, Tom? Yes, three o'clock—and asked them to come and
have a look at his Morgan. They had gone round, and found that the Morgan
wouldn't start, not for toffee. After prolonged investigation and exercise on the
starting-handle, they had diagnosed trouble with the ignition. They had taken
everything out and looked at it, and eventually it had occurred to Mr. Polwhistle
that the fault might be in the H. T. lead. On their removing this and putting in a
new one, the engine had started up at once, sweet as a nut. There could be no
doubt about the time, because Tom had entered it upon his timesheet; 3 p.m.
till 4 p.m.

It was now nearly half-past four, and Wimsey felt that he had a good chance
of finding Mr. Goodrich at home. He was directed to his house—the big place
up the first turning off the Wilvercombe Road—and found the good gentleman
and his family gathered about a table well spread with bread and cakes and
honey and Devonshire cream.

Mr. Goodrich, a stout and hearty squire of the old school, was delighted to
give any assistance in his power. Mr. Martin had turned up at the house at about
seven o'clock on the Tuesday evening and had asked permission to camp at the
bottom of Hinks's Lane. Why Hinks's Lane, by the way? Well, there used to be a
cottage there that belonged to an old fellow called Hinks—a regular character—
used to read the Bible through regularly every year, and it was to be hoped it did
him good, for a graceless old scamp he was and always had been. But that was

donkey's years ago, and the cottage had fallen into disrepair. Nobody ever went down there now, except campers. Mr. Martin had not asked for information about camping-grounds; he had asked straight out for permission to camp in Hinks's Lane, calling it by that name. Mr. Goodrich had never set eyes on Mr. Martin before, and he (Mr. Goodrich) knew pretty well everything that went on in the village. He was almost certain that Mr. Martin had never been in Darley before. No doubt somebody had told him about Hinks's Lane—it was a regular place for campers. They were out of the way down there, and there were no crops for them to damage and no gates for them to leave open, unless they were to go out of their way to trespass on Farmer Newcombe's pasture on the other side of the hedge. But there was no necessity for them to do so, as it didn't lead anywhere. The stream that ran through the pasture came out on to the beach only fifty yards away from the camping-ground and was fresh, except, of course, at flood-tide, when it was brackish. Now Mr. Goodrich came to think about it, he believed there had been some complaint from Mr. Newcombe about a broken hedge, but the story only came through Geary the blacksmith, who was a notorious talker and he (Mr. Goodrich) didn't see that it had anything to do with Mr. Martin. Mr. Newcombe was not altogether a satisfactory tenant in the matter of repairs to hedges and when there were gaps, animals would sometimes stray through them. Apart from this, he (Mr. Goodrich) knew nothing to Mr. Martin's discredit. He seemed to have been quiet enough, and in any case, Hinks's Lane being out of sight and sound of the village, campers couldn't make nuisances of themselves down there. Some of them brought gramophones or concertinas or ukuleles, according to their taste and social position, but Mr. Goodrich had no objection to their amusing themselves, so long as they didn't disturb anybody. He never made any charge for camping on his ground—it didn't hurt *him*, and he didn't see why he should take payment for letting the poor devils who lived in towns help themselves to a mouthful of fresh air and a drink of water. He usually asked them to leave the place as tidy as they could, and as a rule he had found them pretty decent in this respect.

Wimsey thanked Mr. Goodrich and accepted his hospitable invitation to tea. He left at six o'clock, full of buns and cream, with just nice time to pay a visit to the camping-ground and so round off the chapter of Mr. Martin. He drove down the stony little lane, and soon found signs of Mr. Martin's recent presence. The lane led out upon a flat expanse of rough turf, beyond which a belt of heavy stones and shingle sloped down to the edge of the sea. The tide was about a quarter-full, and the beach became progressively less rough as it neared the water; presumably at low tide there would be a narrow strip of sand left uncovered.

The tracks of the Morgan's wheels were still faintly visible upon the coarse grass, and there was a patch of oily drippings to show where it had been parked. Close by, there were the holes where the pole and pegs of a small bell-tent had been driven in. There were the ashes of a burnt-out wood fire, and among them, a ball of greasy newspaper, which had obviously been used to scrub out a frying-pan. Rather reluctantly, Wimsey unfolded the distasteful sheets and glanced at the heading. Thursday's *Morning Star*; nothing particularly exciting about that. Careful search among the ashes of the fire revealed no blood-stained fragments of clothing—not so much as a button of a garment—no half-burnt scraps of paper which might have contained a clue to Mr. Martin's real name and address. The only thing that was in any way remarkable was a piece of thinnish rope about three inches long, heavily blackened by the fire. Wimsey pocketed this, for lack of better occupation, and searched further.

Mr. Martin had been a tidy camper on the whole, leaving no obviously offensive débris. On the right-hand side of the camping-ground there was, however, the remains of a stunted thorn hedge, surrounding the battered remnants of Hinks's Cottage. Half buried at the foot of this hedge, Wimsey discovered a repulsive cache, containing a great number of old tins and bottles, some recent and some obviously abandoned by previous campers, the heels of some loaves, the bones from a neck of mutton, an old dixie with a hole in the bottom, half a neck-tie, a safety-razor blade (still sharp enough to cut one's fingers on) and a very dead gull. An elaborate and back-aching crawl over the whole surface of the camping-ground rewarded the earnest sleuth further with an immoderate quantity of burnt matches, six empty match-boxes of foreign make, the dottles of several pipes, three oat-grains, a broken bootlace (brown), the stalks of about a pound of strawberries, six plum-stones, the stub of a pencil, a drawing-pin business end up, fifteen beer-corks, and an instrument for removing the patent caps of other beer-bottles. The rough grass showed no identifiable footprints.

Weary and hot, Lord Peter gathered his loot together and stretched his cramped limbs. The wind, still blowing heavily in from seaward, was grateful to his perspiring brow, however much it might hold up the Inspector's salvage operations. The sky was cloudy, but so long as the wind held, there was, he felt, not much likelihood of rain, and he was glad, for he didn't want rain. A vague possibility was forming itself in his mind, and he wanted to take a walk next day with Harriet Vane. At the moment, he could do no more. He would go back and change and eat and be normal.

He drove back to Wilvercombe.

After a hot bath and the putting-on of a boiled shirt and dinner-jacket, he felt better and telephoned to the Resplendent to ask Harriet to dine with him.

"I'm sorry, I'm afraid I can't. I'm dining with Mrs. Weldon and her son."

"Her son?"

"Yes; he's just arrived. Why not come round here after grub and be introduced?"

"Dunno. What sort of bloke is he?"

"Oh, yes—he's here, and would like to meet you very much."

"Oh, I see. We are being overheard. I suppose I'd better come and look the blighter over. Is he handsome?"

"Yes, rather! Come along about a quarter to nine."

"Well, you'd better tell him we're engaged, and then I shan't be obliged to assassinate him."

"You will? That's splendid."

"Will you marry me?"

"Of course not. We'll expect you at 8.45."

"All right, and I hope your rabbit dies."

Wimsey ate his solitary dinner thoughtfully. So this was the son, was it? The one who was out of sympathy with his mother. What was he doing here? Had he suddenly become sympathetic? Or had she sent for him and compelled him to come in, by financial or other pressure? Was he perhaps a new factor in the problem? He was the only son of his mother and she a rich widow. Here at last was a person to whom the removal of Paul Alexis might appear in the light of a god-send. Undoubtedly the man must be looked into.

He went round to the Resplendent after dinner and found the party waiting for him in the lounge. Mrs. Weldon, who wore a plain black semi-evening dress and looked her full age in it, greeted Wimsey effusively.

"My dear Lord Peter! I am *so* glad to see you. May I introduce my son Henry? I wrote asking him to come and help us through this terrible time, and he has *most* kindly put his own business aside and come to me. So very sweet of you, Henry dear. I have just been telling Henry how good Miss Vane has been to me, and how *hard* you and she are working to clear poor Paul's memory."

Harriet had merely been mischievous. Henry was certainly not handsome, though he was a good, sturdy specimen of his type. He stood about five foot eleven—a strongly built, heavyish man with a brick-red all-weather face. Evening dress did not suit him, for the breadth of his shoulders and the shortness of his legs gave him a rather top-heavy appearance; one would expect him to look his best in country tweeds and leggings. His hair, rather rough and dull in texture, was mouse-coloured, and offered a pregnant suggestion of what his mother's might once have looked like before it knew the touch of peroxide; indeed, he was, in a curious way, very like his mother, having the same low, narrow forehead and the same long and obstinate chin; though, in the mother the expression was that of a weak, fanciful obstinacy, and, in the son, of stubborn and unimaginative obstinacy. Looking at him, Wimsey felt that he was hardly the sort of man to take kindly to a Paul Alexis for a step father; he would not sympathise with the sterile romance of any woman who was past the age of child-bearing. Wimsey, summing him up with the man of the world's experienced eye, placed him at once as a gentleman-farmer, who was not quite a gentleman and not much of a farmer.

At the moment, the understanding between Henry Weldon and his mother seemed, nevertheless, to be excellent.

"Henry is so delighted," said Mrs. Weldon, "that you are here to help us, Lord Peter. That policeman is so stupid. He doesn't seem to believe a word I tell him. Of course, he's a very well-meaning, honest man, and *most* polite, but how can a person like that possibly understand a nature like Paul's. I *knew* Paul. So did Henry, didn't you, dear?"

"Oh, yes," said Henry, "certainly. Very pleasant fellow."

"Henry knows how utterly devoted Paul was to me. *You* know, don't you, dear, that he *never* would have taken his own life and left me like that without a word. It hurts me so when people say such things—I feel I could—"

"There, there, Mother," muttered Henry, embarrassed by the prospect of emotion and possible break-down in a public place. "You must try to bear up. Of course we know Alexis was all right. Damned fond of you—of course, of course. Police are always silly fools. Don't let 'em worry you."

"No, dear, I'm sorry," said Mrs. Weldon, dabbing her eyes apologetically with a small handkerchief. "It's all been such a shock to me. But I mustn't be weak and silly. We must all be courageous and work hard and *do* something about it."

Wimsey suggested that a spot of something or other might do them all good, and, further, that he and Henry might make a concerted masculine raid on the bar, instructing the waiter to attend upon the ladies. He felt that he could dissect Henry more conveniently in a private interview.

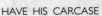
As the two men's backs disappeared in the direction of the bar, Mrs. Weldon turned her anxious eyes on Harriet.

"How nice Lord Peter is," she said, "and what a comforting thing it is for us both to have a man to rely on."

This sentiment was not very well received; Harriet averted her gaze from Lord Peter's back, on which it had been absentmindedly and unaccountably fixed, and frowned; but Mrs. Weldon bleated on, unheeding.

"It's beautiful how kind everybody is when one is in trouble. Henry and I haven't always been as close to one another as a mother and son should be. He takes after his father in a great many ways, though people say he is like me to look at, and when he was a little boy he had the dearest golden curls—just like mine. But he loves sport and out-door life—you can tell that by his looks, can't you? He's always out and about, seeing after his farm, and that's what makes him look a little older than his years. He's really quite a young man—I was a mere child when I married, as I told you before. But though, as I say, we haven't always been as much in harmony as one would have liked, he has been perfectly *sweet* to me about this sad affair. When I wrote to him and told him how much I *felt* the dreadful things they were saying about Paul, he came at *once* to help me, though I know he must be terribly busy just now. I really feel that poor Paul's death has brought us closer together."

Harriet said that that must be a great comfort to Mrs. Weldon. It was the only possible answer.

Henry, meanwhile, had his own view of the matter to put before Lord Peter.

"Bit of a staggerer for the old lady, this," he observed over a glass of Scotch. "Takes it hard. Between you and me, it's all for the best. How's a woman of her age going to be happy with a feller like that? Eh? Don't like these Popoffsky blighters, anyway, and she's fifty-seven if she's a day. I'm thirty-six myself. Consider I'm well out of it. Makes a chap look a bit of a fool when his mother proposes to give him a twenty-year-old lounge lizard for a step-papa. Suppose it's all over the place now. Bet everybody's grinning at me behind my back. Let 'em grin. All over now, anyway. Suppose the chappie did do himself in, didn't he?"

"It looks like it," admitted Wimsey.

"Couldn't face the prospect, eh? All his own fault. Hardup, I suppose, poor devil! The old girl's not a bad sort, really. She'd have given the feller a damn good time if he'd stuck to his bargain. But you can't trust these foreigners. Like collies—lick your boots one minute and bite you the next. Don't like collies, myself. Give me a good bull-terrier any day."

"Oh, yes—so frightfully British and all that, what?"

"Thought I'd better push along and cheer Mother up. Stop all this nonsense about Bolsheviks. Won't do to have her wasting her time with these tom-fool notions. Enough to send the old dear clean off her rocker, you know. Once they get those notions in their heads it's a job to get rid of 'em. Form of mania, don't you think, like women's rights and crystal-gazing?"

Wimsey agreed cautiously that an unreasonable conviction might, in process of time, amount to an obsession.

"That's just what I mean. You've got the word—obsession, that's it. Well, I don't want the old lady to go wasting her time and money on an obsession. Look here, Wimsey, you're a sound sort of fellow—brainy and all that—can't you put her off this Bolshevik idea? She's taken a notion that you and that Vane girl are encouraging her. Now, take it from me, old man, that kind of thing won't do at all."

Lord Peter delicately raised his eyebrows.

"Of course," pursued Mr. Weldon, "I see your game all right. You're nuts on this kind of thing and it's all a darn good advertisement, and it gives you a jolly good excuse for barging round with the girl. That's quite all right. But it's not quite the game to go playing my mother up, if you see what I mean. So I thought I'd just give you a hint. You won't take offence?"

"I am quite ready," said Lord Peter, "to take anything I am offered."

Mr. Weldon looked puzzled for a moment and then burst into a hearty laugh.

"That's good," he said, "dashed good. What was yours? Martell Three-Star? Here, Johnnie, same again for this gentleman."

"Thank you, no," said Wimsey. "You misunderstood me."

"Oh, come—another little spot won't do you any harm. No? Oh, well, if you won't, you won't. Mine's a Scotch-and-soda. Well, now, we understand one another, eh?"

"Oh, yes. I think I understand you perfectly."

"Good. Glad to have this chance of putting you wise. Whole thing's a nuisance, of course. Suppose we shall be stuck here now till they've found the body and held an inquest. Don't like these beastly watering-places. Suits you all right, I daresay. I like a bit more open air and none of this jazz and dinner-jackets."

"Quite right," said Wimsey.

"You think so, eh? I was putting you down for something more in the West-end line. But I suppose you're a bit of a sportsman, too? Huntin', fishin', that sort of thing, eh?"

"I hunted pretty regularly with the Quorn and the Pytchley at one time, and I shoot and fish a bit," said Wimsey. "After all, I was brought up in the country, you know. My people have a place in the shires, and our headquarters is down in Norfolk—Duke's Denver, on the borders of the Fen country."

"Oh, yes, of course. You're Denver's brother. Never seen the place, but I live in that part of the world myself—Huntingdonshire, not far from Ely."

"Oh, yes; I know that part pretty well. Fruit-farming country and all that. Flattish, of course, but uncommonly good sort of soil."

"Nothing in farming these days," grumbled Mr. Weldon. "Look at all this Russian wheat they're dumpin' in. As if things weren't bad enough already, with wages what they are, and taxes, and rates and tithe and insurance. I've got fifty acres of wheat. By the time it's harvested I daresay it'll have cost me £9 an acre. And what shall I get for it? Lucky if I get five. How this damned Government expects the farmer to carry on, I don't know. Damned if I don't feel like chucking it altogether sometimes and clearing out of this bloody country. Nothing much to stick round here for. I'm not married, thank God! Too much sense. If you take my advice you'll do likewise. You must be pretty smart to have escaped so long. Look as if you did yourself pretty well, too. Lucky your brother's still a youngish man. Death-duties and all that. Cripple a place, don't they? But I always thought he was a pretty warm man, for a duke. How's he manage it?"

Wimsey explained that the Denver income was not derived from the Denver estate, which was a liability rather than an asset.

"Oh, I see. Well, you're lucky. Takes a man all he can do to get his living off the land these days."

"Yes; I suppose you have to stick to it uncommonly closely. Up early and late. Nothing escapes the master's eye. That sort of thing, what?"

"Oh, yes—yes."

"It must be trying to be obliged to leave things and come to Wilvercombe. How long do you think you'll be here?"

"Eh? Oh, I don't know. Depends on this inquest, doesn't it? I've left a man in charge, of course."

"Just so. Hadn't we better go back and join the ladies?"

"Ah!" Mr. Weldon dug his elbow into Lord Peter's ribs. "Ladies, eh? You be careful, my boy. Getting to the dangerous age, aren't you? If you ain't careful, you'll find yourself booked one of these days."

"Oh, I daresay I shall manage to keep *my* head out of the noose."

"Out of the—oh, yes—the matrimonial noose. Yes. Ha, ha! All right. I suppose we'd better go."

Mr. Weldon turned away from the bar rather abruptly. Wimsey, reflecting that the ability to swallow insult is a necessary part of the detective's make-up, restrained the temptation to connect his toe with Mr. Weldon's rather massive hinderend, and followed, ruminating.

A message from the waiter informed him that the ladies had adjourned into the dance-lounge. Henry growled, but was relieved to find that his mother was, after all, not dancing. She was watching Harriet who, clad in claret-colour, was revolving smoothly in the practised arm of Antoine. Wimsey politely begged Mrs. Weldon to favour him, but she shook her head.

"I couldn't. Not so soon. In fact, never again—now that Paul—But I begged Miss Vane to enjoy herself and not mind about me. It is such a delight to watch her looking so happy."

Wimsey sat down and did his best to enjoy the spectacle of Harriet's happiness. As the quick-step came to an end, Antoine, with professional tact, contrived to end his progress in the neighbourhood of their table and then, bowing gracefully, melted away. Harriet, a little flushed, smiled amiably upon Lord Peter.

"Oh, there you are," said his lordship.

Harriet became suddenly conscious that every woman in the room was gazing furtively or with frank interest at Wimsey and herself, and the knowledge exhilarated her.

"Yes," she said, "here I am. Frivolling. You didn't know I could do it, did you?"

"I have always taken it for granted that you could do everything."

"Oh, no. I can only do what I like doing."

"We'll see about that."

The orchestra swung gently into a dreamy tune. Wimsey advanced upon Harriet and steered her competently out into the centre of the room. For the first few bars of the music they had the floor to themselves.

"At last," said Wimsey, "we are alone. That is not an original remark, but I am in no condition to invent epigrams. I have been suffering agonies, and my soul is raw. Now that for a brief moment I have you all to myself—"

"Well?" said Harriet. She was aware that the wine-coloured frock became her.

"What," said Wimsey, "do you make of Mr. Henry Weldon?"

"Oh!"

This was not quite the question Harriet had expected. She hastily collected her ideas. It was very necessary that she should be the perfect unemotional sleuth.

"His manners are dreadful," she said, "and I don't think his brains are much to write home about."

"No, that's just it."

"Just what?"

Wimsey countered the question with another.

"Why is he here?"

"She sent for him."

"Yes, but why is he here. Sudden spasm of filial affection?"

"She thinks so."

"Do *you* think so?"

"Possibly. Or, more likely, he doesn't want to get on the wrong side of her. It's her money, you know."

"Quite. Yes. It's funny that that should only just have occurred to him. He's very like her, isn't he?"

"Very. So much so that he gave me an odd feeling just at first, as though I'd met him somewhere. Do you mean that they are too much alike to hit it off together?"

"They seem to be getting along all right at present."

"I expect he's glad to be relieved from the prospect of Paul Alexis, and can't help showing it. He's not very subtle."

"That's what feminine intuition makes of it, is it?"

"Bother feminine intuition. Do *you* find him romantic or obscure?"

"No; I wish I did. I only find him offensive."

"Oh?"

"And I'd like to know why."

Silence for a few moments. Harriet felt that Wimsey ought to be saying, "How well you dance." Since he did not say it, she became convinced that she was dancing like a wax doll with sawdust legs. Wimsey had never danced with her, never held her in his arms before. It should have been an epoch-making moment for him. But his mind appeared to be concentrated upon the dull personality of an East Anglian farmer. She fell a victim to an inferiority complex, and tripped over her partner's feet.

"Sorry," said Wimsey, accepting responsibility like a gentleman.

"It's my fault," said Harriet. "I'm a rotten dancer. Don't bother about me. Let's stop. You haven't got to be polite to me, you know."

Worse and worse. She was being peevish and egotistical. Wimsey glanced down at her in surprise and then suddenly smiled.

"Darling, if you danced like an elderly elephant with arthritis, I would dance the sun and moon into the sea with you. I have waited a thousand years to see you dance in that frock."

"Idiot!" said Harriet.

They made the circuit of the room in silence and harmony. Antoine, guiding an enormous person in jade-green and diamonds, swam comet-like into their orbit and murmured into Harriet's ear across an expanse of fat white shoulder:

"*Qu'est-ce que je vous ai dit? L'élan, c'est trouvé.*"

He slid away dexterously, leaving Harriet flushed.

"What did that blighter say?"

"He said I danced better with you than with him."

"Curse his impudence!" Wimsey scowled over the heads of the intervening couples at Antoine's elegant back.

"Tell me now," said Harriet. The ending of the dance had found them on the opposite side of the room from the Weldons, and it seemed natural to sit down at the nearest table. "Tell me, what is biting you about Henry Weldon?"

"Henry Weldon?" Wimsey jerked his mind back from an immense distance. "Yes, of course. Why is he here? Not to worm himself into his mother's good graces, surely?"

"Why not? Now is his time. Alexis is disposed of and he sees his opportunity. Now that he has nothing to lose by it, he can afford to come along and be frightfully sympathetic and help to investigate things and be filial and affectionate and so on."

"Then why is he trying to drive me out of the place?"

"You?"

"Me."

"How do you mean?"

"Weldon went out of his way in the bar this evening to be as offensive as he possibly could, without using actual violence or bad language. He informed me, in an indirect but unmistakable manner, that I was poking my nose in where I was not wanted, exploiting his mother for my private ends and probably sucking up to her for her money. In fact, he drove me to the indescribable vulgarity of reminding him who I was and why I did not require anybody's money."

"Why didn't you sock him one over the jaw?"

"It was a temptation. I felt that you would love me better if I did. But you would not, in your calmer moments, really wish me to put my love before my detective principles."

"Certainly not. But what's his idea?"

"Oh, that's clear enough. He made it very clear. He wants it to be understood that this detecting business is to stop, and that Mrs. Weldon is to be restrained from lavishing time and money in pursuit of nonexistent Bolsheviks."

"I can understand that. He's looking to inherit the money."

"Of course. But if I were to go and tell Mrs. Weldon the things he's been saying to me, she'd probably disinherit him. And where would be the use of all this display of sympathy then?"

"I knew he was a stupid man."

"He evidently thinks it very important to stop all these inquiries. So much so that he's prepared, not only to risk my splitting on him, but also to spend an indefinite time here hanging round his mother to see that she doesn't make inquiries on her own."

"Well, I daresay he has nothing else to do."

"Nothing else to do? My dear girl, he's a farmer."

"Well?"

"And this is June."

"What about it?"

"Why isn't he attending to his hay-making?"

"I didn't think of that."

"About the last weeks of the year that any decent farmer would be willing to waste are the weeks from hay to harvest. I can understand his running over for a day, but he seems to be prepared to make a session of it. This Alexis business has become so important that he's ready to chuck everything, come down to a place he detests and hang about interminably in a hotel in attendance on a mother with whom he has never had very much in common. I think it's funny."

"Yes, it is rather funny."

"Has he ever been here before?"

"No. I asked him when we met. It's the kind of thing one does ask people. He said he hadn't. I expect he kept away while all the Alexis business was going on —he'd hate it."

"And content himself with forbidding the banns at a distance?"

"Yes—though it doesn't seem the most effective way."

"No? But the banns have been fairly effectively forbidden, haven't they?"

"Yes. But—are you casting Henry for the part of the murderer?"

"I should like to. But I don't feel I can, somehow."

"No."

"That's why I wanted to find out whether you thought Henry was subtle. You don't, and I agree with you. I don't think Henry has the brains to have murdered Paul Alexis."

13

EVIDENCE OF TROUBLE SOMEWHERE

Fool, would thy virtue shame and crush me down;
And make a grateful blushing bond-slave of me?
—*Death's Jest-Book*

TUESDAY, 23 JUNE

Lord Peter Wimsey, reading his *Morning Star* over the eggs and bacon, felt better than he had done for some weeks. The *Morning Star* had come up to scratch nobly, and was offering £100 reward for information about the razor that had slain Paul Alexis. Bunter, returning from his fruitless journey to Eastbourne, had come on to join his master at Wilvercombe, bringing with him a fresh supply of shirts, collars, and other garments. Harriet Vane had danced with Lord Peter in a wine-coloured frock. Wimsey considered, rightly, that when a woman takes a man's advice about the purchase of clothes, it is a sign that she is not indifferent to his opinion. Various women, at various times and in various quarters of the globe, had clothed themselves by Wimsey's advice and sometimes also at his expense —but then, he had fully expected them to do so. He had not expected it of Harriet, and was as disproportionately surprised and pleased as if he had picked up a sovereign in the streets of Aberdeen. Like all male creatures, Wimsey was a simple soul at bottom.

Not only had he this satisfactory past and present to contemplate; he anticipated an interesting day. Harriet had consented to walk with him that afternoon
from the Flat-Iron to Darley in search of clues. Low water being billed to take
place at 4.45, they had arranged to drive out to the Flat-Iron, arriving there at
3.30. After a little light refreshment, the expedition would set out, searching
conscientiously for whatever the shore might have to show them, while Bunter
brought the car back by the road to Hinks's Lane; after which all three would
return to their base at Wilvercombe in their original formation. It was all very
clear, except that Harriet did not see—and said as much—what clues were likely
to remain on the open shore after nearly a week of exceptionally high tides. She
admitted however, that she needed exercise and that walking was better exercise
than most.

And—most immediate of pleasant things to look forward to—Harriet had
further agreed to receive Lord Peter Wimsey after breakfast at the Resplendent,
for a conference. It was necessary, in Wimsey's opinion, that the progress made
so far should be tabulated and brought into some sort of order. Ten o'clock was
the hour fixed for this meeting, and Wimsey was lingering lovingly over his
bacon and eggs, so as to leave no restless and unfilled moment in his morning.
By which it may be seen that his lordship had reached that time of life when a
man can extract an Epicurean enjoyment even from his own passions—the
halcyon period between the self-tormenting exuberance of youth and the fretful
carpe diem of approaching senility.

The great wind had fallen at last. It had rained a little during the night, but
now the sky was fair again, with only the gentlest of breezes ruffling the blue
expanse of sea that was visible from the Bellevue's dining-room windows. Inspector Umpelty had been out with his helpers to explore the Grinders at four
o'clock that morning, and had just looked in on Wimsey to say that they had
found nothing yet.

"And why it hasn't come ashore somewhere before this, I don't know," he
grumbled. "We've had a look-out kept all along the coast from Fishy Ness right
up to Seahampton and on both sides of the estuary. Must have got hooked up
with something. If we don't get it within another week, we'll have to give it up.
Can't waste public money fishing for drowned dagoes. The ratepayers grumble
enough as it is, and we can't keep the witnesses hanging round here for ever.
Well, so long. We shall have another shot at low tide."

At ten o'clock Wimsey and his collaborator sat down before a neat pile of
scribbling paper. Harriet was inclined to be brief and businesslike.

"What system are we going to adopt about this? Do you favour the Michael
Finsbury method by double entry as in *The Wrong Box?* Or one of those charts,
made out in columns, with headings for 'Suspect,' 'Alibi,' 'Witnesses,' 'Motive'
and so on, worked out in percentages?"

"Oh, don't let's have anything that means ruling a lot of lines and
doing arithmetic. Let's behave like your Robert Templeton, and make a
schedule of Things to be Noted and Things to be Done. That only means two
columns."

"Very well, I'm glad you approve of it. I always make Templeton start with the
corpse."

"Right. Here goes—"

PAUL ALEXIS (GOLDSCHMIDT)

THINGS TO BE NOTED	THINGS TO BE DONE
1. Russian by birth; English by adoption, partly American by education. Early history unknown, but claimed to be War refugee of noble descent.	1. Investigate origin. (N.B. The only people who knew much about him are dead, and anyway, this is a job for the police. And does it really matter? Probably not, unless Mrs. Weldon's Bolshevik theory is correct.)
2. Personal characteristics: Said to be delicate (arthritis?); good dancer; vain of his appearance; wore beard on account of tendency to pimples; careful of his dress, but flamboyant in taste. Said to be romantic and emotional.	2. Had he the temperament to commit suicide? Find out if possible from colleagues and/or his mistress.
3. In February last engaged himself to marry Mrs. Weldon, a rich widow. Apparently desirous to secure himself against loss of profession consequent on increasing ill-health. Not anxious to push on marriage on account of opposition put forward by widow's son (or possibly on account of personal reluctance). Marriage fixed for fortnight or so after time of P.A.'s death.	3. Find out if Alexis really took any steps about the marriage at all.
4. Poor, but not mercenary or dishonest, since he refused to soak Mrs. W. Had balance of £320, which he changed into gold about three weeks ago. (N.B. He was only able to do so as result of curious accident. Can we say it was *essential* to any scheme he had in mind?)	4. Find the £300 in gold. Its destination will throw light on his intentions. N.B.—I think I know where it is. (P.W.) Do you? Where? (H.V.) Think it out for yourself. (P.W.)
5. About time of above transaction, his mistress left him for another man. (N.B. He affected distress, but his colleagues seem to think he was an assenting party. If so, did he intend (*a*) to facilitate his marriage with Mrs. W.? (*b*) to start a new liaison with someone else? (*c*) to provide for his mistress in the event of his own disappearance or suicide?)	5. Interview the girl Leila Garland and her new man.

6. Shortly before his death he hinted to Mrs. W. that something pleasing and mysterious was about to happen to him.

7. On the day preceding his death he paid all his bills and burnt his papers. Does this suggest suicide? Or an intention to leave the country?

8. On the morning of his death he took a *return*-ticket to Darley Halt, and thence walked (or, just possibly, was conveyed) to the Flat-Iron Rock. (N.B. He packed no clothes and took his latchkey with him.)

9. At 2.10 p.m. on Thursday, 18 June, he was found dead on the rock with his throat cut. A loud cry was heard at two o'clock, and the condition of the body when found showed that life had been only a few minutes extinct. A razor (which he never used) was found by the body, and he was wearing gloves.

6. Find out if he mentioned this to anyone else. (Query: How does the turning of the £300 into gold bear on this point? It is suggestive of departure from the country rather than suicide.)

7. Find out if he had a passport and visas. (Police.)

8. I think we may take it for granted that none of the persons interviewed by the police took P.A. to the Flat-Iron. Find out whether anybody passed him on the road. He may not have walked alone. (Police.)

9. FIND THE BODY.

"How professional it looks," said Harriet. "A nice little set of problems for Robert Templeton. The only thing I can do much about is interviewing this Leila person and her new young man. I fancy I might get more out of them than the police could."

"There's nothing I can do that the police can't do better," said Wimsey, mournfully. "We'd better go on to the next."

MRS. WELDON

THINGS TO BE NOTED

1. Personal characteristics: Aged fifty-seven; silly; obstinate; genuinely attached to Alexis; incurably romantic.

2. Rich widow; one son; formerly on cool terms with him and complained of lack of sympathy; now has summoned him to her side and seems full of affection for him.

THINGS TO BE DONE

1. Nothing to be done about it.

2. Find out where her money came from; whether it is at her sole disposal; what she proposed to do with it (*a*) before meeting Alexis, (*b*) after marrying Alexis; what she means to do with it now.

3. She attributes death of Alexis to Bolshevik plot.

3. Get information from Scotland Yard about Bolshevik agents. No theory is too silly to be dismissed without investigation.

HENRY WELDON

THINGS TO BE NOTED

1. Personal characteristics: Tallish, broad, powerful, resembles his mother facially: obstinate, ill-mannered, countrified; apparently not very intelligent.

2. He has suddenly left his farm at the busiest time to suck up to his mother and pretend to help her clear P.A.'s memory. But actually he is doing his best to drive P.W. to chucking up the investigation.

3. The news of P.A.'s death was in the papers on Friday morning; H.W. arrived Wilvercombe Monday evening, in answer to letter presumably sent by Mrs. W. on Friday, and addressed to Huntingdonshire.

THINGS TO BE DONE

1. Kick him. (P.W.) Well, no, that wouldn't be politic. String him along and see if he is really as stupid as he makes out. (H.V.) All right, but kick him afterwards. (P.W.)

2. Find out what the state of his finances is, and what his farm is like. Also his local reputation. (Query: Why not give Bunter something to do?)

3. Find out where Henry Weldon was on Thursday.

ESDRAS POLLOCK

THINGS TO BE NOTED

1. Personal characteristics: Aged seventy or more, sturdy for his age; bent, grey, smells of fish; manners none and customs beastly; unpopular with the fishing population.

2. He was in his boat off the Flat-Iron at 2.10 p.m. on Thursday, with his grandson.

3. He is reluctant to say what he was doing there, and the grandson has disappeared to Cork.

4. He states that he hugged the shore between his cottage and the Flat-Iron and saw nobody along the shore; but when questioned about events at the Flat-Iron at two

THINGS TO BE DONE

1. Pump fishing population.

2. A fact.

3. Trace grandson. (Police.)

4. Try the grandson on this when traced. (Police.)

o'clock, contradicts himself and says that he was then in deep water. (N.B. He saw what H.V. was doing all right at 2.10.)

5. When pressed, he says he first saw P.A. on rock about two o'clock, and that he was then alone and already lying down.

5. How about a little Third Degree? Once again, trace and interrogate grandson. (Police.)

6. Curiously enough, when asked if anyone was with him in the boat, says "Nobody"—but when grandson is mentioned, admits grandson. Who did he think was meant?

6. Find out whether P.A. could have reached Flat-Iron in Pollock's boat. Find out what has happened to the £300 in gold. Search boat for blood-stains. (Police.)

————PERKINS (of London)

THINGS TO BE NOTED

THINGS TO BE DONE

1. Personal characteristics: Small, weakish, round-shouldered. Wore spectacles and was apparently shortsighted. Complained of blistered heel. Cockney accent. Appeared to be of timid disposition.

1. Find him.

2. Met H.V. on road at 4.15 about half-a-mile on the far side of Pollock's cottage, i.e. about one and a half miles from Flat-Iron and three miles from Darley. Said he had walked from Wilvercombe.

2. Find out if anybody noticed him on the way. Note: It is only seven miles from Wilvercombe to the place where H.V. met him. When did he start out? Where did he sleep Tuesday night? (Police must have done something about this—ask Umpelty.)

3. On hearing from H.V. about body, turned back and accompanied her, ostensibly to protect her (but was about as useful as a rain-coat under machine-gun fire).

3. Find him and see what he's made of.

4. Went willingly to Pollock's cottage, but was annoyed with H.V. for addressing Martin.

4. Find him! Find Martin!

5. Disappeared mysteriously while H.V. was telephoning police, took car to Wilvercombe station and undiscoverable.

5. Find him! find him! find him, curse you! (Meaning the police.)

Wimsey put his head on one side.
"Really, every character seems more suspicious than the last. Who else is

there? How about the cast-off Leila Garland, for instance? Or this chap Antoine? Or Leila's new man?"

"We can't do much about them till we've seen them."

"No; but either Leila or the man what's his name—da Soto—might have a motive for getting rid of Alexis."

"Well. We've already put down that they've got to be looked into. Is that all? Oh, no!"

"No. We now come to my own pet particular prize suspect, the sinister Mr. Martin."

HAVILAND MARTIN

THINGS TO BE NOTED	THINGS TO BE DONE
1. Personal characteristics: Tall, massive, dark hair: black spectacles; tattoo-mark on right wrist; dressed in khaki shirt and shorts, with wide-brimmed soft hat.	1. Keep your mind on the tattoo-mark! You can fake them, you know. (H.V.) Bah! (P.W.)
2. Arrived Darley six o'clock Tuesday, 16th, with hired Morgan, coming from Heathbury direction.	2. A fact. Why a Morgan?
3. Though no one had ever seen him in the village before, knew all about Hinks's Lane and Mr. Goodrich.	3. Find out if anyone saw him in Heathbury or anywhere else and told him.
4. Seen at Three Feathers about one o'clock on Thursday, 18th, and lunched there.	4. A fact, apparently.
5. Left Feathers not earlier than 1.30.	5. Also a fact, alas!
6. Seen by Mr. Polwhistle and Tom at garage and in Hinks's Lane from 3 p.m. to 4 p.m.	6. Yet another fact, unless they are abominable liars!
7. Obtained car from London garage on previous Friday by means of reference to Cambridge bank. No settled address. Cambridge bank confirms he has had account there for five years.	7. Watch bank. Try to get information out of manager somehow.
8. It is certain that he did not reach the Flat-Iron by road on Thursday. He had not time to walk by the shore before two o'clock. (Aeroplanes are not practical politics.)	8. Bust this alibi if you can, Sherlock!!
9. Search at his camping-ground revealed a number of miscellaneous objects (see the Wimsey Collection). No complaints about him, except that Farmer Newcombe	9. Walk along shore from Flat-Iron to Darley this afternoon—nice little job for H.V. and P.W.

complains of gap made in his
fence.

"And that," said Wimsey, triumphantly adding a flourish at the foot of this
schedule, "rounds off the inquiry charmingly."

"It does." Harriet frowned. Then—

"Have you ever considered this?" she asked, with a not too steady voice. She
scribbled for a moment.

HARRIET VANE
THINGS TO BE NOTED

1. Personal characteristics: Once tried for murder of her lover, and acquitted
   by the skin of her teeth.
2. May have known Paul Alexis in London.
3. Says she found Alexis dead at 2.10, but can bring no evidence to prove that
   she did not see him alive.
4. Took an unconscionable time getting to the Flat-Iron from Lesston Hoe.
5. Took three hours to walk four and a half miles to inform the police.
6. Is the sole witness to the finding of the razor, the time of the death and the
   conditions at the Flat-Iron.
7. Was immediately suspected by Perkins, and is probably still suspected by
   the police, who have been searching her room.

Wimsey's face darkened.

"Have they, by God?"

"Yes. Don't look like that. They couldn't very well do anything else, could
they?"

"I'll have something to say to Umpelty."

"No. You can spare me that."

"But it's absurd."

"It is not. Do you think I have no wits? Do you think I don't know why you
came galloping down here at five minutes' notice? Of course it's very nice of you,
and I ought to be grateful, but do you think I like it?"

Wimsey, with a grey face, got up and walked to the window.

"You thought I was pretty brazen, I expect, when you found me getting
publicity out of the thing. So I was. There's no choice for a person like me to be
anything but brazen. Would it have been better to wait till the papers dragged
the juicy bits out of the dust-bin for themselves? I can't hide my name—it's
what I live by. If I did hide it, that would only be another suspicious circumstance, wouldn't it? But do you think it makes matters any more agreeable to
know that it is only the patronage of Lord Peter Wimsey that prevents men like
Umpelty from being openly hostile?"

"I have been afraid of this," said Wimsey.

"Then why did you come?"

"So that you might not have to send for me."

"Oh!"

There was a strained pause, while Wimsey painfully recalled the terms of the
message that had originally reached him from Salcombe Hardy of the *Morning
Star*—Hardy, a little drunk and wholly derisory, announcing over the telephone,

"I say, Wimsey, that Vane woman of yours has got herself mixed up in another queer story." Then his own furious and terrified irruption into Fleet Street, and the violent bullying of a repentant and sentimental Hardy, till the *Morning Star* report was hammered into a form that set the tone for the comments of the press. Then the return home to find that the Wilvercombe police were already besieging him, in the politest and most restrained manner, for information as to Miss Harriet Vane's recent movements and behaviour. And finally, the certainty that the best way out of a bad situation was to brazen it out—Harriet's word— even if it meant making a public exhibition of his feelings, and the annihilation of all the delicate structure of confidence which he had been so cautiously toiling to build up between this scathed and embittered woman and himself.

He said nothing, but watched the wreck of his fortune in Harriet's stormy eyes.

Harriet, meanwhile, having worked herself up into committing an act of what she obscurely felt to be injustice, was seized by an unreasonable hatred against the injured party. The fact that, until five minutes earlier, she had felt perfectly happy and at ease with this man, before she had placed both him and herself in an intolerable position, she felt somehow as one more added to the list of his offences. She looked round for something really savage to do to him.

"I suppose you think I haven't been humiliated enough already, without all this parade of chivalry. You think you can sit up there all day like King Cophetua being noble and generous and expecting people to be brought to your feet. Of course everybody will say, 'Look what he did for that woman—isn't it marvellous of him!' Isn't that nice for you? You think if you go on long enough I ought to be touched and softened. Well, you're mistaken, that's all. I suppose every man thinks he's only got to go on being superior and any woman will come tumbling into his arms. It's disgusting."

"Thank you," said Wimsey. "I may be everything you say—patronising, interfering, conceited, intolerable and all the rest of it. But do give me credit for a little intelligence. Do you think I don't know all that? Do you think it's pleasant for any man who feels about a woman as I do about you, to have to fight his way along under this detestable burden of gratitude? Damn it, do you think I don't know perfectly well that I'd have a better chance if I was deaf, blind, maimed, starving, drunken or dissolute, so that *you* could have the fun of being magnanimous? Why do you suppose I treat my own sincerest feelings like something out of a comic opera, if it isn't to save myself the bitter humiliation of seeing you try not to be utterly nauseated by them? Can't you understand that this damned dirty trick of fate has robbed me of the common man's right to be serious about his own passions? Is that a position for any man to be proud of?"

"Don't talk like that."

"I wouldn't, if you didn't force me. And you might have the justice to remember that you can hurt me a damned sight more than I can possibly hurt you."

"I know I'm being horribly ungrateful—"

"Hell!"

All endurance has its limits, and Wimsey had reached his.

"Grateful! Good God! Am I never to get away from the bleat of that filthy adjective! I don't want gratitude. I don't want kindness. I don't want sentimentality. I don't even want love—I could make you give me that—of a sort. I want common honesty."

"Do you? But that's what I've always wanted—I don't think it's to be got."

"Listen, Harriet. I do understand. I know you don't want either to give or to take. You've tried being the giver, and you've found that the giver is always fooled. And you won't be the taker, because that's very difficult, and because you know that the taker always ends by hating the giver. You don't want ever again to have to depend for happiness on another person."

"That's true. That's the truest thing you ever said."

"All right. I can respect that. Only you've got to play the game. Don't force an emotional situation and then blame me for it."

"But I don't want any situation. I want to be left in peace."

"Oh! but you are not a peaceful person. You'll always make trouble. Why not fight it out on equal terms and enjoy it? Like Alan Breck, I'm a bonny fighter."

"And you think you're sure to win."

"Not with my hands tied."

"Oh!—well, all right. But it all sounds so dreary and exhausting," said Harriet, and burst idiotically into tears.

"Good Heavens!" said Wimsey, aghast. "Harriet! darling! angel! beast! vixen! don't say that." He flung himself on his knees in a frenzy of remorse and agitation. "Call me anything you like, but not dreary! Not one of those things you find in clubs! Have this one, darling, it's much larger and quite clean. Say you didn't mean it! Great Scott! Have I been boring you interminably for eighteen months on end? A thing any right-minded woman would shudder at. I know you once said that if anybody ever married me it would be for the sake of hearing me piffle on, but I expect that kind of thing palls after a bit. I'm babbling—I know I'm babbling. What on earth am I to do about it?"

"Ass! Oh, it's not fair. You always make me laugh. I can't fight—I'm so tired. You don't seem to know what being tired is. Stop. Let go. I won't be bullied. Thank God! there's the telephone."

"Damn the telephone!"

"It's probably something very important."

She got up and went to the instrument, leaving Wimsey on his knees, looking, and feeling, sufficiently absurd.

"It's you. Somebody wants you over at the Bellevue."

"Let him want."

"Somebody come in answer to the thing in the *Morning Star*."

"Good lord!"

Wimsey shot across the room and snatched the receiver.

"That you, Wimsey? Thought I'd know where to get you. This is Sally Hardy. There's a fellow here claiming the reward. Hurry up! He won't come across without you, and I've got my story to think of. I've got him here in your sitting-room."

"Who is he, and where's he come from?"

"Seahampton. Says his name's Bright."

"Bright? By jove, yes, I'll come along right away. Hear that, my child? The man Bright has materialised! See you this afternoon at 3.30."

He bolted out like a cat that hears the cry of "Meat, meat!"

"Oh! what a fool I am," said Harriet. "What an utter, drivelling fool! And I haven't done a stroke of work since Wednesday."

She pulled out the manuscript of *The Fountain-Pen Mystery*, unscrewed her own pen, and sank into an idle reverie.

14

THE EVIDENCE OF THE THIRD BARBER

Not for him
Blooms my dark Nightshade, nor doth Hemlock brew
Murder for cups within her cavernous root.
Not him is the metal blessed to kill,
Nor lets the poppy her leaves fall for him.
To heroes such are sacred. He may live,
As long as 'tis the Gout and Dropsy's pleasure.
He wished to play at suicide.

—*Death's Jest-Book*

TUESDAY, 23 JUNE

On the doorstep of the Hotel Bellevue, Wimsey encountered Bunter.

"The person that was asking for your lordship is in your lordship's sitting-room," said Bunter. "I had the opportunity of observing him when he was inquiring for your lordship at the reception-counter, but I did not introduce myself to his notice."

"You didn't, eh?"

"No, my lord. I contented myself with privately informing Mr. Hardy of his presence. Mr. Hardy is with him at present, my lord."

"You always have a good reason for your actions, Bunter. May I ask why you have adopted this policy of modest self-effacement?"

"In case of your lordship's subsequently desiring to have the person placed under surveillance," suggested Bunter, "it appeared to me to be preferable that he should not be in a position to recognise me."

"Oh!" said Wimsey. "Am I to infer that the person presents a suspicious appearance? Or is this merely your native caution breaking out in an acute form? Well, perhaps you're right. I'd better go up and interview the bloke. How about the police, by the way? We can't very well keep this from them, can we?"

He reflected for a moment.

"Better hear the story first. If I want you, I'll 'phone down to the office. Have any drinks gone up?"

"I fancy not, my lord."

"Strange self-restraint on Mr. Hardy's part. Tell them to bring up a bottle of Scotch and a siphon and some beer, for malt does more than Milton can to justify God's ways to man. At the moment there seem to be a good many things that call for justification, but perhaps I shall feel better about them when I've heard what Mr. Bright has to tell me. Have at it!"

The moment Wimsey's eyes fell upon the visitor in his sitting-room he felt an interior conviction that his hopes were in a fair way to be realised. Whatever the results, he had, at any rate, been upon the right track in the matter of the razor. Here were the sandy hair, the small stature, the indefinite crookedness of shoulder so graphically described by the Seahampton hairdresser. The man was dressed in a shabby reach-me-down suit of blue serge, and held in his hands a limp felt hat, considerably the worse for wear. Wimsey noticed the soft skin and well-kept finger-nails, and the general air of poverty-stricken gentility.

"Well, Mr. Bright," said Hardy, as Wimsey entered, "here is the gentleman you want to see. Mr. Bright won't come across with his story to anybody but you, Wimsey, though, as I have explained to him, if he's thinking of claiming the *Morning Star* reward, he'll have to let me in on it."

Mr. Bright glanced nervously from one man to the other, and passed the tip of his tongue once or twice across his pallid lips.

"I suppose that's only fair," he said, in a subdued tone, "and I can assure you that the money is a consideration. But I am in a painful position, though I haven't done any wilful harm. I'm sure if I had ever thought what the poor gentleman was going to do with the razor—"

"Suppose we begin from the beginning," said Wimsey, throwing his hat upon a table and himself into a chair. "Come in! Oh, yes, drinks. What will you take, Mr. Bright?"

"It is very kind of your lordship," murmured Mr. Bright, with humility, "but I'm afraid I—the fact is, when I saw that piece in the paper I came away rather hurriedly. In fact, without my breakfast. I—that is to say—I am rather sensitive to alcohol taken upon an empty stomach."

"Bring up some sandwiches," said Wimsey to the waiter. "It is very good of you, Mr. Bright, to have put yourself to so much inconvenience in the interests of justice."

"Justice?"

"I mean, in order to help us with this inquiry. And of course, you must allow us to refund your expenses."

"Thank you, my lord. I won't say no. In fact, I am not in a position to refuse. As a matter of fact," went on Mr. Bright, with more frankness in the absence of the waiter, "as a matter of fact, I had to go without any food in order to pay for my ticket. I don't like making this confession. It's very humiliating for a man who once had a flourishing business of his own. I hope you won't think, gentlemen, that I have been accustomed to this kind of thing."

"Of course not," said Wimsey. "Bad things may happen to anybody. Nobody thinks anything of that nowadays. Now, about this razor. By the way, your full name is—?"

"William Bright, my lord. I'm a hairdresser by profession. I used to have a business up Manchester way. But I lost money by an unfortunate speculation—"

"Whereabouts in Manchester?" put in Salcombe Hardy.

"In Massingbird Street. But it's all been pulled down now. I don't know if anybody would remember about it, I'm sure. It was before the War."

"Any War record?" asked Hardy.

"No." The hairdresser blushed painfully. "I'm not a robust man. I couldn't get passed for active service."

"All right," said Wimsey. "About the razor. What are you doing now?"

"Well, my lord, I am, as you might say, an itinerant hairdresser. I go from one place to the other, especially seaside towns during the season, and take temporary posts."

"Where did you work last?"

The man glanced up at him with his hunted eyes.

"I haven't had anything, really, for a long time. I tried to get work in Seahampton. In fact, I'm still trying. I went back there last Wednesday after trying Wilvercombe and Lesston Hoe. I had a week's employment in Lesston Hoe. Ramage's is the name of the place. I had to leave there—"

"What for?" Hardy was brusque.

"There was trouble with a customer—"

"Theft?"

"Certainly not. He was a very quick-tempered gentleman. I had the misfortune to cut him slightly."

"Drunk and incompetent, eh?" said Hardy.

The small man seemed to shrink together.

"They said so, but on my word of honour—"

"What name were you going by there?"

"Walters."

"Is Bright your real name?"

Under the lash of Hardy's brutality, the story came out in all its sordid triviality. Alias after alias. A week's trial here and there, and then dismissal on the same humiliating grounds. Not his fault. A glass of spirits affected him more than it did the ordinary person. Simpson was his real name, but he had used a great many since then. But to each name, the same reputation had stuck. It was his sad weakness, which he had tried hard to overcome.

Hardy poured himself out a second glass of whisky, and carelessly left the bottle on the window-sill, out of Mr. Bright's reach.

"In the matter of the razor," said Wimsey, patiently.

"Yes, my lord. I got that razor in Seahampton, from the place where I tried to get work. Merryweather, the name was. I needed a new razor, and he was willing to sell this one cheap.

"You'd better describe the razor," suggested Hardy.

"Yes, sir. It was a Sheffield blade with a white handle, and it came originally from a retailer in Jermyn Street. It was a good razor, but a bit worn. I came on to Wilvercombe, but there was nothing doing here, except that Moreton, down on the Esplanade, said he might be requiring help later on. Then I went to Lesston Hoe. I told you about that. After trying one or two other places there, I came back here and tried Moreton again, but he had just engaged somebody. He would tell you about it if you asked him. There was nothing doing anywhere else. I grew very low in my spirits."

Mr. Bright paused and licked his lips again.

"This was last Monday week, gentlemen. On the Tuesday night, I went down to the sea—just out there, at the end of the town, and sat on a seat to think things over. It was getting on for midnight." The words were coming more fluently now, the glass of whisky having no doubt done its work. "I looked at the sea and I felt the razor in my pocket and I wondered whether it was worth while struggling on. I was terrible depressed. I had come quite to the end of my resources. There was the sea, and there was the razor. You might think that the use of a razor would come natural to a hairdresser, but I can assure you gentlemen that the idea of using it for that purpose seems just as horrible to us as it would to you. But the sea—washing up against the wall of the Esplanade—it seemed to call me, if you can understand what I mean. It sounded as if it was saying: 'Chuck it, chuck it, chuck it up, Bill Simpson.' Fascinating and frightening at the same time, as you might say. All the same, I've always had a horror of drowning. Helpless and choking, and the green water in your eyes—we all have our special nightmares, and that one's mine. Well, I'd sat there for a bit, trying to make up my mind, when I heard somebody walking along, and presently this young fellow came and sat down on the seat beside me. He was in evening dress, I remember, with an overcoat and a soft hat. He had a black beard—that was about the first thing I noticed, because it's not very usual on a young man in this country, except he might be an artist, perhaps. Well, we got into conversation— I think he started it by offering me a cigarette. It was one of those Russian ones, with a paper tube to it. He spoke friendly, and, I don't know how it was, I found myself telling him all about the fix I was in. You know how it is, my lord. Sometimes you'll get talking to a stranger where you wouldn't to anybody you knew. It struck me he didn't feel so very happy himself, and we had a long talk about the general damnableness of life. He said he was a Russian and an exile and told me about the hard times he'd had as a kid, and a lot of stuff about 'Holy Russia' and the Soviet. Seemed as if he took it to heart a lot. And women and all that—seemed as though he'd had some trouble with his best girl. And then he said he only wished his difficulties could be solved as easy as mine, and how I ought to pull myself together and make a fresh start. 'You give me that razor,' he said, 'and go away and think it over.' So I said the razor was my livelihood, such as it was, and he laughed and said, 'In the mood you're in, it's more likely to be your deathlihood.' A funny way he had to talking, quick and sort of poetic, you know. So he gave me some money—five pounds it was, in Treasury notes—and I gave him the razor. 'What'll you do with that, sir?' I said, 'it's no good to you.' 'I'll find a use for it,' he said, 'never you fear.' And he laughed and put it away in his pocket. Then he got up and said, 'Funny we should drop across one another to-night,' and something about 'Two minds with but a single thought.' And he clapped me on the shoulder and told me to buck up and gave me a pleasant nod and away he went, and that's the last I saw of him. I wish I'd known what he wanted with the razor, or I wouldn't have given it to him, but there! how was I to know, I ask you, gentlemen?"

"Sounds like Paul Alexis, right enough," said Wimsey, thoughtfully.

"He didn't actually say who he was, I suppose?" suggested Hardy.

"No, he didn't; but he said he was a professional dancing-partner at one of the hotels, and wasn't it one hell of a life for a man that ought to be a prince in his own country—making love to ugly old women at twopence-halfpenny a time. Very bitter he sounded."

"Well," said Wimsey, "we're very much obliged to you, Mr. Bright. That seems to clear the whole thing up quite satisfactorily. I think you'll have to let the police know about it."

Mr. Bright looked uneasy at the mention of the police.

"Better come along now and get it over," said Wimsey, jumping to his feet. "You can't very well get out of it, and, hang it all, man! there's nothing in it for anybody to worry you about."

The hairdresser agreed, reluctantly, and fastened his pale eyes on Sally Hardy.

"It all sounds O.K. to me," said the latter, "but we'll have to check up on your story, you know, old man. You might have invented it. But if the cops can prove what you say about yourself—it's their business, really—then there'll be a good, fat cheque for you, that ought to keep you going for some time, if you'll steer clear of that—er—little weakness of yours. The great thing," added Sally, reaching for the whisky, "is never to let weaknesses interfere with business."

He poured himself out a stiff peg and, as an afterthought, mixed another for the hairdresser.

Superintendent Glaisher was delighted with Bright's story, and so was Inspector Umpelty, who had clung to the suicide theory all along.

"We'll soon get this business cleared up," said the latter, confidently. "We'll check up on this Bright lad's movements, but they're probably right enough. They fit in O.K. with what that man said at Seahampton. And we'll keep an eye on Bright. He's had to give us an address and his promise to stay in Wilvercombe, because, of course, he'll be wanted for the inquest—when we get an inquest. The body's bound to turn up soon. I can't understand why it's not been found before this. It's been five days in the water now, and it can't stay there for ever. They float first, you know, and then they sink, but they have to come up again when the gases start to form. I've seen 'em blown up like balloons. It must have got caught somewhere, that's about the way of it; but we'll be dragging the bay near the Grinders again this afternoon, and we're sure to get something before long. I'll be glad when we do. Makes one feel kind of foolish to be carrying on an investigation without a body to show for it."

"Satisfied?" asked Hardy, as Wimsey returned from the police-station. He had telephoned his story to Town and was absorbing a little refreshment after his labours.

"I ought to be," replied his lordship. "The only thing that worries me, Sally, is that if I'd wanted to invent a story to fit this case, that is exactly the story I should have invented. I wonder where Mr. Bright was at two o'clock on Thursday afternoon."

"What an obstinate devil you are," said Mr. Hardy. "Fact is, you're so damned keen on a murder, you smell murder everywhere. Forget it."

Wimsey was silent, but when he had got rid of Sally Hardy, he drew out of his pocket a small leaflet entitled "Tide Tables," and studied it carefully.

"I thought so," he said.

He took a piece of paper and wrote out a schedule of Things to be Noted and Things to be Done under the name of William Bright. It embodied the substance of Bright's story and of the conversation with the police; but the left-hand column ended with this observation:

He states that the tide, lapping against the Esplanade, seemed to call to him in a very convincing and poetic manner. But at midnight on Tuesday, 16 June the tide was not lapping against the Esplanade. It was the extreme bottom of the ebb.

And in the right-hand column he wrote:

Keep an eye on him.

After a little more thought, he took a fresh sheet of paper and wrote a letter to Chief Inspector Parker of Scotland Yard, asking for information about Bolshevik agents. One never could tell. Queer things had happened before this—queerer things even than Bolshevik conspiracies. Incidentally, he mentioned Mr. Haviland Martin and his banking account. Parker, with the Bolsheviks as an excuse, might find ways and means to unlock even a bank-manager's lips. Superintendent Glaisher might not like this horning in on his province—but Parker had married Lord Peter's sister, and may not a man write a private letter to his own brother-in-law?

15

THE EVIDENCE OF THE LADYLOVE AND THE LANDLADY

You are an adept in these chamber-passions,
And have a heart that's Cupid's arrow-cushion
Worn out with use.
—*Death's Jest-Book*

What's this? Did you not see a white convulsion
Run through his cheek and fling his eyelids up?
There's mischief in the paper.
—*Fragment*

TUESDAY, 23 JUNE

In the meantime, Harriet's novel was not getting along very well. Not only was there the tiresomeness about the town-clock—or ought it to be called the Tolbooth clock? —but also she had arrived at the point where, according to the serial editor who was paying for the first rights, the heroine and the detective's friend were expected to indulge in a spot of lovemaking. Now, a person whose previous experience of love has been disappointing, and who has just been through a harassing scene with another suitor and is, further, busily engaged in investigating the rather sordid love-affairs of a third party who has been brought to a violent and blood-boltered end, is in no mood to sit down and deal competently with the raptures of two innocents holding hands in a rose-garden. Harriet shook her head impatiently, and plunged into her distasteful task.

"I say, Betty, I'm afraid you must think I'm a pretty average sort of idiot."
"But I don't think you're an idiot at all, you idiot."

Would even the readers of the *Daily Message* think that amusing? Harriet feared not. Well, better get on with it. The girl would have to say something encouraging now, or the stammering young imbecile would never come to the point.

"I think it's perfectly wonderful that you should be doing all this to help me."

Here she was, remorselessly binding this hideous load of gratitude on the fortunate girl. But Betty and Jack were a pair of hypocrites, anyway, because they both knew perfectly well that Robert Templeton was doing all the work. However.

"As if there was anything in the world I wouldn't try and do for you—Betty!"

"Well, Jack?"

"Betty—darling—I suppose you couldn't possibly—"

Harriet came to the conclusion that she couldn't—not possibly. She picked up the telephone, got put through to Telegrams, and dictated a brief, snappy message to her long-suffering agent. "Tell Bootle I absolutely refuse introduce love-interest—Vane."

After that she felt better, but the novel was perfectly impossible. Wasn't there anything else she could do? Yes. She again seized the telephone and put an inquiry through to the office. Was it possible to get into touch with M. Antoine?

The management seemed quite used to putting clients in touch with M. Antoine. They had a telephone number which ought to find him. It did. Could M. Antoine put Miss Vane in touch with Miss Leila Garland and Mr. da Soto? Certainly. Nothing was more simple. Mr. da Soto was playing at the Winter Gardens, and the morning concert would be just finishing. Miss Garland would probably be joining him for lunch. In any case, Antoine would charge himself with all that and would, if Miss Vane desired it, call for her and accompany her to the Winter Gardens. It was most good of M. Antoine. On the contrary, it was a pleasure; in a quarter of an hour's time, then? *Parfaitement.*

"Tell me, M. Antoine," said Harriet, as their taxi rolled along the Esplanade. "You who are a person of great experience, is love, in your opinion, a matter of the first importance?"

"It is, alas! of a great importance, mademoiselle, but of the first importance, no!"

"What is of the first importance?"

"Mademoiselle, I tell you frankly that to have a healthy mind in a healthy body is the greatest gift of *le bon Dieu*, and when I see so many people who have clean blood and strong bodies spoiling themselves and distorting their brains with drugs and drink and foolishness, it makes me angry. They should leave that to the people who cannot help themselves because to them life is without hope."

Harriet hardly knew what to reply; the words were spoken with such personal and tragic significance. Rather fortunately, Antoine did not wait.

"*L'amour!* These ladies come and dance and excite themselves and want love and think it is happiness. And they tell me about their sorrows—me—and they have no sorrows at all, only that they are silly and selfish and lazy. Their husbands are unfaithful and their lovers run away and what do they say? Do they say, I have two hands, two feet, all my faculties, I will make a life for myself? No. They say, 'Give me cocaine, give me the cocktail, give me the thrill, give me my gigolo, give me *l'amo-o-ur!*' Like a *mouton* bleating in a field. If they knew!"

Harriet laughed.

"You're right, M. Antoine. I don't believe *l'amour* matters so terribly, after all."

"But understand me," said Antoine who, like most Frenchmen, was fundamentally serious and domestic, "I do not say that love is not important. It is no doubt agreeable to love, and to marry an amiable person who will give you fine, healthy children. This Lord Peter Wimsey, *par exemple*, who is obviously a gentleman of the most perfect integrity—"

"Oh, never mind *him!*" broke in Harriet, hastily. "I wasn't thinking about him. I was thinking about Paul Alexis and these people we are going to see."

"Ah! *c'est différent*. Mademoiselle, I think you know very well the difference between love which is important and love which is not important. But you must remember that one may have an important love for an unimportant person. And you must remember also that where people are sick in their minds or their bodies it does not need even love to make them do foolish things. When I kill myself, for example, it may be out of boredom, or disgust, or because I have the headache or the stomach-ache or because I am no longer able to take a first-class position and do not want to be third-rate."

"I hope you're not thinking of anything of the sort."

"Oh, I shall kill myself one of these days," said Antoine, cheerfully. "But it will not be for love. No. I am not so *détraqué* as all that."

The taxi drew up at the Winter Gardens. Harriet felt a certain delicacy about paying the fare, but soon realised that for Antoine the thing was a commonplace. She accompanied him to the orchestra entrance where, in a few minutes' time, they were joined by Leila Garland and Luis da Soto—the perfect platinum blonde and the perfect lounge-lizard. Both were perfectly self-possessed and incredibly polite; the only difficulty—as Harriet found when they were seated together at a table—was to get any reliable information out of them. Leila had evidently taken up an attitude, and stuck to it. Paul Alexis was "a terribly nice boy," but "too romantic altogether." Leila had been "terribly grieved" to send him away, he "took it so terribly hard"—but, after all, her feeling for him had been no more than pity—he had been "so terribly timid and lonely." When Luis came alone, she realised at once where her affections really lay. She rolled her large periwinkle eyes at Mr. da Soto, who responded by a languishing droop of his fringed lids.

"I was all the more sorry about it," said Leila, "because poor darling Paul—"

"Not darling, honey."

"Of course not, Luis—only the poor thing's dead. Anyway, I was sorry because poor Paul seemed to be so terribly worried about something. But he didn't confide in me, and what is a girl to do when a man won't confide in her? I sometimes used to wonder if he wasn't being blackmailed by somebody."

"Why? did he seem to be short of money?"

"Well, yes, he did. Of course, that wouldn't make any difference to me; I'm not that sort of girl. Still, it's not pleasant, you know, to think that one of your gentleman friends is being blackmailed. I mean, a girl never knows she may not get mixed up in something unpleasant. I mean, it isn't quite nice, is it?"

"Far from it. How long ago did he start being worried?"

"Let me see. I think it was about five months ago. Yes, it was. I mean, that was when the letters started coming."

"Letters?"

"Yes; long letters with foreign stamps on them. I think they came from Czechoslovakia or one of those queer places. It wasn't Russia, anyway, because I asked him and he said no. I thought it was very funny, because he said he'd never been in any foreign country except Russia when he was quite a little boy, and in America, of course."

"Have you told anybody else about these letters?"

"No. You see, Paul always said it would do him harm to have them mentioned. He said the Bolsheviks would kill him if anything got out. I said to him, 'I don't know what you mean by that,' I said, 'I'm not a Bolshie,' I said, 'and I don't know any people of that sort, so what harm would it do to tell me about it?' But now he's dead it can't do any harm, can it? Besides, if you ask me, I don't believe it was Bolshies at all. I mean, it doesn't seem likely, does it? I said to him, 'If you expect me to swallow *that* story, you're expecting a lot,' I said. But he wouldn't tell me, and of course, that did make a little coolness between us. I mean to say, when a girl is friends with a man, like me and Paul, she does expect a little consideration."

"Of course she does," said Harriet, warmly. "It was very wrong of him not to be perfectly frank with you. I really think, in your place, I'd have felt justified in trying to find out who the letters were from."

Leila played delicately with a piece of bread.

"As a matter of fact," she admitted, "I did take a tiny peep once. I thought I owed it to myself. But they were all nonsense. You couldn't make out a word of them."

"Were they in a foreign language?"

"Well, I don't know. They were all in printing letters and some of the words hadn't any vowels in them at all. You couldn't possibly pronounce them."

"It sounds like a cipher," suggested Antoine.

"Yes, that's just what I thought. I did think it was terribly funny."

"But surely," said Harriet, "an ordinary blackmailer wouldn't write letters in cipher."

"Oh, but why shouldn't they? I mean, they might have been a gang, you know, like in that story, *The Trail of the Purple Python*. Have you read it? The Purple Python was a Turkish millionaire, and he had a secret house full of steel-lined rooms and luxurious divans and obelisks—"

"Obelisks?"

"Well, you know. Ladies who weren't quite respectable. And he had agents in every country in Europe, who bought up compromising letters and he wrote to his victims in cipher and signed his missives with a squiggle in purple ink. Only the English detective's young lady found out his secret by disguising herself as an obelisk and the detective who was really Lord Humphrey Chillingfold arrived with the police just in time to rescue her from the loathsome embrace of the Purple Python. It was a terribly exciting book. Paul read lots of books like that—I expect he was trying to pick up ideas for getting the better of the gang. He liked the talkies too. Of course, in those stories, the hero always comes out on top, only poor dear Paul wasn't really a bit like a hero. I said to him one day, 'It's all very well,' I said, 'but I can't see *you* venturing into a Chinese opium den full of gangsters, with a pistol in your pocket, and being gassed and sandbagged and then throwing off your bonds and attacking the Underworld King with an electric lamp. You'd be afraid of getting hurt,' I said. And so he would."

Mr. da Soto snickered appreciatively.

"You said a mouthful, honey. Poor Alexis was a friend of mine, but courage was just what he didn't have. I told him, if he didn't stand out of my way and let little Leila pick her own sweetie, I would give him a sock on the jaw. I give you my word, he was scared stiff."

"So he was," said Leila. "Of course, a girl couldn't feel any respect for a man that didn't stand up for himself."

"Remarkable!" said Antoine. "And this young man, so timid, so complaisant, cuts his throat with a big, ugly gash because you turn him down. *C'est inoui.*"

"I suppose you believe his Bolshie story," said Leila, offended.

"I? I believe nothing. I am agnostic. But I say that your portrait of Alexis is not very logical."

"Antoine always talks about logic," said Leila, "but what I say is, people aren't logical. Look at all the funny things they do. Especially men. I always think men are terribly inconsistent."

"You bet they are," said Mr. da Soto. "You're just dead right, sweetest. They have to be, or they wouldn't be bothered with naughty little girlies like you."

"Yes, but the letters," said Harriet, sticking desperately to her point. "How often did they come?"

"About once a week, sometimes oftener. He kept them locked up in a little box. He used to answer them, too. Sometimes when I went round to see him, he'd have his door locked, and old Ma Lefranc said he was writing letters and wasn't to be disturbed. Naturally, a girl doesn't like her gentleman friend to behave like that. I mean, you do expect him to pay a little attention to you and not shut himself up writing letters when you come to see him. I mean, it wasn't the sort of thing you could expect a girl to put up with."

"Of course you couldn't, baby," said Mr. da Soto.

Antoine smiled, and murmured unexpectedly:

"Mais si quelqu'un venoit de la part de Cassandre,
Ouvre-luy tost la porte, et ne le fais attendre,
Soudain entre dans ma chambre, et me vien accoustrer."

Harriet smiled back at him and then, struck with an idea, asked Leila:

"When did the last of these letters arrive?"

"I don't know. I wasn't friends with him any more after I got friendly with Luis. But I expect Ma Lefranc would tell you. There isn't much goes on that Ma Lefranc doesn't know about."

"Did you and Alexis live together when you were friendly?" demanded Harriet, bluntly.

"Of course not; what a dreadful thing to ask a girl."

"I mean, in the same house."

"Oh, no. We used to go and see each other quite often, but of course, after Luis and me became friends, I said to Paul that it would be better if we didn't see each other any more. You see, Paul was so fond of me, and Luis would have been imagining things—wouldn't you, Luis?"

"You bet your life I would, honey."

"Haven't you told the police about these letters?"

"No, I have not," replied Miss Garland, decidedly. "I don't say I mightn't have told them if they had asked properly, but the way that fat Umpelty went on, you'd have thought I wasn't a respectable girl. So I said to him, 'I know nothing about it,' I said, 'and you've got nothing against me,' I said, 'and you can't make me answer your silly questions unless you take me down to your dirty old police-station and charge me,' I said." Miss Garland's carefully modulated tones escaped from control and became shrill. "And I said, 'It wouldn't be a scrap of good if you did,' I said, 'because I know nothing about Paul Alexis and I haven't seen him for months,' I said, 'and you can ask anybody you like,' I said, 'and what's more, if you get bullying a respectable girl like this,' I said, 'you'll get yourself into trouble, Mr. Rumplety Bumpelty,' I said, 'so now you know where you get off.' That's what I said, and it's a good thing there's a law in this country to protect girls like I."

"Ain't she the snail's ankles?" asked Mr. da Soto, admiringly.

There seemed to be no further information to be gathered from Leila Garland, whom Harriet put down in her own mind as "a regular little gold-digger and as vain as a monkey." As for da Soto, he looked harmless enough, and did not seem to have had any pressing reason for doing away with Alexis. One never knew, of course, with these slinky people of confused nationality. Just as she was thinking this, da Soto drew out his watch.

"You will excuse me, ladies and gentlemen. I have a rehearsal at two o'clock. As always, Tuesdays and Thursdays."

He bowed and left them, with his lithe walk, between a lounge and a swagger. Had he deliberately mentioned Thursdays in order to direct attention to an alibi for Thursday, 18th? And how did he know the time for which an alibi was required? That particular detail had not been allowed to get into the papers, and it was not likely to do so until the inquest. And yet—could one attach any importance to the remark? An alibi depending on an orchestra rehearsal was so easily established or refuted. Then an explanation occurred to her: the police would already have asked da Soto about his movements last Thursday. But surely they would not have emphasised the crucial time to that extent. They had agreed that the less anybody knew about the time the better—it would be helpful in the inquiry if anyone were to come forward ostentatiously flourishing an alibi for two o'clock.

Harriet returned with Antoine, still not quite knowing what to make of da Soto. It was still only a quarter past two; she had time to carry out a new plan which she had formed. She put some clothes in a suit-case and went round to interview Paul Alexis' landlady, Mrs. Lefranc.

The door of the cheap-looking lodging-house was opened to her by an ample personage with brazen hair, who was dressed in a pink wrapper, much-laddered artificial silk stockings and green velvet mules, and wore about her heavily powdered neck a string of synthetic-amber beads like pigeon's eggs.

"Good morning," said Harriet, "I'm looking for a room."

The lady eyed her shrewdly and said:

"Professional, dearie?"

To say "Yes" was tempting but unsafe. Mrs. Lefranc looked as though what she did not know about professionals could have been written on a threepenny bit. Besides, Harriet was becoming well-known in Wilvercombe—she could scarcely hope to hide her identity for ever.

"No," she said. "I write books. In fact, Mrs. Lefranc, I'm the person who found poor Mr. Alexis last week. I've been staying at the Resplendent, but it's terribly expensive, and I thought, if your room was still vacant, I might be able to take it."

"Well, there!" said Mrs. Lefranc. She opened the door a little wider, but seemed to be divided between suspicion and curiosity. "Well, there! I hardly know what to say. You ain't one of these journalists?"

"Oh, dear, no," replied Harriet.

"Because," said Mrs. Lefranc, "with those fellers you never know where you are. Worried to death I've been with them, poking their long noses into my private affairs. But of course *you* can't help but feel an interest, dearie, can you, seeing it was you that found him, poor boy. Come along in. Excuse my negleegy, won't you? If I'm not up and down, up and down, keeping an eye on that girl, I don't know where we'd all be. I don't get time to posh myself up of a morning. How long would you be wanting the room for?"

"I don't quite know. It depends on when they have the inquest."

"Ah, yes—and they've got to find him first, poor lamb, ain't they? You know, I've got such a warm heart, I can't sleep at nights for thinking of him washing about in all that nasty sea. Mind the coal-scuttle, dearie; the times I tell that girl not to leave it on the stairs. It's a lovely room on the first floor—quite the best in the house, and you'll find the bed comfortable. Poor Mr. Alexis always said it was like a home to him and I'm sure he was like a son to me."

Mrs. Lefranc led the way up, her green mules flapping and displaying large holes in the heels of her stockings.

"There, dearie!" said Mrs. Lefranc, throwing open the door. "I'm sure you couldn't find better in Wilvercombe, and it's nice and quiet—you'll be able to do your writing beautiful. I've had it all cleaned up and his clothes and things put away—and if you was to dislike his books and bits of things about, I could easy put them to the one side. But there! I daresay you won't mind them. It's not as if he'd died in this room, is it, poor soul? And I'm sure Mr. Alexis was far too much the gentleman to commit a rash act on anybody's premises. That kind of thing do give a place a bad name, there's no denying it, and one is apt to be blamed for things as aren't in any woman's control, try as she may to make her visitors happy. But as to the books, well, of course, if it had been anything infectious they'd have to have been destroyed, though as to who they belong to now I don't know, I'm sure, and the police can't tell me either, and I daresay they've as much right here as anywhere, with me being like a mother to him this year past and more. But anything infectious there is not, for he never was subject to any such complaint, enjoying good health as a rule, barring the pain in his joints which he had to lay up for at times, and the agony he went through was cruel. I'm sure my heart bled for him, and the amount of antipyrin he took for it would surprise you and he never would have a doctor. But there! I don't blame him. My sister had the rheumatics something cruel and the amount she spent on doctors and electric treatment and nothing to show for it, except her knee swelled up like a pumpkin. And she lost the use of the limb altogether, which was a cruel thing for a woman in her profession. A trapeze-artist, she was; I've got her photograph in my room if you would like to see it one day, dearie, and the wreaths her old pals sent to her funeral was beautiful to see. Covered the hearse, they did, and they had to have an extra carriage on purpose for them. But as I was saying, if you don't care about the books I'll take them away. I'm not going to have that Weldon woman or Leila Garland—the little cat—coming here trying to get hold of them."

The room was pleasant enough—large and airy and much cleaner than Harriet could have hoped from Mrs. Lefranc's appearance. The furniture was, of course, hideous, but, though shabby, solid and in good order. The books were just as Inspector Umplety had described them: mainly novels in cheap editions, with some Russian paper-backs and a few volumes of Russian Court memoirs. The only striking relic of the former tenant was a very beautiful little ikon hung at the head of the bed—certainly old and probably valuable.

For form's sake Harriet entered upon a long haggle with Mrs. Lefranc about terms, emerging victorious with an inclusive charge of two and a half guineas per week, or twelve shillings and find yourself.

"And it's not everybody I'd do that for," said Mrs. Lefranc. "Only I can see you're one of the quiet sort. If there's a thing I don't want in my house it's trouble. Though I'm sure all this dreadful business is trouble enough for anybody. The cruel shock it was to me," said Mrs. Lefranc, gasping a little and sitting down on the bed, as though to demonstrate that the shock had not yet spent its force. "I was that fond of poor Mr. Alexis."

"I'm sure you must have been."

"Such a thoughtful boy," pursued Mrs. Lefranc, "and the manners of a prince, he had. I'm sure, many's the time when I was run off my feet with the girl and the lodgers and all, he'd say, 'Cheer up, ma'—they all call me that, 'cheer up, ma. Have a little cocktail with me and here's to better days.' Just like a son he was to me, I'm sure."

Whatever Harriet may have thought of this touching reminiscence, which sounded quite unlike anything she had heard of Paul Alexis, she did not ignore the hint.

"How about a spot of something now?" she suggested.

"I'm sure," said Mrs. Lefranc, "I wasn't meaning—well, there! It's no end sweet of you, dearie, but I couldn't touch anything this time in the day. Not but what there's the jug-and-bottle at the Dragon just round the corner, which comes very convenient, and there's no doubt as a drop of gin do help your dinner to settle."

Harriet bent her energies to overcoming the resistance of Mrs. Lefranc, who presently put her head over the staircase and called to "the girl" to slip round to the Dragon for a suitable quantity of gin.

"They know me," she added, with a wink. "What with these ridiculous laws about bottles and half-bottles, if they don't know you, they'd get you all locked-up before you knew where you were. You'd think they wanted to make folks drunk by Act of Parliament, wouldn't you? What with one thing and another and the police sticking their noses in and asking questions—as though my house wasn't always as well-conducted as the Archbishop of Canterbury's—and they know it too, for I've been here twenty years and never a complaint—it's hard for a decent woman to keep her head above water these days. And one thing I can say—I've never stinted anybody. My house is just like home to 'em, and so you'll find it, dearie."

Under the influence of gin-and-water, Mrs. Lefranc became less and less guarded. She had her own version of the Leila Garland complication.

"What there might be between those two," she observed, "I couldn't tell you, dearie. It's not my business, so long as my visitors conducts themselves quietly. I always say to my girls, 'I'm not against ladies seeing their gentlemen-friends and contrariwise, provided there's no trouble caused. We've all been young once,' I say to them, 'but you will please to remember we want no trouble here.' That's what I say, and there's never been a mite of trouble in this house till now. But I must say I wasn't sorry when that little cat took herself off. No, I wasn't. Nor I didn't like that dago of hers, either. I hope she's making him pay through the nose. You couldn't give that girl enough. Not but what she didn't make herself pleasant enough, and bring me a bunch of flowers or a little present when she came to see Mr. Alexis, though where the money came from I was not asking. But when poor Mr. Alexis told me that she had taken up with this da Soto fellow, I said, 'You're well rid of her.' That's what I said, and if you ask me, he knew it well enough."

"You don't think he killed himself on her account, then?"

"I do not," said Mrs. Lefranc. "And I'm sure I've puzzled my head often enough wondering why he did it. It wasn't on account of the old lady he was engaged to—I know that. To tell you the truth, dearie, he never expected that to come off. Of course, a young man in his position has to humour his ladies, but her family never would have stood it. Mr. Alexis as good as told me that would never come off—and not so long ago either. 'You see, ma,' he said to me no longer ago than last Sunday week, 'one of these days I may do still better for myself.' 'Oh, yes,' I says to him, 'you'll be marrying the Princess of China, you will, like Aladdin in the Panto.' No. I've thought about it over and over again, and I'll tell you what I think. I think it was his speculations went wrong."

"Speculations?"

"Yes—those speculations of his in foreign countries. The letters he used to get! All stuck over with foreign stamps and addressed in funny handwriting. I used to chaff him about them. Reports, he said they were, and if they came right, he'd be one of the biggest men in the world. He used to say, 'Ma, when my ship comes in, I'll give you a tiara stuck full of diamonds and make you house-keeper to royalty.' Oh, dear, many's the laugh we've had together over it. Not but what there was a time when I could have had tiaras and necklaces if I'd wanted 'em. One of these days I'll show you my newspaper critiques. Airy-fairy-Lilian they used to call me when I was principal boy in old Rosenbaum's shows, though you mightn't think it to look at me now, dearie, for my figure's spread a bit, there ain't no denying."

Harriet admired and sympathised, and led Mrs. Lefranc gently back to the subject of the foreign letters.

"Well, dearie, there was one of them come two days before this dreadful thing happened. It must have been a long one, for he was shut up hours and hours with it. Working out his position, he used to call it. Well, *I* think there must have been bad news in it, though he didn't let on. But he was queer all that day and the next. Seemed as though he didn't see you or hear you when you spoke to him. And laughing—hysterical, I should call it, if he'd been a girl. He kissed me on the Wednesday night when he went up to bed. Joking he was and talking wild, but I didn't pay attention. That was rather his way, you know. 'One of these days,' he said, 'you'll find I've opened my wings and gone.' Little did I think—oh, dear me! Poor boy! I can see now that was just his way of breaking it to me. I heard him about in his room all night. Burning his papers, he was, poor dear lad. He'd had a dreadful disappointment and he didn't want anybody to know. And in the morning he gave me his week's money. 'I know it's a bit early,' he said—because, of course, it wasn't due till Saturday, 'but if I give it to you now, it'll be safe,' he said. 'If I took it out with me, I might spend it.' Of course, I know now what was in his mind, poor dear. He knew he was going out and he didn't want me to suffer; he always was considerate. But when I think now that a word might have saved him—"

Mrs. Lefranc burst into tears.

"I did think he might have been going away sudden to see after his speculations, but he didn't pack up anything, so of course I put that out of my mind. And as for him doing what he did do—how could I have thought it? He seemed in such high spirits. But there! I *might* have guessed, if my mind hadn't been full of other things—only what with the girl giving notice as she did that morning and one thing and another, I didn't pay attention. But they often do seem to be in high spirits before they put an end to themselves. There was poor Billy Carnaby—he was just the same. Gave an oyster-and-champagne party to the whole cast on his last night with his last penny and him the life and soul of it, making us split our sides—and then went off and blew his brains out in the gentlemen's lavatory."

Mrs. Lefranc cried bitterly for a few moments.

"But there!" she exclaimed, suddenly pulling herself together and blowing her nose, "life's a funny thing and you can't account for it, can you? Let's be happy while we can. We'll all be having a little white stone over us before long and it don't matter so much how or when. When was you wanting to take the room, dearie?"

"I'll be coming in to-night," said Harriet. "I don't know whether I'll want my board or not, but if I leave my suit-case and pay you the twelve shillings for the room in advance, that'll be all right, won't it?"

"That's O.K., dearie," said Mrs. Lefranc, obviously cheered. "Just you come when you like, you'll be happy with Ma Lefranc. There, now, you'll think I've been talking enough to fetch the hind leg off a donkey, but what I say is, a good cry now and again does you good when the world ain't using you well. All my young people brings their troubles to me. I only wish poor Mr. Alexis had told me all his worries and he'd be here now. But he was a foreigner, when all's said and done, and they aren't like us, are they? Mind that dust-pan, dearie. Time and again I tell them not to leave things on the stairs, but you might as well talk to the cat. Five mice she left on my door-mat yesterday morning, if you'll believe me, not that they ever come upstairs, dearie, and don't you think it, but the cellars is overrun with them, the dirty little beasts. Well, so long, dearie, and by the way, here's your latch-key. It's lucky I had a new one cut; poor Mr. Alexis took his away with him when he went and goodness knows where it is now. I let my visitors come in when and how they like; you'll find yourself comfortable here."

16

THE EVIDENCE OF THE SANDS

This is the oft-wished hour, when we together
May walk upon the sea-shore.
                              —*Death's Jest-Book*

TUESDAY, 23 JUNE

I f either Harriet Vane or Lord Peter Wimsey felt any embarrassment at meeting again after their burst of free speech, they did not show it. Both had a story to tell, and were thus spared the awkwardness of being gravelled for lack of matter.

"Cipher letters? Is it possible that Mrs. Weldon is all right and that we are all wrong? It makes it look more like murder, anyhow, which is one up to us. I don't think much of Mrs. Lefranc's suggestion about speculations, but it's perfectly obvious that Alexis had some scheme in hand, and it may be that the scheme went wrong. I don't know. . . . I don't know. . . . Were there, perhaps, two different sets of circumstances? Is it an accident that Alexis should have been killed just as his plans were maturing? He seems to have been surrounded by a bunch of curiously unpleasant people—liars and half-wits and prostitutes and dagoes."

"Yes; I can't say we're moving in very exalted circles. Antoine is the decentest of them—but probably you don't approve of Antoine."

"Is that meant for a challenge? I know all about Antoine. Vetted him last night."

"To see if he was nice for me to know?"

"Not altogether. Part of the process of exploring the ground. He seems a modest, sensible fellow. It's not his fault that he suffers from lack of vitality and incipient melancholia. He's supporting a mother in an asylum and looks after an imbecile brother at home."

"Does he?"

"Apparently; but that doesn't mean that his own wits are not quite reliable at the moment. He was a little more frank about Alexis' love-affairs than he could be to you. Alexis seems to have taken a fairly robust view of his association with Mrs. Weldon, and to have got rid of Leila with more than ordinary tact and ability. Da Soto is a bad egg, of course, but good enough for Leila, and he is probably vain enough to believe quite sincerely that he took her from Alexis *vi et armis*. But *why* all this? Well, never mind; let's have our tea. Hullo! Great activity out at sea! Two boats stationed off the Grinders."

"Fishermen?"

"Fishers of men, I fancy," replied Wimsey, grimly. "It's Umpelty and his merry men. Pass me the field glasses, Bunter. Yes. They look very busy. They've got the drags out. Have a squint."

He passed the glasses to Harriet, who exclaimed:

"They're hauling something up. It must be pretty heavy. The Inspector's lending a hand and one of the men is hanging on at the other end for dear life to trim the boat. Oh, oh! you didn't see that. What a pity! Something gave way suddenly, and Inspector Umpelty has gone head over heels backwards into the boat. Now he's sitting up and rubbing himself."

"Dear Umpelty!" Wimsey helped himself to a sandwich.

"They're dragging again; he's left it to the fishermen this time. . . . They've got it—they're hauling—it's coming up!"

"Sit down and have your tea."

"Don't be silly. They're pulling away like anything. There's something black just showing—"

"Here! Let's have a look."

Harriet surrendered the glasses. They were Wimsey's, after all, though if he thought that she would be upset by a distant view of what she had once seen so unpleasantly close—

Wimsey looked and began to laugh.

"Here, take them, quick! It's a bit of old iron. It looks like a boiler or something. Don't miss Umpelty's face; it's worth seeing."

"Yes; that's what it is—a sort of cylinder. I wonder how that got there. They're examining it very carefully. Perhaps they think they'll find the body inside it. No go. They've dropped it back again."

"What a disappointment!"

"Poor Umpelty! I say, these are lovely sandwiches. Did Bunter make them? He's a genius."

"Yes. Hurry up. I want to have another look at that cleft in the rock before we start."

The cleft, however, remained an enigma. Wimsey's attention was concentrated on the ring-bolt.

"I'll swear," he said, "that this hasn't been here more than a fortnight. It looks perfectly new, and the ring isn't worn anywhere. What the devil he can have wanted that for—. Well, let us be going. I'll take the high road and you take the low road; that is, I'll scramble among the loose stuff at high-water mark, and you walk along by the sea's edge, and we'll work to-and-fro between the two. Anybody who finds anything shouts and we compare notes."

"Right-ho!"

To walk along a solitary shore with one's heart's idol in the calm of a summer's afternoon may be classed as an agreeable occupation; but it loses much of its charm when the couple have to proceed, separated by the whole width of the beach, searching with backs bent double and eyes fixed on the ground for something which neither can define and which in all probability is not there. Harriet, mystified, but resolutely believing that Wimsey had some idea in his mind, kept steady to her job; Wimsey, though he searched carefully, paused a good many times to scan sea and shore, and appeared to be computing distances and memorising landmarks. Each explorer carried a satchel in which to store treasure-trove, and the conversation, such as it was, rather resembled the dialogue of a Russian tragedy. Thus:

HARRIET: Oy!

PETER: Hullo!
    (They meet, centre.)

HARRIET: A boot! I've found a boot!

PETER: Alas! alas! What boots it to repeat.

HARRIET: Hobnailed and frightfully ancient.

PETER: Only one boot!

HARRIET: Yes; if it had been two boots, it might mark the place where the murderer started to paddle.

PETER: One foot on sea and one on shore. The tide has risen and fallen ten times since then. It isn't a good boot.

HARRIET: No, it's a bad boot.

PETER: It's a rotten boot.

HARRIET: Can I throw it away?

PETER: No; after all, it *is* a boot.

HARRIET: It's an awfully heavy boot.

PETER: I can't help that; it's a *boot*. Dr. Thorndyke likes boots.

HARRIET: Oh, death! where is thy sting?
(They separate, Harriet carrying the boot.)

PETER: Oy!

HARRIET: Hullo!
(They meet again.)

PETER: Here is an empty sardine-tin, and here is a broken bottle.

HARRIET: Have you the pen of the gardener's aunt?

PETER: No; but my (female) cousin has (some) ink, (some) paper and (some) papers (use du, de la, des, de l' apostrophe).

HARRIET: How long has the bottle been there?

PETER: The edges are much abraded by the action of the water.

HARRIET: Do murderers eat sardines?

PETER: Do cats eat rats?

HARRIET: I have cut my foot on a razor-shell; Paul Alexis had his throat cut with a razor.

PETER: The tide is going out.
(They separate.)

HARRIET (after a long and unproductive pause, meeting Peter with a sodden Gold Flake packet in one hand and half a Bible in the other): Dr. Livingstone, I presume. Do murderers read the Bible?

PETER: Any book had served as well, Any book had stopped the bullet—that may be; I cannot tell.

HARRIET (reading): "Last of all the woman died also"—probably from backache.

PETER: My back aches, and a drowsy numbness stills My brain, as though of hemlock—

HARRIET (suddenly practical): Look at the cigarette-card.

PETER: It belongs to the new series.

HARRIET: Then it may be quite recent.

PETER (wearily): All right; keep it; we'll call it a clue. How about the Holy Writ?

HARRIET (in a marked manner): You can keep that; it might be good for you.

PETER: Very well. (In a still more marked manner): Shall we begin with the Song of Songs?

HARRIET: Get on with your job.

PETER: I am. How far have we come?

HARRIET: How many leagues to Babylon?

PETER: We have walked a mile and a half, and we are still in full view of the Flat-Iron.
(They separate.)

PETER: Oy!

HARRIET: Hullo!

PETER: I just wanted to ask whether you'd given any further thought to that suggestion about marrying me.

HARRIET (sarcastically): I suppose you were thinking how delightful it would be to go through life like this together?

PETER: Well, not quite like this. Hand in hand was more my idea.

HARRIET: What is that in your hand?

PETER: A dead starfish.

HARRIET: Poor fish!

PETER: No ill-feeling, I trust.

HARRIET: Oh, dear no.

They toiled along, presently coming abreast of the spot where the lane led down from Pollock's cottage. Here the beach became more shingly, with a number of biggish stones. Wimsey took the search more seriously here, scrutinising the stones above and around high-water mark very carefully, and even going part of the way up the lane. He seemed not to find anything of importance, and they went on, noticing that the high ground hid the cottages from sight of the beach.

A few hundred yards farther on, Harriet gave tongue again.

"Oy, oy, oy!"

"Hullo!"

"I really have found something this time."

Peter came galloping down the sand.

"If you're pulling my leg, I'll wring your neck. Let your Uncle Peter look. . . . Ah! . . . we are interested, distinctly interested."

"It ought to mean good luck, anyway."

"You're holding it wrong way up; all the luck will drop out if you're not careful, and a black day it will be for—somebody. Hand it over."

He ran his fingers gently round the hoop of metal, clearing the sand away.

"It's a new shoe—and it hasn't been here very long. Perhaps a week, perhaps a little more. Belongs to a nice little cob, about fourteen hands. Pretty little animal, fairly well-bred, rather given to kicking her shoes off, pecks a little with the off-fore."

"Holmes, this is wonderful! How do you do it?"

"Perfectly simple, my dear Watson. The shoe hasn't been worn thin by 'ammer, 'ammer, 'ammer on the 'ard 'igh road, therefore it's reasonably new. It's a little rusty from lying in the water, but hardly at all rubbed by sand and stones, and not at all corroded, which suggests that it hasn't been here long. The size of the shoe gives the size of the nag, and the shape suggests a nice little round, well-bred hoof. Though newish, the shoe isn't fire-new, and it is worn down a little on the inner front edge, which shows that the wearer was disposed to peck a little; while the way the nails are placed and clinched indicates that the smith wanted to make the shoe extra secure—which is why I said that a lost shoe was a fairly common accident with this particular gee. Still, we needn't blame him or her too much. With all these stones about, a slight trip or knock might easily wrench a shoe away."

"Him or her. Can't you go on and tell the sex and colour while you're about it?"

"I am afraid even I have my limitations, my dear Watson."

"Do you think the shoe was lying where it fell? Or would the sea have moved it much? I found it just here, close by the water's edge, buried pretty deep in sand."

"Well, it wouldn't float, but the tide might drag it a bit one way or the other, and each successive tide would tend to bury it farther. It's very lucky you found it at all. But we can't tell exactly at what point the horse passed along, if you mean that. The shoe wouldn't just drop off. It would be thrown and would spin away on one side or other, according to the speed and direction and all that sort of thing."

"So it would. Well, there's quite a pretty little piece of deduction. . . . Peter! Were you looking for a horseshoe?"

"No; I was expecting the horse, but the shoe is a piece of pure, gorgeous luck."

"And observation. I found it."

"You did. And I could kiss you for it. You need not shrink and tremble. I am not going to do it. When I kiss you, it will be an important event—one of those things which stand out among their surroundings like the first time you tasted li-chee. It will not be an unimportant sideshow attached to a detective investigation."

"I think you are a little intoxicated by the excitement of the discovery," said Harriet, coldly. "You say you came here looking for a horse?"

"Naturally. Didn't you?"

"No—I never thought about it."

"You miserable little cockney—no! You never thought of a horse except as something that holds up the traffic. Your knowledge of horses is comprised in the rhyme which says, 'I know two things about the horse and one of them is rather coarse.' Didn't it ever occur to you that a horse is made to R, U, N, *run*, and cover a given distance in a given time. Did you never even have a bob on the Derby? Wretched girl—wait till we are married. You shall fall off a horse every day till you learn to sit on it."

Harriet was silent. She suddenly saw Wimsey in a new light. She knew him to be intelligent, clean, courteous, wealthy, well-read, amusing and enamoured, but he had not so far produced in her that crushing sense of utter inferiority which leads to prostration and hero-worship. But she now realised that there was, after all, something god-like about him. He could control a horse. She had a fleeting vision of him, very sleek, very smart, in a top-hat and pink coat and gleaming white breeches, loftily perched on an immense and fiery animal which pranced and jiggled about without ever disturbing the lofty nonchalance of his demeanour. Her imagination, making a terrific effort, promptly clothed her in a riding-habit of perfect cut, placed her on an animal still larger and fierier and set her at his side, amid the respectful admiration of the assembled nobility and gentry. Then she laughed at this snobbish picture.

"I could do the falling-off part all right. Hadn't we better be getting on?"

"H'm. Yes. I think we'll do the rest by horse-power. I can't see the coast-road from here, but we shall probably find the faithful Bunter in attendance not very far off. We can't hope to find anything more along here. Two horseshoes would be a work of supererogation."

Harriet heartily welcomed this decision.

"We needn't crawl up the cliff," Wimsey went on. "We'll turn up and get to the road by the lane. We'll chuck the Bible and the boot—I don't think they'll get us anywhere."

"Where are we going?"

"To Darley, to find the horse. I fancy we shall find that he belongs to Mr. Newcombe, who had occasion to complain of gaps in his hedges. We shall see."

The two or three miles to Darley were quickly covered, with only the necessary pause while the gates were opened at the Halt. At the top of Hinks's Lane they got out and walked down to the camping-place.

"I would draw your attention," said Wimsey, "to the three grains of oats found at this spot, and also to the two inches of burnt rope found in the ashes. Bunter, have you brought those things?"

"Yes, my lord."

Bunter rummaged in the bowels of the car and brought out a small paper bag and a halter. These he handed over to Wimsey, who immediately undid the bag and from it poured a couple of handfuls of oats into his hat.

"Well," he said, "we've got the halter—now we've only got to find a horse to put in it. Let's go round by the shore to look for the stream our friend Mr. Goodrich spoke of."

The stream was soon found—a small trickle of fresh water emerging through a bank beneath a hedge, some fifty yards from the encampment and wandering away across the sand towards the sea.

"No good looking for marks this side of the hedge—I fancy the tide comes pretty well up to the foot of the grass. Wait a minute, though. Here we are! Yes —on the very edge of the stream, right up against the hedge—a beauty, with nailmarks all complete. Lucky last night's rain didn't wash it out, but the grass overhangs it a bit. But there's no gap in the hedge here. He must—oh, of course, he would. Yes. Now, if we're right, this won't correspond to the shoe we've found —it'll be the other foot. Yes: this is the left fore. Our horse stood here to drink, which means that he (or she) was running loose round here about the ebb of the tide, horses not liking their water salt. The left fore was there—the right should be about here—it *is* here! Look! the print of the naked hoof, without shoe and rather light in the ground—lame, of course, after coming shoeless for nearly three miles over a stony beach. But where is the gap? Let us walk on, my dear Watson. Here, if I mistake not, is the place. Two new stakes driven in and a bunch of dead thorn shoved in and secured with wire. I agree that Mr. Newcombe is not a good hand at mending hedges. Still, he has taken some precautions, so we will hope that our horse is still in the field. We scramble up the bank —we look over the hedge—one, two, three horses, by jove!"

Wimsey let his eye rove meditatively over the large field. At its far side was a thickish clump of spinney, from which the little stream emerged, meandering quietly through the coarse grass.

"Look how nicely those trees screen it from the road and the village. A pleasant, private spot for horse-stealing. How tiresome of Mr. Newcombe to have filled his gap. Aha! What is this, Watson?"

"I'll buy it."

"There is another gap a few yards down, which has been filled in a more workmanlike manner with posts and a rail. Nothing could be better. We approach it—we climb the rail, and we are in the field. Permit me—oh! you are over. Good! Now, which animal will you put your money on?"

"Not the black. He looks too big and heavy."

"No, not the black, certainly. The chestnut might do, as regards size, but he has seen his best days and has hardly got class enough for our work. The jolly little bay cob rather takes my fancy. Coo-op, pretty," said Wimsey, advancing delicately across the field, shaking the oats in the hat. "Coo-op, coo-op."

Harriet had often wondered how people ever managed to catch horses in large fields. It seemed so silly of the creatures to allow themselves to be taken—and indeed, she remembered distinctly having once stayed in a country rectory where it always took at least an hour for "the boy" to catch the pony, with the result that the pony-trap frequently failed to catch the train. Possibly "the boy" had not gone the right way about it, for, as by the miracle by which the needle turns to the pole, all three horses came lolloping steadily across the field to poke soft noses into the hatful of oats. Wimsey stroked the chestnut, patted the black, weeded out the bay from between them and stood for a little talking to it and running a hand gently over its neck and shoulders. Then he stooped, passing his palm down the off-fore leg. The hoof came obediently up into his hand, while the muzzle went round and gently nibbled his ear.

"Hi, you!" said Wimsey, "that's mine. Look here, Harriet."

Harriet edged round to his side and stared at the hoof.

"New shoe." He put the foot down and reached in turn for the other legs. "Better make sure they haven't made an all-round job of it. No; old shoes on three feet and new shoe on off-fore, corresponding exactly to the specimen picked up on the beach. You notice the special arrangement of the nails. The bay mare brings home the bacon all right. Wait a bit, my girl, we'll try your paces."

He slipped the halter neatly over the bay mare's head and swung himself up.

"Come for a ride? Your toe on my foot, and up she comes! Shall we ride away into the sunset and never come back?"

"Better get on with it. Suppose the farmer comes."

"How right you are!" He gave the halter a shake and cantered off. Harriet mechanically picked up his hat and stood squeezing the crown absently in and out, with her eyes on the flying figure.

"Allow me, miss."

Bunter held out his hand for the hat; she relinquished it with a little start. Bunter shook out the remaining oats, dusted the hat with care inside and out and restored it to its proper shape.

"Handy to ride or drive," said Wimsey, coming back and slipping down from his mount. "Might do nine miles an hour on the road—on the shore, through shallow water, say eight. I'd like—my God! how I'd like—to take her along to the Flat-Iron. Better not. We're trespassing."

He pulled the halter off and sent the mare off with a clap on the shoulder.

"It all looks so good," he mourned, "but it won't work. It simply won't work. You see the idea. Here's Martin. He comes and camps here; evidently he knows all about this place beforehand, and knows that horses are kept out in this field in summer. He arranges for Alexis to be at the Flat-Iron at two o'clock—I don't know how, but he works it somehow. At 1.30 he leaves the Feathers, comes down here, gets the mare and rides off along the shore. We see where he spilt the oats with which he got her to come to him and we see the gap he made getting her through the hedge. He rides along through the edge of the water, so as to leave no marks. He tethers the mare to the ring that he has driven into the rock; he kills Alexis and rides back in a deuce of a hurry. In crossing the rough pebbles below Pollock's cottage, the mare casts a shoe. That doesn't worry him, except that it lames the nag a bit and delays him. When he gets back, he doesn't return the mare to the field, but lets her run. Like that, it will look as though she broke out of the field on her own, and will easily explain the gap, the lameness, and the shoe, if anybody finds it. Also, if the horse should be found still blown and sweaty, it will appear perfectly natural. He is back at three o'clock, in time to go round to the garage about his car, and at some subsequent period he burns the halter. It's so convincing, so neat, and it's all wrong."

"Why?"

"The time's too tight, for one thing. He left the inn at 1.30. After that, he had to come down here, catch the mare and ride four and a half miles. We can't very well allow him to do more than eight miles an hour under the conditions of the problem, yet at two o'clock you heard the scream. Are you sure your watch was right?"

"Positive. I compared it with the hotel clock when I got to Wilvercombe; it was dead right, and the hotel clock—"

"Is set by wireless time, naturally. Everything always is."

"Worse than that; all the hotel clocks are controlled by a master-clock which is controlled directly from Greenwich. That was one of the first things I asked about."

"Competent woman."

"Suppose he had had the horse all ready before he went to the Feathers—tied up to the fence, or something?"

"Yes; but if these Darley people are right, he didn't go from here to the Feathers; he came by car from the Wilvercombe side. And even if we allow that, he's still got to make rather over nine miles an hour to get to the Flat-Iron by two o'clock. I doubt if he could do it—though, of course, he *might*, if he leathered the poor beast like fury. That's why I said I'd like to do the ride."

"And the scream I heard may not have been *the* scream. I thought it was a gull, you know—and perhaps it was. I took about five minutes to gather my stuff together and come out into view of the Flat-Iron. You might put the death at 2.5, I think, if you felt you had to."

"All right. But that still leaves it all quite impossible. You see, *you* were there at 2.10 at the very latest. Where was the murderer?"

"In the cleft of the rock. Oh, ah—but not the horse. I see. There wouldn't be room for a horse too. How exasperating! If we put the murder too early, he wouldn't have time to get there, and if we put it too late, he wouldn't have time to get away. It's maddening."

"Yes, and we can't really put the murder earlier than two o'clock because of the blood. Putting the horse's speed and the condition of the blood and the scream all together, we get two o'clock as the earliest possible and on the whole the most probable time for the murder. Right. You come on the scene, at latest, at 2.5. Allow (which is very unlikely) that the murderer dashed up at full gallop, cut Alexis' throat and dashed off again at full speed without wasting a second, and allow him (which is again most unlikely) to do as much as ten miles an hour *through water*. At 2.5 he will have done just under a mile on his way back. But we proved this afternoon that you have a clear view of over a mile and a half from the Flat-Iron in the direction of Darley. If he had been there, you couldn't have failed to see him. Or could you? You didn't start really *looking* till 2.10, when you found the body."

"No, I didn't. But I've got *all* my faculties. If the murder was done at two o'clock, when the scream woke me, I couldn't possibly not have *heard* a horse galloping hell-for-leather along the shore. It would make a pretty good row, wouldn't it?"

"It certainly would. Tramp, tramp along the land they rode, Splash, splash along the sea. It won't do, my girl, it won't do. And yet, that mare went along that bit of beach not so very long ago, or I'll eat my hat. Eh? Oh, thanks, Bunter."

He took the hat which Bunter gravely proffered him.

"And there's the ring-bolt in the rock. That didn't come there by chance. The horse was taken there, but when and why is a puzzle. Never mind. Let's check up on our facts, just as though the thing were coming out all right."

They left the field and walked up Hinks's Lane.

"We won't take the car," said Wimsey. "We'll just wander along chewing straws and looking idle. Yonder is the village green, I fancy, where, as you once informed us, under a spreading chestnut tree the village smithy stands. Let us hope the smith is at work. Smiths, like electric drills, are made to be stared at."

The smith was at work. The cheerful clink of his hammer fell cheerily on their ears as they crossed the green, and the huge dappled quarters of a cart-horse gleamed in the shaft of sunlight that fell across the open door.

Harriet and Wimsey lounged up, Wimsey dangling the horse-shoe in his hand.

"Afternoon, zur," said the yokel in charge of the cart-horse, civilly.

"Noon," replied Wimsey.

"Fine day, zur."

"Ah!" said Wimsey.

The yokel looked Wimsey over thoroughly, and decided that he was a knowledgeable person and no foolish chatterer. He hitched his shoulder a little more comfortably against the door-post and fell into a reverie.

After about five minutes, Wimsey judged that the time had come when a further observation might be well received. He said, jerking his head in the direction of the anvil:

"Not so much of that as there used to be."

"Ah!" said the man.

The smith, who had removed the dull shoe from the anvil and replaced it in the forge for re-heating, must have caught the remark, for he glanced towards the door. He said nothing, however, but put all his energy into working his bellows.

Presently, the shoe being once more on the anvil, the man with horse shifted his shoulders again, pushed his cap back, scratched his head, replaced the cap, spat (but with perfect politeness), thrust his hand deep into the right-hand pocket of his breeches and addressed a brief word of encouragement to the horse.

Silence, punctuated only by the clink of the hammer, followed, till Wimsey remarked:

"You'll get the hay in all right, if this lasts."

"Ah!" said the man, with satisfaction.

The smith, raising the shoe in the tongs and again returning it to the fire, wiped his brow with his leather apron and broke into the conversation. He followed Humpty-Dumpty's method of going back to the last remark but one.

"I recollect," he said, "when thur warn't none of these motor-cars, only the one Squire Goodrich had—what year would that be now, Jem?"

"Mafeking year, that wur."

"Ah! zo it wur."

Silence, while all meditated.

Then Wimsey said:

"I can remember when my father kept twenty-three horses, not counting the farm stock, of course."

"Ah!" said the blacksmith. "That'ud be a big place, zur?"

"Yes; it was a big place. It was a treat for us kids to go down to the smithy and see them shod."

"Ah!"

"I still know a good bit of work when I see one. This young lady and I picked up a cast shoe just now on the beach—you don't get as much of that sort of luck these days as you used to."

He dangled the shoe on his fingers.

"Off-fore," he added, casually; "nice little well-bred cob about fourteen hands; kicks her shoes off, and pecks a bit on this foot—is that right?"

The smith extended a large hand, courteously wiping it first upon his apron.

"Ay," he said. "That's right enough. Bay cob—belongs to Mr. Newcombe—I zhuld know it."

"Your work?"

"Zartain zhure."

"Ah!"

"Not been lying about very long, either."

"No." The smith licked his finger and rubbed the iron lovingly. "What day wur that Mr. Newcombe found the mare loose, Jem?"

Jem appeared to do a complicated arithmetical calculation, and replied:

"Vriday, ay, it did be Vriday morning. That's when it wur. Vriday."

"Ah! to be zhure. So t'wur."

The smith leaned on his hammer and considered the matter. By slow degrees he brought out the rest of the story. It was not much, but it confirmed Wimsey's deductions.

Farmer Newcombe always kept horses in that field during the summer months. No, he never mowed that meadow on account of the (agricultural and botanical detail of which Harriet did not grasp the significance). No, Mr. Newcombe wouldn't be about in that meadow much, no, nor yet the men, on account of it's lying a long way from the rest of his land (interminable historical detail dealing with the distribution of tenancies and glebe round about that district, in which Harriet became completely lost), nor they wouldn't need to, not to water the horses, on account of the stream (lengthy and rather disputatious account, to which Jem contributed, of the original course of the stream in Jem's grandfather's time, before Mr. Grenfell made the pond over to Drake's Spinney), and it wasn't Mr. Newcombe neither that see the mare running wild Friday morning, but Bessie Turvey's youngest, and he came and told Jem's uncle George and him and another of them got her in and tarrible lame she were, but Mr. Newcombe, he did ought to have mended that gap before (prolonged recital of humorous anecdote, ending "and lord! how Old Parson did laugh, to be zhure!").

After which, the explorers drove back in state to Wilvercombe, to hear that the body had not turned up yet, but that Inspector Umpelty had a pretty good idea where it might be. And dinner. And dancing. And so to bed.

17

THE EVIDENCE OF THE MONEY

O ho! here's royal booty, on my soul:
A draught of ducats!

—*Fragment*

WEDNESDAY, 24 JUNE

Faithful to her self-imposed duty, Harriet next morning sought out Mrs. Weldon. It was not altogether easy to get rid of Henry, whose filial affection seemed positively to tie him to his mother's apron-strings. A happy thought made Harriet suggest that she and Mrs. Weldon might go and see what the Resplendent could do for them in the way of a Turkish bath. This was check-mate for Henry. He took himself off, murmuring that he would go and have a haircut.

In the mood of relaxation and confidence that follows on being parboiled, it was easy enough to pump Mrs. Weldon. A little diplomacy was needed, so as not to betray the ulterior object of the inquiry, but no detective could have had a more unsuspecting victim. The matter proved to be very much as Harriet had supposed.

Mrs. Weldon was the only daughter of a wealthy brewer, who had left her a very considerable fortune in her own right. Her parents having died when she was a child, she had been brought up by a strict Nonconformist aunt in the little town of St. Ives in Huntingdonshire. She had been courted by a certain George Weldon, a prosperous farmer owning a considerable property at Leamhurst in the Isle of Ely, and had married him at eighteen, chiefly in order to get away from the aunt. That rigid lady had not altogether opposed the marriage, which was reasonably suitable, though not brilliant; but she had shown sufficient business ability to insist that her niece's money should be tied up in such a manner that Weldon could not touch the capital. Weldon, to do him justice, had made no objection to this. He seemed to have been a perfectly honest, sober and industrious man, farming his land thriftily and well and having, so far as Harriet could make out, no drawbacks beyond a certain lack of imagination in matrimonial matters.

Henry was the only child of the marriage, and had been brought up from the beginning with the idea that he was to follow in his father's footsteps, and here again, Weldon senior took a very proper view of the matter. He would not have the boy brought up in idleness, or to ideas beyond his proper station in life. He was a farmer's son, and a farmer he should be, though Mrs. Weldon herself had often pleaded that the boy should be brought up to one of the professions. But old Weldon was adamant, and indeed Mrs. Weldon was obliged to admit that he had very likely been right after all. Henry showed no special aptitude for anything but the open-air life of the farm; the trouble was that he did not apply himself even to that as well as he should have done, and was inclined to run after girls and race-meetings, leaving his work to be done by his father and the farm-hands. Already, before the elder Weldon's death, there had been a good deal of antagonism between Henry and his mother, and this became intensified later on.

The farmer had died when Henry was twenty-five. He had left the farm and all his own savings to his son, knowing that his wife was well provided for. Under Henry's management the farm had begun to go down. Times had grown harder for farmers. More and more personal supervision was needed to make farming pay; Henry gave it less and less. There were experiments in horse-breeding, which had not turned out well, owing to lack of judgment in buying and handling the stock. Mrs. Weldon had by this time left the farm, which she had always disliked, and was living a nomad life in spas and watering-places. Henry had several times come to her for loans, and had received them; but Mrs. Weldon had steadily refused to make over any of her capital to him, although she might have done so, her trustees being now dead and the trust wound up. She had, after all, learnt something from the Nonconformist aunt. Finally, when she found out that Henry had got himself into rather disgraceful trouble with an innkeeper's wife in a neighbouring village, she quarrelled with Henry, loudly and finally. Since then, she had heard little from him. She understood, however, that

the intrigue with the innkeeper's wife had come to an end, and in February of
the current year she had told him about her forthcoming marriage to Alexis.
Henry had come down to Wilvercombe, stayed for the week-end, met Alexis and
expressed his disapproval of the whole business. This did not mend matters, and
relations had been strained until the death of Alexis had urged the lonely
woman to seek comfort in the ties of blood. Henry had come, expressed contrition for his former waywardness, received forgiveness and shown that he was,
after all, her loving son.

Harriet mentioned Mrs. Lefranc's theory that Alexis had committed suicide
owing to the failure of unknown and important "speculations." Mrs. Weldon
scouted the theory.

"What could it matter to him, my dear? Paul knew perfectly well that when
we were married I should settle my money on him—with the exception, of
course, of a little provision for Henry. Of course, in the ordinary way, Henry
would get everything, and I am afraid he was a little upset when he heard that I
was going to get married, but, you know, it was not right that he should feel like
that. His father left him very well off and always impressed upon him that he
ought not to look for anything from me. After all, I was still quite a young
woman when my husband died, and George—he was a very fair-minded man, I
will say that for him—always said that I should be quite within my rights in
spending my own father's money as I liked and marrying again if I chose. And I
have lent Henry a great deal of money, which he has never repaid. I told Henry,
when I got engaged to Alexis, that I should make him a free gift of everything
that I had lent him, and make a will, giving him the life-interest in £30,000, the
capital of which was to go to Henry's children, if he had any. If he hadn't any,
then the money was to come back to Paul, if Paul outlived Henry, because, of
course, Paul was the younger man."

"Were you going to settle all the rest on Mr. Alexis?"

"Why not, my dear? It was not as though I could have had any more children.
But Paul didn't like that idea—he used to say, so charmingly and absurdly, that
if I did that what would happen to me if he ran away and left me? No, what I was
going to do was this. I was going to settle £30,000 on Paul when we were
married. It would have been his, absolutely, of course—I shouldn't like my
husband to have to come and ask me for permission if he wanted to alter the
investments or anything. Then, at my death, Henry would have had the income
from the other £30,000 and his debts washed out, and Paul would have had all
the rest, which would have been about £100,000 altogether, including his own
£30,000. Because, you see, Paul might have married again and had a family, and
then he would need the money. I don't see that there was anything unfair about
that, do you?"

Harriet felt that a great deal might be said about an arrangement which cut
off the only son with the life-interest on £30,000, with reversion to a young step-
father, and left full control of over three times that sum to the step-father; and
which also placed the hypothetical family of the son in a vastly inferior position
to the equally hypothetical children of the step-father by a hypothetical new
wife. Still, Mrs. Weldon's money was her own, and Alexis had at least stood
between her and the major folly of stripping herself of every farthing in his
favour. One expression had caught her attention, and she returned to it.

"I think you showed considerable judgment," she said—not specifying
whether the judgment was good or bad—"it would be much better for your son,

if he is inclined to squander his money, only to have the life-interest in his share. Then he would always have something to fall back upon. I suppose that arrangement still holds good under your present will."

"Oh, yes," said Mrs. Weldon. "At least, it will do so. I must confess that I have been a little remiss up to the present. I haven't actually made a will. I have always enjoyed such wonderful health—but it will have to be done, of course. You know how one puts things off."

The old story, thought Harriet. If all the wise wills projected in people's minds were actually executed, there would be fewer fortunes inherited only to be thrown away. She reflected that if Mrs. Weldon died the next day, Henry would step into sole control of something over £130,000.

"You know," she said, "I think I should make that will if I were you. Even the youngest and healthiest people may get run over or something."

"Yes, yes—you're so very right. But now that poor Paul is dead, I don't feel that I have the energy for business. It would matter more, of course, if Henry were married and had a family, but he says he doesn't mean to marry, and if so, he may as well have the money first as last. There's nobody else now. But I'm afraid I'm boring you, my dear, with all this chatter. You were asking about poor dear Paul, and I've been led away into telling you all these silly private affairs. What I was trying to say was that Paul simply *couldn't* have been worrying about speculations. He knew he was going to have plenty of money. Besides," added Mrs. Weldon, with perfect justice, "you can't speculate much without capital, can you? Money breeds money, as a stockbroker I once knew used to say, and Paul never had any money to start with. I don't think he would have known anything about speculating either; he was too romantic and unworldly, poor dear boy."

"Maybe," said Harriet to herself, "maybe. But he managed to get on the right side of the person who had it." She was a little surprised. "Wealthy" is a comparative term—she had imagined Mrs. Weldon to possess about three thousand a year. But if her money was decently invested—and she spoke as if it was —she must have at least twice that amount. A pauper like Alexis might be excused for wedding £130,000 at whatever price in convenience and self-respect; had he really intended the marriage after all? And if, on the other hand, he had meant to forgo it and flee the country, what was the enormous threat or inducement which could make him abandon such a golden prospect for the much lesser glitter of three hundred sovereigns, genuine metal though they might be?

And Henry? Even when the death-duties had been subtracted, £130,000 was a pleasant sum, and men had done murder for less. Well, Lord Peter had undertaken to look into Henry's affairs. She became aware that Mrs. Weldon was talking.

"What a curious face that Monsieur Antoine has," she was saying, "he seems to be a nice young man, though I'm sure he is far from robust. He spoke most kindly to me yesterday about Paul. He seems to have been very much attached to him, sincerely so."

"Oh, Antoine!" thought Harriet, a little reproachfully. Then she remembered the mad mother and the imbecile brother and thought instead, "Poor Antoine!" But the thought was still an unpleasant one.

"It's all very well for Lord Peter," she grumbled to herself, "*he's* never wanted for anything." Why Lord Peter should be brought into the matter, she could not explain, but there is undoubtedly something irritating about the favourites of fortune.

In the meantime, that wayward sprig of the nobility was trying not to be idle. He was, in fact, hanging round the police-station, bothering the Inspector. The reports about Bright were coming in, and they fully corroborated his story, so far as they went. He had come to Wilvercombe, as he said, from a lodging-house in Seahampton, and by the train specified, and he was now living peacefully in a cheap room in Wilvercombe, without seeing any strangers and without showing the least sign of wanting to disappear. He had been taken over to Seahampton by the police on the previous day, and had been identified by Merryweather as the man to whom the Endicott razor had been sold some time previously. In the course of a few hours, his movements for the last few weeks had been successfully checked, and were as follows:

May 28th. Arrived in Ilfracombe from London. Four days' employment. Dismissed as incompetent and intoxicated.

June 2nd. Arrived in Seahampton. Called at Merryweather's and purchased razor. Five days in that town looking for employment (details checked).

June 8th. Wilvercombe. Called on Moreton, the barber on the Esplanade. Told that there might be a job later. Recommended to try Ramage's in Lesston Hoe.
Same day went on to Lesston Hoe; taken on by Ramage.

June 15th. Dismissed from Ramage's—drunk and incompetent. Returned to Wilvercombe; informed by Moreton that post was now filled (which it was not; but his reputation had preceded him by telephone). Tried one or two other shops without success. Slept that night in free lodging-house.

June 16th (Tuesday). Again tried for work; no result. Slept that night in workmen's lodgings, where he arrived shortly after midnight. They were reluctant to admit him, but he showed a £1 note to prove that he could pay for his bed.

June 17th. Took 9.57 train to Seahampton. Called on hair-dresser named Lyttleton and asked for work. Was told that Mr. Lyttleton was away, but that he could call the following morning after 11.30. Visited two more hair-dressers. Took a bed in a lodging-house and spent the evening and night there in company with other residents.

June 18th (day of Alexis' death). Left the lodging-house at 10 a.m. and went directly to the Public Library, where he had sat for an hour in the Reading Room, studying the "Situations Vacant" columns in various papers. The guardian of the Reading Room had identified him. He remembered Bright perfectly, on account of some questions he had asked about the dates of publication of the local papers, and also recollected showing him the shelf on which the local directory was kept. At eleven o'clock, Bright had asked whether the library clock was right, as he had an appointment at 11.30. At 11.15 he had left, presumably to keep this appointment.

The appointment was, of course, with Lyttleton, who also had no difficulty in identifying Bright. Lyttleton had returned to Seahampton by the 11.20 train, and, on reaching his shop, had found Bright waiting to see him. He told Bright that he could come and try his hand if he liked, and could start at once. Bright had worked in the toilet-saloon until one o'clock, when he had gone out to lunch. He had returned just after two o'clock and had remained at his job for the rest of the day. The proprietor had then decided that his work was not good enough, and paid him off. It was true that nobody was able to identify him at the small restaurant where he claimed to have lunched, but it was perfectly clear that nothing short of a magic carpet could have transported him forty miles to the Flat-Iron and back in order to commit a murder at two o'clock. Whatever part Bright had played in the tragedy, it was not that of First Murderer.

With regard to Bright's earlier history, they had made very little progress—principally because Bright himself did not even pretend to remember the various aliases under which he had passed from time to time in the last few years. The only statement they had so far succeeded in confirming—up to a point—was that there certainly had at one time been a hair-dresser's establishment in Massingbird Street, Manchester. The proprietor's name had been Simpson, and this agreed with Bright's story; but Massingbird Street had long disappeared in the course of town-improvement and, as Bright himself had warned them, it was difficult to find anybody who remembered what Simpson the hair-dresser had looked like.

"He must have lived in Manchester all right, some time or other," was the Inspector's conclusion, "or he wouldn't know all about Massingbird Street; and it's quite probable he may be Simpson as he says. But what he's been doing with himself between then and now is quite another matter."

A further item of police information concerned old Pollock and his boat. A young constable, who had only recently joined the Wilvercombe force and was therefore likely to be unknown to the local fisher-folk, had been sent, disguised as a holiday-maker, to dawdle about the beach near Darley, in company with his young lady, and persuade Pollock to take them both out for a sail in his boat. The trip had been an uncomfortable one, owing, in the first place, to the old fisherman's extreme surliness and, in the second, to the young lady's unfortunate tendency to mal de mer. They had asked to be taken out as near as possible to the seaward end of the Grinders reef, "as the young lady was that keen to see them drag for the body." Pollock had grumbled a good deal, but had taken them. They had kept the shore in view the whole way, but had finished their outward trip at a point too far from shore to make out clearly the movements of the search-party, who, at that particular moment, seemed to be engaged on shore in the immediate neighbourhood of the Flat-Iron. They had asked Pollock to put in close by the rock, but he had refused very definitely to do so. During the voyage, the constable had examined the boat as closely as he could for signs of anything unusual. He had gone so far as to lose a hypothetical half-crown and insist on having the bottom-boards up to see if it could have slipped below them. He had searched the musty space below thoroughly with a flash light and seen no appearance of bloodstains. For the sake of verisimilitude he had pretended to find the half-crown, and for the sake of peace had handed it to Pollock by way of a tip. On the whole the expedition had been disappointing, having yielded nothing but sea-sickness and a close-up view of a considerable number of lobster-pots.

A question about Alexis' passport found the Inspector very much on his dignity. Did his lordship really suppose they had overlooked that obvious point? Alexis certainly had a passport, and, what was more, had had it visa'd within the last month. Where for? Why, for France, to be sure. But of course he could have got fresh visas from the Consul there, if he had wanted them.

"That offers some support for the theory that our young friend intended to flit, eh?"

"Yes, my lord. And if he was going to some remote place in Central Europe, I daresay he'd have found gold sovereigns a sight handier than notes. Though why he shouldn't have taken currency notes and changed them in Paris I don't know. Still, there it is, and he must have had *some* idea in his mind. I don't mind admitting, my lord, that I'm coming round a bit to your way of thinking. Here's a man with what I might call a purpose in view—and that purpose isn't suicide. And he had £300 in gold on him, and there's plenty as 'ud do murder for less than that. At least, we're supposing he had it on him. We can't tell till we find the body."

"If he was murdered for the sake of the gold, you won't know even then," said Wimsey.

"No, my lord, that's a fact. Unless we was to find the belt or what not he had it in. And even then, likely as not, the murderer would have taken belt and all." The Inspector looked unhappy. "But there might be papers or something to tell us—always supposing the murderer didn't take them as well or the salt water hasn't made pulp of them."

"D'you know," said Wimsey, "I feel inspired to make a prophecy. I think you'll find that Alexis was murdered all right, but not for the sake of the money. I mean, not for the £300."

"Why do you think that, my lord?"

"Because," said Wimsey, "you haven't found the body."

The Inspector scratched his head.

"You don't mean that somebody came and took the body away? What should they want to do that for?"

"What indeed? If my idea's the right one, that's the last thing they would want to do. They'd want the body found."

"Why?"

"Because the murder was not committed for the £300 in gold."

"But you said that was why the body hadn't been found."

"So it is."

"Your proper walk in life," said Inspector Umpelty, "if you'll excuse me, my lord, is setting crossword puzzles. Say that again. They wanted the body found, because they didn't murder him for the £300. And *because* they didn't murder him for the £300, we can't find the body. Is that right?"

"That's right."

The Inspector frowned heavily. Then a radiant smile illumined his broad face. He smacked his hand jubilantly upon his thigh.

"Of course, my lord! By George, you're perfectly right. What mutts we were not to see that before. It's as clear as daylight. It was just your way of putting it that muddled me up. I must try that one on the Super. Bet you *he* won't see through it first go off. They didn't want the body found—no, that's wrong. They did want the body found because they did, didn't—"

"Try it in rhyme," suggested Wimsey.

> "Why did they want the body found?
> They didn't want three hundred pound.
> They didn't want three hundred pound,
> And that's why the body wasn't found."

"Very good, my lord," said the Inspector. "Why, you're quite a poet." He drew out his note-book, and solemnly made an entry of the quatrain.

"You could sing it very nicely to the tune of 'Here we go round the mulberry-bush,'" suggested Wimsey, "with the refrain, 'All on a Thursday morning.' Or it should be 'Thursday afternoon,' but that's just poetic licence. You have my permission to perform it at your next Police-concert. No fee."

"You will have your joke, my lord." The Inspector smiled indulgently, but as Wimsey left the police-station he heard a deep voice laboriously humming:

> "Why did they want the body found, body found,
>   body found,
> Why did they want the body found
> All of a Thur-ursday morning?"

Wimsey went back to the Bellevue and found a note from Harriet, containing the substance of her conversation with Mrs. Weldon. He frowned over it for a moment and then abruptly summoned Bunter.

"Bunter, my man," said he. "I think it is time you took a trip to Huntingdon-shire."

"Very good, my lord."

"You will go to a place called Leamhurst, and find out all about Mr. Henry Weldon, who owns a farm there."

"Certainly, my lord."

"It's only a small village, so you must have some reason for going there. I suggest that you purchase or hire a car and are benighted, owing to some intricate kind of engine-trouble."

"Precisely, my lord."

"Here is £30. If you want more, let me know."

"Very good, my lord."

"You will, naturally, stay at the principal pub and pursue your inquiries in the bar."

"Naturally, my lord."

"You will find out everything you can about Mr. Weldon, and, in particular, what his financial standing and reputation may be."

"Quite so, my lord."

"You will be as quick as you can about it, and return here as soon as possible."

"Very good, my lord."

"You will start immediately."

"Very good, my lord."

"Then be off!"

"Very good, my lord. Your lordship's dress-shirts are in the second drawer and the silk socks in the tray on the right-hand side of the wardrobe, with the dress-ties just above them."

"Very good, Bunter," said Wimsey, mechanically.

Ten minutes later Mr. Bunter, suitcase in hand, was on his way to the railway-station.

18

THE EVIDENCE OF THE SNAKE

There is a little, hairy, green-eyed snake,
Of voice like to the woody nightingale,
And ever singing pitifully sweet,
That nestles in the barry bones of Death,
And is his dearest friend and playfellow.
                    —*Death's Jest-Book*

WEDNESDAY, 24 JUNE

On leaving the Turkish baths, Miss Harriet Vane went out on a shopping expedition. This was her second venture of the kind since her arrival in Wilvercombe, and on both occasions her purchases were dictated by the desire of pleasing a man. On this occasion, she wanted an afternoon frock. And why? She was going out for a picnic.

She had picnicked before, with Lord Peter; and for him the old tweed skirt and well-worn jumper had been good enough. But to-day, these garments would not do. Her appointment was with Mrs. Weldon and Henry.

The curious inhibitions which caused her to be abrupt, harsh, and irritating with Lord Peter did not seem to trouble her in dealing with Henry Weldon. For him she produced a latent strain of sweet womanliness which would have surprised Wimsey. She now selected a slinky garment, composed of what male writers call "some soft, clinging material," with a corsage which outlined the figure and a skirt which waved tempestuously about her ankles. She enhanced its appeal with an oversized hat of which one side obscured her face and tickled her shoulder, while the other was turned back to reveal a bunch of black ringlets, skilfully curled into position by the head hairdresser at the Resplendent. High-heeled beige shoes and sheer silk stockings, with embroidered gloves and a hand-bag completed this alluring toilette, so eminently unsuitable for picnicking. In addition, she made up her face with just so much artful restraint as to suggest enormous experience aping an impossible innocence, and, thus embellished, presently took her place beside Henry in the driving-seat of Mrs. Weldon's large saloon. Mrs. Weldon sat at the back of the car, with a luxurious tea-basket at her feet and a case of liquid refreshment beside her.

Henry seemed gratified by the efforts made to please him, and by Miss Vane's openly expressed admiration of his driving. This was of a showy and ill-tempered kind, and involved "putting the wind up" other users of the road. Harriet had herself driven cars, and suffered as all drivers do when being driven, but even when Henry rounded a corner very wide at fifty miles an hour and crammed a motor-cyclist into the ditch, she merely remarked (with some truth) that the speed made her feel quite nervous.

Mr. Weldon, braking violently at the unexpected sight of a herd of cows nearly under his radiator, and crashing his gears as he changed down, smiled indulgently.

"No point in these damned machines if you don't make 'em move," he said. "Not like a horse—no life in 'em. Only useful for getting from one place to another."

He waited while the cows dawdled by and then let his clutch in with a bang which nearly shot the liquid refreshment to the floor.

"You don't catch me motoring for pleasure," said Mr. Weldon. "I like fresh air —none of these beastly stuffy boxes and stinking petrol. Used to breed gees once—but the bottom's dropped out of the market. Damned shame."

Harriet agreed, and said she was so fond of horses. Life on a farm must be wonderful.

"All right if you don't have to make it pay," growled Mr. Weldon.

"I suppose it *is* rather hard nowadays."

"Damned hard," said Mr. Weldon, adding, however, as though recollecting himself, "not that I have a lot to grumble at as things go."

"No? I'm glad of that. I mean, it's nice for you to be able to leave your work and come down here. I suppose a really well-managed farm runs itself, so to speak."

Mr. Weldon glanced at her almost as though he suspected her of some hidden meaning. She smiled innocently at him, and he said:

"Well—as a matter of fact, it's a beastly nuisance. But what can one do? Couldn't leave my mother all by herself in this hole."

"Of *course* not; I think it's splendid of you to come and stand by her. And besides—well, I mean, it makes such a difference to have somebody really nice to talk to."

"Jolly of you to say that."

"I mean, it must make all the difference to your mother."

"Not to you, eh? Dukes and lords are good enough for you?"

"Oh!" Harriet wriggled her shoulders. "If you mean Lord Peter—he's all *right*, of course, but he's a little—you know what I mean."

"La-di-dah!" said Mr. Weldon. "What's he want to wear that silly thing in his eye for?"

"That's just what I feel. It isn't manly, is it?"

"Lot of affected nonsense," said Mr. Weldon. "Take that fellow away from his valet and his car and his evening togs, and where'd he be? Thinks he can ride, because he's pottered round with a fashionable hunt, trampling down people's crops and leaving the gates open. I'd like to see him—"

He broke off.

"See him what?"

"Oh, nothing. Don't want to be rude to a friend of yours. I say, what's he after down here?"

"Well!" Harriet smirked demurely behind the drooping brim of the preposterous hat. "He *says* he's interested in this crime, or whatever it is."

"But you know better, eh?" He nudged Harriet familiarly in the ribs. "I don't blame the fellow for making the running while he can, but I do wish he wouldn't raise false hopes in the old lady. That's a dashed awkward hat of yours."

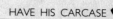
"Don't you like it?"

"It's topping—suits you down to the ground, but it does keep a fellow at a distance. And I don't want to shout, because my mother can hear. I say, Miss Vane."

"Yes?"

"Listen!" Henry pushed his face as far as possible under the guard of the hat and blew his confidences on to Harriet's cheek. "I wish you'd do something for me."

"Of course, I'd do anything I could."

"That's nice of you. Do persuade this Wimsey fellow to drop it. As long as *she* thinks there's anything in that Bolshie idea of hers, she'll hang on here like grim death. It isn't good for her—morbid, you know. Besides, she's making an ass of herself. I want to get her away and go back to my work."

"Yes, I see. I quite understand. I'll do my best."

"Good girl!" Henry patted her encouragingly on the thigh. "I knew you and I'd get on like a house on fire together."

Harriet smiled.

"I don't know if I shall be able to persuade him. He doesn't like taking advice. You know what men are."

"I bet *you* know all right. I don't suppose there's much you don't know, by jove!" Henry was obviously well aware that he was talking to a rather notorious young woman. He chuckled.

"Don't say I've said anything—just try what you can do. I bet you can twist him round your little finger if you try, eh?"

"Oh, Mr. Weldon! I hope I'm not one of those managing sort of women!"

"You don't need to be. You know how to get your own way, I bet. I know you could do anything you liked with *me*."

"You mustn't talk like that."

"Mustn't I? Can't help it. You've got a way with you—haven't you, eh?"

Harriet wished that he would not say "eh?" so often. And she disliked the grossness of his voice and the coarseness of his skin and the little tufts of hair in his ears.

"Don't drive with one hand like that—suppose anything came along suddenly."

Henry laughed and patted her leg again.

"That's all right, don't you worry. I'll look after you, and you'll look after me, eh? Alliance, offensive and defensive—just between you and me, eh?"

"Oh, rather!"

"That's fine. And when all this stupid business is over, you must come and look Mother and me up. She's taken a great fancy to you. Get her to bring you along to my place. You'd like it. What about it?"

"That would be lovely!" (If Henry wanted to be vamped, she would vamp him.) "One gets so tired of the kind of men one meets in London, and the stuffy, restricted, literary kind of surroundings. I don't suppose you ever come to London, Mr. Weldon?"

"Not often. Don't care for the place."

"Oh! Then it's no good asking you to call on me."

"Isn't it, though? Of course I'd come and call on you like a shot. Some inducement, eh? Where do you live?"

"I've got a little flat in Bloomsbury."

"All on your own?"

"Yes."

"Isn't that a bit lonesome?"

"Oh! Well, of course I have plenty of friends. And a woman who comes in for the day. I could give you tea if you cared to come along some time to cheer me up."

"That would be sweet of you. We could go and do a show together or something."

"I should enjoy that."

No—Henry was really too easy. Surely even his colossal vanity could not suppose that he had really made a conquest. Yet there he sat, smiling away and almost audibly purring. No doubt he thought that Harriet Vane was any man's game. He really imagined that, placed between Lord Peter and himself, a woman could possibly—well, why not? How was he to know? It wouldn't be the first time that a woman had made a foolish choice. If anything, he was paying her the compliment of supposing that she was not mercenary. Or, horrid thought, did he expect her to be completely promiscuous?

That was it—he did! He was informing her now, in reasonably plain language, that somebody like himself would be a nice change for her and that he couldn't make out what a fine woman like herself could see in a fellow like Wimsey. Rage rendered her speechless for a moment; then she began to feel amused. If he thought that, he could be made to believe anything. She could twist men round her little finger, could she? Then she would twist *him*. She would fool him to the top of his bent.

She begged him not to talk so loudly; Mrs. Weldon would overhear him.

This reminder had its effect, and Henry "behaved himself" until their arrival at the spot selected for the picnic compelled him to return to his former attitude of ordinary politeness.

The picnic itself passed off without any remarkable incident, and Henry did not succeed in getting Harriet to himself until the meal was over and they went to wash up the plates in a little brook that ran close by. Even then, Harriet was able to avoid his advances by sending him to do the washing while she stood by with a dish-cloth. She ordered him about prettily and he obeyed with delighted willingness, tucking up his sleeves and getting down to the job. However, the inevitable moment arrived when he returned with the clean plates and put them into her hands. Then, seizing his opportunity, he advanced upon her and clasped her with clumsy gallantry about the body. She dropped the plates and wriggled, pushing his arms away and bending her head down, so that the faithful and long-suffering hat was between them.

"Damn it!" said Henry. "You might let a fellow—"

It was then that Harriet became really frightened. She gave a scream which was no mockery, but a really determined yell, and followed it up with a box on the ear that was no butterfly kiss. Henry astonished, relaxed his grasp for a moment. She broke away from him—and at that moment Mrs. Weldon, attracted by the scream, came running to the top of the bank.

"Whatever is the matter?"

"I saw a snake!" said Harriet, wildly. "I'm sure it was a viper."

She screamed again, and so did Mrs. Weldon, who was terrified of snakes. Henry, grunting, picked up the fallen plates and told his mother not to be silly.

"Come back to the car," said Mrs. Weldon. "I won't stay another moment in this horrid place."

They went back to the car. Henry looked glum and injured; he felt that he had been badly treated, as indeed he had. But Harriet's face was white enough to show that she had had a real shock, and she insisted on returning in the back of the car with Mrs. Weldon, who made a great fuss over her with a smelling-bottle and ejaculations of horror and sympathy.

When they got back to Wilvercombe, Harriet was sufficiently recovered to thank Henry properly and apologise for having been so stupid. But she was still not quite herself, refused to come in to the hotel and insisted on walking back to her room at Mrs. Lefranc's. She would not allow Henry to go with her—she wouldn't hear of it—she was quite all right—the walk would do her good. Henry, who was still offended, did not press the point. Harriet walked away, but not to Mrs. Lefranc's. She hastened to the nearest telephone-cabinet and rang up the Bellevue. Was Lord Peter Wimsey there? No, he was out; could they take a message? Yes. Would he please come round and see Miss Vane at once, the minute he came in? It was frightfully urgent. Certainly they would tell him. No, they would not forget.

Harriet went home, sat down on Paul Alexis' chair and stared at Paul Alexis' ikon. She really felt quite upset.

She had sat there for an hour, without removing her hat and gloves—just thinking, when there was a commotion on the staircase. Feet came up two steps at a time and the door burst open so hard upon the preliminary knock as to make the knock superfluous.

"Hullo-ullo-ullo! Here we all are. What's up? Anything exciting? So sorry I was out—Here! I say! Hold up! It's all right, you know—at least, it *is* all right, isn't it?"

He gently extricated his arm from Harriet's frenzied grasp and shut the door.

"Now then! My dear, what's happened? You're all of a doodah!"

"Peter! I believe I've been kissed by a murderer."

"Have you? Well, it serves you right for letting anybody kiss you but me. Good Heavens! You raise all sorts of objections to a perfectly amiable and reasonably virtuous man like myself, and the next thing I hear is that you are wallowing in the disgusting embrace of a murderer. Upon my soul! I don't know what the modern girl is coming to."

"He didn't actually kiss me—he only hugged me."

"That's what I said—I said 'disgusting embraces.' And what is worse, you send urgent messages to my hotel, so that you can get me here to be gloated over. It is abominable. It is repulsive. Sit down. Take off that vulgar and idiotic hat and tell me who this low-down, bone-headed, bird-witted, dissipated murderer is who can't even keep his mind on his murdering, but rushes about the country embracing and hugging painted-faced females that don't belong to him."

"Very well. Prepare for a shock. It was Haviland Martin."

"Haviland Martin?"

"Haviland Martin."

Wimsey walked very deliberately to a table near the window, laid down his hat and stick upon it, drew forward a chair, placed Harriet in it, drew up a second chair, sat down in it himself, and said:

"You win. I am astonished. I am thunderstruck. Kindly explain yourself. I thought you were out this afternoon with the Weldons."

"I was."

"Am I to understand that Haviland Martin is a friend of Henry Weldon's?"

"Haviland Martin is Henry Weldon."

"You have been wallowing in the embraces of Henry Weldon?"

"Only in the interests of justice. Besides, I boxed his ears."

"Go on. Begin from the beginning."

Harriet began from the beginning. Wimsey bore fairly well the story of the vamping of Henry Weldon, merely interjecting that he hoped the man wouldn't make himself a nuisance later on, and listened patiently till she came to the incident of the plate-washing.

"I was sort of wriggling—because I didn't want him actually to kiss me, you know—and I looked down and saw his arm—it was round my waist, you understand—"

"Yes, I grasped that."

"And I saw a snake tattooed all the way up his arm—just as it was up Martin's. And then I suddenly remembered how his face had seemed kind of familiar when I first saw him—and then I realised who he was."

"Did you tell him so?"

"No. I just yelled, and Mrs. Weldon came up and asked what was the matter. So I said I'd seen a snake—it was the only thing I could think of; and of course it was true."

"What did Henry say?"

"Nothing. He was rather grumpy. Of course, he thought I was just making a fuss about his kissing me, only he couldn't tell his mother that."

"No—but do you suppose he put two and two together?"

"I don't *think* he did. I hope not."

"*I* hope not—or he may have bolted."

"I know. I ought to have stuck to him like glue. But I couldn't. I couldn't, Peter. Honestly, I was frightened. It was silly, but I *saw* Alexis with his throat cut and the blood running all over the place—it was horrible. And the idea that— ugh!"

"Wait a moment. Let's think this thing out. You're sure you aren't mistaken about the snake and that. Weldon really *is* Martin?"

"Yes. I'm sure he is. I can see it perfectly now. His profile's the same, now I come to think of it, and his height and size, and his voice too. The hair's different, of course, but he could easily have dyed that."

"So he could. And his hair looks as if it had been dyed recently, for the matter of that, and re-bleached. I thought it looked funny and dead. Well, if Weldon is Martin, there's undoubtedly some funny business somewhere. But Harriet, do put it out of your mind that he's a murderer. We've proved that Martin couldn't possibly have done it. He couldn't get to the place in time. Had you forgotten that?"

"Yes—I believe I had forgotten it. It seemed so obvious, somehow, that if he was there at Darley, in disguise, he must have been up to something or other."

"Of course he was up to something or other. But what? He couldn't be in two places at once, even if he was disguised as Beelzebub."

"No, he couldn't—could he? Oh, what an idiot I am! I've been sitting here having the horrors, and wondering how in the world we could ever break it to Mrs. Weldon."

"We may have to do that in any case, I'm afraid," said Wimsey, gravely. "It looks very much as if he had some hand in it, even if he didn't do the throat-cutting part of it. The only thing is, if he wasn't the actual murderer, why was he at Darley at all?"

"Goodness knows!"

"Something to do with the bay mare, that's a certainty. But what? What was the point of the bay mare at all? It beats me, Harriet; it beats me."

"So it does me."

"Well, there's only one thing to do."

"What's that?"

"To ask him."

"Ask him?"

"Yes. We'll ask him. It's just conceivable that there's some innocent explanation of the thing. And if we ask him about it, he'll have to commit himself one way or another."

"Ye-es. That means open warfare."

"Not necessarily. We needn't tell him all we suspect. I think you'd better leave this one to me."

"I rather think I had. I'm afraid I haven't handled Henry as well as I thought I was going to."

"I don't know. You've got hold of a pretty valuable piece of information, anyhow. Don't worry. We'll turn friend Henry inside-out before we've done with him. I'll just pop round to the Resplendent now, and see that he hasn't taken alarm."

He popped round accordingly, only to find that Henry, so far from bolting, was dining and playing Bridge with a party of other residents. Should he break in on them with his questions? Or should he wait? Better wait, perhaps, and let the matter crop up quietly in conversation the next morning. He made a private arrangement with the night porter to give him the tip if Mr. Weldon showed any signs of departing during the night, and retired to his own quarters to do some hard thinking.

19

THE EVIDENCE OF THE DISGUISED MOTORIST

Confess, or to the dungeon—
Pause!
—*Death's Jest-Book*

THURSDAY, 25 JUNE

Mr. Weldon did not bolt. Wimsey had no difficulty in catching him the following morning, and was rather glad he had waited, for in the meantime he had received a letter from Chief Inspector Parker.

MY DEAR PETER,

What will you want next? I have got a little preliminary information for you, and if anything fresh turns up I will keep you posted.

First of all your Mr. Haviland Martin is not a Bolshevik agent. He has had that account in Cambridge for quite a long time, and owns a small house, complete with lady, in the outskirts of the town. He took it, I believe, in 1925, and makes his appearance there from time to time, dark spectacles and all. He was recommended to the bank by one Mr. Henry Weldon, of Leamhurst, Hunts, and there has never been any trouble with his account—a small one. He is thought to travel in something or other. All this suggests to me that the gentleman may be leading a double life, but you can put the Bolshevik theory out of your head.

I got hold of Morris, the Bolshevik-wallah, this evening. He doesn't know of any Communist or Russian agent who might be knocking about Wilvercombe at the present time and thinks you have got hold of a mare's nest.

By the way, the Cambridge police, from whom I had to wangle the Martin dope by telephone, want to know what is up. First Wilvercombe, then me! Fortunately, knowing their Super pretty well, I was able to get him to put pressure on the bank. I fancy I left them with the impression that it had something to do with bigamy!

Talking of bigamy, Mary sends her love and wants to know whether you are any nearer committing monogamy yet. She says I am to recommend it to you out of my own experience, so I do so—acting strictly under orders.

Affectionately yours,

CHARLES.

Thus armed, Wimsey descended on Henry Weldon, who greeted him with his usual offensive familiarity. Lord Peter bore with this as long as he thought advisable, and then said, carelessly:

"By the way, Weldon—you gave Miss Vane quite a turn yesterday afternoon."
Henry looked at him rather unpleasantly.

"Oh! did I? Well, I don't see why you need to come butting in."

"I wasn't referring to your manners," said Wimsey, "though I admit they are a bit startling. But why didn't you mention that you and she had met before?"

"Met before? For the very simple reason that we never have met before."

"Come, come, Weldon. How about last Thursday afternoon at the top of Hinks's Lane?"

Henry turned an ugly colour.

"I don't know what you're talking about."

"Don't you? Well, it's your own business, of course, but if you want to go about the country incognito, you ought to get rid of that pattern on your arm. I understand that these things can be removed. Re-tattooing in flesh-colour is the simplest method, I believe."

"Oh!" Henry stared for a few moments; then a slow grin spread itself over his face.

"So that's what the little hussy meant when she said she'd seen a snake. Sharp girl, that, Wimsey. Fancy her spotting that."

"Manners, please!" said Wimsey. "You will kindly refer to Miss Vane in a proper way and spare me the boring nuisance of pushing your teeth out at the back of your neck."

"Oh, all right, just as you like. But I'd like to see you try."

"You wouldn't see it. It would happen, that's all. But I've no time to waste in comparative physiology. I want to know what you were doing in Darley in disguise."

"What affair is it of yours?"

"None; but the police might be interested. Anything that happened last Thursday interests them at the moment."

"Oh! I see. You want to fix something on me. Well, just as it so happens, you can't, so you can put that in your pipe and smoke it. It's a fact that I came down here in another name. Why shouldn't I. I didn't want my mother to know I was here."

"Why?"

"Well, you see, I didn't like this Alexis business at all. There's no harm in admitting that. I've said it already and I don't mind saying it again. I wanted to find out what was happening. If this marriage was really going through, I wanted to stop it."

"But couldn't you have done that openly, without blacking your hair and dressing yourself up in dark spectacles?"

"Of course I could. I could have burst in on the lovebirds and made a hell of a row and frightened Alexis off, I dare say. And then what? Had a devil of a scene with my mother, and been cut off with a shilling, I suppose. No. My idea was to snoop around and see whether the job was really being put through, and, if it was, to get hold of the young blighter and buy him off privately."

"You'd have needed some cash to do that," said Wimsey, drily. "I don't know about that. I'd heard some stories about a girl down here, don't you see, and if my mother got to know about that—"

"Ah, yes—a qualified form of blackmail. I begin to see the idea. You were going to pick up information in Wilvercombe about Alexis' previous entanglements, and then present him with the choice between having Mrs. Weldon told about it and possibly getting nothing out of it, and taking your cash in hand and letting his credit as a faithful lover go. Is that it?"

"That's it."

"And why Darley?"

"Because I didn't want to run into the old lady in Wilvercombe. A pair of specs, and a bottle of hair-dye might be all right for the yokels, but to the sharp eye of mother-love, you understand, they might not be as impenetrable as a brick wall."

"Quite so. Do you mind my asking whether you made any progress with this delicate investigation?"

"Not much. I only got to the place on Tuesday evening, and I spent most of Wednesday tinkering with the car. Those fools at the garage sent it out—"

"Ah, yes! One moment. Was it really necessary to hire a car with all that parade of secrecy?"

"It was, rather, because my mother would have recognised my own 'bus. It's rather an unusual colour."

"You seem to have thought it all out very well. Did you have no difficulty about hiring it?—oh, no, how stupid of me! You could give your own name to the garage, naturally."

"I could, but I didn't. To be perfectly frank—well! I don't mind saying that I had another name and address all ready to slip into. Sometimes I slip off to Cambridge on the quiet, see! To visit a lady there. You get me. Nice little woman—devoted and all that. Husband in the background somewhere. He won't divorce her, and I'm not worrying. Suits me all right as it is. Only there again, if my mother got to hear about it—there's been trouble, one way and another, and I didn't want to start it again. We're right as rain in Cambridge—Mr. and Mrs. Haviland Martin—all perfectly respectable, and all that, and it's easy enough to slip over when one wants a spot of domestic bliss and so on. You get me?"

"I get you. Do you also perambulate Cambridge in disguise?"

"I stick on the specs. when I go to the bank. Some of my good neighbours keep an account there."

"So you had this handy little disguise ready to slip into. I do congratulate you on the convenience of your arrangements. They really fill me with admiration, and I'm sure Mrs. Martin must be a very happy woman. It really surprises me that you should be so anxious to pursue Miss Vane with your attentions."

"Ah! But when a young lady asks for it—besides, I rather wanted to find out what the girl—the lady, that is, was after. When your mother's pretty well off, don't you see, you rather get the idea that people are looking out to make a bit out of her."

Wimsey laughed.

"So you thought you'd vamp Miss Vane and find out. How great minds do think alike! She had rather the same idea about you. Wondered why you were so damned anxious to push her and me out of the place. I'm not surprised you each found the other so easy to talk to. Miss Vane said she was afraid you had seen through our little plot and were pulling her leg. Well, well! So now we can come out into the open and be perfectly frank with one another. So much jollier and all that, what?"

Henry Weldon looked at Wimsey suspiciously. He had a dim notion that he had somehow been jockeyed into an absurd position. It was all very well—that damned girl and this chattering lunatic of an amateur detective seemed to be working hand in glove. But it did cross his mind that all this talk about frankness was a little one-sided.

"Oh yes, rather!" he replied, vaguely; adding rather anxiously: "No need to tell my mother all about this, eh? She wouldn't like it."

"Possibly not," said Wimsey. "But you see—the police, what? I don't quite see—British justice—duties of a citizen and all that, don't you know. I can't prevent Miss Vane from going to Inspector Umpelty, can I? Free agent and so on —and she's not over and above pleased with you, from what I can make out."

"Oh, I don't mind the police." Henry's face cleared. "I've nothing to hide from *them*, you know. Not a bit. Rather not. Look here, old man—if I tell you about it, couldn't you just tip them off and get 'em to leave me alone. You're damned thick with that Inspector fellow—if you tell him I'm all right he'll take it from you."

"Oh, yes! Good fellow, the Inspector. Not his business to betray confidences. There's no reason whatever, so far as I can see, that Mrs. Weldon should know anything about it. We men must stick together."

"That's right!" Undeterred by experience, Mr. Weldon instantly entered into another alliance, offensive and defensive. "Well, look here. I came along to Darley on Tuesday evening and got permission to camp in Hinks's Lane."

"You knew the place pretty well, I gather."

"Never been there in my life; why?"

"Sorry—I thought you meant you knew about Hinks's Lane before you got there."

"Eh? Oh! Oh, I see what you mean. I got it from some chap I met in a pub in Heathbury. Don't know his name."

"Oh, quite!"

"I got in some stores and so on and settled in. Then, next day—that was Wednesday—I thought I'd better make a start on my inquiries. Stop a bit. That wasn't till the afternoon. I just loafed round in the morning—it was a grand day, and I was tired with trekking across country, especially as the car hadn't been going any too well. After lunch I had a go at it. It took me a devil of a time to start the 'bus, but I got her to go at last, and ran over to Wilvercombe. I went first of all to the registrar's and found that there was no marriage-notice put up there, so I followed that up by a round of the churches. There was nothing there either, but of course that proved nothing very much, because they might be going to get married in London or somewhere by licence or even by special licence.

"The next thing I did was to get the address of this chap Alexis from the people at the Resplendent. I took good care to dodge the old lady. I rang up the management with a story about a parcel that had gone to the wrong address, and got it out of them. Then I went round to the address they gave me, and tried to pump the old woman there, but she wasn't having any. However, she said I might find Alexis in a restaurant she told me about. I went round; he wasn't there, but I got talking with a fellow who dropped in—some dago, I don't know his name, and he said something which made me think I could find out what I wanted at the Winter Gardens."

Henry paused.

"Of course," he said, "this must look pretty fishy to you—me hanging round there asking about Alexis, and then all this business happening next day, but that was exactly what I did. Well, I went back to where I'd left the car, and had more trouble with it than ever—I began to curse the fool who'd hired it out to me, and I thought I'd better take it to a garage. Well, naturally, having once been started and warmed up, it went all right, and the garage people couldn't find anything wrong with it. They undid a few things and tightened a few things and charged me half a crown and that was all. By the time they'd finished, I was getting fed-up, and thought I'd better take the beastly thing home while she was running. So I went back to Darley, with the engine missing all the way. After that, I went for a walk and that was the end of that day, except that I dropped in a bit later for a pint at the Feathers."

"Which way did you walk?"

"Oh, along the beach for a bit. Why?"

"I just wondered if you'd rambled as far as the Flat-Iron?"

"Four and a half miles? Not likely. As a matter of fact, I haven't seen the place yet and I don't want to. Anyway, Thursday's the day you want to know about. All the details, as they say in the 'tec stories, eh? I had breakfast about nine o'clock —eggs and bacon, if you want to be particular—and then I thought I'd better see about getting along to Wilvercombe. So I went down to the village and flagged a passing car. That was—let me see—just after ten o'clock."

"Whereabouts was this?"

"Where the main road enters Darley—the Wilvercombe side."

"Why didn't you hire a car in the village?"

"Have you seen the cars you can hire in the village? If you had, you wouldn't ask."

"Couldn't you have 'phoned up a Wilvercombe garage and got them to come out and pick you and the Morgan up?"

"I could have, but I didn't. The only garage I knew at Wilvercombe was the place I'd tried the night before, and I knew they weren't any good. Besides, what's wrong about taking a lift?"

"Nothing, if the driver isn't afraid about his insurance."

"Oh! Well, this one wasn't. A very decent sort of woman she seemed to be. Drove a big red open Bentley. Made no bones about it at all."

"You don't know her name, I suppose?"

"I never thought to ask. But I do remember the number of the car—it was a comic one: OI 0101—sort of thing you couldn't help remembering—Oi-oi-oi! I said to this woman what a funny one it was and we laughed about it a good bit."

"Ha ha!" said Wimsey, "that's a good one. Oi-oi-oi!"

"Yes—it made us both laugh. I remember saying it was a bit unfortunate having a number like that, because it 'ud stick in a bobby's mind. Oi-oi-oi!" Mr. Weldon yodelled gleefully.

"So you got to Wilvercombe?"

"Yes."

"And what did you do there?"

"The good lady put me down in the Market Square and asked me if I would like to be taken back. So I said that was very kind of her and when would she be leaving. She said she had to go just before one o'clock because she had an appointment in Heathbury, so I said that would do me all right, and she arranged to meet me in the Market Square again. So then I had a wander round and went down to the Winter Gardens. The chap I'd talked to said that this girl of Alexis' had something to do with the Winter Garden—sung, or something."

"She doesn't, as a matter of fact. Her present young man plays in the orchestra there."

"Yes; I know that now. He'd got it all wrong. Anyhow, that's where I went, and I wasted a good bit of time listening to a tom-fool classical concert—my God! Bach and stuff at eleven in the morning!—and wondering when the real show began."

"Were there many people there?"

"Lord, yes—packed with tabbies and invalids! I soon got fed-up and went round to the Resplendent. I wanted to get hold of the people there, only of course I had the luck to run slap-bang into my mother. She was just going out, and I dodged behind one of these silly palm-trees they have there so that she couldn't see me, and then I thought she might be going off to meet Alexis, so I padded after her."

"And did she meet Alexis?"

"No; she went to some damned milliner's place."

"How provoking!"

"I believe you. I waited a bit, and she came out and went to the Winter Gardens. 'Hullo!' I said to myself, 'what's all this? Is she on the same tack as I am?' So away I toddled again, and dash it! If it wasn't the same infernal concert, and if she didn't sit through it all by herself! I can tell you what they played, too. A thing called the Eroica Symphony. Such stuff!"

"Tut-tut! How wearisome."

"Yes, I was wild, I can tell you. And the funny thing was, Mother looked as if she was waiting for somebody, because she kept looking round and fidgeting. She sat on right through the programme, but when it came to God Save the King, she chucked it and went back to the Resplendent, looking as sick as a cat when you've taken its mouse away. Well, then I looked at my watch, and dashed if it wasn't twenty to one!"

"A sad waste of time! So I suppose you had to give up your drive home with the kindly lady in the Bentley?"

"What, me? Not a bit of it. She was a dashed fine woman. There wasn't such a devil of a hurry about Alexis. I went back to the Market Square, and there she was and we went home. I think that was all. No, it wasn't. I bought some collars at a shop near the War Memorial, and I believe I've got the bill about me somewhere, if that's evidence. Yes, here we are. One stuffs these things into one's pocket, you know. I've got one of the collars on now, if you'd like to look at it."

"Oh, no—I'll believe you."

"Good! Well, that's all, except that I went along and had some lunch at the Feathers. My good lady friend dropped me there and I think she went off up the Heathbury Road. After lunch, that is, at about 1.45, I went and had another go at the car, but couldn't get the slightest sign of a spark. So I thought I'd see if the local man could make anything of it. I went and got him and he came, and after a time they traced the trouble to a fault in the H.T. lead and put it right."

"Well, that seems pretty clear. What time did you and the lady in the Bentley get to the Feathers?"

"Just on one o'clock. I remember hearing the church-clock strike and saying I hoped she wouldn't be late for her tennis-party."

"And what time did you go to the garage?"

"Blest if I know. About three or half-past I should think. But they could probably tell you."

"Oh, yes, they'll be able to check that up all right. It's very lucky you've got so many witnesses to your alibi, isn't it? Otherwise, as you say, it might have looked fishy. Now, here's another thing. While you were in Hinks's Lane on Thursday, did you happen to notice anybody or anything going along the shore?"

"Not a soul. But, as I've been trying to explain, I was only there up to ten o'clock and after 1.45, so it wasn't very likely I should see anything."

"Nobody passed between 1.45 and three o'clock?"

"Oh! between 1.45 and three o'clock? I thought you meant earlier. Yes, there was a chap—a little pip-squeak of a fellow, in shorts, with horn-rimmed goggles on. He came down Hinks's Lane just after I got back—at 1.55, to be exact—and asked the time."

"Did he? Where did he come from?"

"From the village. I mean, from the direction of the village; he seemed to be a stranger. I told him the time, and he went down to the shore and had his lunch on the beach. He cleared off later—at least, he wasn't there after I came back from the garage, and I think he went earlier than that. I didn't have much conversation with him. In fact, he wasn't keen for any, after I'd booted him one in the behind."

"Great Scott! What for?"

"Nosey-parkering. I was struggling with the infernal car, and he stood about asking silly questions. I told him to clear out—standing there bleating 'Won't it start?' Blasted little idiot!"

Wimsey laughed. "He can't be our man, anyhow."

"What man? The murderer? You still want to make out it's murder? Well, I'll swear that little shrimp had nothing to do with it. Sunday-school teacher, that's what he looked like."

"And he was the only person you saw? Nothing else: neither man, woman nor child? Neither bird nor beast?"

"Why, no. No. Nothing."

"H'm. Well, I'm much obliged to you for being so frank. I'll have to tell Umpelty about all this, but I don't imagine he'll bother you much—and I don't see the least need to inform Mrs. Weldon."

"I told you there was nothing in it."

"Exactly. What time did you leave on Friday morning, by the way?"

"Eight o'clock."

"Early start, wasn't it?"

"There was nothing to stay for."

"Why?"

"Well, Alexis was dead, wasn't he?"

"How did you know that?"

Henry broke into a great guffaw.

"Thought you'd got something that time, didn't you? Well, I knew it because I was told it. I went into the Feathers on Thursday night, and of course, they'd all heard about the dead man being found. Presently the local bobby came in— he doesn't live in Darley, but he comes through on his bike from time to time. He'd been over to Wilvercombe for something or the other, and he told us they'd got a photo of the body and had just developed it up and identified it as a fellow called Alexis from the Resplendent. You ask the bobby, and he'll tell you.

So I began to think I'd better pop off home, because that's where my mother would expect condolences to come from. How's that, eh?"

"Overwhelming," said Wimsey.

He left Henry Weldon and made for the police-station.

"Water-tight, water-tight, water-tight," he muttered to himself. "But why did he lie about the horse? He must have seen it, if it was running loose. Unless it broke out of the field after eight o'clock in the morning. And why shouldn't it? Water-tight, water-tight—damned suspiciously water-tight!"

20

THE EVIDENCE OF THE LADY IN THE CAR

Madam, we're strangers:
And yet I knew some while ago a form
Like thine.
—*The Brides' Tragedy*

THURSDAY, 25 JUNE

The Superintendent and the Inspector were perhaps even more surprised than pleased to hear of the identification of Mr. Haviland Martin. They felt that the amateurs had somehow stolen a march on them, although, as they both hastened to point out, the case now remained as obscure as ever, if not more so. That is to say, considered as a murder, it was obscure; on the other hand, the evidence for suicide was perhaps a little strengthened, though only negatively. Instead of the sinister Martin, who might have been anybody, they now had merely Mr. Henry Weldon, whom they knew. True, it was now extremely plain that Henry Weldon had a most cogent reason for wishing Paul Alexis out of the way. But his own explanation of his presence at Darley seemed plausible, if foolish, and there remained the absolute certainty that he could not possibly have been at the Flat-Iron at two o'clock. Moreover, the fact that he had been known for five years as the bespectacled Haviland Martin of the tinted glasses, robbed his latest masquerade of half its significance. The character of Martin had not been invented for the present purpose, and, since it already existed, it was natural enough that Weldon should have assumed it for the purpose of spying on his mother.

As to the outstanding points of Weldon's story, these could be easily checked. The bill for the collars was dated June 18th, and the date did not appear to have been altered in any way. A telephone-call to the shop confirmed it, and brought the additional information that the bill referred to was one of the last half-dozen made out on that day. Since Thursday had been early-closing day, when the shop closed at one o'clock, it was fairly evident that the purchase had been made shortly before that time.

Next, perhaps, in importance was the evidence of the Darley policeman. He was quickly found and interrogated. He admitted that Weldon's account of the matter was perfectly true. He had been in Wilvercombe that evening at about nine o'clock on a visit to his young lady (being then off duty) and had met one of the Wilvercombe Police, Rennie by name, outside the Resplendent. He had asked if there was any news about the body found at the Flat-Iron and Rennie had mentioned the identification. Rennie confirmed this, and there was no reason to doubt it; the photographs had been developed and printed within an hour of their arrival at the police-station; the hotels had been among the first places visited by the police; the identification had been made shortly before nine o'clock, and Rennie had been on duty with Inspector Umpelty while the manager of the Resplendent was being interrogated. The Darley constable further admitted having mentioned the identification in the bar at the Three Feathers. He had gone into the bar, quite legitimately, just before closing-time, in search of a man who was suspected of some trifling misdemeanour, and he distinctly remembered that "Martin" was present at the time. Both constables were reprimanded for talking too freely; but the fact remained that Weldon had been told of the identification that night.

"So what have we got left?" inquired Superintendent Glaisher.

Wimsey shook his head.

"Nothing very much, but still, something. First: Weldon knows something about that horse—I'll swear he does. He hesitated when I asked him if he'd seen any person, thing, or animal, and I am almost certain he was wondering whether to say 'No' or to make up a tarradiddle. Secondly: All his story is so thin. A child would know better than to set about his precious inquiries in the way he did. Why should he twice go into Wilvercombe and twice come away without really doing anything much? Thirdly: His story is so glib, and so full of exact times. Why, if he wasn't deliberately preparing an alibi? Fourthly: Just at the most crucial moment of all, we get an account of his having been seen by an unknown person who asks the time. Why on earth should a man who had just passed through a village full of people and clocks, walk down Hinks's Lane to ask a casual camper for the time? The man who asks the time is part of the regular stock-in-trade of the alibi-maker. The whole thing is so elaborate and fishy—don't you think so?"

Glaisher nodded.

"I agree with you. It is fishy. But what does it mean?"

"There you've got me. I can only suggest that, whatever Weldon was doing that morning in Wilvercombe, it wasn't what he said he was doing, and that he may somehow be in league with the actual murderer. How about this car OI 0101?"

"It's a ——shire number, but that means nothing. Everybody buys second-hand cars these days. Still, naturally, we'll send out an inquiry. A wire to the ——shire authorities will put us on the track. Not that that helps us very much about what Weldon was doing later in the day."

"Not a bit, but there's no harm in getting hold of the lady. And have you asked at the Winter Gardens what the performance was last Thursday morning?"

"Yes: Constable Ormond is down there now—oh! here he is."

Constable Ormond had inquired minutely. It was a classical concert, starting at 10.30. *Eine Kleine Nachtmusik*, by Mozart; two *Leider ohne Worter* by

Mendelssohn; Bach's *Air for G String;* Suite by Handel; Interval; Beethoven's *Eroica.* All present and correct, Bach and Beethoven as per statement and approximately at the correct times. No printed programme that anyone could have taken away or memorised. Further, the *Eroica* had been substituted the last minute for the *Moonlight,* owing to some difficulty about mislaid band-parts. Each piece had been announced from the platform by the conductor. If anyone still nursed a suspicion that Mr. Henry Weldon had not been present at that particular concert, it could only be out of surprise that he should have troubled to remember the items he had heard so exactly. Positive confirmation of his story there was none, though P.C. Ormond had carefully questioned the attendants. Persons in tinted spectacles were, alas! as common in the Winter Gardens as black-beetles in a basement.

Some additional confirmation of Weldon's story was brought in a few minutes later by another constable. He had interviewed Mrs. Lefranc and discovered that a gentleman in dark glasses really had called on Paul Alexis on the Wednesday and tried to get information about Leila Garland. Mrs. Lefranc, scenting "trouble," had packed him off with a flea in his ear to the restaurant where Alexis frequently lunched. Here the proprietor remembered him; yes, there had, he believed, been some talk about the Winter Gardens with a gentleman out of the orchestra who had happened to drop in—no, not Mr. da Soto, but a much humbler gentleman, who played at the fourth desk of second violins. Finally, as sequel to a series of inquiries put round the principal Wilvercombe garages, a mechanic was found who remembered a gent calling on Wednesday evening with a Morgan and complaining of trouble in starting and feeble ignition. The mechanic had been able to find no fault beyond a certain amount of wear on the platinum points, which might have caused bad starting when the engine was cold.

All these things were of little importance as regarded the actual crime, if there was one; they served, however, to support the general accuracy of Weldon's statement.

One of the minor irritations of detective work is the delay which usually occurs in the putting-through of inquiries. Trunk-calls are held up; people urgently required for interviews are absent from home; letters take time to travel. It was, therefore, gratifying and surprising to find the identification of the owner of OI 0101 going along like oiled clockwork. Within an hour, a telegram arrived from the ———shire County Council, stating that OI 0101 had been last transferred to a Mrs. Morecambe, living at 17 Popcorn Street, Kensington. Within ten minutes, the Wilvercombe Exchange had put through a trunk-call. Within fifteen minutes the bell rang and Superintendent Glaisher was learning from Mrs. Morecambe's maid that her mistress was staying at Heathbury Vicarage. A call to the vicarage received immediate attention. Yes, Mrs. Morecambe was staying there; yes, she was at home; yes, they would fetch her; yes, this was Mrs. Morecambe speaking; yes, she distinctly remembered driving a gentleman in dark glasses from Darley to Wilvercombe and back last Thursday; yes, she thought she could remember the times; she must have picked him up about ten o'clock, judging by the time she had started out from Heathbury, and she knew she had dropped him in Darley again at one o'clock because she had consulted her watch to see if she would be in time for her luncheon and tennis-party at Colonel Cranton's, the other side of Heathbury. No, she had never seen the gentleman before and did not know his name, but she thought she could identify him if required. No trouble at all, thanks—she was only glad to know that the police had nothing against *her* (silvery laughter); when the maid said the Superintendent was on the 'phone she had been afraid she might have been trespassing the white lines, or parking in the wrong place or something. She would be staying at the vicarage till next Monday and would be happy to assist the police in any way. She did hope she hadn't been helping a gangster to escape or anything of that sort.

The Superintendent scratched his head. "It's uncanny," he said. "Here we are and we know all about it—not so much as a wrong number! But anyhow, if the lady's a friend of the Rev. Trevor's, she's O.K. He's lived here for fifteen years and is the nicest gentleman you could wish to meet—quite one of the old school. We'll just find out how well he knows this Mrs. Morecambe, but I expect it's all right. As to this identification, I don't know that it's worth while."

"You probably couldn't expect her to identify him without his dark hair and glasses," said Wimsey. "It's astonishing what a difference it makes having the eyes concealed. You could make him put the spectacles on, of course, or you could bring her over and get *him* to identify *her*. I'll tell you what. Ring up again and ask if she can come over here now. I'll get hold of Weldon and park him out on the verandah of the Resplendent, and you can fetch her along casually. If he spots her, all's well; if she spots him, we may feel differently about it."

"I see," said Glaisher. "That's not a bad idea. We'll do that." He rang up Heathbury Vicarage and spoke again.

"It's all right; she's coming."

"Good. I'll toddle round and try to detach Weldon from his mamma. If she's present at the interview the good Henry will be in the soup. If I can't get him, I'll ring you."

Henry Weldon was readily found in the lounge. He was having tea with his mother, but excused himself when Wimsey came up and asked for a word in private. They selected a table about half-way along the verandah, and Weldon ordered drinks, while Wimsey embarked on a rather verbose account of his interview with the police that morning. He harped a good deal on the trouble he had taken to persuade Glaisher not to let the story come to Mrs. Weldon's ears, and Henry expressed a proper sense of gratitude.

Presently a burly figure made his appearance, looking exactly like a police-constable out of uniform, and escorting a rather young-old lady, dressed in the extreme of fashion. They passed slowly along the verandah, which was well filled with people, making for an empty table at the far end. Wimsey watched the lady's glance roam over the assembly; it rested on him, passed on to Weldon and then, without pause or sign of recognition, to a young man in blue glasses who was toying with a chocolate sundae at the next table. Here it paused for a moment—then it moved on again. At the same time Weldon gave quite a convulsive start.

"I beg your pardon," said Wimsey, breaking off short in his monologue. "Did you speak?"

"I—er—no," said Weldon. "I thought I recognised somebody, that's all. Probably a chance resemblance." He followed Mrs. Morecambe with his eyes as she approached them, and raised a tentative hand to his hat.

Mrs. Morecambe saw the movement and looked at Weldon, with a faint expression of puzzlement. She opened her mouth as though to speak, but shut it again. Weldon completed the hat-raising gesture and stood up.

"Good afternoon," he said. "I'm afraid you don't—"

Mrs. Morecambe stared with polite surprise.

"Surely I'm not mistaken," said Weldon. "You were good enough to give me a lift the other day."

"Did I?" said Mrs. Morecambe. She looked more closely and said:

"Yes, I believe I did—but weren't you wearing dark glasses that day?"

"I was—it makes rather a difference, doesn't it?"

"I really shouldn't have known you. But I recognise your voice now. Only I had an idea—But there! I'm not very observant. I carried away an impression that you were quite dark. Probably the glasses put it into my head. So stupid of me. I hope the Morgan has recovered itself."

"Oh, yes, thanks. Fancy meeting you here. The world's a small place, isn't it?"

"Very. I hope you are having an enjoyable holiday."

"Oh, very much so, thanks—now that my car is behaving itself again. I'm tremendously grateful to you for having taken compassion on me that day."

"Not at all; it was a pleasure."

Mrs. Morecambe bowed politely and moved away with her companion. Wimsey grinned.

"So that was your attractive lady. Well, well. You're a gay dog, Weldon. Young or old, they all go down before you, spectacles or no spectacles."

"Chuck it!" said Henry, not displeased. "Lucky thing her turning up like that, wasn't it?"

"Remarkably so," said Wimsey.

"Don't like the hick she's got with her, though," pursued Henry. "One of the local turnip-heads, I suppose."

Wimsey grinned again. Could anybody be as slow-witted as Henry made himself out?

"I ought to have tried to find out who she was," said Henry, "but I thought it would look a bit pointed. Still, I daresay they'll be able to trace her, won't they? It's rather important to me, you know."

"Yes, it is, isn't it? Very good-looking and well-off, too, from the looks of her. I congratulate you, Weldon. Shall I try and trace her for you? I'm a most skilful go-between and an accomplished gooseberry."

"Don't be an ass, Wimsey. She's my alibi, you idiot."

"So she is! Well, here goes!"

Wimsey slipped away, chuckling to himself.

"Well, that's all right," said Glaisher, when all this was reported to him. "We've got the lady taped now all right. She's the daughter of an old school-friend of Mrs. Trevor's and stays with them every summer. Been at Heathbury for the last three weeks. Husband's something in the City; sometimes joins her for week-ends, but hasn't been here this summer. Lunch and tennis at Colonel Cranton's all correct. No funny business there. Weldon's all right."

"That will be a relief to his mind. He's been a bit nervy about this alibi of his. He skipped like a ram when he caught sight of Mrs. Morecambe."

"Did he? Skipping for joy, I expect. After all, you can't be surprised. How's he to know what time the alibi's wanted for? We've managed to keep that part of it out of the papers, and he probably still thinks, as we did at first, that Alexis was dead some time before Miss Vane found the body. He can't help knowing that he had a jolly good motive for killing Alexis, and that he was here under dashed suspicious circumstances. In any case, you've got to let him out, because, if he did the murder or helped to do it, he wouldn't make any mistake about the time. He's scared stiff, and I don't blame him. But his not knowing lets him out as surely and certainly as if he had a really cast-iron alibi for two o'clock."

"Much more surely, my dear man. It's when I find people with cast-iron alibis that I begin to suspect them. Though Weldon's two o'clock alibi seems to be as nearly cast-iron as anything can be. But it's only when somebody comes along and swears himself black in the face that he saw Weldon behaving with perfect innocence at two o'clock precisely that I'll begin seriously to weave a hempen neck-tie for him. Unless, of course—"

"Well?"

"Unless, I was going to say, there was a conspiracy between Weldon and some other person to kill Alexis, and the actual killing was done by the other person. I mean, supposing, for example, Weldon and our friend Bright were both in it, and Bright was scheduled to do the dirty deed at eleven o'clock, for example, while Weldon established his own alibi, and suppose there was some hitch in the arrangements so that the murder didn't come off till two, and suppose Weldon didn't know that and was still sticking to the original time-table—how about that?"

"That's supposing a lot. Bright—or whoever it was—had had plenty of time to communicate with Weldon. He wouldn't be such a fool as not to let him know."

"True; I'm not satisfied with that suggestion. It doesn't seem to fit Bright."

"Besides, Bright really has a cast-iron alibi for two o'clock."

"I know. That's why I suspect him. But what I mean is that Bright is a free agent. Even if it was too dangerous to meet Weldon he could always have written or telephoned, and so could Weldon. You haven't got anybody in jug who would fit the bill, I suppose? Or any sudden deaths? The only thing I can think of is that the accomplice may have been in some place where he couldn't communicate with anybody—quod, or six foot of elm with brass handles."

"Or how about a hospital?"

"Or, as you say, a hospital."

"That's an idea," said Glaisher. "We'll look into that, my lord."

"It can't do any harm—though I haven't much faith in it. I seem to have lost my faith lately, as the good folks say. Well, thank Heaven! it's nearly dinner-time and one can always eat. Hullo—ullo—ullo! What's all the excitement?"

Superintendent Glaisher looked out of the window. There was a noise of trampling feet.

"They're carrying something down to the mortuary. I wonder—"

The door burst open with scant ceremony and Inspector Umpelty surged in, damp and triumphant.

"Sorry, sir," he said. "Good-evening, my lord. We've got the body!"

21

THE EVIDENCE AT THE INQUEST

At the word, "I'm murdered,"
The gaolers of the dead throw back the grave-stone,
Split the deep ocean, and unclose the mountain
To let the buried pass.

—Death's Jest-Book

FRIDAY, 26 JUNE

The inquest upon the body of Paul Alexis was held on June 26th, to the undisguised relief and triumph of Inspector Umpelty. For years (it seemed to him) he had been trying to make an investigation about nothing tangible. But for Harriet's photographs, he might, in his more worried moments, have begun to think that the body was a myth. Now, however, here it definitely was: a real, solid—or comparatively solid—body. True, it was not quite so informative as he had hoped. It was not served out to him complete with a ticket, marked in plain figures: "Suicide, with care," or "This Year's Murder-Model; Body by Bright." However, there was the corpse, and that was something gained. To quote Lord Peter (who seemed to be specialising in the provision of mnemonics), he might now say:

'Twould make a man drink himself dead on gin-toddy
To have neither a corpus delicti nor body;
But now though by destiny scurvily tricked, I
At least have a corpse—though no corpus delicti.

There was some little debate whether the whole matter should be thrashed out at the inquest or the complicated series of clues and suspicions suppressed and the inquest adjourned for further inquiries. In the end, however, it was decided to let matters take their course. Something useful might come out; one never knew. In any case, the possible suspects must know by this time pretty well where they stood. Certain clues—for example, the horseshoe—could, of course, be kept up the sleeves of the police.

The first witness to give evidence was Inspector Umpelty. He explained briefly that the body had been found tightly wedged into a deep crevice at the far end of the Grinders reef, from which it had been recovered with considerable difficulty by means of dredging-tackle and diving. It had apparently been washed into that position by the heavy seas of the previous week. When found, it was considerably distended by internal gases, but had not floated, being heavily weighted down by the presence of a cashbelt containing £300 in gold. (Sensation.)

The Inspector produced the belt and the gold (which the jury inspected with curiosity and awe), and also a passport found on the deceased; this had recently been visa'd for France. Two other items of interest had also been discovered in the dead man's breast-pocket. One was the unmounted photograph of a very beautiful girl of Russian type, wearing a tiara-shaped head-dress of pearls. The photograph was signed in a thin, foreign-looking hand with the name "Feodora." There was no mark of origin on the photograph, which either had never been mounted, or had been skilfully detached from its mount. It was in a fairly good state of preservation, having been kept in one of the compartments of a handsome leather note-case, which had protected it to some extent. The note-case contained nothing further but a few currency notes, some stamps, and the return half of a ticket from Wilvercombe to Darley Halt, dated 18th June.

The second item was more enigmatical. It was a sheet of quarto paper, covered with writing, but so stained with blood and sea-water that it was almost undecipherable. This paper had not been folded in the note-case, but tucked away behind it. Such writing as could be read was in printed capitals and in a purplish ink which, though it had run and smeared a good deal, had stood up reasonably well to its week's immersion. A few sentences could be made out, but they were not of an encouraging nature. There was, for instance, a passage which began musically "SOLFA," but swiftly degenerated into "TGMZ DXL LKKZM VXI" before being lost in the dirty crimson stain. Further down came "AIL AXH NZMLF," "NAGMJU KC KC" and "MULBY MS SZLKO," while the concluding words, which might be the signature, were "UFHA AKTS."

The coroner asked Inspector Umpelty whether he could throw any light on this paper. Umpelty replied that he thought two of the witnesses might be able to do so, and stepped down to make way for Mrs. Lefranc.

The lady of the lodgings, in a great state of nerves, tears and face-powder, was asked if she had identified the body. She replied that she had been able to do so by the clothes, the hair, the beard and by a ring which deceased had always worn on his left hand.

"But as for his poor face," sobbed Mrs. Lefranc, "I couldn't speak to it, not if I was his own mother, and I'm sure I loved him like a son. It's all been nibbled right away by those horrible creatures, and if ever I eat a crab or lobster again, I hope Heaven will strike me dead! Many's the lobster mayonnaise I've ate in the old days, not knowing, and I'm sure it's no wonder if they give you nightmare, knowing where they come from, the brutes!"

The court shuddered, and the managers of the Resplendent and the Bellevue, who were present, despatched hasty notes by messenger to the respective chefs, commanding them on no account whatever to put crab or lobster on the menu for at least a fortnight.

Mrs. Lefranc deposed further that Alexis had been accustomed to receive letters from foreign parts which took him a long time to read and answer. That after receiving the last of these on the Tuesday morning he had become strange and excited in his manner. That on the Wednesday he had paid up all outstanding bills and burnt a quantity of papers, and that that night he had kissed her and referred mysteriously to a possible departure in the near future. That he had gone out on the Thursday morning after making rather a poor breakfast. He had not packed any clothes and had taken his latchkey as though he meant to return.

Shown the photograph: she had never seen it before; she had never seen the original of the portrait; she had never heard Alexis speak of anyone named Feodora; she knew of no ladies in his life except Leila Garland, with whom he

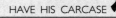
had broken some time ago and Mrs. Weldon, the lady he was engaged to marry at the time of his death.

This, naturally, focused public attention on Mrs. Weldon. Henry handed her a smelling-bottle and said something to her, and she responded by a faint smile.

The next witness was Harriet Vane, who gave a detailed account of the finding of the body. The coroner examined her particularly in the matter of the exact position of the body and the condition of the blood. Harriet was a good witness on these points, her training as a mystery-writer having taught her to assemble details of this kind coherently.

"The body was lying with the knees drawn up, as though it had crumpled together in that position as it fell. The clothes were not disarranged at all. The left arm was doubled so as to bring the hand and wrist directly beneath the throat. The right arm and hand hung over the edge of the rock immediately beneath the head of the corpse. Both hands and both arms, as well as the front part of the body were saturated with blood. The blood had collected in a pool in a hollow of the rock just under the throat, and was still dripping down the face of the rock when I saw it. I cannot say whether there might not have been sea-water as well as blood in the hollow. There was no blood on the upper surface of the rock, or on any part of the body except the front and on the hands and arms. The appearance presented was as though the throat of the deceased had been cut while he was bending forward—as, for example, a person might do over a sink or basin. When I shifted the body the blood flowed freely and copiously from the severed vessels. I did not observe whether any splashes of blood had been dried by the sun. I do not think so, because the pool of blood and the blood beneath the corpse were sheltered from the direct rays of the sun by the corpse itself. When I lifted the corpse, the blood gushed out, as I said before, and ran down the rock. It was quite liquid and ran freely.

"I handled the sleeves and breast of the coat and the gloves which deceased was wearing. They were soaked in blood and felt limp and wet. They were not stiff at all. They were not sticky. They were limp and wet. I have seen bandages which had been soaked in blood some time previously and am acquainted with the stiffness and stickiness of clotted blood. The clothes were not like that at all. They appeared to have been soaked in fresh blood.

"The body felt warm to the touch. The surface of the rock was hot, as it was a hot day. I did not move the body, except when I turned it a little over and lifted the head at first. I am sorry now that I did not attempt to drag it further up the beach. But I did not think I was strong enough to make a good job of it, and supposed that I should be able to get help quickly."

The coroner said he did not think the jury could possibly blame Miss Vane for not having tried to remove the corpse, and complimented her on the presence of mind she had shown in taking photographs and carrying out investigations. The photographs were handed to the jury, and, after Harriet had explained the various difficulties she had encountered before getting into communication with the police, she was allowed to step down.

The next witness was the police-surgeon, Dr. Fenchurch. From his examination of the photographs and of the body, he had formed the opinion that the throat of the deceased had been completely severed by a single blow with a sharp-bladed instrument. The lobsters and crabs had eaten away the greater part of the soft tissues, but the photographs were here of very great value, since they showed definitely that the throat had been cut at the first attempt, without any preliminary surface gashing. This was borne out by the condition of the muscular tissue, which showed no sign of any second cut. All the great vessels and muscles of the neck, including the carotid and jugular veins and the glottis, had been clearly cut through. The wound commenced high up under the left ear, and proceeded in a downward direction to the right side of the throat, extending backwards as far as the vertebral column, which had, however, not been nicked. He concluded that the cut had been made from left to right. This was characteristic of suicidal throat-cutting by a right-handed person; the same appearance would, however, be produced by a homicidal cut, provided the murderer were standing behind his victim at the time.

"Such a wound would, of course, produce a great effusion of blood?"

"It would."

"In the case of a murderer, standing in the position you describe, his hands and clothes would necessarily be very much stained?"

"His right hand and arm, probably. His clothes might not be stained at all, since they would be protected by the body of his victim."

"Did you carry out a post-mortem on the body to ascertain if there was any other possible cause of death?"

The doctor, smiling slightly, said that he had, in the ordinary course of things, opened up the head and body, but had seen nothing of a suspicious nature.

"In your opinion, what was the cause of death?"

Dr. Fenchurch, still smiling slightly, said that in his opinion the cause of death was acute haemorrhage, coupled with the severance of the respiratory canal. In fact, deceased had died of having his throat cut.

The coroner, who was a lawyer and seemed unwilling to let the medical witness have his own way entirely, persisted.

"I am not trying to quibble over absurdities," he remarked, acidly. "I am asking you whether there is any possibility that the deceased was killed in some other way, and the throat cut afterwards to produce the appearance of suicidal throat-cutting?"

"Oh, I see. Well, I can say this: that the throat-cutting was undoubtedly the immediate cause of death. That is, the man was undoubtedly alive when his throat was cut. The body was completely drained of blood. In fact, I have never seen a body drained so completely. There was some very slight clotting about the heart but it was remarkably little. This, however, is no more than one might expect from the great extent of the wound. If the man had been already dead when the wound was inflicted, there would, of course, have been little or no bleeding."

"Quite so. It is as well to have that clear. You said that the throat-cutting was the *immediate* cause of death. What precisely did you mean by that?"

"I meant to exclude the bare possibility that the deceased might also have taken poison. It is not unusual to find suicides doubling their precautions in this way. As a matter of fact, however, the internal organs showed no signs of anything of this nature having taken place. If you wish, I can have an analysis made of the visceral contents."

"Thank you; perhaps it would be as well. It would equally, I suppose, be possible that the man had been previously drugged by some other party before the delivery of the blow, or slash, that cut his throat?"

"Certainly. A soporific might have been administered beforehand in order to make the attack more easy."

Here Inspector Umpelty rose and begged to draw the coroner's attention to the evidence of Harriet and the photographs that the deceased had walked to the rock on his own feet and alone.

"Thank you, Inspector; we shall come to that later. Permit me to finish with the medical evidence. You heard Miss Vane's account of her finding the body, Doctor, and her statement that at ten minutes past two the blood was still liquid. What inference do you draw as regards the time of the death?"

"I should say that it had occurred within a very few minutes of the finding of the body. Not earlier than two o'clock at the outside."

"And would a person die quickly from the effects of having his throat cut in the manner described?"

"He would die immediately. The heart and arteries might continue to pump blood for a few seconds by spasmodic muscular contraction, but the man would be dead from the moment that the great vessels were severed."

"So that we may take it that the wound was actually inflicted certainly not earlier than two o'clock?"

"That is so. Two o'clock is the extreme limit. I myself should incline to put it later."

"Thank you. There is just one more question. You have heard that a razor was found in the proximity of the body. Inspector, would you kindly hand the exhibit to the witness. In your opinion, Doctor, is the appearance of the wound consistent with its having been inflicted by that weapon?"

"Decidedly so. This, or a similar razor, would be an ideal instrument for the purpose."

"In your opinion, would great physical strength be required to deliver such a blow with that, or a similar weapon?"

"Considerable strength, yes. Exceptional strength, no. Much would depend upon the circumstances."

"Will you explain what you mean by that?"

"In the case of a determined suicide, wounds of this kind have been known to be inflicted by persons of quite ordinary or even poor physique. In the case of homicide, much would depend on whether the victim was able to offer any effective resistance to the attack."

"Did you find any other marks of violence on the body?"

"None whatever."

"No signs of throttling or bruising?"

"None. There was nothing remarkable beyond the natural action of the water and the complete absence of post-mortem staining. I attribute the latter to the small amount of blood present in the body and also to the circumstance that the body was not left lying in one position, but was washed from the rock shortly after death and tumbled about in the water."

"In your opinion, does the condition of the body suggest suicide or homicide?"

"In my opinion, and taking all the circumstances into consideration, suicide appears rather more probable. The only point to set against it is the absence of surface cuts. It is rather rare for a suicide to be completely successful at the first attempt, though it is not by any means unknown."

"Thank you."

The next witness was Miss Leila Garland, who confirmed the evidence of Mrs. Lefranc with respect to the cipher letters. That naturally led to an inquiry into the relations between Miss Garland and Mr. Alexis, from which it transpired that their acquaintance had been conducted on a footing of rigid, and even Victorian, propriety; that Mr. Alexis had been terribly distressed when Miss Garland had put an end to the friendship; that Mr. Alexis was not by any means a likely person to commit suicide; that (on the other hand) Miss Garland had been terribly upset to think of his having done anything rash on her account; that Miss Garland had never heard of anybody called Feodora, but did not, of course, know what follies Mr. Alexis might not have committed in a despairing mood after the termination of their friendship; that Miss Garland had not so much as set eyes on Mr. Alexis for ever so long and could not imagine why anybody should think this terrible business had anything to do with her. With regard to the letters, Miss Garland had thought that Mr. Alexis was being blackmailed, but could produce no evidence to prove this.

It now became obvious that nothing on earth could keep Mrs. Weldon out of the witness-box. Attired in near-widow's weeds, she indignantly protested against the suggestion that Alexis could possibly have made away with himself on Leila's account, or on any account whatever. She knew better than anybody that Alexis had had no genuine attachment to anyone but herself. She admitted that she could not explain the presence of the portrait signed "Feodora," but asserted vehemently that, up to the last day of his life, Alexis had been radiant with happiness. She had last seen him on the Wednesday night, and had expected to see him again on the Thursday morning at the Winter Gardens. He had not arrived there, and she was perfectly sure that he must have been lured away to his death by some designing person. He had often said that he was afraid of Bolshevik plots, and in her opinion, the police ought to look for Bolsheviks.

This outburst produced some effect upon the jury, one of whom rose to inquire whether the police were taking any steps to comb out suspicious-looking foreigners residing in, or hanging about, the vicinity. He himself had observed a number of disagreeable-looking tramps on the road. He also noticed with pain that at the very hotel where Alexis had worked, a Frenchman was employed as a professional dancer, and that there were also a number of foreigners in the orchestra at the Winter Gardens. The dead man was also a foreigner. He did not see that naturalisation papers made any difference. With two million British-born workers unemployed, he thought it a scandalous thing that this foreign riff-raff was allowed to land at all. He spoke as an Empire Free-Trader and member of the Public Health Committee.

Mr. Pollock was then called. He admitted having been in the neighbourhood of the Grinders reef with his boat at about two o'clock on the day of the death, but insisted that he had been out in deep water and had seen nothing previous to Harriet's arrival on the scene. He was not looking in that direction; he had his own business to attend to. As to the nature of that business he remained evasive, but nothing could shake his obstinate assertion of complete ignorance. His grandson Jem (having now returned from Ireland) briefly confirmed this evidence, but added that he himself had surveyed the shore with a glass at, he thought, about 1.45. He had then seen someone on the Flat-Iron Rock, either sitting or lying down, but whether dead or alive he could not say.

The last witness was William Bright, who told the story about the razor in almost exactly the same terms that he had used to Wimsey and the police. The

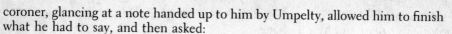
coroner, glancing at a note handed up to him by Umpelty, allowed him to finish what he had to say, and then asked:

"You say this happened at midnight at Tuesday, 16 June?"

"Just after midnight. I heard a clock strike shortly before this man came up to me."

"How was the tide at the time?"

For the first time, Bright faltered. He glanced about him as though he suspected a trap, licked his lips nervously, and replied:

"I know nothing about tides. I don't belong to this part of the country."

"But you mentioned, in your very moving account of this interview, the noise made by the sea lapping against the wall of the Esplanade. That suggests, does it not, that the tide was then full?"

"I suppose so."

"Would you be surprised to learn that at midnight on the 16th of this month the tide was actually at the lowest point of the ebb?"

"I may have sat there longer than I thought."

"Did you sit there for six hours?"

No answer.

"Would it surprise you to know that the sea never comes up to the wall of the Esplanade except at the top of the spring tides which, on that particular date, would occur at about six o'clock in the evening?"

"I can only say that I must have been mistaken. You must allow for the effects of a morbid imagination."

"You still say that the interview took place at midnight?"

"Yes; I am confident about that."

The coroner dismissed Mr. Bright with a warning to be more careful what statements he made in court, and recalled Inspector Umpelty with an inquiry into Bright's movements and character.

He then summed up the evidence. He did not attempt to disguise his own opinion, which was that deceased had taken his own life. (Incoherent protest from Mrs. Weldon.) As to why he should have done so, it was not the jury's business to speculate. Various motives had been suggested, and the jury must bear in mind that deceased was a Russian by birth, and therefore excitable, and liable to be overcome by feelings of melancholy and despair. He himself had read a great deal of Russian literature and could assure the jury that suicide was of frequent occurrence among the members of that unhappy nation. We who enjoyed the blessing of being British might find that difficult to understand, but the jury could take it from him that it was so. They had before them clear evidence of how the razor came into the hands of Alexis, and he thought they need not lay too much stress on Bright's error about the tide. Since Alexis did not shave, what could he have needed a razor for, unless to commit suicide? He (the coroner) would, however, be perfectly fair and enumerate the one or two points which seemed to throw doubt on the hypothesis of suicide. There was the fact that Alexis had taken a return-ticket. There was the passport. There was the belt full of gold. They might perhaps think that deceased had contemplated fleeing the country. Even so, was it not likely that he had lost heart at the last moment and taken the shortest way out of the country and out of life itself? There was the odd circumstance that deceased had apparently committed suicide in gloves, but suicides were notoriously odd. And there was, of course, the evidence of Mrs. Weldon (for whom they must all feel the deepest sympathy) as to deceased's state of mind; but this was contradicted by the evidence of William Bright and Mrs. Lefranc.

In short, here was a man of Russian birth and temperament, troubled by emotional entanglements and by the receipt of mysterious letters, and obviously in an unstable condition of mind. He had wound up his worldly affairs and procured a razor. He had been found in a lonely spot, to which he had obviously proceeded unaccompanied, and had been found dead, with the fatal weapon lying close under his hand. There were no footprints upon the sand but his own, and the person who had discovered the body had come upon it so closely after the time of the death as to preclude the possibility of any murderer having escaped from the scene of the crime by way of the shore. The witness Pollock had sworn that he was out in deep water at the time when the death occurred, and had seen no other boat in the neighbourhood, and his evidence was supported by that of Miss Vane. Further, there was no evidence that anybody had the slightest motive for doing away with the deceased, unless the jury chose to pay attention to the vague suggestion about blackmailers and Bolsheviks, which there was not an atom of testimony to support.

Wimsey grinned at Umpelty over this convenient summary, with its useful suppressions and assumptions. No mention of clefts in the rock or of horseshoes or of the disposal of Mrs. Weldon's money. The jury whispered together. There was a pause. Harriet looked at Henry Weldon. He was frowning heavily and paying no attention to his mother, who was talking excitedly into his ear.

Presently the foreman rose to his feet—a stout person, who looked like a farmer.

"We're all agreed, for certain sure," he said, "as deceased come to his death by cutting of his throat, and most of us thinks he took his own life; but there's some" (he glared at the Empire Free-Trader) "who will have it as it was Bolsheviks."

"A majority verdict is sufficient," said the coroner. "Am I to understand that the majority is for suicide?"

"Yes, sir. I told you so, Jim Cobbley," added the foreman, in a penetrating whisper.

"Then your verdict is that deceased came to his end by cutting his own throat."

"Yes, sir." (A further consultation.) "We should like to add as we think the police regulations about foreigners did ought to be tightened up, like, deceased being a foreigner and suicides and murders being unpleasant in a place where so many visitors come in the summer."

"I can't take that," objected the harassed coroner. "Deceased was a naturalised Englishman."

"That don't make no difference," said the juror, sturdily. "We do think as the regulations ought to be tightened up none the more for that, and that's what we all say. Put it down, sir, as that's our opinion."

"There you are," said Wimsey, "that's the breed that made the Empire. When empire comes in at the door, logic goes out at the window. Well, I suppose that's all. I say, Inspector."

"My lord?"

"What are you doing with that scrap of paper?"

"I don't quite know, my lord. Do you think there's anything to be made of it?"

"Yes; send it up to Scotland Yard and ask them to get the photographic experts on to it. You can do a lot with coloured screens. Get hold of Chief Inspector Parker—he'll see that it's put into the right hands."

The Inspector nodded.

"We'll do that. It's my belief there's something for us in that bit of paper, if we could only get at it. I don't know when I've seen a queerer business than this. It looks just about as clear a case of suicide as you could wish, if it wasn't for one or two things. And yet, when you look into those things separately, they seem to melt away, like. There's that Bright. I thought we'd got him on one point, anyhow. But there! I've noticed that these landsmen, nine times out of ten, haven't the least notion whether the tide's in or out or where it is. I think he was lying; so do you—but you couldn't expect a jury to hang a man for murder on the ground that he didn't know High Water from Low Water. We'll try to keep an eye on the fellow, but I don't see how we're going to detain him. The verdict's suicide (which suits us well enough in a way), and if Bright wants to move on, we can't stop him. Not unless we offer to pay for his board and lodging for an indefinite period, and *that* wouldn't suit the rate-payers. He's got no settled address, and seeing what his business is, we can't hardly expect it. We'll get out a general call to have him kept under observation, but that's about all we *can* do. And of course, he'll change his name again."

"Isn't he on the dole?"

"No." The Inspector snorted. "Says he's got an independent spirit. That's a suspicious circumstance in itself, I should say. Besides—he'll be claiming this reward from the *Morning Star* and won't need any doles for a bit. But we can't force him to stay in Wilvercombe at his own expense, reward or no reward."

"Get hold of Mr. Hardy, and see if the paper can't hold the reward up a bit. Then, if he doesn't turn up to claim it, we'll know for a certainty that there's something wrong with him. A contempt for money, Inspector, is the root—or at any rate, the very definite sign—of all evil."

The Inspector grinned.

"You and me think alike, my lord. There's something fishy about a bloke that doesn't take all he can get. Right you are. I'll speak to Mr. Hardy. And I'll try and fix up with Bright to hang on here a couple of days. If he's up to anything queer, he won't try to bolt for fear of looking suspicious."

"It'll look much more suspicious if he consents to stay."

"Yes, my lord—but he won't reason that way. He won't want to make trouble. He'll stay for a bit, I daresay. Fact is, I was thinking, if we could pull him in over some other little matter. . . . I don't know, but he's a slippery looking customer, and I shouldn't wonder but what we might find some excuse or other to detain him on." He winked.

"Framing him, Inspector?"

"Good lord, no, my lord. Can't do that, in this country. But there's lots of little things a man may do in the way of breaking the law. There's street-betting, and drunk and disorderly, and buying stuff after closing-hours and so on—little odds-and-ends that come in handy at times."

"My conscience!" said Wimsey. "First time I've heard a good word for Dora! Well, I must be getting along. Hullo, Weldon! I didn't know you were there."

"Funny business, all this." Mr. Weldon waved his hand vaguely. "Lots of silly stuff people do talk, eh? You'd think the whole thing was plain as pie, but here's my mother still talking about Bolsheviks. Take more than a coroner's verdict to keep *her* quiet. Women! You can talk yourself black in the face reasoning with 'em and all they do is to go on bleating the same silly nonsense. You can't take any account of what they say, can you?"

"They're not all alike."

"So they say. But that's all part of this equality nonsense. Now, take that Miss Vane. Nice girl, and all that, and decent-looking when she takes the trouble to put her clothes on—"

"What about Miss Vane?" demanded Wimsey, sharply. then he thought: "Damn being in love! I'm losing my lightness of touch." Weldon merely grinned.

"No offence," he said. "I only meant—take that evidence of hers. How's a girl like that to be expected to know about blood and all that—see what I mean? Women always get that idea of blood running about all over the place. Always reading novels. 'Wallowing in gore.' That kind of stuff. No good trying to persuade 'em. They see what they think they ought to see. Get me?"

"You seem to have studied feminine psychology," said Wimsey, gravely.

"Oh, I know women pretty well," said Mr. Weldon, with solemn satisfaction.

"You mean," went on Wimsey, "that they think in clichés."

"Eh?"

"Formulae. 'There's nothing like a mother's instinct.' 'Dogs and children always know.' 'Kind hearts are more than coronets.' 'Suffering refines the character'—that sort of guff, despite all evidence to the contrary."

"Ye-es," replied Mr. Weldon. "What I mean is, you know, they think a thing ought to be so, and they say it is so."

"Yes; I grasped that that was what you meant." Wimsey thought that if ever human being had the air of repeating a formula without a clear idea of its meaning, Mr. Weldon was that human being; yet he pronounced the magic words with a kind of pride, taking credit to himself for a discovery.

"What you really mean," went on Wimsey, "is, I take it, that we can't rely on Miss Vane's evidence at all? You say: She hears a shriek, she finds a man with his throat cut and razor beside him; it looks as though he'd that moment committed suicide, therefore she takes it for granted that he *has* that moment committed suicide. In that case the blood ought to be still flowing. Therefore she persuades herself that it *was* still flowing. Is that it?"

"That's it," said Mr. Weldon.

"Therefore the jury bring in a verdict of suicide. But you and I, who know all about women, know that the evidence about the blood was probably wrong, and that therefore it may quite well have been murder. Is *that* it?"

"Oh, no—I don't mean that," protested Mr. Weldon. "I feel perfectly certain it was suicide."

"Then what are you grumbling at? It seems so obvious. If the man was murdered after two o'clock, Miss Vane would have seen the murderer. She didn't see the murderer. Therefore it was suicide. The proof of the suicide really depends on Miss Vane's evidence, which shows that the man died after two o'clock. Doesn't it?"

Mr. Weldon grappled for some moments with this surprising piece of logic, but failed to detect either the *petitio elenchi*, the undistributed middle or the inaccurate major premise which it contrived to combine. His face cleared.

"Of course," he said. "Yes. I see that. Obviously it must have been suicide, and Miss Vane's evidence proves that it was. So she must be right after all."

This was a syllogistic monstrosity even worse than the last, thought Wimsey.

A man who could reason like that could not reason at all. He constructed a new syllogism for himself.

The man who committed this murder was not a fool.

Weldon is a fool. Therefore Weldon did not commit this murder.

That appeared to be sound, so far as it went. But what was Weldon bothering about, in that case? One could only suppose that he was worried over having no perfect alibi for two o'clock. And indeed that was worrying Wimsey himself. All the best murderers have alibis for the time of the murder.

Then, suddenly, illumination came flooding, stabbing across the dark places of his mind like a searchlight. And, good God! if this was the true solution, Weldon was anything but a fool. He was one of the subtlest criminals a detective had ever encountered. Wimsey studied Weldon's obstinate profile—was it possible? Yes, it was possible—and the scheme might quite well have been successful, if only Harriet Vane had not turned up with her evidence.

Work it out this way; see how it looked. Weldon had murdered Alexis at the Flat-Iron at two o'clock. He had had the mare tethered ready somewhere, and, after leaving the Feathers at 1.30, he had gone down the Lane and got to horse without a moment's delay. Then he must have ridden hell-for-leather. Suppose he had somehow managed to do four miles in twenty-five minutes. That would leave him half a mile from the Flat-Iron at two o'clock. No, that would not do. Strain it a little farther. Let him start from Hinks's Lane at 1.32 and let him wallop a steady nine miles an hour out of the mare—that would almost do it. Let him, in any case, be within five minutes' quick walk of the rock at 1.55. Then what? *He sends the mare home.* Five minutes before Harriet woke, he could send the bay mare galloping back along the sands. Then he walks. He reaches the Flat-Iron at two o'clock. He kills. He hears Harriet coming. He hides in the cleft of the rock. And meanwhile, the bay mare has either run home, or, possibly, has reached the lane by the cottages and run up it, or—

Never mind the mare; she got back to her own field and stream somehow. The times were tight; the whole thing seemed absurdly elaborate, but it was not an absolute impossibility as he had thought at first. Suppose it had been so. Now, if Harriet had not been there, what would have happened? In a few hours the tide would have covered the body. Pause there, Morocco. If Weldon was the murderer, he would not want the body lost. He would want his mother to know that Alexis was dead. Yes; but under ordinary circumstances the body would have turned up sooner. It was the violent south-west wind and the three hundred sovereigns that had combined to keep the body hidden. And the body had been found, even so. Well, then. If Harriet had not found the body when she did, there would have been nothing to show that the death had not occurred earlier —say between 11 and 1.30—the period for which there was the alibi. In fact, the victim's arrival at that early hour at Darley Halt made it look much more likely that the earlier hour was the right one. Why should you tempt your victim to a lonely spot at 11.30 a.m. and then wait two and half hours before polishing him off—except in order to create a presumption that you had really killed him earlier? And then, too, there was that crusty pair, Pollock and his grandson, with their grudging evidence that they had seen Alexis "lying down" on the Flat-Iron at 1.45. They must be in it too. That was it. That must be it. The murder was meant to look like a morning murder—and that was why there had been that curious insistence on the alibi and the journey to Wilvercombe. "Always suspect the man with the cast-iron alibi"—was not that the very first axiom in the detective's book of rules? And here it was—the cast-iron alibi which really was cast-iron; meant to be scrutinised; meant to stand every test—as how should it not, for it was truth! It looked queer—because it was intended to look queer. It was asking, clamouring for investigation. It existed simply and solely to distract attention from the crucial hour of two o'clock. And if only Harriet had not come upon that freshly slain corpse, how well the plan might have succeeded. But Harriet had been there, and the whole structure had collapsed under the shock of her evidence. That must have been a blow indeed. No wonder Weldon was doing his best to discredit that awkward testimony as to the time of the death. He knew better than anyone that death at two o'clock was no proof of suicide, whatever it might appear to a coroner's jury. He was not stupid; he was shamming stupid, and doing it damned well.

Wimsey was vaguely aware that Weldon was bidding him good-bye in some form of words or other. He let him go readily, eagerly. He wanted to think this thing over.

A little concentration in the privacy of his own room brought him to a point from which he could begin to work forward with some assurance.

The original scheme had been smashed to pieces by Harriet's evidence. What would Weldon do next?

He might do nothing. That would be the safest way of all. He might rely on the coroner's verdict and trust that the police and Wimsey and Harriet and everybody else would accept it. But would he have the deadly courage to do that? He might—unless he knew of something in the cipher document which might prove the suicide to be murder. If so, or if he lost his head—then he would have to fall back on his second line of defence, which would be, what? Undoubtedly, an alibi for two o'clock—the real time of the murder.

What had he actually said about this? Wimsey looked up his notes, to which he had added considerably of late. Weldon had vaguely mentioned a possible witness, a man unknown who had been passing through Darley and had asked him the time.

Of course, yes. He had suspected this witness already—that stock character of detective fiction—the man who asks the time. Wimsey laughed. Now he felt sure about it. Everything was provided for and the way discreetly paved for the production of this useful witness in case of necessity. Now that the morning alibi had failed to draw the enemy's fire, the two o'clock alibi would be pushed to the front. Only, this time, it would not be cast-iron. It would be fake. Quite a good fake, very likely, but undoubtedly a fake. And then the shades of the prison-house would begin to close, darkly and coldly over the figure of Mr. Henry Weldon.

"If it were done when it is done, then it were—Weldon," said his lordship to himself. "If I'm right, then that two o'clock witness will turn up pretty quickly now. And if he does turn up, I'll know I'm right."

Which was logic after the manner of Mr. Weldon.

22

THE EVIDENCE OF
THE MANNEQUIN

All honest men, good Melchior, like thyself—
For that thou art, I think, upon my life—
Believe thee too.

—*Torrismond*

SATURDAY, 27 JUNE
SUNDAY, 28 JUNE

Harriet Vane found herself comfortable enough in the quarters of the late Paul Alexis. A polite letter from her literary agent asking "whether the new book would be available for publication in the autumn" had driven her back to the problem of the town-clock, but she found herself giving it a very divided attention. Compared with the remarkable tangle of the Alexis affair, the plot seemed to be thin and obvious, while the ape-like Robert Templeton began to display a tiresome tendency to talk like Lord Peter Wimsey. Harriet continually found herself putting her work aside—"to clear" (as though it were coffee). Novelists who have struck a snag in the working-out of the plot are rather given to handing the problem over in this way to the clarifying action of the sub-conscious. Unhappily, Harriet's sub-conscious had other coffee to clear and refused quite definitely to deal with the matter of the town-clock. Under such circumstances it is admittedly useless to ask the conscious to take any further steps. When she ought to have been writing, Harriet would sit comfortably in an armchair, reading a volume taken from Paul Alexis' bookshelf, with the idea of freeing the sub-conscious for its job. In this way, her conscious imbibed a remarkable amount of miscellaneous information about the Russian Imperial Court and a still more remarkable amount of romantic narrative about love and war in Ruritanian states. Paul Alexis had evidently had a well-defined taste in fiction. He liked stories about young men of lithe and alluring beauty who, blossoming into perfect gentlemen amid the most unpromising surrounding, turned out to be the heirs to monarchies and, in the last chapter, successfully headed the revolts of devoted loyalists, overthrew the machinations of sinister presidents, and appeared on balconies, dressed in blue-and-silver uniforms, to receive the plaudits of their rejoicing and emancipated subjects. Sometimes they were assisted by brave and beautiful English or American heiresses, who placed their wealth at the disposal of the loyalist party; sometimes they remained faithful despite temptation to brides of their own nationality, and rescued them at the last moment from marriages of inconvenience with the sinister presidents of their still more sinister advisers; now and again they were assisted by young Englishmen, Irishmen or Americans with clear-cut profiles and a superabundance of energy, and in every case they went through a series of hair-raising escapes and adventures by land, sea and air. Nobody but the sinister presidents ever thought of anything so sordid as raising money by the usual financial channels or indulging in political intrigue, nor did the greater, European powers or the League of Nations ever have anything to say in the matter. The rise and fall of governments appeared to be a private arrangement, comfortably thrashed out among a selection of small Balkan States, vaguely situated and acknowledging no relationships outside the domestic circle. No literature could have been better suited for the release of the sub-conscious; nevertheless, the sub-conscious obstinately refused to work. Harriet groaned in spirit and turned to crosswords, with the aid of *Chambers's Dictionary*—that Bible of the crossword fan—which she found wedged in between a paper-covered book printed in Russian and *A Bid for the Throne*.

Lord Peter Wimsey had also found something to read, which was occupying both his conscious and his sub-conscious very pleasantly. It was a letter, dated from Leamhurst in Huntingdonshire, and ran thus:

MY LORD,

Agreeably to your lordship's instructions I am residing here for a few days pending repairs to my magneto. I have established friendly relations with an individual called Hogben, who owns a reaper-and-binder, and is well acquainted with the principal farmers in this neighbourhood.

I understand from him that Mr. Henry Weldon's affairs are considered to be in a somewhat involved condition, and that his farm (Fourways) is heavily mortgaged. He is popularly held to have raised a number of loans locally within the last year or two on the strength of his expectations from his mother's estate, but, in view of the fact that Mrs. Weldon had not visited him of late and that relations are rumoured to be somewhat strained between them, some uneasiness is felt as to the value of this security.

The farm management is at present in the hands of a certain Walter Morrison, the head ploughman, a man of no great attainments, and, indeed, little better than an ordinary labourer, though with considerable experience in his own line. It is considered strange that Mr. Weldon should have quitted the farm at this particular time. In view of your lordship's wire of last Wednesday evening, informing me of the identification of Mr. Henry Weldon with Mr. Haviland Martin, I need not tell your lordship that Mr. Weldon left home on Sunday, 14th, returning on Sunday, 21st, only to leave again early the next morning. There have been difficulties and delays of late in the payment of labourers' wages, and, owing partly to this cause, Morrison is finding it no easy matter to get the hay in.

I heard also that there had been some trouble with the mortgages over the upkeep of the farm-buildings, dykes, hedges, etc. Accordingly, I made an expedition to Fourways, in order to inspect the property with my own eyes. I found the conditions to be as stated. Many of the walls and barns are in considerable disrepair, while the field-boundaries display frequent gaps, due to insufficient attention to proper hedging and ditching. The drainage, also (which, as your lordship knows, is of paramount importance in this part of the country) is, in many places very defective. In particular a large field (known as the 16-acre) was allowed to remain (as I am informed) in a water-logged condition all winter. Arrangements for the drainage of this piece of arable were commenced last summer, but proceeded no further than the purchase of the necessary quantity of pantiles, the cost of labour interfering with the progress of the work. In consequence, this piece of land (which adjoins the washes of the 100-foot level) is at present useless and sour.

Personally, Mr. Weldon appears to be fairly well liked in the neighbourhood, except that his manner is said to be somewhat too free with the ladies. He is reckoned as a sportsman, and is frequently seen at Newmarket. It is also rumoured that he supports a lady in a highly desirable little establishment in Cambridge. Mr. Weldon is considered to have a very good knowledge of animals, but to be somewhat ignorant or careless of the agricultural aspect of farming.

His house is kept by an elderly man and his wife, who exercise the respective functions of cowman and dairymaid. They appear respectable and, from the conversation which I had with the woman when requesting the favour of a glass of milk, honest people with nothing to hide. She informed me that Mr. Weldon lived quietly, when at home, keeping himself to himself. He receives few visitors, apart from the local farmers. During the six years that these people have been with him, his mother has visited him on three occasions (all within the first two years of this period). Also, on two occasions he has had a visitor from London, a small gentleman with a beard and said to be an invalid. This gentleman last stayed with him at the end of February this year. The woman (Mrs. Sterne) preserved a perfect discretion on the subject of her employer's financial circumstances, but I have ascertained from Hogben that she and her husband have been privately inquiring after another situation.

This is all that I have been able to discover in the short time at my disposal. (I should have mentioned that I proceeded by train to Cambridge, hiring an automobile there to sustain the character allotted to me and arriving here about Thursday noon.) If your lordship so desires, I can remain and pursue my inquiries further. Your lordship will forgive my reminding you that it is advisable to remove the links from the shirtcuffs before dispatching the garment to the laundry. It gives me great anxiety to feel that I may not be at hand to attend to the matter myself on Monday, and I should feel it deeply if there was any repetition of the disagreeable accident which occurred on the occasion of my last absence. I omitted to inform your lordship before leaving that the pin-stripe lounge suit must on no account be worn again until the slit in the right-hand pocket has been attended to. I cannot account for its presence, except by supposing that your lordship has inadvertently used the pocket for the transport of some heavy and sharp-edged article.

I trust that your lordship is enjoying favourable climatic conditions and that the investigation is progressing according to expectation. My respectful compliments to Miss Vane, and believe me, my lord,

Obediently yours,
MERVYN BUNTER

This document reached Wimsey on the Saturday afternoon, and in the evening he received a visit from Inspector Umpelty, to whom he submitted it.

The inspector nodded.

"We've received much the same information," he observed. "There's a bit more detail in your man's letter—what the deuce are pantiles?—but I think we may take it for granted that our friend Weldon is a bit up the pole financially. However, that's not what I came round about. The fact is, we've found the original of that photo."

"You have? The fair Feodora?"

"Yes," replied the Inspector, with modest triumph, and yet with a kind of mental reservation behind the triumph, "the fair Feodora—only she says she isn't."

Wimsey raised his eyebrows, or, to be more accurate, the one eyebrow which was not occupied in keeping his monocle in place.

"Then if she isn't herself, who is she?"

"She says she's Olga Kohn. I've got her letter here." The Inspector rummaged in his breast pocket. "Writes a good letter, and in a very pretty hand, I must say."

Wimsey took the blue sheet of paper and cocked a knowing eye at it.

"Very dainty. As supplied by Mr. Selfridge's fancy counter to the nobility and gentry. Ornate initial 'O' in royal blue and gilt. A pretty hand, as you say, highly self-conscious. Intensely elegant envelope to match; posted in the Piccadilly district last post on Friday night, and addressed to the Wilvercombe coroner. Well, well. Let us see what the lady has to say for herself."

> 159 Regent Square,
> Bloomsbury.

DEAR SIR,

I read the account of the inquest on Paul Alexis in tonight's paper and was very much surprised to see my photograph. I can assure you that I have nothing to do with the case and I cannot imagine how the photograph came to be on the dead body or signed with a name which is not mine. I never met anybody called Alexis that I know of and it is not my writing on the photograph. I am a mannequin by profession, so there are quite a lot of my photographs about, so I suppose somebody must have got hold of it. I am afraid I know nothing about this poor Mr. Alexis so I cannot be of much help to you, but I thought I ought to write and tell you that it was my photograph which was in the paper.

I cannot say at all how it can have got mixed up with the case, but of course I shall be glad to tell you anything I can. The photograph was taken about a year ago by Messrs. Frith of Wardour Street. I enclose another copy so that you can see it is the same. It is one I used when applying for an engagement as mannequin, and I sent it to a great many heads of big firms, also to some theatrical agents. I am at present engaged as mannequin to Messrs. Doré & Cie, of Hanover Square. I have been six months with them and they would give you references as to my character. I should be very glad to find out how the photograph got into Mr. Alexis' hands, as the gentleman to whom I am engaged is very upset about it all. Excuse me for troubling you, but I thought it right to let you know, though I am afraid I cannot be of much help.

> Yours faithfully,
> OLGA KOHN.

"And what do you make of that, my lord?"

"God knows. The young woman may be lying, of course, but somehow I don't think she is. I feel that the bit about the gentleman who is very upset rings true. Olga Kohn—who sounds like a Russian Jewess—is not precisely out of the top-drawer, as my mother would say, and was obviously not educated at Oxford or

Cambridge, but though she repeats herself a good deal, she is businesslike, and her letter is full of useful facts. Also, if the photograph resembles her, she is easy to look at. What do you say to running up to Town and interviewing the lady? I will provide the transport, and tomorrow being Sunday, we shall probably find her at leisure. Shall we depart, like two gay bachelors, to find Olga Feodora and take her out to tea?"

The Inspector seemed to think that this was a good idea.

"We will ask her if she knows Mr. Henry Weldon, that squire of dames. Have you a photograph of him, by the way?"

The Inspector had an excellent snapshot, taken at the inquest by a press photographer. A wire was sent to Miss Olga Kohn, warning her of the impending visit, and, having made the necessary arrangements at the police-station, the Inspector heaved his large bulk into Wimsey's Daimler and was transported with perilous swiftness to London. They ran up that night, snatched a few hours of repose at Wimsey's flat and, in the morning, set out for Regent Square.

Regent Square is anything but a high-class locality, being chiefly populated by grubby infants and ladies of doubtful calling, but its rents are comparatively cheap for so central a situation. On mounting to the top of a rather dark and dirty stair, Wimsey and his companion were agreeably surprised to discover a freshly-painted green door with the name "Miss O. Kohn" neatly written upon a white card and attached to the panel by drawing-pins. The brass knocker, representing the Lincoln Imp, was highly polished. At its summons the door was opened at once by a handsome young woman, the original of the photograph, who welcomed them in with a smile.

"Inspector Umpelty?"

"Yes, miss. You will be Miss Kohn, I take it? This is Lord Peter Wimsey, who has been kind enough to run me up to Town."

"Very pleased to meet you," said Miss Kohn. "Come in." She ushered them into a pleasantly furnished room, with orange window-curtains and bowls of roses placed here and there on low tables and a general air of semi-artistic refinement. Before the empty fireplace stood a dark-haired young man of Semitic appearance, who acknowledged the introductions with a scowl.

"Mr. Simons, my fiancé," explained Miss Kohn. "Do sit down, and please smoke. Can I offer you any refreshment?"

Declining the refreshment, and heartily wishing Mr. Simons out of the way, the Inspector embarked at once on the subject of the photograph, but it soon became obvious both to Wimsey and himself that Miss Kohn had told in her letter nothing more or less than the exact truth. Sincerity was stamped on every feature of her face as she assured them repeatedly that she had never known Paul Alexis and never given him a photograph under the name of Feodora or any other name. They showed her his photograph, but she shook her head.

"I am perfectly positive that I never saw him in my life."

Wimsey suggested that he might have seen her at a mannequin parade and endeavoured to introduce himself.

"Of course, he may have seen me; so many people see me," replied Miss Kohn, with artless self-importance. "Some of them try to get off with one too, naturally. A girl in my position has to know how to look after herself. But I think I should remember this face if I had ever seen it. You see, a young man with a beard like that is rather noticeable, isn't he?"

She passed the photograph to Mr. Simons, who bent his dark eyes on it disdainfully. Then his expression changed.

"You know, Olga," he said, "I think I have seen this man somewhere."

"You, Lewis?"

"Yes. I don't know where. But there is something familiar about it."

"You never saw him with me," put in the girl, quickly.

"No. I don't know, now I come to think of it, that I ever saw him at all. It's an older face, the one I'm thinking of—it may be a picture I have seen and not a living person. I don't know."

"The photograph has been published in the papers," suggested Umpelty.

"I know; but it isn't that. I noticed a resemblance to—somebody or other, the first time I saw it. I don't know what it is. Something about the eyes, perhaps—"

He paused thoughtfully and the Inspector gazed at him as though he expected him to lay a golden egg there and then, but nothing came of it.

"No, I can't place it," said Simons, finally. He handed the photograph back.

"Well, it means nothing to me," said Olga Kohn. "I do hope you all believe that."

"I believe you," said Wimsey, suddenly, "and I'm going to hazard a suggestion. This Alexis fellow was a romantic sort of blighter. Do you think he can have seen the photograph somewhere and fallen in love with it, as you might say? What I mean is, he might have indulged in an imaginary thingmabob—an ideal passion, so to speak. Kind of fancied he was beloved and all the rest of it, and put a fancy name on to support the illusion if you get what I mean—what?"

"It is possible," said Olga, "but it seems very foolish."

"Seems perfectly cock-eyed to me," pronounced Umpelty with scorn. "Besides, where did he get the picture from, that's what we want to know."

"That wouldn't really be difficult," said Olga. "He was a dancer at a big hotel. He might easily have met many theatrical managers, and one of them might have given the photograph to him. They would get it, you know, from the agents."

Inspector Umpelty asked for particulars of the agents and was supplied with the names of three men, all of whom had offices near Shaftesbury Avenue.

"But I don't suppose they'll remember much about it," said Olga. "They see so many people. Still, you could try. I should be terribly glad to have the thing cleared up. But you do believe me, don't you?"

"We believe in you, Miss Kohn," said Wimsey, solemnly, "as devoutly as in the second law of thermo-dynamics."

"What are you getting at?" said Mr. Simons, suspiciously.

"The second law of thermo-dynamics," explained Wimsey, helpfully, "which holds the universe in its path, and without which time would run backwards like a cinema film wound the wrong way."

"No, would it?" exclaimed Miss Kohn, rather pleased.

"Altars may reel," said Wimsey, "Mr. Thomas may abandon his dress-suit and Mr. Snowden renounce Free Trade, but the second law of thermo-dynamics will endure while memory holds her seat in this distracted globe, by which Hamlet meant his head but which I, with a wider intellectual range, apply to the planet which we have the rapture of inhabiting. Inspector Umpelty appears shocked, but I assure you that I know no more impressive way of affirming my entire belief in your absolute integrity." He grinned. "What I like about your evidence, Miss Kohn, is that it adds the final touch of utter and impenetrable obscurity to

321

the problem which the Inspector and I have undertaken to solve. It reduces it to the complete quintescence of incomprehensible nonsense. Therefore, by the second law of thermo-dynamics, which lays down that we are hourly and momently progressing to a state of more and more randomness, we receive positive assurance that we are moving happily and securely in the right direction. You may not believe me," added Wimsey, now merrily launched on a flight of fantasy, "but I have got to the point now at which the slightest glimmer of commonsense imported into this preposterous case would not merely disconcert me but cut me to the heart. I have seen unpleasant cases, difficult cases, complicated cases and even contradictory cases, but a case founded on stark unreason I have never met before. It is a new experience and, blasé as I am, I confess that I am thrilled to the marrow."

"Well," said Inspector Umpelty, hoisting himself to his feet, "I'm sure we're very much obliged to you, miss, for your information, though at the moment it doesn't seem to get us much farther. If anything should occur to you in connection with this Alexis, or if you, sir, should happen to call to mind where you saw Alexis before, we shall be very greatly obliged. And you mustn't take account of what his lordship here has been saying, because he's a gentleman that makes up poetry and talks a bit humorous at times."

Having thus, as he supposed, restored confidence in the mind of Miss Olga Kohn, the Inspector shepherded his companion away, but it was to Wimsey that the girl turned while Umpelty was hunting in the little hall for his hat.

"The policeman doesn't believe a word I've been saying," she whispered anxiously, "but you do, don't you?"

"I do," replied Wimsey. "But you see, I can believe a thing without understanding it. It's all a matter of training."

23

THE EVIDENCE OF THE THEATRICAL AGENT

Art honest, or a man of many deeds
And many faces to them? Thou'rt a plotter,
a politician.

—*Death's Jest-Book*

MONDAY, 29 JUNE

Wimsey and the Inspector spent Sunday in Town, and on the Monday started out for Shaftesbury Avenue. At the first two names on their list they drew blank; either the agent had given out no photographs of Olga Kohn or he could not remember anything of the circumstances. The third agent, a Mr. Isaac J. Sullivan, had a smaller and dingier office than the other two. Its antechamber was thronged with the usual crowd, patiently waiting for notice. The Inspector sent in his name by a mournful-eyed secretary, who looked as though he had spent all his life saying "No" to people and taking the blame for it. Nothing happened. Wimsey seated himself philosophically on the extreme end of a bench already occupied by eight other people and began to work out a crossword in the morning paper. The Inspector fidgeted. The secretary, emerging from the inner door, was promptly besieged by a rush of applicants. He pushed them away firmly but not harshly, and returned to his desk.

"Look here, young man," said the Inspector, "I've got to see Mr. Sullivan at once. This is a police matter."

"Mr. Sullivan's engaged," said the secretary, impassively.

"He's got to be disengaged then," said the Inspector.

"Presently," said the secretary, copying something into a large book.

"I've no time to waste," said the Inspector, and strode across to the inner door.

"Mr. Sullivan's not there," said the secretary, intercepting him with eel-like agility.

"Oh, yes, he is," replied the Inspector. "Now, don't you go obstructing me in the performance of my duty." He put the secretary aside with one hand and flung the door open, revealing a young lady in the minimum of clothing, who was displaying her charms to a couple of stout gentlemen with large cigars.

"Shut the door, blast you," said one gentleman, without looking round. "Hell of a draught, and you'll let all that lot in."

"Which of you is Mr. Sullivan?" demanded the Inspector, standing his ground, and glaring at a second door on the opposite side of the room.

"Sullivan ain't here. Shut that door, will you?"

The Inspector retired, discomfited, amid loud applause from the ante-room.

"I say, old man," said Wimsey, "what do you think the blighter means by this: 'Bright-eyed after swallowing a wingless biped?' Sounds like the tiger who conveyed the young lady of Riga."

The Inspector snorted.

There was an interval. Presently the inner door opened again and the young lady emerged, clothed and apparently very much in her right mind, for she smiled round and observed to an acquaintance seated next to Wimsey:

"O.K. darling. 'Aeroplane Girl,' first row, song and dance, start next week."

The acquaintance offered suitable congratulations, the two men with cigars came out with their hats on and the assembly surged towards the inner room.

"Now, ladies," protested the secretary, "it's not a bit of use, Mr. Sullivan's engaged."

"Look here," said the Inspector.

At this moment the door opened a fraction of an inch and an impatient voice bellowed: "Horrocks!"

"I'll tell him," said the secretary, hastily, and wormed himself neatly through the crack of the door, frustrating the efforts of a golden-haired sylph to rush the barrier.

Presently the door opened again and the bellowing voice was heard to observe:

"I don't care if he's Godalmighty. He's got to wait. Send that girl in, and—oh, Horrocks—"

The secretary turned back—fatally. The sylph was under his guard in a moment. There was an altercation on the threshold. Then, suddenly, the door opened to its full extent and disgorged, all in a heap, the sylph, the secretary, and an immensely stout man, wearing a benevolent expression entirely at variance with his hectoring voice.

"Now, Grace, my girl, don't you get trying it on. There's nothing for you today. You're wasting my time. Be a good girl. I'll let you know when anything turns up. Hullo, Phyllis, back again? That's right. Might want you next week. No, Mammy, no grey-haired mommas wanted to-day. I—hullo!"

His eye fell on Wimsey, who had got stuck over his crossword and was gazing vaguely round in search of inspiration.

"Here, Horrocks! Why the hell didn't you tell me? What do you think I pay you for? Wasting my time. Here, you, what's your name? Never been here before, have you? I'm wanting your type. Hi! Rosencrantz!"

Another gentleman, slightly less bulky but also inclined to embonpoint, appeared in the doorway.

"Told you we should have something to suit you," bellowed the first gentleman, excitedly.

"Vot for?" demanded Mr. Rosencrantz, languidly.

"What for?" Indignation quivered in the tone. "Why, for the *Worm that Turned*, to be sure! J'ever see such a perfect type? You've got the right thing here, my boy. Knock 'em flat, eh? The nose alone would carry the play for you."

"That's all very well, Sullivan," replied Mr. Rosencrantz, "but can he act?"

"Act?" exploded Mr. Sullivan. "He don't have to act. He's only got to walk on. Look at it! Ain't that the perfect Worm? Here, you, thingummy, speak up, can't you?"

"Well, really, don't you know." Wimsey screwed his monocle more firmly into his eye. "Really, old fellow, you make me feel all of a doo-dah, what?"

"There you are!" said Mr. Sullivan, triumphantly. "Voice like plum. Carries his clothes well, eh! I wouldn't sell you a feller that wasn't the goods, Rosencrantz, you know that."

"Pretty fair," admitted Mr. Rosencrantz, grudgingly. "Walk a bit, will you?"

Wimsey obliged by mincing delicately in the direction of the inner office. Mr. Sullivan purred after him. Mr. Rosencrantz followed. Horrocks, aghast, caught Mr. Sullivan by the sleeve.

"I say," he said, "look out. I think there's a mistake."

"Wotcher mean, mistake?" retorted his employer in a fierce whisper. "I dunno who he is, but he's the goods, all right, so don't you come butting in."

"Ever played lead?" demanded Mr. Rosencrantz of Wimsey.

Lord Peter paused in the inner doorway, raking the petrified audience right and left with impertinent eyes.

"I have played lead," he announced, "before all the crowned heads of Europe. Off with the mask! The Worm has Turned! I am Lord Peter Wimsey, the Piccadilly Sleuth, hot on the trail of Murder."

He drew the two stout gentlemen into the room and shut the door behind them.

"That's a good curtain," said somebody.

"Well!" gasped the Inspector. "Well, I'll be damned!"

He made for the door, and this time Horrocks offered no resistance.

"Well, well, well," said Mr. Sullivan. "Well, *well!*" He turned Wimsey's card over and stared at it. "Dear, dear, what a pity. Such a waste, eh, Rosencrantz? With your face, you ought to be makin' a fortune."

"There ain't nothing in this for me, anyhow," said Mr. Rosencrantz, "so I'd better be pushin' along. The Vorm is a good Vorm, Sullivan, as Shakespeare says, but he ain't on the market. Unless Lord Peter has a fancy for the thing. It 'ud go vell, eh? Lord Peter Vimsey in the title-rôle? The nobility ain't much cop these days, but Lord Peter is vell known. He does somethings. Nowadays, they all vant somebody as does somethings. A lord is nothing, but a lord that flies the Atlantic or keeps a hatshop or detects murders—there might be a draw in that, vot you think?"

Mr. Sullivan looked hopefully at Wimsey.

"Sorry," said his lordship. "Can't be done."

"Times are bad," said Mr. Rosencrantz, who seemed to grow more enthusiastic as the desired article was withdrawn from his grasp, "but I make you a good offer. Vot you say to two hundred a veek, eh?"

Wimsey shook his head.

"Three hundred?" suggested Mr. Rosencrantz.

"Sorry, old horse. I'm not selling."

"Five hundred, then."

"Excuse *me*," said Mr. Umpelty.

"It's no go," said Mr. Sullivan. "Very sad, but it's no go. Suppose you are rich, eh? Great pity. It won't last, you know. Super-tax and death-duties. Better take what you can while you can. No?"

"Definitely, no," said Wimsey.

Mr. Rosencrantz sighed.

"Oh, vell—I'd best be moving. See you to-morrow, Sully. You have something for me then, eh?"

He retired, not through the antechamber, but through the private door on the opposite side of the room. Mr. Sullivan turned to his visitors.

"You want me? Tell me what you want and make it snappy. I'm busy."

The Inspector produced Olga's photograph.

"The Kohn girl, eh? Yes, what about her? No trouble, eh? A good girl. Works hard. Nothing against her here."

The Inspector explained that they wanted to know whether Mr. Sullivan had distributed any photographs of Olga recently.

"Well now, let me think. She hasn't been round here for a good time. Doing mannequin work, I rather think. Better for her. A good girl and a good-looker, but she can't act, poor child. Just a minute, though. Where's Horrocks?"

He surged to the door, set it cautiously ajar and bawled "Horrocks!" through the crack. The secretary sidled in.

"Horrocks! You know this photograph of the little Kohn? Have we sent it out lately?"

"Why, yes, sir. Don't you remember? That fellow who said he wanted Russian types for the provinces."

"That's right, that's right. I knew there was somebody. Tell these gentlemen about him. We didn't know him, did we?"

"No, sir. Said he was starting management on his own. Name of—wait a minute." He pulled a book from a shelf and turned the leaves with a wetted finger. "Yes, here we are. Maurice Vavasour."

"Fine sort of name," grunted Mr. Sullivan. "Not his own, naturally. Never is. Probably called Potts or Spink. Can't run a company as Potts or Spink. Not classy enough. I've got the fellow now. Little chap with a beard. Said he was

casting for romantic drama and wanted a Russian type. We gave him the
Livinsky girl and the little Petrovna and one or two more. He seemed struck with
this photograph, I remember. I told him Petrovna had more experience, but he
said he didn't mind about that. I didn't like the fellow."

"No?"

"No. Never like 'em when they want pretty girls without experience. Old
Uncle Sullivan may be a hard nut, but he ain't standing for anything of that sort.
Told him the girl was fitted up with a job, but he said he'd have a shot at her.
She never came to me about it, though, so I suppose she turned him down. If
she had come, I'd have put her wise. I ain't that keen on my commission, and if
you ask any of the girls they'll tell you so. What's the matter, eh? Has this
Vavasour got her into a hole?"

"Not exactly," said Wimsey. "She's still in her mannequin job. But Vavasour
—show Mr. Sullivan that other photograph, Inspector. Is that the man?"

Mr. Sullivan and Horrocks put their heads together over the photograph of
Paul Alexis and shook them simultaneously.

"No," said Horrocks, "that's not the man."

"Nothing like him," said Mr. Sullivan.

"Sure?"

"Nothing like him," repeated Mr. Sullivan with emphasis. "How old's that
fellow? Well, Vavasour was forty if he was a day. Hollow-cheeked beggar with a
voice like Mother Siegel's Syrup. Make a good Judas, if you were wanting such a
thing."

"Or a Richard III," suggested Mr. Horrocks.

"If you read the part smarmy," said Mr. Sullivan. "Can't see him in Act V,
though. All right for the bit with the citizens. You know. Enter Richard above,
reading, between two monks. Matter of fact," he added, "that's a difficult part
to cast for. Inconsistent, to my mind. You mightn't think it, but I do a bit of
reading and thinking now and again, and what I say is, I don't believe W.
Shakespeare had his mind on the job when he wrote that part. Too slimy at the
beginning and too tough at the end. It ain't nature. Not but what the play
always acts well. Plenty of pep in it, that's why. Keeps moving. But he's made
Richard two men in one, that's what I complain of. One of 'em's a wormy,
plotting sort of fellow and the other's a bold, bustling sort of chap who chops
people's heads off and flies into tempers. It don't seem to fit, somehow, eh?"

Inspector Umpelty began to scrabble with his feet.

"I always think," said Wimsey, "that Shakespeare meant Richard to be one of
those men who are always deliberately acting a part—dramatising things, so to
speak. I don't believe his furies are any more real than his lovemaking. The scene
about the strawberries—that's clearly all put on."

"Maybe. But the scene with Buckingham and the clock—eh? Maybe you're
right. It ain't supposed to be my business to know about Shakespeare, eh?
Chorus-ladies' legs are my department. But I been mixed up with the stage all
my life one way and another, and it ain't all legs and bedroom scenes. That
makes you laugh, um? To hear me go on like this. But I tell you what, it makes
me sick, sometimes, bein' in this business. Half these managers don't want
actors and actresses—they want types. When my old father was runnin' a
repertory company it was actors he wanted—fellows who could be Iago one
night and Brutus the next and do a bit of farce or genteel comedy in the
intervals. But now! If a fellow starts out making his hit with a stammer and an

eyeglass he's got to play stammers and eyeglasses till he's ninety. Poor old Rosencrantz! He sure was fed-up that you weren't thinking of playing his Worm for him. As for getting an experienced actor and giving him a show in the part— nix! I've got the man that could do it—nice chap—clever as you make 'em. But he made a hit as the dear old silver-haired vicar in *Roses Round the Door*, and nobody will look at him now, except for silver-haired vicars. It'll be the end of him as an actor, but who cares? Only old Uncle Sullivan, who's got to take his bread the side it's buttered and look pleasant about it, eh?"

Inspector Umpelty rose to his feet.

"I'm sure we're much obliged to you, Mr. Sullivan," he said. "We won't detain you any longer."

"Sorry I couldn't do more for you. If ever I see that Vavasour fellow again I'll let you know. But he's probably come to grief. Sure it ain't any trouble for little Kohn?"

"We don't think so, Mr. Sullivan."

"She's a good girl," insisted Mr. Sullivan. "I'd hate to think of her going wrong. I know you're thinkin' me an old fool."

"Far from it," said Wimsey.

They were let out through the private door, and picked their way down a narrow staircase in silence.

"Vavasour, indeed!" grunted the Inspector. "I'd like to know who he is and what he's up to. Think that fat idiot was in the game?"

"I'm sure he knows nothing about it," said Wimsey. "And if he says he knows nothing about Vavasour you may be pretty sure he's not really a producer or anything genuinely theatrical. These people all know one another."

"Humph! Fat lot of help that is."

"As you say. I wonder—"

"Well?"

"I wonder what made Horrocks think of Richard III."

"Thought the man looked a bad egg, I suppose. Wasn't that the fellow who made up his mind to be a villain?"

"He was. But I don't somehow think Horrocks is quite the man to read villainy in someone's face. I should say he was quite satisfied with the regrettable practice of typecasting. I've got something at the back of my mind, Inspector, and I can't seem to get it out."

The Inspector grunted and tripped over a packing-case as they emerged into the purlieus of Wardour Street.

24

THE EVIDENCE OF THE L. C. C. TEACHER

Such lily-livered, meek humanity.
—*Death's Jest-Book*

MONDAY, 29 JUNE
TUESDAY, 30 JUNE

Paul Alexis was buried on the Monday, with many flowers and a large crowd of onlookers. Lord Peter was still in London with the Inspector, but he was suitably represented by Bunter, who had returned from Huntingdonshire that morning and, ever efficient, had brought with him a handsome wreath, suitably inscribed. Mrs. Weldon was chief mourner, supported by Henry in solemn black, and the staff of the Resplendent sent a representative contingent and a floral emblem in the shape of a saxophone. The leader of the orchestra, an uncompromising realist, had suggested that the effigy of a pair of dancing-pumps would have been more truly symbolical, but general opinion was against him, and there was, indeed, a feeling that he had been actuated by professional jealousy. Miss Leila Garland made her appearance in restrained and modified weeds, and affronted Mrs. Weldon by casting an enormous bunch of Parma violets into the grave at the most affecting moment and being theatrically overcome and carried away in hysterics. The ceremony was fully reported, with photographs, in the National Press, and the dinner-tables of the Resplendent were so crowded that evening that it became necessary to serve a supplementary dinner in the Louis Quinze Saloon.

"I suppose you will be leaving Wilvercombe now," said Harriet to Mrs. Weldon. "It will always have sad memories for you."

"Indeed, my dear, I shall not. I intend to stay here until the cloud is lifted from Paul's memory. I know positively that he was murdered by a Soviet gang and it's simply a disgrace that the police should let this kind of thing go on."

"I wish you would persuade my mother to leave," said Henry. "Bad for her health to hang on here. You'll be leaving yourself, I expect, before long."

"Probably."

There seemed, in fact, to be little for anyone to stay on for. William Bright applied to the police for leave to depart and was accorded it, subject to an undertaking that he would keep them informed of his whereabouts. He promptly retired to his lodgings at Seahampton, packed up, and started a trek northwards. "And it's to be hoped," said Superintendent Glaisher, "that they'll keep an eye on him, we can't follow him through all the counties in England. We've nothing against him."

Wimsey and the Inspector, returning to Wilvercombe on the Tuesday morning, were greeted with a piece of fresh information.

"We've pulled in Perkins," said Superintendent Glaisher.

It appeared that Mr. Julian Perkins, after leaving Darley and being driven to Wilvercombe in his hired car, had taken the train to Seahampton and resumed his walking-tour at that point. About twenty miles out he had been knocked down by a motor-lorry. As the result, he had lain speechless and senseless for nearly a week in the local hospital. There was nothing in his travelling-pack to indicate his identity, and it was only when he began to sit up and take notice that anything was known about him. As soon as he was well enough for desultory chat, he discovered that his fellow-patients were discussing the Wilvercombe inquest, and he mentioned, with a feeble sense of self-importance, that he had actually been in contact with the young lady who found the body. One of the nurses then called to mind that there had been a broadcast inquiry for somebody called Perkins in connection with that very case. The Wilvercombe police were communicated with, and P.C. Ormond had been sent over to interview Mr. Perkins.

It was now clear enough, of course, why no reply to the S.O.S. message had been received from either Mr. Perkins himself or from his associates at the time of broadcasting. It was now also made clear why nobody had made any inquiry about Mr. Perkins's disappearance. Mr. Perkins was a teacher in an L.C.C. School, and had been granted leave of absence for the term on account of his health. He was unmarried, and an orphan with no near relations, and he lived in a hostel in the neighbourhood of Tottenham Court Road. He had left the hostel in May, announcing that he was going on a tramping holiday and would have no settled address. He would write from time to time, telling the staff of the hostel where to forward letters. As it happened, no letters had arrived for him since the last time he had written (on the 29th May, from Taunton). Consequently, nobody had thought to make any inquiry about him, and the S.O.S. which mentioned only his surname had left it doubtful whether the Mr. Perkins wanted by the police was the Mr. Julian Perkins of the hostel. In any case, since nobody knew where he was supposed to be, there was no information that anybody could have supplied. The police got into touch with the hostel and had Mr. Perkins's mail sent down. It consisted of an advertisement from a cheap tailor, an invitation to secure a last-minute chance in the Irish Sweep, and a letter from a pupil, all about Boy Scout activities.

Mr. Julian Perkins seemed to be an unlikely sort of criminal, but one never knew. He was interviewed, propped up in bed in his little red hospital jacket, with his anxious and unshaven face surrounded with bandages, from which his large horn-rimmed glasses looked out with serio-comic effect.

"So you abandoned your trip and walked back to Darley with this young lady," said Constable Ormond. "Now, why did you do that, sir?"

"I wanted to do my best to help the young lady."

"Quite so, sir, very natural. But as a matter of fact, of course, you couldn't help her much."

"No." Mr. Perkins fumbled with the sheet. "She said something about going along to look for the body, but of course—I didn't see that I was called upon to do that. I'm not a strong man; besides, the tide was coming in. I thought—"

P.C. Ormond waited patiently.

Mr. Perkins suddenly relieved his mind with an outburst of confession.

"I didn't like to go along that road, and that's the truth. I was afraid the murderer might be lurking about somewhere."

"Murderer, eh? What made you think it was a case of murder?"

Mr. Perkins shrank among his pillows.

"The young lady said it might be. I'm not a very courageous person, I'm afraid. You see, since my illness, I've been nervous—nervous, you know. And I'm not physically strong. I didn't like the idea at all."

"I'm sure you can't be blamed for that, sir." The policeman's bluff heartiness seemed to alarm Mr. Perkins, as though he detected something false in the ring of it.

"So when you came to Darley you felt that the young lady was in good hands and needed no further protection. So you went away without saying good-bye."

"Yes. Yes. I—I didn't want to be mixed up in anything, you know. In my position it isn't nice. A teacher has to be careful. And besides—"

"Yes, sir?"

Mr. Perkins had another confessional outburst.

"I'd been thinking it over. I thought it was all rather queer. I wondered if the young lady—one hears of such things—suicide pacts and so on— You see? I felt that I didn't want to be associated with that kind of thing. I am rather timid by nature, I admit, and really *not* strong since my illness, and what with one thing and another—"

P.C. Ormond, who had a touch of imagination and a strong, though elementary, sense of humour, smothered a grin behind his hand. He suddenly saw Mr. Perkins, terrified, hobbling on his blistered feet between the devil and the deep sea; fleeing desperately from the vision of a homicidal maniac at the Flat-Iron only to be pursued by the nightmare that he was travelling in company with a ruthless and probably immoral murderess.

He licked his pencil and started again.

"Quite so, sir. I see your point. Very disagreeable situation. Well, now—just as a matter of routine, you know, sir, we've got to check up on the movements of everybody who passed along the coast-road that day. Nothing to be alarmed at." The pencil happened to be an indelible one and left an unpleasant taste in the mouth. He passed a pink tongue along his purple-stained lips, looking, to Mr. Perkins's goblin-haunted imagination, like a very large dog savouring a juicy bone. "Whereabouts might you have been round about two o'clock, sir?"

Mr. Perkins's mouth dropped open.

"I—I—I—" he began, quavering.

A nurse, hovering near, intervened.

"I hope you won't have to be long, constable," she said, acidly. "I can't have my patient upset. Take a sip of this, No. 22, and you must try not to get excited."

"It's all right." Mr. Perkins sipped and regained his colour. "As a matter of fact I can tell you exactly where I was at two o'clock. It's very fortunate that should be the time. Very fortunate. I was at Darley."

"Oh, indeed," said Mr. Ormond, "that's very satisfactory."

"Yes, and I can prove it. You see, I'd come along from Wilvercombe. I bought some calamine lotion there, and I daresay the chemist would remember me. My skin is very sensitive, you know, and we had a little chat about it. I don't know just where the shop was, but you could find out. No; I don't know quite what time that would be. Then I walked on to Darley. It's four miles. It would take me a bit over an hour, you know, so I must have started from Wilvercombe about one o'clock."

"Where did you stay the night before?"

"In Wilvercombe. At the Trust House. You'll find my name there all right."

"Rather a late start, wasn't it, sir?"

"Yes, it was; but I didn't sleep very well. I was rather feverish. Sunburn, you know; it takes me that way. It does some people. I come out in a rash—most painful. I told you my skin was sensitive. It was the hot sun that last week. I hoped it would get better, but it got worse, and shaving was an agony, really an agony. So I stayed in bed till ten and had a late breakfast at eleven, and got to Darley about two o'clock. I know it was two o'clock, because I asked a man there the time."

"Did you indeed, sir? That was very fortunate. We ought to be able to substantiate that."

"Oh, yes. You'd find him easily enough. It wasn't in the village itself. It was outside. It was a gentleman that was camping in a tent. At least, I call him a gentleman, but I can't say he behaved like one."

P.C. Ormond almost jumped. He was a young man, unmarried and full of enthusiasms, and he had fallen into a state of worshipping admiration for Lord Peter Wimsey. He worshipped his clothes, his car and his uncanny skill in prediction. Wimsey had said that the gold would be found on the body; and lo! it was so. He had said that, as soon as the inquest had established the time of death, Henry Weldon would turn out to have an alibi for two o'clock, and here was the alibi arriving as true to time as moon and tide. He had said that this new alibi would turn out to be breakable. P.C. Ormond set out with determination to break it.

He asked, rather suspiciously, why Mr. Perkins had inquired the time of a casual stranger and not in the village.

"I didn't think about it in the village. I didn't stop anywhere there. When I got out of it I began to think about my lunch. I'd looked at my watch a mile or so back and it said five-and-twenty to two, and I thought I'd push along to the shore and have my meal there. When I looked at it again it still said five-and-twenty to two, and I found it had stopped, so I knew time must be getting on. I saw a kind of little lane going down towards the sea, so I turned down that way. There was an open space at the foot of it with a motor-car and a little tent, and a man doing something to the car. I hailed him and asked what the time was. He was a big man with dark hair and a red face, and he wore coloured spectacles. He told me it was five minutes to two. I set my watch going and thanked him and then I just said something pleasant about what a nice camping-place he had found. He grunted rather rudely, so I thought perhaps he was put out by his car being out of order, so I just asked him—most politely—whether there was anything wrong. That was all. I can't think why he should have taken offence but he did. I expostulated with him and said I only asked out of politeness and to know if I could help him in any way, and he called me a very vulgar name and—" Mr. Perkins hesitated and blushed.

"Well?" said P.C. Ormond.

"He—I am sorry to say he forgot himself so far as to assault me," said Mr. Perkins.

"Oh! what did he do?"

"He—kicked me," said Mr. Perkins, his voice rising up into a squeak, "on my —that is to say, from behind."

"Indeed!"

"Yes, he did. Of course, I did not retaliate. It would not have been—fitting. I just walked away and told him that I hoped he would feel ashamed of himself when he thought it over. I regret to say that he ran at me after that, and I thought it would be better not to associate with such a person any longer. So I went away and had my lunch on the beach."

"On the beach, eh?"

"Yes. He had—that is to say, I was facing in that direction when the assault took place—and I did not wish to pass this unpleasant person again. I knew by my map that it was possible to walk along the shore between Darley and Lesston Hoe, so I thought it better to go that way."

"I see. So you had your lunch on the shore. Whereabouts? And how long did you stay there?"

"Well, I stopped about fifty yards from the lane. I wished to let the man see that he could not intimidate me. I sat down where he could see me and ate my lunch."

P.C. Ormond noted that the kick could not have been a painfully hard one. Mr. Perkins could sit down.

"I think I stayed there for three-quarters of an hour or so."

"And who passed you on the beach during that time?" demanded the constable sharply.

"Who passed me? Why, nobody."

"No man, woman or child? No boat? No horse? Nothing?"

"Nothing whatever. The beach was quite deserted. Even the unpleasant man took himself off in the end, just before I left myself, that would be. I kept an eye on him, just to see that he didn't try any more tricks, you know."

P.C. Ormond bit his lip.

"And what was he doing all that time? Tinkering with his car?"

"No. He seemed to finish that quite quickly. He seemed to be doing something over the fire. I thought he was cooking. Then he went away up the lane."

The constable thought for a moment.

"What did you do then?"

"I walked rather slowly on along the beach till I came to a lane that runs down between stone walls on to the beach. It comes out opposite some cottages. I got on to the road that way, and walked along in the direction of Lesston Hoe till I met the young lady."

"Did you see the man with the dark spectacles again that afternoon?"

"Yes; when I came back with the lady, he was just coming up out of the lane. To my annoyance, she, quite unnecessarily, stopped and spoke to him. I went on, as I did not wish to be subjected to any further incivility."

"I see, sir. That's a very clear account. Now I want to ask you a very important question. When you next had an opportunity of regulating your watch, did you find it fast or slow, and how much?"

"I compared it with the clock in the garage at Darley. It was exactly right at 5:30."

"And you had not altered it in the interval?"

"No—why should I?"

P.C. Ormond looked hard at Mr. Perkins, shut up his note-book with a snap, thrust out his lower jaw and said, quietly but forcefully:

"Now, look here, sir. This is a case of murder. We *know* that somebody passed along that beach between two o'clock and three. Wouldn't it be better to tell the truth?"

Fear flashed up into Mr. Perkins's eyes.

"I don't—I don't—" he began, feebly. His hands clawed at the sheet for a moment. Then he fainted, and the nurse, bustling up, banished P.C. Ormond from the bedside.

25

THE EVIDENCE OF THE DICTIONARY

'Tis but an empty cipher.
—*The Brides' Tragedy*

TUESDAY, 30 JUNE

It was all very well, thought Constable Ormond, to be sure that Perkins's evidence was false: the difficulty was to prove it. There were two possible explanations. Either Perkins was a liar, or Weldon had deliberately deceived him. If the former were the case, then the police would be faced with the notorious difficulty of proving a negative. If the latter, then a reference to Mr. Polwhistle at the Darley Garage would probably clear the matter up.

Mr. Polwhistle and his mechanic were ready and eager to help. They perfectly remembered Mr. Perkins which was not surprising, since the arrival of a complete stranger to hire a car was a rare event in Darley. Mr. Perkins had pulled out his watch, they remembered, and compared it with the garage clock, mentioning as he did so that the watch had run down and that he had had to inquire the time of a passer-by. He had then said: "Oh, yes, it seems to be just right," and had further asked whether their clock was reliable and how long they would take to get to Wilvercombe.

"And *is* your clock reliable?"

"It was reliable that day all right."

"How do you mean, that day?"

"Well, she loses a bit, and that's a fact, but we'd just set her on the Thursday morning, hadn't we, Tom?"

Tom agreed that they had, adding that "she" was an eight-day clock, and that he was accustomed to wind and set her every Thursday morning, Thursday being an important day on account of Heathbury market, the centre about which all local business seemed to revolve.

There seemed to be no shaking this evidence. It was true that neither Mr. Polwhistle nor Tom had actually seen the face of Mr. Perkins's watch, but they both declared that he had said: "It seems to be just right." Therefore, if there was any discrepancy, Perkins must have been intentionally concealing the face. It was, perhaps, a little remarkable that Perkins should so insistently have drawn attention to the rightness of his watch. Constable Ormond remounted his motor-cycle and returned to Wilvercombe more than ever convinced that Perkins was an unconscionable liar.

Inspector Umpelty agreed with him. " 'Tisn't natural," he said, "to my mind, for a man all upset as he was to start bothering about the exact time the minute he gets into a place. Trouble is, if he says he saw Weldon, and we can't prove he didn't, what are we going to do about it?"

"Well, sir," suggested Ormond, with deference, "what I've been thinking is, if Weldon or whoever it was rode along the shore between Darley and the Flat-Iron, somebody ought to have seen him. Have we asked all the people who passed along the top of the cliffs round about that time?"

"You needn't think that hadn't occurred to me, my lad," replied the Inspector, grimly. "I've interrogated everyone that went past between one o'clock and two o'clock, and not a soul of 'em saw hide nor hair of a horse."

"How about those people at the cottages?"

"Them?" The Inspector snorted. "They never saw anything, you bet your life —nor they wouldn't, not if old Pollock was concerned in it, as it's our belief he was—always supposing there was anything to be concerned in. Still, go and try your hand on them again if you like, young 'un, and if you get anything out of 'em I'll hand it to you. Old Pollock's got his back up, and neither him nor that brother-in-law of his, Billy Moggeridge, is out to give anything away to the police. Still, you trot along there. You're a comely young bachelor, and there's no saying but you may be able to get something out of the women-folk."

The blushing Ormond accordingly made his way to the cottages, where, much to his relief, he found the men-folk absent and the women employed at the wash-tub. At first he was none too cordially received, but, after he had stripped off his uniform tunic and given young Mrs. Pollock a hand with the mangle and carried two buckets of water from the well for Mrs. Moggeridge, the atmosphere became less frigid, and he was able to put his questions.

But the results were disappointing. The women were able to give very good reasons for having seen nothing of any horse or rider on Thursday, 18th. The family dinners had been eaten as usual at twelve o'clock, and after dinner there was the ironing to finish. There was a sight of washing, as Mr. Ormond could see for himself, for Mrs. Pollock and Mrs. Moggeridge to deal with. There was Granpa Pollock and Granma Pollock and Jem, what was that particular about his shirts and collars, and young Arthur and Polly and Rosie and Billy Moggeridge and Susie and Fanny and little David and the baby and Jenny Moggeridge's Baby Charles what was a accident what Mrs. Moggeridge was looking after, Jenny being out in service, all of which do make work and often the washing don't get finished till Saturday and you couldn't be surprised, what with the men's jerseys and stockings and one thing and another and every drop of water having to be fetched. Nobody hadn't been out of the house that afternoon, leastways, only at the back, not till after three o'clock for sure, when Susie took the potatoes out into the front garden to peel for supper. Susie see a gentleman then, dressed in shorts and carrying a knapsack, come up the lane from the shore, but it wouldn't be him as Mr. Ormond wanted to know about, because he came in later on with a lady and told them about the body being found. Mr. Ormond was quite pleased to hear about this gentleman, nevertheless. The gentleman was wearing horn-rimmed spectacles and he came up the lane "somewhere between half-past three and four," and went straight off along the road towards Lesston Hoe. This must, of course, have been Perkins, and brief calculation showed that this time fitted in reasonably well both with his own story and Harriet's. Harriet had met him about half-a-mile further on at four o'clock. But that proved nothing, and the crucial period between 1.30 and three o'clock remained as obscure as before.

Puzzled and dissatisfied, Ormond chugged slowly back to Darley, noticing as he went how little of the beach could actually be seen from the road. It was, in fact, only for about a mile on either side of the Flat-Iron that the road ran actually close to the edge of the cliffs. Here there was the breadth of a wide field between them and the height of the cliff hid the sands from view. It would not really have been so risky a business as one might suppose to ride in broad daylight to commit a murder at the Flat-Iron, and it was hardly surprising that no traveller on the road had seen the bay mare pass. But had she passed? There was the horse-shoe to prove it and there was the ring-bolt on the rack to suggest it. It was the ring-bolt that was chiefly bothering Constable Ormond, for if it was not there to hold the horse, what was it for? And Wimsey's latest theory had made it necessary for the horse to be released and sent back before the Flat-Iron was reached.

And that was a very hit-or-miss theory, from the murderer's point of view. How could he be sure that the animal would go back and would not hang about the place attracting attention? In fact, after being galloped violently for four and a half miles, it was far more likely to take matters easy. If one was to ignore the ring-bolt, was it not possible that the bay mare had been tethered somewhere, to be picked up later? There were weighty objections to that. There was no post or groyne along the shore to which she could have been tied, and if the murderer had brought her close in under the cliff, then he would have had to leave two lines of footprints—the mare's in going and his own in returning. But he might have argued that this would not greatly matter if it was at some distance from the Flat-Iron. It might just be worth while to turn back and examine the shore from that point of view.

He did so, riding right up as far as the Flat-Iron itself, scrambling down by the same path that Harriet had used, and working his way along at the foot of the cliff in the direction of Darley. After about half-an-hour's search, he found what he was looking for. There was a recess in the cliff where at some time there had been a fall of rock. Jammed in among the boulders was a large wooden post, which had apparently formed part of a fence—erected, no doubt, to keep men or animals from straying upon the dangerous part of the cliffs. If the bay mare had been brought in there, she might easily have been tethered to the beam, while, owing to the overhang of the cliff and the accumulation of fallen stones, she would have been practically invisible, either from the sea or from the road above.

This discovery was gratifying, but it would have been more gratifying if Ormond could have found any positive indication that this had really happened. The sand was so loose and dry that no recognisable marks could be expected above high-water mark, nor, though he examined the wooden post very carefully with a lens, could he find any indications of its having been used as a horse-post. A strand of rope fibre, a horse-hair or two would have been better than a bank-note to Ormond at that moment, while a bunch of horse-droppings would have been worth its weight in rubies. But none of these simple, homely sights re-warded his anxious gaze. There was the piece of timber and there was the recess in the cliff, and that was all.

Shaking his head, he walked to the edge of the water and set out at a brisk trot for the Flat-Iron. He found that by pelting along as fast as a heavyish, fully-clothed young constable could be expected to pelt on a hot summer's day, he could reach the rock in twelve minutes exactly. It was too far. Five minutes' walk was the most that Weldon could possibly have allowed himself by Wimsey's calculation. Ormond again scrambled up the cliff, remounted his bicycle and began to do sums in his head.

By the time he arrived at the police-station, these sums had taken a definite form.

"The way I look at it is this, sir," he said to Superintendent Glaisher. "We've been going along the line that it was Perkins that was providing the alibi for Weldon. Suppose it was the other way round. Suppose Weldon is providing the alibi for Perkins. What do we know about Perkins? Only that he's a school-teacher and that nobody seems to have kept tabs on him since last May. No, he says he slept at Wilvercombe and didn't start away that morning till one o'clock. That's a bit thick to start with. The only proof he offers of that is that he bought some stuff at a chemist's—he doesn't remember the chemist and he isn't clear about the time. Now we know that Weldon was in Wilvercombe that morning, and *his* time isn't altogether accounted for, either. Supposing those two had met and fixed it all up there. Perkins comes along to Darley and gets the horse."

"We'll have to find out whether anyone saw him pass through the village."

"That's so, sir. We must check that up, naturally. But say he really got there at about 1.15 or so. Then he'd have plenty of time to get along with the mare, tie her up where that there post is, and buzz along on foot to the rock and commit his murder."

"Wait a moment," said Glaisher. "This place is fifteen minutes' quick walk from the rock."

"More like fifteen minutes' run, sir."

"Yes, but over wet sand; through water, actually. Shall we call it just over a mile? Right. Then that leaves three and a half miles for the mare. At eight miles an hour, that needs—eight miles in sixty minutes, one mile in sixty over eight"—Glaisher always had to work these rule-of-three problems out on the corners of blotting-pads; it had been the worst stumbling block he had had to overcome on his way to promotion—"thirty multiplied by seven over eight—oh, dear! divide by two—multiply—divide—"

Ormond, who had the gift of being able to add three columns of figures at once in his head, waited respectfully.

"I make it about twenty-six minutes," said Glaisher.

"Yes, sir."

"That means"—Glaisher gazed at the face of the station-clock with working lips. "Fifteen minutes from two o'clock, 1.45; twenty-six minutes from that again—that's 1.19."

"Yes, sir; and we can allow him four minutes to tie the mare up; 1.15 I make it he'd have to start out from Darley."

"Just so; I was only verifying your figures. In that case he'd have had to be in the village at 1.10 or thereabouts."

"That's right, sir."

"And how and when did he pick the mare up again, Ormond?"

"He didn't, sir, not as I make it out."

"Then what became of it?"

"Well, sir, I look at it like this. Where we've been making the mistake is in thinking as the whole job was done by one person. Supposing now as this Perkins commits his murder at two o'clock and then hides under the Flat-Iron, same as we thought. He can't get away till 2.30; we know that, because Miss Vane was there till that time. Well, then, at 2.30 she clears and *he* clears, and starts to walk back."

"Why should he walk back? Why not go on? Oh, of course—he's got to fix up his times to fit in with Weldon's 1.55 alibi."

"Yes, sir. Well, if he was to walk straight back to Pollock's cottage, which is two miles from the Flat-Iron, doing a steady three mile an hour, he'd be there at 3.10, but Susie Moggeridge says she didn't see him till between 3.30 and four o'clock, and I don't see that she's got any call to lie about it."

"She may be in it too; we've got our doubts about old Pollock."

"Yes, sir; but if she was lying she'd lie the other way. She wouldn't give him more time than he needed to come from the Flat-Iron. No, sir, it's my belief Perkins had to stop on the way for something, and I fancy I know what that was. It's all right for the doctor to say that the man who cut this chap's throat *may* not have got blood on himself, but that's not to say he *didn't* get it—not by a long chalk. I think Perkins had to stop all that time to get his togs changed. He could easily take an extra shirt and pair of shorts in his kit. He may have given the ones he was wearing a bit of a wash, too. Say he did that, and then got to Pollock's place about 3.45. He comes up by the lane, where Susie Moggeridge sees him and he goes along another half-mile or so, and he meets Miss Vane four o'clock—as he did."

"H'm!" Glaisher revolved this idea in his mind. It had its attractive points, but it left a great deal open to question.

"But the mare, Ormond?"

"Well, sir, there's only one person could have brought back the mare that we know of, and that's Weldon, and only one time he could have done it, and that's between four o'clock, when Polwhistle and Tom said good-bye to him, and 5.20, when Miss Vane saw him in Darley. Let's see how that works out, sir. It's three and a half miles from Hinks's Lane to the place where the mare was left; and he could start at four, walk there in an hour or a bit less, ride back quick, and just be back at 5.20 in time to be seen by them two. It all fits in, sir, doesn't it?"

"It fits, as you say, Ormond, but it's what I'd call a tight fit. Why do you suppose Perkins came back with Miss Vane instead of going on to Lesston Hoe?"

"It might be to find out what she was going to do, sir, or it might be just to look innocent-like. He'd be surprised to see her there, I expect—not knowing about her going up to Brennerton—and it's not wonderful he should have seemed a bit put about when she spoke to him. He might think going back with her was the boldest and best thing to do. Or he may have felt anxious and wanted to see for himself whether Weldon had got back with the nag all right. He was very careful not to speak to Weldon when they did meet—went out of his way to have nothing to do with him, as you might say. And as for his clearing off the way he did, that's natural if you come to think of it, supposing he had those pants and things all soiled with blood in his knapsack."

"You've got an answer for everything, Ormond. Here's another for you. Why in the name of goodness, if all this is true, didn't Perkins ride the ruddy horse right up to the rock, while he was about it? He could have taken her back and tethered her up just the same."

"Yes, sir, and I fancy, judging from the ring-bolt, that must have been the first idea. But I was looking at those cliffs today and I noticed that it's just about a mile from the Flat-Iron that the road comes so close to the edge of the cliff as to give you a proper view down on to the beach. When they came to think it over they may have said to themselves that a man riding along that open bit of beach would be conspicuous-like. So Perkins cached the gee where the cover ended and paddled the rest of the way, thinking it would be less noticeable."

"Yes; there's something in that. But all this depends on the time that Perkins passed through Darley. We'll have to get that looked into. Mind, Ormond, I'm not saying you haven't done a good bit of thinking over this, and I like to see you having initiative and striking out a line for yourself; but we can't go behind facts when all's said and done."

"No, sir; certainly not, sir. But of course, sir, even if it wasn't Perkins, that's not to say it wasn't somebody else."

"Who wasn't somebody else?"

"The accomplice, sir."

"That's beginning all over again, Ormond."

"Yes, sir."

"Well, cut along and see what you can make of it."

"Yes, sir."

Glaisher rubbed his chin thoughtfully when Ormond was gone. This business was worrying him. The Chief Constable had been chivvying him that morning and making things unpleasant. The Chief Constable, a military gentleman of the old school, thought that Glaisher was making too much fuss. To him it was obvious that the rather contemptible foreign dancing-fellow had cut his own throat, and he thought that sleeping dogs should be left alone. Glaisher only wished he could leave the thing alone, but he felt a sincere conviction that there was more to it than that. He was not comfortable in his mind—never had been. There were too many odd circumstances. The razor, the gloves, Weldon's incomprehensible movements, the taciturnity of Mr. Pollock, the horseshoe, the ring-bolt, Bright's mistake about the tides and, above all, the cipher letters and the photograph of the mysterious Feodora—each one of these might, separately, have some ordinary and trivial explanation, but not all of them—surely, not all of them. He had put these points to the Chief Constable, and had received a grudging kind of permission to go on with his inquiries. But he was not happy.

He wondered what Umpelty was doing. He had heard the story of his excursion to town with Wimsey, and felt that this had only plunged matters into a still deeper obscurity. Then there was the tiresomeness about Bright. Bright was reported to be working his way towards London. It was going to be a job keeping an eye on him—especially as Glaisher was rather hard put to it to find a good reason for the surveillance. After all, what had Bright done? He was an unsatisfactory character and he had said it was high tide when it was, in fact, low tide—in every other respect he appeared to have been telling the exact truth. Glaisher realised that he was making himself unpopular with the police of half-a-dozen countries, on very insufficient grounds.

He dismissed the case from his mind and applied himself to a quantity of routine business connected with petty theft and motoring offences, and so got through the evening. But after his supper he found the problem of Paul Alexis gnawing at his brain again. Umpelty had reported the result of a few routine inquiries about Perkins, of which the only interesting fact was that Perkins was a member of the Soviet Club and was reported to have Communist sympathies. Just the sort of sympathies he would have, thought Glaisher: it was always these meek, mild, timid-looking people who yearned for revolution and bloodshed. But, taken in connection with the cipher letters, the matter assumed a certain importance. He wondered how soon the photographs of the letters found on Alexis would come to hand. He fretted, was short with his wife, trod on the cat, and decided to go round to the Bellevue and look up Lord Peter Wimsey.

Wimsey was out, and a little further inquiry led Glaisher to Mrs. Lefranc's, where he found, not only Wimsey, but also Inspector Umpelty, seated with Harriet in the bed-sitting-room that had once housed Paul Alexis, all three apparently engaged in a Missing Word Competition. Books were strewn about the place, and Harriet, with *Chambers's Dictionary* in her hand, was reading out words to her companions.

"Hullo, Super!" exclaimed Wimsey. "Come along! I'm sure our hostess will be delighted to see you. We are making discoveries."

"Are you, indeed, my lord? Well, so have we—at least, that lad, Ormond, has been rummaging about, as you might say."

He plunged into his story. He was glad to try it on somebody else. Umpelty grunted. Wimsey took a map and a sheet of paper and began figuring out distances and times. They discussed it. They argued about the speed of the mare. Wimsey was inclined to think that he might have underestimated it. He would borrow the animal—make a test—

Harriet said nothing.

"And what do *you* think?" Wimsey asked her, suddenly.

"I don't believe a word of it," said Harriet.

Glaisher laughed.

"Miss Vane's intuition, as they call it, is against it," said he.

"It's not intuition," retorted Harriet. "There's no such thing. It's common sense. It's artistic sense, if you like. All those theories—they're all wrong. They're artificial—they smell of the lamp."

Glaisher laughed again.

"That's beyond me, that is."

"You men," said Harriet, "have let yourselves be carried away by all these figures and time-tables and you've lost sight of what you're really dealing with. But it's all machine-made. It creaks at every joint. It's like—like a bad plot, built up round an idea that won't work. You've got it into your heads that you must get Weldon and the horse and Perkins into it somehow or other, and when you come up against an inconsistency, you say: 'Oh, well—we'll get over that somehow. We'll make him do this. We'll make him do that.' But you can't make people do things to suit you—not in real life. Why are you obliged to bring all these people into it at all?"

"You won't deny that there's a good deal that needs explaining," said Umpelty.

"Of course there's a lot that needs explaining, but your explanations are more incredible than the problem. It's not possible that anyone should plan a murder like that. You've made them too ingenious in one way and too silly in another. Whatever the explanation is, it must be simpler than that—bigger—not so ramped. Can't you see what I mean? You're simply making up a case, that's all."

"I see what you mean," said Wimsey.

"I daresay it is a bit complicated," admitted Glaisher, "but if we don't make up a case against Weldon and Bright and Perkins, or two of them, or one of them —whom are we to make up a case against? Against Bolshies? Well, but this Perkins is a Bolshie, or a Communist, anyhow, and if he's in it, then Weldon must be, because of their mutual alibi."

"Yes, I know; but your whole case is like that. First you want Weldon to be guilty, because of getting his mother's money, so you say that Perkins must be his accomplice because he's giving an alibi for Weldon. Now you want Perkins to be guilty because he's a Communist, and so you say Weldon must be the accomplice, because he's giving an alibi for Perkins. But it's simply impossible that both those theories should be true. And how did Weldon and Perkins get to know one another?"

"We haven't finished making inquiries yet."

"No; but it does seem unlikely, doesn't it? A Council School teacher from the Tottenham Court Road and a Huntingdonshire farmer. What form? What likelihood? And as for Bright, you have nothing—*nothing* to connect him with either of them. And if his story's true, then there's not an atom of proof that Alexis didn't kill himself. And in any case, if you want to prove murder, you've got to connect Bright with whoever did it, and you certainly haven't found the least trace of communication between him and either Weldon or Perkins."

"Has Bright been receiving any letters?" asked Wimsey of Umpelty.

"Not a line, not since he turned up here, anyway."

"As for Perkins," said Glaisher, "we'll soon get a line on him. Of course, his getting knocked down and laid up like that must have puzzled his accomplices just as much as it puzzled us. There may be a whole correspondence waiting for him at some accommodation address, under another name, in some town or other."

"You will insist on its being Perkins," protested Harriet. "You really think Perkins rode a horse bare-backed along the beach and cut a man's throat to the bone with a razor?"

"Why not?" said Umpelty.

"Does he look like it?"

" 'Do I look like it?' said the Knave. Which he certainly did not, being made entirely of cardboard.' I've never seen the bloke, but I admit that his description isn't encouraging." Wimsey grinned. "But then, you know, friend Henry took *me* for something in the night-club line."

Harriet glanced briefly at his lean limbs and springy build.

"You needn't fish," she said, coldly. "We all know that your appearance of languor is assumed and that you are really capable of tying pokers into knots with your artistic fingers. Perkins is flabby and has a neck like a chicken and those flip-flop hands." She turned to Glaisher. "I can't see Perkins in the rôle of a desperado. Why, your original case against me was a better one."

Glaisher blinked, but took the thrust stolidly.

"Yes, miss. It had a lot to be said for it, that had."

"Of course. Why did you give it up, by the way?"

Some instinct seemed to warn Glaisher that he was treading on thin ice.

"Well," he said, "it seemed a bit too obvious, so to say—and besides, we couldn't trace any connection between you and the deceased."

"It was wise of you to make inquiries. Because, of course, you had only my word for everything, hadn't you? And those photographs were evidence that I was pretty cold-blooded? And my previous history was rather—shall we say, full of incident?"

"Just so, miss." The Superintendent's eyes were expressionless.

"Of whom did you make the inquiries, by the way?"

"Of your charwoman," said Glaisher.

"Oh! you think she would know whether I knew Paul Alexis?"

"In our experience," replied the Superintendent, "charwomen mostly know things of that sort."

"So they do. And you've really given up suspecting me?"

"Oh, dear me, yes."

"On your charwoman's testimony to my character?"

"Supplemented," said the Superintendent, "by our own observation."

"I see." Harriet looked hard at Glaisher, but he was proof against this kind of third degree, and smiled blandly in response. Wimsey, who had listened with his face like a mask, determined to give the stolid policeman the first prize for tact. He now dropped a cold comment into the conversation.

"You and Miss Vane having made short work of each other's theories," he said, "perhaps you would like to hear what we have been doing this evening."

"Very much, my lord."

"We began," said Wimsey, "by making a new search for clues among the corpse's belongings, hoping, of course, to get some light on Feodora or the cipher letters. Inspector Umpelty kindly lent us his sympathetic assistance. In fact, the Inspector has been simply invaluable. He has sat here now for two hours, watching us search, and every time we looked into a hole or corner and found it empty, he has been able to assure us that he had already looked into the hole or corner and found it empty too."

Inspector Umpelty chuckled.

"The only thing we've found," went on Lord Peter, "is *Chambers's Dictionary*, and we didn't find that this evening, because Miss Vane had found it before, while she was engaged in wasting her time on crosswords instead of getting on with her writing. We've found a lot of words marked with pencil. We were engaged in making a collection of them when you came in. Perhaps you'd like to hear a few specimens. Here you are. I'm reeling them off at random: Peculiar, diplomacy, courtesan, furnished, viscount, squander, sunlight, chasuble, clergyman, luminary, thousand, poverty, cherubim, treason, cabriolet, rheumatics, apostle, costumier, viaduct. There are lots more. Do these words say anything to you? Some of them have an ecclesiastical ring about them, but on the other hand, some of them have not. Courtesan, for example. To which I may add tambourine, wrestling and fashion."

Glaisher laughed.

"Sounds to me as though the young fellow was a crossword fan himself. They're nice long words."

"But not the longest. There are many longer, such as supralapsarian, monocotyledenous and diaphragmatic, but he hasn't marked any of the real sesquipedalians. The longest we have found is rheumatics, with ten letters. They all have two peculiarities in common, though, as far as we've gone—that are rather suggestive."

"What's that, my lord?"

"None of them contains any repeated letter, and none of them is less than seven letters long."

Superintendent Glaisher suddenly flung up one hand like a child at school. "The cipher letters!" he cried.

"As you say, the cipher letters. It looks to us as though these might be key-words to a cipher, and from the circumstance that no letters are repeated in any of them, I fancy one might be able to make a guess at the type of cipher. The trouble is that we have already counted a couple of hundred marked words, and haven't finished the alphabet yet. Which leads me to a depressing inference."

"What's that?"

"That they have been changing the key-word in every letter. What I think has happened is this. I think that each letter contained in it the key-word for the next, and that these marks represent a stock of words that Alexis looked up beforehand, so as to be ready with them when it came to his turn to write."

"Couldn't they be the key-words already used?"

"Hardly. I don't believe he has sent out over two hundred code-letters since March, when they first began to be exchanged. Even if he wrote one letter a day, he couldn't have got through that number."

"No more he could, my lord. Still, if the paper we found on him is one of these cipher letters, then the key-word will be one of those marked here. That narrows things a bit."

"I don't think so. I think these are key-words for the letters Alexis sent out. In each letter he would announce *his* key-word for *his* next letter. But his correspondent would do the same, so that the key-word for the paper found on Alexis is much more likely to be one that isn't marked here. Unless, of course, the paper is one of Alexis' own writing, which isn't very likely."

"We can't even say that, then," moaned Glaisher. "Because the correspondent might very well hit on some word that Alexis had marked in advance. It might be anything."

"Perfectly true. Then the only bit of help we get from this is that the cipher used was an English word, and that the letters were probably written in English. That doesn't absolutely follow, because they might be in French or German or Italian, all of which have the same alphabet as English; but they can't be in Russian at any rate, which has an alphabet totally different. So that's one mercy."

"If it's anything to do with Bolsheviks," said Glaisher, thoughtfully, "it's a bit surprising they didn't write in Russian. It would have made it doubly safe if they had. Russian by itself would be bad enough, but a Russian cipher would be a snorter."

"Quite. As I've said before, I can't quite swallow the Bolshevik theory. And yet —dash it all! I simply can*not* fit these letters in with the Weldon side of the business."

"What I want to know," put in the Inspector, "is this. How did the murderers, whoever they were, get Alexis out to the Flat-Iron? Or if it was Bolsheviks that got him there, how did Weldon & Co. know he was going to be there? It must be the same party that made the appointment and did the throat-cutting. Which brings us to the point that either Weldon's party wrote the letters or the foreign party did the murder."

"True, O king."

"And where," asked Harriet, "does Olga Kohn come in?"

"Ah!" said Wimsey, "there you are. That's the deepest mystery of the lot. I'll swear that girl was telling the truth, and I'll swear that the extremely un-Irish Mr. Sullivan was telling the truth too. Little flower in the crannied wall I pluck you out of the crannies, but, as the poet goes on to say, *if* I could understand I should know who the guilty man is. But I don't understand. Who is the mysterious bearded gentleman who asked Mr. Sullivan for the portrait of a Russian-looking girl, and how did the portrait get into the corpse's pocketbook, signed with the name Feodora? These are deep waters, Watson."

"I'm coming back to my original opinion," grumbled the Inspector. "I believe the fellow was dotty and cut his own throat and there's an end of it. He probably had a mania for collecting girls' photographs and sending himself letters in cipher."

"And posting them in Czechoslovakia?"

"Oh, well, somebody must have done that for him. As far as I can see, we've no case against Weldon and no case against Bright, and the case against Perkins is as full of holes as a colander. As for Bolsheviks—where are they? Your friend Chief-Inspector Parker has put out inquiries about Bolshevik agents in this country, and the answer is that none of 'em are known to have been about here lately, and as regards Thursday, 18th, they all seem to be accounted for. You may say it's an unknown Bolshevik agent, but there aren't as many of those going about as you might think. These London chaps know quite a lot more than the ordinary public realises. If there'd been anything funny about Alexis and his crowd, they'd have been on to it like a shot."

Wimsey sighed, and rose.

"I'm going home to bed," he declared. "We must wait till we get the photographs of the paper. Life is dust and ashes. I can't prove my theories and Bunter has deserted me again. He disappeared from Wilvercombe on the same day as William Bright, leaving me a message to say that one of my favourite socks had been lost in the wash and that he had lodged a complaint with the management. Miss Vane, Harriet, if I may call you so, will you marry me and look after my socks, and, incidentally be the only woman-novelist who ever accepted a proposal of marriage in the presence of a superintendent and inspector of police?"

"Not even for the sake of the headlines."

"I thought not. Even publicity isn't what it was. See here, Superintendent, will you take a bet that Alexis didn't commit suicide and that he wasn't murdered by Bolsheviks?"

The Superintendent replied cautiously that he wasn't a sporting man.

"Crushed again!" moaned his lordship. "All the same," he added, with a flash of his old spirit, "I'll break that alibi if I die for it."

26

THE EVIDENCE OF
THE BAY MARE

Hail, shrine of blood!
—The Brides' Tragedy

The photographs of the paper found on the corpse duly arrived next morning, together with the original; and Wimsey, comparing them together in the presence of Glaisher and Umpelty, had to confess that the experts had made a good job of it. Even the original paper was far more legible than it had been before. The chemicals that remove bloodstains and the stains of dyed leather, and the chemicals that restore the lost colour to washed-out ink had done their work well, and the colour-screens that so ingeniously aid the lens to record one colour and cut out the next had produced from the original, thus modified, a result in which only a few letters here and there were irretrievably lost. But to read is one thing; to decipher, another. They gazed sadly at the inextricable jumble of letters.

XNATNX
RBEXMG

PRBFX ALI MKMG BFFY, MGTSQ JMRRY. ZBZE FLOX P.M. MSIU FKX FLDYPC FKAP RPD KL DONA FMKPC FM NOR ANXP.
    SOLFA TGMX DXL LKKZM VXI BWHNZ MBFFY MG, TSQ A NVPD NMM VFYQ. CJU ROGA K.C. RAC RRMTN S.B. IF H.P. HNZ ME? SSPXLZ DFAX LRAEL TLMK XATL RPX BM AEBF HS MPIKATL TO HOKCCI HNRY. TYM VDSM SUSSX GAMKR, BG AIL AXH NZMLF HVUL KNN RAGY QWMCK, MNQS TOIL AXFA AN IHMZS RPT HO KFLTIM. IF MTGNLU H.M. CLM KLZM AHPE ALF AKMSM, ZULPR FHQ—CMZT SXS RSMKRS GNKS FVMP RACY OSS QESBH NAE UZCK CON MGBNRY RMAL RSH NZM, BKTQAP MSH NZM TO ILG MELMS NAGMJU KC KC.
    TQKFX BQZ NMEZLI BM ZLFA AYZ MARS UP QOS KMXBP SUE UMIL PRKBG MSK QD.
    NAP DZMTB N.B. OBE XMG SREFZ DBS AM IMHY GAKY R. MULBY M.S. SZLKO GKG LKL GAW XNTED BHMB XZD NRKZH PSMSKMN A.M. MHIZP DK MIM, XNKSAK C KOK MNRL CFL INXF HDA GAIQ.
    GATLM Z DLFA A QPHND MV AK MV MAG C.P.R. XNATNX PD GUN MBKL I OLKA GLDAGA KQB FTQO SKMX GPDH NW LX SULMY ILLE MKH BEALF MRSK UFHA AKTS.

At the end of a strenuous hour or two, the following facts were established:

1. The letter was written on a thin but tough paper which bore no resemblance to any paper found among the effects of Paul Alexis. The probability was thus increased that it was a letter received, and not written by him.
2. It was written by hand in a purplish ink, which, again, was not like that used by Alexis. The additional inference was drawn that the writer either possessed no typewriter or was afraid that his typewriter might be traced.
3. It was not written in wheel-cipher, or in any cipher which involved the regular substitution of one letter of the alphabet for another.

"At any rate," said Wimsey, cheerfully, "we have plenty of material to work on. This isn't one of those brief, snappy 'Put goods on sundial' messages which leave you wondering whether E really is or is not the most frequently-recurring letter in the English language. If you ask me, it's either one of those devilish codes founded on a book—in which case it must be one of the books in the dead man's possession, and we only have to go through them—or it's a different kind of code altogether—the kind I was thinking about last night, when we saw those marked words in the dictionary."

"What kind's that, my lord?"

"It's a good code," said Wimsey, "and pretty baffling if you don't know the key-word. It was used during the War. I used it myself, as a matter of fact, during a brief interval of detecting under a German alias. But it isn't the exclusive property of the War Office. In fact, I met it not long ago in a detective story. It's just—"

He paused, and the policemen waited expectantly.

"I was going to say, it's just the thing an amateur English plotter might readily get hold of and cotton to. It's not obvious, but it's accessible and very simple to work. It's the kind of thing that young Alexis could easily learn to encode and decode; it doesn't want a lot of bulky apparatus; and it uses practically the same number of letters as the original message, so that it's highly suitable for long epistles of this kind."

"How's it worked?" asked Glaisher.

"Very prettily. You choose a key-word of six letters or more, none of which recurs. Such as, for example, SQUANDER, which was on Alexis' list. Then you make a diagram of five squares each way and write the key-word in the squares like this:

S	Q	U	A	N
D	E	R		

"Then you fill up the remaining spaces with the rest of the alphabet in order, leaving out the ones you've already got."

"You can't put twenty-six letters into twenty-five spaces," objected Glaisher.

"No; so you pretend you're an ancient Roman or a mediaeval monk and treat I and J as one letter. So you get this."

S	Q	U	A	N
D	E	R	B	C
F	G	H	IJ	K
L	M	O	P	T
V	W	X	Y	Z

"Now, let's take a message—What shall we say? 'All is known, fly at once'— that classic hardy perennial. We write it down all of a piece and break it into groups of two letters, reading from left to right. It won't do to have two of the same letters coming together, so where that happens we shove in Q or Z or something which won't confuse the reader. So now our message runs AL QL IS KN OW NF LY AT ON CE."

"Suppose there was an odd letter at the end?"

"Well, then we'd add on another Q or Z or something to square it up. Now, we take our first group, AL. We see that they come at the corners of a rectangle in which the other corners are SP. So we put down SP for the first two letters of the coded message. In the same way QL becomes SM and IS becomes FA."

"Ah!" cried Glaisher, "but here's KN. They both come on the same vertical line. What happens then?"

"You take the letter next below each—TC. Next comes OW, which you can do for yourself by taking the corners of the square."

"MX?"

"MX it is. Go on."

"SK," said Glaisher, happily taking diagonals from corner to corner, "PV, NP, UT—"

"No, TU. If your first diagonal went from bottom to top, you must take it the same way again. ON = TU, NO would be UT."

"Of course, of course. TU. Hullo!"

"What's the matter?"

"CE come on the same horizontal line."

"In that case you take the next letter to the *right* of each."

"But there isn't a letter to the right of C."

"Then start again at the beginning of the line."

This confused the Superintendent for a moment, but he finally produced DR.

"That's right. So your coded message stands now: SP SM FA TC MX SK PV NP TU DR. To make it look prettier and not give the method away, you can break it up into any lengths you like. For instance: SPSM FAT CMXS KPV NPTUDR. Or you can embellish it with punctuation as haphazard. S.P. SMFA. TCMXS, KPVN, PT! UDR. It doesn't matter. The man who gets it will ignore all that. He will simply break it up into pairs of letters again and read it with the help of the code diagram. Taking the diagonals as before, and the next letter *above*, where they come on the same vertical line, and the next to the *left* where they come on the same horizontal."

The two policemen pored over the diagram. Then Umpelty said:

"I see, my lord. It's very ingenious. You can't guess it by way of the most frequent letter, because you get a different letter for it each time, according as it's grouped to the next letter. And you can't guess individual words, because you don't know where the words begin and end. Is it at all possible to decode it without the key-word?"

"Oh dear, yes," said Wimsey. "Any code ever coded can be decoded with pains and patience—except possibly some of the book codes. I know a man who spent years doing nothing else. The code diagram got so bitten into him that when he caught measles he came out in checks instead of spots."

"Then he could decode this," said Glaisher, eagerly.

"On his head. We'll send him a copy if you like. I don't know where he is, but I know those that do. Shall I bung it off? It would save us a lot of time."

"I wish you would, my lord."

Wimsey took a copy of the letter, pushed it into an envelope and enclosed a brief note.

DEAR CLUMPS,— Here's a cipher message. Probably Playfair, but old Bungo will know. Can you push it off to him and say I'd be grateful for a construe? Said to hail from Central Europe, but ten to one it's in English. How goes?

Yours,

WIMBLES.

Seen anything of Trotters lately?

He addressed the envelope to an official at the Foreign Office, and picked up another copy of the cipher.

"I'll take this if I may. We'll try it out with some of Alexis' selected words. It'll be a nice job for Miss Vane, and a healthy change from crosswords. Now, what's the next item?"

"Nothing very much yet, my lord. We haven't found anybody who saw Perkins pass through Darley at any time, but we've found the chemist who served him in Wilvercombe. He says Perkins was there at eleven o'clock, which gives him ample time to be at Darley by 1.15. And Perkins has had a bad relapse and can't be interrogated. And we've seen Newcombe, the farmer, who corroborates finding the mare wandering on the shore on Friday morning. He says, too, that she was in the field O.K. when his man was down there on the Wednesday, and that he is quite sure she couldn't have got through the gap in the hedge by herself. But then, naturally, nobody ever believes his own neglect is to blame for anything."

"Naturally not. I think I'll run over and see Farmer Newcombe. In the meantime, Miss Vane is going to do her damnedest with the cipher—trying out all the marked words on it. Aren't you?"

"If you like."

"Noble woman! It would be fun if we got ahead of the official interpreter. I suppose the Weldons show no signs of moving."

"Not the slightest. But I haven't seen much of them since the funeral. Henry seems a bit stand-offish—can't get over the snake episode, I suppose. And his mother—"

"Well?"

"Oh, nothing. But she seems to be trying to get fresh information out of Antoine."

"Indeed?"

"Yes. Antoine is being very sympathetic."

"Good luck to him. Well, cheerio!"

Wimsey drove over to Darley, interviewed the farmer and asked for the loan of the bay mare and a bridle. Mr. Newcombe not only granted the loan most cordially, but expressed his intention of accompanying Wimsey to watch the experiment. Wimsey was at first not best pleased; it is perhaps easier to wallop another man's horse over a four-mile course if the owner is not looking on. On reflection, however, he thought he saw a use to which he could put Mr. Newcombe. He asked that gentleman to be good enough to precede him to the Flat-Iron, and make a note of the exact moment at which he himself should come into view, and thence time his progress. The farmer, surmising with a wink that the loosing of the mare and the tragedy at the Flat-Iron had some connection with one another, readily agreed, and, himself mounting a sturdy white nag, took his departure along the shore, while Wimsey, glancing at his watch, set out in pursuit of the bay mare.

She came up to be caught with remarkable readiness, no doubt connecting Wimsey in her simple equine mind with oats. The gap in the hedge had been opened again, by permission, and Wimsey, having bridled her, rode her through it and stirred her up to a canter.

The mare, though willing enough, had, as he expected, no exceptional turn of speed, and since their progress had to be made actually through the water, it was a trifle impeded and remarkably noisy. As he rode, Wimsey kept his eye on the cliffs above. Nobody and nothing was in sight, with the exception of a few grazing animals. The road was hidden. He made good time to the cottages, and then began to look about for Ormond's break in the cliff. He recognised it when he came to it by the fallen rocks and the fragments of broken fence above, and looked at his watch. He was a little ahead of time. Glancing along the shore, he saw the Flat-Iron well in view, with Farmer Newcombe seated upon it, a little dark lump at a mile's distance. He left the break in the cliff to be explored on the return journey, and urged the mare to her best pace. She responded vigorously, and they made the final mile in fine style, the water spraying about them. Wimsey could see the farmer clearly now; he had the white horse tethered to the famous ring-bolt and was standing on the rock, watch conscientiously in hand, to time them.

It was not till they were within a few score paces of the rock that the bay mare seemed to realise what was happening. Then she started as if she had been shot, flung up her head and slewed round so violently that Wimsey, jerked nearly on to her neck by the plunge, was within an ace of being spun off altogether. He dug his knees into her bare sides and hauled hard upon the bridle, but, like many farm nags, she had a mouth of iron, and the snaffle made little impression upon her. She was off, tearing back in her tracks as if the devil was after her. Wimsey, cynically telling himself that he had underestimated her power of speed, clung grimly to her withers and concentrated on shortening his left-hand rein so as to wrench her head round to the sea. Presently, finding it hard to go forward against this determined drag, she slacked pace, skirmishing sideways.

"Bless and save you, my girl," said Wimsey, mildly, "what's the matter with you?"

The mare panted and shuddered.

"But this'll never do," said Wimsey. He stroked her sweaty shoulder reassuringly. "Nobody's going to hurt you, you know."

She stood quietly enough, but shook as she stood.

"There, there," said Wimsey.

He turned her head once more in the direction of the Flat-Iron, and was aware of the hurried approach of Mr. Newcombe on the white horse.

"Lord a'mighty," exclaimed Mr. Newcombe, "what's come to the mare? I thought she'd have you off sure-ly. Done a bit of riding, ain't you?"

"Something must have frightened her," said Wimsey. "Has she ever been there before?"

"Not as I know on," said the farmer.

"You weren't waving your arms or anything, were you?"

"Not I. I was looking at my watch—and there! Dang me if I haven't clean forgot what time I made it. I was fair mazed with her taking fright so all of a sudden."

"Is she given to shying?"

"Never known her take and do such a thing before."

"Queer," said Wimsey. "I'll try her again. Keep behind us, and we'll know it wasn't you that startled her."

He urged the mare back towards the rock at a gentle trot. She moved forward uneasily, chucking her head about. Then, as before, she stopped dead and stood trembling.

They tried her half-a-dozen times, cajoling and encouraging her, but to no purpose. She would not go near the Flat-Iron—not even when Wimsey dismounted and led her step by step. She flatly refused to budge, standing with her shaking legs rooted to the sand, and rolling white and terrified eyes. Out of sheer mercy for her they had to give up the attempt.

"I'll be damned," said Mr. Newcombe.

"And so will I," said Wimsey.

"What can have come over her—" said Mr. Newcombe.

"I know what's come over her all right," said Wimsey, "but—Well, never mind, we'd better go back."

They rode slowly homeward. Wimsey did not stay to examine the break in the cliff. He did not need to. He knew now exactly what had happened between Darley and the Flat-Iron Rock. As he went, he put the whole elaborate structure of his theories together, line by line, and like Euclid, wrote at the bottom of it:

WHICH IS IMPOSSIBLE.

In the meantime, Constable Ormond was also feeling a little blue. He had suddenly bethought him of the one person in Darley who was likely to have kept tabs on Mr. Perkins. This was old Gaffer Gander who, every day, rain or shine, sat on the seat at the little shelter built about the village oak in the centre of the green. He had unaccountably overlooked Gaffer Gander the previous day, owing to the fact that—by a most unusual accident—the Gaffer had not been in his accustomed seat when Ormond was making his inquiries. It turned out that Mr. Gander had actually been in Wilvercombe, celebrating his youngest grandson's wedding to a young woman of that town, but now he was back again and ready to be interviewed. The old gentleman was in high spirits. He was eighty-five come Martinmas, hale and hearty, and boasted that, though he might perhaps be a trifle hard of hearing, his eyes, thank God, were as good as ever they were.

Why, yes, he remembered Thursday, 18th. Day as the poor young man was found dead at the Flat-Iron. A beautiful day, surely, only a bit blowy towards evening. He always notices any strangers that came through. He remembered seeing a big open car come past at ten o'clock. A red one it was, and he even knew the number of it, because his great-grandson, little Johnnie—ah! and a bright lad he was—had noticed what a funny number it was. OI 0101—just like you might be saying Oy, oy, oy. Mr. Gander could call to mind the day when there wasn't none o' them things about, and folks was none the worse for it, so far as he could see. Not that Mr. Gander was agin' progress. He'd always voted Radical in his young days, but these here Socialists was going too far, he reckoned. Too free with other folks' money, that's what they were. It was Mr. Lloyd George as give him the Old Age Pension, which was only right, seeing he had worked hard all his life, but he didn't hold with no dole for boys of eighteen. When Mr. Gander was eighteen, he was up at four o'clock every morning and on the land till sunset and after for five shillings a week and it hadn't done him no harm as he could see. Married at nineteen he was, and ten children, seven of them still alive and hearty. Why, yes, the car had come back at one o'clock. Mr. Gander had just come out from the Feathers after having a pint to his dinner, and he sees the car stop and the gentleman as was camping in the lane get out of it. There was a lady in the car, very finely rigged out, but mutton dressed as lamb in Gaffer's opinion. In his day, women weren't ashamed of their age. Not that he minded a female making the best of herself, he was all for progress, but he thought they were going a bit too far nowadays. Mr. Martin, that was the gentleman's name, had said good-morning to him and gone into the Feathers, and the car had taken the Heathbury road. Why, yes, he'd seen Mr. Martin leave. Half-past one it were by the church-clock. A good clock, that was. Vicar, he'd had it put in order at his own expense two years ago and when they turned the wireless on, you might hear Big Ben and the church-clock striking together quite beautiful. There hadn't been no wireless in Mr. Gander's day, but he thought it was a great thing and a fine bit of progress. His grandson Willy, the one that was married on a woman over to Taunton, had given him a beautiful set. It was that loud, he could hear it beautiful, even though his hearing was getting a little hard. He'd heard tell as they were going to show you pictures by wireless soon, and he hoped the Lord might spare him long enough to see it. He hadn't nothing against wireless, though some people thought it was going a bit far to have the Sunday services laid on like gas, as you might say. Not but what it might be a good thing for them as was ailing, but he thought it made the young folks lazy and disrespectful-like. He himself hadn't missed going to Sunday church for twenty year, not since he broke his leg falling off the hayrick, and while he had his strength, please God, he would sit under vicar. Why, yes, he did remember a strange young man coming through the village that afternoon. Of course he could describe him; there wasn't nothing wrong with his eyes, nor his memory neither, praise be! It was only his hearing as wasn't so good but, as Mr. Ormond might have noticed, you had only to speak up clear and not mumble as these young people did nowadays and Mr. Gander could hear you well enough. One of these rickety-looking town-bred fellows it was, in big glasses, with a little bag strapped to his back and a long stick to walk with, same as they all had. Hikers, they called them. They all had long sticks, like these here Boy Scouts, though, as anybody with experience could have told them, there was nothing like a good crutch-handled ash-plan to give you a help along when you were walking. Because, it stood to reason, you got a better holt on it than on one of them long sticks. But young folks never listened to reason, especially the fe-males, and he thought they was going a bit far, too, with their bare legs and short pants like football players. Though Mr. Gander wasn't so old neither that he didn't like to look at a good pair of female legs. In his days females didn't show their legs, but he'd known men as would go a mile to look at a pretty ankle.

Constable Ormond put all his energy into his last question.

"What time did this young man go through?"

"What time? You needn't shout, young man—I may be a bit hard of hearing, but I'm not deaf. I says to vicar only last Monday, 'That was a good sermon you give us yesterday,' I says. And he says, 'Can you hear all right where you sit?' And I says to him, 'I may not have my hearing as good as it was when I was a young man,' I says, 'but I can still hear you preach, vicar,' I says, 'from My Text is Taken to Now to God the Father.' And he says, 'You're a wonderful man for your age, Gander,' he says. And so I be, surely."

"So you are, indeed," said Ormond. "I was just asking you when you saw this fellow with the glasses and the long stick pass through the village."

"Nigh on two o'clock it was," replied the old gentleman, triumphantly, "nigh on two o'clock. Because why? I says to myself, 'You'll be wanting a wet to your whistle, my lad,' I says, 'and the Feathers shuts at two, so you'd better hurry up a bit.' But he goes right on, coming from Wilvercombe and walking straight through towards Hinks's Lane. So I says 'Bah!' I says, 'you're one o' them pussy-footin' slop-swallowers, and you looks it, like as if you was brought up on them gassy lemonades, all belch and no body' (if you'll excuse me), that's what I says to myself. And I says, 'Gander,' I says, 'that comes like a reminder as you've just got time for another pint.' So I has my second pint, and when I gets into the bar I see as it's two o'clock by the clock in the bar, as is always kept five minutes fast, on account of getting the men out legal."

Constable Ormond took the blow in silence. Wimsey was wrong; wrong as sin. The two o'clock alibi was proved up to the hilt. Weldon was innocent; Bright was innocent; Perkins was innocent as day. It now only remained to prove that the mare was innocent, and the whole Weldon-theory would collapse like a pack of cards.

He met Wimsey on the village green and communicated this depressing intelligence.

Wimsey looked at him.

"Do you happen to have a railway time-table on you?" he said at last.

"Time-table? No, my lord. But I could get one. Or perhaps I could tell your lordship—"

"Don't bother," said Wimsey. "I only wanted to look up the next train to Colney Hatch."

The constable stared in his turn.

"The mare is guilty," said Wimsey. "She was at the Flat-Iron, and she saw the murder done."

"But I thought, my lord, you proved that was impossible."

"So it is. But it's true."

Wimsey returned to report his conclusions to Superintendent Glaisher, whom he found suffering from nerves and temper.

"Those London fellows have lost Bright," he remarked, curtly. "They traced him to the *Morning Star* office, where he drew his reward in the form of an open cheque. He cashed it at once in currency notes and then skipped off to a big multiple outfitter's—one of those places all lifts and exits. To cut a long story short, he diddled them there, and now he's vanished. I thought you could rely on these London men, but it seems I was mistaken. I wish we'd never come up against this qualified case," added the Superintendent bitterly. "And now you say that the mare was there and that she wasn't there, and that none of the people who ought to have ridden her did ride her. Are you going to say next that she cut the bloke's throat with her own shoe and turned herself into a sea-horse?"

Saddened, Wimsey went home to the Bellevue and found a telegram waiting for him. It had been despatched from a West-end office that afternoon, and ran:

DOING BRIGHT WORK HERE. EXPECT RESULTS SHORTLY. COMMUNICATING CHIEF INSPECTOR PARKER. HOPE FIND OPPORTUNITY DESPATCH LOVAT TWEEDS FROM FLAT.—BUNTER.

27

THE EVIDENCE OF THE FISHERMAN'S GRANDSON

Has it gone twelve?—
   This half-hour. Here I've set
A little clock, that you may mark the time.
          —*Death's Jest-Book*

WEDNESDAY, 1 JULY

"There's one thing that stands out a mile," said Inspector Umpelty. "If there was any hanky-panky with that horse round about two o'clock at the Flat-Iron, Pollock and his precious grandson must have seen it. It's not a mite of use saying they didn't. I always did think that lot was in it up to the eyes. A quiet, private, heart-to-heart murder they might have overlooked, but a wild horse careering about they couldn't, and there you are."

Wimsey nodded.

"I've seen that all along—but how are you going to get it out of them? Shall I have a go at it, Umpelty? That young fellow, Jem—he doesn't look as surly as his grandpa—how about him? Has he got any special interests or hobbies?"

"Well, I don't know, my lord, not without it might be football. He's reckoned a good player, and I know he's hoping to get taken on by the Westshire Tigers."

"H'm. Wish it had been cricket—that's more in my line. Still, we can but try. Think one might find him anywhere about this evening? How about the Three Feathers?"

"If he's not out with his boat, you'd most likely find him there."

Wimsey did find him there. It is always reasonably easy to get conversation going in a pub, and it will be a black day for detectives when beer is abolished. After an hour's entertaining discussion about football and the chances of various teams in the coming season, Wimsey found Jem becoming distinctly more approachable. With extreme care and delicacy he then set out to work the conversation round to the subject of fishing, the Flat-Iron and the death of Paul Alexis. At first, the effect was disappointing. Jem lost his loquacity, his smile vanished, and he fell into a brooding gloom. Then, just as Wimsey was deciding to drop the dangerous subject, the young man seemed to make up his mind. He edged a little closer to Wimsey, glanced over his shoulder at the crowd about the bar, and muttered:

"See here, sir, I'd like a word with you about that."

"By all means. Outside? Right! Dashed interesting," he added, more loudly. "Next time I'm down this way I'd like to come along and see you play. Well, I must be barging along. You going home? I can run you over in the car if you like —won't take a minute."

"Thank'ee, sir. I'd be glad of it."

"And you could show me those photographs you were talking about."

The two pushed their way out. Good-nights were exchanged, but Wimsey noticed that none of the Darley inhabitants seemed particularly cordial to Jem. There was a certain air of constraint about their farewells.

They got into the car, and drove in silence till they were past the level crossing. Then Jem spoke:

"About that business, sir. I told Grand-dad he'd better tell the police how it were, but he's that obstinate, and it's a fact there'd be murder done if it was to get out. None the more for that, he did ought to speak, because this here's a hanging matter and there's no call as I see to get mixed up with it. But Grand-dad, he don't trust that Umpelty and his lot, and he'd leather the life out of Mother or me if we was to let on. Once tell the police, he says, and it 'ud be all about the place."

"Well—it depends what it is," said Wimsey, a little mystified. "Naturally, the police can't hide anything—well, anything criminal, but—"

"Oh, 'tis not that, sir. Leastways, not as you might take notice on. But if they Bainses was to hear tell on it and was to let Gurney know—but there! I've always told Grand-dad as it wur a fool thing to do, never mind if Tom Gurney did play a dirty trick over them there nets."

"If it's nothing criminal," said Wimsey, rather relieved, "you may be sure *I* shan't let anybody know."

"No, sir. That's why I thought I'd like to speak to you, sir. You see, Grand-dad left a bad impression, the way he wouldn't let on what we was doing off the

Grinders, and I reckon I did ought to have spoke up at the time, only for
knowing as Grand-dad 'ud take it out of Mother the moment my back was
turned."

"I quite understand. But, what was it you were doing at the Grinders?"

"Taking lobsters, sir."

"Taking lobsters? What's the harm in that?"

"None, sir; only, you see, they was Tom Gurney's pots."

After a little interrogation, the story became clear. The unfortunate Tom
Gurney, who lived in Darley, was accustomed to set out his lobster-pots near the
Grinders, and drove a very thriving trade with them. But, some time previously,
he had offended old Pollock in the matter of certain nets, alleged to have
sustained wilful damage. Mr. Pollock, unable to obtain satisfaction by constitu-
tional methods, had adopted a simple method of private revenge. He chose
suitable moments when Tom Gurney was absent, visited the lobster-pots, abstracted the greater part of their live contents and replaced the pots. It was not,
Jem explained, that Mr. Pollock really hoped to take out the whole value of the
damaged net in lobsters; the relish of the revenge lay in the thought of "doing
that Gurney down" and in hearing "that Gurney" swearing from time to time
about the scarcity of lobsters in the bay. Jem thought the whole thing rather
foolish and didn't care for having a hand in it, because it would have suited his
social ambitions better to keep on good terms with his neighbours, but what
with one thing and another (meaning, Wimsey gathered, what with old Pollock's
surly temper and the possibility of his leaving his very considerable savings to
some other person, if annoyed), Jem had humoured his grandfather in this
matter of lobster-snatching.

Wimsey was staggered. It was as simple as that, then. All this mystification,
and nothing behind it but a trivial local feud. He glanced sharply at Jem. It was
getting dark, and the young man's face was nothing but an inscrutable profile.

"Very well, Jem," he said. "I quite see. But now, about this business on the
shore. Why did you and your grandfather persist in saying you saw nobody
there?"

"But that was right, sir. We didn't see nobody. You see, it was like this, sir. We
had the boat out, and we brings her along there round 'bout the slack, knowin'
as the other boats 'ud be comin' home with the tide, see? And Grand-dad says,
'Have a look along the shore, Jem,' he said, 'and see as there's none o' them
Gurneys a-hanging about.' So I looks, an' there weren't a soul to be seen, leaving
out this chap on the Flat-Iron. And I looks at him and I sees as he's asleep or
summat, and he's none of us by the looks of him, so I says to Grand-dad as he's
some fellow from the town, like."

"He was asleep, you say?"

"Seemingly. So Grand-dad takes a look at him and says 'He's doin' no harm,'
he says, 'but keep your eyes skinned for the top of the cliffs.' So I did, and there
wasn't a single soul come along that there shore before we gets to the Grinders,
and that's the truth if I was to die for it."

"Now, see here, Jem," said Wimsey. "You heard all the evidence at the
inquest, and you know that this poor devil was killed round about two o'clock."

"That's true, sir; and as sure as I'm sitting here, he must ha' killed himself, for
there was nobody come a-nigh him—barring the young lady, of course. Unless it
might be while we was taking them pots up. I won't say but what we might
a-missed summat them. We finished that job around two o'clock—I couldn't

say just when it were, not to the minute, but the tide had turned nigh on three-quarters of an hour, and that's when I looks at this fellow again and I says to Grand-dad, 'Grand-dad,' I says, 'that chap there on the rock looks queer-like,' I says, 'I wonder if there's summat wrong.' So we brings the boat in shore a bit, and then, all of a sudden, out comes the young lady from behind them rocks and starts caperin' about. And Grand-dad, he says, 'Let un bide,' he says, 'let un bide. Us have no call to be meddlin' wi' they,' he says. And so we puts about again. Because, you see, sir, if we'd gone a-meddling and it was to come out as we was thereabouts with the boat full of Tom Gurney's lobsters, Tom Gurney'd a-had summat to say about it."

"Your grandfather said you saw Alexis first about 1.45."

"It 'ud be before that, sir. But I'll not say as we kept our eyes on un all the time, like."

"Suppose someone had come along, say, between 1.45 and two o'clock, would you have seen him?"

"Reckon so. No, sir; that poor gentleman made away with himself, there's no doubt of it. Just cut his throat quiet-like as he sat there. There's no manner of doubt about that."

Wimsey was puzzled. If this was lying, it was done with a surprising appearance of sincerity. But if it was truth, it made the theory of murder still harder to substantiate than before. Every fragment of evidence there was pointed to the conclusion that Alexis had died alone upon his rock and by his own hand.

And yet—why wouldn't the bay mare go near the Flat-Iron? Was it possible—Wimsey was no friend to superstition, but he had known such things happen before—was it possible that the uneasy spirit of Paul Alexis still hung about the Flat-Iron, perceptible to the brute though not to self-conscious man? He had known another horse that refused to pass the scene of an age-old crime.

He suddenly thought of another point that he might incidentally verify.

"Will anybody be up and about at your home, Jem?"

"Oh, yes, sir. Mother's sure to be waiting up for me."

"I'd like to see her."

Jem offered no objection, and Wimsey went in with him to Pollock's cottage. Mrs. Pollock, stirring soup for Jem in a saucepan, received him politely, but shook her head at his question.

"No sir. We heard no horse on the beach this afternoon."

That settled that, then. If Wimsey could ride past the cottages unnoticed, so could any other man.

"The wind's off-shore today," added Mrs. Pollock.

"And you're still sure you heard nothing of the sort last Thursday week?"

"Ah!" Mrs. Pollock removed the saucepan. "Not in the afternoon, what the police was asking about. But Susie have called to mind as she did hear something like a trampling round about dinner-time. Happen it might be twelve o'clock. But being at her work, she didn't run out to look."

"Twelve o'clock?"

"Thereabout, sir. It come back to her all of a sudden, when we was talkin' over what that young Ormond wur askin' about."

Wimsey left the cottage with his ideas all in disorder. If someone had been riding on the shore at twelve o'clock, it accounted for the horseshoe, but it did not account for the murder. Had he, after all, been quite wrong in attaching so much importance to the horseshoe? Might not some mischievous lad, finding the bay mare at large, have ridden her along the beach for a lark? Might she not even have strayed away on her account?

But that brought him back to her strange behaviour of that afternoon, and to the problem of the ring-bolt. Had the ring-bolt been used for some other purpose? Or suppose the murderer had come to the rock on horseback at twelve o'clock and remained talking there with Alexis till two o'clock? But Jem said that there had been only the one figure on the Flat-Iron. Had the murderer lurked hidden in the rocky cleft till the time came to strike the blow? But why? Surely the sole reason for riding thither could only have been the establishment of an alibi, and an alibi is thrown away if one lingers for two hours before taking advantage of it. And how had the mare got home? She was not on the shore between one o'clock and two o'clock if—again—Jem was to be trusted. Wimsey played for a few moments with the idea of two men riding on one horse—one to do the murder and one to take the animal back, but the thing seemed far-fetched and absurd.

Then an entirely new thought struck him. In all the discussions about the crime, it has been taken for granted that Alexis had walked along the coast-road to the Flat-Iron; but had this been proved? He had never thought to ask. Why might not Alexis have been the rider?

In that case, the time of the mare's passing might be explained, but other problems bristled up thick as thorns in a rose-garden. At what point had he taken horse? He had been seen to leave Darley Halt by road in the direction of Lesston Hoe. Had he subsequently returned and fetched the mare from the field, and so ridden? If not, who had brought her and to what rendezvous? And again, how had she returned?

He determined to hunt out Inspector Umpelty and face him with these problems.

The Inspector was just going to bed, and his welcome was not a hearty one, but he showed signs of animation on hearing Wimsey's fresh information.

"Them Pollocks and Moggeridges are the biggest liars in creation," he observed, "and if there's been murder done, it's good proof that they're all concerned in it," said he. "But as to how Alexis got there, you can set your mind at rest. We've found six witnesses who saw him at various points along the road between 10.15 and 11.45, and unless there's some other fellow been going about in a black beard, you can take it as proved that he went by the coast-road and no other way."

"Did none of the witnesses know him personally?"

"Well, no," the Inspector admitted, "but it isn't likely there'd be more than one young fellow in a blue suit and a beard going about at that time, unless somebody was deliberately disguised as him, and where'd be the point of that? I mean to say, the only reasons for anybody impersonating him would be to make out either that he was in that neighbourhood at that particular time when he was really elsewhere, or that he was really alive some time after he was supposed to be killed. Now, we know that he was in that neighbourhood all right, so that disposes of number one; and we know that he really was killed at two o'clock and not earlier, and that disposes of number two. Unless, of course," said the Inspector, slowly, "the real Alexis was up to some funny business between 10.15 and two o'clock, and this other fellow was making an alibi for him. I hadn't thought of that."

"I suppose," said Wimsey, "that it really *was* Alexis who was killed. His face was gone, you know, and we've only the clothes and a photograph to go upon."

"Well, it was somebody else with a real beard, anyhow," said the Inspector. "And who would Alexis be wanting to kill, do you suppose?"

"Bolsheviks," suggested Wimsey, lightly. "He might make an appointment with a Bolshevik who meant to murder him, and then murder the Bolshevik."

"So he might—but that doesn't make things any easier. Whoever it was did the murder, he had to get away from the Flat-Iron. And how could he have managed to change clothes with the victim? There wasn't time."

"Not after the murder, certainly."

"Then where are you? It's only making things more complicated. If you ask me, I think your notion of the mare having been ridden down there at some other time by some mischievous young fellow is a good one. There's nothing against it except that ring-bolt, and that might quite well have been put there for a quite different purpose. That washes the mare out of the thing altogether and makes it all a lot easier. Then we can say that either Alexis did away with himself or else he was murdered by some person we don't know of yet, who just walked along the coast on his two feet. It doesn't matter that those Pollocks didn't see him. He could have been hiding under the rock, like you said. The only trouble is, who was he? It wasn't Weldon, it wasn't Bright, and it wasn't Perkins. But they're not the only people in the world."

Wimsey nodded.

"I'm feeling a bit depressed," he said. "I seem to have fallen down a bit over this case."

"It's a nuisance," said Umpelty, "but there! We've only been at it a fortnight, and what's a fortnight? We'll have to be patient, my lord, and wait for the translation of that letter to come through. The explanation may be all in that."

28

THE EVIDENCE OF THE CIPHER

I know not whether
I see your meaning: if I do, it lies
Upon the wordy wavelets of your voice,
Dim as an evening shadow in a brook.
—*Fragment*

FRIDAY, 3 JULY

The letter from "Clumps" at the Foreign Office did not arrive till the Friday, and then was a disappointment. It ran:—

DEAR WIMBLES,

Got your screed. Old Bungo is in China, dealing with the mess-up there, so have posted enclosure off to him as per instructions. He may be up-country, but he'll probably get it in a few weeks. How's things? Saw Trotters last week at the Carlton. He has got himself into a bit of a mess with his old man, but seems to bear up. You remember the Newton-Carberry business? Well, it's settled, and Flops has departed for the Continent. What-ho!

Yours ever,

CLUMPS.

"Young idiot!" said Wimsey, wrathfully. He threw the letter into the waste-paper basket, put on his hat and went round to Mrs. Lefranc's. Here he found Harriet industriously at work upon the cipher. She reported, however, total failure.

"I don't think it's a scrap of good going on with these marked words," said Wimsey. "And Bungo has failed us. Let's put our great brains to the business. Now, look here. Here is a problem to start with. What is in this letter, and why wasn't it burnt with the rest?"

"Now you mention it, that is rather odd."

"Very. This letter came on the Tuesday morning. On the Wednesday, bills were settled up, and on the Wednesday night, papers were burned. On Thursday morning, Alexis set out to catch his train. Is it too much to suppose that the instructions to do all this were in the letter?"

"It looks likely."

"It does. That means that this letter probably made the appointment for the meeting at the Flat-Iron. Now why wasn't this letter burnt with the rest?"

Harriet let her mind range over the field of detective fiction, with which she was moderately well acquainted.

"In my own books," she remarked, "I usually make the villain end up by saying 'Bring this letter with you.' The idea is, from the villain's point of view, that he can then make certain that the paper is destroyed. From *my* point of view, of course, I put it in so that the villain can leave a fragment of paper clutched in the victim's stiffened hand to assist Robert Templeton."

"Just so. Now, suppose our villain didn't quite grasp the duplicity of your motives. Suppose he said to himself: 'Harriet Vane and other celebrated writers of mystery fiction always make the murderer tell the victim to bring the letter with him. That is evidently the correct thing to do.' That would account for the paper's being here."

"He'd have to be rather an amateur villain."

"Why shouldn't he be? Unless this is really the work of a trained Bolshevik agent, he probably is. I suggest that somewhere in this letter, perhaps at the end, we shall find the words 'Bring this letter with you'—and that will account for its presence."

"I see. Then why do we find it tucked away in an inner pocket and not in the victim's hand as per schedule?"

"Perhaps the victim didn't play up?"

"Then the murderer ought to have searched him and found the paper."

"He must have forgotten."

"How inefficient!"

"I can't help that. Here *is* the paper. And no doubt it's full of dangerous and important information. If it made an appointment, it must be because it would then almost amount to a proof that Alexis didn't commit suicide but was murdered."

"Look here, though! Suppose the letter was brought simply because it contained instructions for reaching the Flat-Iron and so on, which Alexis didn't want to forget."

"Can't be that. For one thing, he'd have had it handy, in an outer pocket—not tucked away in a case. And besides—"

"Not necessarily. He'd keep it handy till he got to the place and then he'd tuck it away safely. After all, he sat at the Flat-Iron alone for an hour or so, didn't he?"

"Yes, but I was going to say something else. If he wanted to keep on referring to the letter, he'd take—not the cipher, which would be troublesome to read, but the de-coded copy."

"Of course—but—don't you see, that solves the whole thing! He did take the copy, and the villain said: 'Have you brought the letter?' And Alexis, without thinking, handed him the copy, and the villain took that and destroyed that, forgetting that the original might be on the body too."

"You're right," said Wimsey, "you're dead right. That's exactly what must have happened. Well, that's that, but it doesn't get us very much farther. Still, we've got some idea of what must have been in the letter, and that will be a great help with the de-coding. We've also got the idea that the villain may have been a bit of an amateur, and that is borne out by the letter itself."

"How?"

"Well, there are two lines here at the top, of six letters apiece. Nobody but an amateur would present us with six isolated letters, let alone two sets of six. He'd run the whole show together. There are just about two things these words might be. One: they might be a key to the cipher—a letter-substitution key, but they're not, because I've tried them, and anyway, nobody would be quite fool enough to send key-word and cipher together on the same sheet of paper. They might, of course, be a key-word or words for the *next* letter, but I don't think so. Six letters is very short for the type of code I have in mind, and words of twelve letters with no repeating letter are very rare in any language."

"Wouldn't any word do, if you left out the repeated letters?"

"It would; but judging by Alexis' careful marking of his dictionary, that simple fact does not seem to have occurred to these amateurs. Well, then, if these words are not keys to a cipher, I suggest that they represent an address, or, more probably, an address and date. They're in the right place for it. I don't mean a whole address, of course—just the name of a town—say Berlin or London—and the date below it."

"That's possible."

"We can try. Now we don't know much about the town, except that the letters are said to have come from Czechoslovakia. But we might get the date."

"How would that be written?"

"Let's see. The letters may just represent the figures of the day, month and year. That means that one of them is an arbitrary fill-up letter, because you can't have an odd number of letters, and a double figure for the number of the month is quite impossible, since the letter arrived here on June 17th. I don't quite know how long the post takes from places in Central Europe, but surely not more than three or four days at the very outside. That means it must have been posted after the 10th of June. If the letters do not stand for numbers, then I suggest that RBEXMG stands either for somethingteen June or June somethingteen. Now, to represent figures our code-merchant may have taken 1 = A, 2 = B, 3 = C, and so on, or he may have taken 1 as the first letter of the code-word and so on. The first would be more sensible, because it wouldn't give the code away.[1] So we'll suppose that 1 = A, so that he originally wrote A? JUNE or JUNE A? and then coded the letters in the ordinary way, the ? standing for the unknown figure, which must be less than 5. Very good. Now, is he more likely to have written June somethingteen or somethingteen June?"

"Most English people write the day first and the month second. Business people at any rate, though old-fashioned ladies still stick to putting the month first."

"All right. We'll try somethingteen June first and say that RBEXMG stands for A? JUNE. Very good. Now we'll see what we can make of that. Let's write it out in pairs. We'll leave out RB for the moment and start with EX. Now EX = JU. Now there's one point about this code that is rather helpful in decoding. Supposing two letters come next door to one another in the code-diagram, either horizontally or vertically, you'll find that the code pair and the clear pair have a letter in common. You don't get that? Well, look! Take our old key-word SQUANDER, written in the diagram like this:

S	Q	U	A	N
D	E	R		

If you're coding the pair of letters DE, then, by taking the letters to the right of them (by the horizontal rule) you get DE = ER; the letter E appears both in code and clear. And the same for letters that *immediately* follow one another in a vertical line. Now, in our first pair EX = JU, this doesn't happen, so we may provisionally write them down in diagonal form.

$$\frac{J \mid E}{X \mid U}$$

---

[1] The hypothesis that RBEXMG represented a date written entirely in numerals proved to be untenable, and for brevity's sake, the calculations relating to this supposition are omitted.

Taking these letters as forming the corners of a parallelogram, we can tell ourselves that JX must come on the same line in the diagram either vertically or horizontally; the same with JE, the same with EU, and the same with UX."

"But suppose JU follows the horizontal rule or the vertical rule without the two letters actually coming together?"

"It doesn't matter; it would only mean then that *all four of them* come on the same line, like this ?J E U X, or X U E ? J or some arrangement of that kind. So, taking all the letters we have got and writing them in diagonals we get this:

J	E	N	M	A	R
X	U	G	E	B	?

Unfortunately there are no side-by-side letters at all. It would be very helpful if there were, but we can't have everything.

"Now the first striking thing is this: that U and X have to come on the same line. That very strongly suggests that they both come in the bottom line. There are five letters that follow U in the alphabet, and only four spaces in which to put them. One of them, therefore, must be in the key-word. We'll take a risk with it and assume that it isn't Z. If it is, we'll have to start all over again, but one must make a start somewhere. We'll risk Z. That gives us three possibilities for our last line: UVXYZ with W in the key-word, or UWXYZ with V in the key-word, or UVWXZ with Y in the key-word. But in any case, U might be in the bottom left-hand corner. Now, looking again at our diagonals, we find that E and U must come in the same line. We can't suppose that E comes immediately above U, because it would be a frightful great key-word that only left us with four spaces between E and U, so we must put E in one of the top three spaces of the left-hand column, like this:

e				
e				
e				
U				Z

"That's not much, but it's a beginning. Now let's tackle X. There's one square in which we know it *can't* be. It can't come next to U, or there would be two spaces between X and Z with only one letter to fill them; so X must come in either the third or the fourth square of the bottom line. So now we have two possible diagrams.

"Looking at our diagonal pairs again, we find that J and X come in the same line and so do J and E. That means that J can't come immediately above X, so we will again enter it on both our diagrams in the top three squares in the X line.

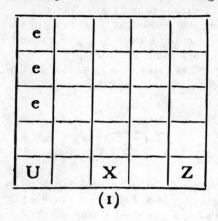

(1)

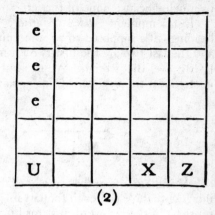

(2)

Now we come to an interesting point. M and N have got to come in the same line. In Diagram 1 it looks fearfully tempting to put them into the two empty-spaces on the right of J, leaving K and L for the key-word; but you can't do that in Diagram 2, because there's not room in the line. If Diagram 2 is the right one, then M or N or both of them must come in the key-word. M and E come in the same line, but N can't come next-door to E. That warns us against a few arrangements, but still leaves a devil of a lot of scope. Our key-word can't begin with EN, that's a certainty. But now, wait! If E is rightly placed in the third square down, then N can't come at the right-hand extremity of the same line, for that would bring it next to E by the horizontal rule; so in Diagram 1 that washes out the possibility of JMN or JLN for that line. It would give us JLM, which is impossible unless N is in the key-word, because N can't come next to E and yet must be in the same line with it and also with M."

Wimsey clawed a little at his hair and sat muttering.

"It looks as though we'd sucked our five letters rather dry," said Harriet. "How about trying the rest of the message? I've got it all ready sorted out into pairs. Hullo! Here's our old friend EXMG appearing again in the body of it."

"Is there?" Wimsey sat up. "Then, if we're right, that will be another date in June. I can't believe it's part of two words, one of which ends in J, or I, or JU or IU or IUN or JUN. If the letter was making an appointment for June 18th, why shouldn't the two letters before it be the letters for 18, that is AH? We'll try it, anyway; what are they?"

"O B."

"OB = AH. That's a fat lot of use. Well, we'll stick 'em down.

$$\frac{O \mid A}{H \mid B}$$

O and A in the same line, O and H in the same line, and A and B we knew about before. That looks as though we might be on the right track, but it doesn't help us much, because none of the letters we've already placed comes into it."

"Just a moment," put in Harriet. "I've got a brainwave. That town in the heading—it's supposed to be something in Central Europe. It's got six letters, and the last two are the first two reversed. How about Warsaw?"

"By jove! that's bright! We can but try it. Let's see—that gives us this." He wrote down the new pairs of diagonals.

W	X
N	A

R	A
T	S

"W and X come in the same line," he observed, "and it's terribly tempting to imagine that W comes in the last line, next door to X. Otherwise, of course, it must be in the key-word. Just for fun, let's enter it in the last line in both our diagrams. Now, this becomes interesting. W and N are also in the same line. We can't place N in the fourth line down, because it's got to be in line with E. Nor can we put it in the third line down, because there are only six letters that come between N and U, and we should have eight spaces left to put them in. Therefore, if W is rightly placed, N has got to go in the top two lines, which means that it definitely does belong to the key-word."

Harriet filled the letters in tentatively.

e	n	i		
e	n	i		
e				
U	W	X	Y	Z

(1)

e		n	i	
e		n	i	
e			i	
U		W	X	Z

(2)

"That makes Diagram 1 look wrong," she said. "Why? What have we done? Oh, I know. E and N can't come together, so if that's the right diagram, E must come in the third line. I *say!* That would mean a key-word of eleven letters!"

"Not necessarily. E may be in its proper alphabetical place. But if Diagram 1 is right, then the beginning of Line 3 is the only place for it. Let's get on. S and T come in one line, and so do R and T, but RST don't follow one another, or RS would become ST, which it doesn't. I should like ST to go in the two places next before U, but we can't be sure that that is the right place for them. Well, dash it! stick 'em down—if we're wrong we must do it again, that's all. There! Now, in that case, R must be in the key-word and therefore in one of the top two spaces on the right of the diagram. That means that RS will be something-T."

"But we know RS! If AT = RS, then RS = AT."

"Good lord! so it does! That's fine! That practically proves that our S and T are correct. And now we know that AR must come next to one another in the key-word."

Harriet pored over the diagrams again.

"Can't we do something now with NX = AW? Yes—look! If we put A into either of the squares in Diagram 1, so as to make NX = AW, then A won't come next to R! So either we're all wrong, or we can wash out Diagram 1 altogether."

"Hurray! Brilliant woman! I always hated Diagram 1, so we'll stack it. That leaves us with a very hopeful-looking Diagram 2."

e		N	i a	r
e		N	i a	r
e			i	
			S	T
U	V	W	X	Z

"I'm glad you think it's hopeful! How about this business of M and N coming in the same line? Can we do anything with that now?"

"Why not? Let's try. Put M immediately below the N-spaces. That leaves five spaces between it and S and only three letters to fill them, because we know that N and R are in the key-word. So that M must come in one of the four spaces in the top left-hand corner. Now we do know that NE = MG. Obviously G can't come immediately between E and N anywhere, because that would give us a key-word with MNG in it, which sounds almost incredible. But that still leaves us with several possible arrangements. Is there anything else we can do?"

"We can fill in Q in the space before S. It isn't likely to be in the key-word without its U, and we know roughly what has become of R."

"Yes. All right. There it is. Do any of these pairs of letters make sense in the letter itself, by the way?"

"No, I've been trying to fit them in, but they're remarkably unhelpful. There's a group AT GM which works out as RS EN, but that might be anything. And quite near the beginning there's TS followed by QJ. TS = SQ, and you'd expect the next group to be U-something, but it isn't. QJ must be S-something."

"So it is; that shows we're on the right track. Q is an arbitrary letter stuck in to separate the two S's. It's curious how little one can get out of the actual text at this stage. Shows what an ingenious beast of a code it is, doesn't it? Wait a jiff—the group before that is MG = NE—that gives us NESS. Perfectly possible and even probable, but it might be anything. Here it comes again! Whatever it is, it appears to be important—it's the same word, BFFY followed by NESS, but

BFFY is simply baffling, I can see nothing for it but to go on struggling with the top left-hand corner. Let's write out all the possible positions for NE = MG."

E		G
M		N

(1)

E		G
	M		N

(2)

M		N
E		G

(3)

"I can see one thing," said Harriet, "and that is that we have got to have a vowel of some kind between M and N, and that vowel can't be A, E, I or U, because we've placed those elsewhere. Therefore it's got to be either O or Y."

"O for preference. The number of words with MYN in them must be limited. But Y has got to be in the key-word somewhere. The end would be the likeliest place for it. Perhaps it ends in MONY. That gives us MONY in Diagram (1), and a word of nine letters. That's quiet plausible. And it's got to begin with E—G. That's less pleasant. EBG, ECG—let's run through the alphabet. EHG—I think not. EIG—pronounceable, but we've got I elsewhere. ELG—where's the dictionary? Nothing there. ENG is impossible, we know where N is—same with ERG. My child, you can wash out all words ending in—MONY—they won't work in Diagram (1) or on Diagram (3), and as for Diagram (2), I refuse to believe in a fourteen-letter word until I'm absolutely forced to."

"In that case, you can wash out Diagram (2) altogether."

"Right-ho! I don't mind, though a thirteen-letter word ending in MON is not absolutely inconceivable. In that case, either our word begins with MON, or it doesn't."

"But it does! We couldn't find any words beginning E—G."

"Nor we could. *Now* then! We've got our E and our G fixed as well as our MON. Now we shan't be long! Fill them in! Oh! and look here! I'm sure the F must go between the E and the G—it's so obviously the place for it."

Harried filled the diagram in with a quivering pencil.

M	O	N	i a	r
			i a	r
E	F	G	i	
		Q	S	T
U	V	W	X	Z

"That *does* look better," she admitted. "Now, let's see if it helps to get any sense out of the letter. Bother! What a lot of groups that we still haven't got! Still no sense for BFFY. Oh! wait! Here's something! MZ TS XS RS. Now, MZ is something-U, and quite possibly RU; it's a 50-50 chance, anyway. TS is SQ and XS is S-something, which means that the Q is just a fill-in letter. Now suppose XS = SI—there's no reason why it shouldn't. Then RS might quite likely be AT—there's nothing against it. And suppose—suppose all these supposes are right, then MZTSXSRS is RUSQSIAT. Knock out the Q and we've got RUSSIAT. *Why* couldn't that be RUSSIA?"

"Why not, indeed? Let's make it so. Write the letters down. M O N A R—oh, Harriet!"

"Don't joggle!"

"I must joggle! We've got the key-word. MONARCH. Wait a jiff. That leaves three spaces before E, and we've only got B and D to put in. Oh, no, I forgot! Y—dear old Y! MONARCHY! Three loud cheers! There you are. All done by kindness! There! There's your square complete. And jolly pretty it looks, I must say."

M	O	N	A	R
C	H	Y	B	D
E	F	G	I J	K
L	P	Q	S	T
U	V	W	X	Z

"Oh, Peter! How marvellous! Let's dance or do something!"

"Nonsense! Let's get on with the job. None of your frivolling now. Start away. PR BF XA LI MK MG BF FY MG TS QJ—and let's get to the bottom of this BF FY business, once and for all. I'll read out the diagonals and you write 'em down."

"Very well. T—O—H—I—'To His Serene'—can that be right?"

"It's English. Hurry up—let's get to BFFY."

" 'To His Serene Highness'—Peter! what *is* all this about?"

Lord Peter turned pale.

"My God!" he exclaimed, melodramatically, "can it be? Have we been wrong and the preposterous Mrs. Weldon right? Shall I be reduced, at my time of life, to hunting for a Bolshevik gang? Read on!"

29

THE EVIDENCE OF THE LETTER

In one word hear, what soon they all shall hear:
A king's a man, and I will be no man
Unless I am a king.

—*Death's Jest-Book*

"To His Serene Highness Grand-Duke Pavlo Alex-eivitch heir to the throne of the Romanovs.

FRIDAY, 3 JULY

"Papers entrusted to us by your Highness now thoroughly examined and marriage of your illustrious ancestress to Tsar Nicholas First proved beyond doubt."

Harriet paused. "What does that mean?"

"God knows. Nicholas I was no saint, but I didn't think he ever *married* anybody except Charlotte-Louise of Prussia. Who the deuce is Paul Alexis' illustrious ancestress?"

Harriet shook her head and went on reading.

"All is in readiness. Your people groaning under oppression of brutal Soviets eagerly welcome return of imperial rule to Holy Russia."

Wimsey shook his head.

"If so, that's one in the eye for my Socialist friends. I was told only the other day that Russian Communism was doing itself proud and that the Russian standard of living, measured in boot-consumption, had risen from zero to one pair of boots in three years per head of population. Still, there may be Russians so benighted as not to be content with that state of things."

"Alexis did always say he was of noble birth, didn't he?"

"He did, and apparently found somebody to believe him. Carry on."

"Treaty with Poland happily concluded. Money and arms at your disposal. Your presence alone needed."

"Oho!" said Wimsey. "Now we're coming to it. Hence the passport and the three hundred gold sovereigns."

"Spies at work. Use caution. Burn all papers all clues to identity."

"He obeyed that bit all right, blow him!" interjected Wimsey. "It looks as though we were now getting down to brass tacks."

"On Thursday 18 June take train reaching Darley Halt ten-fifteen walk by coast-road to Flat-Iron Rock. There await Rider from the Sea who brings instructions for your journey to Warsaw. The word is Empire."

"The Rider from the Sea? Good gracious! Does that mean that Weldon—that the mare—that—?"

"Read on. Perhaps Weldon is the hero of the piece instead of the villain. But if so, why didn't he tell us about it?"

Harriet read on.

"Bring this paper with you. Silence, secrecy imperative. BORIS."

"Well!" said Wimsey. "In all this case, from beginning to end, I only seem to have got one thing right. I said that the letter would contain the words: 'Bring this paper with you' and it does. But the rest of it beats me. 'Pavlo Alexeivitch, heir to the throne of the Romanovs.' Can your landlady produce anything in the shape of a drink?"

After an interval for refreshment, Wimsey hitched his chair closer to the table and sat staring at the decoded message.

"Now," he said, "let's get this straight. One thing is certain. This is the letter that brought Paul Alexis to the Flat-Iron. Boris sent it, whoever he is. Now, is Boris a friend or an enemy?"

He rumpled his hair wildly, and went on, speaking slowly.

"The first thing one is inclined to think is that Boris was a friend and that the Bolshevik spies mentioned in the letter got to the Flat-Iron before he did and murdered Alexis and possibly Boris as well. In that case, what about Weldon's mare? Did she bring the 'Rider from the Sea' to his appointment? And was Weldon the rider, and the imperialist friend of Alexis? It's quite possible, because—no, it isn't. That's funny, if you like."

"What?"

"I was going to say, that in that case Weldon could have ridden to the Flat-Iron at twelve o'clock, when Mrs. Pollock heard the sound of hoofs. But he didn't. He was in Wilvercombe. But somebody else may have done so—some friend to whom Weldon lent the mare."

"Then how did the murderer get there?"

"He walked through the water and escaped the same way, after hiding in the niche till you had gone. It was only while Weldon or Bright or Perkins was supposed to be the murderer that the time-scheme presented any real difficulty. But who was the Rider from the Sea? Why does he not come forward and say: 'I had an appointment with this man. I saw him alive at such a time?'"

"Why, because he is afraid that the man who murdered Alexis will murder him too. But it's all very confusing. We've now got two unknown people to look for instead of one: the Rider from the Sea, who stole the mare and was at the Flat-Iron about midday, and the murderer, who was there at two o'clock."

"Yes. How difficult it all is. At any rate, all this explains Weldon and Perkins. Naturally they said nothing about the mare, because she had gone and come again long before either of them was at the camping-ground. Wait a moment, though; that's odd. How did the Rider from the Sea know that Weldon was going to be away in Wilvercombe that morning? It seems to have been pure accident."

"Perhaps the Rider damaged Weldon's car on purpose."

"Yes, but even then, how could he be sure that Weldon would go away? On the face of it, it was far more likely that Weldon would be there, tinkering with his car."

"Suppose he knew that Weldon meant to go to Wilvercombe that morning in any case. Then the damaged H.T. lead would be pure bad luck for him, and the fact that Weldon did, after all, get to Wilvercombe, a bit of compensating good luck."

"And how did he know about Weldon's plans?"

"Possibly he knew nothing about Weldon at all. Weldon only arrived at Darley on the Tuesday, and all this business was planned long before that, as the date of the letter shows. Possibly whoever it was was horrified to find Weldon encamped in Hinks's Lane and frightfully relieved to see him barge off on the Thursday morning."

Wimsey shook his head.

"Talk about coincidence! Well, maybe so. Now let's go on and see what happened. The Rider made the appointment with Alexis, who would get to the Flat-Iron about 11.45. The Rider met him there, and gave him his instructions —verbally, we may suppose. He then rode back to Darley, loosed the mare and went about his business. Right. The whole thing may have been over by 12.30 or 12.45, and it must have been over by 1.30, or Weldon would have seen him on his return. Meanwhile, what does Alexis do? Instead of getting up and going about *his* business, he sits peacefully on the rock, waiting for someone to come along and murder him at two o'clock!"

"He may have been told to sit on a bit, so as not to leave at the same time as the Rider. Or here's a better idea. When the Rider has gone, Alexis waits for a little bit—say five minutes—at any rate, till his friend is well out of reach. Then up pops the murderer from the niche in the rock, where he has been eavesdropping, and has an interview with Alexis. At two o'clock, the interview ends in murder. Then I turn up, and the murderer pops back into hiding. How's that? The murderer didn't show himself while the Rider was there, because he didn't feel equal to tackling two men at once."

"That seems to cover the facts. I only wonder, though, that he didn't murder you too, while he was about it."

"That would make it look much less like suicide."

"Very true. But how was it you didn't see these two people talking animatedly on the Flat-Iron when you arrived and looked over the cliff at one o'clock?"

"Goodness knows! But if the murderer was standing on the seaward side of the rock—or if they both were—I shouldn't have seen anything. And they may have been, because it was quite low tide then, and the sand would have been dry."

"Yes, so it would. And as the discussion prolonged itself, they saw the tide turn, so they scrambled up on to the rock to keep their feet dry. That would be while you were asleep. But I wonder you didn't hear the chattage and talkery going on while you were having your lunch. Voices carry well by the sea-shore."

"Perhaps they heard me scrambling down the cliff and shut up."

"Perhaps. And then the murderer, knowing that you were there, deliberately committed his murder under your very nose, so to speak."

"He may have thought I had gone. He knew I couldn't see him at the moment, because he couldn't see me."

"And Alexis yelled, and you woke up, and he had to hide."

"That's about it. It seems to hang together reasonably well. And that means we've got to look for a quite new murderer who had an opportunity of knowing about the appointment between Boris and Alexis. And," added Harriet, hopefully, "it needn't be a Bolshevik. It might be somebody with a private motive for doing away with Alexis. How about the da Soto gentleman who got the reversion of Leila Garland? Leila may have told him some nasty story about Alexis."

Wimsey was silent; his thoughts seemed to be wandering. Presently he said.

"Yes. Only we happen to know that da Soto was playing at the Winter Gardens all that time. But now I want to look at the thing from a quite different point of view. What about the letter? Is it genuine? It's written on ordinary sort of paper, without a water-mark, which might come from anywhere, so that proves nothing, but if it really comes from a foreign gentleman of the name of Boris, why is it written in English? Surely Russian would be safer and more likely, if Boris was really a Russian imperialist. Then again—all that opening stuff about brutal Soviets and Holy Russia is so vague and sketchy. Does it look like the letter of a serious conspirator doing a real job of work? No names mentioned; no details about the Treaty with Poland; and, on the other hand, endless wasted words about an 'illustrious ancestress' and 'His Serene Highness.' It doesn't ring true. It doesn't look like business. It looks like somebody with a very sketchy idea of the way revolutions really work, trying to flatter that poor boob's monomania about his birth."

"I'll tell you what it does look like," said Harriet. "It's like the kind of thing I should put into a detective story if I didn't know a thing about Russia and didn't care much, and only wanted to give a general idea that somebody was a conspirator."

"That's it!" said Wimsey. "You're absolutely right. It might have come straight out of one of those Ruritanian romances that Alexis was so fond of."

"Of course—and now we know why he was fond of them. No wonder! They were all part of the mania. I suppose we ought to have guessed all that."

"And here's another thing. Do you notice that the first two paragraphs of the letter are very casually coded. The sentences all run together anyhow, as though the writer didn't much care whether Alexis got them right or wrong. But the minute the good Boris gets down to specific instructions, he starts marking off the ends of his sentences with extra Q's and X's, so as to make sure there will be no mistake in decoding. The Flat-Iron loomed much larger in his mind than Holy Russia and disgruntled Poland."

"In fact, you think the letter looks like a lure."

"Yes. But it's difficult to be quite sure, even then, who sent it and why. If Weldon is at the bottom of it, as we originally thought, then we are still bothered by all these alibis. If it isn't Weldon, who is it? If we're really investigating a political plot, then who was Alexis? Why should anybody want to get rid of him? Unless, of course, he genuinely was somebody important, which seems hard to believe. He can't even have imagined himself to be one of the Russian Imperial house—his age is all wrong. I know we're always hearing tales about the Tsarevitch's having survived the Revolution, but *his* name was Alexei Nicholaivitch, not Pavlo Alexeivitch. And his age would be quite different—and besides, there never was any doubt about *his* descent from Nicholas I. There isn't any note in any of Alexis' books anywhere, is there?—that would tell us who he imagined he might have been."

"Not a thing."

Wimsey gathered up the papers from the table and rose to his feet.

"I shall hand these over to Glaisher," he said. "They will give him something to think about. I like to see other people doing a spot of work from time to time. Do you realise that it's nearly tea-time and we haven't had any lunch?"

"Time passes when one is pleasantly occupied," said Harriet, sententiously.

Wimsey put his hat and papers down on the table, opened his mouth to speak, changed his mind, took up his belongings again and marched to the door.

"Cheerio!" he said, amiably.

"Cheerio!" replied Harriet

He went out, Harriet sat looking at the closed door.

"Well," she said, "thank goodness he's given up asking me to marry him. It's much better he should put it out of his mind."

She must have felt strongly about it, for she repeated the remark several times.

Wimsey absorbed an anomalous meal in the Grill Room, went round to the police-station, handed the decoded letter to the Superintendent, whom it surprised very much, and then ran his car out to Darley. He was still worried by the coincidence about Weldon, and his absence from Hinks's Lane during the crucial period. He approached Mr. Polwhistle.

"Why, yes, my lord," said that worthy. "The fault was in the H.T. leads all right. We tried the mag, and she was working top-hole, and there wasn't nothing wrong with the plugs, so after we'd fiddled about a bit more, young Tom here says, 'Well,' he says, 'only thing I can think of is the leads,' he says. Didn't you, Tom?"

"That's right. Me having a motor-bike, and having had trouble with the leads before, on account of the insulation having got worked through, like, against the radiator-fins, I said, 'How about the H.T. leads?' And Mr. Martin, he says, 'That's an idea,' and before I could say 'knife' he whips the leads out of the clip and gets them off. 'Let's have a look, sir,' I says. 'Never mind looking at the blasted things,' he says, 'you can't do no bloody good'—begging your pardon—'by looking at 'em,' he says. 'Shove a new pair in and look smart.' So I got a bit of H.T. wire out of my bag and I fixes up a new pair of leads and connects 'em up, and no sooner I done so than up she starts, sweet as a nut. What I think, my lord, there must have been a fault in the insulation, see?—what were giving an intermittent short the day before when Mr. Martin complained of bad running and starting, and somehow or other the wires might ha' got fused together, and that made a dead short on the Thursday."

"Very likely," said Wimsey. "Did you actually examine the leads afterwards?"

Tom scratched his head.

"Now you ask me," he said, "I don't rightly know what happened to them leads. I recollect seein' of Mr. Martin a dangling of them in his hand, but whether he took 'em away or whether he left 'em I couldn't say for certain."

"Ah!" said Mr. Polwhistle, triumphantly, "but I can, though. When Mr. Martin went to start up the engine, he pushed them leads into his pocket, careless-like, and when he pulled out his handkercher to wipe the oil off his fingers, them leads falls out on the grass. And I picks 'em up, seeing as he wasn't likely to be a-wantin' of 'em and I drops 'em into my little bag, what I always carried, being a tidy-minded man and thinkin' as a bit on 'em might come in useful one day for a motor-bike or such-like. And there they lays to this day, if they ain't been used for nothin' since."

"I'd like to have a look at them."

"Nothing easier," said Mr. Polwhistle, producing a small tool-bag and routing among a quantity of miscellaneous odds and ends. "Nothing easier, and here they do be, which just shows you what it is to be a tidy-minded man."

Wimsey took the pair of leads from his hands.

"H'm—yes—they seem to be fused together just where they pass under the clip." He jerked the wires apart. "Nothing wrong with the insulation, though, apparently. Hullo! hullo!"

He ran a finger lightly along one of the leads.

"Here's your trouble," he said.

Mr. Polwhistle also ran his finger along and then withdrew it with a hasty exclamation.

"That's pretty sharp," he muttered. "What is it?"

"I suggest that it's the business end of a sewing-needle," said Wimsey. "Give us a sharp pen-knife, and we'll soon see."

When the insulation was opened up the cause of the short-circuit was abundantly plain. A needle had been passed through the lead and broken off short, so as to leave no visible trace of its presence. When the two leads were in place side by side, it was clear that the needle would pass through both, thus effectively bridging the circuit and shorting the spark.

"Well, there now!" said Mr. Polwhistle. "To think of that! That's a nice, dirty trick to play on a gentleman. Who could a-done it beats me. How was it you missed seeing them two leads skewered together that way, Tom?"

"Nobody could possibly see it when it was in place," said Wimsey. "It would be pushed up under the clip."

"And Mr. Martin jerking the leads out that sudden," put in Tom, "it stands to reason I couldn't a-seen it. Of course, if I'd had 'em in my hands afterwards—"

He gazed reproachfully at Mr. Polwhistle, who ignored the gaze.

"It's a wonder to me," said Mr. Polwhistle, "how you came to think of such a thing, my lord."

"I've seen it done before. It's a very handy way of holding up a motor-cyclist at the beginning of a race, for example."

"And when you came here asking about them leads, did you expect to find that needle there, my lord?"

"I didn't, Tom. I'd made sure I shouldn't find it. I came here on purpose to prove it wasn't there. Look here, you two, don't say a word about this to anybody."

"Not, my lord? But we did surely ought to find out what young devil it is that was monkeying about with the gentleman's car."

"No, I'll take the thing up myself if it's necessary. But it's possible that this— trick may have been played by somebody connected with that business up at the Flat-Iron, and it's best not talked about. You see? Somebody who didn't want Mr. Martin to go to Wilvercombe that morning."

"I see, my lord. Very good. We won't say a word. But that's a queer thing, none the more for that."

"It is," said Wimsey, "very queer."

It was rather queerer than Mr. Polwhistle quite realised, though a peculiar glint in Tom's eye suggested that he at least was beginning to appreciate its full oddity. A needle thrust through the H.T. leads of a two-cylinder car does not produce intermittent firing or erratic running: it stops the ignition dead. Yet on the Wednesday, Mr. Martin's Morgan had been running (though not well) up to the moment of his return to Hinks's Lane. And to Wimsey, who knew that Martin was Weldon, the whole thing seemed doubly inexplicable. Why had Weldon gone out of his way to hire a Morgan for his little trip when, with a tent and luggage to carry, he would surely have found a larger vehicle more convenient? Was it another coincidence that he should have particularly asked for a two-cylinder vehicle, which could be put completely out of action with one sewing-needle? True, a Morgan pays a smaller tax than a four-wheeled car, but then, Weldon was not paying the tax. It might cost a little less to hire, but, under the circumstances, why should Weldon skimp himself on a week's car-hire?

And yet—and yet—whichever way you took it, it was obviously to everybody's interest to get Mr. Weldon away to Wilvercombe, and not keep him hanging about Hinks's Lane. Could it be a coincidence that some practical joker had chosen to put the Morgan out of action at that particular moment? Surely not. But then, who had done it? Somebody who wanted a witness at Darley? Somebody who did not want Weldon to carry out his investigations in Wilvercombe? And why had Weldon complained of bad running the day before? Another coincidence? An intermittent choke, perhaps, which had blown itself out since? Perhaps.

One thing was certain: that Henry Weldon, arriving incognito in dyed hair and dark spectacles to carry on a bit of detective work on his own, had contrived to involve himself in a tangle of coincidence and conjecture which looked almost like the work of a malignant and interfering demon.

Another thing seemed certain, too: that every theory Wimsey had so far formed about the case was utterly and madly wide of the mark.

30

THE EVIDENCE OF THE GENTLEMAN'S GENTLEMAN

Just so they crossed, and turned, and came again.
—*The Second Brother*

SATURDAY, 4 JULY

Mr. Mervyn Bunter sat in the bedroom of a cheap hotel in Bloomsbury, keeping his eye on a rather dusty window, adorned with a rather grubby curtain, which he could see just across a very dingy courtyard. It was Mr. Bunter's fourth residence in as many days, and he felt that, if this went on much longer, it would be very difficult for him to keep out of view. His first night had been spent in the street, watching the door of a common lodging-house in the Whitechapel district. Thence he had followed his quarry to a gloomy little boarding-house in Brixton. On this occasion he had found a night's lodging over a tobacconist's opposite, and by dint of returning very late and getting up very early, had contrived to keep on Mr. Bright's trail the following morning. The chase had then led him all round the more dreary parts of London, following a continual succession of trams and omnibuses. This had been very difficult. Once or twice he had ventured on the same vehicle with Bright, but a dread of being spotted had obliged him to do most of his sleuthing in taxis, which, in that part of the town, were apt to be hard to find and painfully conspicuous when found. The night had been dismally spent in the crypt of St. Martin's-in-the-Fields. Now here they were, and Bunter hoped that the ordeal would not last much longer. He had bought himself a suit of horrible cheap serge, which it gave him acute agony to wear, and he had also purchased a disgusting bowler of curly shape and heavy quality—also a check cap, a soft hat and a subfusc overcoat. Each day he had endeavoured to alter his appearance by successively assuming these repellent garments, carrying the others about with him in paper parcels, until at last he had felt that the perpetual presence of a man with a paper parcel would alarm the fugitive, and had relieved his arm and his mind by depositing the loathly bowler under the table in an eating-house and leaving it to its fate. Now, with a pair of pyjamas in one pocket of the overcoat and a razor and tooth-brush in the other along with the cap, he sat, felt hat in hand, ready to dart out as soon as Bright showed any signs of moving.

During these last four days, Bright had merely wandered. He had entered no hairdresser's shop and made no attempt to get work. He seemed to be merely filling in time, or else deliberately confusing his trail. He had gone to a Talkie once or twice, had visited the British Museum, sat for a whole afternoon on a bench in Hyde Park. He had spoken to nobody, except to 'bus-conductors, tram-conductors, waitresses and other harmless, necessary persons. At present he was sitting at his bedroom window, reading a book by Edgar Wallace which Bunter had seen him purchase the day before at Leicester Square Tube Station.

Suddenly, as Bunter watched him, he shut up the book and stepped back from the window. Peering across the courtyard, Bunter saw him stooping, moving about, raising and lowering his arms in a familiar series of actions. Bunter, who had performed these actions many hundreds of times, was not at a loss. The man was folding and packing pyjamas and other wearing apparel. Bunter hastened down to the office, handed over the key of his room (there was no bill for, being without luggage, he had paid for his bed and breakfast in advance), and stepped out into the street. Here he was fortunate enough to find a cruising taxi with an intelligent-looking driver, who was ready enough to engage in a little detective work. The street was a cul-de-sac and Bunter, getting into the taxi, was driven out into the main road. Here he got out and entered a newspaper shop, leaving the taximan to watch the entrance to the cul-de-sac. Presently, while Bunter, standing just within the doorway, pretended to be absorbed in the morning paper, he saw the driver raise his hand as a signal. A green taxi had driven into the cul-de-sac. So far, so good.

"Go slowly along to the corner," said Bunter, "and stand there till the taxi comes out again. If it's the right man, I'll tap on the glass. Then follow him, but not too close. Only don't lose him in the traffic."

"Right you are. Divorce, eh?"

"Murder," said Bunter.

"Crikey!" said the driver. "Police, eh?"

Bunter nodded.

"Gorblimey," said the driver. "You don't look it. P'raps you don't mean to. Here we are. Taxi's at the 'otel door. Keep your 'ed down—I'll tell you when 'e comes out."

So saying, the taximan descended in a leisurely way from his perch and pulled open the bonnet of his machine. A passing policeman gave him a glance, nodded and strode heavily by.

"Just a-coming out now," said the driver, thrusting his head in at the window, and then, in a louder tone: "All right, guv'nor—jest a loose connection. She'll start first swing now."

He crawled up, just as the green taxi swung out of the cul-de-sac. Bunter, peering from behind his newspaper, recognised the pale face of Mr. Bright and tapped on the glass. The green taxi passed within a foot of them. Bunter's taxi circled in the road and swung in thirty yards behind.

The green taxi wriggled through some dismal by-streets, emerged into Judd Street and went ahead through Brunswick Square into Guilford Street and down Lamb's Conduit Street and Red Lion Street. It turned to the right into Holborn, then to the left again into Kingsway, and then circled across into Great Queen Street and Long Acre. The following taxi kept it in view without very great difficulty till at last it turned to the left down one of the narrow streets, encumbered with huge drays and stationary carts, which lead down into Covent Garden. At the entrance to the market the green taxi pulled up.

Bunter's taxi was one of the new and superior sort, which have an electric speaking-tube which really works. Bunter pressed the button and addressed his driver.

"If he gets out here, drive past very slowly round that big cart. I shall slip out. Don't look round or take any notice. I'm leaving a ten-bob note on the seat. Go straight on through the market."

The driver's head nodded assent. From the left-hand window, Bunter saw Bright standing on the pavement, settling his fare. Bunter went on his way, and as the taxi passed on the far side of the big cart, he slipped quickly to the pavement. A fruiterer's man, observing this manoeuvre, turned sharply to shout to the driver that his fare was bilking him, but at that moment the hand of the faithful taximan came round and slammed the door shut. The fruiterer's man stood staring, while Bunter, who had exchanged the felt hat for the cap in the taxi, dodged round in front of the cart to look for Bright.

To his great delight he saw Bright standing on the kerb, watching with a pleased air the steady retreat of Bunter's taxi. After a quick scrutiny of his surroundings, the man appeared satisfied that he was not being followed and set off, briskly, suitcase in hand, towards the market. Bunter took up the trail, squelching his way among the oddments of fruit and cabbage-leaves. The chase led through the market, out into Tavistock Street and down towards the Strand. Here Bright took a 'bus going West, Bunter pursuing in a fresh taxi. The new trail led only as far as Charing Cross, where Bright got out and hastened into the station-yard. Bunter, hurriedly flinging a florin to his driver, dived in after him.

Bright led the way into the Charing Cross Hotel; Bunter was forced this time to follow closely, lest he should lose his prey. Bright went up to the desk and spoke to the reception-clerk. After a short pause and the display of a visiting-card, a parcel was handed over. Upon receiving it and putting it away in his suit-case, Bright turned sharp round and walked back to the door, passing Bunter within a couple of feet. Their eyes met, but Bright's showed no recognition. He went straight out into the station-yard again.

From now onwards it was hit or miss for Bunter. He had been seen once and it was now more than ever his business to keep out of sight. He waited for a few agonising moments before following, and was just in time to see Bright vanishing down the subway to the Underground.

At this moment, Bunter would have given much for his trusty bowler. He did his best, by again exchanging the cap for the hat as he ran across the yard, and struggling into the subfusc overcoat. It is not necessary to pursue the involved underground journey that occupied the next hour. At the end of it, hare and hound emerged in good order at Piccadilly, having boxed the compass pretty successfully in the interval. The next move was to the Corner House, where Bright took the lift.

Now, at the Corner House there are three large floors, and each large floor has two doorways. Yet to get into the same lift as Bright was to challenge disaster. Bunter, like a baffled cat that sees its mouse vanish down a hole, stood and watched the ascending lift. Then he moved to the centre counter and stood, apparently inspecting the array of cakes and sweetmeats, but in reality keeping a sharp look-out on all the lift-doors and the two marble staircases. After ten minutes he felt that he might assume Bright's purpose to be genuinely that of getting refreshment. He made for the nearest staircase and went up it like a lamp-lighter. The lift passed him on a downward journey before he reached the first floor, and he was assailed by a horrible conviction that it was bearing Bright away with it. No matter, the die was cast now. He pushed open the swing door on the first floor and began his slow stroll among the crowded tables.

The sight of bewildered customers looking for a seat is no unusual one in the Corner House. Nobody paid any attention to Bunter until he had made the circuit of the big room and satisfied himself that Bright was not among those present. He went out by the farther door, where he was challenged by the inquiry whether he had been served. He replied that he was looking for a friend and ran on up to the second floor.

This room was the exact twin of the first, except that, instead of a male orchestra in evening dress playing *My Canary has Circles under His Eyes*, it possessed a female orchestra in blue playing excerpts from *The Gondoliers*. Bunter pushed his way slowly through the throng until—his staid heart giving a sudden leap beneath the deplorable blue serge waistcoat—he caught sight of a familiar sandy head and crooked pair of shoulders. Bright was there, seated at a table containing three elderly women, and peacefully eating a grilled chop.

Bunter gazed desperately about him. At first it seemed hopeless to find a seat anywhere near, but at length he espied a girl making-up her face and dabbling at her hair preparatory to leaving. He made a dart for the table and secured the reversion of her chair. He was some time catching the eye of the waitress and ordering a cup of coffee; fortunately Bright seemed to be in no particular hurry with his chop. Bunter asked for the bill as soon as the coffee was brought, and sat patiently, his useful newspaper well spread out before him.

After what seemed an interminable delay, Bright finished his lunch, looked at his watch, called for his bill and rose. Bunter was four behind him in the queue at the pay-desk, and squeezed through the door in time to see the sandy head disappearing down the stairs. At this happy moment, the lift arrived. Bunter bundled into it, and was shot out on the ground floor well ahead of the quarry. He watched Bright out, took up the trail and, after a few minutes of hectic traffic-dodging, found himself in a cinema in the Haymarket, purchasing a ticket for the stalls.

Bright took a seat in the third row of the three-and-six pennies. Bunter, hastily whispering to the attendant that he didn't care to be too far forward, managed to slip in a couple of rows behind him. Now he could breathe again. From where he sat, he could see the top of Bright's head, outlined against the comparative brightness at the foot of the screen. Ignoring the drama of Love and Passion which shimmered and squeaked its mechanical way from the first misunderstanding to the last lingering kiss, Bunter fixed his eyes on that head with such concentration that the tears stole down his cheeks.

The film shuddered to its close. The lights went up. Bright stood suddenly upright and pushed his way out into the gangway. Bunter prepared to follow, but Bright, instead of making for the nearest exit, merely walked across and passed behind a discreet curtain over which was blazoned in blue fire the legend GENTLEMEN.

Bunter sank down again and waited. Other gentlemen passed in and out, but no Bright returned. Fear smote Bunter. Was there a way out through the cloak-room? The lights dimmed and blacked out, and a Comic started. Bunter rose up, tripping over the feet of three sniggering girls and an irritable old man, and sneaked gently down the gangway.

As he did so the curtain leading to "GENTLEMEN" was drawn aside and a man came out. Bunter stared at him as he passed in the soft, thick twilight, but the sharp peak of the silhouette told him that this was a bearded man. He passed Bunter with a muttered apology and went on up the gangway. Bunter proceeded on his way down but, by some instinct, turned at the curtained door and looked back.

He saw the back of the bearded man, outlined against the sudden blue daylight, passing through an exit, and remembered how Wimsey had once said to him: "Any fool can disguise his face, but it takes a genius to disguise a back." He had not followed that back through London for five days without knowing every line of it. In a moment he was hurrying up the gangway and out through the exit. Beard or no beard, this was his man.

Two more taxis and then a clear run out to Kensington. This time, Bright appeared to be really going somewhere. His taxi drew up at a neat house in a good quarter; he got out and let himself in with a latch-key. Bunter went on to the next corner and there interrogated his driver.

"Did you see the number of the house they stopped at?"

"Yes, sir. Number 17."

"Thanks."

"Divorce, sir?" asked the man, with a grin.

"Murder," said Bunter.

"Crikey!" This appeared to be the natural reaction to murder. "Well," said the taximan, " 'ope 'e swings for it," and drove off.

Bunter glanced about him. He dared not pass Number 17. Bright might still be on the watch, and both the cap and the felt hat were now, he felt, war-worn veterans of whom nothing more could be asked in the way of disguise. He saw a chemist's shop and went in.

"Can you tell me," he asked, "who lives at No. 17?"

"Why, yes," said the chemist, "gentleman of the name of Morecambe."

"Morecambe?" A great piece of jig-saw seemed to fall into place in Bunter's mind with an almost audible click. "Littlish gentleman with one shoulder a bit higher than the other?"

"That's right."

"Reddish hair."

"Yes, sir; reddish hair and beard."

"Oh, he wears a beard?"

"Oh, yes, sir. Gentleman in the City, he is. Lived here as long as I can remember. Very pleasant gentleman. Did you want to know—?"

"Yes," said Bunter. "The fact is, I heard there might be a vacancy for a gentleman's personal attendant at No. 17, and I thought I'd like to know what the family was like before applying for it."

"Oh, I see. Yes. You'd find it a nice family. Quiet. No children. Mrs. Morecambe is a nice lady. Good-looking in her time I should say. Used to be on the stage, I'm told, but that must have been a good long time ago. Two maids kept and everything quite as you might wish to find it."

Bunter expressed his gratitude and left the shop to send a telegram to Lord Peter.

The chase was ended.

31

THE EVIDENCE OF THE HABERDASHER'S ASSISTANT

Ha! well! what next?
You are the cupbearer of richest joy—
But it was a report, a lie.
—*The Second Brother*

MONDAY, 6 JULY

"I look at it this way," said Superintendent Glaisher. "If this here Bright is Morecambe, and Mrs. Morecambe is in cahoots with Weldon, then, likewise, Weldon and Bright—so to call him—are in cahoots together."

"Undoubtedly," said Wimsey, "but if you think that this identification is going to make life one grand, sweet song for you, you are mistaken. All it has done so far is to bust up every conclusion we have so far come to."

"Yes, my lord; undoubtedly the thing still has a hitch in it. Still, every little helps, and this time we've got more than a little to go on with. Suppose we work out where we stand. First of all, if Bright is Morecambe, he isn't a hairdresser; therefore he had no legitimate call to buy that razor; therefore his tale about the razor is all eyewash, like we always thought it was; therefore, humanly speaking there's not much doubt that Paul Alexis didn't commit suicide, but was murdered."

"Exactly," said Wimsey, "and since we have devoted a great deal of time and thought to the case on the assumption that it was a murder, it's a convenience to know that the assumption is probably correct."

"So it is. Well, now, if Weldon and Morecambe are both in this together, it's likely that the motive for the murder is what we thought—getting hold of Mrs. W.'s money—or isn't it?"

"It's likely," agreed Wimsey.

"Then what's all this Bolshevik business got to do with it?" demanded Inspector Umpelty.

"Lots," said Wimsey. "Look here; I'm going to offer you two more identifications. First of all, I suggest that Morecambe was the bearded friend who came to stay with Weldon at Fourways Farm at the end of February. And secondly, I suggest that Morecambe was the bearded gentleman who approached Mr. Sullivan of Wardour Street and asked him for the photograph of a Russian-looking girl. It is interesting that Mr. Horrock's cultivated theatrical mind should have associated him immediately with Richard III."

Inspector Umpelty looked puzzled, but the Superintendent smacked his hand on the table.

"The hunchback!" he cried.

"Yes—but they seldom play Richard as a real hunchback nowadays. A slight suggestion of crookedness is what they usually give you—just that scarcely perceptible twistiness of shoulder that Morecambe has about him."

"Of course, that's plain enough, now we know about the beard," said Glaisher. "But why the photograph?"

"Let's try and put the story together in the right order, as far as we've got it," suggested Wimsey. "First of all, here is Weldon, over head and ears in debt, and raising money against his expectations from his mother. Very well. Now, early this year, Mrs. Weldon comes to Wilvercombe, and begins to take a great deal of interest in Paul Alexis. In February, she definitely announces that she means to marry Alexis, and possibly she is foolish enough to admit that, if she does marry him, she will leave him all her money. Almost immediately after this announcement, Morecambe comes to stay at Weldon's farm. And within a week or two, the strange coded letters with the foreign stamps begin to arrive for Alexis."

"That's clear enough."

"Now, Alexis has always hinted to people that there is a mystery about his birth. He fancies that he is of noble Russian descent. I suggest that the first letter—"

"One minute, my lord. Who do you suppose wrote those letters?"

"I *think* Morecambe wrote them, and got them posted by some friend in Warsaw. As I see it, Morecambe is the brains of the conspiracy. He writes his first letter, no doubt in plain English, hinting at Imperialist activities in Russia and grandiose prospects for Paul Alexis, if he can prove his descent—but, of course, there must be complete secrecy about the whole thing."

"Why the secrecy?"

"To preserve the romantic atmosphere. Alexis, poor egg, swallows this, hook, line and sinker. He promptly writes back telling the so-called Boris everything he knows or imagines about himself. The code is henceforth used, of course, to keep Alexis in the proper frame of mind and give him a nice toy to play with. Then, from the little bits of family tradition that Alexis supplies, 'Boris' (that is, Morecambe) builds up a suitable genealogical fantasy to fit in with these data, and outlines a marvellous plot to place Alexis on the Imperial throne of Russia. Meanwhile, Alexis reads books about Russian history, and obligingly assists his murderer to bait and arm the trap. Eventually, Boris tells him that the conspiracy is nearly ready to take effect; and that is when we find Alexis indulging in mysterious hints and prophecies of his forthcoming apotheosis."

"Just a minute," said Glaisher. "I should have thought that the simplest way for Morecambe would have been to get Alexis to break off with Mrs. Weldon on the grounds that he had to go to Russia and be a Tsar. Surely that would have attained the object of the plot without bumping off the poor little blighter."

"Well, would it?" said Wimsey. "In the first place, I rather imagine that Mrs. Weldon's romantic reaction to a notion of that kind would have been to hand over large sums of money to Alexis for the Imperial war-chest, which would hardly have suited Messrs. Weldon and Morecambe. Secondly, if Alexis did break off the engagement and they trusted to that—what would happen next? They couldn't go on for the remainder of all their lives writing code-letters about imaginary conspiracies. Some time or other, Alexis would wake up to the fact that the plot was never going to materialise. He would tell Mrs. Weldon and in all probability the *status quo* would be restored. And the lady would be keener than ever on the marriage if she thought her fiancé really was the unacknowledged Tsar of all the Russias. No; the safest way was to tell Alexis to keep the whole thing absolutely secret, and then, when the time came, they could wipe him out finally and completely."

"Yes—I see that."

"Now we come to Leila Garland. I don't think there is any doubt that Alexis deliberately pushed her off on to our conceited young friend, da Soto—though naturally neither da Soto nor she would admit that possibility for a moment. I fancy Antoine has got the right idea about that; he is probably an observer of considerable experience in these matters. Leila would be a very dangerous person if she were allowed to know anything about the pretended plot. She would be bound to talk, and they didn't want talk. We've got to remember that the object of all this business was to stage a suicide. Young emperors on the point of leading successful revolutions do not commit suicide. To tell Leila about the plot was to tell the world: therefore, Leila must be got rid of, because, if she remained closely in contact with Alexis, it would be almost impossible to keep her in ignorance."

"Sounds as though young Alexis was a bit of a blackguard," said Inspector Umpelty. "First, he chucks his girl. Secondly, he leads poor old Mrs. Weldon up the garden, by pretending to go on with an engagement he doesn't mean to carry out."

"No," said Wimsey. "You don't allow for the Imperial outlook. A prince in exile may form irregular attachments, but, when the call comes to him to take up his imperial station, all personal ties must be sacrificed to his public duty. A mere kept woman, like Leila, can be simply dismissed or handed over to somebody else. A person to whom he is bound by more honourable ties will also have to be sacrificed, but with more ceremony. We do not know, and we never shall know, exactly what Alexis meant to do about Mrs. Weldon. We have her word for it that he tried to prepare her for some grand and surprising development in the near future, though, naturally, she put the wrong interpretation on the thing. I imagine that what Alexis intended to do was to write her a letter, after his departure for Warsaw, telling her what had happened to him and offering her his hospitality at his Imperial court. The whole affair would have been surrounded with a halo of romance and splendour and self-sacrifice, and no doubt Mrs. Weldon would have enjoyed it down to the ground. There's one thing: although, before all this Russian business started, Alexis had Mrs. Weldon completely under his thumb, he apparently always refused to take any large sums of money from her—and that, I think, is greatly to his credit, and shows that he had the instincts of a gentleman, if not necessarily of a prince."

"That's true," said Glaisher. "I suppose, if the plot had never been started, he would have married her."

"Oh, yes, I should think so. He'd have married her and done his duty by her according to his own lights, which were probably—well, continental. He would have been a charming husband to her and kept a mistress in a discreet and decent manner."

Inspector Umpelty seemed disposed to quarrel with the term "decent," but Wimsey hurried on with his argument.

"I fancy, too, that Alexis may have shown a little reluctance to take this course with Leila and Mrs. Weldon. He may have been really fond of Leila; or he may have felt uncomfortable about letting Mrs. Weldon down. So that was why they invented Feodora."

"And who was Feodora?"

"Feodora was no doubt supposed to be the lady of lofty lineage destined to be the bride of the new Tsar Pavlo Alexeivitch. What was easier than to go to a theatrical agent, find the photograph of a not-too-well-known lady of Russian extraction, and send it to Alexis as the portrait of the Princess Feodora, the lovely lady who was waiting and working for him in exile until the time should come for her to take her place beside him on the Imperial throne? Those blessed romances that Alexis was so fond of are full of that kind of thing. There would be letters, perhaps, from Feodora, full of tender anticipation. She would be already in love with the Grand-Duke Pavlo from all she had heard of him. The glamour of the whole idea would bewitch him. And besides, it would be his duty to his people to marry Feodora. How could he hesitate? A glance at that very beautiful face, crowned with its regal head-dress of pearls—"

"Oh!" said Glaisher. "Yes, of course. That would be one reason why they hit on that particular photograph."

"Of course. No doubt the pearls were merely the best Woolworth, like the whole pathetic illusion, but these things serve their purpose, Glaisher, they serve their purpose. My God, Glaisher—when you think of that poor silly devil, going to his death on a lonely rock, with his brain spinning with the idea of being crowned Emperor—"

Wimsey broke off, shaken by an unwonted vehemence of feeling. The two policemen shuffled their feet sympathetically.

"Well, it does seem a shame, my lord, and that's a fact," said Glaisher. "Let's hope he died quick, without knowing any better."

"Ah!" said Wimsey, "but how did he die? That's the snag, you know. Well, never mind that for the moment. What next? Oh, the three hundred pounds in gold. That's a funny little incident, and very nearly upset the conspiracy altogether.

"I can't believe that that was any part of the plot as originally worked out. Morecambe couldn't have foreseen the opportunity of collecting that gold. I think that must have been Paul Alexis' own contribution to the romance. He had probably read in books about gold—and about its passing current everywhere, and all that—and thought it would somehow be a fine thing to set out to conquer a throne with a beltful of gold. It was ridiculous, of course—an absurd little sum, bulky and awkward to carry about—but it was Gold. Gold has its glitter, you know. As somebody says, 'the glitter is the gold.' That sounds like relativity physics, but it's psychological fact. If you were a romantic young prince, Glaisher, or thought you were, would you rather pay your bills with a few dirty bits of paper, or with this?"

He put his hand in his pocket and drew out a handful of gold sovereigns. They rolled ringing over the table as he threw them down, and Glaisher and Umpelty flung out eager hands to catch them as they spun away in the lamplight. They picked them up and weighed them in their palms; they held them between their fingers, passing inquisitive fingers along the milled edges and over the smooth relief of the gleaming George and Dragon.

"Yes," said Wimsey, "they feel pleasant, don't they? There are ten of them there, and they're worth no more than paper pounds,[1] and to me they're actually worth nothing, because, being a tom-fool, I can't bring myself to spend them. But they're gold. I wouldn't mind possessing £300 worth of them, though they might weigh five pounds avoirdupois and be an infernal nuisance. But the queer thing is this—that that extra five pounds of weight just disturbed the very delicate balance between the corpse and the water. The specific gravity of a dead body is *just* less than sufficient to sink it—but only just. A very heavy pair of boots or a belt stuffed with gold is enough to carry it down and wedge it among the Grinder rocks—as you know to your cost, Umpelty. It would have been uncommonly awkward for the conspirators if Alexis had never been found. In time, Mrs. Weldon would have come to believe in his death, I daresay—but she might have squandered a fortune first, in hunting for him."

"It's a queer story altogether," said Glaisher, "and what nobody that hadn't been through it all from the beginning as you might say would hardly be disposed to believe. But now, my lord, allowing that it was all worked out as you say, how about the murder?"

"Exactly. As regards the murder I frankly admit we're not much further on than before. The preliminaries are all easy enough. First of all, somebody must have come along to have a look at the place. I don't quite know who that was, but I think I can guess. Somebody who already knew the lie of the land, from having stayed here before. Somebody who had a car to spin about the country in. Somebody who had a very good excuse for being in the neighbourhood and respectable friends whose guests were above suspicion."

"Mrs. Morecambe!"

"Just so. Mrs. Morecambe. Possibly Mr. Morecambe also. We can soon find out whether that delightful couple spent a week-end at the Heathbury Vicarage any time within the last few months."

---

[1] The acute reader will discern that at the date of this story, Great Britain had not yet gone off the Gold Standard.

"Yes, they did," put in Umpelty. "The lady was here for a fortnight at the end of February and her husband came down for one week-end. They told us that when we made our inquiries, but we didn't attach any importance to it at the time."

"Of course not. Very well. Then, at the moment when everything is ready to poop off, the rest of the gang arrive. Morecambe gets himself up as a hairdresser and establishes his identity round about the neighbourhood. He has to do that, because he wants to purchase a razor in a way which it is difficult to trace. You may say, why a razor at all, when they must have known that Alexis didn't shave? Well, I can imagine why. It's quieter than a pistol and it's a typical suicide's weapon. And it's very safe and sure, and much handier to carry about than, say a carving-knife. And if any question was raised about it, Morecambe could always come forward with a convincing story about how he had given the razor to Alexis."

"Ah! I was thinking about that. Would he have come forward, do you suppose, if you hadn't put that bit in the paper?"

"Difficult to say. But I imagine that he would have waited to see how things went. He would probably have attended the inquest, as a casual spectator, and then if the coroner showed any signs of not accepting the suicide theory, he would have risen up and put the matter beyond doubt with a few well-chosen words. You see, the beauty of his itinerant hairdresser impersonation was that it afforded him an excellent excuse for appearing and disappearing like a Cheshire cat, and also changing his name. By the way, I think we shall find that he really did live in Manchester at some time or another, and so knew just how much dope to dole out about derelict streets and departed hairdressers' shops in that city."

"I take it, then, that he wears a beard in ordinary life."

"Oh, yes. He just shaved it off when he began his impersonation. Then, when he went back to London, he had only to get a false beard sent to him at a hotel under a different name, and wear it for the brief period of his taxi-ride to Kensington. If the attendant at the picture-palace happened to notice a gentleman putting on a false beard in the cloak-room—which he may not have done—it would not be his business to interfere, and Morecambe had done his very best to throw off any shadowers. If Bunter hadn't been uncommonly persevering and uncommonly quick, he'd have lost the trail twenty times over. As it was, he very nearly missed Morecambe in the cinema. Supposing Bunter had followed Morecambe into the cloak-room. Morecambe would have postponed the beard business and there would have been another chase, but by having the wits to keep outside, he gave Morecambe the impression that the coast was clear. Scotland Yard is keeping an eye on Morecambe's house now, but I expect they will find that the gentleman is ill in bed, being attended by his devoted wife. When his beard has grown again, he will emerge; and meantime Mrs. Morecambe, who was an actress and knows something about make-up, will see to it that there is always a beard fit for inspection when the maid comes in to do the room."

"So much for Morecambe," said Glaisher. "Now, how about Weldon? We'd pretty well put him out of the thing. Now we've got to bring him back. He comes along in his Morgan, two days before the murder is due to take place, and he camps in Hinks's Lane, which somebody's been good enough to find out all about beforehand. Mrs. Morecambe, I suppose—very good. He accounts for his presence on the scene by a cock-and-bull tale about keeping an eye on his mother's love-affairs. All right. But what I want to know is, why did he come and mix himself up in the thing at all, taking all those risks? He wasn't there to do the murder, because we know where he was at 1.30, if not at 1.55, and we can't fit the times in anyhow, even supposing Perkins is a liar, which we can't prove. And he wasn't there to ride the mare down to the Flat-Iron, because we know where he was at twelve o'clock—"

"Do we?" said Harriet, gently.

She had joined the committee-meeting half-way through the session, and had been sitting quietly in an armchair, smoking with her hat on her knee.

"Yes, do we?" said Wimsey. "We thought we did when Mrs. Morecambe was supposed to be an unimpeachable witness, but do we now? I think I see a gleam in Miss Vane's eye that suggests she is about to put one over on us. Speak, I am bound to hear! What has Robert Templeton been discovering?"

"Mr. Weldon," said Harriet, "was not doing anything nefarious in Wilvercombe on Thursday, 18th. He wasn't doing anything in Wilvercombe. He never was in Wilvercombe. He didn't buy collars. He didn't go to the Winter Gardens. Mrs. Morecambe arrived alone and she left alone, and there's no evidence that Mr. Weldon was with her at any point of the journey."

"O my prophetic soul! There goes my reputation! I said that the two o'clock alibi would be broken, and it's standing like the Flat-Iron Rock. I said the Wilvercombe alibi would stand, and it has broken in pieces like a potter's vessel. I'll go no more a-sleuthing with you, fair maid. Oh, now, for ever farewell the tranquil mind! Farewell content! Farewell, Othello's occupation's gone. Are you sure about it?"

"Pretty well. I went to the men's outfitting and asked for collars like the ones my husband bought on the 18th. Had I the bill? No. What kind of collars? Well, collars, just ordinary collars. What was my husband like? I described Henry Weldon and his dark spectacles. Nobody remembered him. Would they look up the day-book? Well, they looked up the paper thing that twizzles round in the till, and found the item. Oh, yes—the assistant remembered *those* collars. Sold to a lady. A lady? Oh, yes, my sister-in-law, no doubt. I described Mrs. Morecambe. Yes, that was the lady. Was that the only sale of collars that morning? It was. Then those must be the collars. So I bought six of them—here they are— and asked whether the gentleman had been outside in the car. Gentlemen are funny about going into shops. No, no gentleman. The assistant had taken the parcel out to the car, which was empty. So then I went to the Winter Gardens. I knew, of course, that they had been asked about Weldon, but *I* asked them about Mrs. Morecambe, and I found an attendant who remembered her by her appearance and get-up, and by the fact that she had taken notes of the programme. For Weldon, naturally. After that I tried the bobby on point-duty in the Market Square. Such a nice, intelligent bobby. He remembered the car, because of the funny number, and he'd noticed there was no one in it except the lady who was driving. He'd noticed it again when it came away: still only the lady in it. So that's that. Of course, Mrs. Morecambe may have dropped Henry Weldon at some point between Darley and Wilvercombe, but as for being *in* Wilvercombe—that I'll swear he wasn't; at any rate, he didn't arrive in the Square with her, as he said."

"No," said Glaisher. "And it's pretty clear now where he was. He was riding that damned mare along the beach—out at eleven o'clock and back at 12.30, or thereabouts. But why?"

"That's clear, too. He was the Rider from the Sea. But he still didn't kill Paul Alexis. Who did?"

"Well, my lord," said Umpelty, "we'll have to go back to our first idea. Weldon brought bad news about this here conspiracy, and Alexis killed himself."

"With Morecambe's razor? No, it's all wrong, Inspector. It's all *wrong*."

"Hadn't we better ask Weldon what he knows about it all? If we confront him with what we know about Morecambe and the letter and all that, he may come clean. If he was along there at 12.15, he must have seen Alexis, anyhow."

Wimsey shook his head.

"Deep waters," he said, "deep waters. Look here! I've an idea we've been working this thing from the wrong end. If only we knew more about those papers that Alexis sent to 'Boris,' they might tell us something. Where do you suppose they are? You may say, in Warsaw—but I don't think so. I fancy Warsaw was only an accommodation address. Everything that went there probably came back to Morecambe."

"Then perhaps we'll find them in London," suggested Glaisher, hopefully.

"Very much perhaps. The man who planned this show is no fool. If he told Alexis to destroy all his papers, he'll hardly have risked keeping anything of that sort himself. But we could try. Have we enough evidence against him to justify a search-warrant?"

"Why, yes." Glaisher pondered. "If Morecambe's identified as Bright, then he's been giving false information to the police. We could detain him on suspicion and go through his place in Kensington. The London fellows are keeping tabs on him now, but we didn't want to be in too much of a hurry. We thought, maybe, the real murderer might be getting in touch with him. You see, there must be another party to the business—the chap who did the actual job, and we don't know who he is from Adam. But of course, there's this to it—the longer we leave Morecambe to himself, the more time he's got to make away with the evidence. It may be you're right, my lord, and we ought to pull him in. Only you'll bear in mind, my lord, that if we do detain him, we'll have to make a charge. There's such a thing as Habeas Corpus."

"All the same," said Wimsey, "I think you'll have to risk that. I don't suppose you'll find any papers, but you may find something else. The paper and ink used to write the letters, perhaps, and books of reference about Russia. Books aren't as easy to get rid of as papers. And we've got to find out the exact connection between Morecambe and Weldon."

"They're working on that now, my lord."

"Good. After all, people don't conspire to commit murder for the fun of the thing. Does Mrs. Weldon know anything about the Morecambes?"

"No," said Harriet. "I asked her. She's never heard of them."

"Then the connection won't go too far back. It'll belong to London or Huntingdonshire. What *is* Morecambe, by the way?"

"Described as a Commission Agent, my lord."

"Oh, is he? That's a description that hides a multitude of sins. Well, go to it, Superintendent. As for me, I'll have to do something drastic to restore my self-respect. Seeking the bubble reputation even in the cannon's mouth."

"Oh yeah?" Harriet grinned impishly. "When Lord Peter gets these fits of quotation he's usually on to something."

"Sez you," retorted Wimsey. "I am going, straight away, to make love to Leila Garland."

"Well, look out for da Soto."

"I'll chance da Soto," said Wimsey. "Bunter!"

"My lord?"

Bunter emerged from Wimsey's bedroom, looking as prim as though he had never sleuthed in a bad bowler through the purlieus of South London.

"I wish to appear in my famous impersonation of the perfect Lounge Lizard —*imitation très difficile.*"

"Very good, my lord. I suggest the fawn-coloured suit we do not care for, with the autumn-leaf socks and our out-size amber cigarette-holder."

"As you will, Bunter; as you will. We must stoop to conquer."

He kissed his hand gallantly to the assembly and vanished into his inner chamber.

32

THE EVIDENCE OF THE FAMILY TREE

A hundred years hence, or, it may be, more,
I shall return and take my dukedom back.
—*Death's Jest-Book*

MONDAY, 6 JULY

The conquest of Leila Garland followed the usual course. Wimsey pursued her into a tea-shop, cut her out neatly from the two girl-friends who accompanied her, fed her, took her to the pictures and carried her off to the Bellevue for a cocktail.

The young lady showed an almost puritanical discretion in clinging to the public rooms of that handsome hotel, and drove Wimsey almost to madness by the refinement of her table-manners. Eventually, however, he manoeuvred her into an angle of the lounge behind a palm-tree, where they could not be overlooked and where they were far enough from the orchestra to hear each other speak. The orchestra was one of the more infuriating features of the Bellevue, and kept up an incessant drivel of dance-tunes from four in the afternoon till ten at night. Miss Garland awarded it a moderate approval, but indicated that it did not quite reach the standard of the orchestra in which Mr. da Soto played a leading part.

Wimsey gently led the conversation to the distressing publicity which Miss Garland had been obliged to endure in connection with the death of Alexis. Miss Garland agreed that it had not been nice at all. Mr. da Soto had been very much upset. A gentleman did not like his girl-friend to have to undergo so much unpleasant questioning.

Lord Peter Wimsey commended Miss Garland on the discretion she had shown throughout.

Of course, said Leila, Mr. Alexis was a dear boy, and always a perfect gentleman. And most devoted to her. But hardly a manly man. A girl could not help preferring manly men, who had *done* something. Girls were like that! Even though a man might be of very good family and not *obliged* to do anything he might still *do* things, might he not? (Languishing glance at Lord Peter.) That was the kind of man Miss Garland liked. It was, she thought, much finer to be a nobly-born person who *did* things than a nobly-born person who only *talked* about nobility.

"But was Alexis nobly born?" inquired Wimsey.

"Well, he *said* he was—but how is a girl to know? I mean, it's easy to talk, isn't it? Paul—that is, Mr. Alexis—used to tell wonderful stories about himself, but it's *my* belief he was making it all up. He was such a boy for romances and story-books. But I said to him, 'What's the good of it?' I said. 'Here you are,' I said, 'not earning half as much money as some people I could name, and what good does it do, even if you're the Tsar of Russia?' I said."

"Did he say he was the Tsar of Russia?"

"Oh, no—he only said that if his great-great grandmother or somebody had married somebody he might have been somebody very important, but what I said was 'What's the good of saying If,' I said. 'And anyhow,' I said, 'they've done away with all these royalties now,' I said, 'so what are you going to get out of it anyway?' He made me tired, talking about his great-grandmother, and in the end he shut up and didn't say anything more about it. I suppose he tumbled to it that a girl couldn't be terribly interested in people's great-grandmothers."

"Who did he think his great-grandmother was, then?"

"I'm sure *I* don't know. He did go on so. He wrote it all down for me one day, but I said to him, 'You make my head ache,' I said, 'and besides, from what you say, none of your people were any better than they should have been,' I said, 'so I don't see what you've got to boast about. It doesn't sound very respectable to me,' I said, 'and if princesses with plenty of money can't keep respectable,' I said, 'I don't see why anybody should put any blame on girls who have to earn their own living.' That's what I told him."

"Very true indeed," said Wimsey. "He must have had a bit of a mania about it."

"Loopy," said Miss Garland, allowing the garment of refinement to slip aside for a moment. "I mean to say, I think he must have been a little silly about it, don't you?"

"He seems to have given more thought to the thing than it was worth. Wrote it all down, did he?"

"Yes, he did. And then one day he came bothering about it again. Asked me if I'd still got the paper he'd written. 'I'm sure I don't know,' I said, 'I'm not so frightfully interested in it as all that,' I said. 'Do you think I keep every bit of your handwriting?' I said, 'like the heroines in story-books?' I said. 'Because,' I said, 'let me tell you I don't,' I said. 'Anything that's *worth* keeping, I'll keep, but not rubbishing bits of paper.'"

Wimsey remembered that Alexis had offended Leila towards the end of their connection by a certain lack of generosity.

" 'If you want things kept,' I said, 'why don't you give them to that old woman that's so struck on you?' I said. 'If you're going to marry her,' I said, 'she's the right person to give things to,' I said, 'if you want them kept.' And he said he particularly didn't want the paper kept, and I said, 'Well, then, what are you worrying about?' I said. So he said, if I hadn't kept it, that was all right, then, and I said I reely didn't know if I'd kept it or not, and he said, yes, but he wanted the paper burnt and I wasn't to tell anybody about what he'd said—about his great-grandmother, I mean—and I said, 'If you think I've nothing better to talk to my friends about than you and your great-grandmother,' I said, 'you're mistaken,' I said. Only fancy! Well, of course, after that, we weren't such friends as we had been—at least, I wasn't, though I will say he always was very fond of me. But I couldn't stand the way he went on. Silly, I call it."

"And *had* you burnt the paper?"

"Why, I'm sure I don't know. You're nearly as bad as he is, going on about the paper. What does the stupid paper matter, anyhow?"

"Well," said Wimsey, "I'm inquisitive about papers. Still, if you've burnt it, you've burnt it. It's a pity. If you could have found that paper, it might be worth—"

The beautiful eyes of Leila directed their beams upon him like a pair of swivelling head-lamps rounding a corner on a murky night.

"Yes?" breathed Leila.

"It might be worth having a look at," replied Wimsey, coolly. "Perhaps if you had a hunt among your odds-and-ends, you know—"

Leila shrugged her shoulders. This sounded troublesome.

"I can't see what you want that old bit of paper for."

"Nor do I, till I see it. But we might have a shot at looking for it, eh, what?" He smiled. Leila smiled. She felt she had grasped the idea.

"What? You and me? Oh, *well!*—but I don't see that I could exactly take you round to my place, *could* I? I mean to say—"

"Oh, that'll be all right," said Wimsey, swiftly. "You're surely not afraid of *me*. You see, I'm trying to *do* something, and I want your help."

"I'm sure, anything I can do—provided it's nothing Mr. da Soto would object to. He's a terribly jealous boy, you know."

"I should be just the same in his place. Perhaps he would like to come too and help hunt for the paper?"

Leila smiled and said she did not think that would be necessary, and the interview ended, where it was in any case doomed to end, in Leila's crowded and untidy apartment.

Drawers, bags, boxes, overflowing with intimate and multifarious litter which piled itself on the bed, streamed over the chairs and swirled ankle-deep upon the floor! Left to herself Leila would have wearied of the search in ten minutes, but Wimsey, bullying, cajoling, flattering, holding out golden baits, kept her remorselessly to her task. Mr. da Soto, arriving suddenly to find Wimsey holding an armful of lingerie, while Leila ferreted among a pile of crumpled bills and picture postcards which had been bundled into the bottom of a trunk, thought the scene was set for a little genteel blackmail and started to bluster. Wimsey told him curtly not to be a fool, pushed the lingerie into his reluctant hands and started to hunt through a pile of magazines and gramophone records.

Curiously enough, it was da Soto who found the paper. Leila's interest in the business seemed rather to cool after his arrival—was it possible that she had had other designs upon Lord Peter, with which Luis' sulky presence interfered?—whereas da Soto, suddenly tumbling to the notion that the production of the paper might turn out to be of value to somebody, gradually became more and more interested.

"I wouldn't be that surprised, honey-bunch," he observed, "if you left it in one of those story-books you're always reading, same like you always do with your 'bus-tickets."

"That's an idea," said Wimsey, eagerly.

They turned their attention to a shelf stacked with cheap fiction and penny novelettes. The volumes yielded quite a surprising collection, not only of 'bus-tickets, but also of cinema-ticket counterfoils, bills, chocolate-papers, envelopes, picture-cards, cigarette-cards and other assorted book-markers, and at length da Soto, taking *The Girl who gave All* by the spine and administering a brisk shake, shot out from between its passionate leaves a folded sheet of writing-paper.

"What do you say to that?" he inquired, picking it up quickly. "If that isn't the fellow's handwriting you can call me a deaf-and-dumb elephant with four left feet."

Leila grabbed the paper from him.

"Yes, that's it, all right," she observed. "A lot of stuff, if you ask me. I never could make head or tail of it, but if it's any good to you, you're welcome to it."

Wimsey cast a rapid glance at the spidery lines of the family tree which sprawled from top to bottom of the sheet.

"So that's who he thought he was. Yes—I'm glad you didn't chuck this away, Miss Garland. It may clear things up quite a lot."

Here Mr. da Soto was understood to say something about dollars.

"Ah, yes," said Wimsey. "It's lucky it's me and not Inspector Umpelty, isn't it? Umpelty might run you in for suppressing important evidence." He grinned in da Soto's baffled face. "But I won't say—seeing that Miss Garland has turned her place upside-down to oblige me—that she mightn't get a new frock out of it if she's a good girl. Now, listen to me, my child. When did you say Alexis gave you this?"

"Oh, ages ago. When him and me were first friends. I can't remember exactly. But I know it's donkey's years since I read that silly old book."

"Donkey's years being, I take it, rather less than a year ago—unless you knew Alexis before he came to Wilvercombe."

"That's right. Wait a minute. Look! Here's a bit of a cinema-ticket stuck in at another page, with the date on it. Ooh, yes! November 15th—that's right. I remember now. We went to the pictures and then Paul came round to see me afterwards and told me a lot about himself. It was the same evening. He expected me to be terribly excited about it all."

"November; you're sure?"

"Yes, sure."

"At any rate, it was some time before those funny letters started to come for him?"

"Oh, yes, ages. And after the letters started to come, he shut up about it, and wanted his silly old paper back. I told you that before."

"I know you did. All right. Now, sit down. I want to look at this."

This was the paper:

Francis Josias
D. of Saxe-Coburg-Gotha (1678–1735)

Charles Marie Levannier   =   Anastasia (illegitimate)
(of the French Legation)   b.1728

Nicholas I   =   Charlotte, *b.* 1770
Tsar of Russia   (youngest of seven children)
(morganatically in
1815)

Nicolaevna (Nicole)   =   Gaston, natural son of
                                      Louis-Philippe,
                                      b. 1820, m. 1847

Capt. Stefan Ivanovitch Krasky   =   Louis, *b.* 1848
       m. 1871

Alexis Gregorovitch Vorodin   =   Mélanie, *b.* 1883

Pavlo Alexeivitch Vorodin, *b.* 1909.

"H'm!" said Wimsey. "I wonder where he got this from. I never knew that Nicholas I married anybody but Charlotte-Louise of Prussia."

"I remember about that," said Leila. "Paul said that that marriage couldn't be proved. He kept on about that. He said, if only it could be proved he'd be a prince or something. He was always worrying over that Charlotte-person—horrid old wretch she must have been, too. Why, she was forty-five if she was a day, and then she went and had a baby. I wonder it didn't kill her. It ought to have, I'm sure."

"Nicholas I must have been quite a kid at the time. Let's see—1815—that would be when he was in Paris after the Waterloo business. Yes, I see—Charlotte's father was something to do with the French legation; that fits in all right. I suppose he had this illegitimate daughter of Duke Francis pushed off on to him when he was in Saxe-Coburg. She went back and lived with him in Paris and had seven children, and the youngest of them was Charlotte, who, I suppose, somehow got hold of the young Emperor and cradle-snatched him."

" 'The old beast!' I said to Paul, when he took up with this Mrs. Weldon. 'Well,' I said, 'marrying old hags must run in your family,' I said. But he wouldn't hear anything against Great-Great-Grandma Charlotte. She was something quite out of the way, by his account of it. A sort of what's-her-name."

"Ninon de l'Enclos?"

"Yes, I daresay—if that's the old wretch who went on having lovers till she was about a hundred and fifty. I don't think it's nice at all. I can't think what the men were thinking about. Potty, they must have been, if you ask me. Anyway, what you said is about right. She was a widow several times over—Charlotte, I mean. She married some Count or other or General Somebody—I forget—and had something to do with politics."

"Everybody in Paris in 1815 had to do with politics," said Wimsey. "I can see Charlotte all right, playing her cards carefully among the new nobility. Well, this elderly beauty marries, or doesn't marry, the young Tsar and produces a daughter and calls her Nicolaevna after her illustrious papa. Being in France, they call the child Nicole. What happens next? Old Charlotte goes on playing her cards well, and, having tasted royal blood, so to speak, thinks she'll worm herself in on the Bourbons. There are no legitimate princes she can beg for her daughter, but she thinks the wrong side of the blanket better than being left out in the cold, and marries the girl off to some little accident of Louis-Philippe's."

"A nice set of people they must have been in those days!"

"So-so. I daresay Charlotte may really have thought she *was* married to Nicholas, and been frightfully disappointed at finding her claims set aside. They must have been one too many for her there—Nicholas and his diplomats. Just when she thought she had hooked her fish so well—the fading beauty, with her wit and charm, pulling off the biggest coup of her life—making herself Empress. France was in confusion, the Empire broken, and those who had climbed to power on the eagle's wings falling with his fall—who knew what would happen to the intriguing widow of one of Napoleon's counts or generals?—but Russia! The double-headed eagle still had all his pinions—"

"How you do go on!" said Miss Garland, impatiently. "It doesn't sound a bit likely to me. If you ask me, I think Paul made it all up out of those books he was so fond of."

"Very probably," admitted Wimsey. "I only mean that it was a very good story. Colourful, vivid stuff, with costume effects and plenty of human interest. And it fits in reasonably well from the historical point of view. You're quite sure you heard all about it in November?"

"Yes, of course I'm sure."

"My opinion of Paul Alexis' powers of invention is going up. Romantic fiction should have been his line. Anyhow, we'll pass all that. Here's Charlotte, still clinging to this idea about morganatic marriages and thrones, and marrying her daughter Nicole to this Bourbon fellow, Gaston. Nothing unlikely about that. He'd come in between the Prince de Joinville and the Duc d'Aumale as regards age, and there's no reason why he shouldn't. Now, what happens to Nicole? She has a daughter—the family seems to have run to daughters—called Louise. I wonder what happened to Gaston and Nicole under the second Empire. Nothing is said about Gaston's profession. Probably he accepted the fait accompli and kept his royalist leanings and origin quiet. At any rate, in 1871, his daughter Louise marries a Russian—that's a throw-back to the old stock. Let's see—1871. What do I connect with 1871? Of course—the Franco-Prussian War, and Russia's behaving rather unkindly to France about the Treaty of Paris. Alas! I fear Louise went over, horse, foot and artillery, to the enemy! Possibly this Stefan Ivanovitch came to Paris in some diplomatic connection about the time of the Treaty of Berlin. Goodness knows!"

Leila Garland yawned dreadfully.

"Louise has a daughter, anyhow," pursued Wimsey, wrapped up in his speculations. "And she married another Russian. Presumably they are living in Russia again now. Mélanie is the daughter's name, and the husband is Alexis Gregorovitch, and they are the parents of Paul Alexis, otherwise Goldschmidt, who is rescued from the Russian revolution, brought over to England and naturalised, becomes a hotel gigolo and is murdered on the Flat-Iron Rock—why?"

"Goodness knows," said Leila, and yawned again.

Wimsey, making sure that Leila had really told him all she knew, gathered up his precious piece of paper and carried the whole problem away to Harriet.

"But it's simply silly," said that practical young woman when she saw it. "Even if Alexis' great-great-grandmother had been married to Nicholas I fifty times over, he wouldn't have been the heir to the throne. Why, there are heaps and heaps of people nearer than he was—the Grand-Duke Dimitri, for instance, and all sorts of people."

"Oh? of course. But you can always persuade people into believing what they want to, you know. Some sort of tradition about it must have been handed down in the family from old Charlotte—you know what people are when they get these genealogical bugs in their heads. I know a fellow who's a draper's assistant in Leeds, who very earnestly told me once that he ought really to be King of England, if he could only find the record of somebody's marriage to Perkin Warbeck. The trifling accident of a few intervening changes of dynasty didn't worry him at all. He really thought he had only to state his case in the House of Lords to have the crown handed to him on a gold plate. And as for all the other claimants, Alexis would probably be told that they'd all abdicated in his favour. Besides, if he really believed in this family tree of his, he'd say that his claim was better than theirs, and that his great-great-grandmother was the only legitimate descendant of Nicholas I. I don't think there was a Salic Law in Russia to prevent his claiming through the female line. Anyhow, it's perfectly clear now how the trap was baited. If only we could get hold of the papers that Alexis sent to 'Boris'! But they'll have been destroyed, as sure as eggs is eggs."

Inspector Umpelty, accompanied by Chief Inspector Parker, of Scotland Yard, rang the bell at No. 17 Popcorn Street, Kensington, and was admitted without difficulty. It was obliging of Chief Inspector Parker to be taking a personal interest in the matter, though Umpelty felt he could have done with a less distinguished escort—but the man was Lord Peter's brother-in-law and no doubt felt a peculiar interest in the case. At any rate, Mr. Parker seemed disposed to leave the provincial inspector a free hand with his inquiries.

Mrs. Morecambe tripped into the room, smiling graciously.

"Good morning. Won't you sit down? Is it something about this Wilvercombe business again?"

"Well, yes, madam. There appears to be some slight misunderstanding." The Inspector brought out a notebook and cleared his throat. "About this gentleman, Mr. Henry Weldon, to whom you gave a lift on the Thursday morning. I think you said that you drove him in to the Market Square?"

"Why, yes. It is the Market Square, isn't it? Just outside the town, with a sort of green and a building with a clock on it?"

"Oh!" said Umpelty, disconcerted. "No; that's not the Market Square—it's the fair-ground, where they have the football-matches and the flower-show. Was that where you put him down?"

"Why, yes. I'm so sorry. I quite thought it was the Market Square."

"Well, it's called the Old Market. But what they call the Market Square now is the square in the centre of the town, where the point-constable stands."

"Oh, I see. Well, I'm afraid I've been giving you misleading information." Mrs. Morecambe smiled. "Is that a very dreadful offence?"

"It might have serious consequences, of course," said the Inspector, "but nobody can't help a genuine mistake. Still, I'm glad to have it cleared up. Now, just as a matter of routine, madam, what did you yourself do that morning in Wilvercombe?"

Mrs. Morecambe considered, with her head on one side.

"Oh, I did some shopping, and I went to the Winter Gardens, and I had a cup of coffee at the Oriental Café—nothing very special."

"Did you happen to buy any gentleman's collars?"

"Collars?" Mrs. Morecambe looked surprised. "Really, Inspector, you seem to have been going into my movements very thoroughly. Surely I'm not suspected of anything?"

"Matter of routine, madam," replied the Inspector, stolidly; he licked his pencil.

"Well, no, I didn't *buy* any collars. I looked at some."

"Oh, you looked at some?"

"Yes; but they hadn't the sort my husband wanted."

"Oh, I see. Do you remember the name of the shop?"

"Yes—Rogers & something—Rogers & Peabody, I think."

"Now, madam." The Inspector looked up from his notebook and stared sternly at her. "Would it surprise you to learn that the assistant at Rogers & Peabody's says that a lady dressed in the same style as yourself and answering your description, bought collars there that morning and had the parcel taken out to the car?"

"It wouldn't surprise me at all. He was a very stupid young man. He did take a parcel out to the car, but it wasn't collars. It was ties. I went in twice—once for the ties, and then I remembered the collars and went back; but as they hadn't got what I wanted, I left them. That would be about half-past twelve, I think, if the time is of any importance."

The Inspector hesitated. It might—it might *just* be true. The most honest witness makes a mistake sometimes. He decided to let it go for the moment.

"And you picked Mr. Weldon up at the Old Market again?"

"Yes. But when you say it was this Mr. Weldon, Inspector, you're putting words into my mouth. I picked up somebody—a man with dark spectacles—but I didn't know his name till he told it me, and I didn't recognise the man afterwards when I saw him without the spectacles. In fact I thought then, and I still think, that the man I picked up had dark hair. The other man's voice sounded much the same—but, after all, that isn't a lot to go upon. I thought it must be he, because he seemed to remember all about it, and knew the number of my car, but of course, if it came to swearing to his identity—well!" She shrugged her shoulders.

"Quite so, madam." It was clear enough to the Inspector what was happening. Since the discovery of the real time of the murder had made the morning alibi more dangerous than useful, it was being ruthlessly jettisoned. More trouble, he thought sourly, and more checking-up of times and places. He thanked the lady politely for her helpful explanation, and then asked whether he might have a word with Mr. Morecambe.

"With my husband?" Mrs. Morecambe registered surprise. "I don't think he will be able to tell you anything. He was not staying at Heathbury at the time, you know."

The Inspector admitted that he was aware of the fact, and added, vaguely, that this was a purely formal inquiry. "Part of our system," he explained, and obscurely connected with the fact that Mr. Morecambe was the legal owner of the Bentley.

Mrs. Morecambe smiled graciously. Well, Mr. Morecambe was at home, as it happened. He had not been very well, lately, but no doubt he would be ready to assist the Inspector if it was really necessary. She would ask him to come down.

Inspector Umpelty indicated that this was not really necessary. He would be happy to accompany Mrs. Morecambe to her husband's room. At which precaution Chief Inspector Parker smiled: any necessary arrangements between the Morecambes would surely have been perfected by this time.

Mrs. Morecambe led the way to the door, followed by Mr. Umpelty. She glanced round as though expecting Parker to follow, but he kept his seat. After a momentary hesitation, Mrs. Morecambe went out, leaving her second guest to his own devices. She went upstairs, with the Inspector padding behind her, murmuring apologies and trying to keep his boots from making a noise.

The room they entered on the first floor was furnished as a study, and beyond it, another door, half-open, led into a bedroom. At a table in the study sat a small, red-bearded man, who turned sharply to face them at their entrance.

"My dear," said Mrs. Morecambe, "this is Inspector Umpelty of the Wilvercombe police. He wants to know something about the car."

"Oh, yes, Inspector, what is it?" Mr. Morecambe spoke genially, but his geniality was as nothing compared to the geniality of the Inspector.

"Hullo, Bright, my man!" said he. "Risen a bit in the world since I last saw you, haven't you?"

Mr. Morecambe raised his eyebrows, glanced at his wife, and then broke into a hearty laugh.

"Well done, Inspector!" said he. "What did I tell you, dear? You can't deceive our fine British police-force. With his usual acumen, the man had spotted me! Well, sit down, Inspector and have a drink, and I'll tell you all about it."

Umpelty cautiously lowered his large form into a chair and accepted a whisky-and-soda.

"First of all, congratulations on your sleuthing," said Mr. Morecambe, cheerfully. "I thought I'd got rid of that fellow in Selfridge's, but I suppose the other fellow with the quick change headgear managed to keep on the scent, in spite of my artistic camouflage in the Cinema. Well, now, I suppose you want to know why Alfred Morecambe, commission-agent of London, was going about at Wilvercombe disguised as William Bright, that seedy and unsatisfactory tonsorial artist. I don't blame you. I daresay it does look queerish. Well, to start with —here's the explanation."

He gathered up a number of sheets of paper from his writing-table and pushed them across to Umpelty.

"I'm writing a play for my wife," he said. "You have no doubt discovered that she was the famous Tillie Tulliver before she married. I've written a play or two before, under the name of Cedric St. Denis—spare-time work, you know—and this new one deals with the adventures of an itinerant hair-dresser. The best way to pick up local colour is to go and get it personally."

"I see, sir."

"I ought to have told you all this at the time," said Mr. Morecambe, with a frank air of apology, "but it really didn't seem necessary. As a matter of fact, I felt it would make me look a bit of a fool in the City. I was supposed to be taking a holiday for my health, you see, and if my partner had known what I was really up to, he might have been a little annoyed. In any case, you had my evidence, which was all that was really necessary—and I must admit that I rather enjoyed playing the ne'er-do-weel to all you people. I did it rather well, don't you think? Thanks to my wife's coaching, of course."

"I see, sir." Inspector Umpelty fastened promptly on the salient point of all this. "Your account of your meeting with Paul Alexis was a fact, then?"

"Absolutely true in every particular. Except, of course, that I never really had the slightest intention of committing suicide. As a matter of fact, the idea of passing the night in one of the lodging-houses appropriate to my impersonation didn't greatly appeal to me at that moment, and I was putting off the evil hour as long as possible. It's quite true that I made up a hard-luck story for Alexis— though I didn't actually take any money from the poor fellow. I drew the line at that. The pound-note I paid out that night was my own. But you nearly tied me up over the business about the tide. I rather over-reached myself there with all that picturesque detail." He laughed again.

"Well, well," said the Inspector, "You've led us a fine dance, sir." He glanced at the manuscript sheets in his hands, which appeared, so far as he could make out, to substantiate Morecambe's story. "It's a pity you didn't take us into your confidence, sir. We could probably have arranged for nothing to come out about it in the press. However—if I take a fresh statement from you now, that will clear that up all right."

He cocked his head for a moment as though listening, and then went on rapidly:

"I take it, that statement will just confirm the evidence you gave at the inquest? Nothing to add to it in any way?"

"Nothing at all."

"You never, for instance, came across this Mr. Henry Weldon at any time?"

"Weldon?"

"The man I gave the lift to," prompted Mrs. Morecambe, "whose mother was engaged to the dead man."

"Oh, him? Never saw him in my life. Don't suppose I'd recognise him now if I saw him. He didn't give evidence, did he?"

"No sir. Very good, then. If you like, I will take a statement from you now. I'll just call in my colleague, if you don't mind, to witness it."

The Inspector threw open the door. Chief Inspector Parker must have been waiting on the landing, for he marched in at once, followed by a respectable-looking working-woman and a large, stout man smoking a cigar. The Inspector kept his eye on the Morecambes. The wife looked merely surprised, but Morecambe's face changed.

"Now, Mrs. Sterne," said Parker, "have you ever seen this gentleman before?"

"Why, yes, sir; this is Mr. Field, as was staying with Mr. Weldon down at Fourways in February. I'd know him anywhere."

"That's who he is, is he?" said the stout gentleman. "I thought it might be Potts or Spink. Well, Mr. Maurice Vavasour, did you give the little Kohn girl a show after all?"

Mr. Morecambe opened his mouth, but no sound came. Inspector Umpelty consulted the Scotland Yard man by a glance, cleared his throat, took his courage in both hands, and advanced upon his prey:

"Alfred Morecambe," he said, "alias William Bright, alias William Simpson, alias Field, alias Cedric St. Denis, alias Maurice Vavasour, I arrest you for being

concerned in the murder of Paul Alexis Goldschmidt, otherwise Pavlo Alexeivitch, and I warn you that anything you say may be taken down and used in
evidence at your trial."

He wiped his forehead.

Alibi or no alibi, he had burnt his boats.

33

EVIDENCE OF WHAT SHOULD HAVE HAPPENED

Now see you how this dragon egg of ours
Swells with its ripening plot?
—*Death's Jest-Book*

WEDNESDAY, 8 JULY

"Turning my hair grey, that's what it is," said Inspector
Umpelty.

"Not a book, not a scrap of paper, not so much as a
line on the blotting pad. . . .

"No, not even a bottle of purple ink. . . .

"He's an artful one if you like. Always posted his own letters, or so the girl
says. . . .

"Yes, I know, it's all very well saying he must have been up to mischief—the
job is to prove it. You know what juries are. . . .

"Weldon's the fool of the two, but he's not talking. And we shan't find
anything at his place—Morecambe never trusted *him* with anything. . . .

"No; we haven't traced his friend in Warsaw—not yet. . . .

"Oh, I know; but meantime we've got to charge them with something that
looks like something. And do it quick. There's such a thing as Habeas
Corpus. . . .

"It's absolutely positive that neither of them could have been at the Flat-Iron
cutting throats, nor yet the lady. And it's a bit awkward to fetch up three people
and charge 'em with being accomplices to a murder which you can't even prove
is a murder. . . .

"Thank you, my lord, I don't mind if I do."

"I freely admit," said Wimsey, "that it's the queerest case I ever struck. We've
got all the evidence—at least, not all, but overwhelming evidence—of an elaborate conspiracy to do something or the other. And we've got a corpse which
looks like the victim of a conspiracy to murder. But when we come to put the
two together, they don't fit. Everything in the garden is lovely except the
melancholy fact that none of the people engaged in the conspiracy could possibly have done the murder. Harriet! It's your business to work out problems of
this sort—how do you propose to tackle this one?"

"I don't know," said Harriet. "I can only suggest a few methods and precedents. There's the Roger Sheringham method, for instance. You prove elaborately and in detail that A did the murder; then you give the story one final shake, twist it round a fresh corner, and find that the real murderer is B—the person you suspected first and then lost sight of."

"That's no good; the cases aren't parallel. We can't even plausibly fix anything on A, let alone B."

"No; well, there's the Philo Vance method. You shake your head and say: 'There's worse yet to come,' and then the murderer kills five more people, and that thins the suspects out a bit and you spot who it is."

"Wasteful, wasteful," said Wimsey. "And too slow."

"True. There's the Inspector French method—you break the unbreakable alibi."

Wimsey groaned.

"If anybody says 'Alibi' to me again, I'll—I'll—"

"All right. There are plenty of methods left. There's the Thorndyke type of solution, which, as Thorndyke himself says, can be put in a nut-shell. 'You have the wrong man, you have got the wrong box, and you have got the wrong body.' Suppose, for instance, that Paul Alexis is really—"

"The Emperor of Japan! Thank you."

"Well, that might not be so far off. He thought he was an Emperor, or next door to it, anyhow. Though even if he had fifty kinds of Imperial blood in his veins instead of only two or three, it wouldn't help us to explain how he managed to get killed with nobody near him. The real difficulty—"

"Wait a moment," said Wimsey. "Say that again."

Harriet said it again. "The real difficulty," she persisted, "is that one can't see how *anybody*—let alone Morecambe or Henry Weldon—could have done the murder. Even if Pollock—"

"The real difficulty," interrupted Wimsey, in a suddenly high-pitched and excited voice, "is the time of the death, isn't it?"

"Well, yes, I suppose it is."

"Of course it is. If it wasn't for that, we could explain everything." He laughed. "You know, I *always* thought it was funny, if Henry Weldon did the murder, that he shouldn't seem to know what time he did it at. Look! Let's pretend we've planned this murder ourselves and have timed it for twelve o'clock, shall we?"

"What's the good of that? We know it wasn't actually done till two o'clock. You can't get round that, my lord."

"Ah! but I want to look at the original murder as it was planned. It's true that the murderers later on found themselves faced with an unexpected alteration in the time-scheme, but just for the moment we'll work out the time-scheme as it originally stood. Do you mind? I want to."

The Inspector grunted, and Wimsey sat for a few minutes, apparently thinking hard. Then he spoke, without any trace of his former excitement.

"It's February," he said. "You're Henry Weldon. You have just heard that your elderly and foolish mother is going to marry a dancing dago thirty-five years younger than herself, and disinherit you. You are badly in need of money and you want to stop this at all costs. You make yourself unpleasant, but you find it's no good: you'll only lose all the money instead of only part. You are not an inventive man yourself, but you consult—yes, why do you consult Morecambe, Inspector?"

"Well, my lord, it seems that when Weldon came down here to see his mother, he picked up with Mrs. Morecambe somewhere or other. He's a great man with the ladies, and she probably thought there was money to be made out of him, seeing his mother was a rich woman. He pretty soon put her right about that, I fancy, and she got the idea of bringing her husband in on the job. That's all speculative, as you might say, though we've checked up that Mrs. M. was staying at Heathbury about the time Weldon was in Wilvercombe. Anyhow, we have made sure of one thing, and that is that Morecambe's 'Commission Agency' is a pretty vague sort of affair and uncommonly rocky on its pins. Our idea was that the lady brought the two men together, and that Morecambe promised to do what he could for Weldon on a fifty-fifty basis."

"Fifty-fifty of what?" asked Harriet.

"Of his mother's money—when he raked it in."

"But that wouldn't be till she died."

"No, miss, it wouldn't."

"Oh—do you think—?"

"I think those two might have been in it for what they could get out of it, miss," said the Inspector, stolidly.

"I agree," said Wimsey. "Anyway, the next thing that happens is that Mr. Morecambe goes to Leamhurst and stays a few days with Weldon. All through this business, Morecambe has been far too smart to put anything on paper, except all that rubbish in cipher, so I imagine the plot was more or less worked out then. Weldon mentions to Morecambe the romantic tale of Alexis' Imperial descent, and that gives them the idea for luring their victim to the Flat-Iron. Immediately after this, the mysterious letters begin to go out. I wonder, by the way, what was the excuse for not writing that first letter in Russian. Because, of course, that must have gone out in clear and not in code."

"I've got an idea about that," said Harriet. "Didn't you say you knew of an English novel that had an explanation of the Playfair cipher?"

"Yes—one of John Rhode's. Why?"

"I suggest that the first letter merely gave the title of the book and the chapters concerned and added the code-word for the next message. Since the book was English it would be quite natural to make the whole message English."

"Ingenious beast," said Wimsey. "Meaning you. But it's quite a possible explanation. We needn't go into all that story again. Obviously, Mrs. Morecambe was the source of information about the topography and fauna of Wilvercombe and Darley. Weldon was chosen to do the throat-cutting and horse-riding part of it, which needed brawn only, while Morecambe buzzed about despatching letters and photographs and working Alexis up to the topnotch of excitement. Then, when everything is about ready, Morecambe goes off to take up his rôle of travelling hairdresser."

"But why all that incredible elaboration?" demanded Harriet. "Why didn't they just buy an ordinary razor or knife in an ordinary way? Surely it would be less traceable."

"You'd think so. In fact, I daresay it might have been. But it's surprising how things do get traced. Look at Patrick Mahon and the chopper, for instance. The plan was to make the thing really impregnable by double and triple lines of defence. First, it was to look like suicide; secondly, if that was questioned and the razor traced, there was to be a convincing origin for the razor; thirdly, if by any chance Morecambe's disguise was seen through, there was to be an explanation for that."

"I see. Well, go on. Morecambe had the courage of his own convictions, anyhow—he did the thing very thoroughly."

"Wise man. I admit that he took me in absolutely. Well, now—Weldon. He had his character of Haviland Martin all ready to slip into. Acting under instructions, he hired a Morgan, crammed it uncomfortably with a small tent and his personal belongings, and went to camp at Darley, next door to Farmer Newcombe's field. Morecambe arrived at Wilvercombe the same day. Whether and when those two met I don't know. It's my impression that the whole thing was scheduled beforehand as far as possible, and that there was next to no communication after the plot had once got going."

"Very likely," said Umpelty. "That would account for its getting hitched-up over the times."

"Possibly. Well, on the Thursday, Alexis starts off for the Flat-Iron according to instructions. By the way, it was necessary that the body should be found and recognised—hence, I fancy, the fact that Alexis was told to go openly to the rock by the coast-road. In case the body got lost, there would be witnesses to say that he had been last seen going in that direction, and to suggest a possible area for search. It would never have done for him simply to disappear like snow upon the desert's dusty face.

"So Alexis goes off to look for a crown. Meanwhile, Henry Weldon has run a needle through the H.T. leads of the Morgan, so as to provide a very good reason for asking for a lift into Wilvercombe. And now you see why a Morgan. It had to be something with only two cylinders, if the whole ignition was to be put out of action with one needle: that is, a Morgan, a Belsize-Bradshaw or a motorbike. He probably avoided the bike on the ground of exposure to weather, and chose the Morgan as the next most handy and numerous two-cylinder 'bus."

Inspector Umpelty smacked his thigh, and then, remembering that none of all this did away with the central snag in the case, blew his nose mournfully.

"Shortly after ten o'clock, along comes Mrs. Morecambe in the Bentley with the conspicuous number-plate. That number-plate was pure bunce for them—they can scarcely have picked or wangled it on purpose, but it came in very convenient as a means of identifying the 'bus. What more natural than that Weldon, if questioned, should remember a number so screamingly funny as that? Oi, oi, oi! Highly humorous, wasn't it, Inspector?"

"Where did she put him down, then?" asked Umpelty, scowling.

"Anywhere, out of sight of the village and the passing throng. At some point where he can cut across the fields to the shore again. The road turns in rather sharply from the coast between Darley and Wilvercombe, which doubtless accounts for their having left him so much time for his walk back. In any case, by, say, 11.15, he has walked back to Darley and is cocking an eye over the fence at Farmer Newcombe's bay mare. He pulls a stake out of the hedge and goes into the field, with oats in one hand and a rope-bridle in the other."

"What did he want to take oats for? Surely the horse would have come up to him if he just said 'Coop' or whatever it is and shaken his hat about? It seems silly of him to scatter oats all over the place like that."

"Yes, my child," said Wimsey. "But there was a reason for that. I think the oats he scattered were from the day before, when he first started to make friends with the mare. Teach an animal to come for food once and it'll come twice as fast the second time; but once disappoint it, and it won't come at all."

"Yes, of course. You're quite right."

"Now," said Wimsey, "I *think*, I can't prove it, but I *think*, our hero left most of his clothes behind him. I'm not certain, but it seems an obvious precaution. At any rate, he bridled the mare and mounted her and rode off. You've got to remember that between Darley and Pollock's cottage the shore is hidden from the road, so that the only risk he ran of being seen was by somebody straying on the edge of the cliff itself. And they would probably not worry much about a man exercising a horse along the shore. His real awkward moment was the passing of the cottages, but he had carefully chosen the very time when the working-classes have their dinner. I fancy he went past there just before mid-day."

"They heard hoofs about that time."

"Yes. And a little later, Paul Alexis heard them too, as he sat on his rock and dreamed of the Imperial purple. He looked and saw the Rider from the Sea."

"Quite so," said Umpelty, unmoved. "And what then?"

"Ah?—you recollect that we are merely describing an ideal crime, in which everything works out as planned."

"Oh, yes—of course."

"Then—in the ideal crime—Weldon rides up to the rock through the water— and by the way, you will bear in mind that it is fully an hour before low tide and that there is a foot and a half of water at the foot of the Flat-Iron. He ties the mare close by the head to the ring-bolt put there the day before, and he climbs up on to the rock. Alexis may or may not have recognised him. If he did . . ."

Wimsey paused, and his eyes grew angry.

"Whether he did or not, he hadn't much time for disappointment. Weldon asked him to sit down, I think; emperors sit, while respectful commoners stand behind them, you see. Weldon asked for the letter, and Alexis gave him the decoded translation. Then he leaned over him from behind with the razor. . . ."

"Weldon, of course, was a fool. He did everything wrong that he could do. He ought to have removed those gloves, and he ought to have seen to it that he had the original letter. Perhaps he ought to have searched the body. But I think that would have been worse still. It might have destroyed the suicidal appearance. Once move a body and you never can recapture the first, fine, careless rapture, don't you know. And besides, the mare was struggling and nearly breaking away. That would have been fatal. . . .

"Do you know, I rather take my hat off to Weldon about this. Ever seen a horse that has suddenly had fresh blood splashed all over it? Not pretty. Definitely not. Cavalry horses have to get used to it, of course—but the bay mare could never have smelt blood before. When I realise that Weldon had to mount that squealing, plunging, terrified brute bareback from the top of a rock, and ride her away without letting her once plunge on to the sand, I tell you, I take off my hat."

"You mean, you would have had to, if it had happened that thick way."

"Exactly. A man who could seriously contemplate bringing that scheme off knew something about horses. He may even have known too much. I mean . . . there are ways and ways of subduing violent animals, and some ways are crueller than others. . . .

"We'll suppose he did it. That he somehow got the mare untied from the rock and forced her straight out to sea. That would be the best way. That would tire her out, and at the same time wash the blood away. Then, having got control of her, he rides back as he came. But she has loosened a shoe in her frantic plunging and kicking, and on the way back she wrenches it off altogether. Probably he doesn't notice that. He rides on past his camp to wherever he left his clothes, looses the mare, gets dressed and hurries out to flag the Bentley on the return journey. I don't suppose he gets there much before, say, 12.55. He's picked up and set down at the Feathers at one o'clock. Here we leave romance and come back to the facts. Then, after lunch, he goes down to his own place, burns the rope-bridle, which is bloody, and kicks out our friend Perkins, who seems disposed to take too much interest in the rope."

"He hadn't the rope with him at the Feathers, had he?"

"No; I expect he threw it down in some handy spot on his way back from the Flat-Iron—somewhere near the stream, I should imagine. Well, all he has to do after that is to get Polwhistle to come along and deal with the Morgan. He made another mistake there, of course. When he was putting those leads in his pocket he should have *put* them in his pocket and seen that they stayed put.

"But you see that he, too, was intended to have three lines of defence. First, of course, the death was to look like suicide; secondly, the camper at Darley Halt was to be Mr. Martin of Cambridge, having no connection with anybody; and thirdly, if Mr. Martin was proved to be Henry Weldon, there was the alibi in Wilvercombe, with all the details about Bach and shirt-collars, and an absolutely independent witness in a Bentley car to swear to the story."

"Yes, but—" said Umpelty.

"I know, I know—bear with me. I know the plan went all wrong, but I want you to realise what it was meant to be. Suppose all this had worked properly— what would have happened? The body would have been left on the rock at about noon, with the razor lying below it. By 12.30, the murderer was well away, nearly at Darley. By one o'clock, he was at the Feathers, eating and drinking, with a witness to swear that he had spent the whole morning in Wilvercombe. If the body was found before the tide turned, there would be no footprints, other than those of the corpse, and suicide would probably be presumed without a second thought—especially when the razor turned up. If the body was not found till later, the footprints would be less important, but the medical evidence would probably establish the time of death, and then the alibi would come in.

"It sounds a very risky plan, but it sounds riskier than it was. Its boldness was its strength. From the Flat-Iron and for a mile or more before you come to it, the coast-road is visible from the shore. He could keep an eye on it and bide his time. If it looked dangerous, he could put it off to a more convenient season. Actually, the only real risk he ran was of being seen at the very moment of the murder and chased by car along the coast. Otherwise, even if it turned out later that a horseman had been seen on the shore about noon, who could prove who the horseman was? It could certainly not be Mr. Haviland Martin, who had no connection with anybody and had spent the morning musically in Wilvercombe. And in any case, how many people did pass along that road? What were the odds that the body would be discovered under a few hours? Or that the death would be supposed to be anything except suicide?"

"What are the odds now that it wasn't suicide?" said Inspector Umpelty. "By your own showing it can't have been anything else. But I see what you mean, my lord. You mean that all this plan was made out, and then, when Weldon got along to the Flat-Iron, something made him change his mind. How's this? When Alexis sees his Rider from the Sea, he recognises Weldon and asks him to explain. Weldon tells him how they've made a fool of him and somehow gets him to promise to chuck Mrs. Weldon. Maybe he threatens him with the razor. Then Weldon goes away and Alexis is so disappointed that, after thinking it over a bit, he cuts his throat."

"Weldon having thoughtfully armed him with the razor for that purpose?"

"Well, yes—I suppose so."

"And what did the bay mare see?" asked Harriet.

"Ghosts," replied Inspector Umpelty, with a snort of incredulity. "Anyhow, you can't put horses in the witness-box."

"Weldon made a mistake afterwards in coming to Wilvercombe," went on Wimsey. "With that identification mark on his arm, he should have kept away, mother or no mother. But he *had* to poke his nose in and see what was happening. And Morecambe—well, his possible appearance as a witness was foreseen, of course. I wonder, though, if he was really wise to answer that advertisement of ours. I suppose it was the best thing he could do—but he ought to have smelt the trap, I think. But my private impression is that he wanted to keep an eye on Weldon, who was blundering about all over the place."

"Excuse me, my lord," said Inspector Umpelty, "but we've wasted a good hour now speculating about what these people might have done or meant to do. That's very interesting to you, no doubt, but meanwhile we're no nearer to knowing what they did do, and here's three people in prison for doing something they can't have done. If Alexis cut his own throat, we've either got to release these people with apologies, or get up a case against them for conspiring to procure by menaces or something. If some accomplice of theirs killed him, we've got to find that accomplice. In either case, I mustn't waste any more time about it. I only wish I'd never touched the bleeding case."

"But you're so hasty, Inspector," bleated Wimsey. "I only said the plan went wrong; I never said they didn't carry it out."

Inspector Umpelty looked sadly at Wimsey, and his lips silently formed the word "loopy." But aloud he merely observed:

"Well, my lord, whatever they did, they didn't murder Alexis at two o'clock, because they weren't there to do it; and they didn't murder him at twelve o'clock, because he didn't die till two. Those are facts, aren't they?"

"No."

"No?"

"No."

"You mean, one or other of them was there at two o'clock?"

"No."

"You mean, they did murder Alexis at twelve o'clock?"

"Yes."

"By cutting his throat?"

"Yes."

"Right through?"

"Right through."

"Then how is it he didn't die till two o'clock?"

"We have no evidence at all," said Wimsey, "as to the time Alexis died."

34

EVIDENCE OF
WHAT DID HAPPEN

Take thou this flower to strew upon *his* grave,
A lily of the valley; it bears bells,
For even the plants, it seems, must have their fool,
So universal is the spirit of folly;
And whisper, to the nettles of *his* grave,
"King Death hath asses' ears."

—*Death's Jest-Book*

WEDNESDAY, 8 JULY

"**D**o you mean to say," demanded Inspector Umpelty, with slow indignation, "that the young lady finds herself mistaken all this time?"

Harriet shook her head, and Wimsey said, "No."

"Well, my lord, I don't think you can go against the doctor. I've asked other doctors about it, and they say there's no doubt about it."

"You didn't tell them the whole of the facts," said Wimsey. "I don't blame you," he added, kindly, "I've only just thought of the rest of the facts myself. Something you said about blood put it in my head, Harriet. Suppose we put down a few things we know about this supposed heir of the Romanovs."

1. He is known to have been very ill as a child, through being knocked down in the playground.
2. At the age of twenty-one he wore a beard, and had never used a razor. He was also
3. Extraordinarily timid about using sharp weapons or visiting the dentist.
4. Moreover, he had had at least one molar crowned—the last resort to avoid extraction.
5. On Thursday 18th, when scrambling over rocks, he wore gloves.
6. Periodic pains in the joints caused him acute suffering.
7. He used antipyrin to relieve this condition.
8. In no circumstances would he see a doctor, though he anticipated that the trouble would eventually cripple him.
9. Lack of the usual post-mortem stains was remarked on at the inquest.
10. Inquest also established that the great vessels were almost completely drained of blood.
11. And, finally, one may inherit other things besides Imperial crowns through the female line.

Harriet and the Inspector stared at this for a moment or two. Then Harriet laughed:

"Of course!" she said. "I thought your style was a little laboured in places! But as an impromptu effort it's creditable."

"I don't see what you get from all that," said Umpelty. And then, suspiciously: "Is it a joke? Is it another of these ciphers?" He snatched up the paper and ran a large thumb down the lines. "Here!" he said, "what are you playing at? Is it a riddle?"

"No, it's the answer," said Harriet. "You're right, Peter, you're right—you must be. It would explain such a lot. Only I didn't know about antipyrin."

"I'm almost sure that is right; I remember reading about it somewhere."

"Did it come through the Romanovs?"

"Possibly. It doesn't prove that he really was a Romanov, if you mean that. Though he may have been, for young Simons recognised something familiar in his face, which may have been a family resemblance. But it may quite likely have been the other way: the fact that he had it may have lent colour to the tradition. It often occurs spontaneously."

"What *is* all this?" asked the Inspector.

"Don't tease him, Peter. Try the initial letters, Mr. Umpelty."

"Ah—oh! You *will* have your fun, my lord! H, A, E—Haemophilia. What in the name of blazes is that, when it's at home?"

"It's a condition of the blood," said Wimsey, "due to a lack of something-or-the-other, calcium or what not. It is inherited, like colour-blindness, through the female, and shows itself only, or practically only, in the male, and then only in alternate generations. That is to say, it might lie hidden in generation after generation of daughters, and then, by some malignant chance, pop suddenly up in a son born of a perfectly healthy father and an apparently quite healthy mother. And so far as is known it is incurable."

"And what is it? And why do you think Alexis had it? And what does it matter if he did?"

"It's a condition in which the blood doesn't clot properly; if you get even a tiny little scratch, you may bleed to death from it. You may die of having a tooth drawn or from cutting your chin with a razor, unless you know how to deal with it—and in any case, you will go on bleeding like a stuck pig for hours. And if you get a fall or a blow, you have internal bleeding, which comes out in great lumps and swellings and is agonisingly painful. And even if you are terribly careful, you may get internal bleeding at the joints for no reason at all. It comes on from time to time and is horribly painful and gives you a hell of a fever. Hence, if I remember rightly, the antipyrin. And what's more, it generally ends up by ankylosing your joints and making you a permanent cripple."

"The Tsarevitch had it, of course," said Harriet. "I read about it in those books of Alexis—but like a fool, I never thought about it in connection with the murder."

"I don't know that I see it now," said the Inspector, "except that it explains why Alexis was such a namby-pamby and all that. Do you mean it proves that Alexis really was a royalty of sorts and that the Bolshies—"

"It may or may not prove any of that," said Wimsey. "But don't you see, my dear old goat, that it completely busts up and spifflicates the medical evidence? We timed the death for two o'clock because the blood hadn't clotted—but if Alexis was a haemophilic, you might wait till Kingdom Come, and his blood would never clot at all. Therefore, he may have died at noon or dawn for all we know. As a matter of fact, the blood might end by clotting very slightly after some hours—it depends how badly he had the disease—but as evidence for the time of death, the blood is a simple washout."

"Good lord!" said Umpelty.

He sat open-mouthed.

"Yes," he said, when he'd recovered himself a little, "but here's a snag. If he might have died any time, how are we to prove he died at twelve o'clock?"

"Easy. First of all, we know it must have been then, because that's the time these people have an alibi for. As Sherlock Holmes says somewhere: 'Only a man with a criminal enterprise desires to establish an alibi.' I must say, this case is really unique in one thing. It's the only one I have ever known in which a murderer didn't know the time he was supposed to have done the murder at. No wonder the evidence at the inquest gave Henry Weldon such a jolt!"

"Yes—but—" the Inspector seemed worried. "That's all right for us, but I mean to say, that doesn't prove it was a murder—I mean, you've got to prove it was a murder first, before you prove anything else. I mean to say—"

"Quite right," said Wimsey. "Unlike Mr. Weldon, you can spot the *petitio elenchi*. But look here, if Alexis was seen alive on the road between half-past ten and half-past eleven and was dead at two o'clock, then he must have died during the period covered by the alibis; that's certain. And I think we can get it down a bit closer. Jem Pollock and his grand-dad puzzled us by saying that they thought they saw the man lying down on the rock well before two o'clock. In that case, he was probably dead already. We now know that they were in all likelihood speaking the truth, and so we need not now imagine them to be accomplices in the crime. You can whittle the period during which death must have occurred down to about two hours—say from 11.30, when Alexis could have reached the rock, to about 1.30, when the Pollocks first set eyes on the body. That ought to be near enough for you—especially as you can trace the weapon quite definitely to the hands of one of the accomplices. I suppose you can't find that the razor was sent anywhere by post for Weldon to get hold of?"

"We've tried that, but we couldn't find anything."

"No. I shouldn't wonder if Weldon's trip to Wilvercombe on the Wednesday was made for the purpose of picking up the razor. It could so easily have been left somewhere for him. Of course, Morecambe took good care not to be in Wilvercombe that day himself, the cunning devil—but what could be easier than to deposit a little parcel at a tobacconist's or somewhere to be called for by his friend Mr. Jones? I suggest that you look into that, Inspector."

"I will, my lord. There's just one thing. I can't see why Weldon and Morecambe should have been so surprised about the inquest evidence. Wouldn't Alexis have told them about this disability of his? If he thought it proved his descent from the Romanovs, you'd think he'd have mentioned it first thing."

"Oh, no, you wouldn't. It's pretty clear that Alexis disguised that little matter very jealously. It's not a recommendation to a man who wants to lead a successful revolution that he is liable to be laid up at any moment by a painful and incurable disease. Nor would it be exactly an inducement to 'Feodora' to marry him, if he was known to be a 'bleeder.' No, poor devil, he must have been terrified the whole time for fear they should find it out."

"Yes, I see. It's natural, when you come to think of it."

"If you exhume the body," said Wimsey, "you will very likely find the characteristic thickening of the joints that accompanies haemophilia. And I daresay

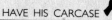
you might get conclusive evidence by inquiring among the people who knew Alexis in London and America. I'm pretty sure he had the disease."

"It's funny," said Harriet, "the way all this worked out for Weldon & Co. They had such good luck in one way and such bad luck in another. I mean: first of all they laid a fairly good plot, which turned on an alibi and a disguise. Then I came along unexpectedly and busted up the disguise. That was bad luck. But at the same time I produced a lot of unnecessary cleverness and observation which gave them a far better alibi for a totally different time, which was good luck. Then they lost the body, owing to the £300 in gold, which would have been a beastly nuisance for them. But again I barged in with evidence and photographs, and so drew attention to the death and got the body found again. Then, when, to their horror, their original lovely alibi turned out to be useless and dangerous, along comes poor little Perkins—who of course is as innocent as any sucking-pig —to give them a cast-iron alibi for the wrong time. We found the horseshoe, which would have pretty well cooked their goose, but for the astonishing bit of luck over the blood-clotting affair. And so on. It's been an incredible muddle. And it's all my fault, really. If I hadn't been so bright and brainy nobody would ever have known anything about the condition of the blood at all, and we should have taken it for granted that Alexis had died long before I came on the scene. It's so complicated, I really don't know whether my being there helped or hindered."

"It's so complicated," said the Inspector with a groan, "that I don't believe we'll ever get any jury to believe it. Besides there's the Chief Constable. I'll bet you anything you like he'll pooh-pooh the whole thing. He'll still say that after all we haven't *proved* it wasn't suicide, and we'd better let it go at that. He's as mad as a dog with us for arresting those people anyhow, and if I come along with this story about hemo-what-you-call, he'll have fifty thousand fits. See here, my lord, if we do prosecute, d'you really think we've a hope in Hades?"

"I'll tell you this," said Harriet. "Last night, Mrs. Weldon consented to dance with M. Antoine, and Henry didn't like it at all. If you let Henry Weldon and Morecambe loose again, what premium would you take on those two lives— Antoine's and Mrs. Weldon's?"

There was silence after the Inspector left them.

"Well!" said Harriet at last.

"Well," said Wimsey, "isn't that a damned awful, bitter, bloody farce? The old fool who wanted a lover and the young fool who wanted an empire. One throat cut and three people hanged, and £130,000 going begging for the next man who likes to sell his body and soul for it. God! What a jape! King Death has asses' ears with a vengeance."

He got up.

"Let's clear out of this," he said. "Get your things packed and leave your address with the police and come on up to Town. I'm fed to the back teeth."

"Yes, let's go. I'm terrified of meeting Mrs. Weldon. I don't want to see Antoine. It's all frightening and disgusting. We'll go home."

"Right-ho! We'll go home. We'll dine in Piccadilly. Damn it," said Wimsey, savagely, "I always did hate watering places!"

UNNATURAL
DEATH

ROGER DAWSON
b. 1710 *Blacksmith of unknown family. M.1749 Susan Pethick, with £500 after her seduction by Lord Matherford, and had by her*

BARNABAS DAWSON
Grocer. b. 1760; d. 1840

BARNABAS DAWSON
b. 1786. Killed at Waterloo, 1815
<u>No Issue</u>

ROGER DAWSON
b. 1789; d. of the Small-pox 1801
<u>No Issue</u>

JOHN WHITTAKER
b. 1824, m. 1849 & had issue

NO DESCENDANTS OF AUNT SOPHIE DESMOULINS STILL LIVING, BEING KIN OF 6TH DEGREE

HENRY DAWSON
b. 1830; m. 1852, Sophie Desmoulins, one of 3 sisters (of whom the other 2 entered a convent and died unmarried) d. 1884

2 DAUGHTERS
<u>d. in infancy</u>

CLARA WHITTAKER
f. 1850; d. 1923; unmarried
<u>No Issue</u>

JAMES WHITTAKER
b. 1852; m. 1873; d. 1913

HARRIET DAWSON
b. 1854; m. 1873; d. 1910

TWIN SONS
b. 1858, Survived only 2 days

*NB ALBERTA ALLCOCK LEFT AS SOLE KIN AN ORPHAN NEPHEW, FIRST COUSIN TO MARY WHITTAKER AND HER SOLE HEIR

REV. CHARLES WHITTAKER
*b. 1875; m. Alberta * Allcock 1895; killed with his wife while motoring 1924*

MARY WHITTAKER
b. 1898 Only surviving kin of 4th. degree

RUPERT DANBY
*Yeoman; only survivor of 4
brothers, of whom the
remainder were killed or fled
the country after the '45,
leaving no heirs*

HENRIETTA DANBY
b. 1758; m.1785; d. 1822

ELIZABETH DANBY
*b. 1754-m.1779 Stephen
Armstrong; descendents of the
4th generation still living.
(Kin of 8th. degree)*

AGATHA DAWSON
*b. 1791; d. of the
Small-pox 1801*
<u>No Issue</u>

FREDERICK DAWSON
*b. 1798; m. Lucy, daughter
of Geo. Marston, orphan
without kin.
Killed by falling from his
horse 1833.*

SIMON DAWSON
*b. 1794. Sailed to the West
Indies.*
<u>No Legitimate issue</u>

MARY ANN DAWSON
*b. 1831; d. of a decline
1848, unmarried*
<u>No Issue</u>

PAUL DAWSON
*b. 1832. Turned R.C.
& entered a monastery
d. 1922*
<u>No Issue</u>

BOSUN DAWSON
*Natural son of Simon by
a W. Indian woman.
b. 1842 m. 1887, Gloria,
a woman of his mother's
nationality.*

AGATHA DAWSON
b. 1852, d. unmarried 1925.
<u>No Issue</u>

STEPHEN DAWSON
*b. 1859; m. 1891; Rosa,
natural daughter of
J. Fairbanks d. 1917.*

REV. HALLELUJAH DAWSON
b. 1869.

JOHN DAWSON
*b. 1893. Killed in the Great
War, 1916 unmarried.*

CONTENTS

PART I

THE MEDICAL PROBLEM

"But how I caught it, found it, came by it,
What stuff 'tis made of, whereof it is born,
I am to learn."

Merchant of Venice

1

OVERHEARD

"The death was certainly sudden, unexpected, and to me mysterious."

Letter from Dr. Paterson to the Registrar
in the case of Reg. v. Pritchard

"**B**ut if he thought the woman was being murdered—"

"My dear Charles," said the young man with the monocle, "it doesn't do for people, especially doctors, to go about 'thinking' things. They may get into frightful trouble. In Pritchard's case, I consider Dr. Paterson did all he reasonably could by refusing a certificate for Mrs. Taylor and sending that uncommonly disquieting letter to the Registrar. He couldn't help the man's being a fool. If there had only been an inquest on Mrs. Taylor, Pritchard would probably have been frightened off and left his wife alone. After all, Paterson hadn't a spark of real evidence. And suppose he'd been quite wrong—what a dust-up there'd have been!"

"All the same," urged the nondescript young man, dubiously extracting a bubbling-hot Helix Pomatia from its shell, and eyeing it nervously before putting it in his mouth, "surely it's a clear case of public duty to voice one's suspicions."

"Of *your* duty—yes," said the other. "By the way, it's not a public duty to eat snails if you don't like 'em. No, I thought you didn't. Why wrestle with a harsh fate any longer? Waiter, take the gentleman's snails away and bring oysters instead. . . . No—as I was saying, it may be part of *your* duty to have suspicions and invite investigation and generally raise hell for everybody, and if you're mistaken nobody says much, beyond that you're a smart, painstaking officer though a little overzealous. But doctors, poor devils! are everlastingly walking a kind of social tight-rope. People don't fancy calling in a man who's liable to bring out accusations of murder on the smallest provocation."

"Excuse me."

The thin-faced young man sitting alone at the next table had turned round eagerly.

"It's frightfully rude of me to break in, but every word you say is absolutely true, and mine is a case in point. A doctor—you can't have any idea how dependent he is on the fancies and prejudices of his patients. They resent the most elementary precautions. If you dare to suggest a post-mortem, they're up in arms at the idea of 'cutting poor dear So-and-so up,' and even if you only ask permission to investigate an obscure disease in the interests of research, they imagine you're hinting at something unpleasant. Of course, if you let things go, and it turns out afterwards there's been any jiggery-pokery, the coroner jumps down your throat and the newspapers make a butt of you, and, whichever way it is, you wish you'd never been born."

"You speak with personal feeling," said the man with the monocle, with an agreeable air of interest.

"I do," said the thin-faced man, emphatically. "If I had behaved like a man of the world instead of a zealous citizen, I shouldn't be hunting about for a new job to-day."

The man with the monocle glanced round the little Soho restaurant with a faint smile. The fat man on their right was unctuously entertaining two ladies of the chorus; beyond him, two elderly habitués were showing their acquaintance with the fare at the "Au Bon Bourgeois" by consuming a Tripes à la Mode de Caen (which they do very excellently there) and a bottle of Chablis Moutonne 1916; on the other side of the room a provincial and his wife were stupidly clamouring for a cut off the joint with lemonade for the lady and whisky and soda for the gentleman, while at the adjoining table, the handsome silver-haired proprietor, absorbed in fatiguing a salad for a family party, had for the moment no thoughts beyond the nice adjustment of the chopped herbs and garlic. The head waiter, presenting for inspection a plate of Blue River Trout, helped the monocled man and his companion and retired, leaving them in the privacy which unsophisticated people always seek in genteel tea-shops and never, never find there.

"I feel," said the monocled man, "exactly like Prince Florizel of Bohemia. I am confident that you, sir, have an interesting story to relate, and shall be greatly obliged if you will favour us with the recital. I perceive that you have finished your dinner, and it will therefore perhaps not be disagreeable to you to remove to this table and entertain us with your story while we eat. Pardon my Stevensonian manner—my sympathy is none the less sincere on that account."

"Don't be an ass, Peter," said the nondescript man. "My friend is a much more rational person than you might suppose to hear him talk," he added, turning to the stranger, "and if there's anything you'd like to get off your chest, you may be perfectly certain it won't go any farther."

The other smiled a little grimly.

"I'll tell you about it with pleasure if it won't bore you. It just happens to be a case in point, that's all."

"On *my* side of the argument," said the man called Peter, with triumph. "Do carry on. Have something to drink. It's a poor heart that never rejoices. And begin right at the beginning, if you will, please. I have a very trivial mind. Detail delights me. Ramifications enchant me. Distance no object. No reasonable offer refused. Charles here will say the same."

"Well," said the stranger, "to begin from the very beginning, I am a medical man, particularly interested in the subject of cancer. I had hoped, as so many people do, to specialise on the subject, but there wasn't money enough, when I'd done my exams., to allow me to settle down to research work. I had to take a country practice, but I kept in touch with the important men up here, hoping to be able to come back to it some day. I may say I have quite decent expectations from an uncle, and in the meanwhile they agreed it would be quite good for me to get some all-round experience as a G.P. Keeps one from getting narrow and all that.

"Consequently, when I bought a nice little practice at . . . —I'd better not mention any names, let's call it X, down Hampshire way, a little country town of about 5,000 people—I was greatly pleased to find a cancer case on my list of patients. The old lady—"

"How long ago was this?" interrupted Peter.

"Three years ago. There wasn't much to be done with the case. The old lady was seventy-two, and had already had one operation. She was a game old girl, though, and was making a good fight of it, with a very tough constitution to back her up. She was not, I should say, and had never been, a woman of very powerful intellect or strong character as far as her dealings with other people went, but she was extremely obstinate in certain ways and was possessed by a positive determination not to die. At this time she lived alone with her niece, a young woman of twenty-five or so. Previously to that, she had been living with another old lady, the girl's aunt on the other side of the family, who had been her devoted friend since their school days. When this other old aunt died, the girl, who was their only living relative, threw up her job as a nurse at the Royal Free Hospital to look after the survivor—my patient—and they had come and settled down at X about a year before I took over the practice. I hope I am making myself clear."

"Perfectly. Was there another nurse?"

"Not at that time. The patient was able to get about, visit acquaintances, do light work about the house, flowers and knitting and reading and so on, and to drive about the place—in fact, most of the things that old ladies do occupy their time with. Of course, she had her bad days of pain from time to time, but the niece's training was quite sufficient to enable her to do all that was necessary."

"What was the niece like?"

"Oh, a very nice, well-educated, capable girl, with a great deal more brain than her aunt. Self-reliant, cool, all that sort of thing. Quite the modern type. The sort of woman one can trust to keep her head and not forget things. Of course, after a time, the wretched growth made its appearance again, as it always does if it isn't tackled at the very beginning, and another operation became necessary. That was when I had been in X about eight months. I took her up to London, to my own old chief, Sir Warburton Giles, and it was performed very successfully as far as the operation itself went, though it was then only too evident that a vital organ was being encroached upon, and that the end could only be a matter of time. I needn't go into details. Everything was done that could be done. I wanted the old lady to stay in town under Sir Warburton's eye, but she was vigorously opposed to this. She was accustomed to a country life and could not be happy except in her own home. So she went back to X, and I was able to keep her going with visits for treatment at the nearest large town, where there is an excellent hospital. She rallied amazingly after the operation and eventually was able to dismiss her nurse and go on in the old way under the care of the niece."

"One moment, doctor," put in the man called Charles, "you say you took her to Sir Warburton Giles and so on. I gather she was pretty well off."

"Oh, yes, she was quite a wealthy woman."

"Do you happen to know whether she made a will?"

"No. I think I mentioned her extreme aversion to the idea of death. She had always refused to make any kind of will because it upset her to think about such things. I did once venture to speak of the subject in the most casual way I could, shortly before she underwent her operation, but the effect was to excite her very undesirably. Also she said, which was quite true, that it was quite unnecessary.

'You, my dear,' she said to the niece, 'are the only kith and kin I've got in the world, and all I've got will be yours some day, whatever happens. I know I can trust you to remember my servants and my little charities.' So, of course, I didn't insist.

"I remember, by the way—but that was a good deal later on and has nothing to do with the story—"

"*Please*," said Peter, "*all* the details."

"Well, I remember going there one day and finding my patient not so well as I could have wished and very much agitated. The niece told me that the trouble was caused by a visit from her solicitor—a family lawyer from her home town, not our local man. He had insisted on a private interview with the old lady, at the close of which she had appeared terribly excited and angry, declaring that everyone was in a conspiracy to kill her before her time. The solicitor, before leaving, had given no explanation to the niece, but had impressed upon her that if at any time her aunt expressed a wish to see him, she was to send for him at any hour of the day or night and he would come at once."

"And was he ever sent for?"

"No. The old lady was deeply offended with him, and almost the last bit of business she did for herself was to take her affairs out of his hands and transfer them to the local solicitor. Shortly afterwards, a third operation became necessary, and after this she gradually became more and more of an invalid. Her head began to get weak, too, and she grew incapable of understanding anything complicated, and indeed she was in too much pain to be bothered about business. The niece had a power of attorney, and took over the management of her aunt's money entirely."

"When was this?"

"In April, 1925. Mind you, though she was getting a bit 'gaga'—after all, she was getting on in years—her bodily strength was quite remarkable. I was investigating a new method of treatment and the results were extraordinarily interesting. That made it all the more annoying to me when the surprising thing happened.

"I should mention that by this time we were obliged to have an outside nurse for her, as the niece could not do both the day and night duty. The first nurse came in April. She was a most charming and capable young woman—the ideal nurse. I placed absolute dependence on her. She had been specially recommended to me by Sir Warburton Giles, and though she was not then more than twenty-eight, she had the discretion and judgment of a woman twice her age. I may as well tell you at once that I became deeply attached to this lady and she to me. We are engaged, and had hoped to be married this year—if it hadn't been for my damned conscientiousness and public spirit."

The doctor grimaced wryly at Charles, who murmured rather lamely that it was very bad luck.

"My fiancée, like myself, took a keen interest in the case—partly because it was my case and partly because she was herself greatly interested in the disease. She looks forward to being of great assistance to me in my life work if I ever get the chance to do anything at it. But that's by the way.

"Things went on like this till September. Then, for some reason, the patient began to take one of those unaccountable dislikes that feeble-minded patients do take sometimes. She got it into her head that the nurse wanted to kill her— the same idea she'd had about the lawyer, you see—and earnestly assured her

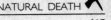
niece that she was being poisoned. No doubt she attributed her attacks of pain to this cause. Reasoning was useless—she cried out and refused to let the nurse come near her. When that happens, naturally, there's nothing for it but to get rid of the nurse, as she can do the patient no possible good. I sent my fiancée back to town and wired to Sir Warburton's Clinic to send me down another nurse.

"The new nurse arrived the next day. Naturally, after the other, she was a second-best as far as I was concerned, but she seemed quite up to her work and the patient made no objection. However, now I began to have trouble with the niece. Poor girl, all this long-drawn-out business was getting on her nerves, I suppose. She took it into her head that her aunt was very much worse. I said that of course she must gradually get worse, but that she was putting up a wonderful fight and there was no cause for alarm. The girl wasn't satisfied, however, and on one occasion early in November sent for me hurriedly in the middle of the night because her aunt was dying.

"When I arrived, I found the patient in great pain, certainly, but in no immediate danger. I told the nurse to give her a morphia injection, and administered a dose of bromide to the girl, telling her to go to bed and not to do any nursing for the next few days. The following day I overhauled the patient very carefully and found that she was doing even better than I supposed. Her heart was exceptionally strong and steady, she was taking nourishment remarkably well and the progress of the disease was temporarily arrested.

"The niece apologised for her agitation, and said she really thought her aunt was going. I said that, on the contrary, I could now affirm positively that she would live for another five or six months. As you know, in cases like hers, one can speak with very fair certainty.

" 'In any case,' I said, 'I shouldn't distress yourself too much. Death, when it does come, will be a release from suffering.'

" 'Yes,' she said, 'poor Auntie. I'm afraid I'm selfish, but she's the only relative I have left in the world.'

"Three days later, I was just sitting down to dinner when a telephone message came. Would I go over at once? The patient was dead."

"Good gracious!" cried Charles, "it's perfectly obvious—"

"Shut up, Sherlock," said his friend, "the doctor's story is not going to be obvious. Far from it, as the private said when he aimed at the bull's-eye and hit the gunnery instructor. But I observe the waiter hovering uneasily about us while his colleagues pile up chairs and carry away the cruets. Will you not come and finish the story in my flat? I can give you a glass of very decent port. You will? Good. Waiter, call a taxi . . . 110A Piccadilly."

2

MICHING MALLECHO

"By the pricking of my thumbs
Something evil this way comes."
Macbeth

The April night was clear and chilly, and a brisk wood fire burned in a welcoming manner on the hearth. The bookcases which lined the walls were filled with rich old calf bindings, mellow and glowing in the lamp-light. There was a grand piano, open, a huge chesterfield piled deep with cushions and two arm-chairs of the build that invites one to wallow. The port was brought in by an impressive man-servant and placed on a very beautiful little Chippendale table. Some big bowls of scarlet and yellow parrot tulips beckoned, banner-like, from dark corners.

The doctor had just written his new acquaintance down as an aesthete with a literary turn, looking for the ingredients of a human drama, when the man-servant re-entered.

"Inspector Sugg rang up, my lord, and left this message, and said would you be good enough to give him a call as soon as you came in."

"Oh, did he?—well, just get him for me, would you? This is the Worplesham business, Charles. Sugg's mucked it up as usual. The baker has an alibi—naturally—he would have. Oh, thanks. . . . Hullo! that you, Inspector? What did I tell you?—Oh, routine be hanged. Now, look here. You get hold of that gamekeeper fellow, and find out from him what he saw in the sand-pit. . . . No, I know, but I fancy if you ask him impressively enough he will come across with it. No, of course not—if you ask if he was there, he'll say no. Say you know he was there and what did he see—and, look here! if he hums and haws about it, say you're sending a gang down to have the stream diverted. . . . All right. Not at all. Let me know if anything comes of it."

He put the receiver down.

"Excuse me, doctor. A little matter of business. Now go on with your story. The old lady was dead, eh? Died in her sleep, I suppose. Passed away in the most innocent manner possible. Everything all ship-shape and Bristol-fashion. No struggle, no wounds, haemorrhages, or obvious symptoms, naturally, what?"

"Exactly. She had taken some nourishment at 6 o'clock—a little broth and some milk pudding. At eight, the nurse gave her a morphine injection and then went straight out to put some bowls of flowers on the little table on the landing for the night. The maid came to speak to her about some arrangements for the next day, and while they were talking, Miss . . . that is, the niece—came up and went into her aunt's room. She had only been there a moment or two when she cried out, 'Nurse! Nurse!' The nurse rushed in, and found the patient dead.

"Of course, my first idea was that by some accident a double dose of morphine had been administered—"

"Surely that wouldn't have acted so promptly."

"No—but I thought that a deep coma might have been mistaken for death. However, the nurse assured me that this was not the case, and, as a matter of fact, the possibility was completely disproved, as we were able to count the ampullae of morphine and found them all satisfactorily accounted for. There were no signs of the patient having tried to move or strain herself, or of her having knocked against anything. The little night-table was pushed aside, but that had been done by the niece when she came in and was struck by her aunt's alarmingly lifeless appearance."

"How about the broth and the milk pudding?"

"That occurred to me, also—not in any sinister way, but to wonder whether she'd been having too much—distended stomach—pressure on the heart, and that sort of thing. However, when I came to look into it, it seemed very unlikely. The quantity was so small, and on the face of it, two hours were sufficient for digestion—if it had been that, death would have taken place earlier. I was completely puzzled, and so was the nurse. Indeed, she was very much upset."

"And the niece?"

"The niece could say nothing but 'I told you so, I told you so—I knew she was worse than you thought.' Well, to cut a long story short, I was so bothered with my pet patient going off like that, that next morning, after I had thought the matter over, I asked for a post-mortem."

"Any difficulty?"

"Not the slightest. A little natural distaste, of course, but no sort of opposition. I explained that I felt sure there must be some obscure morbid condition which I had failed to diagnose and that I should feel more satisfied if I might make an investigation. The only thing which seemed to trouble the niece was the thought of an inquest. I said—rather unwisely, I suppose, according to general rules—that I didn't think an inquest would be necessary."

"You mean you offered to perform the post-mortem yourself."

"Yes—I made no doubt that I should find a sufficient cause of death to enable me to give a certificate. I had one bit of luck, and that was that the old lady had at some time or the other expressed in a general way an opinion in favour of cremation, and the niece wished this to be carried out. This meant getting a man with special qualifications to sign the certificate with me, so I persuaded this other doctor to come and help me to do the autopsy."

"And did you find anything?"

"Not a thing. The other man, of course, said I was a fool to kick up a fuss. He thought that as the old lady was certainly dying in any case, it would be quite enough to put in, Cause of death, cancer; immediate cause, heart failure, and leave it at that. But I was a damned conscientious ass, and said I wasn't satisfied. There was absolutely nothing about the body to explain the death naturally, and I insisted on an analysis."

"Did you actually suspect—?"

"Well, no, not exactly. But—well, I wasn't satisfied. By the way, it was very clear at the autopsy that the morphine had nothing to do with it. Death had occurred so soon after the injection that the drug had only partially dispersed from the arm. Now I think it over, I suppose it must have been shock, some-how."

"Was the analysis privately made?"

"Yes; but of course the funeral was held up and things got round. The coroner heard about it and started to make inquiries, and the nurse, who got it into her head that I was accusing her of neglect or something, behaved in a very unpro-fessional way and created a lot of talk and trouble."

"And nothing came of it?"

"Nothing. There was no trace of poison or anything of that sort, and the analysis left us exactly where we were. Naturally, I began to think I had made a ghastly exhibition of myself. Rather against my own professional judgment, I signed the certificate—heart failure following on shock, and my patient was finally got into her grave after a week of worry, without an inquest."

"Grave?"

"Oh, yes. That was another scandal. The crematorium authorities, who are pretty particular, heard about the fuss and refused to act in the matter, so the body is filed in the church-yard for reference if necessary. There was a huge attendance at the funeral and a great deal of sympathy for the niece. The next day I got a note from one of my most influential patients, saying that my professional services would no longer be required. The day after that, I was avoided in the street by the Mayor's wife. Presently I found my practice drop-ping away from me, and discovered I was getting known as 'the man who practically accused that charming Miss So-and-so of murder.' Sometimes it was the niece I was supposed to be accusing. Sometimes it was 'that nice Nurse—not the flighty one who was dismissed, the other one, you know.' Another version was, that I had tried to get the nurse into trouble because I resented the dismissal of my fiancée. Finally, I heard a rumour that the patient had discov-ered me 'canoodling'—that was the beastly word—with my fiancée, instead of doing my job, and had done away with the old lady myself out of revenge—though why, in that case, I should have refused a certificate, my scandal-mon-gers didn't trouble to explain.

"I stuck it out for a year, but my position became intolerable. The practice dwindled to practically nothing, so I sold it, took a holiday to get the taste out of my mouth—and here I am, looking for another opening. So that's that—and the moral is, Don't be officious about public duties."

The doctor gave an irritated laugh, and flung himself back in his chair.

"I don't care," he added, combatantly, "the cats! Confusion to 'em!" and he drained his glass.

"Hear, hear!" agreed his host. He sat for a few moments looking thoughtfully into the fire.

"Do you know," he said, suddenly, "I'm feeling rather interested by this case. I have a sensation of internal gloating which assures me that there is something to be investigated. That feeling has never failed me yet—I trust it never will. It warned me the other day to look into my income-tax assessment, and I discov-ered that I had been paying about £900 too much for the last three years. It urged me only last week to ask a bloke who was preparing to drive me over the Horseshoe Pass whether he had any petrol in the tank, and he discovered he had just about a pint—enough to get us nicely half-way round. It's a very lonely spot. Of course, I knew the man, so it wasn't *all* intuition. Still, I always make it a rule to investigate anything I feel like investigating. I believe," he added, in a reminiscent tone, "I was a terror in my nursery days. Anyhow, curious cases are rather a hobby of mine. In fact, I'm not just being the perfect listener. I have deceived you. I have an ulterior motive, said he, throwing off his side-whiskers and disclosing the well-known hollow jaws of Mr. Sherlock Holmes."

"I was beginning to have my suspicions," said the doctor, after a short pause. "I think you must be Lord Peter Wimsey. I wondered why your face was so familiar, but of course it was in all the papers a few years ago when you disentangled the Riddlesdale Mystery."

"Quite right. It's a silly kind of face, of course, but rather disarming, don't you think? I don't know that I'd have chosen it, but I do my best with it. I do hope it isn't contracting a sleuth-like expression, or anything unpleasant. This is the real sleuth—my friend Detective-Inspector Parker of Scotland Yard. He's the one who really does the work. I make imbecile suggestions and he does the work of elaborately disproving them. Then, by a process of elimination, we find the right explanation, and the world says, 'My god, what intuition that young man has!' Well, look here—if you don't mind, I'd like to have a go at this. If you'll entrust me with your name and address and the names of the parties concerned, I'd like very much to have a shot at looking into it."

The doctor considered a moment, then shook his head.

"It's very good of you, but I think I'd rather not. I've got into enough bothers already. Anyway, it isn't professional to talk, and if I stirred up any more fuss, I should probably have to chuck this country altogether and end up as one of those drunken ship's doctors in the South Seas or somewhere, who are always telling their life-history to people and delivering awful warnings. Better to let sleeping dogs lie. Thanks very much, all the same."

"As you like," said Wimsey. "But I'll think it over, and if any useful suggestion occurs to me, I'll let you know."

"It's very good of you," replied the visitor, absently, taking his hat and stick from the man-servant, who had answered Wimsey's ring. "Well, good night, and many thanks for hearing me so patiently. By the way, though," he added, turning suddenly at the door, "how do you propose to let me know when you haven't got my name and address?"

Lord Peter laughed.

"I'm Hawkshaw, the detective," he answered, "and you shall hear from me anyhow before the end of the week."

3

A USE FOR SPINSTERS

"There are two million more females than males in England and Wales! And this is an awe-inspiring circumstance."

Gilbert Frankau

"**W**hat do you really think of that story?" inquired Parker. He had dropped in to breakfast with Wimsey the next morning, before departing in the Notting Dale direction, in quest of an elusive anonymous letter-writer. "I thought it sounded rather as though our friend had been a bit too cocksure about his grand medical specialising. After all, the old girl might so easily have had some sort of heart attack. She was very old and ill."

"So she might, though I believe as a matter of fact cancer patients very seldom pop off in that unexpected way. As a rule, they surprise everybody by the way they cling to life. Still, I wouldn't think much of that if it wasn't for the niece. She prepared the way for the death, you see, by describing her aunt as so much worse than she was."

"I thought the same when the doctor was telling his tale. But what did the niece do? She can't have poisoned her aunt or even smothered her, I suppose, or they'd have found signs of it on the body. And the aunt *did* die—so perhaps the niece was right and the opinionated young medico wrong."

"Just so. And of course, we've only got his version of the niece and the nurse—and he obviously had what the Scotch call ta'en a scunner at the nurse. We mustn't lose sight of her, by the way. She was the last person to be with the old lady before her death, and it was she who administered that injection."

"Yes, yes—but the injection had nothing to do with it. If anything's clear, that is. I say, do you think the nurse can have said anything that agitated the old lady and gave her a shock that way. The patient was a bit gaga, but she may have had sense enough to understand something really startling. Possibly the nurse just said something stupid about dying—the old lady appears to have been very sensitive on the point."

"Ah!" said Lord Peter, "I was waiting for you to get on to that. Have you realised that there really is one rather sinister figure in the story, and that's the family lawyer."

"The one who came down to say something about the will, you mean, and was so abruptly sent packing."

"Yes. Suppose he'd wanted the patient to make a will in favour of somebody quite different—somebody outside the story as we know it. And when he found he couldn't get any attention paid to him, he sent the new nurse down as a sort of substitute."

"It would be rather an elaborate plot," said Parker, dubiously. "He couldn't know that the doctor's fiancée was going to be sent away. Unless he was in

422

league with the niece, of course, and induced her to engineer the change of nurses."

"That cock won't fight, Charles. The niece wouldn't be in league with the lawyer to get herself disinherited."

"No, I suppose not. Still, I think there's something in the idea that the old girl was either accidentally or deliberately startled to death."

"Yes—and whichever way it was, it probably wasn't legal murder in that case. However, I think it's worth looking into. That reminds me." He rang the bell. "Bunter, just take a note to the post for me, would you?"

"Certainly, my lord."

Lord Peter drew a writing pad towards him.

"What are you going to write?" asked Parker, looking over his shoulder with some amusement.

Lord Peter wrote:

"Isn't civilisation wonderful?"

He signed this simple message and slipped it into an envelope.

"If you want to be immune from silly letters, Charles," he said, "don't carry your monomark in your hat."

"And what do you propose to do next?" asked Parker. "Not, I hope, to send me round to Monomark House to get the name of a client. I couldn't do that without official authority, and they would probably kick up an awful shindy."

"No," replied his friend, "I don't propose violating the secrets of the confessional. Not in that quarter at any rate. I think, if you can spare a moment from your mysterious correspondent, who probably does not intend to be found, I will ask you to come and pay a visit to a friend of mine. It won't take long. I think you'll be interested. I—in fact, you'll be the first person I've ever taken to see her. She will be very much touched and pleased."

He laughed a little self-consciously.

"Oh," said Parker, embarrassed. Although the men were great friends, Wimsey had always preserved a reticence about his personal affairs—not so much by concealing as by ignoring them. This revelation seemed to mark a new stage of intimacy, and Parker was not sure that he liked it. He conducted his own life with an earnest middle-class morality which he owed to his birth and upbringing, and, while theoretically recognising that Lord Peter's world acknowledged different standards, he had never contemplated being personally faced with any result of their application in practice.

"—rather an experiment," Wimsey was saying a trifle shyly; "anyway, she's quite comfortably fixed in a little flat in Pimlico. You can come, can't you, Charles? I really should like you two to meet."

"Oh, yes, rather," said Parker, hastily, "I should like to very much. Er—how long—I mean—"

"Oh, the arrangement's only been going a few months," said Wimsey, leading the way to the lift, "but it really seems to be working out quite satisfactorily. Of course, it makes things much easier for me."

"Just so," said Parker.

"Of course, as you'll understand—I won't go into it all till we get there, and then you'll see for yourself," Wimsey chattered on, slamming the gates of the lift with unnecessary violence—"but, as I was saying, you'll observe it's quite a new departure. I don't suppose there's ever been anything exactly like it before.

Of course, there's nothing new under the sun, as Solomon said, but after all, I daresay all those wives and porcupines, as the child said, must have soured his disposition a little, don't you know."

"Quite," said Parker. "Poor fish," he added to himself, "they *always* seem to think it's different."

"Outlet," said Wimsey, energetically, "hi! taxi! . . . outlet—everybody needs an outlet—97A, St. George's Square—and after all, one can't really blame people if it's just that they need an outlet. I mean, why be bitter? They can't help it. I think it's much kinder to give them an outlet than to make fun of them in books—and, after all, it isn't really difficult to write books. Especially if you either write a rotten story in good English or a good story in rotten English, which is as far as most people seem to get nowadays. Don't you agree?"

Mr. Parker agreed, and Lord Peter wandered away along the paths of literature, till the cab stopped before one of those tall, awkward mansions which, originally designed for a Victorian family with fatigue-proof servants, have lately been dissected each into half a dozen inconvenient band-boxes and let off in flats.

Lord Peter rang the top bell, which was marked CLIMPSON, and relaxed negligently against the porch.

"Six flights of stairs," he explained; "it takes her some time to answer the bell, because there's no lift, you see. She wouldn't have a more expensive flat, though. She thought it wouldn't be suitable."

Mr. Parker was greatly relieved, if somewhat surprised, by the modesty of the lady's demands, and, placing his foot on the door-scraper in an easy attitude, prepared to wait with patience. Before many minutes, however, the door was opened by a thin, middle-aged woman, with a sharp, sallow face and very vivacious manner. She wore a neat, dark coat and skirt, a high-necked blouse and a long gold neck-chain with a variety of small ornaments dangling from it at intervals, and her iron-grey hair was dressed under a net, in the style fashionable in the reign of the late King Edward.

"Oh, Lord Peter! How *very* nice to see you. Rather an *early* visit, but I'm sure you will excuse the sitting-room being a trifle in disorder. *Do* come in. The lists are *quite* ready for you. I finished them last night. In fact, I was just about to put on my hat and bring them round to you. I do *hope* you don't think I have taken an *unconscionable* time, but there was a quite *surprising* number of entries. It is *too* good of you to trouble to call."

"Not at all, Miss Climpson. This is my friend, Detective-Inspector Parker, whom I have mentioned to you."

"How do you do, Mr. Parker—or ought I to say Inspector? Excuse me if I make mistakes—this is really the first time I have been in the hands of the police. I hope it's not rude of me to say that. Please come up. A great many stairs, I am afraid, but I hope you do not mind. I do so like to be *high up*. The air is so much better, and you know, Mr. Parker, thanks to Lord Peter's great kindness, I have such a *beautiful*, *airy* view, right over the houses. I think one can work so much *better* when one doesn't feel cribbed, cabined and confined, as Hamlet says. Dear me! Mrs. Winbottle *will* leave the pail on the stairs, and always in that very dark corner. I am *continually* telling her about it. If you keep close to the banisters you will avoid it nicely. Only one more flight. Here we are. Please overlook the untidiness. I always think breakfast things look so *ugly* when one has finished with them—almost sordid, to use a nasty word for a nasty subject.

What a pity that some of these clever people can't invent *self-cleaning* and *self-clearing* plates, is it not? But please *do* sit down; I won't keep you a moment. And I know, Lord Peter, that you will not hesitate to smoke. I do so enjoy the smell of your cigarettes—quite delicious—and you are so *very* good about extinguishing the ends."

The little room was, as a matter of fact, most exquisitely neat, in spite of the crowded array of knick-knacks and photographs that adorned every available inch of space. The sole evidences of dissipation were an empty eggshell, a used cup and a crumby plate on a breakfast tray. Miss Climpson promptly subdued this riot by carrying the tray bodily on to the landing.

Mr. Parker, a little bewildered, lowered himself cautiously into a small armchair, embellished with a hard, fat little cushion which made it impossible to lean back. Lord Peter wriggled into the window-seat, lit a Sobriane and clasped his hands above his knees. Miss Climpson, seated upright at the table, gazed at him with a gratified air which was positively touching.

"I have gone *very* carefully into all these cases," she began, taking up a thick wad of type-script. "I'm afraid, indeed, my notes are rather *copious*, but I trust the typist's bill will not be considered too heavy. My handwriting is very clear, so I don't think there can be any errors. Dear me! such *sad* stories some of these poor women had to tell me! But I have investigated most fully, with the kind assistance of the clergyman—a very nice man and so helpful—and I feel sure that in the majority of the cases your assistance will be *well bestowed*. If you would like to go through—"

"Not at the moment, Miss Climpson," interrupted Lord Peter, hurriedly. "It's all right, Charles—nothing whatever to do with Our Dumb Friends or supplying Flannel to Unmarried Mothers. I'll tell you about it later. Just now, Miss Climpson, we want your help on something quite different."

Miss Climpson produced a business-like notebook and sat at attention.

"The inquiry divides itself into two parts," said Lord Peter. "The first part, I'm afraid, is rather dull. I want you (if you will be so good) to go down to Somerset House and search, or get them to search, through all the death-certificates for Hampshire in the month of November, 1925. I don't know the town and I don't know the name of the deceased. What you are looking for is the death-certificate of an old lady of 73; cause of death, cancer; immediate cause, heart failure; and the certificate will have been signed by two doctors, one of whom will be either a Medical Officer of Health, Police Surgeon, Certifying Surgeon under the Factory and Workshops Act, Medical Referee under the Workmen's Compensation Act, Physician or Surgeon in a big General Hospital, or a man specially appointed by the Cremation authorities. If you want to give any excuse for the search, you can say that you are compiling statistics about cancer; but what you really want is the names of the people concerned and the name of the town."

"Suppose there are more than one answering to the requirements?"

"Ah! that's where the second part comes in, and where your remarkable tact and shrewdness are going to be so helpful to us. When you have collected all the "possibles," I shall ask you to go down to each of the towns concerned and make very, very skilful inquiries, to find out which is the case we want to get on to. Of course, you mustn't appear to be inquiring. You must find some good gossipy lady living in the neighbourhood and just get her to talk in a natural way. You must pretend to be gossipy yourself—it's not in your nature, I know, but I'm sure you can make a little pretense about it—and find out all you can. I fancy you'll find it pretty easy if you once strike the right town, because I know for a certainty that there was a terrible lot of ill-natured talk about this particular death, and it won't have been forgotten yet by a long chalk."

"How shall I know when it's the right one?"

"Well, if you can spare the time, I want you to listen to a little story. Mind you, Miss Climpson, when you get to wherever it is, you are not supposed ever to have heard a word of this tale before. But I needn't tell you that. Now, Charles, you've got an official kind of way of puttin' these things clearly. Will you just weigh in and give Miss Climpson the gist of that rigmarole our friend served out to us last night?"

Pulling his wits into order, Mr. Parker accordingly obliged with a digest of the doctor's story. Miss Climpson listened with great attention, making notes of the dates and details. Parker observed that she showed great acumen in seizing on the salient points; she asked a number of very shrewd questions, and her grey eyes were intelligent. When he had finished, she repeated the story, and he was able to congratulate her on a clear head and retentive memory.

"A dear old friend of mine used to say that I should have made a very good lawyer," said Miss Climpson, complacently, "but of course, when I was young, girls didn't have the education or the *opportunities* they get nowadays, Mr. Parker. I should have liked a good education, but my dear father didn't believe in it for women. Very old-fashioned, you young people would think him."

"Never mind, Miss Climpson," said Wimsey, "you've got just exactly the qualifications we want, and they're rather rare, so we're in luck. Now we want this matter pushed forward as fast as possible."

"I'll go down to Somerset House at once," replied the lady, with great energy, "and let you know the minute I'm ready to start for Hampshire."

"That's right," said his lordship, rising. "And now we'll just make a noise like a hoop and roll away. Oh! and while I think of it, I'd better give you something in hand for traveling expenses and so on. I think you had better be just a retired lady in easy circumstances looking for a nice little place to settle down in. I don't think you'd better be wealthy—wealthy people don't inspire confidence. Perhaps you would oblige me by living at the rate of about £800 a year—your own excellent taste and experience will suggest the correct accessories and so on for creating that impression. If you will allow me, I will give you a cheque for £50 now, and when you start on your wanderings you will let me know what you require."

"Dear me," said Miss Climpson, "I don't—"

"This is a pure matter of business, of course," said Wimsey, rather rapidly, "and you will let me have a note of the expenses in your usual business-like way."

"Of course." Miss Climpson was dignified. "And I will give you a proper receipt immediately.

"Dear, dear," she added, hunting through her purse, "I do not appear to have any penny stamps. How extremely remiss of me. It is most *unusual* for me not to have my little book of stamps—so handy I always think they are—but only last night Mrs. Williams borrowed my last stamps to send a very urgent letter to her son in Japan. If you will excuse me a moment—"

"I think I have some," interposed Parker.

"Oh, thank you very much, Mr. Parker. Here is the two-pence. I *never* allow myself to be without pennies—on account of the bathroom geyser, you know. Such a very *sensible* invention, most *convenient*, and prevents *all* dispute about hot water among the tenants. Thank you so much. And now I sign my name *across* the stamps. That's right, isn't it? My dear father would be surprised to find his daughter so business-like. He always said a woman should never *need* to know anything about money matters, but times have changed so greatly, have they not?"

Miss Climpson ushered them down all six flights of stairs, volubly protesting at their protests, and the door closed behind them.

"May I ask—?" began Parker.

"It is not what you think," said his lordship, earnestly.

"Of course not," agreed Parker.

"There, I knew you had a nasty mind. Even the closest of one's friends turn out to be secret thinkers. They think in private thoughts which they publicly repudiate."

"Don't be a fool. Who *is* Miss Climpson?"

"Miss Climpson," said Lord Peter, "is a manifestation of the wasteful way in which this country is run. Look at electricity. Look at water-power. Look at the tides. Look at the sun. Millions of power units being given off into space every minute. Thousands of old maids, simply bursting with useful energy, forced by our stupid social system into hydros and hotels and communities and hostels and posts as companions, where their magnificent gossip-powers and units of inquisitiveness are allowed to dissipate themselves or even become harmful to the community, while the ratepayers' money is spent on getting work for which these women are providentially fitted, inefficiently carried out by ill-equipped policemen like you. My god! it's enough to make a man write to *John Bull*. And then bright young men write nasty little patronising books called 'Elderly Women,' and 'On the Edge of the Explosion'—and the drunkards make songs upon 'em, poor things."

"Quite, quite," said Parker. "You mean that Miss Climpson is a kind of inquiry agent for you."

"She is my ears and tongue," said Lord Peter, dramatically, "and especially my nose. She asks questions which a young man could not put without a blush. She is the angel that rushes in where fools get a clump on the head. She can smell a rat in the dark. In fact, she is the cat's whiskers."

"That's not a bad idea," said Parker.

"Naturally—it is mine, therefore brilliant. Just think. People want questions asked. Whom do they send? A man with large flat feet and a notebook—the sort of man whose private life is conducted in a series of inarticulate grunts. I send a lady with a long, woolly jumper on knitting-needles and jingly things round her neck. Of course she asks questions—everyone expects it. Nobody is surprised. Nobody is alarmed. And so-called superfluity is agreeably and usefully disposed of. One of these days you will put up a statue to me, with an inscription:

" 'To the Man who Made
Thousands of Superfluous Women
Happy
without Injury to their Modesty
or Exertion to Himself.' "

"I wish you wouldn't talk so much," complained his friend. "And how about all those type-written reports? Are you turning philanthropist in your old age?"

"No—no," said Wimsey, rather hurriedly hailing a taxi. "Tell you about that later. Little private pogrom of my own—Insurance against the Socialist Revolution—when it comes. 'What did you do with your great wealth, comrade?' 'I bought First Editions.' 'Aristocrat! à la lanterne!' 'Stay, spare me! I took proceedings against 500 money-lenders who oppressed the workers.' 'Citizen, you have done well. We will spare your life. You shall be promoted to cleaning out the sewers.' Voilà! We must move with the times. Citizen taxi-driver, take me to the British Museum. Can I drop you anywhere? No? So long. I am going to collate a 12th century manuscript of Tristan, while the old order lasts."

Mr. Parker thoughtfully boarded a westward-bound 'bus and was rolled away to do some routine questioning, on his own account, among the female population of Notting Dale. It did not appear to him to be a milieu in which the talents of Miss Climpson could be usefully employed.

4

A BIT MENTAL

"A babbled of green fields."
King Henry V

*L*etter from Miss Alexandra Katherine Climpson to Lord Peter Wimsey.

C/o Mrs. Hamilton Budge,
Fairview, Nelson Avenue,
Leahampton, Hants.
April 29th, 1927.

MY DEAR LORD PETER,

You will be happy to hear, after my *two previous* bad shots (!), that I have found the *right* place at last. The Agatha Dawson certificate is the *correct* one, and the dreadful *scandal* about Dr. Carr is still very much alive, I am sorry to say for the sake of *human nature*. I have been fortunate enough to secure rooms in the *very next street* to Wellington Avenue, where Miss Dawson used to live. My landlady seems a very nice woman, though a *terrible gossip!*—which is *all to the good!!* Her charge for a very pleasant bedroom and sitting-room with *full board* is 3½ guineas weekly. I trust you will not think this *too extravagant*, as the situation is *just* what you wished me to look for. I enclose a careful statement of my expenses up-to-date. You will *excuse* the mention of *underwear*, which is, I fear, a somewhat large item! but wool is so expensive nowadays, and it is necessary that every detail of my equipment should be suitable to my (supposed!) position in life. I have been careful to *wash* the garments through, so that they do not look *too new*, as this might have a *suspicious* appearance!!

But you will be anxious for me to (if I may use a vulgar expression) 'cut the cackle, and come to the horses' (!!). On the day after my arrival, I informed Mrs. Budge that I was a great sufferer from *rheumatism* (which is quite true, as I have a sad legacy of that kind left me by, alas! my *port-drinking* ancestors!)—and inquired what *doctors* there were in the neighbourhood. This at once brought forth a *long catalogue*, together with a *grand panegyric* of the sandy soil and healthy situation of the town. I said I should prefer an *elderly* doctor, as the *young men*, in my opinion, were *not to be depended on*. Mrs. Budge heartily agreed with me, and a little discreet questioning brought out the *whole story* of Miss Dawson's illness and the 'carryings-on' (as she termed them) of Dr. Carr and *the nurse!* "I never did trust that first nurse," said Mrs. Budge, "for all she had her training at Guy's and ought to have been trustworthy. A sly, red-headed, *baggage*, and it's my belief that all Dr. Carr's fussing over Miss Dawson and his visits all day and every day were just to get love-making with Nurse Philliter. No wonder poor Miss Whittaker couldn't stand it any longer and gave the girl the sack—none too soon, in my opinion. Not quite so attentive after that, Dr. Carr wasn't—why, up to the last minute, he was pretending the old lady was quite all right, when Miss Whittaker had only said the day before that she felt sure she was going to be taken from us."

I asked if Mrs. Budge knew Miss Whittaker personally. Miss Whittaker is *the niece*, you know.

Not personally, she said, though she had met her in a social way at the Vicarage working-parties. But she knew all about it, because her maid was own sister to the maid at Miss Dawson's. Now is not that a *fortunate* coincidence, for you know how these girls *talk!*

I also made careful inquiries about the *Vicar*, Mr. Tredgold, and was much gratified to find that he teaches *sound Catholic* doctrine, so that I shall be able to attend the Church (S. Onesimus) without doing *violence* to my religious beliefs—a thing I could *not* undertake to do, *even in your interests*. I am sure you will *understand* this. As it happens, *all is well*, and I have written to my *very good friend*, the Vicar of S. Edfrith's, Holborn, to ask for an introduction to Mr. Tredgold. By this means, I feel sure of meeting *Miss Whittaker* before long, as I hear she is quite a "pillar of the Church"! I do hope it is not wrong to make use of the Church of God to a *worldly* end; but after all, you are only seeking to establish *Truth* and *Justice!*—and in so good a cause, we may *perhaps* permit ourselves to be a little bit *JESUITICAL!!!*

This is all I have been able to do as yet, but I shall not be *idle*, and will write to you again as soon as I have *anything to report*. By the way, the *pillar-box* is most *conveniently* placed just at the corner of Wellington Avenue, so that I can easily *run out* and post my letters to you *myself* (away from *prying* eyes!!) —and just take a little peep at Miss *Dawson's*—now Miss *Whittaker's*— house, "The Grove," at the same time.

> Believe me,
> Sincerely yours,
> ALEXANDRA KATHERINE CLIMPSON.

The little red-headed nurse gave her visitor a quick, slightly hostile look-over.

"It's quite all right," he said apologetically, "I haven't come to sell you soap or gramophones, or to borrow money or enroll you in the Ancient Froth-blowers or anything charitable. I really am Lord Peter Wimsey—I mean, that really is my title, don't you know, not a Christian name like Sanger's Circus or Earl Derr Biggers. I've come to ask you some questions, and I've no real excuse, I'm afraid, for butting in on you—do you ever read the *News of the World?*"

Nurse Philliter decided that she was to be asked to go to a mental case, and that the patient had come to fetch her in person.

"Sometimes," she said, guardedly.

"Oh—well, you may have noticed my name croppin' up in a few murders and things lately. I sleuth, you know. For a hobby. Harmless outlet for natural inquisitiveness, don't you see, which might otherwise strike inward and produce introspection an' suicide. Very natural, healthy pursuit—not too strenuous, not too sedentary; trains and invigorates the mind."

"I know who you are now," said Nurse Philliter, slowly. "You—you gave evidence against Sir Julian Freke. In fact, you traced the murder to him, didn't you?"

"I did—it was rather unpleasant," said Lord Peter, simply, "and I've got another little job of the same kind in hand now, and I want your help."

"Won't you sit down?" said Nurse Philliter, setting the example. "How am I concerned in the matter?"

"You know Dr. Edward Carr, I think—late of Leahampton—conscientious but a little lackin' in worldly wisdom—not serpentine at all, as the Bible advises, but far otherwise."

"What!" she cried, "do *you* believe it was murder, then?"

Lord Peter looked at her for a few seconds. Her face was eager, her eyes gleaming curiously under her thick, level brows. She had expressive hands, rather large and with strong, flat joints. He noticed how they gripped the arms of her chair.

"Haven't the faintest," he replied, nonchalantly, "but I wanted your opinion."

"Mine?"—she checked herself. "You know, I am not supposed to give opinions about my cases."

"You have given it to me already," said his lordship, grinning. "Though possibly I ought to allow for a little prejudice in favour of Dr. Carr's diagnosis."

"Well, yes—but it's not merely personal. I mean, my being engaged to Dr. Carr wouldn't affect my judgment of a cancer case. I have worked with him on a great many of them, and I know that his opinion is really trustworthy—just as I know that, as a motorist, he's exactly the opposite."

"Right. I take it that if he says the death was inexplicable, it really was so. That's one point gained. Now about the old lady herself. I gather she was a little queer towards the end—a bit mental, I think you people call it?"

"I don't know that I'd say that either. Of course, when she was under morphia, she would be unconscious, or only semi-conscious, for hours together. But up to the time when I left, I should say she was quite—well, quite all there. She was obstinate, you know, and what they call a character, at the best of times."

"But Dr. Carr told me she got odd fancies—about people poisoning her?"

The red-haired nurse rubbed her fingers slowly along the arm of the chair, and hesitated.

"If it will make you feel any less unprofessional," said Lord Peter, guessing what was in her mind, "I may say that my friend Detective-Inspector Parker is looking into this matter with me, which gives me a sort of right to ask questions."

"In that case—yes—in that case I think I can speak freely. I never understood about that poisoning idea. I never saw anything of it—no aversion, I mean, or fear of me. As a rule, a patient will show it, if she's got any queer ideas about the nurse. Poor Miss Dawson was always most kind and affectionate. She kissed me when I went away and gave me a little present, and said she was sorry to lose me."

"She didn't show any sort of nervousness about taking food from you?"

"Well, I wasn't allowed to give her any food that last week. Miss Whittaker said her aunt had taken this funny notion, and gave her all her meals herself."

"Oh! that's very interestin'. Was it Miss Whittaker, then, who first mentioned this little eccentricity to you?"

"Yes. And she begged me not to say anything about it to Miss Dawson, for fear of agitating her."

"And did you?"

"I did not. I wouldn't mention it in any case to a patient. It does no good."

"Did Miss Dawson ever speak about it to anyone else? Dr. Carr, for instance?"

"No. According to Miss Whittaker, her aunt was frightened of the doctor too, because she imagined he was in league with me. Of course, that story rather lent colour to the unkind things that were said afterwards. I suppose it's just possible that she saw us glancing at one another or speaking aside, and got the idea that we were plotting something."

"How about the maids?"

"There were new maids about that time. She probably wouldn't talk about it to them, and anyhow, I wouldn't be discussing my patient with her servants."

"Of course not. Why did the other maids leave? How many were there? Did they all go at once?"

"Two of them went. They were sisters. One was a terrible crockery-smasher, and Miss Whittaker gave her notice, so the other left with her."

"Ah, well! one can have too much of seeing the Crown Derby rollin' round the floor. Quite. Then it had nothing to do with—it wasn't on account of any little—"

"It wasn't because they couldn't get along with the nurse, if you mean that," said Nurse Philliter, with a smile. "They were very obliging girls, but not very bright."

"Quite. Well, now, is there any little odd, out-of-the-way incident you can think of that might throw light on the thing. There was a visit from a lawyer, I believe, that agitated your patient quite a lot. Was that in your time?"

"No. I only heard about it from Dr. Carr. And he never heard the name of the lawyer, what he came about, or anything."

"A pity," said his lordship. "I have been hoping great things of the lawyer. There's such a sinister charm, don't you think, about lawyers who appear unexpectedly with little bags, and alarm people with mysterious conferences, and then go away leaving urgent messages that if anything happens they are to be sent for. If it hadn't been for the lawyer, I probably shouldn't have treated Dr. Carr's medical problem with the respect it deserves. He never came again, or wrote, I suppose?"

"I don't know. Wait a minute. I do remember one thing. I remember Miss

Dawson having another hysterical attack of the same sort, and saying just what she said then—'that they were trying to kill her before her time.' "

"When was that?"

"Oh, a couple of weeks before I left. Miss Whittaker had been up to her with the post, I think, and there were some papers of some kind to sign, and it seems to have upset her. I came in from my walk and found her in a dreadful state. The maids could have told you more about it than I could, really, for they were doing some dusting on the landing at the time and heard her going on, and they ran down and fetched me up to her. I didn't ask them about what happened myself, naturally—it doesn't do for nurses to gossip with the maids behind their employers' backs. Miss Whittaker said that her aunt had had an annoying communication from a solicitor."

"Yes, it sounds as though there might be something there. Do you remember what the maids were called?"

"What was the name now? A funny one, or I shouldn't remember it— Gotobed, that was it—Bertha and Evelyn Gotobed. I don't now where they went, but I daresay you could find out."

"Now one last question, and I want you to forget all about Christian kindliness and the law of slander when you answer it. What is Miss Whittaker like?"

An indefinable expression crossed the nurse's face.

"Tall, handsome, very decided in manner," she said, with an air of doing strict justice against her will, "an extremely competent nurse—she was at the Royal Free, you know, till she went to live with her aunt. I think she would have made a perfectly wonderful theatre nurse. She did not like me, nor I her, you know, Lord Peter—and it's better I should be telling you so at once, that way you can take everything I say about her with a grain of charity added—but we both knew good hospital work when we saw it, and respected one another."

"Why in the world didn't she like you, Miss Philliter? I really don't know when I've seen a more likeable kind of person, if you'll 'scuse my mentionin' it."

"I don't know." The nurse seemed a little embarrassed. "The dislike seemed to grow on her. You—perhaps you heard the kind of things people said in the town? when I left?—that Dr. Carr and I—Oh! it really was damnable, and I had the most dreadful interview with Matron when I got back here. She *must* have spread those stories. Who else could have done it?"

"Well—you *did* become engaged to Dr. Carr, didn't you?" said his lordship, gently. "Mind you, I'm not sayin' it wasn't a very agreeable occurrence and all that, but—"

"But she said I neglected the patient. I *never* did. I wouldn't think of such a thing."

"Of course not. No. But, do you suppose that possibly getting engaged was an offence in itself? Is Miss Whittaker engaged to anyone, by the way?"

"No. You mean, was she jealous? I'm sure Dr. Carr never gave the slightest, not the *slightest*—"

"Oh, *please*," cried Lord Peter, "please don't be ruffled. Such a nice word, ruffled—like a kitten, I always think—so furry and nice. But even without the least what-d'ye-call-it on Dr. Carr's side, he's a very prepossessin' person and all that. Don't you think there *might* be something in it?"

"I did think so once," admitted Miss Philliter, "but afterwards, when she got him into such awful trouble over the post-mortem, I gave up the idea."

"But she didn't object to the post-mortem?"

"She did not. But there's such a thing as putting yourself in the right in the eyes of your neighbours, Lord Peter, and then going off to tell people all about it at Vicarage tea-parties. I wasn't there, but you ask someone who was. I know those tea-parties."

"Well, it's not impossible. People can be very spiteful if they think they've been slighted."

"Perhaps you're right," said Nurse Philliter, thoughtfully. "But," she added suddenly, "that's no motive for murdering a perfectly innocent old lady."

"That's the second time you've used that word," said Wimsey, gravely. "There's no proof yet that it was murder."

"I know that."

"But you think it was?"

"I do."

"And you think she did it?"

"Yes."

Lord Peter walked across to the aspidistra in the bow-window and stroked its leaves thoughtfully. The silence was broken by a buxom nurse who, entering precipitately first and knocking afterwards, announced with a giggle:

"Excuse me, I'm sure, but you're in request this afternoon, Philliter. Here's Dr. Carr come for you."

Dr. Carr followed hard upon his name. The sight of Wimsey struck him speechless.

"I told you I'd be turnin' up again before long," said Lord Peter, cheerfully. "Sherlock is my name and Holmes is my nature. I'm delighted to see you, Dr. Carr. Your little matter is well in hand, and seein' I'm not required any longer I'll make a noise like a bee and buzz off."

"How did *he* get here?" demanded Dr. Carr, not altogether pleased.

"Didn't you send him? I think he's very nice," said Nurse Philliter.

"He's mad," said Dr. Carr.

"He's clever," said the red-haired nurse.

5

GOSSIP

"With vollies of eternal babble."
Butler, Hudibras

"So you are thinking of coming to live in Leahampton," said Miss Murgatroyd. "How *very nice.* I do hope you will be settling down in the parish. We are *not* too well off for week-day congregations—there is so much indifference and so much *Protestantism* about. There! I have dropped a stitch. Provoking! Perhaps it was meant as a little reminder to me not to think uncharitably about Protestants. All is well—I have retrieved it. Were you thinking of taking a house, Miss Climpson?"

"I am not quite sure," replied Miss Climpson. "Rents are so very high nowadays, and I fear that to buy a house would be almost beyond my means. I must look round very carefully, and view the question from *all sides*. I should certainly *prefer* to be in this parish—and close to the Church, if possible. Perhaps the Vicar would know whether there is likely to be anything suitable."

"Oh, yes, he would doubtless be able to suggest something. It is such a very nice, residential neighbourhood. I am sure you would like it. Let me see—you are staying in Nelson Avenue, I think Mrs. Tredgold said?"

"Yes—with Mrs. Budge at Fairview."

"I am sure she makes you comfortable. Such a nice woman, though I'm afraid she never stops talking. Hasn't she got any ideas on the subject? I'm sure if there's any news going about, Mrs. Budge never fails to get hold of it."

"Well," said Miss Climpson, seizing the opening with a swiftness which would have done credit to Napoleon, "she did say something about a house in Wellington Avenue which she thought might be to let before long."

"Wellington Avenue? You surprise me! I thought I knew almost everybody there. Could it be the Parfitts—really moving at last! They have been talking about it for at least seven years, and I really had begun to think it was *all talk*. Mrs. Peasgood, do you hear that? Miss Climpson says the Parfitts are really leaving that house at last!"

"Bless me," cried Mrs. Peasgood, raising her rather prominent eyes from a piece of plain needlework and focusing them on Miss Climpson like a pair of opera-glasses. "Well, that *is* news. It must be that brother of hers who was staying with them last week. Possibly he is going to live with them permanently, and that would clinch the matter, of course, for they couldn't get on without another bedroom when the girls come home from school. A very sensible arrangement, I should think. I believe he is quite well off, you know, and it will be a very good thing for those children. I wonder where they will go. I expect it will be one of the new houses out on the Winchester Road, though of course that would mean keeping a car. Still, I expect he would want them to do that in any case. Most likely he will have it himself, and let them have the use of it."

"I don't think Parfitt was the name," broke in Miss Climpson hurriedly, "I'm sure it wasn't. It was a Miss somebody—a Miss Whittaker, I think, Mrs. Budge mentioned."

"Miss Whittaker?" cried both the ladies in chorus. "Oh, no! *surely* not?"

"I'm sure Miss Whittaker would have told me if she thought of giving up her house," pursued Miss Murgatroyd. "We are such great friends. I think Mrs. Budge must have run away with a wrong idea. People do build up such amazing stories out of nothing at all."

"I wouldn't go so far as that," put in Mrs. Peasgood, rebukingly. "There *may* be something in it. I know dear Miss Whittaker has sometimes spoken to me about wishing to take up chicken-farming. I daresay she has not mentioned the matter *generally*, but then she always confides in *me*. Depend on it, that is what she intends to do."

"Mrs. Budge didn't actually say Miss Whittaker was moving," interposed Miss Climpson. "She said, I think, that Miss Whittaker had been left alone by some relation's death, and she wouldn't be surprised if she found the house lonely."

"Ah! that's Mrs. Budge all over!" said Mrs. Peasgood, nodding ominously. "A most excellent woman, but she sometimes gets hold of the wrong end of the stick. Not but what I've often thought the same thing myself. I said to poor Mary Whittaker only the other day, 'Don't you find it very lonely in that house, my dear, now that your poor dear Aunt is no more?' I'm sure it would be a very good thing if she did move, or got someone to live with her. It's not a natural life for a young woman, all alone like that, and so I told her. I'm one of those that believe in speaking their mind, you know, Miss Climpson."

"Well, now, so am I, Mrs. Peasgood," rejoined Miss Climpson promptly, "and that is what I said to Mrs. Budge at the time. I said, 'Do I understand that there was anything *odd* about the old lady's death?'—because she had spoken of the *peculiar circumstances* of the case, and you know, I should not *at all like* to live in a house which could be called in any way *notorious*. I should really feel quite *uncomfortable* about it." In saying which, Miss Climpson no doubt spoke with perfect sincerity.

"But not at all—not at all," cried Miss Murgatroyd, so eagerly that Mrs. Peasgood, who had paused to purse up her face and assume an expression of portentous secrecy before replying, was completely crowded out and left at the post. "There never was a more wicked story. The death was natural—perfectly natural, and a most happy release, poor soul, I'm sure, for her sufferings at the last were truly terrible. It was all a scandalous story put about by that young Dr. Carr (whom I'm sure I never liked) simply to aggrandise himself. As though any doctor would pronounce so definitely upon what exact date it would please God to call a poor sufferer to Himself! Human pride and vanity make a most shocking exhibition, Miss Climpson, when they lead us to cast suspicion on innocent people, simply because we are wedded to our own presumptuous opinions. Poor Miss Whittaker! She went through a most terrible time. But it was proved—absolutely *proved*, that there was nothing in the story at all, and I hope that young man was properly ashamed of himself."

"There may be two opinions about that, Miss Murgatroyd," said Mrs. Peasgood. "I say what I think, Miss Climpson, and in my opinion there should have been an inquest. I try to be up-to-date, and I believe Dr. Carr to have been a very able young man, though of course, he was not the kind of old-fashioned family doctor that appeals to elderly people. It was a great pity that nice Nurse Philliter was sent away—that woman Forbes was no more use than a headache —to use my brother's rather vigorous expression. I don't think she knew her job, and that's a fact."

"Nurse Forbes was a charming person," snapped Miss Murgatroyd, pink with indignation at being called elderly.

"That may be," retorted Mrs. Peasgood, "but you can't get over the fact that she nearly killed herself one day by taking nine grains of calomel by mistake for three. She told me that herself, and what she did in one case she might do in another."

"But Miss Dawson wasn't given anything," said Miss Murgatroyd, "and at any rate, Nurse Forbes' mind was on her patient, and not on flirting with the doctor. I've always thought that Dr. Carr felt a spite against her for taking his young woman's place, and nothing would have pleased him better than to get her into trouble."

"You don't mean," said Miss Climpson, "that he would refuse a certificate and cause all that trouble, just to annoy the nurse. *Surely* no doctor would dare to do that."

"Of course not," said Mrs. Peasgood, "and nobody with a grain of sense would suppose it for a moment."

"Thank you very much, Mrs. Peasgood," cried Miss Murgatroyd, "thank you very much, I'm sure—"

"I say what I think," said Mrs. Peasgood.

"Then I'm glad I haven't such uncharitable thoughts," said Miss Murgatroyd.

"I don't think your own observations are so remarkable for their charity," retorted Mrs. Peasgood.

Fortunately, at this moment Miss Murgatroyd, in her agitation, gave a vicious tweak to the wrong needle and dropped twenty-nine stitches at once. The Vicar's wife, scenting battle from afar, hurried over with a plate of scones, and helped to bring about a diversion. To her, Miss Climpson, doggedly sticking to her mission in life, broached the subject of the house in Wellington Avenue.

"Well, I don't know, I'm sure," replied Mrs. Tredgold, "but there's Miss Whittaker just arrived. Come over to my corner and I'll introduce her to you, and you can have a nice chat about it. You will like each other so much, she is such a keen worker. Oh! and Mrs. Peasgood, my husband is so anxious to have a word with you about the choirboys' social. He is discussing it now with Mrs. Findlater. I wonder if you'd be so very good as to come and give him your opinion? He values it so much."

Thus tactfully the good lady parted the disputants and, having deposited Mrs. Peasgood safely under the clerical wing, towed Miss Climpson away to an arm-chair near the tea-table.

"Dear Miss Whittaker, I so want you to know Miss Climpson. She is a near neighbour of yours—in Nelson Avenue, and I hope we shall persuade her to make her home among us."

"That will be delightful," said Miss Whittaker.

The first impression which Miss Climpson got of Mary Whittaker was that she was totally out of place among the tea-tables of S. Onesimus. With her handsome, strongly-marked features and quiet air of authority, she was of the type that "does well" in City offices. She had a pleasant and self-possessed manner, and was beautifully tailored—not mannishly, and yet with a severe fineness of outline that negatived the appeal of a beautiful figure. With her long and melancholy experience of frustrated womanhood, observed in a dreary succession of cheap boarding-houses, Miss Climpson was able to dismiss one theory which had vaguely formed itself in her mind. This was no passionate nature, cramped by association with an old woman and eager to be free to mate before youth should depart. *That* look she knew well—she could diagnose it with dreadful accuracy at the first glance, in the tone of a voice saying, "How do you do?" But meeting Mary Whittaker's clear, light eyes under their well-shaped brows, she was struck by a sudden sense of familiarity. She had seen that look before, though the where and the when escaped her. Chatting volubly about her arrival in Leahampton, her introduction to the Vicar and her approval of the Hampshire air and sandy soil, Miss Climpson racked her shrewd brain for a clue. But the memory remained obstinately somewhere at the back of her head. "It will come to me in the night," thought Miss Climpson, confidently, "and meanwhile I won't say anything about the house; it would seem so pushing on a first acquaintance."

Whereupon, fate instantly intervened to overthrow this prudent resolve, and very nearly ruined the whole effect of Miss Climpson's diplomacy at one fell swoop.

The form which the avenging Erinyes assumed was that of the youngest Miss Findlater—the gushing one—who came romping over to them, her hands filled with baby-linen, and plumped down on the end of the sofa beside Miss Whittaker.

"Mary my *dear!* Why didn't you tell me? You really are going to start your chicken-farming scheme at once. I'd no *idea* you'd got on so far with your plans. How *could* you let me hear it first from somebody else? You promised to tell me before anybody."

"But I didn't know it myself," replied Miss Whittaker, coolly. "Who told you this wonderful story?"

"Why, Mrs. Peasgood said that she heard it from . . ." Here Miss Findlater was in a difficulty. She had not yet been introduced to Miss Climpson and hardly knew how to refer to her before her face. "This lady" was what a shop-girl would say; "Miss Climpson" would hardly do, as she had, so to speak, no official cognisance of the name; "Mrs. Budge's new lodger" was obviously impossible in the circumstances. She hesitated—then beamed a bright appeal at Miss Climpson, and said: "Our new helper—may I introduce myself? I do so detest formality, don't you, and to belong to the Vicarage work-party is a sort of introduction in itself, don't you think? Miss Climpson, I believe? How do you do? It is true, isn't it, Mary?—that you are letting your house to Miss Climpson, and starting a poultry-farm at Alford."

"Certainly not that I know of. Miss Climpson and I have only just met one another." The tone of Miss Whittaker's voice suggested that the first meeting might very willingly be the last so far as she was concerned.

"Oh dear!" cried the youngest Miss Findlater, who was fair and bobbed and rather coltish, "I believe I've dropped a brick. I'm *sure* Mrs. Peasgood understood that it was all settled." She appealed to Miss Climpson again.

"*Quite* a mistake!" said that lady, energetically, "what *must* you be thinking of me, Miss Whittaker? *Of course*, I could not *possibly* have said such a thing. I only happened to mention—in the most *casual* way, that I was looking—that is, *thinking* of looking about—for a house in the neighbourhood of the Church—so convenient, you know, for *Early Services* and *Saints' Days*—and it was suggested —just *suggested*, I really forget by *whom*, that you *might*, just *possibly*, at *some* time, consider letting your house. I assure you, that was *all*." In saying which, Miss Climpson was not wholly accurate or disingenuous, but excused herself to her conscience on the rather jesuitical grounds that where so much responsibility was floating about, it was best to pin it down in the quarter which made for peace. "Miss Murgatroyd," she added, "put me right at once, for she said you were *certainly* not thinking of any such thing, or you would have told her before anybody else."

Miss Whittaker laughed.

"But I shouldn't," she said, "I should have told my house-agent. It's quite true, I did have it in mind, but I certainly haven't taken any steps."

"You really are thinking of doing it, then?" cried Miss Findlater. "I do hope so —because, if you do, I mean to apply for a job on the farm! I'm simply longing to get away from all these silly tennis-parties and things, and live close to the Earth and the fundamental crudities. Do you read Sheila Kaye-Smith?"

Miss Climpson said no, but she was very fond of Thomas Hardy.

"It really is terrible, living in a little town like this," went on Miss Findlater, "so full of aspidistras, you know, and small gossip. You've no idea what a dreadfully gossipy place Leahampton is, Miss Climpson. I'm sure, Mary dear, you must have had more than enough of it, with that tiresome Dr. Carr and the things people said. I don't wonder you're thinking of getting rid of that house. I shouldn't think you could ever feel comfortable in it again."

"Why on earth not?" said Miss Whittaker, lightly. Too lightly? Miss Climpson was startled to recognise in eye and voice the curious quick defensiveness of the neglected spinster who cries out that she has no use for men.

"Oh well," said Miss Findlater, "I always think it's a little sad, living where people have died, you know. Dear Miss Dawson—though of course it really was merciful that she should be released—all the same—"

Evidently, thought Miss Climpson, she was turning the matter off. The atmosphere of suspicion surrounding the death had been in her mind, but she shied at referring to it.

"There are very few houses in which somebody hasn't died sometime or other," said Miss Whittaker. "I really can't see why people should worry about it. I suppose it's just a question of not realising. We are not sensitive to the past lives of people we don't know. Just as we are much less upset about epidemics and accidents that happen a long way off. Do you really suppose, by the way, Miss Climpson, that this Chinese business is coming to anything? Everybody seems to take it very casually. If all this rioting and Bolshevism was happening in Hyde Park, there'd be a lot more fuss made about it."

Miss Climpson made a suitable reply. That night she wrote to Lord Peter:

Miss Whittaker has asked me to tea. She tells me that, *much as she would enjoy* an active, country life, with something definite to do, she has a *deep affection* for the house in Wellington Avenue, and *cannot tear herself* away. She seems *very anxious* to give this impression. Would it be *fair* for me to say "The lady doth protest *too much*, methinks"? The *Prince of Denmark* might even add: "Let the galled jade wince"—if one can use that expression of a *lady*. How wonderful Shakespeare is! One can *always* find a phrase in his works for *any* situation!

6

FOUND DEAD

"Blood, though it sleep a time, yet never dies."
Chapman, The Widow's Tears

"You know, Wimsey, I think you've found a mare's nest," objected Mr. Parker. "I don't believe there's the slightest reason for supposing that there was anything odd about the Dawson woman's death. You've nothing to go on but a conceited young doctor's opinion and a lot of silly gossip."

"You've got an official mind, Charles," replied his friend. "Your official passion for evidence is gradually sapping your brilliant intellect and smothering your instincts. You're overcivilised, that's your trouble. Compared with you, I am a child of nature. I dwell among the untrodden ways beside the springs of Dove, a maid whom there are (I am shocked to say) few to praise, likewise very few to love, which is perhaps just as well. I *know* there is something wrong about this case."

"How?"

"How?—well, just as I know there is something wrong about that case of reputed Lafite '76 which that infernal fellow Pettigrew-Robinson had the nerve to try out on me the other night. It has a nasty flavour."

"Flavour be damned. There's no indication of violence or poison. There's no motive for doing away with the old girl. And there's no possibility of proving anything against anybody."

Lord Peter selected a Villar y Villar from his case, and lighted it with artistic care.

"Look here," he said, "will you take a bet about it? I'll lay you ten to one that Agatha Dawson was murdered, twenty to one that Mary Whittaker did it, and fifty to one that I bring it home to her within the year. Are you on?"

Parker laughed. "I'm a poor man, your Majesty," he temporised.

"There you are," said Lord Peter, triumphantly, "you're not comfortable about it yourself. If you were, you'd have said, 'It's taking your money, old chap,' and closed like a shot, in the happy assurance of a certainty."

"I've seen enough to know that nothing is a certainty," retorted the detective, "but I'll take you—in—half-crowns," he added, cautiously.

"Had you said ponies," replied Lord Peter, "I would have taken your alleged poverty into consideration and spared you, but seven-and-sixpence will neither make nor break you. Consequently, I shall proceed to make my statements good."

"And what step do you propose taking?" inquired Parker, sarcastically. "Shall you apply for an exhumation order and search for poison, regardless of the analyst's report? Or kidnap Miss Whittaker and apply the third-degree in the Gallic manner?"

"Not at all. I am more modern. I shall use up-to-date psychological methods. Like the people in the Psalms, I lay traps; I catch men. I shall let the alleged criminal convict herself."

"Go on! You are a one, aren't you?" said Parker, jeeringly.

"I am indeed. It is a well-established psychological fact that criminals cannot let well alone. They—"

"Revisit the place of the crime?"

"Don't interrupt, blast you. They take unnecessary steps to cover the traces which they haven't left, and so invite, seriatim, Suspicion, Inquiry, Proof, Conviction and the Gallows. Eminent legal writers—no, pax! don't chuck that S. Augustine about, it's valuable. Anyhow, not to cast the jewels of my eloquence into the pig-bucket, I propose to insert this advertisement in all the morning papers. Miss Whittaker must read *some* product of our brilliant journalistic age, I suppose. By this means, we shall kill two birds with one stone."

"Start two hares at once, you mean," grumbled Parker. "Hand it over."

"Bertha and Evelyn Gotobed, formerly in the service of Miss Agatha Dawson, of 'The Grove,' Wellington Avenue, Leahampton, are requested to communicate with J. Murbles, solicitor, of Staple Inn, when they will hear of something to their advantage."

"Rather good, I think, don't you?" said Wimsey. "Calculated to rouse suspicion in the most innocent mind. I bet you Mary Whittaker will fall for that."

"In what way?"

"I don't know. That's what's so interesting. I hope nothing unpleasant will happen to dear old Murbles. I should hate to lose him. He's such a perfect type of the family solicitor. Still, a man in his profession must be prepared to take risks."

"Oh, bosh!" said Parker. "But I agree that it might be as well to get hold of the girls, if you really want to find out about the Dawson household. Servants always know everything."

"It isn't only that. Don't you remember that Nurse Philliter said the girls were sacked shortly before she left herself? Now, passing over the odd circumstances of the Nurse's own dismissal—the story about Miss Dawson's refusing to take food from her hands, which wasn't at all borne out by the old lady's own attitude to her nurse—isn't it worth considerin' that these girls should have been pushed off on some excuse just about three weeks after one of those hysterical attacks of Miss Dawson's? Doesn't it rather look as though everybody who was likely to remember anything about that particular episode had been got out of the way?"

"Well, there was a good reason for getting rid of the girls."

"Crockery?—well, nowadays it's not so easy to get good servants. Mistresses put up with a deal more carelessness than they did in the dear dead days beyond recall. Then, about that attack. Why did Miss Whittaker choose just the very moment when the highly-intelligent Nurse Philliter had gone for her walk, to bother Miss Dawson about signin' some tiresome old lease or other? If business was liable to upset the old girl, why not have a capable person at hand to calm her down?"

"Oh, but Miss Whittaker is a trained nurse. She was surely capable enough to see to her aunt herself."

"I'm perfectly sure she was a very capable woman indeed," said Wimsey, with emphasis.

"Oh, all right. You're prejudiced. But stick the ad. in by all means. It can't do any harm."

Lord Peter paused, in the very act of ringing the bell. His jaw slackened, giving his long, narrow face a faintly foolish and hesitant look, reminiscent of the heroes of Mr. P. G. Wodehouse.

"You don't think—" he began. "Oh! rats!" He pressed the button. "It *can't* do any harm, as you say. Bunter, see that this advertisement appears in the personal columns of all this list of papers, every day until further notice."

The advertisement made its first appearance on the Tuesday morning. Nothing of any note happened during the week, except that Miss Climpson wrote in some distress to say that the youngest Miss Findlater had at length succeeded in persuading Miss Whittaker to take definite steps about the poultry farm. They had gone away together to look at a business which they had seen advertised in the *Poultry News*, and proposed to be away for some weeks. Miss Climpson feared that under the circumstances she would not be able to carry on any investigations of sufficient importance to justify her *far too generous* salary. She had, however, become friendly with Miss Findlater, who had promised to tell her *all about* their doings. Lord Peter replied in reassuring terms.

On the Tuesday following, Mr. Parker was just wrestling in prayer with his charlady, who had a tiresome habit of boiling his breakfast kippers till they resembled heavily pickled loofahs, when the telephone whirred aggressively.

"Is that you, Charles?" asked Lord Peter's voice. "I say, Murbles has had a letter about that girl, Bertha Gotobed. She disappeared from her lodgings last Thursday, and her landlady, getting anxious, and having seen the advertisement, is coming to tell us all she knows. Can you come round to Staple Inn at eleven?"

"Dunno," said Parker, a little irritably. "I've got a job to see to. Surely you can tackle it by yourself."

"Oh, yes!" The voice was peevish. "But I thought you'd like to have some of the fun. What an ungrateful devil you are. You aren't taking the faintest interest in this case."

"Well—I don't believe in it, you know. All right—don't use language like that —you'll frighten the girl at the Exchange. I'll see what I can do. Eleven?—right! —Oh, I say!"

"Cluck!" said the telephone.

"Rung off," said Parker, bitterly. "Bertha Gotobed. H'm! I could have sworn—"

He reached across to the breakfast-table for the *Daily Yell*, which was propped against the marmalade jar, and read with pursed lips a paragraph whose heavily leaded headlines had caught his eye, just before the interruption of the kipper episode.

"NIPPY" FOUND DEAD
IN EPPING FOREST

—

£5 Note in Hand-bag.

—

He took up the receiver again and asked for Wimsey's number. The man-servant answered him.

"His lordship is in his bath, sir. Shall I put you through?"

"Please," said Parker.

The telephone clucked again. Presently Lord Peter's voice came faintly, "Hullo!"

"Did the landlady mention where Bertha Gotobed was employed?"

"Yes—she was a waitress at the Corner House. Why this interest all of a sudden? You snub me in my bed, but you woo me in my bath. It sounds like a music-hall song of the less refined sort. Why, oh why?"

"Haven't you seen the papers?"

"No. I leave those follies till breakfast-time. What's up? Are we ordered to Shanghai? or have they taken sixpence off the income-tax?"

"Shut up, you fool, it's serious. You're too late."

"What for?"

"Bertha Gotobed was found dead in Epping Forest this morning."

"Good God! Dead? How? What of?"

"No idea. Poison or something. Or heart failure. No violence. No robbery. No clue. I'm going down to the Yard about it now."

"God forgive me, Charles. D'you know, I had a sort of awful feeling when you said that ad. could do no harm. Dead. Poor girl! Charles, I feel like a murderer. Oh, damn! and I'm all wet. It does make one feel so helpless. Look here, you spin down to the Yard and tell 'em what you know and I'll join you there in half a tick. Anyway, there's no doubt about it now."

"Oh, but, look here. It may be something quite different. Nothing to do with your ad."

"Pigs *may* fly. Use your common sense. Oh! and Charles, does it mention the sister?"

"Yes. There was a letter from her on the body, by which they identified it. She got married last month and went to Canada."

"That's saved her life. She'll be in absolutely horrible danger, if she comes back. We must get hold of her and warn her. And find out what she knows. Good-bye. I *must* get some clothes on. Oh, hell!"

Cluck! the line went dead again, and Mr. Parker, abandoning the kippers without regret, ran feverishly out of the house and down Lamb's Conduit Street to catch a diver tram to Westminster.

The Chief of Scotland Yard, Sir Andrew Mackenzie, was a very old friend of Lord Peter's. He received that agitated young man kindly and listened with attention to his slightly involved story of cancer, wills, mysterious solicitors and advertisements in the agony column.

"It's a curious coincidence," he said, indulgently, "and I can understand your feeling upset about it. But you may set your mind at rest. I have the police-surgeon's report, and he is quite convinced that the death was perfectly natural. No signs whatever of any assault. They will make an examination, of course, but I don't think there is the slightest reason to suspect foul play."

"But what was she doing in Epping Forest?"

Sir Andrew shrugged gently.

"That must be inquired into, of course. Still—young people *do* wander about, you know. There's a fiancé somewhere. Something to do with the railway, I believe. Collins has gone down to interview him. Or she may have been with some other friend."

"But if the death was natural, no one would leave a sick or dying girl like that?"

"*You* wouldn't. But say there had been some running about—some horse-play —and the girl fell dead, as these heart cases sometimes do. The companion may well have taken fright and cleared out. It's not unheard of."

Lord Peter looked unconvinced.

"How long has she been dead?"

"About five or six days, our man thinks. It was quite by accident that she was found then at all; it's quite an unfrequented part of the Forest. A party of young people were exploring with a couple of terriers, and one of the dogs nosed out the body."

"Was it out in the open?"

"Not exactly. It lay among some bushes—the sort of place where a frolicsome young couple might go to play hide-and-seek."

"Or where a murderer might go to play hide and let the police seek," said Wimsey.

"Well, well. Have it your own way," said Sir Andrew, smiling. "If it was murder, it must have been a poisoning job, for, as I say, there was not the slightest sign of a wound or a struggle. I'll let you have the report of the autopsy. In the meanwhile, if you'd like to run down there with Inspector Parker, you can of course have any facilities you want. And if you discover anything, let me know."

Wimsey thanked him, and collecting Parker from an adjacent office, rushed him briskly down the corridor.

"I don't like it," he said, "that is, of course, it's very gratifying to know that our first steps in psychology have led to action, so to speak, but I wish to God it hadn't been quite such decisive action. We'd better trot down to Epping straight away, and see the landlady later. I've got a new car, by the way, which you'll like."

Mr. Parker took one look at the slim black monster, with its long rakish body and polished-copper twin exhausts, and decided there and then that the only hope of getting down to Epping without interference was to look as official as possible and wave his police authority under the eyes of every man in blue along the route. He shoe-horned himself into his seat without protest, and was more unnerved than relieved to find himself shoot suddenly ahead of the traffic—not with the bellowing roar of the ordinary racing engine, but in a smooth, uncanny silence.

"The new Daimler Twin-Six," said Lord Peter, skimming dexterously round a lorry without appearing to look at it. "With a racing body. Specially built . . . useful . . . gadgets . . . no row—hate row . . . like Edmund Sparkler . . .

very anxious there should be no row . . . Little Dorrit . . . remember . . . call her Mrs. Merdle . . . for that reason . . . presently we'll see what she can do."

The promise was fulfilled before their arrival at the spot where the body had been found. Their arrival made a considerable sensation among the little crowd which business or curiosity had drawn to the spot. Lord Peter was instantly pounced upon by four reporters and a synod of Press photographers, whom his presence encouraged in the hope that the mystery might turn out to be a three-column splash after all. Parker, to his annoyance, was photographed in the undignified act of extricating himself from "Mrs. Merdle." Superintendent Walmisley came politely to his assistance, rebuked the onlookers, and led him to the scene of action.

The body had been already removed to the mortuary, but a depression in the moist ground showed clearly enough where it had lain. Lord Peter groaned faintly as he saw it.

"Damn this nasty warm spring weather," he said, with feeling. "April showers —sun and water—couldn't be worse. Body much altered, Superintendent?"

"Well, yes, rather, my lord, especially in the exposed parts. But there's no doubt about the identity."

"I didn't suppose there was. How was it lying?"

"On the back, quite quiet and natural-like. No disarrangement of clothing, or anything. She must just have sat down when she felt herself bad and fallen back."

"M'm. The rain has spoilt any footprints or signs on the ground. And it's grassy. Beastly stuff, grass, eh, Charles?"

"Yes. These twigs don't seem to have been broken at all, Superintendent."

"Oh, no," said the officer, "no signs of a struggle, as I pointed out in my report."

"No—but if she'd sat down here and fallen back as you suggest, don't you think her weight would have snapped some of these young shoots?"

The Superintendent glanced sharply at the Scotland Yard man.

"You don't suppose she was brought and put here, do you, sir?"

"I don't suppose anything," retorted Parker, "I merely drew attention to a point which I think you should consider. What are these wheel-marks?"

"That's our car, sir. We backed it up here and took her up that way."

"And all this trampling is your men too, I suppose?"

"Partly that, sir, and partly the party as found her."

"You noticed no other person's tracks, I suppose?"

"No, sir. But it's rained considerably this last week. Besides, the rabbits have been all over the place, as you can see, and other creatures too, I fancy. Weasels, or something of that sort."

"Oh! Well, I think you'd better take a look round. There might be traces of some kind a bit further away. Make a circle, and report anything you see. And you oughtn't to have let all that bunch of people get so near. Put a cordon round and tell 'em to move on. Have you seen all you want, Peter?"

Wimsey had been poking his stick aimlessly into the bole of an oak-tree at a few yards' distance. Now he stooped and lifted out a package which had been stuffed into a cleft. The two policemen hurried forward with eager interest, which evaporated somewhat at sight of the find—a ham sandwich and an empty Bass bottle, roughly wrapped up in a greasy newspaper.

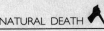
"Picnickers," said Walmisley, with a snort. "Nothing to do with the body, I daresay."

"I think you're mistaken," said Wimsey, placidly. "When did the girl disappear, exactly?"

"Well, she went off duty at the Corner House at five a week ago to-morrow, that's Wednesday, 27th," said Parker.

"And this is the *Evening Views* of Wednesday, 27th," said Wimsey. "Late Final edition. Now that edition isn't on the streets till about 6 o'clock. So unless somebody brought it down and had supper here, it was probably brought by the girl herself or her companion. It's hardly likely anyone would come and picnic here afterwards, not with the body there. Not that bodies need necessarily interfere with one's enjoyment of one's food. À la guerre comme à la guerre. But for the moment there isn't a war on."

"That's true, sir. But you're assuming the death took place on the Wednesday or Thursday. She may have been somewhere else—living with someone in town or anywhere."

"Crushed again," said Wimsey. "Still, it's a curious coincidence."

"It is, my lord, and I'm very glad you found the things. Will you take charge of 'em, Mr. Parker, or shall I?"

"Better take them along and put them with the other things," said Parker, extending his hand to take them from Wimsey, whom they seemed to interest quite disproportionately. "I fancy his lordship's right and that the parcel came here along with the girl. And that certainly looks as if she didn't come alone. Possibly that young man of hers was with her. Looks like the old, old story. Take care of that bottle, old man, it may have finger-prints on it."

"You can have the bottle," said Wimsey. "May we ne'er lack a friend or a bottle to give him, as Dick Swiveller says. But I earnestly beg that before you caution your respectable young railway clerk that anything he says may be taken down and used against him, you will cast your eye, and your nose, upon this ham sandwich."

"What's wrong with it?" inquired Parker.

"Nothing. It appears to be in astonishingly good preservation, thanks to this admirable oak-tree. The stalwart oak—for so many centuries Britain's bulwark against the invader! Heart of oak are our ships—not hearts, by the way, as it is usually misquoted. But I am puzzled by the incongruity between the sandwich and the rest of the outfit."

"It's an ordinary ham sandwich, isn't it?"

"Oh, gods of the wine-flask and the board, how long? how long?—it is a ham sandwich, Goth, but not an ordinary one. Never did it see Lyons' kitchen, or the counter of the multiple store or the delicatessen shop in the back street. The pig that was sacrificed to make this dainty titbit fattened in no dull style, never knew the daily ration of pig-wash or the not unmixed rapture of the domestic garbage-pail. Observe the hard texture, the deep brownish tint of the lean; the rich fat, yellow as a Chinaman's cheek; the dark spot where the black treacle cure has soaked in, to make a dish fit to lure Zeus from Olympus. And tell me, man of no discrimination and worthy to be fed on boiled cod all the year round, tell me how it comes that your little waitress and her railway clerk come down to Epping Forest to regale themselves on sandwiches made from coal-black, treacle-cured Bradenham ham, which long ago ran as a young wild boar about the woodlands, till death translated it to an incorruptible and more glorious body? I may add that it costs about 3*s*. a pound uncooked—an argument which you will allow to be weighty."

"That's odd, certainly," said Parker. "I imagine that only rich people—"

"Only rich people or people who understand eating as a fine art," said Wimsey. "The two classes are by no means identical, though they occasionally overlap."

"It may be very important," said Parker, wrapping the exhibits up carefully. "We'd better go along now and see the body."

The examination was not a very pleasant matter, for the weather had been damp and warm and there had certainly been weasels. In fact, after a brief glance, Wimsey left the two policemen to carry on alone, and devoted his attention to the dead girl's handbag. He glanced through the letter from Evelyn Gotobed—(now Evelyn Cropper)—and noted down the Canadian address. He turned the cutting of his own advertisement out of an inner compartment, and remained for some time in consideration of the £5 note which lay, folded up, side by side with a 10*s*. Treasury note, 7*s*., 8*d*. in silver and copper, a latch-key and a powder compacte.

"You're having this note traced, Walmisley, I suppose?"

"Oh, yes, my lord, certainly."

"And the latch-key, I imagine, belongs to the girl's lodgings."

"No doubt it does. We have asked her landlady to come and identify the body. Not that there's any doubt about it, but just as a matter of routine. She may give us some help. Ah!"—the Superintendent peered out of the mortuary door—"I think this must be the lady."

The stout and motherly woman who emerged from a taxi in charge of a youthful policeman identified the body without difficulty, and amid many sobs, as that of Bertha Gotobed. "Such a nice young lady," she mourned. "What a terrible thing, oh, dear! who would go to do a thing like that? I've been in such a state of worriment ever since she didn't come home last Wednesday. I'm sure many's the time I've said to myself I wished I'd had my tongue cut out before I ever showed her that wicked advertisement. Ah, I see you've got it there, sir. A dreadful thing it is that people should be luring young girls away with stories about something to their advantage. A sinful old devil—calling himself a lawyer, too! When she didn't come back and didn't come back I wrote to the wretch, telling him I was on his track and was coming round to have the law on him as sure as my name's Dorcas Gulliver. He wouldn't have got round me—not that I'd be the bird he was looking for, being sixty-one come Mid-Summer Day—and so I told him."

Lord Peter's gravity was somewhat upset by this diatribe against the highly respectable Mr. Murbles of Staple Inn, whose own version of Mrs. Gulliver's communication had been decently expurgated. "How shocked the old boy must have been," he murmured to Parker. "I'm for it next time I see him."

Mrs. Gulliver's voice moaned on and on.

"Such respectable girls, both of them, and Miss Evelyn married to that nice young man from Canada. Deary me, it will be a terrible upset for her. And there's poor John Ironsides, was to have married Miss Bertha, the poor lamb, this very Whitsuntide as ever is. A very steady, respectable man—a clurk on the Southern, which he always used to say, joking like, 'Slow but safe, like the Southern—that's me, Mrs. G.' T'ch, t'ch—who'd a' believed it? And it's not as if she was one of the flighty sort. I give her a latch-key gladly, for she'd sometimes be on late duty, but never any staying out after her time. That's why it worried me so, her not coming back. There's many nowadays as would wash one's hands and glad to be rid of them, knowing what they might be up to. No. When the time passed and she didn't come back, I said, Mark my words, I said, she's bin kidnapped, I said, by that Murbles."

"Had she been long with you, Mrs. Gulliver?" asked Parker.

"Not above a fifteen month or so, she hadn't, but bless you, I don't have to know a young lady fifteen days to know if she's a good girl or not. You gets to know by the look of 'em almost, when you've 'ad my experience."

"Did she and her sister come to you together?"

"They did. They come to me when they was lookin' for work in London. And they could a' fallen into a deal worse hands I can tell you, two young things from the country, and them that fresh and pretty looking."

"They were uncommonly lucky, I'm sure, Mrs. Gulliver," said Lord Peter, "and they must have found it a great comfort to be able to confide in you and get your good advice."

"Well, I think they did," said Mrs. Gulliver, "not that young people nowadays seems to want much guidance from them as is older. Train up a child and away she go, as the Good Book says. But Miss Evelyn, that's now Mrs. Cropper—she'd had this London idea put into her head, and up they comes with the idea of bein' made ladies of, havin' only been in service before, though what's the difference between serving in one of them tea-shops at the beck of all the nasty tagrag and bobtail and serving in a lady's home, I *don't* see, except that you works harder and don't get your meals so comfortable. Still, Miss Evelyn, she was always the go-ahead one of the two, and she did very well for herself, I will say, meetin' Mr. Cropper as used to take his breakfast regular at the Corner House every morning and took a liking to the girl in the most honourable way."

"That was very fortunate. Have you any idea what gave them the notion of coming to town?"

"Well, now, sir, it's funny you should ask that, because it was a thing I never could understand. The lady as they used to be in service with, down in the country, she put it into Miss Evelyn's head. Now, sir, wouldn't you think that with good service that 'ard to come by, she'd have done all she could to keep them with her? But no! There was a bit of trouble one day, it seems, over Bertha —this poor girl here, poor lamb—it do break one's 'eart to see her like that, don't it, sir?—over Bertha 'avin' broke an old teapot—a very valuable one by all accounts, and the lady told 'er she couldn't put up with 'avin' her things broke no more. So she says: 'You'll 'ave to go,' she says, 'but,' she says, 'I'll give you a very good character and you'll soon get a good place. And I expect Evelyn'll want to go with you,' she says, 'so I'll have to find someone else to do for me,' she says. 'But,' she says, 'why not go to London? You'll do better there and have a much more interesting life than what you would at home,' she says. And the end of it was, she filled 'em up so with stories of how fine a place London was and how grand situations was to be had for the asking, that they was mad to go, and she give them a present of money and behaved very handsome, take it all round."

"H'm," said Wimsey, "she seems to have been very particular about her teapot. Was Bertha a great crockery-breaker?"

"Well, sir, she never broke nothing of mine. But this Miss Whittaker—that was the name—she was one of these opinionated ladies, as will 'ave their own way in everythink. A fine temper she 'ad, or so poor Bertha said, though Miss Evelyn—her as is now Mrs. Cropper—*she* always 'ad an idea as there was somethink at the back of it. Miss Evelyn was always the sharp one, as you might say. But there, sir, we all 'as our peculiarities, don't we? It's my own belief as the lady had somebody of her own choice as she wanted to put in the place of Bertha —that's this one—and Evelyn—as is now Mrs. Cropper, you understand me— and she jest trampled up an excuse, as they say, to get rid of 'em."

"Very possibly," said Wimsey. "I suppose, Inspector, Evelyn Gotobed—"

"Now Mrs. Cropper," put in Mrs. Gulliver with a sob.

"Mrs. Cropper, I should say—has been communicated with?"

"Oh, yes, my lord. We cabled her at once."

"Good. I wish you'd let me know when you hear from her."

"We shall be in touch with Inspector Parker, my lord, of course."

"Of course. Well, Charles, I'm going to leave you to it. I've got a telegram to send. Or will you come with me?"

"Thanks, no," said Parker. "To be frank, I don't like your methods of driving. Being in the Force, I prefer to keep on the windy side of the law."

"Windy is the word for you," said Peter. "I'll see you in Town, then."

7

HAM AND BRANDY

"Tell me what you eat and I will tell you what you are."
Brillat-Savarin

"Well," said Wimsey, as Parker was ushered in that same evening by Bunter, "have you got anything fresh?"

"Yes, I've got a new theory of the crime, which knocks yours into a cocked hat. I've got evidence to support it, too."

"Which crime, by the way?"

"Oh, the Epping Forest business. I don't believe the old Dawson person was murdered at all. That's just an idea of yours."

"I see. And you're now going to tell me that Bertha Gotobed was got hold of by the White Slave people."

"How did you know?" asked Parker, a little peevishly.

"Because Scotland Yard have two maggots which crop up whenever anything happens to a young woman. Either it's White Slavery or Dope Dens—sometimes both. You are going to say it's both."

"Well, I was, as a matter of fact. It so often is, you know. We've traced the £5 note."

"That's important, anyhow."

"Yes. It seems to me to be the clue to the whole thing. It is one of a series paid out to a Mrs. Forrest, living in South Audley Street. I've been round to make some inquiries."

"Did you see the lady?"

"No, she was out. She usually is, I'm told. In fact, her habits seem to be expensive, irregular and mysterious. She has an elegantly furnished flat over a flower-shop."

"A service flat?"

"No. One of the quiet kind, with a lift you work yourself. She only turns up occasionally, mostly in the evenings, spends a night or two and departs. Food ordered in from Fortnum and Mason's. Bills paid promptly by note or cheque. Cleaning done by an elderly female who comes in about eleven, by which time Mrs. Forrest has usually gone out."

"Doesn't anybody ever see her?"

"Oh dear, yes! The people in the flat below and the girl at the flower-shop were able to give me quite a good description of her. Tall, over-dressed, musquash and those abbreviated sort of shoes with jewelled heels and hardly any uppers—you know the sort of thing. Heavily peroxided; strong aroma of origan wafted out upon the passer-by; powder too white for the fashion and mouth heavily obscured with sealing-wax red; eyebrows painted black to startle, not deceive; finger-nails a monument to Kraska—the pink variety."

"I'd no idea you studied the Woman's Page to such good purpose, Charles."

"Drives a Renault Four-seater, dark green with tapestry doings. Garages just round the corner. I've seen the man, and he says the car was out on the night of the 27th. Went out at 11:30. Returned about 8 the next morning."

"How much petrol had been used?"

"We worked that out. Just about enough for a run to Epping and back. What's more, the charwoman says that there had been supper for two in the flat that night, and three bottles of champagne drunk. Also, there is a ham in the flat."

"A Bradenham ham?"

"How do you expect the charwoman to know that? But I think it probably is, as I find from Fortnum & Mason's that a Bradenham ham was delivered to Mrs. Forrest's address about a fortnight ago."

"That sounds conclusive. I take it you think Bertha Gotobed was inveigled there for some undesirable purpose by Mrs. Forrest, and had supper with her—"

"No; I should think there was a man."

"Yes, of course. Mrs. F. brings the parties together and leaves them to it. The poor girl is made thoroughly drunk—and then something untoward happens."

"Yes—shock, perhaps, or a shot of dope."

"And they bustle her off and get rid of her. It's quite possible. The post-mortem may tell us something about it. Yes, Bunter, what is it?"

"The telephone, my lord, for Mr. Parker."

"Excuse me," said Parker, "I asked the people at the flower-shop to ring me up here, if Mrs. Forrest came in. If she's there, would you like to come round with me?"

"Very much."

Parker returned from the telephone with an air of subdued triumph.

"She's just gone up to her flat. Come along. We'll take a taxi—not that death-rattle of yours. Hurry up, I don't want to miss her."

The door of the flat in South Audley Street was opened by Mrs. Forrest in person. Wimsey recognised her instantly from the description. On seeing Parker's card, she made no objection whatever to letting them in, and led the way into a pink and mauve sitting-room, obviously furnished by contract from a Regent Street establishment.

"Please sit down. Will you smoke? And your friend?"

"My colleague, Mr. Templeton," said Parker, promptly.

Mrs. Forrest's rather hard eyes appeared to sum up in a practised manner the difference between Parker's seven-guinea "fashionable lounge suiting, tailored in our own workrooms, fits like a made-to-measure suit," and his "colleague's" Savile Row outlines, but beyond a slight additional defensiveness of manner she showed no disturbance. Parker noted the glance. "She's summing us up professionally," was his mental comment, "and she's not quite sure whether Wimsey's an outraged brother or husband or what. Never mind. Let her wonder. We may get her rattled."

"We are engaged, Madam," he began, with formal severity, "on an inquiry relative to certain events connected with the 26th of last month. I think you were in Town at that time?"

Mrs. Forrest frowned slightly in the effort to recollect. Wimsey made a mental note that she was not as young as her bouffant apple-green frock made her appear. She was certainly nearing the thirties, and her eyes were mature and aware.

"Yes, I think I was. Yes, certainly. I was in Town for several days about that time. How can I help you?"

"It is a question of a certain bank-note which has been traced to your possession," said Parker, "a £5 note numbered x/y58929. It was issued to you by Lloyds Bank in payment of a cheque on the 19th."

"Very likely. I can't say I remember the number, but I think I cashed a cheque about that time. I can tell in a moment by my cheque-book."

"I don't think it's necessary. But it would help us very much if you can recollect to whom you paid it."

"Oh, I see. Well, that's rather difficult. I paid my dressmaker's about that time—no, that was by cheque. I paid cash to the garage, I know, and I think there was a £5 note in that. Then I dined at Verry's with a woman friend—that took the second £5 note, I remember, but there was a third. I drew out £25— three fives and ten ones. Where did the third note go? Oh, of course, how stupid of me! I put it on a horse."

"Through a Commission Agent?"

"No. I had nothing much to do one day, so I went down to Newmarket. I put the £5 on some creature called Brighteye or Attaboy or some name like that, at 50 to 1. Of course the wretched animal didn't win, they never do. A man in the train gave me the tip and wrote the name down for me. I handed it to the nearest bookie I saw—a funny little grey-haired man with a hoarse voice—and that was the last I saw of it."

"Could you remember which day it was?"

"I think it was Saturday. Yes. I'm sure it was."

"Thank you very much, Mrs. Forrest. It will be a great help if we can trace those notes. One of them has turned up since in—other circumstances."

"May I know what the circumstances are, or is it an official secret?"

Parker hesitated. He rather wished now, that he had demanded point-blank at the start how Mrs. Forrest's £5 note had come to be found on the dead body of the waitress at Epping. Taken by surprise, the woman might have got flustered. Now, he had let her entrench herself securely behind this horse story. Impossible to follow up the history of a bank-note handed to an unknown bookie at a race-meeting. Before he could speak, Wimsey broke in for the first time, in a high, petulant voice which quite took his friend aback.

"You're not getting anywhere with all this," he complained. "I don't care a continental curse about the beastly note, and I'm sure Sylvia doesn't."

"Who is Sylvia?" demanded Mrs. Forrest with considerable amazement.

"Who is Sylvia? What is she?" gabbled Wimsey, irrepressibly. "Shakespeare always has the right word, hasn't he? But, God bless my soul, it's no laughing matter. It's very serious and you've no business to laugh at it. Sylvia is very much upset, and the doctor is afraid it may have an effect on her heart. You may not know it, Mrs. Forrest, but Sylvia Lyndhurst is my cousin. And what she wants to know, and what we all want to know—don't interrupt me, Inspector, all this shilly-shallying doesn't get us anywhere—I want to know, Mrs. Forrest, who was it dining here with you on the night of April 26th. Who was it? Who was it? Can you tell me that?"

This time, Mrs. Forrest was visibly taken aback. Even under the thick coat of powder they could see the red flush up into her cheeks and ebb away, while her eyes took on an expression of something more than alarm—a kind of vicious fury, such as one may see in those of a cornered cat.

"On the 26th?" she faltered. "I can't—"

"I knew it!" cried Wimsey. "And that girl Evelyn was sure of it too. Who was it, Mrs. Forrest? Answer me that!"

"There—there was no one," said Mrs. Forrest, with a thick gasp.

"Oh, come, Mrs. Forrest, think again," said Parker, taking his cue promptly, "you aren't going to tell us that you accounted by yourself for three bottles of Veuve Clicquot and two people's dinners."

"Not forgetting the ham," put in Wimsey, with fussy self-importance, "the Bradenham ham specially cooked and sent up by Fortnum & Mason. Now, Mrs. Forrest—"

"Wait a moment. Just a moment. I'll tell you everything."

The woman's hands clutched at the pink silk cushions, making little hot, tight creases. "I—would you mind getting me something to drink? In the dining-room, through there—on the sideboard."

Wimsey got up quickly and disappeared into the next room. He took rather a long time, Parker thought. Mrs. Forrest was lying back in a collapsed attitude, but her breathing was more controlled, and she was, he thought, recovering her wits. "Making up a story," he muttered savagely to himself. However, he could not, without brutality, press her at the moment.

Lord Peter, behind the folding doors, was making a good deal of noise, chinking the glasses and fumbling about. However, before very long, he was back.

" 'Scuse my taking such a time," he apologised, handing Mrs. Forrest a glass of brandy and soda. "Couldn't find the syphon. Always was a bit wool-gathering, y'know. All my friends say so. Starin' me in the face all the time, what? And then I sloshed a lot of soda on the sideboard. Hand shakin'. Nerves all to pieces and so on. Feelin' better? That's right. Put it down. That's the stuff to pull you to-gether. How about another little one, what? Oh, rot, it can't hurt you. Mind if I have one myself? I'm feelin'· a bit flustered. Upsettin', delicate business and all that. Just another spot. That's the idea."

He trotted out again, glass in hand, while Parker fidgeted. The presence of amateur detectives was sometimes an embarrassment. Wimsey clattered in again, this time, with more common sense, bringing decanter, syphon and three glasses, bodily, on a tray.

"Now, now," said Wimsey, "now we're feeling better, do you think you can answer our question, Mrs. Forrest?"

"May I know, first of all, what right you have to ask it?"

Parker shot an exasperated glance at his friend. This came of giving people time to think.

"Right?" burst in Wimsey. "Right? Of course, we've a right. The police have a right to ask questions when anything's the matter. Here's murder the matter! Right, indeed?"

"Murder?"

A curious intent look came into her eyes. Parker could not place it, but Wimsey recognised it instantly. He had seen it last on the face of a great financier as he took up his pen to sign a contract. Wimsey had been called to witness the signature, and had refused. It was a contract that ruined thousands of people. Incidentally, the financier had been murdered soon after, and Wimsey had declined to investigate the matter, with a sentence from Dumas: "Let pass the justice of God."

"I'm afraid," Mrs. Forrest was saying, "that in that case I can't help you. I *did* have a friend dining with me on the 26th, but he has not, so far as I know, been murdered, nor has he murdered anybody."

"It was a man, then?" said Parker.

Mrs. Forrest bowed her head with a kind of mocking ruefulness. "I live apart from my husband," she murmured.

"I am sorry," said Parker, "to have to press for this gentleman's name and address."

"Isn't that asking rather much? Perhaps if you would give me further details—"

"Well, you see," cut in Wimsey again, "if we could just know for certain it wasn't Lyndhurst. My cousin is so frightfully upset, as I said, and that Evelyn girl is making trouble. In fact—of course one doesn't want it to go any further—but actually Sylvia lost her head very completely. She made a savage attack on poor old Lyndhurst—with a revolver, in fact, only fortunately she is a shocking bad shot. It went over his shoulder and broke a vase—most distressin' thing—a Famille Rose jar, worth thousands—and of course it was smashed to atoms. Sylvia is really hardly responsible when she's in a temper. And, we thought, as Lyndhurst was actually traced to this block of flats—if you could give us definite proof it wasn't him, it might calm her down and prevent murder being done, don't you know. Because, though they might call it Guilty but Insane, still, it would be awfully awkward havin' one's cousin in Broadmoor —a first cousin, and really a very nice woman, when she's not irritated."

Mrs. Forrest gradually softened into a faint smile.

"I think I understand the position, Mr. Templeton," she said, "and if I give you a name, it will be in strict confidence, I presume?"

"Of course, of course," said Wimsey. "Dear me, I'm sure it's uncommonly kind of you."

"You'll swear you aren't spies of my husband's?" she said, quickly. "I am trying to divorce him. How do I know this isn't a trap?"

"Madam," said Wimsey, with intense gravity, "I swear to you on my honour as a gentleman that I have not the slightest connection with your husband. I have never even heard of him before."

Mrs. Forrest shook her head.

"I don't think, after all," she said, "it would be much good my giving you the name. In any case, if you asked him whether he'd been here, he would say no, wouldn't he? And if you've been sent by my husband, you've got all the evidence you want already. But I give you my solemn assurance, Mr. Templeton, that I know nothing about your friend, Mr. Lyndhurst—"

"Major Lyndhurst," put in Wimsey, plaintively.

"And if Mrs. Lyndhurst is not satisfied, and likes to come round and see me, I will do my best to satisfy her of the fact. Will that do?"

"Thank you very much," said Wimsey. "I'm sure it's as much as any one could expect. You'll forgive my abruptness, won't you? I'm rather—er—nervously constituted, and the whole business is exceedingly upsetting. *Good* afternoon. Come on, Inspector, it's quite all right—you see it's quite all right. I'm really very much obliged—uncommonly so. Please don't trouble to see us out."

He teetered nervously down the narrow hall-way, in his imbecile and well-bred way, Parker following with a policemanlike stiffness. No sooner, however, had the flat-door closed behind them than Wimsey seized his friend by the arm and bundled him helter-skelter into the lift.

"I thought we should never get away," he panted. "Now quick—how do we get round to the back of these flats?"

"What do you want with the back?" demanded Parker, annoyed. "And I wish you wouldn't stampede me like this. I've no business to let you come with me on a job at all, and if I do, you might have the decency to keep quiet."

"Right you are," said Wimsey, cheerfully, "just let's do this little bit and you can get all the virtuous indignation off your chest later on. Round here, I fancy, up this back alley. Step lively and mind the dust-bin. One, two, three, four— here we are! Just keep a look-out for the passing stranger, will you?"

Selecting a back window which he judged to belong to Mrs. Forrest's flat, Wimsey promptly grasped a drain-pipe and began to swarm up it with the agility of a cat-burglar. About fifteen feet from the ground he paused, reached up, and appeared to detach something with a quick jerk, and then slid very gingerly to the ground again, holding his right hand at a cautious distance from his body, as though it were breakable.

And indeed, to his amazement, Parker observed that Wimsey now held a long-stemmed glass in his fingers, similar to those from which they had drunk in Mrs. Forrest's sitting-room.

"What on earth—?" said Parker.

"Hush! I'm Hawkshaw the detective—gathering finger-prints. Here we come a-wassailing and gathering prints in May. That's why I took the glass back. I brought a different one in the second time. Sorry I had to do this athletic stunt, but the only cotton-reel I could find hadn't much on it. When I changed the glass, I tip-toed into the bathroom and hung it out of the window. Hope she hasn't been in there since. Just brush my bags down, will you, old man? Gently —don't touch the glass."

"What the devil do you want finger-prints for?"

"You're a grateful sort of person. Why, for all you know, Mrs. Forrest is someone the Yard has been looking for for years. And anyway, you could compare the prints with those on the Bass bottle, if any. Besides, you never know when finger-prints mayn't come in handy. They're excellent things to have about the house. Coast clear? Right. Hail a taxi, will you? I can't wave my hand with this glass in it. Look so silly, don't you know. I say!"

"Well?"

"I saw something else. The first time I went out for the drinks, I had a peep into her bedroom."

"Yes?"

"What do you think I found in the wash-stand drawer?"

"What?"

"A hypodermic syringe!"

"Really?"

"Oh, yes, and an innocent little box of ampullae, with a doctor's prescription headed 'The injection, Mrs. Forrest. One to be injected when the pain is very severe.' What do you think of that?"

"Tell you when we've got the results of that post-mortem," said Parker, really impressed. "You didn't bring the prescription, I suppose?"

"No, and I didn't inform the lady who we were or what we were after or ask her permission to carry away the family crystal. But I made a note of the chemist's address."

"Did you?" ejaculated Parker. "Occasionally, my lad, you have some glimmerings of sound detective sense."

8

CONCERNING CRIME

"Society is at the mercy of a murderer who is remorseless,
who takes no accomplices and who keeps his head."
Edmund Pearson, Murder at Smutty Nose

*L*etter from Miss Alexandra Katherine Climpson to Lord Peter Wimsey.

"Fair View,"
Nelson Avenue,
Leahampton.
12 May, 1927.

MY DEAR LORD PETER,

I have not *yet* been able to get ALL the information you ask for, as Miss Whittaker has been away for some weeks, inspecting *chicken-farms!!* With a view to purchase, I mean of course, and not in any *sanitary capacity*(!). I *really think* she means to set up farming *with Miss Findlater*, though what Miss Whittaker can see in that very gushing and really *silly* young woman I cannot think. However, Miss Findlater has evidently quite a "pash" (as we used to call it at school) for Miss Whittaker, and I am afraid none of us are being *flattered* by such outspoken admiration. I must say, I think it rather *unhealthy* —you may remember Miss Clemence Dane's *very clever book* on the subject? —I have seen so *much* of that kind of thing in my rather WOMAN-RIDDEN existence! It has such a bad effect, as a rule, upon the *weaker character* of the two—But I must not take up your time with my TWADDLE!!

Miss Murgatroyd, who was quite a friend of old *Miss Dawson*, however, has been able to tell me a *little* about her past life.

It seems that, until five years ago, Miss Dawson lived in Warwickshire with her cousin, a Miss Clara Whittaker, Mary Whittaker's great-aunt on the *father's* side. This Miss Clara was evidently rather a "character," as my dear father used to call it. In her day she was considered very "advanced" and *not quite nice* (!) because she *refused* several *good offers*, cut her hair short(!!) and set up in business for herself as a HORSE-BREEDER!!! Of course, *nowadays*, nobody would think anything of it, but *then* the old lady—or *young* lady as she was when she embarked on this *revolutionary* proceeding, was quite a PIONEER.

Agatha Dawson was a school-fellow of hers, and *deeply attached* to her. And as a result of this friendship, Agatha's *sister*, HARRIET, married Clara Whittaker's brother JAMES! But *Agatha* did not care about marriage, any more than *Clara*, and the two ladies lived together in a big old house, with immense stables, in a village in Warwickshire—Crofton, I think the name was. Clara Whittaker turned out to be a remarkably *good business woman*, and worked up a big connection among the *hunting folk* in those parts. Her hunters became quite *famous*, and from a capital of a few thousand pounds with which she started she made quite a *fortune*, and was a *very rich woman* before her death! Agatha Dawson never had anything to do with the *horsey* part of the business. She was the "domestic" partner, and looked after the *house* and the *servants*.

When Clara Whittaker died, she left *all her money* to Agatha, passing over her *own family*, with whom she was *not on very good terms*—owing to the narrow-minded attitude they had taken up about her horse-dealing!! Her nephew, Charles Whittaker, who was a clergyman, and the father of *our* Miss Whittaker, resented very much not getting the money, though, as he had kept up the feud in a very *un-Christian* manner, he had really *no right* to complain, especially as Clara had built up her fortune *entirely* by her own exertions. But, of course, he inherited the *bad, old-fashioned* idea that women *ought not* to be their own mistresses, or make money for themselves, or do what they liked with their own!

He and his family were the only surviving Whittaker relations, and when *he and his wife* were killed in a motor-car accident, Miss Dawson asked Mary to leave her work as a nurse and make her home with her. So that, you see, Clara Whittaker's money was destined to *come back* to James Whittaker's daughter in the end!! Miss Dawson made it *quite* CLEAR that this was her intention, provided Mary would come and *cheer the declining days* of a lonely old lady!

Mary accepted, and as her aunt—or, to speak more *exactly*, her great-aunt —had given up the big old Warwickshire house after Clara's death, they lived in London for a short time and then moved to Leahampton. As you know, poor old Miss Dawson was then already suffering from the *terrible disease* of which she died, so that Mary did not have to wait very long for Clara Whittaker's money!!

I hope this information will be of *use* to you. Miss Murgatroyd did not, of course, know anything about the rest of the family, but she always understood that there were no *other* surviving relatives, either on the Whittaker or the Dawson side.

When Miss Whittaker returns, I hope to *see more* of her. I enclose my *account* for expenses up to date. I do *trust* you will not consider it *extravagant*. How are your money-lenders progressing? I was sorry not to see more of those *poor women* whose cases I investigated—their stories were *so* PATHETIC!

I am,

Very sincerely yours,

ALEXANDRA K. CLIMPSON.

P.S.—I *forgot* to say that Miss Whittaker has a little motorcar. I do not, of course, know anything about these matters, but Mrs. Budge's maid tells me that Miss Whittaker's maid says it is an Austin 7 (is this right?). It is grey, and the number is XX9917.

Mr. Parker was announced, just as Lord Peter finished reading this document, and sank rather wearily in a corner of the chesterfield.

"What luck?" inquired his lordship, tossing the letter over to him. "Do you know, I'm beginning to think you were right about the Bertha Gotobed business, and I'm rather relieved. I don't believe one word of Mrs. Forrest's story, for reasons of my own, and I'm now hoping that the wiping out of Bertha was a pure coincidence and nothing to do with my advertisement."

"Are you?" said Parker, bitterly, helping himself to whisky and soda. "Well, I hope you'll be cheered to learn that the analysis of the body has been made, and that there is not the slightest sign of foul play. There is no trace of violence or of poisoning. There was a heart weakness of fairly long standing, and the verdict is syncope after a heavy meal."

"That doesn't worry me," said Wimsey. "We suggested shock, you know. Amiable gentleman met at flat of friendly lady suddenly turns funny after dinner and makes undesirable overtures. Virtuous young woman is horribly shocked. Weak heart gives way. Collapse. Exit. Agitation of amiable gentleman and friendly lady, left with corpse on their hands. Happy thought: motor-car; Epping Forest; *exeunt omnes*, singing and washing their hands. Where's the difficulty?"

"Proving it is the difficulty, that's all. By the way, there were no finger-marks on the bottle—only smears."

"Gloves, I suppose. Which looks like camouflage, anyhow. An ordinary picnicking couple wouldn't put on gloves to handle a bottle of Bass."

"I know. But we can't arrest all the people who wear gloves."

"I weep for you, the Walrus said, I deeply sympathise. I see the difficulty, but it's early days yet. How about those injections?"

"Perfectly O.K. We've interrogated the chemist and interviewed the doctor. Mrs. Forrest suffers from violent neuralgic pains, and the injections were duly prescribed. Nothing wrong there, and no history of doping or anything. The prescription is a very mild one, and couldn't possibly be fatal to anybody. Besides, haven't I told you that there was no trace of morphia or any other kind of poison in the body?"

"Oh, well!" said Wimsey. He sat for a few minutes looking thoughtfully at the fire.

"I see the case has more or less died out of the papers," he resumed, suddenly.

"Yes. The analysis has been sent to them, and there will be a paragraph to-morrow and a verdict of natural death, and that will be the end of it."

"Good. The less fuss there is about it the better. Has anything been heard of the sister in Canada?"

"Oh, I forgot. Yes. We had a cable three days ago. She's coming over."

"Is she? By Jove! What boat?"

"The *Star of Quebec*—due in next Friday."

"H'm! We'll have to get hold of her. Are you meeting the boat?"

"Good heavens, no! Why should I?"

"I think someone ought to. I'm reassured—but not altogether happy. I think I'll go myself, if you don't mind. I want to get that Dawson story—and this time I want to make sure the young woman doesn't have a heart attack before I interview her."

"I really think you're exaggerating, Peter."

"Better safe than sorry," said his lordship. "Have another peg, won't you? Meanwhile, what do you think of Miss Climpson's latest?"

"I don't see much in it."

"No?"

"It's a bit confusing, but it all seems quite straightforward."

"Yes. The only thing we know now is that Mary Whittaker's father was annoyed about Miss Dawson's getting his aunt's money and thought it ought to have come to him."

"Well, you don't suspect *him* of having murdered Miss Dawson, do you? He died before her, and the daughter's got the money, anyhow."

"Yes, I know. But suppose Miss Dawson had changed her mind? She might have quarrelled with Mary Whittaker and wanted to leave her money else-where."

"Oh, I see—and been put out of the way before she could make a will?"

"Isn't it possible?"

"Yes, certainly. Except that all the evidence we have goes to show that will-making was about the last job anybody could persuade her to do."

"True—while she was on good terms with Mary. But how about that morning Nurse Philliter mentioned, when she said people were trying to kill her before her time? Mary may really have been impatient with her for being such an unconscionable time a-dying. If Miss Dawson became aware of that, she would certainly have resented it and may very well have expressed an intention of making her will in someone else's favour—as a kind of insurance against prema-ture decease!"

"Then why didn't she send for her solicitor?"

"She may have tried to. But after all, she was bed-ridden and helpless. Mary may have prevented the message from being sent."

"That sounds quite plausible."

"Doesn't it? That's why I want Evelyn Cropper's evidence. I'm perfectly certain those girls were packed off because they had heard more than they should. Or why such enthusiasm over sending them to London?"

"Yes. I thought that part of Mrs. Gulliver's story was a bit odd. I say, how about the other nurse?"

"Nurse Forbes? That's a good idea. I was forgetting her. Think you can trace her?"

"Of course, if you really think it important."

"I do. I think it's damned important. Look here, Charles, you don't seem very enthusiastic about this case."

"Well, you know, I'm not so certain it is a case at all. What makes you so fearfully keen about it? You seem dead set on making it a murder, with practically nothing to go upon. Why?"

Lord Peter got up and paced the room. The light from the solitary reading-lamp threw his lean shadow, diffused and monstrously elongated, up to the ceiling. He walked over to a book-shelf, and the shadow shrank, blackened, settled down. He stretched his hand, and the hand's shadow flew with it, hovering over the gilded titles of the books and blotting them out one by one.

"Why?" repeated Wimsey. "Because I believe this is the case I have always been looking for. The case of cases. The murder without discernible means, or motive or clue. The norm. All these"—he swept his extended hand across the book-shelf, and the shadow outlined a vaster and more menacing gesture—"all these books on this side of the room are books about crimes. But they only deal with the abnormal crimes."

"What do you mean by abnormal crimes?"

"The failures. The crimes that have been found out. What proportion do you suppose they bear to the successful crimes—the ones we hear nothing about?"

"In this country," said Parker, rather stiffly, "we manage to trace and convict the majority of criminals—"

"My good man, I know that where a crime is known to have been committed, you people manage to catch the perpetrator in at least sixty per cent of the cases. But the moment a crime is even suspected, it falls, *ipso facto*, into the category of failures. After that, the thing is merely a question of greater or less efficiency on the part of the police. But how about the crimes which are never even suspected?"

Parker shrugged his shoulders.

"How can anybody answer that?"

"Well—one may guess. Read any newspaper to-day. Read the *News of the World*. Or, now that the Press has been muzzled, read the divorce court lists. Wouldn't they give you the idea that marriage is a failure? Isn't the sillier sort of journalism packed with articles to the same effect? And yet, looking round among the marriages you know of personally, aren't the majority of them a success, in a hum-drum, undemonstrative sort of way? Only you don't hear of them. People don't bother to come into court and explain that they dodder along very comfortably on the whole, thank you. Similarly, if you read all the books on this shelf, you'd come to the conclusion that murder was a failure. But bless you, it's always the failures that make the noise. Successful murderers don't write to the papers about it. They don't even join in imbecile symposia to tell an inquisitive world 'What Murder means to me,' or 'How I became a Successful Poisoner.' Happy murders, like happy wives, keep quiet tongues. And they probably bear just about the same proportion to the failures as the divorced couples do to the happily mated."

"Aren't you putting it rather high?"

"I don't know. Nor does anybody. That's the devil of it. But you ask any doctor, when you've got him in an unbuttoned, well-lubricated frame of mind, if he hasn't often had grisly suspicions which he could not and dared not take steps to verify. You see by our friend Carr what happens when one doctor is a trifle more courageous than the rest."

"Well, he couldn't prove anything."

"I know. But that doesn't mean there's nothing to be proved. Look at the scores and scores of murders that have gone unproved and unsuspected till the fool of a murderer went too far and did something silly which blew up the whole show. Palmer, for instance. His wife and brother and mother-in-law and various illegitimate children, all peacefully put away—till he made the mistake of polishing Cook off in that spectacular manner. Look at George Joseph Smith. Nobody'd have thought of bothering any more about those first two wives he drowned. It was only when he did it the third time that he aroused suspicion. Armstrong, too, is supposed to have got away with many more crimes than he was tried for—it was being clumsy over Martin and the Chocolates that stirred up the hornets' nest in the end. Burke and Hare were convicted of murdering an old woman, and then brightly confessed that they'd put away sixteen people in two months and no one a penny the wiser."

"But they *were* caught."

"Because they were fools. If you murder someone in a brutal, messy way, or poison someone who had previously enjoyed rollicking health, or choose the very day after a will's been made in your favour to extinguish the testator, or go on killing everyone you meet till people begin to think you're first cousin to a upas tree, naturally you're found out in the end. But choose somebody old and ill, in circumstances where the benefit to yourself isn't too apparent, and use a sensible method that looks like natural death or accident, and don't repeat your effects too often, and you're safe. I swear all the heart-diseases and gastric enteritis and influenzas that get certified are not nature's unaided work. Murder's so easy, Charles, so damned easy—even without special training."

Parker looked troubled.

"There's something in what you say. I've heard some funny tales myself. We all do, I suppose. But Miss Dawson—"

"Miss Dawson fascinates me, Charles. Such a beautiful subject. So old and ill. So likely to die soon. Bound to die before long. No near relations to make inquiries. No connections or old friends in the neighbourhood. And so rich. Upon my soul, Charles, I lie in bed licking my lips over ways and means of murdering Miss Dawson."

"Well, anyhow, till you can think of one that defies analysis and doesn't seem to need a motive, you haven't found the right one," said Parker, practically, rather revolted by this ghoulish conversation.

"I admit that," replied Lord Peter, "but that only shows that as yet I'm merely a third-rate murderer. Wait till I've perfected my method and then I'll show you —perhaps. Some wise old buffer has said that each of us holds the life of one other person between his hands—but only one, Charles, only one."

9

THE WILL

"Our wills are ours to make them thine."
Tennyson, In Memoriam

"Hullo! hullo—ullo! oh, operator, shall I call thee bird or but a wandering voice? . . . Not at all, I had no intention of being rude, my child, that was a quotation from the poetry of Mr. Wordsworth . . . well, ring him again . . . thank you, is that Dr. Carr? . . . Lord Peter Wimsey speaking . . . oh, yes . . . yes . . . aha! . . . not a bit of it . . . We are about to vindicate you and lead you home, decorated with triumphal wreaths of cinnamon and senna-pods . . . No, really. . . . we've come to the conclusion that the thing is serious. . . . Yes. . . . I want Nurse Forbes' address. . . . Right, I'll hold on. . . . Luton? . . . oh, Tooting, yes, I've got that. . . . Certainly, I've no doubt she's a tartar, but I'm the Grand Panjandrum with the little round button a-top. . . . Thanks awfully . . . cheer-frightfully-ho!—oh! I say!—hullo!—I say, she doesn't do maternity work, does she? Maternity work?—M for Mother-in-law—Maternity? —No—You're sure? . . . It would be simply awful if she did and came along. . . . I couldn't possibly produce a baby for her. . . . As long as you're quite sure. . . . Right—right—yes—not for the world—nothing to do with you at all. Good-bye, old thing, good-bye."

Lord Peter hung up, whistling cheerfully, and called for Bunter.

"My lord?"

"What is the proper suit to put on, Bunter, when one is an expectant father?"

"I regret, my lord, to have seen no recent fashions in paternity wear. I should say, my lord, whichever suit your lordship fancies will induce a calm and cheerful frame of mind in the lady."

"Unfortunately I don't know the lady. She is, in fact, only the figment of an over-teeming brain. But I think the garments should express bright hope, self-congratulations, and a tinge of tender anxiety."

"A newly married situation, my lord, I take it. Then I would suggest the lounge suit in pale grey—the willow-pussy cloth, my lord—with a dull amethyst tie and socks and a soft hat. I would not recommend a bowler, my lord. The anxiety expressed in a bowler hat would be rather of the financial kind."

"No doubt you are right, Bunter. And I will wear those gloves that got so unfortunately soiled yesterday at Charing Cross. I am too agitated to worry about a clean pair."

"Very good, my lord."

"No stick, perhaps."

"Subject to your lordship's better judgment, I should suggest that a stick may be suitably handled to express emotion."

"You are always right, Bunter. Call me a taxi, and tell the man to drive to Tooting."

Nurse Forbes regretted very much. She would have liked to oblige Mr. Simms-Gaythorpe, but she never undertook maternity work. She wondered who could have misled Mr. Simms-Gaythorpe by giving him her name.

"Well, y'know, I can't say I was misled," said Mr. Simms-Gaythorpe, dropping his walking-stick and retrieving it with an ingenuous laugh. "Miss Murgatroyd—you know Miss Murgatroyd of Leahampton, I think—yes—she—that is, I heard about you through her" (this was a fact), "and she said what a charming person—excuse my repeatin' these personal remarks, won't you?—what a charmin' person you were and all that, and how nice it would be if we could persuade you to come, don't you see. But she said she was afraid perhaps you *didn't* do maternity work. Still, y'know, I thought it was worth tryin', what? Bein' so anxious, what?—about my wife, that is, you see. So necessary to have someone young and cheery at these—er—critical times, don't you know. Maternity nurses often such ancient and ponderous sort of people—if you don't mind my sayin' so. My wife's highly nervous—naturally—first effort and all that—doesn't like middle-aged people tramplin' round—you see the idea."

Nurse Forbes, who was a bony woman of about forty, saw the point perfectly, and was very sorry she really could not see her way to undertaking the work.

"It was very kind of Miss Murgatroyd," she said. "Do you know her well? Such a delightful woman, is she not?"

The expectant father agreed.

"Miss Murgatroyd was so very much impressed by your sympathetic way—don't you know—of nursin' that poor old lady, Miss Dawson, y'know. Distant connection of my own as a matter of fact—er, yes—somewhere about fifteenth cousin twelve times removed. So nervous, wasn't she? A little bit eccentric, like the rest of the family, but a charming old lady, don't you think?"

"I became very much attached to her," said Nurse Forbes. "When she was in full possession of her faculties, she was a most pleasant and thoughtful patient. Of course, she was in great pain, and we had to keep her under morphia a great part of the time."

"Ah, yes! poor old soul! I sometimes think, Nurse, it's a great pity we aren't allowed just to help people off, y'know, when they're so far gone. After all, they're practically dead already, as you might say. What's the point of keepin' them sufferin' on like that?"

Nurse Forbes looked rather sharply at him.

"I'm afraid that wouldn't do," she said, "though one understands the lay person's point of view, of course. Dr. Carr was not of your opinion," she added, a little acidly.

"I think all that fuss was simply shockin'," said the gentleman warmly. "Poor old soul! I said to my wife at the time, why couldn't they let the poor old thing rest. Fancy cuttin' her about, when obviously she'd just mercifully gone off in a natural way! My wife quite agreed with me. She was quite upset about it, don't you know."

"It was very distressing to everybody concerned," said Nurse Forbes, "and of course, it put me in a very awkward position. I ought not to talk about it, but as you are one of the family, you will quite understand."

"Just so. Did it ever occur to you, Nurse"—Mr. Simms-Gaythorpe leaned forward, crushing his soft hat between his hands in a nervous manner—"that there might be something behind all that?"

Nurse Forbes primmed up her lips.

"You know," said Mr. Simms-Gaythorpe, "there *have* been cases of doctors tryin' to get rich old ladies to make wills in their favour. You don't think—eh?"

Nurse Forbes intimated that it was not her business to think things.

"No, of course not, certainly not. But as man to man—I mean, between you and me, what?—wasn't there a little—er—friction, perhaps, about sending for the solicitor-johnnie, don't you know? Of course, my Cousin Mary—I call her cousin, so to speak, but it's no relation at all really—of course, I mean, she's an awfully nice girl and all that sort of thing, but I'd got a sort of idea perhaps she wasn't altogether keen on having the will-making wallah sent for, what?"

"Oh, Mr. Simms-Gaythorpe, I'm sure you're quite wrong there. Miss Whittaker was most anxious that her aunt should have every facility in that way. In fact —I don't think I'm betraying any confidence in telling you this—she said to me, 'If at any time Miss Dawson should express a wish to see a lawyer, be sure you send for him at once.' And so, of course, I did."

"You did? And didn't he come, then?"

"Certainly he came. There was no difficulty about it at all."

"There! That just shows, doesn't it? how wrong some of these gossipy females can be! Excuse me, but y'know, I'd got absolutely the wrong impression about the thing. I'm quite *sure* Mrs. Peasgood said that no lawyer had been sent for."

"I don't know what Mrs. Peasgood could have known about it," said Nurse Forbes with a sniff, "her permission was not asked in the matter."

"Certainly not—but you know how these ideas get about. But, I say—if there was a will, why wasn't it produced?"

"I didn't say that, Mr. Simms-Gaythorpe. There was no will. The lawyer came to draw up a power of attorney, so that Miss Whittaker could sign cheques and so on for her aunt. That was very necessary, you know, on account of the old lady's failing powers."

"Yes—I suppose she was pretty woolly towards the end."

"Well, she was quite sensible when I took over from Nurse Philliter in September, except, of course, for that fancy she had about poisoning."

"She really was afraid of that?"

"She said once or twice, 'I'm not going to die to please anybody, Nurse.' She had great confidence in me. She got on better with me than with Miss Whittaker, to tell you the truth, Mr. Simms-Gaythorpe. But during October, her mind began to give way altogether, and she rambled a lot. She used to wake up sometimes all in a fright and say, 'Have they passed it yet, Nurse?'—just like that. I'd say, 'No, they haven't got that far yet,' and that would quiet her. Thinking of her hunting days, I expect she was. They often go back like that, you know, when they're being kept under drugs. Dreaming, like, they are, half the time."

"Then in the last month or so, I suppose she could hardly have made a will, even if she had wanted to."

"No, I don't think she could have managed it then."

"But earlier on, when the lawyer was there, she could have done so if she had liked?"

"Certainly she could."

"But she didn't?"

"Oh no. I was there with her all the time, at her particular request."

"I see. Just you and Miss Whittaker."

"Not even Miss Whittaker most of the time. I see what you mean, Mr. Simms-Gaythorpe, but indeed you should clear your mind of any unkind suspicions of Miss Whittaker. The lawyer and Miss Dawson and myself were alone together for nearly an hour, while the clerk drew up the necessary papers in the next room. It was all done then, you see, because we thought that a second visit would be too much for Miss Dawson. Miss Whittaker only came in quite at the end. If Miss Dawson had wished to make a will, she had ample opportunity to do so."

"Well, I'm glad to hear that," said Mr. Simms-Gaythorpe, rising to go. "These little doubts are so apt to make unpleasantness in families, don't you know. Well, I must be toddlin' now. I'm frightfully sorry you can't come with us, Nurse —my wife will be so disappointed. I must try to find somebody else equally charmin' if possible. Good-bye."

Lord Peter removed his hat in the taxi and scratched his head thoughtfully.

"Another good theory gone wrong," he murmured. "Well, there's another string to the jolly old bow yet. Cropper first and then Crofton—that's the line to take, I fancy."

PART II

THE LEGAL PROBLEM

"The gladsome light of jurisprudence."
Sir Edward Coke

NOTE—A genealogical table is printed at the front of the book

10

THE WILL AGAIN

"The will! the will! We will hear Caesar's will!"
Julius Caesar

"Oh, Miss Evelyn, my dear, oh, poor dear!"

The tall girl in black started, and looked round.

"Why, Mrs. Gulliver—how very, very kind of you to come and meet me!"

"And glad I am to have the chance, my dear, all owing to these kind gentlemen," cried the landlady, flinging her arms round the girl and clinging to her to the great annoyance of the other passengers pouring off the gangway. The elder of the two gentlemen referred to gently put his hand on her arm, and drew them out of the stream of traffic.

"Poor lamb!" mourned Mrs. Gulliver, "coming all this way by your lonesome, and poor dear Miss Bertha in her grave and such terrible things said, and her such a good girl always."

"It's poor Mother I'm thinking about," said the girl. "I couldn't rest. I said to my husband, 'I must go,' I said, and he said, 'My honey, if I could come with you I would, but I can't leave the farm, but if you feel you ought to go, you shall,' he said."

"Dear Mr. Cropper—he was always that good and kind," said Mrs. Gulliver, "but here I am, forgittin' all about the good gentlemen as brought me all this way to see you. This is Lord Peter Wimsey, and this is Mr. Murbles, as put in that unfortnit advertisement, as I truly believes was the beginin' of it all. 'Ow I wish I'd never showed it to your poor sister, not but wot I believe the gentleman acted with the best intentions, 'avin' now seen 'im, which at first I thought 'e was a wrong 'un."

"Pleased to meet you," said Mrs. Cropper, turning with the ready address derived from service in a big restaurant. "Just before I sailed I got a letter from poor Bertha enclosing your ad. I couldn't make anything of it, but I'd be glad to know anything which can clear up this shocking business. What have they said it is—murder?"

"There was a verdict of natural death at the inquiry," said Mr. Murbles, "but we feel that the case presents some inconsistencies, and shall be exceedingly grateful for your co-operation in looking into the matter, and also in connection with another matter which may or may not have some bearing upon it."

"Righto," said Mrs. Cropper. "I'm sure you're proper gentlemen, if Mrs. Gulliver answers for you, for I've never known her mistaken in a person yet, have I, Mrs. G? I'll tell you anything I know, which isn't much, for it's all a horrible mystery to me. Only I don't want you to delay me, for I've got to go straight on down to Mother. She'll be in a dreadful way, so fond as she was of Bertha, and she's all alone except for the young girl that looks after her, and that's not much comfort when you've lost your daughter so sudden."

"We shall not detain you a moment, Mrs. Cropper," said Mr. Murbles. "We propose, if you will allow us, to accompany you to London, and to ask you a few questions on the way, and then—again with your permission—we should like to see you safely home to Mrs. Gotobed's house, wherever that may be."

"Christchurch, near Bournemouth," said Lord Peter. "I'll run you down straight away, if you like. It will save time."

"I say, you know all about it, don't you?" exclaimed Mrs. Cropper with some admiration. "Well, hadn't we better get a move on, or we'll miss this train?"

"Quite right," said Mr. Murbles. "Allow me to offer you my arm."

Mrs. Cropper approving of this arrangement, the party made its way to the station, after the usual disembarkation formalities. As they passed the barrier on to the platform Mrs. Cropper gave a little exclamation and leaned forward as though something had caught her eye.

"What is it, Mrs. Cropper?" said Lord Peter's voice in her ear. "Did you think you recognised somebody?"

"You're a noticing one, aren't you?" said Mrs. Cropper. "Make a good waiter —you would—not meaning any offence, sir, that's a real compliment from one who knows. Yes, I did think I saw someone, but it couldn't be, because the minute she caught my eye she went away."

"Who did you think it was?"

"Why, I thought it looked like Miss Whittaker, as Bertha and me used to work for."

"Where was she?"

"Just down by that pillar there, a tall dark lady in a crimson hat and grey fur. But she's gone now."

"Excuse me."

Lord Peter unhitched Mrs. Gulliver from his arm, hitched her smartly on to the unoccupied arm of Mr. Murbles, and plunged into the crowd. Mr. Murbles, quite unperturbed by this eccentric behaviour, shepherded the two women into an empty first-class carriage which, Mrs. Cropper noted, bore a large label, "Reserved for Lord Peter Wimsey and party." Mrs. Cropper made some pro-testing observation about her ticket, but Mr. Murbles merely replied that every-thing was provided for, and that privacy could be more conveniently secured in this way.

"Your friend's going to be left behind," said Mrs. Cropper as the train moved out.

"That would be very unlike him," replied Mr. Murbles, calmly unfolding a couple of rugs and exchanging his old-fashioned top-hat for a curious kind of travelling cap with flaps to it. Mrs. Cropper, in the midst of her anxiety, could not help wondering where in the world he had contrived to purchase this Victorian relic. As a matter of fact, Mr. Murbles' caps were specially made to his own design by an exceedingly expensive West End hatter, who held Mr. Murbles in deep respect as a real gentleman of the old school.

Nothing, however, was seen of Lord Peter for something like a quarter of an hour, when he suddenly put his head in with an amiable smile and said:

"One red-haired woman in a crimson hat; three dark women in black hats; several nondescript women in those pull-on sort of dust-coloured hats; old women with grey hair, various; sixteen flappers without hats—hats on rack, I mean, but none of 'em crimson; two obvious brides in blue hats; innumerable fair women in hats of all colours; one ash-blonde dressed as a nurse, none of 'em our friend as far as I know. Thought I'd best just toddle along the train to make sure. There's just one dark sort of female whose hat I can't see because it's tucked down beside her. Wonder if Mrs. Cropper would mind doin' a little stagger down the corridor to take a squint at her."

Mrs. Cropper, with some surprise, consented to do so.

"Right you are. 'Splain later. About four carriages along. Now, look here, Mrs. Cropper, if it *should* be anybody you know, I'd rather on the whole she didn't spot you watching her. I want you to walk along behind me, just glancin' into the compartments but keepin' your collar turned up. When we come to the party I have in mind, I'll make a screen for you, what?"

These manoeuvres were successfully accomplished, Lord Peter lighting a cigarette opposite the suspected compartment, while Mrs. Cropper viewed the hatless lady under cover of his raised elbows. But the result was disappointing. Mrs. Cropper had never seen the lady before, and a further promenade from end to end of the train produced no better results.

"We must leave it to Bunter, then," said his lordship, cheerfully, as they returned to their seats. "I put him on the trail as soon as you gave me the good word. Now, Mrs. Cropper, we really get down to business. First of all, we should be glad of any suggestions you may have to make about your sister's death. We don't want to distress you, but we have got an idea that there might, just possibly, be something behind it."

"There's just one thing, sir—your lordship, I suppose I should say. Bertha was a real good girl—I can answer for that absolutely. There wouldn't have been any carryings-on with her young man—nothing of that. I know people have been saying all sorts of things, and perhaps, with lots of girls as they are, it isn't to be wondered at. But, believe me, Bertha wouldn't go for to do anything that wasn't right. Perhaps you'd like to see this last letter she wrote me. I'm sure nothing could be nicer and properer from a girl just looking forward to a happy marriage. Now, a girl as wrote like that wouldn't be going larking about, sir, would she? I couldn't rest, thinking they was saying that about her."

Lord Peter took the letter, glanced through it, and handed it reverently to Mr. Murbles.

"We're not thinking that at all, Mrs. Cropper, though of course we're very glad to have your point of view, don't you see. Now, do you think it possible your sister might have been—what shall I say?—got hold of by some woman with a plausible story and all that, and—well—pushed into some position which shocked her very much? Was she cautious and up to the tricks of London people and all that?"

And he outlined Parker's theory of the engaging Mrs. Forrest and the supposed dinner in the flat.

"Well, my lord, I wouldn't say Bertha was a very quick girl—not as quick as me, you know. She'd always be ready to believe what she was told and give people credit for the best. Took more after her father, like. I'm Mother's girl, they always said, and I don't trust anybody further than I can see them. But I'd warned her very careful against taking up with women as talks to a girl in the street, and she did ought to have been on her guard."

"Of course," said Peter, "it may have been somebody she'd got to know quite well—say, at the restaurant, and she thought she was a nice lady and there'd be no harm in going to see her. Or the lady might have suggested taking her into good service. One never knows."

"I think she'd have mentioned it in her letters if she'd talked to the lady much, my lord. It's wonderful what a lot of things she'd find to tell me about the customers. And I don't think she'd be for going into service again. We got real fed up with service, down in Leahampton."

"Ah, yes. Now that brings us to quite a different point—the thing we wanted to ask you or your sister about before this sad accident took place. You were in service with this Miss Whittaker whom you mentioned just now. I wonder if you'd mind telling us just exactly why you left. It was a good place, I suppose?"

"Yes, my lord, quite a good place as places go, though of course a girl doesn't get her freedom the way she does in a restaurant. And naturally there was a good deal of waiting on the old lady. Not as we minded that, for she was a very kind, good lady, and generous too."

"But when she became so ill, I suppose Miss Whittaker managed everything, what?"

"Yes, my lord; but it wasn't a hard place—lots of the girls envied us. Only Miss Whittaker was very particular."

"Especially about the china, what?"

"Ah, they told you about that, then?"

"I told 'em, dearie," put in Mrs. Gulliver. "I told 'em all about how you come to leave your place and go to London."

"And it struck us," put in Mr. Murbles, "that it was, shall we say, somewhat rash of Miss Whittaker to dismiss so competent and, if I may put it so, so well-spoken and personable a pair of maids on so trivial a pretext."

"You're right there, sir. Bertha—I told you she was the trusting one—she was quite ready to believe as she done wrong, and thought how good it was of Miss Whittaker to forgive her breaking the china, and take so much interest in sending us to London, but I always thought there was something more than met the eye. Didn't I, Mrs. Gulliver?"

"That you did, dear; something more than meets the eye, that's what you says to me, and what I agrees with."

"And did you, in your own mind," pursued Mr. Murbles, "connect this sudden dismissal with anything which had taken place?"

"Well, I did then," replied Mrs. Cropper, with some spirit. "I said to Bertha—but she would hear nothing of it, taking after her father as I tell you—I said, 'Mark my words,' I said, 'Miss Whittaker don't care to have us in the house after the row she had with the old lady."

"And what row was that?" inquired Mr. Murbles.

"Well, I don't know as I ought rightly to tell you about it, seeing it's all over now and we promised to say nothing about it."

"That, of course," said Mr. Murbles, checking Lord Peter, who was about to burst in impetuously, "depends upon your own conscience. But, if it will be of any help to you in making up your mind, I think I may say, in the strictest confidence, that this information may be of the utmost importance to us—in a roundabout way which I won't trouble you with—in investigating a very singular set of circumstances which have been brought to our notice. And it is just barely possible—again in a very roundabout way—that it may assist us in throwing some light on the melancholy tragedy of your sister's decease. Further than that I cannot go at the moment."

"Well, now," said Mrs. Cropper, "if that's so—though, mind you, I don't see what connection there could be—but if you think that's so, I reckon I'd better come across with it, as my husband would say. After all, I only promised I wouldn't mention about it to the people in Leahampton, as might have made mischief out of it—and a gossipy lot they is, and no mistake."

"We've nothing to do with the Leahampton crowd," said his lordship, "and it won't be passed along unless it turns out to be necessary."

"Righto. Well, I'll tell you. One morning early in September Miss Whittaker comes along to Bertha and I, and says, 'I want you girls to be just handy on the landing outside Miss Dawson's bedroom,' she says, 'because I may want you to come in and witness her signature to a document. We shall want two witnesses,' she says, 'and you'll have to see her sign; but I don't want to flurry her with a lot of people in the room, so when I give you the tip, I want you to come just inside the door without making a noise, so that you can see her write her name, and then I'll bring it straight across to you and you can write your names where I show you. It's quite easy,' she says, 'nothing to do but just put your names opposite where you see the word Witnesses.'

"Bertha was always a bit the timid sort—afraid of documents and that sort of thing, and she tried to get out of it. 'Couldn't Nurse sign instead of me?' she says. That was Nurse Philliter, you know, the red-haired one as was the doctor's fiancée. She was a very nice woman, and we liked her quite a lot. 'Nurse has gone out for her walk,' says Miss Whittaker, rather sharp, 'I want you and Evelyn to do it,' meaning me, of course. Well, we said we didn't mind, and Miss Whittaker goes upstairs to Miss Dawson with a whole heap of papers, and Bertha and I followed and waited on the landing, like she said."

"One moment," said Mr. Murbles, "did Miss Dawson often have documents to sign?"

"Yes, sir, I believe so, quite frequently, but they was usually witnessed by Miss Whittaker or the nurse. There was some leases and things of that sort, or so I heard. Miss Dawson had a little house-property. And then there'd be the cheques for the housekeeping, and some papers as used to come from the Bank, and be put away in the safe."

"Share coupons and so on, I suppose," said Mr. Murbles.

"Very likely, sir, I don't know much about those business matters. I did have to witness a signature once, I remember, a long time back, but that was different. The paper was brought down to me with the signature ready wrote. There wasn't any of this to-do about it."

"The old lady was capable of dealing with her own affairs, I understand?"

"Up till then, sir. Afterwards, as I understood, she made it all over to Miss Whittaker—that was just before she got feeble-like, and was kept under drugs. Miss Whittaker signed the cheques then."

"The power of attorney," said Mr. Murbles, with a nod. "Well now, did you sign this mysterious paper?"

"No, sir, I'll tell you how that was. When me and Bertha had been waiting a little time, Miss Whittaker comes to the door and makes us a sign to come in quiet. So we comes and stands just inside the door. There was a screen by the head of the bed, so we couldn't see Miss Dawson nor she us, but we could see her reflection quite well in a big looking-glass she had on the left side of the bed."

Mr. Murbles exchanged a significant glance with Lord Peter.

"Now be sure you tell us every detail," said Wimsey, "no matter how small and silly it may sound. I believe this is goin' to be very excitin'."

"Yes, my lord. Well, there wasn't much else, except that just inside the door, on the left-hand side as you went in, there was a little table, where Nurse mostly used to set down trays and things that had to go down, and it was cleared, and a piece of blotting-paper on it and an inkstand and pen, all ready for us to sign with."

"Could Miss Dawson see that?" asked Mr. Murbles.

"No, sir, because of the screen."

"But it was inside the room."

"Yes, sir."

"We want to be quite clear about this. Do you think you could draw—quite roughly—a little plan of the room, showing where the bed was and the screen and the mirror, and so on?"

"I'm not much of a hand at drawing," said Mrs. Cropper dubiously, "but I'll try."

Mr. Murbles produced a notebook and fountain pen, and after a few false starts, the following rough sketch was produced.

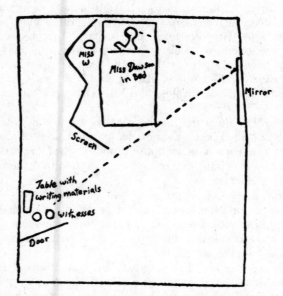

"Thank you, that is very clear indeed. You notice, Lord Peter, the careful arrangements to have the document signed in presence of the witnesses, and witnessed by them in the presence of Miss Dawson and of each other. I needn't tell you for what kind of document that arrangement is indispensable."

"Was that it, sir? We couldn't understand why it was all arranged like that."

"It might have happened," explained Mr. Murbles, "that in case of some dispute about this document, you and your sister would have had to come into court and give evidence about it. And if so, you would have been asked whether you actually saw Miss Dawson write her signature, and whether you and your sister and Miss Dawson were all in the same room together when you signed your names as witnesses. And if that had happened, you could have said yes, couldn't you, and sworn to it?"

"Oh, yes."

"And yet, actually, Miss Dawson would have known nothing about your being there."

"No, sir."

"That was it, you see."

"I see now, sir, but at the time Bertha and me couldn't make nothing of it."

"But the document, you say, was never signed."

"No, sir. At any rate, we never witnessed anything. We saw Miss Dawson write her name—at least, I suppose it was her name—to one or two papers, and then Miss Whittaker puts another lot in front of her and says, 'Here's another little lot, auntie, some more of those income-tax forms.' So the old lady says, 'What are they exactly, dear, let me see?' So Miss Whittaker says, 'Oh, only the usual things.' And Miss Dawson says, 'Dear, dear, what a lot of them. How complicated they do make these things to be sure.' And we could see that Miss Whittaker was giving her several papers, all laid on top of one another, with just the places for the signatures left showing. So Miss Dawson signs the top one, and then lifts up the paper and looks underneath at the next one, and Miss Whittaker says, 'They're all the same,' as if she was in a hurry to get them signed and done with. But Miss Dawson takes them out of her hand and starts looking through them, and suddenly she lets out a screech, and says, 'I won't have it, I won't have it! I'm not dying yet. How dare you, you wicked girl! Can't you wait till I'm dead?—you want to frighten me into my grave before my time. Haven't you got everything you want?' And Miss Whittaker says, 'Hush, auntie, you won't let me explain—' and the old lady says, 'No, I won't, I don't want to hear anything about it. I hate the thought of it. I won't talk about it. You leave me be. I can't get better if you keep frightening me so.' And then she begins to take and carry on dreadful, and Miss Whittaker comes over to us looking awful white and says, 'Run along, you girls,' she says, 'my aunt's taken ill and can't attend to business. I'll call you if I want you,' she says. And I said, 'Can we help with her, miss?' and she says, 'No, it's quite all right. It's just the pain come on again. I'll give her her injection and then she'll be all right.' And she pushes us out of the room, and shuts the door, and we heard the poor old lady crying fit to break anybody's heart. So we went downstairs and met Nurse just coming in, and we told her Miss Dawson was took worse again, and she runs up quick without taking her things off. So we was in the kitchen, just saying it seemed rather funny-like, when Miss Whittaker comes down again and says, 'It's all right now, and auntie's sleeping quite peaceful, only we'll have to put off business till another day.' And she says, 'Better not say anything about this to anybody, because when the pain comes on Aunt gets frightened and talks a bit wild. She don't mean what she says, but if people was to hear about it they might think it odd.' So I up and says, 'Miss Whittaker,' I says, 'me and Bertha was never ones to talk'; rather stiff, I said it, because I don't hold by gossip and never did. And Miss Whittaker says, 'That's quite all right,' and goes away. And the next day she gives us an afternoon off and a present—ten shillings each, it was, because it was her aunt's birthday, and the old lady wanted us to have a little treat in her honour."

"A very clear account indeed, Mrs. Cropper, and I only wish all witnesses were as sensible and observant as you are. There's just one thing. Did you by any chance get a sight of this paper that upset Miss Dawson so much?"

"No, sir—only from a distance, that is, and in the looking-glass. But I think it was quite short—just a few lines of typewriting."

"I see. Was there a typewriter in the house, by the way?"

"Oh, yes, sir. Miss Whittaker used one quite often for business letters and so on. It used to stand in the sitting-room."

"Quite so. By the way, do you remember Miss Dawson's solicitor calling shortly after this?"

"No, sir. It was only a little time later Bertha broke the teapot and we left. Miss Whittaker gave her her month's warning, but I said no. If she could come down on a girl like that for a little thing, and her such a good worker, Bertha should go at once and me with her. Miss Whittaker said, 'Just as you like,' she said—she never was one to stand any back-chat. So we went that afternoon. But afterwards I think she was sorry, and came over to see us at Christchurch, and suggested why shouldn't we try for a better job in London. Bertha was a bit afraid to go so far—taking after Father, as I mentioned, but Mother, as was always the ambitious one, she says, 'If the lady's kind enough to give you a good start, why not go? There's more chances for a girl in Town.' And I said to Bertha, private-like, afterwards, I says, 'Depend on it, Miss Whittaker wants to see the back of us. She's afraid we'll get talking about the things Miss Dawson said that morning. But,' I says, 'if she's willing to pay us to go, why not go,' I says. 'A girl's got to look out for herself these days, and if we go off to London she'll give us a better character than what she would if we stayed. And anyway,' I said, 'if we don't like it we can always come home again.' So the long and short was, we came to Town, and after a bit we got good jobs with Lyons, what with the good character Miss Whittaker gave us, and I met my husband there and Bertha met her Jim. So we never regretted having taken the chance—not till this dreadful thing happened to Bertha."

The passionate interest with which her hearers had received this recital must have gratified Mrs. Cropper's sense of the dramatic. Mr. Murbles was very slowly rotating his hands over one another with a dry, rustling sound—like an old snake, gliding through the long grass in search of prey.

"A little scene after your own heart, Murbles," said Lord Peter, with a glint under his dropped eyelids. He turned again to Mrs. Cropper.

"This is the first time you've told this story?"

"Yes—and I wouldn't have said anything if it hadn't been—"

"I know. Now, if you'll take my advice, Mrs. Cropper, you won't tell it again. Stories like that have a nasty way of bein' dangerous. Will you consider it an impertinence if I ask you what your plans are for the next week or two?"

"I'm going to see Mother and get her to come back to Canada with me. I wanted her to come when I got married, but she didn't like going so far away from Bertha. She was always Mother's favourite—taking so much after Father, you see. Mother and me was always too much alike to get on. But now she's got nobody else, and it isn't right for her to be all alone, so I think she'll come with me. It's a long journey for an ailing old woman, but I reckon blood's thicker than water. My husband said, 'Bring her back first-class, my girl, and I'll find the money.' He's a good sort, is my husband."

"You couldn't do better," said Wimsey, "and if you'll allow me, I'll send a friend to look after you both on the train journey and see you safe on to the boat. And don't stop long in England. Excuse me buttin' in on your affairs like this, but honestly I think you'd be safer elsewhere."

"You don't think that Bertha—?"

Her eyes widened with alarm.

"I don't like to say quite what I think, because I don't know. But I'll see you and your mother are safe, whatever happens."

"And Bertha? Can I do anything about that?"

"Well, you'll have to come and see my friends at Scotland Yard, I think, and tell them what you've told me. They'll be interested."

"And will something be done about it?"

"I'm sure, if we can prove there's been any foul play, the police won't rest till it's been tracked down to the right person. But the difficulty is, you see, to prove that the death wasn't natural."

"I observe in to-day's paper," said Mr. Murbles, "that the local superintendent is now satisfied that Miss Gotobed came down alone for a quiet picnic and died of a heart attack."

"That man would say anything," said Wimsey. "We know from the post-mortem that she had recently had a heavy meal—forgive these distressin' details, Mrs. Cropper—so why the picnic?"

"I suppose they had the sandwiches and the beer-bottle in mind," said Mr. Murbles, mildly.

"I see. I suppose she went down to Epping alone with a bottle of Bass and took out the cork with her fingers. Ever tried doing it, Murbles? No? Well, when they find the corkscrew I'll believe she went there alone. In the meantime, I hope the papers will publish a few more theories like that. Nothin' like inspiring criminals with confidence, Murbles—it goes to their heads, you know."

11

CROSS-ROADS

"Patience—and shuffle the cards."
Don Quixote

Lord Peter took Mrs. Cropper down to Christchurch and returned to town to have a conference with Mr. Parker. The latter had just listened to his recital of Mrs. Cropper's story, when the discreet opening and closing of the flat-door announced the return of Bunter.

"Any luck?" inquired Wimsey.

"I regret exceedingly to have to inform your lordship that I lost track of the lady. In fact, if your lordship will kindly excuse the expression, I was completely done in the eye."

"Thank God, Bunter, you're human after all. I didn't know anybody could do you. Have a drink."

"I am much obliged to your lordship. According to instructions, I searched the platform for a lady in a crimson hat and a grey fur, and at length was fortunate enough to observe her making her way out by the station entrance towards the big bookstall. She was some way ahead of me, but the hat was very conspicuous, and, in the words of the poet, if I may so express myself, I followed the gleam."

"Stout fellow."

"Thank you, my lord. The lady walked into the Station Hotel, which, as you know, has two entrances, one upon the platform, and the other upon the street. I hurried after her for fear she should give me the slip, and made my way through the revolving doors just in time to see her back disappearing into the Ladies' Retiring Room."

"Whither, as a modest man, you could not follow her. I quite understand."

"Quite so, my lord. I took a seat in the entrance hall, in a position from which I could watch the door without appearing to do so."

"And discovered too late that the place had two exits, I suppose. Unusual and distressin'."

"No, my lord. That was not the trouble. I sat watching for three quarters of an hour, but the crimson hat did not reappear. Your lordship will bear in mind that I had never seen the lady's face."

Lord Peter groaned.

I foresee the end of this story, Bunter. Not your fault. Proceed."

"At the end of this time, my lord, I felt bound to conclude either that the lady had been taken ill or that something untoward had occurred. I summoned a female attendant who happened to cross the hall and informed her that I had been entrusted with a message for a lady whose dress I described. I begged her to ascertain from the attendant in the Ladies' Room whether the lady in question was still there. The girl went away and presently returned to say that the lady had changed her costume in the cloak-room and had gone out half an hour previously."

"Oh, Bunter, Bunter. Didn't you spot the suitcase or whatever it was when she came out again?"

"Excuse me, my lord. The lady had come in earlier in the day and had left an attaché-case in charge of the attendant. On returning, she had transferred her hat and fur to the attaché-case and put on a small black felt hat and a light-weight raincoat which she had packed there in readiness. So that her dress was concealed when she emerged and she was carrying the attaché-case, whereas, when I first saw her, she had been empty-handed."

"Everything foreseen. What a woman!"

"I made immediate inquiries, my lord, in the region of the hotel and the station, but without result. The black hat and raincoat were entirely inconspicuous, and no one remembered having seen her. I went to the Central Station to discover if she had travelled by any train. Several women answering to the description had taken tickets for various destinations, but I could get no definite information. I also visited all the garages in Liverpool, with the same lack of success. I am greatly distressed to have failed your lordship."

"Can't be helped. You did everything you could do. Cheer up. Never say die. And you must be tired to death. Take the day off and go to bed."

"I thank your lordship, but I slept excellently in the train on the way up."

"Just as you like, Bunter. But I did hope you sometimes got tired like other people."

Bunter smiled discreetly and withdrew.

"Well, we've gained this much, anyhow," said Parker. "We know now that this Miss Whittaker has something to conceal, since she takes such precautions to avoid being followed."

"We know more than that. We know that she was desperately anxious to get hold of the Cropper woman before anybody else could see her, no doubt to stop her mouth by bribery or by worse means. By the way, how did she know she was coming by that boat?"

"Mrs. Cropper sent a cable, which was read at the inquest."

"Damn these inquests. They give away all the information one wants kept quiet, and produce no evidence worth having."

"Hear, hear," said Parker, with emphasis, "not to mention that we had to sit through a lot of moral punk by the Coroner, about the prevalence of jazz and the immoral behaviour of modern girls in going off alone with young men to Epping Forest."

"It's a pity these busy-bodies can't be had up for libel. Never mind. We'll get the Whittaker woman yet."

"Always provided it was the Whittaker woman. After all, Mrs. Cropper may have been mistaken. Lots of people do change their hats in cloak-rooms without any criminal intentions."

"Oh, of course. Miss Whittaker's supposed to be in the country with Miss Findlater, isn't she? We'll get the invaluable Miss Climpson to pump the girl when they turn up again. Meanwhile, what do you think of Mrs. Cropper's story?"

"There's no doubt about what happened there. Miss Whittaker was trying to get the old lady to sign a will without knowing it. She gave it to her all mixed up with the income-tax papers, hoping she'd put her name to it without reading it. It must have been a will, I think, because that's the only document I know of which is invalid unless it's witnessed by two persons in the presence of the testatrix and of each other."

"Exactly. And since Miss Whittaker couldn't be one of the witnesses herself, but had to get the two maids to sign, the will must have been in Miss Whittaker's favour."

"Obviously. She wouldn't go to all that trouble to disinherit herself."

"But that brings us to another difficulty. Miss Whittaker, as next of kin, would have taken all the old lady had to leave in any case. As a matter of fact, she did. Why bother about a will?"

"Perhaps, as we said before, she was afraid Miss Dawson would change her mind, and wanted to get a will made out before—no, that won't work."

"No—because, anyhow, any will made later would invalidate the first will. Besides, the old lady sent for her solicitor some time later, and Miss Whittaker put no obstacle of any kind in her way."

"According to Nurse Forbes, she was particularly anxious that every facility should be given."

"Seeing how Miss Dawson distrusted her niece, it's a bit surprising, really, that she didn't will the money away. Then it would have been to Miss Whittaker's advantage to keep her alive as long as possible."

"I don't suppose she really distrusted her—not to the extent of expecting to be made away with. She was excited and said more than she meant—we often do."

"Yes, but she evidently thought there'd be other attempts to get a will signed."

"How do you make that out?"

"Don't you remember the power of attorney? The old girl evidently thought that out and decided to give Miss Whittaker authority to sign everything for her so that there couldn't possibly be any jiggery-pokery about papers in future."

"Of course. Cute old lady. How very irritating for Miss Whittaker. And after that very hopeful visit of the solicitor, too. So disappointing. Instead of the expected will, a very carefully planted spoke in her wheel."

"Yes. But we're still brought up against the problem, why a will at all?"

"So we are."

The two men pulled at their pipes for some time in silence.

"The aunt evidently intended the money to go to Mary Whittaker all right," remarked Parker at last. "She promised it so often—besides, I daresay she was a just-minded old thing, and remembered that it was really Whittaker money which had come to her over the head of the Rev. Charles, or whatever his name was."

"That's so. Well, there's only one thing that could prevent that happening, and that's—oh, lord! old son. Do you know what it works out at? The old, old story, beloved of novelists—the missing heir!"

"Good lord, yes, you're right. Damn it all, what fools we were not to think of it before. Mary Whittaker possibly found out that there was some nearer relative left, who would scoop the lot. Maybe she was afraid that if Miss Dawson got to know about it, she'd divide the money or disinherit Mary altogether. Or perhaps she just despaired of hammering the story into the old lady's head, and so hit on the idea of getting her to make the will unbeknownst to herself in Mary's favour."

"What a brain you've got, Charles. Or, see here, Miss Dawson may have known all about it, sly old thing, and determined to pay Miss Whittaker out for her indecent urgency in the matter of will-makin' by just dyin' intestate in the other chappie's favour."

"If she did, she deserved anything she got," said Parker, rather viciously. "After taking the poor girl away from her job under promise of leaving her the dibs."

"Teach the young woman not to be so mercenary," retorted Wimsey, with the cheerful brutality of the man who has never in his life been short of money.

"If this bright idea is correct," said Parker, "it rather messes up your murder theory, doesn't it? Because Mary would obviously take the line of keeping her aunt alive as long as possible, in hopes she might make a will after all."

"That's true. Curse you, Charles, I see that bet of mine going west. What a blow for friend Carr, too. I did hope I was going to vindicate him and have him played home by the village band under a triumphal arch with 'Welcome, Champion of Truth!' picked out in red-white-and-blue electric bulbs. Never mind. It's better to lose a wager and see the light than walk in ignorance bloated with gold. —Or stop!—why shouldn't Carr be right after all? Perhaps it's just my choice of a murderer that's wrong. Aha! I see a new and even more sinister villain step upon the scene. The new claimant, warned by his minions—"

"What minions?"

"Oh, don't be so pernickety, Charles. Nurse Forbes, probably. I shouldn't wonder if she's in his pay. Where was I? I wish you wouldn't interrupt."

"Warned by his minions—" prompted Parker.

"Oh, yes—warned by his minions that Miss Dawson is hob-nobbing with solicitors and being tempted into making wills and things, gets the said minions to polish her off before she can do any mischief."

"Yes, but how?"

"Oh, by one of those native poisons which slay in a split second and defy the skill of the analyst. They are familiar to the meanest writer of mystery stories. I'm not going to let a trifle like that stand in my way."

"And why hasn't this hypothetical gentleman brought forward any claim to the property so far?"

"He's biding his time. The fuss about the death scared him, and he's lying low till it's all blown over."

"He'll find it much more awkward to dispossess Miss Whittaker now she's taken possession. Possession is nine points of the law, you know."

"I know, but he's going to pretend he wasn't anywhere near at the time of Miss Dawson's death. He only read about it a few weeks ago in a sheet of newspaper wrapped round a salmon-tin, and now he's rushing home from his distant farm in thing-ma-jig to proclaim himself as the long-lost Cousin Tom. . . . Great Scott! that reminds me."

He plunged his hand into his pocket and pulled out a letter.

"This came this morning just as I was going out, and I met Freddy Arbuthnot on the doorstep and shoved it into my pocket before I'd read it properly. But I do believe there was something in it about a Cousin Somebody from some god-forsaken spot. Let's see."

He unfolded the letter, which was written in Miss Climpson's old-fashioned flowing hand, and ornamented with such a variety of underlinings and exclamation marks as to look like an exercise in musical notation.

"Oh, lord!" said Parker.

"Yes, it's worse than usual, isn't it?—it must be of desperate importance. Luckily it's comparatively short."

My Dear Lord Peter,

I heard something this morning which MAY be of *use*, *so* I HASTEN to communicate it!! You remember I *mentioned before* that Mrs. Budge's *maid* is the SISTER of the *present* maid at Miss *Whittaker's?* WELL!!! The AUNT of these two girls came to *pay a visit* to Mrs. Budge's girl this afternoon, and was *introduced to me*—of course, as *boarder* at Mrs. Budge's I am naturally an *object of local interest*—and, bearing *your instructions* in mind, I *encourage* this to an extent I should not otherwise do!!

It appears that this *aunt* was well acquainted with a *former housekeeper* of Miss Dawson's—*before* the time of the Gotobed girls, I mean. The *aunt* is a highly *respectable* person of FORBIDDING ASPECT!—with a *bonnet* (!) and to my mind, a most *disagreeable* CENSORIOUS woman. However!—We got to speaking of Miss Dawson's death, and this aunt—her name is Timmins—*primmed* up her mouth and said: "No unpleasant scandal would surprise me about *that* family, Miss Climpson. They were *most* UNDESIRABLY connected! You recollect, Mrs. Budge, that I felt *obliged to leave* after the appearance of that *most*

EXTRAORDINARY person who announced himself as Miss Dawson's cousin." Naturally, I asked *who* this *might be,* not having heard of any *other relations!* She said that this person, whom she described as a *nasty,* DIRTY NIGGER (!!!) arrived one morning, dressed up as a CLERGYMAN!!!—and sent her—Miss Timmins—to announce him to Miss Dawson as her COUSIN HALLELUJAH!!! Miss Timmins showed him up, *much against her will,* she said, into the *nice,* CLEAN, drawing-room! Miss Dawson, she said, actually *came down* to see this "creature" instead of sending him about his "black business" (!), and as a *crowning scandal,* asked him to *stay to lunch!*—"with her niece there, too," Miss Timmins said, "and this horrible *blackamoor* ROLLING his dreadful eyes at her." Miss Timmins said that it "regularly turned her stomach"—that was her phrase, and I trust you will excuse it—I understand that these *parts of the body* are frequently referred to in polite (!) society nowadays. In fact, it appears she *refused to cook the lunch* for the poor black man—after all, even *blacks* are *God's creatures* and we might *all* be *black* OURSELVES if He had not in His infinite kindness seen fit to *favour us* with *white* skins!!)—and walked straight out of the house!!! So that unfortunately she cannot tell us anything *further* about this *remarkable* incident! She is *certain,* however, that the "nigger" had a *visiting-card,* with the name "Rev. H. Dawson" upon it, and an address in foreign parts. It does seem *strange,* does it not, but I believe many of these *native preachers* are called to do *splendid work* among their own people, and no doubt a MINISTER is entitled to have *visiting-card,* even when black!!!

> In great haste,
> Sincerely yours,
> A. K. CLIMPSON.

"God bless my soul," said Lord Peter, when he had disentangled this screed—"here's our claimant ready made."

"With a hide as black as his heart, apparently," replied Parker. "I wonder where the Rev. Hallelujah has got to—and where he came from. He—er—he wouldn't be in 'Crockford,' I suppose."

"He would be, probably, if he's Church of England," said Lord Peter, dubiously, going in search of that valuable work of reference. "Dawson—Rev. George, Rev. Gordon, Rev. Gurney, Rev. Habbakuk, Rev. Hadrian, Rev. Hammond—no, there's no Rev. Hallelujah. I was afraid the name hadn't altogether an established sound. It would be easier if we had an idea what part of the world the gentleman came from. 'Nigger,' to a Miss Timmins, may mean anything from a high-caste Brahmin to Sambo and Raustus at the Coliseum—it may even, at a pinch, be an Argentine or an Esquimaux."

"I suppose other religious bodies have their Crockfords," suggested Parker, a little hopelessly.

"Yes, no doubt—except perhaps the more exclusive sects—like the Agapemonites and those people who gather together to say OM. Was it Voltaire who said that the English had three hundred and sixty-five religions and only one sauce?"

"Judging from the War Tribunals," said Parker, "I should say that was an under-statement. And then there's America—a country, I understand, remarkably well supplied with religions."

"Too true. Hunting for a single dog-collar in the States must be like the proverbial needle. Still, we could make a few discreet inquiries, and meanwhile I'm going to totter up to Crofton with the jolly old 'bus."

"Crofton?"

"Where Miss Clara Whittaker and Miss Dawson used to live. I'm going to look for the man with the little black bag—the strange, suspicious solicitor, you remember, who came to see Miss Dawson two years ago, and was so anxious that she should make a will. I fancy he knows all there is to know about the Rev. Hallelujah and his claim. Will you come too?"

"Can't—not without special permission. I'm not officially on this case, you know."

"You're on the Gotobed business. Tell the Chief you think they're connected. I shall need your restraining presence. No less ignoble pressure than that of the regular police force will induce a smoke-dried family lawyer to spill the beans."

"Well, I'll try—if you'll promise to drive with reasonable precaution."

"Be thou as chaste as ice and have a license as pure as snow, thou shalt not escape calumny. I am *not* a dangerous driver. Buck up and get your leave. The snow-white horsepower foams and frets and the blue bonnet—black in this case —is already, in a manner of speaking, over the border."

"You'll drive me over the border one of these days," grumbled Parker, and went to the 'phone to call up Sir Andrew Mackenzie at Scotland Yard.

Crofton is a delightful little old-world village tucked away amid the maze of criss-cross country roads which fills the triangle of which Coventry, Warwick and Birmingham mark the angles. Through the falling night, "Mrs. Merdle" purred her way delicately round hedge-blinded corners and down devious lanes, her quest made no easier by the fact that the Warwick County Council had pitched upon that particular week for a grand repainting of signposts and had reached the preliminary stage of laying a couple of thick coats of gleaming white paint over all the lettering. At intervals the patient Bunter unpacked himself from the back seat and climbed one of these uncommunicative guides to peer at its blank surface with a torch—a process which reminded Parker of Alan Quartermaine trying to trace the features of the departed Kings of the Kukuanas under their calcareous shrouds of stalactite. One of the posts turned out to be in the wet-paint stage, which added to the depression of the party. Finally, after several misdirections, blind alleys, and reversings back to the main road, they came to a fourways. The signpost here must have been in extra need of repairs, for its arms had been removed bodily; it stood, stark and ghastly—a long, livid finger erected in wild protest to the unsympathetic heavens.

"It's starting to rain," observed Parker, conversationally.

"Look here, Charles, if you're going to bear up cheerfully and be the life and soul of the expedition, say so and have done with it. I've got a good, heavy spanner handy under the seat, and Bunter can help to bury the body."

"I think this must be Brushwood Cross," resumed Parker, who had the map on his knee. "If so, and if it's not Covert Corner, which I thought we passed half an hour ago, one of those roads leads directly to Crofton."

"That would be highly encouraging if we only knew which road we were on."

"We can always try them in turn, and come back if we find we're going wrong."

"They bury *suicides* at cross-roads," replied Wimsey, dangerously.

"There's a man sitting under that tree," pursued Parker. "We can ask him."

"He's lost his way too, or he wouldn't be sitting there," retorted the other. "People don't sit about in the rain for fun."

At this moment the man observed their approach and, rising, advanced to meet them with raised, arresting hand.

Wimsey brought the car to a standstill.

"Excuse me," said the stranger, who turned out to be a youth in motor-cycling kit, "but could you give me a hand with my 'bus?"

"What's the matter with her?"

"Well, she won't go."

"I guessed as much," said Wimsey. "Though why she should wish to linger in a place like this beats me." He got out of the car, and the youth, diving into the hedge, produced the patient for inspection.

"Did you tumble there or put her there?" inquired Wimsey, eyeing the machine distastefully.

"I put her there. I've been kicking the starter for hours but nothing happened, so I thought I'd wait till somebody came along."

"I see. What is the matter, exactly?"

"I don't know. She was going beautifully and then she conked out suddenly."

"Have you run out of petrol?"

"Oh, no. I'm sure there's plenty in."

"Plug all right?"

"I don't know." The youth looked unhappy. "It's only my second time out, you see."

"Oh! well—there can't be much wrong. We'll just make sure about the petrol first," said Wimsey, more cheerfully. He unscrewed the filler-cap and turned his torch upon the interior of the tank. "Seems all right." He bent over again, whistling, and replaced the cap. "Let's give her another kick for luck and then we'll look at the plug."

The young man, thus urged, grasped the handle-bars, and with the energy of despair delivered a kick which would have done credit to an army mule. The engine roared into life in a fury of vibration, racing heart-rendingly.

"Good God!" said the youth, "it's a miracle."

Lord Peter laid a gentle hand on the throttle-lever and the shattering bellow calmed into a grateful purr.

"What did you do to it?" demanded the cyclist.

"Blew through the filler-cap," said his lordship with a grin. "Air-lock in the feed, old son, that's all."

"I'm frightfully grateful."

"That's all right. Look here, can you tell us the way to Crofton?"

"Sure. Straight down here. I'm going there, as a matter of fact."

"Thank Heaven. Lead and I follow, as Sir Galahad says. How far?"

"Five miles."

"Decent inn?"

"My governor keeps the 'Fox-and-Hounds.' Would that do? We'd give you awfully decent grub."

"Sorrow vanquished, labour ended, Jordan passed. Buzz off, my lad. No, Charles I will *not* wait while you put on a Burberry. Back and side go bare, go bare, hand and foot go cold, so belly-god send us good ale enough, whether it be new or old."

The starter hummed—the youth mounted his machine and led off down the lane after one alarming wobble—Wimsey slipped in the clutch and followed in his wake.

The "Fox-and-Hounds" turned out to be one of those pleasant, old-fashioned inns where everything is upholstered in horse-hair and it is never too late to obtain a good meal of cold roast sirloin and home-grown salad. The landlady, Mrs. Piggin, served the travellers herself. She wore a decent black satin dress and a front of curls of the fashion favoured by the Royal Family. Her round, cheerful face glowed in the firelight, seeming to reflect the radiance of the scarlet-coated huntsmen who galloped and leapt and fell on every wall through a series of sporting prints. Lord Peter's mood softened under the influence of the atmosphere and the house's excellent ale, and by a series of inquiries directed to the hunting-season, just concluded, the neighbouring families and the price of horseflesh, he dexterously led the conversation round to the subject of the late Miss Clara Whittaker.

"Oh, dear, yes," said Mrs. Piggin, "to be sure, we knew Miss Whittaker. Everybody knew her in these parts. A wonderful old lady she was. There's a many of her horses still in the country. Mr. Cleveland, he bought the best part of the stock, and is doin' well with them. Fine honest stock she bred, and they all used to say she was a woman of wonderful judgment with a horse—or a man either. Nobody ever got the better of her twice, and very few, once."

"Ah!" said Lord Peter, sagaciously.

"I remember her well, riding to hounds when she was well over sixty," went on Mrs. Piggin, "and she wasn't one to wait for a gap, neither. Now Miss Dawson—that was her friend as lived with her—over at the Manor beyond the stone bridge—she was more timid-like. She'd go by the gates, and we often used to say she'd never be riding at all, but for bein' that fond of Miss Whittaker and not wanting to let her out of her sight. But there, we can't all be alike, can we, sir?—and Miss Whittaker was altogether out of the way. They don't make them like that nowadays. Not but what these modern girls are good goers, many of them, and does a lot of things as would have been thought very fast in the old days, but Miss Whittaker had the knowledge as well. Bought her own horses and physicked 'em and bred 'em, and needed no advice from anybody."

"She sounds a wonderful old girl," said Wimsey, heartily. "I'd have liked to know her. I've got some friends who knew Miss Dawson quite well—when she was living in Hampshire, you know."

"Indeed, sir? Well, that's strange, isn't it? She was a very kind, nice lady. We heard she'd died, too. Of this cancer, was it? That's a terrible thing, poor soul. And fancy you being connected with her, so to speak. I expect you'd be interested in some of our photographs of the Crofton Hunt. Jim?"

"Hullo!"

"Show these gentlemen the photographs of Miss Whittaker and Miss Dawson. They're acquainted with some friends of Miss Dawson down in Hampshire. Step this way—if you're sure you won't take anything more, sir."

Mrs. Piggin led the way into a cosy little private bar, where a number of hunting-looking gentlemen were enjoying a final glass before closing-time. Piggin, stout and genial as his wife, moved forward to do the honours.

"What'll you have, gentlemen?—Joe, two pints of the winter ale. And fancy you knowing our Miss Dawson. Dear me, the world's a very small place, as I often says to my wife. Here's the last group as was ever took of them, when the meet was held at the Manor in 1918. Of course, you'll understand, it wasn't a regular meet, like, owing to the War and the gentlemen being away and the horses too—we couldn't keep things up regular like in the old days. But what with the foxes gettin' so terrible many, and the packs all going to the dogs—ha! ha!—that's what I often used to say in this bar—the 'ounds is going to the dogs, I says. Very good, they used to think it. There's many a gentleman has laughed at me sayin' that—the 'ounds, I says, is goin' to the dogs—well, as I was sayin', Colonel Fletcher and some of the older gentlemen, they says, we must carry on somehow, they says, and so they 'ad one or two scratch meets as you might say, just to keep the pack from fallin' to pieces, as you might say. And Miss Whittaker, she says, "Ave the meet at the Manor, Colonel,' she says, 'it's the last meet I'll ever see, perhaps,' she says. And so it was, poor lady, for she 'ad a stroke in the New Year. She died in 1922. That's 'er, sitting in the pony-carriage and Miss Dawson beside 'er. Of course, Miss Whittaker 'ad 'ad to give up riding to 'ounds some years before. She was gettin' on, but she always followed in the trap, up to the very last. 'Andsome old lady, ain't she, sir?"

Lord Peter and Parker looked with considerable interest at the rather grim old woman sitting so uncompromisingly upright with the reins in her hand. A dour, weather-beaten old face, but certainly handsome still, with its large nose and straight, heavy eyebrows. And beside her, smaller, plumper and more feminine, was the Agatha Dawson whose curious death had led them to this quiet country place. She had a sweet, smiling face—less dominating than that of her redoubtable friend, but full of spirit and character. Without doubt they had been a remarkable pair of old ladies.

Lord Peter asked a question or two about the family.

"Well, sir, I can't say as I knows much about that. We always understood as Miss Whittaker had quarrelled with her people on account of comin' here and settin' up for herself. It wasn't usual in them days for girls to leave home the way it is now. But if you're particularly interested, sir, there's an old gentleman here as can tell you all about the Whittakers and the Dawsons too, and that's Ben Cobling. He was Miss Whittaker's groom for forty years, and he married Miss Dawson's maid as come with her from Norfolk. Eighty-six 'e was, last birthday, but a grand old fellow still. We thinks a lot of Ben Cobling in these parts. 'Im and his wife lives in the little cottage what Miss Whittaker left them when she died. If you'd like to go round and see them to-morrow, sir, you'll find Ben's memory as good as ever it was. Excuse me, sir, but it's time. I must get 'em out of the bar.—Time, gentlemen, please! Three and eightpence, sir, thank you, sir. Hurry up, gentlemen, please. Now then, Joe, look sharp."

"Great place, Crofton," said Lord Peter, when he and Parker were left alone in a great, low-ceilinged bedroom, where the sheets smelt of lavender. "Ben Cobling's sure to know all about Cousin Hallelujah. I'm looking forward to Ben Cobling."

12

A TALE OF TWO SPINSTERS

"The power of perpetuating our property in our families is
one of the most valuable and interesting circumstances
belonging to it."

Burke, Reflections on the Revolution

The rainy night was followed by a sun-streaked morning.
Lord Peter, having wrapped himself affectionately
round an abnormal quantity of bacon and eggs, strolled
out to bask at the door of the "Fox-and-Hounds." He filled a pipe slowly and
meditated. Within, a cheerful bustle in the bar announced the near arrival of
opening time. Eight ducks crossed the road in Indian file. A cat sprang up upon
the bench, stretched herself, tucked her hind legs under her and coiled her tail
tightly round them as though to prevent them from accidentally working loose.
A groom passed, riding a tall bay horse and leading a chestnut with a hogged
mane; a spaniel followed them, running ridiculously, with one ear flopped inside-out over his foolish head.

Lord Peter said, "Hah!"

The inn-door was set hospitably open by the barman, who said, "Good morning, sir; fine morning, sir," and vanished within again.

Lord Peter said, "Umph." He uncrossed his right foot from over his left and
straddled happily across the threshold.

Round the corner by the church-yard wall a little bent figure hove into sight—
an aged man with a wrinkled face and legs incredibly bowed, his spare shanks
enclosed in leather gaiters. He advanced at a kind of brisk totter and civilly bared
his ancient head before lowering himself with an audible creak on to the bench
beside the cat.

"Good morning, sir," said he.

"Good morning," said Lord Peter. "A beautiful day."

"That it be, sir, that it be," said the old man, heartily. "When I sees a
beautiful May day like this, I pray the Lord He'll spare me to live in this
wonderful world of His a few years longer. I do indeed."

"You look uncommonly fit," said his lordship, "I should think there was every
chance of it."

"I'm still very hearty, sir, thank you, though I am eighty-seven next Michaelmas."

Lord Peter expressed a proper astonishment.

"Yes, sir, eighty-seven, and if it wasn't for the rheumatics I'd have nothin' to
complain on. I'm stronger maybe than what I look. I knows I'm a bit bent, sir,
but that's the 'osses, sir, more than age. Regular brought up with 'osses I've been

all my life. Worked with 'em, slept with 'em—lived in a stable, you might say, sir."

"You couldn't have better company," said Lord Peter.

"That's right, sir, you couldn't. My wife always used to say she was jealous of the 'osses. Said I preferred their conversation to hers. Well, maybe she was right, sir. A 'oss never talks no foolishness, I says to her, and that's more than you can always say of women, ain't it, sir?"

"It is indeed," said Wimsey. "What are you going to have?"

"Thank you, sir, I'll have my usual pint of bitter. Jim knows. Jim! Always start the day with a pint of bitter, sir. It's 'olesomer than tea to my mind and don't fret the coats of the stomach."

"I dare say you're right," said Wimsey. "Now you mention it, there is something fretful about tea. Mr. Piggin, two pints of bitter, please, and will you join us?"

"Thank you, my lord," said the landlord. "Joe! Two large bitters and a Guinness. Beautiful morning, my lord—'morning, Mr. Cobling—I see you've made each other's acquaintance already."

"By Jove! So this is Mr. Cobling. I'm delighted to see you. I wanted particularly to have a chat with you."

"Indeed, sir?"

"I was telling this gentleman—Lord Peter Wimsey his name is—as you could tell him all about Miss Whittaker and Miss Dawson. He knows friends of Miss Dawson's."

"Indeed? Ah! There ain't much I *couldn't* tell you about them ladies. And proud I'd be to do it. Fifty years I was with Miss Whittaker. I come to her as under-groom in old Johnny Blackthorne's time, and stayed on as headgroom after he died. A rare young lady she was in them days. Deary me. Straight as a switch, with a fine, high colour in her cheeks and shiny black hair—just like a beautiful two-year-old filly she was. And very sperrited. Wonnerful sperrited. There was a many gentlemen as would have been glad to hitch up with her, but she was never broke to harness. Like dirt, she treated 'em. Wouldn't look at 'em, except it might be the grooms and stablehands in a matter of 'osses. And in the way of business, of course. Well, there is some creatures like that. I 'ad a terrier-bitch that way. Great ratter she was. But a business woman—nothin' else. I tried 'er with all the dogs I could lay 'and to, but it weren't no good. Bloodshed there was an' sich a row—you never 'eard. The Lord makes a few on 'em that way to suit 'Is own purposes, I suppose. There ain't no arguin' with females."

Lord Peter said "Ah!"

The ale went down in silence.

Mr. Piggin roused himself presently from contemplation to tell a story of Miss Whittaker in the hunting-field. Mr. Cobling capped this by another. Lord Peter said "Ah!" Parker then emerged and was introduced, and Mr. Cobling begged the privilege of standing a round of drinks. This ritual accomplished, Mr. Piggin begged the company would be his guests for a third round, and then excused himself on the plea of customers to attend to.

He went in, and Lord Peter, by skilful and maddeningly slow degrees, began to work his way back to the history of the Dawson family. Parker—educated at Barrow-in-Furness grammar school and with his wits further sharpened in the London police service—endeavoured now and again to get matters along faster by a brisk question. The result, every time, was to make Mr. Cobling lose the thread of his remarks and start him off into a series of interminable side-tracks. Wimsey kicked his friend viciously on the anklebone to keep him quiet, and with endless patience worked the conversation back to the main road again.

At the end of an hour or so, Mr. Cobling explained that his wife could tell them a great deal more about Miss Dawson than what he could, and invited them to visit his cottage. This invitation being accepted with alacrity, the party started off, Mr. Cobling explaining to Parker that he was eighty-seven come next Michaelmas, and hearty still, indeed, stronger than he appeared, bar the rheumatics that troubled him. "I'm not saying as I'm not bent," said Mr. Cobling, "but that's more the work of the 'osses. Regular lived with 'osses all my life—"

"Don't look so fretful, Charles," murmured Wimsey in his ear, "it must be the tea at breakfast—it frets the coats of the stomach."

Mrs. Cobling turned out to be a delightful old lady, exactly like a dried-up pippin and only two years younger than her husband. She was entranced at getting an opportunity to talk about her darling Miss Agatha. Parker, thinking it necessary to put forward some reason for the inquiry, started on an involved explanation, and was kicked again. To Mrs. Cobling, nothing could be more natural than that all the world should be interested in the Dawsons, and she prattled gaily on without prompting.

She had been in the Dawson family service as a girl—almost born in it as you might say. Hadn't her mother been housekeeper to Mr. Henry Dawson, Miss Agatha's papa, and to his father before him? She herself had gone to the big house as stillroom maid when she wasn't but fifteen. That was when Miss Harriet was only three years old—her as afterwards married Mr. James Whittaker. Yes, and she'd been there when the rest of the family was born. Mr. Stephen —him as should have been the heir—ah, dear! only the trouble came and that killed his poor father and there was nothing left. Yes, a sad business that was. Poor Mr. Henry speculated with something—Mrs. Cobling wasn't clear what, but it was all very wicked and happened in London where there were so many wicked people—and the long and the short was, he lost it all, poor gentleman, and never held up his head again. Only fifty-four he was when he died; such a fine upright gentleman with a pleasant word for everybody. And his wife didn't live long after him, poor lamb. She was a Frenchwoman and a sweet lady, but she was very lonely in England, having no family and her two sisters walled up alive in one of them dreadful Romish Convents.

"And what did Mr. Stephen do when the money went?" asked Wimsey.

"Him? Oh, he went into business—a strange thing that did seem, though I have heard tell as old Barnabas Dawson, Mr. Henry's grandfather that was, was nought but a grocer or something of that—and they do say, don't they, that from shirtsleeves to shirtsleeves is three generations? Still, it was very hard on Mr. Stephen, as had always been brought up to have everything of the best. And engaged to be married to a beautiful lady, too, and a very rich heiress. But it was all for the best, for when she heard Mr. Stephen was a poor man after all, she threw him over, and that showed she had no heart in her at all. Mr. Stephen never married till he was over forty, and then it was a lady with no family at all— not lawful, that is, though she was a dear, sweet girl and made Mr. Stephen a most splendid wife—she did indeed. And Mr. John, he was their only son. They thought the world of him. It was a terrible day when the news came that he was killed in the War. A cruel business that was, sir, wasn't it?—and nobody the better for it as as I can see, but all these shocking hard taxes, and the price of everything gone up so, and so many out of work."

"So he was killed? That must have been a terrible grief to his parents."

"Yes, sir, terrible. Oh, it was an awful thing altogether, sir, for poor Mr. Stephen, as had had so much trouble all his life, he went out of his poor mind and shot hisself. Out of his mind he must have been, sir, to do it—and what was more dreadful still, he shot his dear lady as well. You may remember it, sir. There was pieces in the paper about it."

"I seem to have some vague recollection of it," said Peter, quite untruthfully, but anxious not to seem to belittle the local tragedy. "And young John—he wasn't married, I suppose."

"No, sir. That was very sad, too. He was engaged to a young lady—a nurse in one of the English hospitals, as we understood, and he was hoping to get back and be married to her on his next leave. Everything did seem to go all wrong together them terrible years."

The old lady sighed, and wiped her eyes.

"Mr. Stephen was the only son, then?"

"Well, not exactly, sir. There was the darling twins. Such pretty children, but they only lived two days. They come four years after Miss Harriet—her as married Mr. James Whittaker."

"Yes, of course. That was how the families became connected."

"Yes, sir. Miss Agatha and Miss Harriet and Miss Clara Whittaker was all at the same school together, and Mrs. Whittaker asked the two young ladies to go and spend their holidays with Miss Clara, and that was when Mr. James fell in love with Miss Harriet. She wasn't as pretty as Miss Agatha, to my thinking, but she was livelier and quicker—and then, of course, Miss Agatha was never one for flirting and foolishness. Often she used to say to me, 'Betty,' she said, 'I mean to be an old maid and so does Miss Clara, and we're going to live together and be ever so happy, without any stupid, tiresome gentlemen.' And so it turned out, sir, as you know, for Miss Agatha, for all she was so quiet, was very determined. Once she'd said a thing, you couldn't turn her from it—not with reasons, nor with threats, nor with coaxings—nothing! Many's the time I've tried when she was a child—for I used to give a little help in the nursery sometimes, sir. You might drive her into a temper or into the sulks, but you couldn't make her change her little mind, even then."

There came to Wimsey's mind the picture of the stricken, helpless old woman, holding to her own way in spite of her lawyer's reasoning and her niece's subterfuge. A remarkable old lady, certainly, in her way.

"I suppose the Dawson family has practically died out, then," he said.

"Oh, yes, sir. There's only Miss Mary now—and she's a Whittaker, of course. She is Miss Harriet's grand-daughter, Mr. Charles Whittaker's only child. She was left all alone, too, when she went to live with Miss Dawson. Mr. Charles and his wife was killed in one of these dreadful motors—dear, dear—it seemed we was fated to have nothing but one tragedy after another. Just to think of Ben and me outliving them all."

"Cheer up, Mother," said Ben, laying his hand on hers. "The Lord have been wonderful good to us."

"That He have. Three sons we have, sir, and two daughters, and fourteen grandchildren and three great-grandchildren. Maybe you'd like to see their pictures, sir."

Lord Peter said he should like to very much, and Parker made confirmatory noises. The life-histories of all the children and descendants were detailed at suitable length. Whenever a pause seemed discernible, Parker would mutter hopefully in Wimsey's ear, "How about Cousin Hallelujah?" but before a question could be put, the interminable family chronicle was resumed.

"And for God's sake, Charles," whispered Peter, savagely, when Mrs. Cobling had risen to hunt for the shawl which Grandson William had sent home from the Dardanelles, "don't keep saying Hallelujah at me! I'm not a revival meeting."

The shawl being duly admired, the conversation turned upon foreign parts, natives and black people generally, following on which, Lord Peter added carelessly:

"By the way, hasn't the Dawson family got some sort of connections in those foreign countries, somewhere?"

Well, yes, said Mrs. Cobling, in rather a shocked tone. There had been Mr. Paul, Mr. Henry's brother. But he was not mentioned much. He had been a terrible shock to his family. In fact—a gasp here, and a lowering of the voice—he had *turned Papist* and become—a monk! (Had he become a murderer, apparently, he could hardly have done worse.) Mr. Henry had always blamed himself very much in the matter.

"How was it his fault?"

"Well, of course, Mr. Henry's wife—my dear mistress, you see, sir—she was French, as I told you, and of course, *she* was a Papist. Being brought up that way, she wouldn't know any better, naturally, and she was very young when she was married. But Mr. Henry soon taught her to be a Christian, and she put away her idolatrous ideas and went to the parish church. But Mr. Paul, *he* fell in love with one of her sisters, and the sister had been vowed to religion, as they called it, and had shut herself up in a nunnery." And then Mr. Paul had broken his heart and "gone over" to the Scarlet Woman and—again the pause and the hush— become a monk. A terrible to-do it made. And he'd lived to be a very old man, and for all Mrs. Cobling knew was living yet, still in the error of his ways.

"If he's alive," murmured Parker, "he's probably the real heir. He'd be Agatha Dawson's uncle and her nearest relation."

Wimsey frowned and returned to the charge.

"Well, it couldn't have been Mr. Paul I had in mind," he said, "because this sort of relation of Miss Agatha Dawson's that I heard about was a real foreigner —in fact, a very dark-complexioned man—almost a black man or so I was told."

"Black?" cried the old lady—"oh, no, sir—that couldn't be. Unless—dear Lord a' mercy, it couldn't be that, surely! Ben, do you think it could be that?— Old Simon, you know?"

Ben shook his head. "I never heard tell much about him."

"Nor nobody did," replied Mrs. Cobling, energetically. "He was a long way back, but they had tales of him in the family. 'Wicked Simon,' they called him. He sailed away to the Indies, many years ago, and nobody knew what became of him. Wouldn't it be a queer thing, like, if he was to have married a black wife out in them parts, and this was his—oh, dear—his grandson it 'ud have to be, if not his great-grandson, for he was Mr. Henry's uncle, and that's a long time ago."

This was disappointing. A grandson of "old Simon's" would surely be too distant a relative to dispute Mary Whittaker's title. However:

"That's very interesting," said Wimsey. "Was it the East Indies or the West Indies he went to, I wonder?"

Mrs. Cobling didn't know, but she believed it was something to do with America.

"It's a pity as Mr. Probyn ain't in England any longer. He could have told you more about the family than what I can. But he retired last year and went away to Italy or some such place."

"Who was he?"

"He was Miss Whittaker's solicitor," said Ben, "and he managed all Miss Dawson's business, too. A nice gentleman he was, but uncommon sharp—ha, ha! Never gave nothing away. But that's lawyers all the world over," added he, shrewdly, "take all and give nothing."

"Did he live in Crofton?"

"No, sir, in Croftover Magna, twelve miles from here. Pointer & Winkin have his business now, but they're young men, and I don't know much about them."

Having by this time heard all the Coblings had to tell, Wimsey and Parker gradually disentangled themselves and took their leave.

"Well, Cousin Hallelujah's a wash-out," said Parker.

"Possibly—possibly not. There may be some connection. Still, I certainly think the disgraceful and papistical Mr. Paul is more promising. Obviously Mr. Probyn is the bird to get hold of. You realise who he is?"

"He's the mysterious solicitor, I suppose."

"Of course he is. He knows why Miss Dawson ought to have made her will. And we're going straight off to Croftover Magna to look up Messrs. Pointer & Winkin, and see what they have to say about it."

Unhappily, Messrs. Pointer & Winkin had nothing to say whatever. Miss Dawson had withdrawn her affairs from Mr. Probyn's hands and had lodged all the papers with her new solicitor. Messrs. Pointer & Winkin had never had any connection with the Dawson family. They had no objection, however, to furnishing Mr. Probyn's address—Villa Bianca, Fiesole. They regretted that they could be of no further assistance to Lord Peter Wimsey and Mr. Parker. Good morning.

"Short and sour," was his lordship's comment. "Well, well—we'll have a spot of lunch and write a letter to Mr. Probyn and another to my good friend Bishop Lambert of the Orinoco Mission to get a line on Cousin Hallelujah, Smile, smile, smile. As Ingoldsby says: 'The breezes are blowing a race, a race! The breezes are blowing—we near the chase!' Do ye ken John Peel? Likewise, know'st thou the land where blooms the citron-flower? Well, never mind if you don't— you can always look forward to going there for your honeymoon."

13

HALLELUJAH

"Our ancestors are very good kind of folks, but they are the last people I should choose to have a visiting acquaintance with."

Sheridan, The Rivals

That excellent prelate, Bishop Lambert of the Orinoco Mission, proved to be a practical and kind man. He did not personally know the Rev. Hallelujah Dawson, but thought he might belong to the Tabernacle Mission—a Nonconformist body which was doing a very valuable work in those parts. He would himself communicate with the London Headquarters of this community and let Lord Peter know the result. Two hours later, Bishop Lambert's secretary had duly rung up the Tabernacle Mission and received the very satisfactory information that the Rev. Hallelujah Dawson was in England, and, indeed, available at their Mission House in Stepney. He was an elderly minister, living in very reduced circumstances—in fact, the Bishop rather gathered that the story was a sad one—Oh, not at all, pray, no thanks. The Bishop's poor miserable slave of a secretary did all the work. Very glad to hear from Lord Peter, and was he being good? Ha, ha! and when was he coming to dine with the Bishop?

Lord Peter promptly gathered up Parker and swooped down with him upon the Tabernacle Mission, before whose dim and grim frontage Mrs. Merdle's long black bonnet and sweeping copper exhaust made an immense impression. The small fry of the neighbourhood had clustered about her and were practising horn solos almost before Wimsey had rung the bell. On Parker's threatening them with punishment and casually informing them that he was a police officer, they burst into ecstasies of delight, and joining hands, formed a ring-o'-roses round him, under the guidance of a sprightly young woman of twelve years old or thereabouts. Parker made a few harassed darts at them, but the ring only broke up, shrieking with laughter, and reformed, singing. The Mission door opened at the moment, displaying this undignified exhibition to the eyes of a lank young man in spectacles, who shook a long finger disapprovingly and said, "Now, you children," without the slightest effect and apparently without the faintest expectation of producing any.

Lord Peter explained his errand.

"Oh, come in, please," said the young man, who had one finger in a book of theology. "I'm afraid your friend—er—this is rather a noisy district."

Parker shook himself free from his tormentors, and advanced, breathing threatenings and slaughter, to which the enemy responded by a derisive blast of the horn.

"They'll run those batteries down," said Wimsey.

"You can't do anything with the little devils," growled Parker.

"Why don't you treat them as human beings?" retorted Wimsey. "Children are creatures of like passions with politicians and financiers. Here, Esmeralda!" he added, beckoning to the ringleader.

The young woman put her tongue out and made a rude gesture, but observing the glint of coin in the outstretched hand, suddenly approached and stood challengingly before them.

"Look here," said Wimsey, "here's half a crown—thirty pennies, you know. Any use to you?"

The child promptly proved her kinship with humanity. She became abashed in the presence of wealth, and was silent, rubbing one dusty shoe upon the calf of her stocking.

"You appear," pursued Lord Peter, "to be able to keep your young friends in order if you choose. I take you, in fact, for a woman of character. Very well, if you keep them from touching my car while I'm in the house, you get this half-crown, see? But if you let 'em blow the horn, I shall hear it. Every time the horn goes, you lose a penny, got that? If the horn blows six times, you only get two bob. If I hear it thirty times, you don't get anything. And I shall look out from time to time, and if I see anybody mauling the car about or sitting in it, *then* you don't get anything. Do I make myself clear?"

"I takes care o' yer car fer 'arf a crahn. An' ef the 'orn goes, you docks a copper 'orf of it."

"That's right."

"Right you are, mister. I'll see none on 'em touches it."

"Good girl. Now, sir."

The spectacled young man led them into a gloomy little waiting-room, suggestive of a railway station and hung with Old Testament prints.

"I'll tell Mr. Dawson you're here," said he, and vanished, with the volume of theology still clutched in his hand.

Presently a shuffling step was heard on the coconut matting, and Wimsey and Parker braced themselves to confront the villainous claimant.

The door, however, opened to admit an elderly West Indian, of so humble and inoffensive an appearance that the hearts of the two detectives sank into their boots. Anything less murderous could scarcely be imagined, as he stood blinking nervously at them from behind a pair of steel-rimmed spectacles, the frames of which had at one time been broken and bound with twine.

The Rev. Hallelujah Dawson was undoubtedly a man of colour. He had the pleasant, slightly aquiline features and brown-olive skin of the Polynesian. His hair was scanty and greyish—not woolly, but closely curled. His stooping shoulders were clad in a threadbare clerical coat. His black eyes, yellow about the whites and slightly protruding, rolled amiably at them, and his smile was open and frank.

"You asked to see me?" he began, in perfect English, but with the soft native intonation. "I think I have not the pleasure—?"

"How do you do, Mr. Dawson? Yes. We are—er—makin' certain inquiries—er—in connection with the family of the Dawsons of Crofton in Warwickshire, and it has been suggested that you might be able to enlighten us, what? as to their West Indian connections—if you would be so good."

"Ah, yes!" The old man drew himself up slightly. "I am myself—in a way—a descendant of the family. Won't you sit down?"

"Thank you. We thought you might be."

"You do not come from Miss Whittaker?"

There was something eager, yet defensive in the tone. Wimsey, not quite knowing what was behind it, chose the discreeter part.

"Oh, no. We are—preparin' a work on County Families, don't you know. Tombstones and genealogies and that sort of thing."

"Oh!—yes—I hoped perhaps—" The mild tones died away in a sigh. "But I shall be very happy to help you in any way."

"Well, the question now is, what became of Simon Dawson? We know that he left his family and sailed for the West Indies in—ah!—in seventeen—"

"Eighteen hundred and ten," said the old man, with surprising quickness. "Yes. He got into trouble when he was a lad of sixteen. He took up with bad men older than himself, and became involved in a very terrible affair. It had to do with gaming, and a man was killed. Not in a duel—in those days that would not have been considered disgraceful—though violence is always displeasing to the Lord—but the man was foully murdered and Simon Dawson and his friends fled from justice. Simon fell in with the press-gang and was carried off to sea. He served fifteen years and was then taken by a French privateer. Later on he escaped and—to cut a long story short—got away to Trinidad under another name. Some English people there were kind to him and gave him work on their sugar plantation. He did well there and eventually became owner of a small plantation of his own."

"What was the name he went by?"

"Harkaway. I suppose he was afraid that they would get hold of him as a deserter from the Navy if he went by his own name. No doubt he should have reported his escape. Anyway, he liked plantation life and was quite satisfied to stay where he was. I don't suppose he would have cared to go home, even to claim his inheritance. And then, there was always the matter of the murder, you know—though I dare say they would not have brought that trouble up against him, seeing he was so young when it happened and it was not his hand that did the awful deed."

"His inheritance? Was he the eldest son, then?"

"No. Barnabas was the eldest, but he was killed at Waterloo and left no family. Then there was a second son, Roger, but he died of smallpox as a child. Simon was the third son."

"Then it was the fourth son who took the estate?"

"Yes, Frederick. He was Henry's Dawson's father. They tried, of course, to find out what became of Simon, but in those days it was very difficult, you understand, to get information from foreign places, and Simon had quite disappeared. So they had to pass him over."

"And what happened to Simon's children?" asked Parker. "Did he have any?"

The clergyman nodded, and a deep, dusky flush showed under his dark skin.

"I am his grandson," he said, simply. "That is why I came over to England. When the Lord called me to feed His lambs among my own people, I was in quite good circumstances. I had the little sugar plantation which had come down to me through my father, and I married and was very happy. But we fell on bad times—the sugar crop failed, and our little flock became smaller and poorer and could not give so much support to their minister. Besides, I was getting too old and frail to do my work—and I have a sick wife, too, and God has blessed us with many daughters, who needed our care. I was in great straits. And then I came upon some old family papers belonging to my grandfather, Simon, and learned that his name was not Harkaway but Dawson, and I thought, maybe I had a family in England and that God would yet raise up a table in the wilderness. Accordingly, when the time came to send a representative home to our London Headquarters, I asked permission to resign my ministry out there and come over to England."

"Did you get into touch with anybody?"

"Yes. I went to Crofton—which was mentioned in my grandfather's letters—and saw a lawyer in the town there—a Mr. Probyn of Croftover. You know him?"

"I've heard of him."

"Yes. He was very kind, and very much interested to see me. He showed me the genealogy of the family, and how my grandfather should have been the heir to the property."

"But the property had been lost by that time, had it not?"

"Yes. And, unfortunately—when I showed him my grandmother's marriage certificate, he—he told me that it was no certificate at all. I fear that Simon Dawson was a sad sinner. He took my grandmother to live with him, as many of the planters did take women of colour, and he gave her a document which was supposed to be a certificate of marriage signed by the Governor of the country. But when Mr. Probyn inquired into it, he found that it was all a sham, and no such governor had ever existed. It was distressing to my feelings as a Christian, of course—but since there was no property, it didn't make any actual difference to us."

"That was bad luck," said Peter, sympathetically.

"I called resignation to my aid," said the old Indian, with a dignified little bow. "Mr. Probyn was also good enough to send me with a letter of introduction to Miss Agatha Dawson, the only surviving member of our family."

"Yes, she lived at Leahampton."

"She received me in the most charming way, and when I told her who I was—acknowledging, of course, that I had not the slightest claim upon her—she was good enough to make me an allowance of £100 a year, which she continued till her death."

"Was that the only time you saw her?"

"Oh, yes. I would not intrude upon her. It could not be agreeable to her to have a relative of my complexion continually at her house," said the Rev. Hallelujah, with a kind of proud humility. "But she gave me lunch, and spoke very kindly."

"And—forgive my askin'—hope it isn't impertinent—but does Miss Whittaker keep up the allowance?"

"Well, no—I—perhaps I should not expect it, but it would have made a great difference to our circumstances. And Miss Dawson rather led me to hope that it might be continued. She told me that she did not like the idea of making a will, but, she said, 'It is not necessary at all, Cousin Hallelujah, Mary will have all my money when I am gone, and she can continue the allowance on my behalf.' But perhaps Miss Whittaker did not get the money after all?"

"Oh, yes, she did. It is very odd. She may have forgotten about it."

"I took the liberty of writing her a few words of spiritual comfort when her aunt died. Perhaps that did not please her. Of course, I did not write again. Yet I am loath to believe that she has hardened her heart against the unfortunate. No doubt there is some explanation."

"No doubt," said Lord Peter. "Well, I'm very grateful to you for your kindness. That has quite cleared up the little matter of Simon and his descendants. I'll just make a note of the names and dates, if I may."

"Certainly. I will bring you the paper which Mr. Probyn kindly made out for me, showing the whole of the family. Excuse me."

He was not gone long, and soon reappeared with a genealogy, neatly typed out on a legal-looking sheet of blue paper.

Wimsey began to note down the particulars concerning Simon Dawson and his son, Bosun, and his grandson, Hallelujah. Suddenly he put his finger on an entry further along.

"Look here, Charles," he said. "Here is our Father Paul—the bad boy who turned R.C. and became a monk."

"So he is. But—he's dead, Peter—died in 1922, three years before Agatha Dawson."

"Yes. We must wash him out. Well, these little setbacks will occur."

They finished their notes, bade farewell to the Rev. Hallelujah, and emerged to find Esmeralda valiantly defending Mrs. Merdle against all comers. Lord Peter handed over the half-crown and took delivery of the car.

"The more I hear of Mary Whittaker," he said, "the less I like her. She might at least have given poor old Cousin Hallelujah his hundred quid."

"She's a rapacious female," agreed Parker. "Well, anyway, Father Paul's safely dead, and Cousin Hallelujah is illegitimately descended. So there's an end of the long-lost claimant from overseas."

"Damn it all!" cried Wimsey, taking both hands from the steering-wheel and scratching his head, to Parker's extreme alarm, "that strikes a familiar chord. Now where in thunder have I heard those words before?"

14

SHARP QUILLETS OF THE LAW

"Things done without example—in their issue
Are to be feared."

Henry VIII, *I, 2*

"**M**urbles is coming round to dinner to-night, Charles," said Wimsey. "I wish you'd stop and have grub with us too. I want to put all this family history business before him."

"Where are you dining?"

"Oh, at the flat. I'm sick of restaurant meals. Bunter does a wonderful bloody steak and there are new peas and potatoes and genuine English grass. Gerald sent it up from Denver specially. You can't buy it. Come along. Ye olde English fare, don't you know, and a bottle of what Pepys calls Ho Bryon. Do you good."

Parker accepted. But he noticed that, even when speaking on his beloved subject of food, Wimsey was vague and abstracted. Something seemed to be worrying at the back of his mind, and even when Mr. Murbles appeared, full of mild legal humour, Wimsey listened to him with extreme courtesy indeed, but with only half his attention.

They were partly through dinner when, a propos of nothing, Wimsey suddenly brought his fist down on the mahogany with a crash that startled even Bunter, causing him to jerk a great crimson splash of the Haut Brion over the edge of the glass upon the tablecloth.

"Got it!" said Lord Peter.

Bunter in a low shocked voice begged his lordship's pardon.

"Murbles," said Wimsey, without heeding him, "isn't there a new Property Act?"

"Why, yes," said Mr. Murbles, in some surprise. He had been in the middle of a story when the interruption occurred, and was a little put out.

"I knew I'd read that sentence somewhere—you know, Charles—about doing away with the long-lost claimant from overseas. It was in some paper or other about a couple of years ago, and it had to do with the new Act. Of course, it said what a blow it would be to romantic novelists. Doesn't the Act wash out the claims of distant relatives, Murbles?"

"In a sense, it does," replied the solicitor. "Not, of course, in the case of entailed property, which has its own rules. But I understand you to refer to ordinary personal property or real estate not entailed."

"Yes—what happens to that, now, if the owner of the property dies without making a will?"

"It is rather a complicated matter," began Mr. Murbles.

"Well, look here, first of all—before the jolly old Act was passed, the next-of-kin got it all, didn't he—no matter if he was only a seventh cousin fifteen times removed?"

"In a general way, that is correct. If there was a husband or wife—"

"Wash out the husband and wife. Suppose the person is unmarried and has no near relations living. It would have gone—"

"To the next-of-kin, whoever that was, if he or she could be traced."

"Even if you had to burrow back to William the Conqueror to get at the relationship?"

"Always supposing you could get a clear record back to so very early a date," replied Mr. Murbles. "It is, of course, in the highest degree improbable—"

"Yes, yes, I know, sir. But what happens now in such a case?"

"The new Act makes inheritance on intestacy very much simpler," said Mr. Murbles, setting his knife and fork together, placing both elbows on the table and laying the index-finger of his right hand against his left thumb in a gesture of tabulation.

"I bet it does," interpolated Wimsey. "I know what an Act to make things simpler means. It means that the people who drew it up don't understand it themselves and that every one of its clauses needs a law-suit to disentangle it. But do go on."

"Under the new Act," pursued Mr. Murbles, "one half of the property goes to the husband and wife, if living, and subject to his or her life-interest, then all to the children equally. But if there be no spouse and no children, then it goes to the father or mother of the deceased. If the father and mother are both dead, then everything goes to the brothers and sisters of the whole blood who are living at the time, but if any brother or sister dies before the intestate, then to his or her issue. In case there are no brothers or sisters of the—"

"Stop, stop! you needn't go any further. You're absolutely sure of that? It goes to the brothers' or sisters' issue?"

"Yes. That is to say, if it were you that died intestate and your brother Gerald and your sister Mary were already dead, your money would be equally divided among your nieces and nephews."

"Yes, but suppose they were already dead too—suppose I'd gone tediously living on till I'd nothing left but great-nephews and great-nieces—would they inherit?"

"Why—why, yes, I suppose they would," said Mr. Murbles, with less certainty, however. "Oh, yes, I think they would."

"Clearly they would," said Parker, a little impatiently, "if it says to the issue of the deceased's brothers and sisters."

"Ah! but we must not be precipitate," said Mr. Murbles, rounding upon him. "To the lay mind, doubtless, the word 'issue' appears a simple one. But in law"—(Mr. Murbles, who up till this point had held the index-finger of the right hand poised against the ring-finger of the left, in recognition of the claims of the brothers and sisters of the half-blood, now placed his left palm upon the table and wagged his right index-finger admonishingly in Parker's direction)—"in *law* the word may bear one of two, or indeed several, interpretations according to the nature of the document in which it occurs and the date of that document."

"But in the new Act—" urged Lord Peter.

"I am not, particularly," said Mr. Murbles, "a specialist in the law concerning property, and I should not like to give a decided opinion as to its interpretation, all the more as, up to the present, no case has come before the Courts bearing on the present issue—no pun intended, ha, ha, ha! But my immediate and entirely tentative opinion—which, however, I should advise you not to accept without the support of some weightier authority—would be, I *think*, that issue in this case means issue *ad infinitum*, and that therefore the great-nephews and great-nieces would be entitled to inherit."

"But there might be another opinion?"

"Yes—the question is a complicated one—"

"What did I tell you?" groaned Peter. "I *knew* this simplifying Act would cause a shockin' lot of muddle."

"May I ask," said Mr. Murbles, "exactly why you want to know all this?"

"Why, sir," said Wimsey, taking from his pocket-book the genealogy of the Dawson family which he had received from the Rev. Hallelujah Dawson, "here is the point. We have always talked about Mary Whittaker as Agatha Dawson's niece; she was always called so and she speaks of the old lady as her aunt. But if you look at this, you will see that actually she was no nearer to her than great-niece: she was the grand-daughter of Agatha's sister Harriet."

"Quite true," said Mr. Murbles, "but still, she was apparently the nearest surviving relative, and since Agatha Dawson died in 1925, the money passed without any question to Mary Whittaker under the old Property Act. There's no ambiguity there."

"No," said Wimsey, "none whatever, that's the point. But—"

"Good God!" broke in Parker, "I see what you're driving at. When did the new Act come into force, sir?"

"In January, 1926," replied Mr. Murbles.

"And Miss Dawson died, rather unexpectedly, as we know, in November, 1925," went on Peter. "But supposing she had lived, as the doctor fully expected her to do, till February or March, 1926—are you absolutely positive, sir, that Mary Whittaker would have inherited then?"

Mr. Murbles opened his mouth to speak—and shut it again. He rubbed his hands very slowly the one over the other. He removed his eyeglasses and resettled them more firmly on his nose. Then:

"You are quite right, Lord Peter," he said in a grave tone, "this is a very serious and important point. Much too serious for me to give an opinion on. If I understand you rightly, you are suggesting that any ambiguity in the interpretation of the new Act might provide an interested party with a very good and sufficient motive for hastening the death of Agatha Dawson."

"I do mean exactly that. Of course, if the great-niece inherits anyhow, the old lady might as well die under the new Act as under the old. But if there was any doubt about it—how tempting, don't you see, to give her a little push over the edge, so as to make her die in 1925. Especially as she couldn't live long anyhow, and there were no other relatives to be defrauded."

"That reminds me," put in Parker, "suppose the great-niece is excluded from the inheritance, where does the money go?"

"It goes to the Duchy of Lancaster—or in other words, to the Crown."

"In fact," said Wimsey, "to no one in particular. Upon my soul, I really can't see that it's very much of a crime to bump a poor old thing off a bit previously when she's sufferin' horribly, just to get the money she intends you to have. Why the devil should the Duchy of Lancaster have it? Who cares about the Duchy of Lancaster? It's like defrauding the Income Tax."

"Ethically," observed Mr. Murbles, "there may be much to be said for your point of view. Legally, I am afraid, murder is murder, however frail the victim or convenient the result."

"And Agatha Dawson didn't want to die," added Parker, "she said so."

"No," said Wimsey, thoughtfully, "and I suppose she had a right to an opinion."

"I think," said Mr. Murbles, "that before we go any further, we ought to consult a specialist in this branch of the law. I wonder whether Towkington is at home. He is quite the ablest authority I could name. Greatly as I dislike that modern invention, the telephone, I think it might be advisable to ring him up."

Mr. Towkington proved to be at home and at liberty. The case of the great-niece was put to him over the 'phone. Mr. Towkington, taken at a disadvantage without his authorities, and hazarding an opinion on the spur of the moment, thought that in all probability the great-niece would be excluded from the succession under the new Act. But it was an interesting point, and he would be glad of an opportunity to verify his references. Would not Mr. Murbles come round and talk it over with him? Mr. Murbles explained that he was at that moment dining with two friends who were interested in the question. In that case, would not the two friends also come round and see Mr. Towkington?

"Towkington has some very excellent port," said Mr. Murbles, in a cautious aside, and clapping his hand over the mouthpiece of the telephone.

"Then why not go and try it?" said Wimsey, cheerfully.

"It's only as far as Gray's Inn," continued Mr. Murbles.

"All the better," said Lord Peter.

Mr. Murbles released the telephone and thanked Mr. Towkington. The party would start at once for Gray's Inn. Mr. Towkington was heard to say, "Good, good," in a hearty manner before ringing off.

On their arrival at Mr. Towkington's chambers the oak was found to be hospitably unsported, and almost before they could knock, Mr. Towkington himself flung open the door and greeted them in a loud and cheerful tone. He was a large, square man with a florid face and a harsh voice. In court, he was famous for a way of saying, "Come now," as a preface to tying recalcitrant witnesses into tight knots, which he would then proceed to slash open with a brilliant confutation. He knew Wimsey by sight, expressed himself delighted to meet Inspector Parker, and bustled his guests into the room with jovial shouts.

"I've been going into this little matter while you were coming along," he said. "Awkward, eh? ha! Astonishing thing that people can't say what they mean when they draw Acts, eh? ha! Why do you suppose it is, Lord Peter, eh? ha! Come now!"

"I suspect it's because Acts are drawn up by lawyers," said Wimsey with a grin.

"To make work for themselves, eh? I daresay you're right. Even lawyers must live, eh? ha! Very good. Well now, Murbles, let's just have this case again, in greater detail, d'you mind?"

Mr. Murbles explained the matter again, displaying the genealogical table and putting forward the point as regards a possible motive for murder.

"Eh, ha!" exclaimed Mr. Towkington, much delighted, "that's good—very good—your idea, Lord Peter? Very ingenious. Too ingenious. The dock at the Old Bailey is peopled by gentlemen who are too ingenious. Ha! Come to a bad end one of these days, young man. Eh! Yes—well, now, Murbles, the question here turns on the interpretation of the word 'issue'—you grasp that, eh, ha! Yes. Well, *you* seem to think it means issue *ad infinitum*. How do you make that out, come now?"

"I didn't say I thought it did; I said I thought it might," remonstrated Mr. Murbles, mildly. "The general intention of the Act appears to be to exclude any remote kin where the common ancestor is further back than the grandparents—not to cut off the descendants of the brothers and sisters."

"Intention?" snapped Mr. Towkington. "I'm astonished at you, Murbles! The law has nothing to do with good intentions. What does the Act *say*? It says, 'To the brothers and sisters of the whole blood and their issue.' Now, in the absence of any new definition, I should say that the word is here to be construed as before the Act it was construed on intestacy—in so far, at any rate, as it refers to personal property, which I understand the property in question to be, eh?"

"Yes," said Mr. Murbles.

"Then I don't see that you and your great-niece have a leg to stand on—come now!"

"Excuse me," said Wimsey, "but d'you mind—I know lay people are awful ignorant nuisances—but if you *would* be so good as to explain what the beastly word did or does mean, it would be frightfully helpful, don't you know."

"Ha! Well, it's like this," said Mr. Towkington, graciously. "Before 1837—"

"Queen Victoria, I know," said Peter, intelligently.

"Quite so. At the time when Queen Victoria came to the throne, the word 'issue' had no legal meaning—no legal meaning at all."

"You surprise me!"

"You are too easily surprised," said Mr. Towkington. "Many words have no legal meaning. Others have a legal meaning very unlike their ordinary meaning. For example, the word 'daffy-down-dilly.' It is a criminal libel to call a lawyer a daffy-down-dilly. Ha! Yes, I advise you never to do such a thing. No, I certainly advise you *never* to do it. Then again, words which are quite meaningless in your ordinary conversation may have a meaning in law. For instance, I might say to a young man like yourself, 'You wish to leave such-and-such property to so-and-so.' And you would very likely reply, 'Oh, yes, absolutely'—meaning nothing in particular by that. But if you were to write in your will, 'I leave such-and-such property to so-and-so *absolutely*,' then that word would bear a definite legal meaning, and would condition your bequest in a certain manner, and might even prove an embarrassment and produce results very far from your actual intentions. Eh, ha! You see?"

"Quite."

"Very well. Prior to 1837, the word 'issue' meant nothing. A grant 'to A. and his issue' merely gave A. a life estate. Ha! But this was altered by the Wills Act of 1837."

"As far as a will was concerned," put in Mr. Murbles.

"Precisely. After 1837, in a will, 'issue' meant 'heirs of the body'—that is to say, 'issue *ad infinitum.*' In a deed, on the other hand, 'issue' retained its old meaning—or lack of meaning, eh, ha! You follow?"

"Yes," said Mr. Murbles, "and on intestacy of personal property—"

"I am coming to that," said Mr. Towkington.

"—the word 'issue' continued to mean 'heirs of the body,' and that held good till 1926."

"Stop!" said Mr. Towkington, "issue of the child or children of the deceased certainly meant 'issue *ad infinitum*'—but—issue of any person *not* a child of the deceased only meant the child of that person and did not include other descendants. And that undoubtedly held good till 1926. And since the new Act contains no statement to the contrary, I think we must presume that it continues to hold good. Ha! Come now! In the case before us, you observe that the claimant is *not* the child of the deceased nor issue of the child of the deceased; nor is she the child of the deceased's sister. She is merely the grandchild of the deceased sister of the deceased. Accordingly, I think she is debarred from inheriting under the new Act, eh? ha!"

"I see your point," said Mr. Murbles.

"And moreover," went on Mr. Towkington, "after 1925, 'issue' in a will or deed does *not* mean 'issue *ad infinitum.*' That at least is clearly stated, and the Wills Act of 1837 is revoked on that point. Not that that has any direct bearing on the question. But it may be an indication of the tendency of modern interpretation, and might possibly affect the mind of the court in deciding how the word 'issue' was to be construed for the purposes of the new Act."

"Well," said Mr. Murbles, "I bow to your superior knowledge."

"In any case," broke in Parker, "any uncertainty in the matter would provide as good a motive for murder as the certainty of exclusion from inheritance. If

Mary Whittaker only *thought* she might lose the money in the event of her great-aunt's surviving into 1926, she might quite well be tempted to polish her off a little earlier, and make sure."

"That's true enough," said Mr. Murbles.

"Shrewd, very shrewd, ha!" added Mr. Towkington. "But you realise that all this theory of yours depends on Mary Whittaker's having known about the new Act and its probable consequences as early as October, 1925, eh, ha!"

"There's no reason why she shouldn't" said Wimsey. "I remember reading an article in the *Evening Banner*, I think it was, some months earlier—about the time when the Act was having its second reading. That's what put the thing into my head—I was trying to remember all evening where I'd seen that thing about washing out the long-lost heir, you know. Mary Whittaker may easily have seen it too."

"Well, she'd probably have taken advice about it if she did," said Mr. Murbles. "Who is her usual man of affairs?"

Wimsey shook his head.

"I don't think she'd have asked him," he objected. "Not if she was wise, that is. You see, if she did, and he said she probably wouldn't get anything unless Miss Dawson either made a will or died before January, 1926, and if after that the old lady did unexpectedly pop off in October, 1925, wouldn't the solicitor-johnnie feel inclined to ask questions? It wouldn't be safe, don't y'know. I 'xpect she went to some stranger and asked a few innocent little questions under another name, what?"

"Probably," said Mr. Towkington. "You show a remarkable disposition for crime, don't you, eh?"

"Well, if I did go in for it, I'd take reasonable precautions," retorted Wimsey. " 'S wonderful, of course, the tomfool things murderers *do* do. But I have the highest opinion of Miss Whittaker's brains. I bet she covered her tracks pretty well."

"You don't think Mr. Probyn mentioned the matter," suggested Parker, "the time he went down and tried to get Miss Dawson to make her will."

"I *don't*," said Wimsey, with energy, "but I'm pretty certain he tried to explain matters to the old lady, only she was so terrified of the very idea of a will she wouldn't let him get a word in. But I fancy old Probyn was too downy a bird to tell the heir that her only chance of gettin' the dollars was to see that her great-aunt died off before the Act went through. Would *you* tell anybody that, Mr. Towkington?"

"Not if I knew it," said that gentleman, grinning.

"It would be highly undesirable," agreed Mr. Murbles.

"Anyway," said Wimsey, "we can easily find out. Probyn's in Italy—I was going to write to him, but perhaps you'd better do it, Murbles. And, in the meanwhile, Charles and I will think up a way to find whoever it was that did give Miss Whittaker an opinion on the matter."

"You're not forgetting, I suppose," said Parker, rather dryly, "that before pinning down a murder to any particular motive, it is usual to ascertain that a murder has been committed? So far, all we know is that, after a careful post-mortem analysis, two qualified doctors have agreed that Miss Dawson died a natural death."

"I wish you wouldn't keep on saying the same thing, Charles. It bores me so. It's like the Raven never flitting which, as the poet observes, still is sitting, still is

502

sitting, inviting one to heave the pallid bust of Pallas at him and have done with it. You wait till I publish my epoch-making work: *The Murderer's Vade-Mecum, or 101 Ways of Causing Sudden Death.* That'll show you I'm not a man to be trifled with."

"Oh, well!" said Parker.

But he saw the Chief Commissioner next morning and reported that he was at last disposed to take the Dawson case seriously.

15

TEMPTATION OF ST. PETER

PIERROT: "Scaramel, I am tempted."
SCARAMEL: "Always yield to temptation."
L. Housman, Prunella

A s Parker came out from the Chief Commissioner's room, he was caught by an officer.

"There's been a lady on the 'phone to you," he said. "I told her to ring up at 10:30. It's about that now."

"What name?"

"A Mrs. Forrest. She wouldn't say what she wanted."

"Odd," thought Parker. His researches in the matter had been so unfruitful that he had practically eliminated Mrs. Forrest from the Gotobed mystery— merely keeping her filed, as it were, in the back of his mind for future reference. It occurred to him, whimsically, that she had at length discovered the absence of one of her wine-glasses and was ringing him up in a professional capacity. His conjectures were interrupted by his being called to the telephone to answer Mrs. Forrest's call.

"Is that Detective-Inspector Parker?—I'm so sorry to trouble you, but could you give me Mr. Templeton's address?"

"Templeton?" said Parker, momentarily puzzled.

"Wasn't it Templeton—the gentleman who came with you to see me?"

"Oh, yes, of course—I beg your pardon—I—the matter had slipped my memory. Er—you want his address?"

"I have some information which I think he will be glad to hear."

"Oh, yes. You can speak quite freely to me, you know, Mrs. Forrest."

"Not *quite* freely," purred the voice at the other end of the wire, "you are rather official, you know. I should prefer just to write to Mr. Templeton privately, and leave it to him to take up with you."

"I see." Parker's brain worked briskly. It might be inconvenient to have Mrs. Forrest writing to Mr. Templeton at 110A, Piccadilly. The letter might not be delivered. Or, if the lady were to take it into her head to call and discovered that Mr. Templeton was not known to the porter, she might take alarm and bottle up her valuable information.

"I think," said Parker, "I ought not, perhaps, to give you Mr. Templeton's address without consulting him. But you could 'phone him—"

"Oh, yes, that would do. Is he in the book?"

"No—but I can give you his private number."

"Thank you very much. You'll forgive my bothering you."

"No trouble at all." And he named Lord Peter's number.

Having rung off, he waited a moment and then called the number himself.

"Look here, Wimsey," he said, "I've had a call from Mrs. Forrest. She wants to write to you. I wouldn't give the address, but I've given her your number, so if she calls and asks for Mr. Templeton, you will remember who you are, won't you?"

"Righty-ho! Wonder what the fair lady wants."

"It's probably occurred to her that she might have told a better story, and she wants to work off a few additions and improvements on you."

"Then she'll probably give herself away. The rough sketch is frequently so much more convincing than the worked-up canvas."

"Quite so. I couldn't get anything out of her myself."

"No. I expect she's thought it over and decided that it's rather unusual to employ Scotland Yard to ferret out the whereabouts of errant husbands. She fancies there's something up, and that I'm a nice soft-headed imbecile whom she can easily pump in the absence of the official Cerberus."

"Probably. Well, you'll deal with the matter. I'm going to make a search for that solicitor."

"Rather a vague sort of search, isn't it?"

"Well, I've got an idea which may work out. I'll let you know if I get any results."

Mrs. Forrest's call duly came through in about twenty minutes' time. Mrs. Forrest had changed her mind. Would Mr. Templeton come round and see her that evening—about 9 o'clock, if that was convenient? She had thought the matter over and preferred not to put her information on paper.

Mr. Templeton would be very happy to come round. He had no other engagement. It was no inconvenience at all. He begged Mrs. Forrest not to mention it.

Would Mr. Templeton be so very good as not to tell anybody about his visit? Mr. Forrest and his sleuths were continually on the watch to get Mrs. Forrest into trouble, and the decree absolute was due to come up in a month's time. Any trouble with the King's Proctor would be positively disastrous. It would be better if Mr. Templeton would come by Underground to Bond Street, and proceed to the flats on foot, so as not to leave a car standing outside the door or put a taxi-driver into a position to give testimony against Mrs. Forrest.

Mr. Templeton chivalrously promised to obey these directions.

Mrs. Forrest was greatly obliged, and would expect him at nine o'clock.

"Bunter!"

"My lord."

"I am going out to-night. I've been asked not to say where, so I won't. On the other hand, I've got a kind of feelin' that it's unwise to disappear from mortal ken, so to speak. Anything might happen. One might have a stroke, don't you know. So I'm going to leave the address in a sealed envelope. If I don't turn up before to-morrow mornin', I shall consider myself absolved from all promises, what?"

"Very good, my lord."

"And if I'm not to be found at that address, there wouldn't be any harm in tryin'—say Epping Forest, or Wimbledon Common."

"Quite so, my lord."

"By the way, you made the photographs of those fingerprints I brought you some time ago?"

"Oh, yes, my lord."

"Because possibly Mr. Parker may be wanting them presently for some inquiries he will be making."

"I quite understand, my lord."

"Nothing whatever to do with my excursion to-night, you understand."

"Certainly not, my lord."

"And now you might bring me Christie's catalogue. I shall be attending a sale there and lunching at the club."

And, detaching his mind from crime, Lord Peter bent his intellectual and financial powers to outbidding and breaking a ring of dealers, an exercise very congenial to his mischievous spirit.

Lord Peter duly fulfilled the conditions imposed upon him, and arrived on foot at the block of flats in South Audley Street. Mrs. Forrest, as before, opened the door to him herself. It was surprising, he considered, that, situated as she was, she appeared to have neither maid nor companion. But then, he supposed, a chaperon, however disarming of suspicion in the eyes of the world, might prove venal. On the whole, Mrs. Forrest's principle was a sound one: no accomplices. Many transgressors, he reflected, had

> "died because they never knew
> These simple little rules and few."

Mrs. Forrest apologised prettily for the inconvenience to which she was putting Mr. Templeton.

"But I never know when I am not spied upon," she said. "It is sheer spite, you know. Considering how my husband has behaved to me, I think it is monstrous —don't you?"

Her guest agreed that Mr. Forrest must be a monster, jesuitically, however, reserving the opinion that the monster might be a fabulous one.

"And now you will be wondering why I have brought you here," went on the lady. "Do come and sit on the sofa. Will you have whisky or coffee?"

"Coffee, please."

"The fact is," said Mrs. Forrest, "that I've had an idea since I saw you. I—you know, having been much in the same position myself" (with a slight laugh) "I felt *so much* for your friend's wife."

"Sylvia," put in Lord Peter with commendable promptitude. "Oh, yes. Shocking temper and so on, but possibly some provocation. Yes, yes, quite. Poor woman. Feels things—extra sensitive—highly-strung and all that, don't you know."

"Quite so." Mrs. Forrest nodded her fantastically turbanned head. Swathed to the eyebrows in gold tissue, with only two flat crescents of yellow hair plastered over her cheekbones, she looked, in an exotic smoking-suit of embroidered tissue, like a young prince out of the Arabian Nights. Her heavily ringed hands busied themselves with the coffee-cups.

"Well—I felt that your inquiries were really serious, you know, and though, as I told you, it had nothing to do with me, I was interested and mentioned the matter in a letter to—to my friend, you see, who was with me that night."

"Just so," said Wimsey, taking the cup from her, "yes—er—that was very—er —it was kind of you to be interested."

"He—my friend—is abroad at the moment. My letter had to follow him, and I only got his reply to-day."

Mrs. Forrest took a sip or two of coffee as though to clear her recollection.

"His letter rather surprised me. He reminded me that after dinner he had felt the room rather close, and had opened the sitting-room window—that window, there—which overlooks South Audley Street. He noticed a car standing there— a small closed one, black or dark blue or some such colour. And while he was looking idly at it—the way one does, you know—he saw a man and woman come out of this block of flats—not this door, but one or two along to the left—and get in and drive off. The man was in evening dress and he thought it might have been your friend."

Lord Peter, with his coffee-cup at his lips, paused and listened with great attention.

"Was the girl in evening dress, too?"

"No—that struck my friend particularly. She was in just a plain little dark suit, with a hat on."

Lord Peter recalled to mind as nearly as possible Bertha Gotobed's costume. Was this going to be real evidence at last?

"Th—that's very interesting," he stammered. "I suppose your friend couldn't give any more exact details of the dress?"

"No," replied Mrs. Forrest, regretfully, "but he said the man's arm was round the girl as though she was feeling tired or unwell, and he heard him say, 'That's right—the fresh air will do you good.' But you're not drinking your coffee."

"I beg your pardon—" Wimsey recalled himself with a start. "I was dreamin' —puttin' two and two together, as you might say. So he *was* along here at the time—the artful beggar. Oh, the coffee. D'you mind if I put this away and have some without sugar?"

"I'm *so* sorry. Men always seem to take sugar in black coffee. Give it to me— I'll empty it away."

"Allow me." There was no slop-basin on the little table, but Wimsey quickly got up and poured the coffee into the window-box outside. "That's all right. How about another cup for you?"

"Thank you—I oughtn't to take it really, it keeps me awake."

"Just a drop."

"Oh, well, if you like." She filled both cups and sat sipping quietly. "Well— that's all, really, but I thought perhaps I ought to let you know."

"It was very good of you," said Wimsey.

They sat talking a little longer—about plays in Town ("I go out very little, you know, it's better to keep oneself out of the limelight on these occasions"), and books ("I adore Michael Arlen"). Had she read *Young Men in Love* yet? No—she had ordered it from the library. Wouldn't Mr. Templeton have something to eat or drink? Really? A brandy? A liqueur?

No, thank you. And Mr. Templeton felt he really ought to be slippin' along now.

"No—don't go yet—I get so lonely, these long evenings."

There was a desperate kind of appeal in her voice. Lord Peter sat down again.

She began a rambling and rather confused story about her "friend." She had given up so much for the friend. And now that her divorce was really coming off, she had a terrible feeling that perhaps the friend was not as affectionate as he used to be. It was very difficult for a woman, and life was very hard.

And so on.

As the minutes passed, Lord Peter became uncomfortably aware that she was watching him. The words tumbled out—hurriedly, yet lifelessly, like a set task, but her eyes were the eyes of a person who expects something. Something alarming, he decided, yet something she was determined to have. It reminded him of a man waiting for an operation—keyed up to it—knowing that it will do him good—yet shrinking from it with all his senses.

He kept up his end of the fatuous conversation. Behind a barrage of small-talk, his mind ran quickly to and fro, analysing the position, getting the range . . .

Suddenly he became aware that she was trying—clumsily, stupidly and as though in spite of herself—to get him to make love to her.

The fact itself did not strike Wimsey as odd. He was rich enough, well-bred enough, attractive enough and man of the world enough to have received similar invitations fairly often in his thirty-seven years of life. And not always from experienced women. There had been those who sought experience as well as those qualified to bestow it. But so awkward an approach by a woman who admitted to already possessing a husband and a lover was a phenomenon outside his previous knowledge.

Moreover, he felt that the thing would be a nuisance. Mrs. Forrest was handsome enough, but she had not a particle of attraction for him. For all her make-up and her somewhat outspoken costume, she struck him as spinsterish—even epicene. That was the thing which puzzled him during their previous interview. Parker—a young man of rigid virtue and limited worldly knowledge—was not sensitive to these emanations. But Wimsey had felt her as something essentially sexless, even then. And he felt it even more strongly now. Never had he met a woman in whom "the great It," eloquently hymned by Mrs. Elinor Glyn, was so completely lacking.

Her bare shoulder was against him now, marking his broadcloth with white patches of powder.

Blackmail was the first explanation that occurred to him. The next move would be for the fabulous Mr. Forrest, or someone representing him, to appear suddenly in the doorway, aglow with virtuous wrath and outraged sensibilities.

"A very pretty little trap," thought Wimsey, adding aloud, "Well, I really must be getting along."

She caught him by the arm.

"Don't go."

There was no caress in the touch—only a kind of desperation.

He thought, "If she really made a practice of this, she would do it better."

"Truly," he said, "I oughtn't to stay longer. It wouldn't be safe for you."

"I'll risk it," she said.

A passionate woman might have said it passionately. Or with a brave gaiety. Or challengingly. Or alluringly. Or mysteriously.

She said it grimly. Her fingers dug at his arm.

"Well, damn it all, *I'll* risk it," thought Wimsey. "I must and will know what it's all about."

"Poor little woman." He coaxed into his voice the throaty, fatuous tone of the man who is preparing to make an amorous fool of himself.

He felt her body stiffen as he slipped his arm round her, but she gave a little sigh of relief.

He pulled her suddenly and violently to him, and kissed her mouth with a practised exaggeration of passion.

He knew then. No one who has ever encountered it can ever again mistake that awful shrinking, that uncontrollable revulsion of the flesh against a caress that is nauseous. He thought for a moment that she was going to be actually sick.

He released her gently, and stood up—his mind in a whirl, but somehow triumphant. His first instinct had been right, after all.

"That was very naughty of me," he said, lightly. "You made me forget myself. You will forgive me, won't you?"

She nodded, shaken.

"And I really must toddle. It's gettin' frightfully late and all that. Where's my hat? Ah, yes, in the hall. Now, good-bye, Mrs. Forrest, an' take care of yourself. An' thank you ever so much for telling me about what your friend saw."

"You are really going?"

She spoke as though she had lost all hope.

"In God's name," thought Wimsey, "what does she want? Does she suspect that Mr. Templeton is not everything that he seems? Does she want me to stay the night so that she can get a look at the laundry-mark on my shirt? Should I suddenly save the situation for her by offering her Lord Peter Wimsey's visiting-card?"

His brain toyed freakishly with the thought as he babbled his way to the door. She let him go without further words.

As he stepped into the hall he turned and looked at her. She stood in the middle of the room, watching him, and on her face was such a fury of fear and rage as turned his blood to water.

16

A CAST-IRON ALIBI

> "Oh, Sammy, Sammy, why vorn't there an alleybi?"
> Pickwick Papers

Miss Whittaker and the youngest Miss Findlater had returned from their expedition. Miss Climpson, most faithful of sleuths, and carrying Lord Peter's letter of instructions in the pocket of her skirt like a talisman, had asked the youngest Miss Findlater to tea.

As a matter of fact, Miss Climpson had become genuinely interested in the girl. Silly affectation and gush, and a parrot-repetition of the shibboleths of the modern school were symptoms that the experienced spinster well understood. They indicated, she thought, a real unhappiness, a real dissatisfaction with the narrowness of life in a country town. And besides this, Miss Climpson felt sure that Vera Findlater was being "preyed upon," as she expressed it to herself, by the handsome Mary Whittaker. "It would be a mercy for the girl," thought Miss Climpson, "if she could form a genuine attachment to a young man. It is natural for a schoolgirl to be *schwärmerisch*—in a young woman of twenty-two it is thoroughly undesirable. That Whittaker woman encourages it—she would, of course. She likes to have someone to admire her and run her errands. And she prefers it to be a stupid person, who will not compete with her. If Mary Whittaker were to marry, she would marry a rabbit." (Miss Climpson's active mind quickly conjured up a picture of the rabbit—fair-haired and a little paunchy, with a habit of saying, "I'll ask the wife." Miss Climpson wondered why Providence saw fit to create such men. For Miss Climpson, men were intended to be masterful, even though wicked or foolish. She was a spinster made and not born —a perfectly womanly woman.)

"But," thought Miss Climpson, "Mary Whittaker is not of the marrying sort. She is a professional woman by nature. She has a profession, by the way, but she does not intend to go back to it. Probably nursing demands too much sympathy —and one is under the authority of the doctors. Mary Whittaker prefers to control the lives of chicken. 'Better to reign in hell than serve in heaven.' Dear me! I wonder if it is uncharitable to compare a fellow-being to Satan. Only in poetry, of course—I daresay that makes it not so bad. At any rate, I am certain that Mary Whittaker is doing Vera Findlater no good."

Miss Climpson's guest was very ready to tell about their month in the country. They had toured round at first for a few days, and then they had heard of a delightful poultry farm which was for sale, near Orpington in Kent. So they had gone down to have a look at it, and found that it was to be sold in about a fortnight's time. It wouldn't have been wise, of course, to take it over without some inquiries, and by the greatest good fortune they found a dear little cottage to let, furnished, quite close by. So they had taken it for a few weeks, while Miss Whittaker "looked round" and found out about the state of the poultry business in that district, and so on. They *had* enjoyed it so, and it was delightful keeping house together, right away from all the silly people at home.

"Of course, I don't mean you, Miss Climpson. You come from London and are so much more broadminded. But I simply can't stick the Leahampton lot, nor can Mary."

"It is very delightful," said Miss Climpson, "to be *free* from the conventions, I'm sure—especially if one is in company with a *kindred spirit.*"

"Yes—of course Mary and I are tremendous friends, though she is so much cleverer than I am. It's absolutely settled that we're to take the farm and run it together. Won't it be wonderful?"

"Won't you find it rather dull and lonely—just you two girls together? You mustn't forget that you've been accustomed to see quite a lot of young people in Leahampton. Shan't you miss the tennis-parties, and the young men, and so on?"

"Oh, no! If you only knew what a stupid lot they are! Anyway, I've no use for men!" Miss Findlater tossed her head. "They haven't got any ideas. And they always look on women as sort of pets or playthings. As if a woman like Mary wasn't worth fifty of them! You should have heard that Markham man the other day—talking politics to Mr. Tredgold, so that nobody could get a word in edgeways, and then saying, 'I'm afraid this is a very dull subject of conversation for you, Miss Whittaker,' in his condescending way. Mary said in that quiet way of hers, 'Oh, I think the *subject* is anything but dull, Mr. Markham.' But he was so stupid, he couldn't even grasp that and said, 'One doesn't expect ladies to be interested in politics, you know. But perhaps you are one of the modern young ladies who want the flapper's vote.' Ladies, indeed! Why are men so insufferable when they talk about ladies?"

"I think men are apt to be *jealous* of women," replied Miss Climpson, thoughtfully, "and jealousy *does* make people rather *peevish* and *ill-mannered.* I suppose that when one would *like* to despise a set of people and yet has a horrid suspicion that one *can't* genuinely despise them, it makes one *exaggerate* one's contempt for them in conversation. That is why, my dear, I am always *very* careful not to speak sneeringly about men—even though they *often deserve* it, you know. But if I did, everybody would think I was an *envious old maid,* wouldn't they?"

"Well, I mean to be an old maid, anyhow," retorted Miss Findlater. "Mary and I have quite decided that. We're interested in things, not in men."

"You've made a good start at finding out how it's going to work," said Miss Climpson. "Living with a person for a month is an *excellent* test. I suppose you had somebody to do the housework for you."

"Not a soul. We did every bit of it, and it was great fun. I'm ever so good at scrubbing floors and laying fires and things, and Mary's a simply marvellous cook. It was such a change from having the servants always bothering round like they do at home. Of course, it was quite a modern, labour-saving cottage—it belongs to some theatrical people, I think."

"And what did you do when you weren't inquiring into the poultry business?"

"Oh, we ran round in the car and saw places and attended markets. Markets are frightfully amusing, with all the funny old farmers and people. Of course, I'd often been to markets before, but Mary made it all so interesting—and then, too, we were picking up hints all the time for our own marketing later on."

"Did you run up to Town at all?"

"No."

"I should have thought you'd have taken the opportunity for a little jaunt."

"Mary hates Town."

"I thought *you* rather enjoyed a run up now and then."

"I'm not keen. Not now. I used to think I was, but I expect that was only the sort of spiritual restlessness one gets when one hasn't an object in life. There's nothing in it."

Miss Findlater spoke with the air of a disillusioned rake, who has sucked life's orange and found it dead sea fruit. Miss Climpson did not smile. She was accustomed to the rôle of confidante.

"So you were together—just you two—all the time?"

"Every minute of it. And we weren't bored with one another a bit."

"I hope your experiment will prove very successful," said Miss Climpson. "But when you really start on your life together, don't you think it would be wise to arrange for a few *breaks* in it? A little *change of companionship* is good for *everybody*. I've known so many *happy friendships* spoilt by people seeing *too much* of one another."

"They couldn't have been *real* friendships, then," asserted the girl, dogmatically. "Mary and I are *absolutely* happy together."

"Still," said Miss Climpson, "if you don't mind an *old woman* giving you a word of warning, I should be inclined not to keep the bow *always* bent. Suppose Miss Whittaker, for instance, wanted to go off and have a day in Town on her own, say—or go to stay with friends—you would have to learn not to mind that."

"Of course I shouldn't mind. Why—" she checked herself. "I mean, I'm quite sure that Mary would be every bit as loyal to me as I am to her."

"That's right," said Miss Climpson. "The longer I live, my dear, the more *certain* I become that *jealousy* is the most *fatal* of feelings. The Bible calls it 'cruel as the grave,' and I'm sure that is so. *Absolute* loyalty, without jealousy, is the essential thing."

"Yes. Though naturally one would hate to think that the person one was really friends with was putting another person in one's place . . . Miss Climpson, you do believe, don't you, that a friendship ought to be 'fifty-fifty'?"

"That is the ideal friendship, I suppose," said Miss Climpson, thoughtfully, "but I think it is a *very rare thing*. Among women, that is. I doubt very much if I've ever seen an example of it. *Men*, I believe, find it easier to give and take in that way—probably because they have so many outside interests."

"Men's friendships—oh yes! I know one hears a lot about them. But half the time, I don't believe they're *real* friendships at all. Men can go off for years and forget all about their friends. And they don't really confide in one another. Mary and I tell each other all our thoughts and feelings. Men seem just content to think each other good sorts without ever bothering about their inmost selves."

"Probably that's why their friendships last so well," replied Miss Climpson. "They don't make such demands on one another."

"But a great friendship does make demands," cried Miss Findlater eagerly. "It's got to be just everything to one. It's wonderful the way it seems to colour all one's thoughts. Instead of being centred in oneself, one's centred in the other person. That's what Christian love means—one's ready to die for the other person."

"Well, I don't know," said Miss Climpson. "I once heard a sermon about that from a most *splendid* priest—and he said that that kind of love might become *idolatry* if one wasn't very careful. He said that Milton's remark about Eve—you know, 'he for God only, she for God in him'—was not congruous with Catholic doctrine. One must get the *proportions* right, and it was *out of proportion* to see everything through the eyes of another fellow-creature."

"One must put God first, of course," said Miss Findlater, a little formally. "But if the friendship is mutual—that was the point—quite unselfish on both sides, it *must* be a good thing."

"Love is always good, when it's the *right kind*," agreed Miss Climpson, "but I don't think it ought to be too *possessive*. One has to *train* oneself—" she hesitated, and went on courageously—"and in any case, my dear, I cannot help feeling that it is more natural—more proper, in a sense—for a man and woman to be all in all to one another than for two persons of the same sex. Er—after all, it is a—a *fruitful* affection," said Miss Climpson, boggling a trifle at this idea, "and—and all that, you know, and I am sure that when the *right* MAN comes along for you—"

"Bother the right man!" cried Miss Findlater, crossly. "I do hate that kind of talk. It makes one feel dreadful—like a prize cow or something. Surely, we have got beyond that point of view in these days."

Miss Climpson perceived that she had let her honest zeal outrun her detective discretion. She had lost the goodwill of her informant, and it was better to change the conversation. However, she could assure Lord Peter now of one thing. Whoever the woman was that Mrs. Cropper had seen at Liverpool, it was not Miss Whittaker. The attached Miss Findlater, who had never left her friend's side, was sufficient guarantee of that.

17

THE COUNTRY LAWYER'S STORY

"And he that gives us in these days new lords may give us new laws."

Wither, Contented Man's Morrice

Letter from Mr. Probyn, retired Solicitor, of Villa Bianca, Fiesole, to Mr. Murbles, Solicitor, of Staple Inn.

Private and confidential.

Dear Sir,

I was much interested in your letter relative to the death of Miss Agatha Dawson, late of Leahampton, and will do my best to answer your inquiries as briefly as possible, always, of course, on the understanding that all information as to the affairs of my late client will be treated as strictly confidential. I make an exception, of course, in favor of the police officer you mention in connection with the matter.

You wish to know (1) whether Miss Agatha Dawson was aware that it might possibly prove necessary, under the provisions of the new Act, for her to make a testamentary disposition, in order to ensure that her greatniece, Miss Mary Whittaker, should inherit her personal property. (2) Whether I ever urged her to make this testamentary disposition and what her reply was. (3) Whether I had made Miss Mary Whittaker aware of the situation in which she might be placed, supposing her great-aunt to die intestate later than December 31, 1925.

In the course of the Spring of 1925, my attention was called by a learned friend to the ambiguity of the wording of certain clauses in the Act, especially in respect of the failure to define the precise interpretation to be placed on the word "Issue." I immediately passed in review the affairs of my various clients, with a view to satisfying myself that the proper dispositions had been made in each case to avoid misunderstanding and litigation in case of intestacy. I at once realised that Miss Whittaker's inheritance of Miss Dawson's property entirely depended on the interpretation given to the clauses in question. I was aware that Miss Dawson was extremely averse from making a will, owing to that superstitious dread of decease which we meet with so frequently in our profession. However, I thought it my duty to make her understand the question and to do my utmost to get a will signed. Accordingly, I went down to Leahampton and laid the matter before her. This was on March the 14th, or thereabouts—I am not certain to the precise day.

Unhappily, I encountered Miss Dawson at a moment when her opposition to the obnoxious idea of making a will was at its strongest. Her doctor had informed her that a further operation would become necessary in the course of the next few weeks, and I could have selected no more unfortunate occasion for intruding the subject of death upon her mind. She resented any such suggestion—there was a conspiracy, she declared, to frighten her into dying under the operation. It appears that that very tactless practitioner of hers had frightened her with a similar suggestion before her previous operation. But she had come through that and she meant to come through this, if only people would not anger and alarm her.

Of course, if she *had* died under the operation, the whole question would have settled itself and there would have been no need of any will. I pointed out that the very reason why I was anxious for the will to be made was that I fully expected her to live on into the following years, and I explained the provisions of the Act once more, as clearly as I could. She retorted that in that case I had no business to come and trouble her about the question at all. It would be time enough when the Act was passed.

Naturally, the fool of a doctor had insisted that she was not to be told what her disease was—they always do—and she was convinced that the next operation would make all right and that she would live for years. When I ventured to insist—giving as my reason that we men of laws always preferred to be on the safe and cautious side, she became exceedingly angry with me, and practically ordered me out of the house. A few days afterwards I received a letter from her, complaining of my impertinence, and saying that she could no longer feel any confidence in a person who treated her with such inconsiderate rudeness. At her request, I forwarded all her private papers in my possession to Mr. Hodgson, of Leahampton, and I have not held any communication with any member of the family since that date.

This answers your first and second questions. With regard to the third: I certainly did not think it proper to inform Miss Whittaker that her inheritance might depend upon her great-aunt's either making a will or else dying before December 31, 1925. While I know nothing to the young lady's disadvantage, I have always held it inadvisable that persons should know too exactly how much they stand to gain by the unexpected decease of other persons. In case of any unforeseen accident, the heirs may find themselves in an equivocal position, where the fact of their possessing such knowledge might—if made public—be highly prejudicial to their interests. The most that I thought it proper to say was that if at any time Miss Dawson should express a wish to see me, I should like to be sent for without delay. Of course, the withdrawal of Miss Dawson's affairs from my hands put it out of my power to interfere any further.

In October 1925, feeling that my health was not what it had been, I retired from business and came to Italy. In this country the English papers do not always arrive regularly, and I missed the announcement of Miss Dawson's death. That it should have occurred so suddenly and under circumstances somewhat mysterious, is certainly interesting.

You say further that you would be glad of my opinion on Miss Agatha Dawson's mental condition at the time when I last saw her. It was perfectly clear and competent—in so far as she was ever competent to deal with business. She was in no way gifted to grapple with legal problems, and I had extreme difficulty in getting her to understand what the trouble was with regard to the new Property Act. Having been brought up all her life to the idea that property went of right to the next of kin, she found it inconceivable that this state of things should ever alter. She assured me that the law would never permit the Government to pass such an Act. When I had reluctantly persuaded her that it would, she was quite sure that no court would be wicked enough to interpret the Act so as to give the money to anybody but Miss Whittaker, when she was clearly the proper person to have it. "Why should the Duchy of Lancaster have any right to it?" she kept on saying. "I don't even know the Duke of Lancaster." She was not a particularly sensible woman, and in the end I was not at all sure that I had made her comprehend the situation —quite apart from the dislike she had of pursuing the subject. However, there is no doubt that she was then quite *compos mentis*. My reason for urging her to make the will before her final operation was, of course, that I feared she might subsequently lose the use of her faculties, or—which comes to the same thing from a business point of view—might have to be kept continually under the influence of opiates.

Trusting that you will find here the information you require,

I remain,

Yours faithfully,

Thos. Probyn.

Mr. Murbles read this letter through twice, very thoughtfully. To even his cautious mind, the thing began to look like the makings of a case. In his neat, elderly hand, he wrote a little note to Detective-Inspector Parker, begging him to call at Staple Inn at his earliest convenience.

Mr. Parker, however, was experiencing nothing at that moment but inconvenience. He had been calling on solicitors for two whole days, and his soul sickened at the sight of a brass plate. He glanced at the long list in his hand, and distastefully counted up the scores of names that still remained unticked.

Parker was one of those methodical, painstaking people whom the world could so ill spare. When he worked with Wimsey on a case, it was an understood thing that anything lengthy, intricate, tedious and soul-destroying was done by Parker. He sometimes felt that it was irritating of Wimsey to take this so much for granted. He felt so now. It was a hot day. The pavements were dusty. Pieces of paper blew about the streets. Buses were grilling outside and stuffy inside. The Express Dairy, where Parker was eating a hurried lunch, seemed full of the odours of fried plaice and boiling tea-urns. Wimsey, he knew, was lunching at his club, before running down with Freddy Arbuthnot to see the New Zealanders at somewhere or other. He had seen him—a vision of exquisite pale grey, ambling gently along Pall Mall. Damn Wimsey! Why couldn't he have let Miss Dawson rest quietly in her grave? There she was, doing no harm to anybody— and Wimsey must insist on prying into her affairs and bringing the inquiry to such a point that Parker simply had to take official notice of it. Oh well! he supposed he must go on with these infernal solicitors.

He was proceeding on a system of his own, which might or might not prove fruitful. He had reviewed the subject of the new Property Act, and decided that if and when Miss Whittaker had become aware of its possible effect on her own expectations, she would at once consider taking legal advice.

Her first thought would no doubt be to consult a solicitor in Leahampton, and unless she already had the idea of foul play in her mind, there was nothing to deter her from doing so. Accordingly, Parker's first move had been to run down to Leahampton and interview the three firms of solicitors there. All three were able to reply quite positively that they had never received such an inquiry from Miss Whittaker, or from anybody, during the year 1925. One solicitor, indeed—the senior partner of Hodgson & Hodgson, to whom Miss Dawson had entrusted her affairs after her quarrel with Mr. Probyn—looked a little oddly at Parker when he heard the question.

"I assure you, Inspector," he said, "that if the point had been brought to my notice in such a way, I should certainly have remembered it, in the light of subsequent events."

"The matter never crossed your mind, I suppose," said Parker, "when the question arose of winding up the estate and proving Miss Whittaker's claim to inherit?"

"I can't say it did. Had there been any question of searching for next-of-kin it might—I don't say it would—have occurred to me. But I had a very clear history of the family connections from Mr. Probyn, the death took place nearly two months before the Act came into force, and the formalities all went through more or less automatically. In fact, I never thought about the Act one way or another in that connection."

Parker said he was not surprised to hear it, and favoured Mr. Hodgson with Mr. Towkington's learned opinion on the subject, which interested Mr.

Hodgson very much. And that was all he got at Leahampton, except that he fluttered Miss Climpson very much by calling upon her and hearing all about her interview with Vera Findlater. Miss Climpson walked to the station with him, in the hope that they might meet Miss Whittaker—"I am sure you would be *interested* to *see* her"—but they were unlucky. On the whole, thought Parker, it might be just as well. After all, though he would like to see Miss Whittaker, he was not particularly keen on her seeing him, especially in Miss Climpson's company. "By the way," he said to Miss Climpson, "you had better explain me in some way to Mrs. Budge, or she may be a bit inquisitive."

"But I *have*," replied Miss Climpson, with an engaging giggle, "when Mrs. Budge said there was a Mr. Parker to see me, of course I realised at *once* that she mustn't know *who* you were, so I said, quite quickly, 'Mr. Parker! Oh, that must be my nephew Adolphus.' You don't mind being Adolphus, do you? It's funny, but that was the *only* name that came into my mind at the moment. I can't *think* why, for I've never known an Adolphus."

"Miss Climpson," said Parker, solemnly, "you are a marvellous woman, and I wouldn't mind even if you'd called me Marmaduke."

So here he was, working out his second line of inquiry. If Miss Whittaker did not go to a Leahampton solicitor, to whom would she go? There was Mr. Probyn, of course, but he did not think she would have selected him. She would not have known him at Crofton, of course—she had never actually lived with her great-aunts. She had met him the day he came down to Leahampton to see Miss Dawson. He had not then taken her into his confidence about the object of his visit, but she must have known from what her aunt said that it had to do with the making of a will. In the light of her new knowledge, she would guess that Mr. Probyn had then had the Act in his mind, and had not thought fit to trust her with the facts. If she asked him now, he would probably reply that Miss Dawson's affairs were no longer in his hands, and refer her to Mr. Hodgson. And besides, if she asked the question and anything were to happen—Mr. Probyn might remember it. No, she would not have approached Mr. Probyn.

What then?

To the person who has anything to conceal—to the person who wants to lose his identity as one leaf among the leaves of a forest—to the person who asks no more than to pass by and be forgotten, there is one name above others which promises a haven of safety and oblivion. London. Where no one knows his neighbour. Where shops do not know their customers. Where physicians are suddenly called to unknown patients whom they never see again. Where you may lie dead in your house for months together unmissed and unnoticed till the gas-inspector comes to look at the meter. Where strangers are friendly and friends are casual. London, whose rather untidy and grubby bosom in the repository of so many odd secrets. Discreet, incurious and all-enfolding London.

Not that Parker put it that way to himself. He merely thought, "Ten to one she'd try London. They mostly think they're safer there."

Miss Whittaker knew London, of course. She had trained at the Royal Free. That meant she would know Bloomsbury better than any other district. For nobody knew better than Parker how rarely Londoners move out of their own particular little orbit. Unless, of course, she had at some time during her time at the hospital been recommended to a solicitor in another quarter, the chances were that she would have gone to a solicitor in the Bloomsbury or Holborn district.

Unfortunately for Parker, this is a quarter which swarms with solicitors. Gray's Inn Road, Gray's Inn itself, Bedford Row, Holborn, Lincoln's Inn—the brass plates grow all about as thick as blackberries.

Which was why Parker was feeling so hot, tired and fed-up that June afternoon.

With an impatient grunt he pushed away his eggy plate, paid-at-the-desk-please, and crossed the road towards Bedford Row, which he had marked down as his portion for the afternoon.

He started at the first solicitor's he came to, which happened to be the office of one J. F. Trigg. He was lucky. The youth in the outer office informed him that Mr. Trigg had just returned from lunch, was disengaged, and would see him. Would he walk in?

Mr. Trigg was a pleasant, fresh-faced man in his early forties. He begged Mr. Parker to be seated and asked what he could do for him.

For the thirty-seventh time, Parker started on the opening gambit which he had devised to suit his purpose.

"I am only temporarily in London, Mr. Trigg, and finding I needed legal advice, I was recommended to you by a man I met in a restaurant. He did give me his name, but it has escaped me, and anyway, it's of no great importance, is it? The point is this. My wife and I have come up to Town to see her great-aunt, who is in a very bad way. In fact, she isn't expected to live.

"Well, now, the old lady has always been fond of my wife, don't you see, and it has always been an understood thing that Mrs. Parker was to come into her money when she died. It's quite a tidy bit, and we have been—I won't say looking forward to it, but in a kind of mild way counting on it as something for us to retire upon later on. You understand. There aren't any other relations at all, so, though the old lady has often talked about making a will, we didn't worry much, one way or the other, because we took it for granted my wife would come in for anything there was. But we were talking about it to a friend yesterday, and he took us rather aback by saying that there was a new law or something, and that if my wife's great-aunt hadn't made a will we shouldn't get anything at all. I think he said it would all go to the Crown. I didn't think that could be right and told him so, but my wife is a bit nervous—there are the children to be considered, you see—and she urged me to get legal advice, because her great-aunt may go off at any minute, and we don't know whether there is a will or not. Now, how does a great-niece stand under the new arrangements?"

"The point has not been made very clear," said Mr. Trigg, "but my advice to you is, to find out whether a will has been made and if not, to get one made without delay if the testatrix is capable of making one. Otherwise I think there is a very real danger of your wife's losing her inheritance."

"You seem quite familiar with the question," said Parker, with a smile; "I suppose you are always being asked it since this new Act came in?"

"I wouldn't say 'always.' It is comparatively rare for a great-niece to be left as sole next-of-kin."

"Is it? Well, yes, I should think it must be. Do you remember being asked that question in the summer of 1925, Mr. Trigg?"

A most curious expression came over the solicitor's face—it looked almost like alarm.

"What makes you ask that?"

"You need have no hesitation in answering," said Parker, taking out his official card. "I am a police officer and have a good reason for asking. I put the legal point to you first as a problem of my own, because I was anxious to have your professional opinion first."

"I see. Well, Inspector, in that case I suppose I am justified in telling you all about it. I *was* asked that question in June, 1925."

"Do you remember the circumstances?"

"Clearly. I am not likely to forget them—or rather, the sequel to them."

"That sounds interesting. Will you tell the story in your own way and with all the details you can remember?"

"Certainly. Just a moment." Mr. Trigg put his head out into the outer office. "Badcock, I am engaged with Mr. Parker and can't see anybody. Now, Mr. Parker, I am at your service. Won't you smoke?"

Parker accepted the invitation and lit up his well-worn briar, while Mr. Trigg, rapidly smoking cigarette after cigarette, unfolded his remarkable story.

18

THE LONDON LAWYER'S STORY

"I who am given to novel-reading, how often have I gone
out with the doctor when the stranger has summoned
him
to visit the unknown patient in the lonely house. . . .
This
Strange Adventure may lead, in a later chapter, to the
revealing of a mysterious crime."

The Londoner

"I think," said Mr. Trigg, "that it was on the 15th, or 16th June, 1925, that a lady called to ask almost exactly the same question that you have done—only that she represented herself as inquiring on behalf of a friend whose name she did not mention. Yes—I think I can describe her pretty well. She was tall and handsome, with a very clear skin, dark hair and blue eyes—an attractive girl. I remember that she had very fine brows, rather straight, and not much colour in her face, and she was dressed in something summery but very neat. I should think it would be called an embroidered linen dress—I am not an expert on those things—and a shady white hat of panama straw."

"Your recollection seems very clear," said Parker.

"It is; I have rather a good memory; besides, I saw her on other occasions, as you shall hear.

"At this first visit she told me—much as you did—that she was only temporarily in Town, and had been casually recommended to me. I told her that I should not like to answer her question off-hand. The Act, you may remember, had only recently passed its Final Reading, and I was by no means up in it. Besides, from just skimming through it, I had convinced myself that various important questions were bound to crop up.

"I told the lady—Miss Grant was the name she gave, by the way—that I should like to take counsel's opinion before giving her any advice, and asked if she could call again the following day. She said she could, rose and thanked me, offering me her hand. In taking it, I happened to notice rather an odd scar, running across the backs of all the fingers—rather as though a chisel or something had slipped at some time. I noticed it quite idly, of course, but it was lucky for me I did.

"Miss Grant duly turned up the next day. I had looked up a very learned friend in the interval, and gave her the same opinion that I gave you just now. She looked rather concerned about it—in fact, almost more annoyed than concerned.

" 'It seems rather unfair,' she said, 'that people's family money should go away to the Crown like that. After all, a great-niece is quite a near relation, really.'

"I replied that, provided the great-niece could call witnesses to prove that the deceased had always had the intention of leaving her the money, the Crown would, in all probability, allot the estate, or a suitable proportion of it, in accordance with the wishes of the deceased. It would, however, lie entirely within the discretion of the court to do so or not, and, of course, if there had been any quarrel or dispute about the matter at any time, the judge might take an unfavourable view of the great-niece's application.

" 'In any case,' I added, 'I don't *know* that the great-niece is excluded under the Act—I only understand that she *may* be. In any case, there are still six months before the Act comes into force, and many things may happen before then.'

" 'You mean that Auntie may die,' she said, 'but she's not really dangerously ill —only mental, as Nurse calls it.'

"Anyhow, she went away then after paying my fee, and I noticed that the 'friend's great-aunt' had suddenly become 'Auntie,' and decided that my client felt a certain personal interest in the matter."

"I fancy she had," said Parker. "When did you see her again?"

"Oddly enough, I ran across her in the following December. I was having a quick and early dinner in Soho, before going on to a show. The little place I usually patronise was very full, and I had to sit at a table where a woman was already seated. As I muttered the usual formula about 'Was anybody sitting there,' she looked up, and I promptly recognised my client.

" 'Why, how do you do, Miss Grant?' I said.

" 'I beg your pardon,' she replied, rather stiffly. 'I think you are mistaken.'

" 'I beg *your* pardon,' said I, stiffer still, 'My name is Trigg, and you came to consult me in Bedford Row last June. But if I am intruding, I apologise and withdraw.'

"She smiled then, and said, 'I'm sorry, I did not recognise you for the moment.'

"I obtained permission to sit at her table.

"By way of starting a conversation, I asked whether she had taken any further advice in the matter of the inheritance. She said no, she had been quite content with what I had told her. Still to make conversation, I inquired whether the great-aunt had made a will after all. She replied, rather briefly, that it had not been necessary; the old lady had died. I noticed that she was dressed in black, and was confirmed in my opinion that she herself was the great-niece concerned.

"We talked for some time, Inspector, and I will not conceal from you that I found Miss Grant a very interesting personality. She had an almost masculine understanding. I may say I am not the sort of a man who prefers women to be brainless. No, I am rather modern in that respect. If ever I was to take a wife, Inspector, I should wish her to be an intelligent companion."

Parker said Mr. Trigg's attitude did him great credit. He also made the mental observation that Mr. Trigg would probably not object to marrying a young woman who had inherited money and was unencumbered with relations.

"It is rare," went on Mr. Trigg, "to find a woman with a legal mind. Miss Grant was unusual in that respect. She took a great interest in some case or other that was prominent in the newspapers at the time—I forget now what it was—and asked me some remarkably sensible and intelligent questions. I must say that I quite enjoyed our conversation. Before dinner was over, we had got on to more personal topics, in the course of which I happened to mention that I lived in Golder's Green."

"Did she give you her own address?"

"She said she was staying at the Peveril Hotel in Bloomsbury, and that she was looking for a house in Town. I said that I might possibly hear of something out Hampstead way, and offered my professional services in case she should require them. After dinner I accompanied her back to her hotel, and bade her good-bye in the lounge."

"She was really staying there, then?"

"Apparently. However, about a fortnight later, I happened to hear of a house in Golder's Green that had fallen vacant suddenly. It belonged, as a matter of fact, to a client of mine. In pursuance of my promise, I wrote to Miss Grant at the Peveril. Receiving no reply, I made inquiries there, and found that she had left the hotel the day after our meeting, leaving no address. In the hotel register, she had merely given her address as Manchester. I was somewhat disappointed, but thought no more about the matter.

"About a month later—on January 26th, to be exact, I was sitting at home reading a book, preparatory to retiring to bed. I should say that I occupy a flat, or rather maisonette, in a small house which has been divided to make two establishments. The people on the ground floor were away at that time, so that I was quite alone in the house. My housekeeper only comes in by the day. The telephone rang—I noticed the time. It was a quarter to eleven. I answered it, and a woman's voice spoke, begging me to come instantly to a certain house on Hampstead Heath, to make a will for someone who was at the point of death."

"Did you recognise the voice?"

"No. It sounded like a servant's voice. At any rate, it had a strong cockney accent. I asked whether to-morrow would not be time enough, but the voice urged me to hurry or it might be too late. Rather annoyed, I put my things on and went out. It was a most unpleasant night, cold and foggy. I was lucky enough to find a taxi on the nearest rank. We drove to the address, which we had great difficulty in finding, as everything was pitch-black. It turned out to be a small house in a very isolated position on the Heath—in fact, there was no proper approach to it. I left the taxi on the road, about a couple of hundred yards off, and asked the man to wait for me, as I was very doubtful of ever finding another taxi in that spot at that time of night. He grumbled a good deal, but consented to wait if I promised not to be very long.

"I made my way to the house. At first I thought it was quite dark, but presently I saw a faint glimmer in a ground-floor room. I rang the bell. No answer, though I could hear it trilling loudly. I rang again and knocked. Still no answer. It was bitterly cold. I struck a match to be sure I had come to the right house, and then I noticed that the front door was ajar.

"I thought that perhaps the servant who had called me was so much occupied with her sick mistress as to be unable to leave her to come to the door. Thinking that in that case I might be of assistance to her, I pushed the door open and went in. The hall was perfectly dark, and I bumped against an umbrella-stand in entering. I thought I heard a faint voice calling or moaning, and when my eyes had become accustomed to the darkness, I stumbled forward, and saw a dim light coming from a door on the left."

"Was that the room which you had seen to be illuminated from outside?"

"I think so. I called out, 'May I come in?' and a very low, weak voice replied, 'Yes, please.' I pushed the door open and entered a room furnished as a sitting-room. In one corner there was a couch, on which some bed-clothes appeared to have been hurriedly thrown to enable it to be used as a bed. On the couch lay a woman, all alone.

"I could only dimly make her out. There was no light in the room except a small oil-lamp, with a green shade so tilted as to keep the light from the sick woman's eyes. There was a fire in the grate, but it had burnt low. I could see, however, that the woman's head and face were swathed in white bandages. I put out my hand and felt for the electric switch, but she called out:

"No light, please—it hurts me."

"How did she see you put your hand to the switch?"

"Well," said Mr. Trigg, "that was an odd thing. She didn't speak, as a matter of fact, till I had actually clicked the switch down. But nothing happened. The light didn't come on."

"Really?"

"No. I supposed that the bulb had been taken away or had gone phut. However, I said nothing, and came up to the bed. She said in a sort of half-whisper, 'Is that the lawyer?'

"I said, 'Yes,' and asked what I could do for her.

"She said, 'I have had a terrible accident. I can't live. I want to make my will quickly.' I asked whether there was nobody with her. 'Yes, yes,' she said in a hurried way, 'my servant will be back in a moment. She has gone to look for a doctor.' 'But,' I said, 'couldn't she have rung up? You are not fit to be left alone.' 'We couldn't get through to one,' she replied, 'it's all right. She will be here soon. Don't waste time. I must make my will.' She spoke in a dreadful, gasping way, and I felt that the best thing would be to do what she wanted, for fear of agitating her. I drew a chair to the table where the lamp was, got out my fountain pen and a printed will-form with which I had provided myself, and expressed myself ready to receive her instructions.

"Before beginning, she asked me to give her a little brandy and water from a decanter which stood on the table. I did so, and she took a small sip, which seemed to revive her. I placed the glass near her hand, and at her suggestion mixed another glass for myself. I was very glad of it, for, as I said, it was a beast of a night, and the room was cold. I looked round for some extra coals to put on the fire, but could see none."

"That," said Parker, "is extremely interesting and suggestive."

"I thought it queer at the time. But the whole thing was queer. Anyway, I then said I was ready to begin. She said, 'You may think I am a little mad, because my head has been so hurt. But I am quite sane. But he shan't have a penny of the money.' I asked her if someone had attacked her. She replied, 'My husband. He thinks he has killed me. But I am going to live long enough to will the money away.' She then said that her name was Mrs. Marion Mead, and proceeded to make a will, leaving her estate, which amounted to about £10,000, among various legatees, including a daughter and three or four sisters. It was rather a complicated will, as it included various devices for tying up the daughter's money in a trust, so as to prevent her from ever handing over any of it to the father."

"Did you make a note of the names and addresses of the people involved?"

"I did, but, as you will see later on, I could make no use of them. The testatrix was certainly clear-headed enough about the provisions of the will, though she seemed terribly weak, and her voice never rose above a whisper after that one time when she had called to me not to turn on the light.

"At length I finished my notes of the will, and started to draft it out on to the proper form. There were no signs of the servant's return, and I began to be really anxious. Also the extreme cold—or something else—added to the fact that it was now long past my bed-time, was making me appallingly sleepy. I poured out another stiff little dose of the brandy to warm me up, and went on writing out the will.

"When I had finished I said:

" 'How about signing this? We need another witness to make it legal.'

"She said, 'My servant must be here in a minute or two. I can't think what has happened to her.'

" 'I expect she has missed her way in the fog,' I said. 'However, I will wait a little longer. I can't go and leave you like this.'

"She thanked me feebly, and we sat for some time in silence. As time went on, I began to feel the situation to be increasingly uncanny. The sick woman breathed heavily, and moaned from time to time. The desire for sleep overpowered me more and more. I could not understand it.

"Presently it occurred to me, stupefied though I felt, that the most sensible thing would be to get the taxi-man—if he was still there—to come in and witness the will with me, and then to go myself to find a doctor. I sat, sleepily revolving this in my mind, and trying to summon energy to speak. I felt as though a great weight of inertia was pressing down upon me. Exertion of any kind seemed almost beyond my powers.

"Suddenly something happened which brought me back to myself. Mrs. Mead turned a little over upon the couch and peered at me intently, as it seemed, in the lamp-light. To support herself, she put both her hands on the edge of the table. I noticed, with a vague sense of something unexpected, that the left hand bore no wedding-ring. And then I noticed something else.

"Across the back of the fingers of the right hand went a curious scar—as though a chisel or some such thing had slipped and cut them."

Parker sat upright in his chair.

"Yes," said Mr. Trigg, "that interests you. It startled me. Or rather, startled isn't quite the word. In my oppressed state, it affected me like some kind of nightmare. I struggled upright in my chair, and the woman sank back upon her pillows.

"At that moment there came a violent ring at the bell."

"The servant?"

"No—thank Heaven it was my taxi-driver, who had become tired of waiting. I thought—I don't quite know what I thought—but I was alarmed. I gave some kind of shout or groan, and the man came straight in. Happily, I had left the door open as I had found it.

"I pulled myself together sufficiently to ask him to witness the will. I must have looked queer and spoken in a strange way, for I remember how he looked from me to the brandy-bottle. However, he signed the paper after Mrs. Mead, who wrote her name in a weak, straggling hand as she lay on her back.

" 'Wot next, guv'nor?' asked the man, when this was done.

"I was feeling dreadfully ill by now. I could only say, 'Take me home.'

"He looked at Mrs. Mead and then at me, and said, 'Ain't there nobody to see to the lady, sir?'

"I said, 'Fetch a doctor. But take me home first.'

"I stumbled out of the house on his arm. I heard him muttering something about its being a rum start. I don't remember the drive home. When I came back to life, I was in my own bed, and one of the local doctors was standing over me.

"I'm afraid this story is getting very long and tedious. To cut matters short, it seems the taxi-driver, who was a very decent, intelligent fellow, had found me completely insensible at the end of the drive. He didn't know who I was, but he hunted in my pocket and found my visiting card and my latch-key. He took me home, got me upstairs and, deciding that if I was drunk, I was a worse drunk that he had ever encountered in his experience, humanely went round and fetched a doctor.

"The doctor's opinion was that I had been heavily drugged with veronal or something of that kind. Fortunately, if the idea was to murder me, the dose had been very much under-estimated. We went into the matter thoroughly, and the upshot was that I must have taken about 30 grains of the stuff. It appears that it is a difficult drug to trace by analysis, but that was the conclusion the doctor came to, looking at the matter all round. Undoubtedly the brandy had been doped.

"Of course, we went round to look at the house next day. It was all shut up, and the local milkman informed us that the occupiers had been away for a week and were not expected home for another ten days. We got into communication with them, but they appeared to be perfectly genuine, ordinary people, and they declared they knew nothing whatever about it. They were accustomed to go away every so often, just shutting the house and not bothering about a caretaker or anything. The man came along at once, naturally, to investigate matters, but couldn't find that anything had been stolen or disturbed, except that a pair of sheets and some pillows showed signs of use, and a scuttle of coal had been used in the sitting-room. The coal-cellar, which also contained the electric meter, had been left locked and the meter turned off before the family left—they apparently had a few grains of sense—which accounts for the chill darkness of the house when I entered it. The visitor had apparently slipped back the catch of the pantry window—one of the usual gimcrack affairs—with a knife or something, and had brought her own lamp, siphon and brandy. Daring, but not really difficult.

"No Mrs. Mead or Miss Grant was to be heard of anywhere, as I needn't tell you. The tenants of the house were not keen to start expensive inquiries—after all, they'd lost nothing but a shilling's worth of coals—and on consideration, and seeing that I hadn't actually been murdered or anything, I thought it best to let the matter slide. It was a most unpleasant adventure."

"I'm sure it was. Did you ever hear from Miss Grant again?"

"Why, yes. She rang me up twice—once, after three months, and again only a fortnight ago, asking for an appointment. You may think me cowardly, Mr. Parker, but each time I put her off. I didn't quite know what might happen. As a matter of fact, the opinion I formed in my own mind was that I had been entrapped into that house with the idea of making me spend the night there and afterwards blackmailing me. That was the only explanation I could think of which would account for the sleeping-draught. I thought discretion was the better part of valour, and gave my clerks and my housekeeper instructions that if Miss Grant should call at any time I was out and not expected back."

"H'm. Do you suppose she knew you had recognised the scar on her hand?"

"I'm sure she didn't. Otherwise she would hardly have made advances to me in her own name again."

"No. I think you are right. Well, Mr. Trigg, I am much obliged to you for this information, which may turn out to be very valuable. And if Miss Grant should ring you up again—where did she call from, by the way?"

"From call-boxes, each time. I know that, because the operator always tells one when the call is from a public box. I didn't have the calls traced."

"No, of course not. Well, if she does it again, will you please make an appointment with her, and then let me know about it at once? A call to Scotland Yard will always find me."

Mr. Trigg promised that he would do this, and Parker took his leave.

"And now we know," thought Parker as he returned home, "that somebody— an odd unscrupulous somebody—was making inquiries about great-nieces in 1925. A word to Miss Climpson, I fancy, is indicated—just to find out whether Mary Whittaker has a scar on her right hand, or whether I've got to hunt up any more solicitors."

The hot streets seemed less oppressively oven-like than before. In fact, Parker was so cheered by his interview that he actually bestowed a cigarette-card upon the next urchin who accosted him.

PART III

THE MEDICO-LEGAL PROBLEM

"There's not a crime
But takes its proper change out still in crime
If once rung on the counter of this world."
E. B. Browning, Aurora Leigh

19

GONE AWAY

"There is nothing good or evil save in the will."
Epictetus

"You will not, I imagine, deny," observed Lord Peter, "that very odd things seem to happen to the people who are in a position to give information about the last days of Agatha Dawson. Bertha Gotobed dies suddenly, under suspicious circumstances; her sister thinks she sees Miss Whittaker lying in wait for her at Liverpool docks; Mr. Trigg is inveigled into a house of mystery and is semi-poisoned. I wonder what would have happened to Mr. Probyn, if he had been careless enough to remain in England."

"I deny nothing," replied Parker. "I will only point out to you that during the month in which these disasters occurred to the Gotobed family, the object of your suspicions was in Kent with Miss Vera Findlater, who never left her side."

"As against that undoubted snag," rejoined Wimsey, "I bring forward a letter from Miss Climpson, in which—amid a lot of rigmarole with which I will not trouble you—she informs me that upon Miss Whittaker's right hand there is a scar, precisely similar to the one which Mr. Trigg describes."

"Is there? That does seem to connect Miss Whittaker pretty definitely with the Trigg business. But is it your theory that she is trying to polish off all the people who know anything about Miss Dawson? Rather a big job, don't you think, for a single-handed female? And if so, why is Dr. Carr spared? and Nurse Philliter? and Nurse Forbes? And the other doctor chappie? And the rest of the population of Leahampton, if it comes to that?"

"That's an interesting point which had already occurred to me. I think I know why. Up to the present, the Dawson case has presented two different problems, one legal and one medical—the motive and the means, if you like that better. As far as opportunity goes, only two people figure as possibles—Miss Whittaker and Nurse Forbes. The Forbes woman had nothing to gain by killin' a good patient, so for the moment we can wash her out.

"Well now, as to the medical problem—the means. I must say that up to now that appears completely insoluble. I am baffled, Watson (said he, his hawk-like eyes gleaming angrily from under the half-closed lids). Even I am baffled. But not for long! (he cried, with a magnificent burst of self-confidence). My Honour (capital H) is concerned to track this Human Fiend (capitals) to its hidden source, and nail the whited sepulchre to the mast even though it crush me in the attempt! Loud applause. His chin sank broodingly upon his dressing-gown, and he breathed a few guttural notes into the bass saxophone which was the cherished companion of his solitary hours in the bathroom."

Parker ostentatiously took up the book which he had laid aside on Wimsey's entrance.

"Tell me when you've finished," he said, caustically.

"I've hardly begun. The means, I repeat, seems insoluble—and so the criminal evidently thinks. There has been no exaggerated mortality among the doctors and nurses. On that side of the business the lady feels herself safe. No. The motive is the weak point—hence the hurry to stop the mouths of the people who knew about the legal part of the problem."

"Yes, I see. Mrs. Cropper has started back to Canada, by the way. She doesn't seem to have been molested at all."

"No—and that's why I still think there was somebody on the watch in Liverpool. Mrs. Cropper was only worth silencing so long as she had told nobody her story. That is why I was careful to meet her and accompany her ostentatiously to Town."

"Oh, rot, Peter! Even if Miss Whittaker had been there—which we know she couldn't have been—how was she to know that you were going to ask about the Dawson business? She doesn't know you from Adam."

"She might have found out who Murbles was. The advertisement which started the whole business was in his name, you know."

"In that case, why hasn't she attacked Murbles or you?"

"Murbles is a wise old bird. In vain are nets spread in his sight. He is seeing no female clients, answering no invitations, and never goes out without an escort."

"I didn't know he took it so seriously."

"Oh, yes. Murbles is old enough to have learnt the value of his own skin. As for me—have you noticed the remarkable similarity in some ways between Mr. Trigg's adventure and my own little adventurelet, as you might say, in South Audley Street?"

"What, with Mrs. Forrest?"

"Yes. The secret appointment. The drink. The endeavour to get one to stay the night at all costs. I'm positive there was something in that sugar, Charles, that no sugar should contain—see Public Health (Adulteration of Food) Acts, various."

"You think Mrs. Forrest is an accomplice?"

"I do. I don't know what she has to gain by it—probably money. But I feel sure there is some connection. Partly because of Bertha Gotobed's £5 note; partly because Mrs. Forrest's story was a palpable fake—I'm certain the woman's never had a lover, let alone a husband—you can't mistake real inexperience; and chiefly because of the similarity of method. Criminals always tend to repeat their effects. Look at George Joseph Smith and his brides. Look at Neill Cream. Look at Armstrong and his tea-parties."

"Well, if there's an accomplice, all the better. Accomplices generally end up by giving the show away."

"True. And we are in a good position because up till now I don't think they know that we suspect any connection between them."

"But I still think, you know, we ought to get some evidence that actual crimes have been committed. Call me finicking, if you like. If you *could* suggest a means of doing away with these people so as to leave no trace, I should feel happier about it."

"The means, eh?—Well, we do know something about it."

"As what?"

"Well—take the two victims—"

"Alleged."

"All right, old particular. The two alleged victims and the two (alleged) intended victims. Miss Dawson was ill and helpless; Bertha Gotobed possibly stupefied by a heavy meal and an unaccustomed quantity of wine; Trigg was given a sufficient dose of veronal to send him to sleep, and I was offered something of probably the same kind—I wish I could have kept the remains of that coffee. So we deduce from that, what?"

"I suppose that it was a means of death which could only be used on somebody more or less helpless or unconscious."

"Exactly. As for instance, a hypodermic injection—only nothing appears to have been injected. Or a delicate operation of some kind—if we could only think of one to fit the case. Or the inhalation of something—such as chloroform —only we could find no traces of suffocation."

"Yes. That doesn't get us very far, though."

"It's something. Then again, it may very well be something that a trained nurse would have learnt or heard about. Miss Whittaker was trained, you know —which, by the way, was what made it so easy for her to bandage up her own head and provide a pitiful and unrecognisable spectacle for the stupid Mr. Trigg."

"It wouldn't have to be anything very out of the way—nothing, I mean, that only a trained surgeon could do, or that required very specialised knowledge."

"Oh, no. Probably something picked up in conversation with a doctor or the other nurses. I say, how about getting hold of Dr. Carr again? Or, no—if he'd got any ideas on the subject he'd have trotted 'em out before now. I know! I'll ask Lubbock, the analyst. He'll do. I'll get in touch with him to-morrow."

"And meanwhile," said Parker, "I suppose we just sit round and wait for somebody else to be murdered."

"It's beastly, isn't it? I still feel poor Bertha Gotobed's blood on my head, so to speak. I say!"

"Yes?"

"We've practically got clear proof on the Trigg business. Couldn't you put the lady in quod on a charge of burglary while we think out the rest of the dope? It's often done. It *was* a burglary, you know. She broke into a house after dark and appropriated a scuttleful of coal to her own use. Trigg could identify her—he seems to have paid the lady particular attention on more than one occasion— and we could rake up his taxi-man for corroborative detail."

Parker pulled at his pipe for a few minutes.

"There's something in that," he said finally. "I think perhaps it's worth while putting it before the authorities. But we mustn't be in too much of a hurry, you know. I wish we were further ahead with our other proofs. There's such a thing as Habeas Corpus—you can't hold on to people indefinitely just on a charge of stealing coal—"

"There's the breaking and entering, don't forget that. It's burglary, after all. You can get penal servitude for life for burglary."

"But it all depends on the view the law takes of the coal. It might decide that there was no original intention of stealing coal, and treat the thing as a mere misdemeanour or civil trespass. Anyhow, we don't really *want* a conviction for stealing coal. But I'll see what they think about it at our place, and meanwhile I'll get hold of Trigg again and try and find the taxi-driver. And Trigg's doctor.

We might get it as an attempt to murder Trigg, or at least to inflict grievous bodily harm. But I should like some more evidence about—"

"Cuckoo! So should I. But I can't manufacture evidence out of nothing. Dash it all, be reasonable. I've built you up a case out of nothing. Isn't that handsome enough? Base ingratitude—that's what's the matter with you."

Parker's inquiries took some time, and June lingered into its longest days.

Chamberlin and Levine flew the Atlantic, and Segrave bade farewell to Brooklands. The *Daily Yell* wrote anti-Red leaders and discovered a plot, somebody laid claim to a marquisate, and a Czecho-Slovakian pretended to swim the Channel. Hammond out-graced Grace, there was an outburst of murder at Moscow, Foxlaw won the Gold Cup and the earth opened at Oxhey and swallowed up somebody's front garden. Oxford decided that women were dangerous, and the electric hare consented to run at the White City. England's supremacy was challenged at Wimbledon, and the House of Lords made the gesture of stooping to conquer.

Meanwhile, Lord Peter's projected *magnum opus* on a-hundred-and-one ways of causing sudden death had advanced by the accumulation of a mass of notes which flowed all over the library at the flat, and threatened to engulf Bunter, whose task it was to file and cross-reference and generally to produce order from chaos. Oriental scholars and explorers were button-holed in clubs and strenuously pumped on the subject of abstruse native poisons; horrid experiments performed in German laboratories were communicated in unreadable documents; and the life of Sir James Lubbock, who had the misfortune to be a particular friend of Lord Peter's, was made a burden to him with daily inquiries as to the post-mortem detection of such varying substances as chloroform, curare, hydrocyanic acid gas and diethylsulphonmethylethylmetane.

"But surely there *must* be something which kills without leaving a trace," pleaded Lord Peter, when at length informed that the persecution must cease. "A thing in such universal demand—surely it is not beyond the wit of scientists to invent it. It must exist. Why isn't it properly advertised? There ought to be a company to exploit it. It's simply ridiculous. Why, it's a thing one might be wantin' one's self any day."

"You don't understand," said Sir James Lubbock. "Plenty of poisons leave no particular post-mortem appearances. And plenty of them—especially the vegetable ones—are difficult to find by analysis, unless you know what you are looking for. For instance, if you're testing for arsenic, that test won't tell you whether strychnine is present or not. And if you're testing for strychnine, you won't find morphia. You've got to try one test after another till you hit the right one. And of course there are certain poisons for which no recognised tests exist."

"I know all that," said Wimsey. "I've tested things myself. But these poisons with no recognised test—how do you set about proving that they're there?"

"Well, of course, you'd take the symptoms into account, and so on. You would look at the history of the case."

"Yes—but I want a poison that doesn't produce any symptoms. Except death, of course—if you call that a symptom. Isn't there a poison with no symptoms and no test? Something that just makes you go off, Pouf! like that?"

"Certainly not," said the analyst, rather annoyed—for your medical analyst lives by symptoms and tests, and nobody likes suggestions that undermine the very foundations of his profession—"not even old age or mental decay. There are always symptoms."

Fortunately, before symptoms of mental decay could become too pronounced in Lord Peter, Parker sounded the call to action.

"I'm going down to Leahampton with a warrant," he said. "I may not use it, but the chief thinks it might be worth while to make an inquiry. What with the Battersea mystery and the Daniels business, and Bertha Gotobed, there seems to be a feeling that there have been too many unexplained tragedies this year, and the Press have begun yelping again, blast them! There's an article in *John Citizen* this week, with a poster: 'Ninety-six Murderers at Large,' and the *Evening Views* is starting its reports with 'Six weeks have now passed, and the police are no nearer the solution—' you know the kind of thing. We'll simply have to get some sort of move on. Do you want to come?"

"Certainly—a breath of country air would do me good, I fancy. Blow away the cobwebs, don't you know. It might even inspire me to invent a good way of murderin' people. 'O Inspiration, solitary child, warbling thy native wood-notes wild—' Did somebody write that, or did I invent it? It sounds reminiscent, somehow."

Parker, who was out of temper, replied rather shortly, and intimated that the police car would be starting for Leahampton in an hour's time.

"I will be there," said Wimsey, "though, mind you, I hate being driven by another fellow. It feels so unsafe. Never mind. I will be bloody, bold and resolute, as Queen Victoria said to the Archbishop of Canterbury."

They reached Leahampton without any incident to justify Lord Peter's fears. Parker had brought another officer with him, and on the way they picked up the Chief Constable of the County, who appeared very dubiously disposed towards their errand. Lord Peter, observing their array of five strong men, going out to seize upon one young woman, was reminded of the Marquise de Brinvilliers— ("What! all that water for a little person like me?")—but this led him back to the subject of poison, and he remained steeped in thought and gloom till the car drew up before the house in Wellington Avenue.

Parker got out, and went up the path with the Chief Constable. The door was opened to them by a frightened-looking maid, who gave a little shriek at sight of them.

"Oh, sir! have you come to say something's happened to Miss Whittaker?"

"Isn't Miss Whittaker at home, then?"

"No, sir. She went out in the car with Miss Vera Findlater on Monday—that's four days back, sir, and she hasn't come home, nor Miss Findlater neither, and I'm frightened something's happened to them. When I see you, sir, I thought you was the police come to say there had been an accident. I didn't know what to do, sir."

"Skipped, by God!" was Parker's instant thought, but he controlled his annoyance, and asked:

"Do you know where they were going?"

"Crow's Beach, Miss Whittaker said, sir."

"That's a good fifty miles," said the Chief Constable. "Probably they've just decided to stay there a day or two."

"More likely gone in the opposite direction," thought Parker.

"They didn't take no things for the night, sir. They went off about ten in the morning. They said they was going to have lunch there and come home in the evening. And Miss Whittaker hasn't written nor nothing. And her always so particular. Cook and me, we didn't know what—"

"Oh, well, I expect it's all right," said the Chief Constable. "It's a pity, as we particularly wanted to see Miss Whittaker. When you hear from her, you might say Sir Charles Pillington called with a friend."

"Yes, sir. But please, sir, what ought we to do, sir?"

"Nothing. Don't worry. I'll have inquiries made. I'm the Chief Constable, you know, and I can soon find out whether there's been an accident or anything. But if there had been, depend upon it we should have heard about it. Come, my girl, pull yourself together, there's nothing to cry about. We'll let you know as soon as we hear anything."

But Sir Charles looked disturbed. Coming on top of Parker's arrival in the district, the thing had an unpleasant look about it.

Lord Peter received the news cheerfully.

"Good," said he, "joggle 'em up. Keep 'em moving. That's the spirit. Always like it when somethin' happens. My worst suspicions are goin' to be justified. That always makes one feel so important and virtuous, don't you think? Wonder why she took the girl with her, though. By the way, we'd better look up the Findlaters. They may have heard something."

This obvious suggestion was acted upon at once. But at the Findlaters' house they drew blank. The family were at the seaside, with the exception of Miss Vera, who was staying in Wellington Avenue with Miss Whittaker. No anxiety was expressed by the parlour-maid and none, apparently, felt. The investigators took care not to arouse any alarm, and, leaving a trivial and polite message from Sir Charles, withdrew for a consultation.

"There's nothing for it, so far as I can see," said Parker, "but an all-stations call to look out for the car and the ladies. And we must put inquiries through to all the ports, of course. With four days' start, they may be anywhere by now. I wish to Heaven I'd risked a bit and started earlier, approval or no approval. What's this Findlater girl like? I'd better go back to the house and get photographs of her and the Whittaker woman. And, Wimsey, I wish you'd look in on Miss Climpson and see if she has any information."

"And you might tell 'em at the Yard to keep an eye on Mrs. Forrest's place," said Wimsey. "When anything sensational happens to a criminal it's a good tip to watch the accomplice."

"I feel sure you are both quite mistaken about this," urged Sir Charles Pillington. "Criminal—accomplice—bless me! I have had considerable experience in the course of a long life—longer than either of yours—and I really feel convinced that Miss Whittaker, whom I know quite well, is as good and nice a girl as you could wish to find. But there has undoubtedly been an accident of some kind, and it is our duty to make the fullest investigation. I will get on to Crow's Beach police immediately, as soon as I know the description of the car."

"It's an Austin Seven and the number is XX9917," said Wimsey, much to the Chief Constable's surprise. "But I doubt very much whether you'll find it at Crow's Beach, or anywhere near it."

"Well, we'd better get a move on," snapped Parker. "We'd better separate. How about a spot of lunch in an hour's time at the George?"

Wimsey was unlucky. Miss Climpson was not to be found. She had had her lunch early and gone out, saying she felt that a long country walk would do her good. Mrs. Budge was rather afraid she had had some bad news—she had seemed so upset and worried since yesterday evening.

"But indeed, sir," she added, "if you was quick, you might find her up at the church. She often drops in there to say her prayers like. Not a respectful way to approach a place of worship to my mind, do you think so yourself, sir? Popping in and out on a week-day, the same as if it was a friend's house. And coming home from Communion as cheerful as anything and ready to laugh and make jokes. I don't see as how we was meant to make an ordinary thing of religion that way—so disrespectful and nothing uplifting to the 'art about it. But there! we all 'as our failings, and Miss Climpson is a nice lady and that I must say, even if she is a Roaming Catholic or next door to one."

Lord Peter thought that Roaming Catholic was rather an appropriate name for the more ultramontane section of the High Church party. At the moment, however, he felt he could not afford time for religious discussion, and set off for the church in quest of Miss Climpson.

The doors of S. Onesimus were hospitably open, and the red Sanctuary lamp made a little spot of welcoming brightness in the rather dark building. Coming in from the June sunshine, Wimsey blinked a little before he could distinguish anything else. Presently he was able to make out a dark, bowed figure kneeling before the lamp. For a moment he hoped it was Miss Climpson, but presently saw to his disappointment that it was merely a Sister in a black habit, presumably taking her turn to watch before the Host. The only other occupant of the church was a priest in a cassock, who was busy with the ornaments on the High Altar. It was the Feast of S. John, Wimsey remembered suddenly. He walked up the aisle, hoping to find his quarry hidden in some obscure corner. His shoes squeaked. This annoyed him. It was a thing which Bunter never permitted. He was seized with a fancy that the squeak was produced by diabolic possession—a protest against a religious atmosphere on the part of his own particular besetting devil. Pleased with this thought, he moved forward more confidently.

The priest's attention was attracted by the squeak. He turned and came down towards the intruder. No doubt, thought Wimsey, to offer his professional services to exorcise the evil spirit.

"Were you looking for anybody?" inquired the priest, courteously.

"Well, I was looking for a lady," began Wimsey. Then it struck him that this sounded a little odd under the circumstances, and he hastened to explain more fully, in the stifled tones considered appropriate to consecrated surroundings.

"Oh, yes," said the priest, quite unperturbed, "Miss Climpson was here a little time ago, but I fancy she has gone. Not that I usually keep tabs on my flock," he added, with a laugh, "but she spoke to me before she went. Was it urgent? What a pity you should have missed her. Can I give any kind of message or help you in any way?"

"No, thanks," said Wimsey. "Sorry to bother you. Unseemly to come and try to haul people out of church, but—yes, it was rather important. I'll leave a message at the house. Thanks frightfully."

He turned away; then stopped and came back.

"I say," he said, "you give advice on moral problems and all that sort of thing, don't you?"

"Well, we're supposed to try," said the priest. "Is anything bothering you in particular?"

"Ye-es," said Wimsey, "nothing religious, I don't mean—nothing about infallibility or the Virgin Mary or anything of that sort. Just something I'm not comfortable about."

The priest—who was, in fact, the vicar, Mr. Tredgold—indicated that he was quite at Lord Peter's service.

"It's very good of you. Could we come somewhere where I didn't have to whisper so much. I never can explain things in a whisper. Sort of paralyses one, don't you know."

"Let's go outside," said Mr. Tredgold.

So they went out and sat on a flat tombstone.

"It's like this," said Wimsey. "Hypothetical case, you see, and so on. S'posin' one knows somebody who's very, very ill and can't last long anyhow. And they're in awful pain and all that, and kept under morphia—practically dead to the world, you know. And suppose that by dyin' straight away they could make something happen which they really wanted to happen and which couldn't happen if they lived on a little longer (I can't explain exactly how, because I don't want to give personal details and so on)—you get the idea? Well, supposin' somebody who knew all that was just to give 'em a little push off so to speak—hurry matters on—why should that be a very dreadful crime?"

"The law—" began Mr. Tredgold.

"Oh, the law says it's a crime, fast enough," said Wimsey. "But do you honestly think it's very bad? I know you'd call it a sin, of course, but why is it so very dreadful? It doesn't do the person any harm, does it?"

"We can't answer that," said Mr. Tredgold, "without knowing the ways of God with the soul. In those last weeks or hours of pain and unconsciousness, the soul may be undergoing some necessary part of its pilgrimage on earth. It isn't our business to cut it short. Who are we to take life and death into our hands?"

"Well, we do it all day, one way and another. Juries—soldiers—doctors—all that. And yet I do feel, somehow, that it isn't a right thing in this case. And yet, by interfering—finding things out and so on—one may do far worse harm. Start all kinds of things."

"I think," said Mr. Tredgold, "that the sin—I won't use that word—the damage to Society, the wrongness of the thing lies much more in the harm it does the killer than in anything it can do to the person who is killed. Especially, of course, if the killing is to the killer's own advantage. The consequence you mention—this thing which the sick person wants done—does the other person stand to benefit by it, may I ask?"

"Yes. That's just it. He—she—they do."

"That puts it at once on a different plane from just hastening a person's death out of pity. Sin is in the intention, not the deed. That is the difference between divine law and human law. It is bad for a human being to get to feel that he has any right whatever to dispose of another person's life to his own advantage. It leads him to think himself above all laws—Society is never safe from the man who has deliberately committed murder with impunity. That is why—or one reason why—God forbids private vengeance."

"You mean that one murder leads to another."

"Very often. In any case it leads to a readiness to commit others."

"It has. That's the trouble. But it wouldn't have if I hadn't started trying to find things out. Ought I to have left it alone?"

"I see. That is very difficult. Terrible, too, for you. You feel responsible."

"Yes."

"You yourself are not serving a private vengeance?"

"Oh, no. Nothing really to do with me. Started in like a fool to help somebody who'd got into trouble about the thing through having suspicions himself. And my beastly interference started the crimes all over again."

"I shouldn't be too troubled. Probably the murderer's own guilty fears would have led him into fresh crimes even without your interference."

"That's true," said Wimsey, remembering Mr. Trigg.

"My advice to you is to do what you think is right, according to the laws which we have been brought up to respect. Leave the consequences to God. And try to think charitably, even of wicked people. You know what I mean. Bring the offender to justice, but remember that if we all got justice, you and I wouldn't escape either."

"I know. Knock the man down but don't dance on the body. Quite. Forgive my troublin' you—and excuse my bargin' off, because I've got a date with a friend. Thanks so much. I don't feel quite so rotten about it now. But I was gettin' worried."

Mr. Tredgold watched him as he trotted away between the graves. "Dear, dear," he said, "how nice they are. So kindly and scrupulous and so vague outside their public-school code. And much more nervous and sensitive than people think. A very difficult class to reach. I must make a special intention for him at Mass to-morrow."

Being a practical man, Mr. Tredgold made a knot in his handkerchief to remind himself of this pious resolve.

"The problem—to interfere or not to interfere—God's law and Caesar's. Policemen, now—it's no problem to them. But for the ordinary man—how hard to disentangle his own motives. I wonder what brought him here. Could it possibly be—No!" said the vicar, checking himself, "I have no right to specu-late." He drew out his handkerchief again and made another mnemonic knot as a reminder against his next confession that he had fallen into the sin of inquisi-tiveness.

20

MURDER

SIEGFRIED: "What does this mean?"
ISBRAND: "A pretty piece of kidnapping, that's all."
Beddoes, Death's Jest-Book

Parker, too, had spent a disappointing half-hour. It appeared that Miss Whittaker not only disliked having her photograph taken, but had actually destroyed all the existing portraits she could lay hands on, shortly after Miss Dawson's death. Of course, many of Miss Whittaker's friends might be in possession of one—notably, of course, Miss Findlater. But Parker was not sure that he wanted to start a local hue-and-cry at the moment. Miss Climpson might be able to get one, of course. He went round to Nelson Avenue. Miss Climpson was out; there had been another gentleman asking for her. Mrs. Budge's eyes were beginning to bulge with curiosity—evidently she was becoming dubious about Miss Climpson's "nephew" and his friends. Parker then went to the local photographers. There were five. From two of them he extracted a number of local groups, containing unrecognisable portraits of Miss Whittaker at church bazaars and private theatricals. She had never had a studio portrait made in Leahampton.

Of Miss Findlater, on the other hand, he got several excellent likenesses—a slight, fair girl, with a rather sentimental look—plump and prettyish. All these he despatched to Town, with directions that they should be broadcast to the police, together with a description of the girl's dress when last seen.

The only really cheerful members of the party at the "George" were the second policeman, who had been having a pleasant gossip with various garage-proprietors and publicans, with a view to picking up information, and the Chief Constable, who was vindicated and triumphant. He had been telephoning to various country police-stations, and had discovered that XX9917 had actually been observed on the previous Monday by an A.A. scout on the road to Crow's Beach. Having maintained all along that the Crow's Beach excursion was a genuine one, he was inclined to exult over the Scotland Yard man. Wimsey and Parker dispiritedly agreed that they had better go down and make inquiries at Crow's Beach.

Meanwhile, one of the photographers, whose cousin was on the staff of the *Leahampton Mercury*, had put a call through to the office of that up-to-date paper, which was just going to press. A stop-press announcement was followed by a special edition; somebody rang up the London *Evening Views* which burst out into a front-page scoop; the fat was in the fire, and the *Daily Yell*, *Daily Views*, *Daily Wire* and *Daily Tidings*, who were all suffering from lack of excitement, came brightly out next morning with bold headlines about disappearing young women.

Crow's Beach, indeed, that pleasant and respectable watering-place, knew nothing of Miss Whittaker, Miss Findlater, or car XX9917. No hotel had received them; no garage had refuelled or repaired them; no policeman had observed them. The Chief Constable held to his theory of an accident, and scouting parties were sent out. Wires arrived at Scotland Yard from all over the place. They had been seen at Dover, at Newcastle, at Sheffield, at Winchester, at Rugby. Two young women had had tea in a suspicious manner at Folkestone; a car had passed noisily through Dorchester at a late hour on Monday night; a dark-haired girl in an "agitated condition" had entered a public-house in New Alresford just before closing-time and asked the way to Hazelmere. Among all these reports, Parker selected that of a boy-scout, who reported on the Saturday morning that he had noticed two ladies with a car having a picnic on the downs on the previous Monday, not far from Shelly Head. The car was an Austin Seven—he knew that, because he was keen on motors (an unanswerable reason for accuracy in a boy of his age), and he had noticed that it was a London number, though he couldn't say positively what the number was.

Shelly Head lies about ten miles along the coast from Crow's Beach, and is curiously lonely, considering how near it lies to the watering-place. Under the cliffs is a long stretch of clear sandy beach, never visited, and overlooked by no houses. The cliffs themselves are chalk, and covered with short turf, running back into a wide expanse of downs, covered with gorse and heather. Then comes a belt of pine-trees, beyond which is a steep, narrow and rutty road, leading at length into the tarmac high-road between Ramborough and Ryders Heath. The downs are by no means frequented, though there are plenty of rough tracks which a car can follow, if you are not particular about comfort or fussy over your springs.

Under the leadership of the boy-scout, the police-car bumped uncomfortably over these disagreeable roads. It was hopeless to look for any previous car-tracks, for the chalk was dry and hard, and the grass and heath retained no marks. Everywhere, little dells and hollows presented themselves—all exactly alike, and many of them capable of hiding a small car, not to speak of the mere signs and remains of a recent picnic. Having arrived at what their guide thought to be approximately the right place, they pulled up and got out. Parker quartered the ground between the five of them and they set off.

Wimsey took a dislike to gorse-bushes that day. There were so many of them and so thick. Any of them might hold a cigarette package or a sandwich paper or a scrap of cloth or a clue of some kind. He trudged along unhappily, back bent and eyes on the ground, over one ridge and down into the hollow—then circling to right and to left, taking his bearings by the police-car; over the next ridge and down into the next hollow; over the next ridge—

Yes. There was something in the hollow.

He saw it first sticking out round the edge of a gorse-bush. It was light in colour, and pointed, rather like a foot.

He felt a little sick.

"Somebody has gone to sleep here," he said aloud.

Then he thought:

"Funny—it's always the feet they leave showing."

He scrambled down among the bushes, slipping on the short turf and nearly rolling to the bottom. He swore irritably.

The person was sleeping oddly. The flies must be a nuisance all over her head like that.

It occurred to him that it was rather early in the year for flies. There had been an advertising rhyme in the papers. Something about "Each fly you swat now means, remember, Three hundred fewer next September." Or was it a thousand fewer? He couldn't get the metre quite right.

Then he pulled himself together and went forward. The flies rose up in a little cloud.

It must have been a pretty heavy blow, he thought, to smash the back of the skull in like that. The shingled hair was blonde. The face lay between the bare arms.

He turned the body on its back.

Of course, without the photograph, he could not—he need not—be certain that this was Vera Findlater.

All this had taken him perhaps thirty seconds.

He scrambled up to the rim of the hollow and shouted.

A small black figure at some distance stopped and turned. He saw its face as a white spot with no expression on it. He shouted again, and waved his arms in wide gestures of explanation. The figure came running; it lurched slowly and awkwardly over the heathy ground. It was the policeman—a heavy man, not built for running in the heat. Wimsey shouted again, and the policeman shouted too. Wimsey saw the others closing in upon him. The grotesque figure of the boy-scout topped a ridge, waving its staff—then disappeared again. The policeman was quite near now. His bowler hat was thrust back on his head, and there was something on his watch-chain that glinted in the sun as he ran. Wimsey found himself running to meet him and calling—explaining at great length. It was too far off to make himself heard, but he explained, wordily, with emphasis, pointing, indicating. He was quite breathless when the policeman and he came together. They were both breathless. They wagged their heads and gasped. It was ludicrous. He started running again, with the man at his heels. Presently they were all there, pointing, measuring, taking notes, grubbing under the gorse-bushes. Wimsey sat down. He was dreadfully tired.

"Peter," said Parker's voice, "come and look at this."

He got up wearily.

There were the remains of a picnic lunch a little farther down the hollow. The policeman had a little bag in his hand—he had taken it from under the body, and was now turning over the trifles it contained. On the ground, close to the dead girl's head, was a thick, heavy spanner—unpleasantly discoloured and with a few fair hairs sticking to its jaws. But what Parker was calling his attention to was none of these, but a man's mauve-grey cap.

"Where did you find that?" asked Wimsey.

"Alf here picked it up at the top of the hollow," said Parker.

"Tumbled off into the gorse it was," corroborated the scout, "just up here, lying upside down just as if it had fallen off somebody's head."

"Any footmarks?"

"Not likely. But there's a place where the bushes are all trodden and broken. Looks as if there'd been some sort of struggle. What's become of the Austin? Hi! don't touch that spanner, my lad. There may be finger-prints on it. This looks like an attack by some gang or other. Any money in that purse? Ten-shilling note, sixpence and a few coppers—oh! Well, the other woman may have had more on her. She's very well off, you know. Held up for ransom, I shouldn't wonder." Parker bent down and very gingerly enfolded the spanner in a silk handkerchief, carrying it slung by the four corners. "Well, we'd better spread about and have a look for the car. Better try that belt of trees over there. Looks a likely spot. And, Hopkins—I think you'd better run back with our car to Crow's Beach and let 'em know at the station, and come back with a photographer. And take this wire and send it to the Chief Commissioner at Scotland Yard, and find a doctor and bring him along with you. And you'd better hire another car while you're about it, in case we don't find the Austin—we shall be too many to get away in this one. Take Alf back with you if you're not sure of finding the place again. Oh! and Hopkins, fetch us along something to eat and drink, will you, we may be at it a long time. Here's some money—that enough?"

"Yes, thank you, sir."

The constable went off, taking Alf, who was torn between a desire to stay and do some more detecting, and the pride and glory of being first back with the news. Parker gave a few words of praise for his valuable assistance which filled him with delight, and then turned to the Chief Constable.

"They obviously went off in this direction. Would you bear away to the left, sir, and enter the trees from that end, and Peter, will you bear to the right and work through from the other end, while I go straight up the middle?"

The Chief Constable, who seemed a good deal shaken by the discovery of the body, obeyed without a word. Wimsey caught Parker by the arm.

"I say," he said, "have you looked at the wound? Something funny, isn't there? There ought to be more mess, somehow. What do you think?"

"I'm not thinking anything for the moment," said Parker, a little grimly. "We'll wait for the doctor's report. Come on, Steve! We want to dig out that car."

"Let's have a look at the cap. H'm. Sold by a gentleman, resident in Stepney. Almost new. Smells strongly of California Poppy—rather a swell sort of gangsman, apparently. Quite one of the lads of the village."

"Yes—we ought to be able to trace that. Thank Heaven, they always overlook something. Well, we'd better get along."

The search for the car presented no difficulties. Parker stumbled upon it almost as soon as he got in under the trees. There was a clearing, with a little rivulet of water running through it, beside which stood the missing Austin. There were other trees here, mingled with the pines, and the water made an elbow and spread into a shallow pool, with a kind of muddy beach.

The hood of the car was up, and Parker approached with an uncomfortable feeling that there might be something disagreeable inside, but it was empty. He tried the gears. They were in neutral and the handbrake was on. On the seat was a handkerchief—a large linen handkerchief, very grubby and with no initials or laundry-mark. Parker grunted a little over the criminal's careless habit of strewing his belongings about. He came round in front of the car and received immediate further proof of carelessness. For on the mud there were footmarks—two men's and a woman's, it seemed.

The woman had got out of the car first—he could see where the left heel had sunk heavily in as she extricated herself from the low seat. Then the right foot—less heavily—then she had staggered a little and started to run. But one of the men had been there to catch her. He had stepped out of the bracken in shoes with new rubbers on them, and there were some scuffling marks as though he had held her and she had tried to break away. Finally, the second man, who seemed to possess rather narrow feet and to wear the long-toed boots affected by town boys of the louder sort—had come after her from the car—the marks of his feet were clear, crossing and half-obliterating hers. All three had stood together for a little. Then the tracks moved away, with those of the woman in the middle, and led up to where the mark of a Michelin balloon tyre showed clearly. The tyres of the Austin were ordinary Dunlops—besides, this was obviously a bigger car. It had apparently stood there for some little time, for a little pool of engine-oil had dripped from the crank-case. Then the bigger car had moved off, down a sort of ride that led away through the trees. Parker followed it for a little distance, but the tracks soon became lost in a thick carpet of pine-needles. Still, there was no other road for a car to take. He turned to the Austin to investigate further. Presently shouts told him that the other two were converging upon the centre of the wood. He called back and before long Wimsey and Sir Charles Pillington came crashing towards him through the bracken which fringed the pines.

"Well," said Wimsey, "I imagine we may put down this elegant bit of purple headgear to the gentleman in the slim boots. Bright yellow, I fancy, with buttons. He must be lamenting his beautiful cap. The woman's footprints belong to Mary Whittaker, I take it."

"I suppose so. I don't see how they can be the Findlater girl's. This woman went or was taken off in the car."

"They are certainly not Vera Findlater's—there was no mud on her shoes when we found her."

"Oh! you were taking notice, then. I thought you were feeling a bit dead to the world."

"So I was, old dear, but I can't help noticin' things, though moribund. Hullo! what's this?"

He put his hand down behind the cushions of the car and pulled out an American magazine—that monthly collection of mystery and sensational fiction published under the name of *The Black Mask*.

"Light reading for the masses," said Parker.

"Brought by the gentleman in the yellow boots, perhaps," suggested the Chief Constable.

"More likely by Miss Findlater," said Wimsey.

"Hardly a lady's choice," said Sir Charles, in a pained tone.

"Oh, I dunno. From all I hear, Miss Whittaker was dead against sentimentality and roses round the porch, and the other poor girl copied her in everything. They might have a boyish taste in fiction."

"Well, it's not important," said Parker.

"Wait a bit. Look at this. Somebody's been making marks on it."

Wimsey held out the cover for inspection. A thick pencil-mark had been drawn under the first two words of the title.

"Do you think it's some sort of message? Perhaps the book was on the seat, and she contrived to make the marks unnoticed and shove it away here before they transferred her to the other car."

"Ingenious," said Sir Charles, "but what does it mean? The Black. It makes no sense."

"Perhaps the long-toed gentleman was a black man," suggested Parker. "Or possibly a Hindu or Parsee of sorts."

"God bless my soul," said Sir Charles, horrified, "an English girl in the hands of a black man. How abominable!"

"Well, we'll hope it isn't so. Shall we follow the road out or wait for the doctor to arrive?"

"Better go back to the body, I think," said Parker. "They've got a long start of us, and half an hour more or less in following them up won't make much odds."

They turned from the translucent cool greenness of the little wood back on to the downs. The streamlet clacked merrily away over the pebbles, running out to the southwest on its way to the river and the sea.

"It's all very well your chattering," said Wimsey to the water. "Why can't you say what you've seen?"

21

BY WHAT MEANS?

"Death hath so many doors to let out life."
Beaumont and Fletcher, Custom of the Country

The doctor turned out to be a plumpish, fussy man—and what Wimsey impatiently called a "Tutster." He tutted over the mangled head of poor Vera Findlater as though it was an attack of measles after a party or a self-provoked fit of the gout.

"Tst, tst, tst. A terrible blow. How did we come by that, I wonder? Tst, tst. Life extinct? Oh, for several days, you know. Tst, tst—which makes it so much more painful, of course. Dear me, how shocking for her poor parents. And her sisters. They are very agreeable girls; you know them, of course, Sir Charles. Yes. Tst, tst."

"There is no doubt, I suppose," said Parker, "that it is Miss Findlater."

"None whatever," said Sir Charles.

"Well, as you can identify her, it may be possible to spare the relatives the shock of seeing her like this. Just a moment, doctor—the photographer wants to record the position of the body before you move anything. Now, Mr.—Andrews?—yes—have you ever done any photographs of this kind before? No?—well, you mustn't be upset by it! I know it's rather unpleasant. One from here, please, to show the position of the body—now from the top of the bank—that's right—now one of the wound itself—a close-up view, please. Yes. Thank you. Now, doctor, you can turn her over, please—I'm sorry, Mr. Andrews—I know exactly how you are feeling, but these things have to be done. Hullo! look how her arms are all scratched about. Looks as if she'd put up a bit of a fight. The right wrist and left elbow—as though someone had been trying to hold her down. We must have a photograph of the marks, Mr. Andrews—they may be important. I say, doctor, what do you make of this on the face?"

The doctor looked as though he would have preferred not to make so much as an examination of the face. However, with many tuts he worked himself up to giving an opinion.

"As far as one can tell, with all these post-mortem changes," he ventured, "it looks as though the face had been roughened or burnt about the nose and lips. Yet there is no appearance of the kind on the bridge of the nose, neck or forehead. Tst, tst—otherwise I should have put it down to severe sunburn."

"How about chloroform burns?" suggested Parker.

"Tst, tst," said the doctor, annoyed at not having thought of this himself—"I wish you gentlemen of the police force would not be quite so abrupt. You want everything decided in too great a hurry. I was about to remark—if you had not anticipated me—that since I could *not* put the appearance down to sunburn, there remains some such possibility as you suggest. I can't possibly say that it *is* the result of chloroform—medical pronouncements of that kind cannot be hastily made without cautious investigation—but I was about to remark that it *might* be."

"In that case," put in Wimsey, "could she have died from the effects of the chloroform? Supposing she was given too much or that her heart was weak?"

"My good sir," said the doctor, deeply offended this time, "look at that blow upon the head, and ask yourself whether it is necessary to suggest any other cause of death. Moreover, if she had died of the chloroform, where would be the necessity for the blow?"

"That is exactly what I was wondering," said Wimsey.

"I suppose," went on the doctor, "you will hardly dispute my medical knowledge?"

"Certainly not," said Wimsey, "but as you say, it is unwise to make any medical pronouncement without cautious investigation."

"And this is not the place for it," put in Parker, hastily. "I think we have done all there is to do here. Will you go with the body to the mortuary, doctor. Mr. Andrews, I shall be obliged if you will come and take a few photographs of some footmarks and so on up in the wood. The light is bad, I'm afraid, but we must do our best."

He took Wimsey by the arm.

"The man is a fool, of course," he said, "but we can get a second opinion. In the meantime, we had better let it be supposed that we accept the surface explanation of all this."

"What is the difficulty?" asked Sir Charles, curiously.

"Oh, nothing much," replied Parker. "All the appearances are in favour of the girls having been attacked by a couple of ruffians, who have carried Miss Whittaker off with a view to ransom, after brutally knocking Miss Findlater on the head when she offered resistance. Probably that is the true explanation. Any minor discrepancies will doubtless clear themselves up in time. We shall know better when we have had a proper medical examination."

They returned to the wood, where photographs were taken and careful measurements made of the footprints. The Chief Constable followed these activities with intense interest, looking over Parker's shoulder as he entered the particulars in his notebook.

"I say," he said, suddenly, "isn't it rather odd—"

"Here's somebody coming," broke in Parker.

The sound of a motor-cycle being urged in second gear over the rough ground proved to be the herald of a young man armed with a camera.

"Oh, God!" groaned Parker. "The damned Press already."

He received the journalist courteously enough, showing him the wheel-tracks and the footprints, and outlining the kidnapping theory as they walked back to the place where the body was found.

"Can you give us any idea, Inspector, of the appearance of the two wanted men?"

"Well," said Parker, "one of them appears to be something of a dandy; he wears a loathsome mauve cap and narrow pointed shoes and, if those marks on the magazine cover mean anything, one or other of the men may possibly be a coloured man of some kind. Of the second man, all we can definitely say is that he wears number 10 shoes, with rubber heels."

"I was going to say," said Pillington, "that, à propos de bottes, it is rather remarkable—"

"And this is where we found the body of Miss Findlater," went on Parker, ruthlessly. He described the injuries and the position of the body, and the journalist gratefully occupied himself with taking photographs, including a group of Wimsey, Parker and the Chief Constable standing among the gorse-bushes, while the latter majestically indicated the fatal spot with his walking-stick.

"And now you've got what you want, old son," said Parker, benevolently, "buzz off, won't you, and tell the rest of the boys. You've got all we can tell you, and we've got other things to do beyond granting special interviews."

The reporter asked no better. This was tantamount to making his information exclusive, and no Victorian matron could have a more delicate appreciation of the virtues of exclusiveness than a modern newspaper man.

"Well now, Sir Charles," said Parker, when the man had happily chugged and popped himself away, "what were you about to say in the matter of the foot-prints?"

But Sir Charles was offended. The Scotland Yard man had snubbed him and thrown doubt on his discretion.

"Nothing," he replied. "I feel sure that my conclusions would appear very elementary to you."

And he preserved a dignified silence throughout the return journey.

The Whittaker case had begun almost imperceptibly, in the overhearing of a casual remark dropped in a Soho restaurant; it ended amid a roar of publicity that shook England from end to end and crowded even Wimbledon into the second place. The bare facts of the murder and kidnapping appeared exclusively that night in a Late Extra edition of the *Evening Views*. Next morning it sprawled over the Sunday papers with photographs and full details, actual and imaginary. The idea of two English girls—the one brutally killed, the other carried off for some end unthinkably sinister, by a black man—aroused all the passion of horror and indignation of which the English temperament is capable. Reporters swarmed down upon Crow's Beach like locusts—the downs near Shelly Head were like a fair with motors, bicycles and parties on foot, rushing out to spend a happy week-end amid surroundings of mystery and bloodshed. Parker, who with Wimsey had taken rooms at the Green Lion, sat answering the telephone and receiving the letters and wires which descended upon him from all sides, with a stalwart policeman posted at the end of the passage to keep out all intruders.

Wimsey fidgeted about the room, smoking cigarette after cigarette in his excitement.

"This time we've got them," he said. "They've overreached themselves, thank God!"

"Yes. But have a little patience, old man. We can't lose them—but we must have all the facts first."

"You're sure those fellows have got Mrs. Forrest safe?"

"Oh, yes. She came back to the flat on Monday night—or so the garage man says. Our men are shadowing her continually and will let us know the moment anybody comes to the flat."

"Monday night!"

"Yes. But that's no proof in itself. Monday night is quite a usual time for week-enders to return to Town. Besides, I don't want to frighten her till we know whether she's the principal or merely the accomplice. Look here, Peter, I've had a message from another of our men. He's been looking into the finances of Miss Whittaker and Mrs. Forrest. Miss Whittaker has been drawing out big sums, ever since last December year in cheques to Self, and these correspond almost exactly, amount for amount, with sums which Mrs. Forrest has been paying into her own account. That woman has had a big hold over Miss Whittaker, ever since old Miss Dawson died. She's in it up to the neck, Peter."

"I knew it. She's been doing the jobs while the Whittaker woman held down her alibi in Kent. For God's sake, Charles, make no mistake. Nobody's life is safe for a second while either of them is at large."

"When a woman is wicked and unscrupulous," said Parker, sententiously, "she is the most ruthless criminal in the world—fifty times worse than a man, because she is always so much more single-minded about it."

"They're not troubled with sentimentality, that's why," said Wimsey, "and we poor mutts of men stuff ourselves up with the idea that they're romantic and emotional. All punk, my son. Damn that 'phone!"

Parker snatched up the receiver.

"Yes—yes—speaking. Good God, you don't say so. All right. Yes. Yes, of course you must detain him. I think myself it's a plant, but he must be held and questioned. And see that all the papers have it. Tell 'em you're sure he's the man. See? Soak it well into 'em that that's the official view. And—wait a moment—I want photographs of the cheque and of any finger-prints on it. Send 'em down immediately by a special messenger. It's genuine, I suppose? The Bank people say it is? Good! What's his story? . . . Oh! . . . any envelope? — Destroyed?—Silly devil. Right. Right. Good-bye."

He turned to Wimsey with some excitement.

"Hallelujah Dawson walked into Lloyds Bank in Stepney yesterday morning and presented Mary Whittaker's cheque for £10,000, drawn on their Leahampton branch to Bearer, and dated Friday 24th. As the sum was such a large one and the story of the disappearance was in Friday night's paper, they asked him to call again. Meanwhile, they communicated with Leahampton. When the news of the murder came out yesterday evening, the Leahampton manager remembered about it and 'phoned the Yard, with the result that they sent round this morning and had Hallelujah up for a few inquiries. His story is that the cheque arrived on Saturday morning, all by itself in an envelope, without a word of explanation. Of course the old juggins chucked the envelope away, so that we can't verify his tale or get a line on the post-mark. Our people thought the whole thing looked a bit fishy, so Hallelujah is detained pending investigation—in other words, arrested for murder and conspiracy!"

"Poor old Hallelujah! Charles, this is simply devilish! That innocent, decent old creature, who couldn't harm a fly."

"I know. Well, he's in for it and will have to go through with it. It's all the better for us. Hell's bells, there's somebody at the door. Come in."

"It's Dr. Faulkner to see you, sir," said the constable, putting his head in.

"Oh, good. Come in, doctor. Have you made your examination?"

"I have, Inspector. Very interesting. You were quite right. I'll tell you that much straight away."

"I'm glad to hear that. Sit down and tell us all about it."

"I'll be as brief as possible," said the doctor. He was a London man, sent down by Scotland Yard, and accustomed to police work—a lean, grey badger of a man, business-like and keen-eyed, the direct opposite of the "tutster" who had annoyed Parker the evening before.

"Well, first of all, the blow on the head had, of course, nothing whatever to do with the death. You saw yourself that there had been next to no bleeding. The wound was inflicted some time after death—no doubt to create the impression of an attack by a gang. Similarly with the cuts and scratches on the arms. They are the merest camouflage."

"Exactly. Your colleague—"

"My colleague, as you call him, is a fool," snorted the doctor. "If that's a specimen of his diagnosis, I should think there would be a high death-rate in Crow's Beach. That's by the way. You want the cause of death?"

"Chloroform?"

"Possibly. I opened the body but found no special symptoms suggestive of poisoning or anything. I have removed the necessary organs and sent them to Sir James Lubbock for analysis at your suggestion, but candidly I expect nothing from that. There was no odour of chloroform on opening the thorax. Either the time elapsed since the death was too long, as is very possible, seeing how volatile the stuff is, or the dose was too small. I found no indications of any heart weakness, so that, to produce death in a healthy young girl, chloroform would have had to be administered over a considerable time."

"Do you think it was administered at all?"

"Yes, I think it was. The burns on the face certainly suggest it."

"That would also account for the handkerchief found in the car," said Wimsey.

"I suppose," pursued Parker, "that it would require considerable strength and determination to administer chloroform to a strong young woman. She would probably resist strenuously."

"She would," said the doctor, grimly, "but the odd thing is, she didn't. As I said before, all the marks of violence were inflicted post-mortem."

"Suppose she had been asleep at the time," suggested Wimsey, "couldn't it have been done quietly then?"

"Oh, yes—easily. After a few long breaths of the stuff she would become semi-conscious and then could be more firmly dealt with. It is quite possible, I suppose, that she fell asleep in the sunshine, while her companion wandered off and was kidnapped, and that the kidnappers then came along and got rid of Miss Findlater."

"That seems a little unnecessary," said Parker. "Why come back to her at all?"

"Do you suggest that they both fell asleep and were both set on and chloroformed at the same time? It sounds rather unlikely."

He outlined the history of their suspicions about Mary Whittaker, to which the doctor listened in horrified amazement.

"What happened," said Parker, "as we think, is this. We think that for some reason Miss Whittaker had determined to get rid of this poor girl who was so devoted to her. She arranged that they should go off for a picnic and that it should be known where they were going to. Then, when Vera Findlater was dozing in the sunshine, our theory is that she murdered her—either with chloroform or—more likely, I fancy—by the same method that she used upon her other victims, whatever that was. Then she struck her on the head and produced the other appearances suggestive of a struggle, and left on the bushes a cap which she had previously purchased and stained with brilliantine. I am, of course, having the cap traced. Miss Whittaker is a tall, powerful woman—I don't think it would be beyond her strength to inflict that blow on an unresisting body."

"But how about those footmarks in the wood?"

"I'm coming to that. There are one or two very odd things about them. To begin with, if this was the work of a secret gang, why should they go out of their way to pick out the one damp, muddy spot in twenty miles of country to leave their footprints in, when almost anywhere else they could have come and gone without leaving any recognisable traces at all?"

"Good point," said the doctor. "And I add to that, that they must have noticed they'd left a cap behind. Why not come back and remove it?"

"Exactly. Then again. Both pairs of shoes left prints entirely free from the marks left by wear and tear. I mean that there were no signs of the heels or soles being worn at all, while the rubbers on the larger pair were obviously just out of the shop. We shall have the photographs here in a moment, and you will see. Of course, it's not impossible that both men should be wearing brand new shoes, but on the whole it's unlikely."

"It is," agreed the doctor.

"And now we come to the most suggestive thing of all. One of the supposed men had very much bigger feet than the other, from which you would expect a taller and possibly heavier man with a longer stride. But on measuring the footprints, what do we find? In all three cases—the big man, the little man and the woman—we have exactly the same length of stride. Not only that, but the footprints have sunk into the ground to precisely the same depth, indicating that all three people were of the same weight. Now, the other discrepancies might pass, but that is absolutely beyond the reach of coincidence."

Dr. Faulkner considered this for a moment.

"You've proved your point," he said at length. "I consider that absolutely convincing."

"It struck even Sir Charles Pillington, who is none too bright," said Parker. "I had the greatest difficulty in preventing him from blurting out the extraordinary agreement of the measurements to that *Evening Views* man."

"You think, then, that Miss Whittaker had come provided with these shoes and produced the tracks herself."

"Yes, returning each time through the bracken. Cleverly done. She had made no mistake about superimposing the footprints. It was all worked out to a nicety —each set over and under the two others, to produce the impression that three people had been there at the same time. Intensive study of the works of Mr. Austin Freeman, I should say."

"And what next?"

"Well, I think we shall find that this Mrs. Forrest, who we think has been her accomplice all along, had brought her car down—the big car, that is—and was waiting there for her. Possibly she did the making of the footprints while Mary Whittaker was staging the assault. Anyhow, she probably arrived there after Mary Whittaker and Vera Findlater had left the Austin and departed to the hollow on the downs. When Mary Whittaker had finished her part of the job, they put the handkerchief and the magazine called *The Black Mask* into the Austin and drove off in Mrs. Forrest's car. I'm having the movements of the car investigated, naturally. It's a dark blue Renault fourseater, with Michelin bal-loon-tyres, and the number is XO4247. We know that it returned to Mrs. Forrest's garage on the Monday night with Mrs. Forrest in it."

"But where is Miss Whittaker?"

"In hiding somewhere. We shall get her all right. She can't get money from her own bank—they're warned. If Mrs. Forrest tries to get money for her, she will be followed. So if the worst comes to the worst, we can starve her out in time with any luck. But we've got another clue. There has been a most determined attempt to throw suspicion on an unfortunate relative of Miss Whittaker's—a black Nonconformist parson, with the remarkable name of Hallelujah Dawson. He has certain pecuniary claims on Miss Whittaker—not legal claims, but claims which any decent and humane person should have respected. She didn't respect them, and the poor old man might very well have been expected to nurse a grudge against her. Yesterday morning he tried to cash a Bearer cheque of hers for £10,000, with a lame-sounding story to the effect that it had arrived by the first post, without explanation, in an envelope. So, of course, he's had to be detained as one of the kidnappers."

"But that is very clumsy, surely. He's almost certain to have an alibi."

"I fancy the story will be that he hired some gangsters to do the job for him. He belongs to a Mission in Stepney—where that mauve cap came from—and no doubt there are plenty of tough lads in his neighbourhood. Of course we shall make close inquiries and publish details broadcast in all the papers."

"And then?"

"Well then, I fancy, the idea is that Miss Whittaker will turn up somewhere in an agitated condition with a story of assault and holding to ransom made to fit the case. If Cousin Hallelujah has not produced a satisfactory alibi, we shall learn that he was on the spot directing the murderers. If he has definitely shown that he wasn't there, his name will have been mentioned, or he will have turned up at some time which the poor dear girl couldn't exactly ascertain, in some dreadful den to which she was taken in a place which she won't be able to identify."

"What a devilish plot."

"Yes. Miss Whittaker is a charming young woman. If there's anything she'd stop at, I don't know what it is. And the amiable Mrs. Forrest appears to be another of the same kidney. Of course, doctor, we're taking you into our confi-dence. You understand that our catching Mary Whittaker depends on her be-lieving that we've swallowed all these false clues of hers."

"I'm not a talker," said the doctor. "Gang you call it, and gang it is, as far as I'm concerned. And Miss Findlater was hit on the head and died of it. I only hope my colleague and the Chief Constable will be equally discreet. I warned them, naturally, after what you said last night."

"It's all very well," said Wimsey, "but what positive evidence have we, after all, against this woman? A clever defending counsel would tear the whole thing to rags. The only thing we can absolutely *prove* her to have done is the burgling that house on Hampstead Heath and stealing the coal. The other deaths were returned natural deaths at the inquest. And as for Miss Findlater—even if we show it to be chloroform—well, chloroform isn't difficult stuff to get hold of—it's not arsenic or cyanide. And even if there were finger-prints on the span-ner—"

"There were not," said Parker, gloomily. "This girl knows what she's about."

"What did she want to kill Vera Findlater for, anyway?" asked the doctor, suddenly. "According to you, the girl was the most valuable bit of evidence she had. She was the one witness who could prove that Miss Whittaker had an alibi for the other crimes—if they were crimes."

"She may have found out too much about the connection between Miss Whittaker and Mrs. Forrest. My impression is that she had served her turn and become dangerous. What we're hoping to surprise now is some communication between Forrest and Whittaker. Once we've got that—"

"Humph!" said Dr. Faulkner. He had strolled to the window. "I don't want to worry you unduly, but I perceive Sir Charles Pillington in conference with the Special Correspondent of the *Wire*. The *Yell* came out with the gang story all over the front page this morning, and a patriotic leader about the danger of encouraging coloured aliens. I needn't remind you that the *Wire* would be ready to corrupt the Archangel Gabriel in order to kill the *Yell*'s story."

"Oh, hell!" said Parker, rushing to the window.

"Too late," said the doctor. "The *Wire* man has vanished into the post office. Of course, you can 'phone up and try to stop it."

Parker did so, and was courteously assured by the editor of the *Wire* that the story had not reached him, and that if it did, he would bear Inspector Parker's instructions in mind.

The editor of the *Wire* was speaking the exact truth. The story had been received by the editor of the *Evening Banner*, sister paper to the *Wire*. In times of crisis, it is sometimes convenient that the left hand should not know what the right hand does. After all, it was an exclusive story.

22

A CASE OF CONSCIENCE

"I know thou art religious,
And hast a thing within thee called conscience,
With twenty popish tricks and ceremonies
Which I have seen thee careful to observe."

Titus Andronicus

Thursday, June 23rd, was the Eve of S. John. The sober green workaday dress in which the church settles down to her daily duties after the bridal raptures of Pentecost, had been put away, and the altar was white and shining once again. Vespers were over in the Lady Chapel at S. Onesimus—a faint reek of incense hung cloudily under the dim beams of the roof. A very short acolyte with a very long brass extinguisher snuffed out the candles, adding the faintly unpleasant yet sanctified odour of hot wax. The small congregation of elderly ladies rose up lingeringly from their devotions and slipped away in a series of deep genuflections.

Miss Climpson gathered up a quantity of little manuals, and groped for her gloves. In doing so, she dropped her office-book. It fell, annoyingly, behind the long kneeler, scattering as it went a small pentecostal shower of Easter cards, book-markers, sacred pictures, dried palms and Ave Marias into the dark corner behind the confessional.

Miss Climpson gave a little exclamation of wrath as she dived after them— and immediately repented this improper outburst of anger in a sacred place. "Discipline," she murmured, retrieving the last lost sheep from under a hassock, "discipline. I must learn self-control." She crammed the papers back into the office-book, grasped her gloves and handbag, bowed to the Sanctuary, dropped her bag, picked it up this time in a kind of glow of martyrdom, bustled down the aisle and across the church to the south door, where the sacristan stood, key in hand, waiting to let her out. As she went, she glanced up at the High Altar, unlit and lonely, with the tall candles like faint ghosts in the twilight of the apse. It had a grim and awful look she thought, suddenly.

"Good night, Mr. Stanniforth," she said, quickly.

"Good night, Miss Climpson, good night."

She was glad to come out of the shadowy porch into the green glow of the June evening. She had felt a menace. Was it the thought of the stern Baptist, with his call to repentance? the prayer for grace to speak the truth and boldly rebuke vice? Miss Climpson decided that she would hurry home and read the Epistle and Gospel—curiously tender and comfortable for the festival of that harsh and uncompromising Saint. "And I can tidy up these cards at the same time," she thought.

Mrs. Budge's first-floor front seemed stuffy after the scented loveliness of the walk home. Miss Climpson flung the window open and sat down by it to rearrange her sanctified oddments. The card of the Last Supper went in at the Prayer of Consecration; the Fra Angelico Annunciation had strayed out of the office for March 25th and was wandering among the Sundays after Trinity; the Sacred Heart with its French text belonged to Corpus Christi; the . . .

"Dear me!" said Miss Climpson, "I must have picked this up in church."

Certainly the little sheet of paper was not in her writing. Somebody must have dropped it. It was natural to look and see whether it was anything of importance.

Miss Climpson was one of those people who say: "I am not the kind of person who reads other people's postcards." This is clear notice to all and sundry that they are, precisely, that kind of person. They are not untruthful; the delusion is real to them. It is merely that Providence has provided them with a warning rattle, like that of the rattlesnake. After that, if you are so foolish as to leave your correspondence in their way, it is your own affair.

Miss Climpson perused the paper.

In the manuals for self-examination issued to the Catholic-minded, there is often included an unwise little paragraph which speaks volumes for the innocent unworldliness of the compilers. You are advised, when preparing for confession, to make a little list of your misdeeds, lest one or two peccadilloes should slip your mind. It is true that you are cautioned against writing down the names of other people or showing your list to your friends, or leaving it about. But accidents may happen—and it may be that this recording of sins is contrary to the mind of the church, who bids you whisper them with fleeting breath into the ear of a priest and bids him, in the same moment that he absolves, forget them as though they had never been spoken.

At any rate, somebody had been recently shriven of the sins set forth upon the paper—probably the previous Saturday—and the document had fluttered down unnoticed between the confession-box and the hassock, escaping the eye of the cleaner. And here it was—the tale that should have been told to none but God —lying open upon Mrs. Budge's round mahogany table under the eye of a fellow-mortal.

To do Miss Climpson justice, she would probably have destroyed it instantly unread, if one sentence had not caught her eye:

"The lies I told for M. W.'s sake."

At the same moment she realised that this was Vera Findlater's handwriting, and it "came over her like a flash"—as she explained afterwards, exactly what the implication of the words was.

For a full half-hour Miss Climpson sat alone, struggling with her conscience. Her natural inquisitiveness said "Read"; her religious training said, "You must not read"; her sense of duty to Wimsey, who employed her, said, "Find out"; her own sense of decency said, "Do no such thing"; a dreadful, harsh voice muttered gratingly, "Murder is the question. Are you going to be the accomplice of Murder?" She felt like Lancelot Gobbo between conscience and the fiend—but which was the fiend and which was conscience?

"To speak the truth and boldly rebuke vice."

Murder.

There was a real possibility now.

But *was* it a possibility? Perhaps she had read into the sentence more than it would bear.

In that case, was it not—almost—a duty to read further and free her mind from this horrible suspicion?

She would have liked to go to Mr. Tredgold and ask his advice. Probably he would tell her to burn the paper promptly and drive suspicion out of her mind with prayer and fasting.

She got up and began searching for the match-box. It would be better to get rid of the thing quickly.

What, exactly, was she about to do?—To destroy the clue to the discovery of a Murder?

Whenever she thought of the word, it wrote itself upon her brain in large capitals, heavily underlined. MURDER—like a police-bill.

Then she had an idea. Parker was a policeman—and probably also he had no particular feelings about the sacred secrecy of the Confessional. He had a Protestant appearance—or possibly he thought nothing of religion one way or the other. In any case, he would put his professional duty before everything. Why not send him the paper, without reading it, briefly explaining how she had come upon it? Then the responsibility would be his.

On consideration, however, Miss Climpson's innate honesty scouted this scheme as jesuitical. Secrecy was violated by this open publication as much as if she had read the thing—or more so. The old Adam, too, raised his head at this point, suggesting that if anybody was going to see the confession, she might just as well satisfy her own reasonable curiosity. Besides—suppose she was quite mistaken. After all, the "lies" might have nothing whatever to do with Mary Whittaker's alibi. In that case, she would have betrayed another person's secret wantonly, and to no purpose. If she *did* decide to show it, she was bound to read it first—in justice to all parties concerned.

Perhaps—if she just glanced at another word or two, she would see that it had nothing to do with—MURDER—and then she could destroy it and forget it. She knew that if she destroyed it unread she never would forget it, to the end of her life. She would always carry with her that grim suspicion. She would think of Mary Whittaker as—perhaps—a Murderess. When she looked into those hard blue eyes, she would be wondering what sort of expression they had when the soul behind them was plotting—MURDER. Of course, the suspicions had been there before, planted by Wimsey, but now they were her own suspicions. They crystallised—became real to her.

"What shall I do?"

She gave a quick, shamefaced glance at the paper again. This time she saw the word "London."

Miss Climpson gave a kind of little gasp, like a person stepping under a cold shower-bath.

"Well," said Miss Climpson, "if this is a sin I am going to do it, and may I be forgiven."

With a red flush creeping over her cheeks as though she were stripping something naked, she turned her attention to the paper.

The jottings were brief and ambiguous. Parker might not have made much of them, but to Miss Climpson, trained in this kind of devotional shorthand, the story was clear as print.

"Jealousy"—the word was written large and underlined. Then there was a reference to a quarrel, to wicked accusations and angry words and to a pre-occupation coming between the penitent's soul and God. "Idol"—and a long dash.

From these few fossil bones, Miss Climpson had little difficulty in reconstructing one of those hateful and passionate "scenes" of slighted jealousy with which a woman-ridden life had made her only too familiar. "I do everything for you—you don't care a bit for me—you treat me cruelly—you're simply sick of me, that's what it is!" And "Don't be so ridiculous. Really, I can't stand this. Oh, stop it, Vera! I hate being slobbered over." Humiliating, degrading, exhausting, beastly scenes. Girls' school, boarding-house, Bloomsbury-flat scenes. Damnable selfishness wearying of its victim. Silly *schwärmerei* swamping all decent self-respect. Barren quarrels ending in shame and hatred.

"Beastly, blood-sucking woman," said Miss Climpson, viciously. "It's too bad. She's only making use of the girl."

But the self-examiner was now troubled with a more difficult problem. Piecing the hints together, Miss Climpson sorted it out with practised ease. Lies had been told—that was wrong, even though done to help a friend. Bad confessions had been made, suppressing those lies. This ought to be confessed and put right. But (the girl asked herself) had she come to this conclusion out of hatred of the lies or out of spite against the friend? Difficult, this searching of the heart. And ought she, not content with confessing the lies to the priest, also to tell the truth to the world?

Miss Climpson had here no doubt what the priest's ruling would be. "You need not go out of your way to betray your friend's confidence. Keep silent if you can, but if you speak you must speak the truth. You must tell your friend that she is not to expect any more lying from you. She is entitled to ask for secrecy—no more."

So far, so good. But there was a further problem.

"Ought I to connive at her doing what is wrong?"—and then a sort of explanatory aside—"the man in South Audley Street."

This was a little mysterious . . . No!—on the contrary, it explained the whole mystery, jealousy, quarrel and all.

In those weeks of April and May, when Mary Whittaker had been supposed to be all the time in Kent with Vera Findlater, she had been going up to London. And Vera had promised to say that Mary was with her the whole time. And the visits to London had to do with a man in South Audley Street, and there was something sinful about it. That probably meant a love-affair. Miss Climpson pursed her lips virtuously, but she was more surprised than shocked. Mary Whittaker! she would never have suspected it of her, somehow. But it so explained the jealousy and the quarrel—the sense of desertion. But how had Vera found out? Had Mary Whittaker confided in her?—No; that sentence again, under the heading "Jealousy"—what was it—"following M. W. to London." She had followed then, and seen. And then, at some moment, she had burst out with her knowledge—reproached her friend. Yet this expedition to London must have happened before her own conversation with Vera Findlater, and the girl had then seemed so sure of Mary's affection. Or had it been that she was trying to persuade herself, with determined self-deception, that there was "nothing in" this business about the man? Probably. And probably some brutality of Mary's had brought all the miserable suspicions boiling to the surface, vocal, reproachful and furious. And so they had gone on to the row and the break.

"Queer," thought Miss Climpson, "that Vera has never come and told me about her trouble. But perhaps she is ashamed, poor child. I haven't seen her for nearly a week. I think I'll call and see her and perhaps she'll tell me all about it. In which case"—cried Miss Climpson's conscience, suddenly emerging with a bright and beaming smile from under the buffets of the enemy—"in which case I shall know the whole history of it legitimately and can *quite honourably* tell Lord Peter about it."

The next day—which was the Friday—she woke, however, with an unpleasant ache in the conscience. The paper—still tucked into the office-book—worried her. She went round early to Vera Findlater's house, only to hear that she was staying with Miss Whittaker. "Then I suppose they've made it up," she said. She did not want to see Mary Whittaker, whether her secret was murder or mere immorality; but she was tormented by the desire to clear up the matter of the alibi for Lord Peter.

In Wellington Avenue she was told that the two girls had gone away on the Monday and had not yet returned. She tried to reassure the maid, but her own heart misgave her. Without any real reason, she was uneasy. She went round to the church and said her prayers, but her mind was not on what she was saying. On an impulse, she caught Mr. Tredgold as he pottered in and out of the Sacristy, and asked if she might come the next evening to lay a case of conscience before him. So far, so good, and she felt that a "good walk" might help to clear the cob-webs from her brain.

So she started off, missing Lord Peter by a quarter of an hour, and took the train to Guildford and then walked and had lunch in a wayside tea-shop and walked back into Guildford and so came home, where she learnt that "Mr. Parker and ever so many gentlemen had been asking for her all day, and what a dreadful thing, miss, here was Miss Whittaker and Miss Findlater disappeared and the police out looking for them, and them motor-cars was such dangerous things, miss, wasn't they? It was to be hoped there wasn't an accident."

And into Miss Climpson's mind there came, like an inspiration, the words, "South Audley Street."

Miss Climpson did not, of course, know that Wimsey was at Crow's Beach. She hoped to find him in Town. For she was seized with a desire, which she could hardly have explained even to herself, to go and look at South Audley Street. What she was to do when she got there she did not know, but go there she must. It was the old reluctance to make open use of that confession paper. Vera Findlater's story at first hand—that was the idea to which she obscurely clung. So she took the first train to Waterloo, leaving behind her, in case Wimsey or Parker should call again, a letter so obscure and mysterious and so lavishly underlined and interlined that it was perhaps fortunate for their reason that they were never faced with it.

In Piccadilly she saw Bunter, and learned that his lordship was at Crow's Beach with Mr. Parker, where he, Bunter, was just off to join him. Miss Climpson promptly charged him with a message to his employer slightly more involved and mysterious than her letter, and departed for South Audley Street. It was only when she was walking up it that she realised how vague her quest was and how little investigation one can do by merely walking along a street. Also, it suddenly occurred to her that if Miss Whittaker was carrying on anything of a secret nature in South Audley Street, the sight of an acquaintance patrolling the pavement would put her on her guard. Much struck by this reflection, Miss Climpson plunged abruptly into a chemist's shop and bought a toothbrush, by way of concealing her movements and gaining time. One can while away many minutes comparing the shapes, sizes and bristles of toothbrushes, and sometimes chemists will be nice and gossipy.

Looking round the shop for inspiration, Miss Climpson observed a tin of nasal snuff labelled with the chemist's own name.

"I will take a tin of that, too, please," she said. "What *excellent* stuff it is— quite *wonderful*. I have used it for *years* and am really *delighted* with it. I recommend it to all my friends, particularly for *hay fever*. In fact, there's a friend of mine who often passes your shop, who told me only *yesterday* what a *martyr* she was to that complaint. 'My dear,' I said to her, 'you have only to get a tin of this *splendid* stuff and you will be *quite* all right *all* summer.' She was so *grateful* to me for telling her about it. Has she been in for it yet?" And she described Mary Whittaker closely.

It will be noticed, by the way, that in the struggle between Miss Climpson's conscience and what Wilkie Collins calls "detective fever," conscience was getting the worst of it and was winking at an amount of deliberate untruth which a little time earlier would have staggered it.

The chemist, however, had seen nothing of Miss Climpson's friend. Nothing, therefore, was to be done but to retire from the field and think what was next to be done. Miss Climpson left, but before leaving she neatly dropped her latchkey into a large basket full of sponges standing at her elbow. She felt she might like to have an excuse to visit South Audley Street again.

Conscience sighed deeply, and her guardian angel dropped a tear among the sponges.

Retiring into the nearest tea-shop she came to, Miss Climpson ordered a cup of coffee and started to think out a plan for honey-combing South Audley Street. She needed an excuse—and a disguise. An adventurous spirit was welling up in her elderly bosom, and her first dozen or so ideas were more lurid than practical.

At length a really brilliant notion occurred to her. She was (she did not attempt to hide it from herself) precisely the type and build of person one associates with the collection of subscriptions. Moreover, she had a perfectly good and genuine cause ready to hand. The church which she attended in London ran a slum mission, which was badly in need of funds, and she possessed a number of collecting cards, bearing full authority to receive subscriptions on its behalf. What more natural than that she should try a little house-to-house visiting in a wealthy quarter?

The question of disguise, also, was less formidable than it might appear. Miss Whittaker had only known her well-dressed and affluent in appearance. Ugly, clumping shoes, a hat of virtuous ugliness, a shapeless coat and a pair of tinted glasses would disguise her sufficiently at a distance. At close quarters, it would not matter if she was recognised, for if once she got to close quarters with Mary Whittaker, her job was done and she had found the house she wanted.

Miss Climpson rose from the table, paid her bill and hurried out to buy the glasses, remembering that it was Saturday. Having secured a pair which hid her eyes effectively without looking exaggeratedly mysterious, she made for her rooms in St. George's Square, to choose suitable clothing for her adventure. She realised, of course, that she could hardly start work till Monday—Saturday afternoon and Sunday are hopeless from the collector's point of view.

The choice of clothes and accessories occupied her for the better part of the afternoon. When she was at last satisfied she went downstairs to ask her landlady for some tea.

"Certainly, miss," said the good woman. "Ain't it awful, miss, about this murder?"

"What murder?" asked Miss Climpson, vaguely.

She took the *Evening Views* from her landlady's hand, and read the story of Vera Findlater's death.

Sunday was the most awful day Miss Climpson had ever spent. An active woman, she was condemned to inactivity, and she had time to brood over the tragedy. Not having Wimsey's or Parker's inside knowledge, she took the kidnapping story at its face value. In a sense, she found it comforting, for she was able to acquit Mary Whittaker of any share in this or the previous murders. She put them down—except, of course, in the case of Miss Dawson, and that might never have been a murder after all—to the mysterious man in South Audley Street. She formed a nightmare image of him in her mind—blood-boltered, sinister, and—most horrible of all—an associate and employer of debauched and brutal assassins. To Miss Climpson's credit be it said that she never for one moment faltered in her determination to track the monster to his lurking-place.

She wrote a long letter to Lord Peter, detailing her plans. Bunter, she knew, had left 110A Piccadilly, so, after considerable thought, she addressed it to Lord Peter Wimsey, c/o Inspector Parker, The Police-Station, Crow's Beach. There was, of course, no Sunday post from Town. However, it would go with the midnight collection.

On the Monday morning she set out early, in her old clothes and her spectacles, for South Audley Street. Never had her natural inquisitiveness and her hard training in third-rate boarding-houses stood her in better stead. She had learned to ask questions without heeding rebuffs—to be persistent, insensitive and observant. In every flat she visited she acted her natural self, with so much sincerity and such limpet-like obstinacy that she seldom came away without a subscription and almost never without some information about the flat and its inmates.

By tea-time, she had done one side of the street and nearly half the other, without result. She was just thinking of going to get some food, when she caught sight of a woman, about a hundred yards ahead, walking briskly in the same direction as herself.

Now it is easy to be mistaken in faces, but almost impossible not to recognise a back. Miss Climpson's heart gave a bound. "Mary Whittaker!" she said to herself, and started to follow.

The woman stopped to look into a shop window. Miss Climpson hesitated to come closer. If Mary Whittaker was at large, then—why then the kidnapping had been done with her own consent. Puzzled, Miss Climpson determined to play a waiting game. The woman went into the shop. The friendly chemist's was almost opposite. Miss Climpson decided that this was the moment to reclaim her latchkey. She went in and asked for it. It had been put aside for her and the assistant produced it at once. The woman was still in the shop over the way. Miss Climpson embarked upon a long string of apologies and circumstantial details about her carelessness. The woman came out. Miss Climpson gave her a longish start, brought the conversation to a close, and fussed out again, replacing the glasses which she had removed for the chemist's benefit.

The woman walked on without stopping, but she looked into the shop windows from time to time. A man with a fruiterer's barrow removed his cap as she passed and scratched his head. Almost at once, the woman turned quickly and came back. The fruiterer picked up the handles of his barrow and trundled it away into a side street. The woman came straight on, and Miss Climpson was obliged to dive into a doorway and pretend to be tying a bootlace, to avoid a face to face encounter.

Apparently the woman had only forgotten to buy cigarettes. She went into a tobacconist's and emerged again in a minute or two, passing Miss Climpson again. That lady had dropped her bag and was agitatedly sorting its contents. The woman passed her without a glance and went on. Miss Climpson, flushed from stooping, followed again. The woman turned in at the entrance to a block of flats next door to a florist's. Miss Climpson was hard on her heels now, for she was afraid of losing her.

Mary Whittaker—if it was Mary Whittaker—went straight through the hall to the lift, which was one of the kind worked by the passenger. She stepped in and shot up. Miss Climpson—gazing at the orchids and roses in the florist's window—watched the lift out of sight. Then, with her subscription card prominently in her hand, she too entered the flats.

There was a porter on duty in a little glass case. He at once spotted Miss Climpson as a stranger and asked politely if he could do anything for her. Miss Climpson, selecting a name at random from the list of occupants in the entrance, asked which was Mrs. Forrest's flat. The man replied that it was on the fourth floor, and stepped forward to bring the lift down for her. A man, to whom he had been chatting, moved quietly from the glass case and took up a position in the doorway. As the lift ascended, Miss Climpson noticed that the fruiterer had returned. His barrow now stood just outside.

The porter had come up with her, and pointed out the door of Mrs. Forrest's flat. His presence was reassuring. She wished he would stay within call till she had concluded her search of the building. However, having asked for Mrs. Forrest, she must begin there. She pressed the bell.

At first she thought the flat was empty, but after ringing a second time she heard footsteps. The door opened, and a heavily over-dressed and peroxided lady made her appearance, whom Lord Peter would at once—and embarrassingly—have recognised.

"I have come," said Miss Climpson, wedging herself briskly in at the doorway with the skill of the practised canvasser, "to try if I can enlist your help for our Mission Settlement. May I come in? I am sure you—"

"No thanks," said Mrs. Forrest, shortly, and in a hurried, breathless tone, as if there was somebody behind her who she was anxious should not overhear her, "I'm not interested in Missions."

She tried to shut the door. But Miss Climpson had seen and heard enough.

"Good gracious!" she cried, staring, "why, it's—"

"Come in." Mrs. Forrest caught her by the arm almost roughly and pulled her over the threshold, slamming the door behind them.

"How extraordinary!" said Miss Climpson, "I hardly recognised you, Miss Whittaker, with your hair like that."

"You!" said Mary Whittaker. "You—of all people!" They sat facing one another in the sitting-room with its tawdry pink silk cushions. "I knew you were a meddler. How did you get here? Is there anyone with you?"

"No—yes—I just happened," began Miss Climpson vaguely. One thought was uppermost in her mind. "How did you get free? What happened? Who killed Vera?" She knew she was asking her questions crudely and stupidly. "Why are you disguised like that?"

"Who sent you?" reiterated Mary Whittaker.

"Who is the man with you?" pursued Miss Climpson. "Is he here? Did he do the murder?"

"What man?"

"The man Vera saw leaving your flat. Did he—?"

"So that's it. Vera told you. The liar. I thought I had been quick enough."

Suddenly, something which had been troubling Miss Climpson for weeks crystallised and became plain to her. The expression in Mary Whittaker's eyes. A long time ago, Miss Climpson had assisted a relative to run a boarding-house, and there had been a young man who paid his bill by cheque. She had had to make a certain amount of unpleasantness about the bill, and he had written the cheque unwillingly, sitting, with her eye upon him, at the little plush-covered table in the drawing-room. Then he had gone away—slinking out with his bag when no one was about. And the cheque had come back, like the bad penny that it was. A forgery. Miss Climpson had had to give evidence. She remembered now the odd, defiant look with which the young man had taken up his pen for his first plunge into crime. And to-day she was seeing it again—an unattractive mingling of recklessness and calculation. It was with the look which had once warned Wimsey and should have warned her. She breathed more quickly.

"Who was the man?"

"The man?" Mary Whittaker laughed suddenly. "A man called Templeton— no friend of mine. It's really funny that you should think he was a friend of mine. I would have killed him if I could."

"But where is he? What are you doing? Don't you know that everybody is looking for you? Why don't you—?"

"That's why!"

Mary Whittaker flung her ten o'clock edition of the *Evening Banner*, which was lying on the sofa. Miss Climpson read the glaring headlines.

AMAZING NEW DEVELOPMENTS
IN CROW'S BEACH CRIME.

———

WOUNDS ON BODY INFLICTED AFTER DEATH.

———

FAKED FOOTPRINTS.

———

Miss Climpson gasped with amazement, and bent over the smaller type. "How extraordinary!" she said, looking up quickly.

Not quite quickly enough. The heavy brass lamp missed her head indeed, but fell numbingly on her shoulder. She sprang to her feet with a loud shriek, just as Mary Whittaker's strong white hands closed upon her throat.

23

—AND SMOTE HIM, THUS

" 'Tis not so deep as a well, nor so wide as a church-door; but 'tis enough, 'twill serve."

Romeo and Juliet

Lord Peter missed both Miss Climpson's communications. Absorbed in the police inquiry, he never thought to go back to Leahampton. Bunter had duly arrived with "Mrs. Merdle" on the Saturday evening. Immense police activity was displayed in the neighbourhood of the downs, and at Southampton and Portsmouth, in order to foster the idea that the authorities supposed the "gang" to be lurking in those districts. Nothing, as a matter of fact, was farther from Parker's thoughts. "Let her think she is safe," he said, "and she'll come back. It's the cat-

and-mouse act for us, old man." Wimsey fretted. He wanted the analysis of the body to be complete and loathed the thought of the long days he had to wait. And he had small hope of the result.

"It's all very well sitting round with your large disguised policemen outside Mrs. Forrest's flat," he said irritably, over the bacon and eggs on Monday morning, "but you do realise, don't you, that we've still got no proof of murder. Not in one single case."

"That's so," replied Parker, placidly.

"Well, doesn't it make your blood boil?" said Wimsey.

"Hardly," said Parker. "This kind of thing happens too often. If my blood boiled every time there was a delay in getting evidence, I should be in a perpetual fever. Why worry? It may be that perfect crime you're so fond of talking about—the one that leaves no trace. You ought to be charmed with it."

"Oh, I daresay. O Turpitude, where are the charms that sages have seen in thy face? Time's called at the Criminals' Arms, and there isn't a drink in the place. Wimsey's Standard Poets, with emendations by Thingummy. As a matter of fact, I'm not at all sure that Miss Dawson's death wasn't the perfect crime—if only the Whittaker girl had stopped at that and not tried to cover it up. If you notice, the deaths are becoming more and more violent, elaborate and unlikely in appearance. Telephone again. If the Post Office accounts don't show a handsome profit on telephones this year it won't be your fault."

"It's the cap and shoes," said Parker, mildly. "They've traced them. They were ordered from an outfitter's in Stepney, to be sent to the Rev. H. Dawson, Peveril Hotel, Bloomsbury, to await arrival."

"The Peveril again!"

"Yes. I recognise the hand of Mr. Trigg's mysterious charmer. The Rev. Hallelujah Dawson's card, with message 'Please give parcel to bearer,' was presented by a District Messenger next day, with a verbal explanation that the gentleman found he could not get up to Town after all. The messenger, obeying instructions received by telephone, took the parcel to a lady in a nurse's dress on the platform at Charing Cross. Asked to describe the lady, he said she was tall and wore blue glasses and the usual cloak and bonnet. So that's that."

"How were the goods paid for?"

"Postal order, purchased at the West Central office at the busiest moment of the day."

"And when did all this happen?"

"That's the most interesting part of the business. Last month, shortly before Miss Whittaker and Miss Findlater returned from Kent. This plot was well thought out beforehand."

"Yes. Well, that's something more for you to pin on to Mrs. Forrest. It looks like proof of conspiracy, but whether it's proof of murder—"

"It's meant to look like a conspiracy of Cousin Hallelujah's, I suppose. Oh, well, we shall have to trace the letters and the typewriter that wrote them and interrogate all these people, I suppose. God! what a grind! Hullo! Come in! Oh, it's you, doctor?"

"Excuse my interrupting your breakfast," said Dr. Faulkner, "but early this morning, while lying awake, I was visited with a bright idea. So I had to come and work it off on you while it was fresh. About the blow on the head and the marks on the arms, you know. Do you suppose they served a double purpose? Besides making it look like the work of a gang, could they be hiding some other, smaller mark? Poison, for instance, could be injected, and the mark covered up by scratches and cuts inflicted after death."

"Frankly," said Parker, "I wish I could think it. It's a very sound idea and may be the right one. Our trouble is, that in the two previous deaths which we have been investigating, and which we are inclined to think form a part of the same series as this one, there have been no signs or traces of poison discoverable in the bodies at all by any examination or analysis that skill can devise. In fact, not only no proof of poison, but no proof of anything but natural death."

And he related the cases in fuller detail.

"Odd," said the doctor. "And you think this may turn out the same way. Still, in this case the death can't very well have been natural—or why these elaborate efforts to cover it up?"

"It wasn't," said Parker; "the proof being that—as we now know—the plot was laid nearly two months ago."

"But the method!" cried Wimsey, "the method! Hang it all—here are all we people with our brilliant brains and our professional reputations—and this half-trained girl out of a hospital can beat the lot of us. How was it done?"

"It's probably something so simple and obvious that it's never occurred to us," said Parker. "The sort of principle you learn when you're in the fourth form and never apply to anything. Rudimentary. Like that motor-cycling imbecile we met up at Crofton, who sat in the rain and prayed for help because he'd never heard of an air-lock in his feed. Now I daresay that boy had learnt—What's the matter with you?"

"My God!" cried Wimsey. He smashed his hand down among the breakfast things, upsetting his cup. "My God! But that's it! You've got it—you've done it —Obvious? God Almighty—it doesn't need a doctor. A garage hand could have told you. People die of it every day. Of course, it was an air-lock in the feed."

"Bear up, doctor," said Parker, "he's always like this when he gets an idea. It wears off in time. D'you mind explaining yourself, old thing?"

Wimsey's pallid face was flushed. He turned on the doctor.

"Look here," he said, "the body's a pumping engine, isn't it? The jolly old heart pumps the blood round the arteries and back through the veins and so on, doesn't it? That's what keeps things working, what? Round and home again in two minutes—that sort of thing?"

"Certainly."

"Little valve to let the blood out; 'nother little valve to let it in—just like an internal combustion engine, which it is?"

"Of course."

"And s'posin' that stops?"

"You die."

"Yes. Now, look here. S'posin' you take a good big hypodermic, empty, and dig it into one of the big arteries and push the handle—what would happen? What would happen, doctor? You'd be pumpin' a big air-bubble into your engine feed, wouldn't you? What would become of your circulation, then?"

"It would stop it," said the doctor, without hesitation. "That is why nurses have to be particular to fill the syringe properly, especially when doing an intra-venous injection."

"I *knew* it was the kind of thing you learnt in the fourth form. Well, go on. Your circulation would stop—it would be like an embolism in its effect, wouldn't it?"

"Only if it was in a main artery, of course. In a small vein the blood would find a way round. That is why" (this seemed to be the doctor's favourite opening) "that is why it is so important that embolisms—blood-clots—should be dispersed as soon as possible and not left to wander about the system."

"Yes—yes—but the air-bubble, doctor—in a main artery—say the femoral or the big vein in the bend of the elbow—that would stop the circulation, wouldn't it? How soon?"

"Why, at once. The heart would stop beating."

"And then?"

"You would die."

"With what symptoms?"

"None to speak of. Just a gasp or two. The lungs would make a desperate effort to keep things going. Then you'd just stop. Like heart failure. It would *be* heart failure."

"How well I know it . . . That sneeze in the carburettor—a gasping, as you say. And what would be the post-mortem symptoms?"

"None. Just the appearances of heart failure. And, of course, the little mark of the needle, if you happened to be looking for it."

"You're sure of all this, doctor?" said Parker.

"Well, it's simple, isn't it? A plain problem in mechanics. Of course that would happen. It must happen."

"Could it be proved?" insisted Parker.

"That's more difficult."

"We must try," said Parker. "It's ingenious, and it explains a lot of things. Doctor, will you go down to the mortuary again and see if you can find any puncture mark on the body. I really think you've got the explanation of the whole thing, Peter. Oh, dear! Who's on the 'phone now? . . . What?—*what?*—oh, hell!—Well, that's torn it. She'll never come back now. Warn all the ports—send out an all-stations call—watch the railways and go through Bloomsbury with a toothcomb—that's the part she knows best. I'm coming straight up to Town now—yes, immediately. Right you are." He hung up the receiver with a few brief, choice expressions.

"That adjectival imbecile, Pillington, has let out all he knows. The whole story is in the early editions of the *Banner*. We're doing no good here. Mary Whittaker will know the game's up, and she'll be out of the country in two twos, if she isn't already. Coming back to Town, Wimsey?"

"Naturally. Take you up in the car. Lose no time. Ring the bell for Bunter, would you? Oh, Bunter, we're going up to Town. How soon can we start?"

"At once, my lord. I have been holding your lordship's and Mr. Parker's things ready packed from hour to hour, in case a hurried adjournment should be necessary."

"Good man."

"And there is a letter for you, Mr. Parker, sir."

"Oh, thanks. Ah, yes. The finger-prints off the cheque. H'm. Two sets only—besides those of the cashier, of course—Cousin Hallelujah's and a female set, presumably those of Mary Whittaker. Yes, obviously—here are the four fingers of the left hand, just as one would place them to hold the cheque flat while signing."

"Pardon me, sir—but might I look at that photograph?"

"Certainly. Take a copy for yourself. I know it interests you as a photographer. Well, cheerio, doctor. See you in Town some time. Come on, Peter."

Lord Peter came on. And that, as Dr. Faulkner would say, was why Miss Climpson's second letter was brought up from the police-station too late to catch him.

They reached Town at twelve—owing to Wimsey's brisk work at the wheel—and went straight to Scotland Yard, dropping Bunter, at his own request, as he was anxious to return to the flat. They found the Chief Commissioner in rather a brusque mood—angry with the *Banner* and annoyed with Parker for having failed to muzzle Pillington.

"God knows where she will be found next. She's probably got a disguise and a get-away all ready."

"Probably gone already," said Wimsey. "She could easily have left England on the Monday or Tuesday and nobody a penny the wiser. If the coast had seemed clear, she'd have come back and taken possession of her goods again. Now she'll stay abroad. That's all."

"I'm very much afraid you're right," agreed Parker, gloomily.

"Meanwhile, what is Mrs. Forrest doing?"

"Behaving quite normally. She's been carefully shadowed, of course, but not interfered with in any way. We've got three men out there now—one as a coster —one as a dear friend of the hall-porter's who drops in every so often with racing tips, and an odd-job man doing a spot of work in the back-yard. They report that she has been in and out, shopping and so on, but mostly having her meals at home. No one has called. The men deputed to shadow her away from the flat have watched carefully to see if she speaks to anyone or slips money to anyone. We're pretty sure the two haven't met yet."

"Excuse me, sir." An officer put his head in at the door. "Here's Lord Peter Wimsey's man, sir, with an urgent message."

Bunter entered, trimly correct in bearing, but with a glitter in his eye. He laid down two photographs on the table.

"Excuse me, my lord and gentlemen, but would you be so good as to cast your eyes on these two photographs?"

"Finger-prints?" said the chief, interrogatively.

"One of them is our own official photograph of the prints on the £10,000 cheque," said Parker. "The other—where did you get this, Bunter? It looks like the same set of prints, but it's not one of ours."

"They appeared similar, sir, to my uninstructed eye. I thought it better to place the matter before you."

"Send Dewsby here," said the Chief Commissioner.

Dewsby was the head of the finger-print department, and he had no hesitation at all.

"They are undoubtedly the same prints," he said.

A light was slowly breaking in on Wimsey.

"Bunter—did these come off that wine-glass?"

"Yes, my lord."

"But they are Mrs. Forrest's!"

"So I understood you to say, my lord, and I have filed them under that name."

"Then, if the signature on the cheque is genuine—"

"We haven't far to look for our bird," said Parker, brutally. "A double identity;

damn the woman, she's made us waste a lot of time. Well, I think we shall get her now, on the Findlater murder at least, and possibly on the Gotobed business."

"But I understood there was an alibi for that," said the Chief.

"There was," said Parker, grimly, "but the witness was the girl that's just been murdered. Looks as though she had made up her mind to split and was got rid of."

"Looks as though several people had had a near squeak of it," said Wimsey. "Including you. That yellow hair was a wig, then."

"Probably. It never looked natural, you know. When I was there that night she had on one of those close turban affairs—she might have been bald for all one could see."

"Did you notice the scar on the fingers of the right hand?"

"I did not—for the very good reason that her fingers were stiff with rings to the knuckles. There was pretty good sense behind her ugly bad taste. I suppose I was to be drugged—or, failing that, caressed into slumber and then—shall we say, put out of circulation! Highly distressin' incident. Amorous clubman dies in a flat. Relations very anxious to hush matter up. I was selected, I suppose, because I was seen with Evelyn Cropper at Liverpool. Bertha Gotobed got the same sort of dose, too, I take it. Met by old employer, accidentally, on leaving work—£5 note and nice little dinner—lashings of champagne—poor kid as drunk as a blind fiddler—bundled into the car—finished off there and trundled out to Epping in company with a ham sandwich and a bottle of Bass. Easy, ain't it—when you know how?"

"That being so," said the Chief Commissioner, "the sooner we get hold of her the better. You'd better go at once, Inspector; take a warrant for Whittaker or Forrest—and any help you may require."

"May I come?" asked Wimsey, when they were outside the building.

"Why not? You may be useful. With the men we've got there already we shan't need any extra help."

The car whizzed swiftly through Pall Mall, up St. James's Street and along Piccadilly. Half-way up South Audley Street they passed the fruit-seller, with whom Parker exchanged an almost imperceptible signal. A few doors below the entrance to the flats they got out and were almost immediately joined by the hall-porter's sporting friend.

"I was just going out to call you up," said the latter. "She's arrived."

"What, the Whittaker woman?"

"Yes. Went up about two minutes ago."

"Is Forrest there too?"

"Yes. She came in just before the other woman."

"Queer," said Parker. "Another good theory gone west. Are you sure it's Whittaker?"

"Well, she's made up with old-fashioned clothes and greyish hair and so on. But she's the right height and general appearance. And she's running the old blue spectacle stunt again. I think it's the right one—though of course I didn't get close to her, remembering your instructions."

"Well, we'll have a look, anyhow. Come along."

The coster had joined them now, and they all entered together.

"Did the old girl go up to Forrest's flat all right?" asked the third detective of the porter.

"That's right. Went straight to the door and started something about a subscription. Then Mrs. Forrest pulled her in quick and slammed the door. Nobody's come down since."

"Right. We'll take ourselves up—and mind you don't let anybody give us the slip by the staircase. Now then, Wimsey, she knows you as Templeton, but she may still not know for certain that you're working with us. Ring the bell, and when the door's opened, stick your foot inside. We'll stand just round the corner here and be ready to rush."

This manoeuvre was executed. They heard the bell trill loudly.

Nobody came to answer it, however. Wimsey rang again, and then bent his ear to the door.

"Charles," he cried suddenly, "there's something going on here." His face was white. "Be quick! I couldn't stand *another*—!"

Parker hastened up and listened. Then he caught Peter's stick and hammered on the door, so that the hollow liftshaft echoed with the clamour.

"Come on there—open the door—this is the police."

And all the time, a horrid, stealthy thumping and gurgling sounded inside—dragging of something heavy and a scuffling noise. Then a loud crash, as though a piece of furniture had been flung to the floor—and then a loud hoarse scream, cut brutally off in the middle.

"Break in the door," said Wimsey, the sweat pouring down his face.

Parker signalled to the heavier of the two policemen. He came along, shoulder first, lunging. The door shook and cracked. They stamped and panted in the narrow space.

The door gave way, and they tumbled into the hall. Everything was ominously quiet.

"Oh, quick!" sobbed Peter.

A door on the right stood open. A glance assured them that there was nothing there. They sprang to the sitting-room door and pushed it. It opened about a foot. Something bulky impeded its progress. They shoved violently and the obstacle gave. Wimsey leapt over it—it was a tall cabinet, fallen, with broken china strewing the floor. The room bore signs of a violent struggle—tables flung down, a broken chair, a smashed lamp. He dashed for the bedroom, with Parker hard at his heels.

The body of a woman lay limply on the bed. Her long, grizzled hair hung in a dark rope over the pillow and blood was on her head and throat. But the blood was running freely, and Wimsey could have shouted for joy at the sight. Dead men do not bleed.

Parker gave only one glance at the injured woman. He made promptly for the dressing-room beyond. A shot sang past his head—there was a snarl and a shriek —and the episode was over. The constable stood shaking his bitten hand, while Parker put the come-along-o'-me grip on the quarry. He recognised her readily, though the peroxide wig had fallen awry and the blue eyes were bleared with terror and fury.

"That'll do," said Parker, quietly, "the game's up. It's not a bit of use. Come, be reasonable. You don't want us to put the bracelets on, do you? Mary Whittaker, alias Forrest, I arrest you on the charge—" he hesitated for a moment and she saw it.

"On what charge? What have you got against me?"

"Of attempting to murder this lady, for a start," said Parker.

"The old fool!" she said, contemptuously, "she forced her way in here and attacked me. Is that all?"

"Very probably not," said Parker. "I warn you that anything you say may be taken down and used in evidence at your trial."

Indeed, the third officer had already produced a notebook and was imperturbably writing down: "When told the charge, the prisoner said 'Is that all?' " The remark evidently struck him as an injudicious one, for he licked his pencil with an air of satisfaction.

"Is the lady all right—who is it?" asked Parker, coming back to a survey of the situation.

"It's Miss Climpson—God knows how she got here. I think she's all right, but she's had a rough time."

He was anxiously sponging her head as he spoke, and at that moment her eyes opened.

"Help!" said Miss Climpson, confusedly. "The syringe—you shan't—oh!" She struggled feebly, and then recognised Wimsey's anxious face. "Oh, dear!" she exclaimed, "Lord Peter. Such an upset. Did you get my letter? Is it all right? . . . Oh, dear! What a state I'm in. I—that woman—"

"Now, don't worry, Miss Climpson," said Wimsey, much relieved, "everything's quite all right and you mustn't talk. You must tell us about it later."

"What was that about a syringe?" said Parker, intent on his case.

"She'd got a syringe in her hand," panted Miss Climpson, trying to sit up, and fumbling with her hands over the bed. "I fainted, I think—such a struggle—and something hit me on the head. And I saw her coming at me with the thing. And I knocked it out of her hand and I can't remember what happened afterwards. But I have *remarkable* vitality," said Miss Climpson, cheerfully. "My dear father always used to say 'Climpsons take a lot of killing'!"

Parker was groping on the floor.

"Here you are," said he. In his hand was a hypodermic syringe.

"She's mental, that's what she is," said the prisoner. "That's only the hypodermic I use for my injections when I get neuralgia. There's nothing in that."

"That is quite correct," said Parker, with a significant nod at Wimsey. "There is—nothing in it."

On the Tuesday night, when the prisoner had been committed for trial on the charges of murdering Bertha Gotobed and Vera Findlater, and attempting to murder Alexandra Climpson, Wimsey dined with Parker. The former was depressed and nervous.

"The whole thing's been beastly," he grumbled. They had sat up discussing the case into the small hours.

"Interesting," said Parker, "interesting. I owe you seven and six, by the way. We ought to have seen through that Forrest business earlier, but there seemed no real reason to suspect the Findlater girl's word as to the alibi. These mistaken loyalties make a lot of trouble.

"I think the thing that put us off was that it all started so early. There seemed no reason for it, but looking back on Trigg's story it's as plain as a pike-staff. She took a big risk with that empty house, and she couldn't always expect to find empty houses handy to do away with people in. The idea was, I suppose, to build up a double identity, so that, if Mary Whittaker was ever suspected of anything, she could quietly disappear and become the frail but otherwise innocent Mrs.

Forrest. The real slip-up was forgetting to take back that £5 note from Bertha Gotobed. If it hadn't been for that, we might never have known anything about Mrs. Forrest. It must have rattled her horribly when we turned up there. After that, she was known to the police in both her characters. The Findlater business was a desperate attempt to cover up her tracks—and it was bound to fail, because it was so complicated."

"Yes. But the Dawson murder was beautiful in its ease and simplicity."

"If she had stuck to that and left well alone, we could never have proved anything. We can't prove it now, which is why I left it off the charge-sheet. I don't think I've ever met a more greedy and heartless murderer. She probably really thought that anyone who inconvenienced her had no right to exist."

"Greedy and malicious. Fancy tryin' to shove the blame on poor old Hallelujah. I suppose he'd committed the unforgivable sin of askin' her for money."

"Well, he'll get it, that's one good thing. The pit digged for Cousin Hallelujah has turned into a gold-mine. That £10,000 cheque has been honoured. I saw to that first thing, before Whittaker could remember to try and stop it. Probably she couldn't have stopped it anyway, as it was duly presented last Saturday."

"Is the money legally hers?"

"Of course it is. We know it was gained by a crime, but we haven't charged her with the crime, so that legally no such crime was committed. I've not said anything to Cousin Hallelujah, of course, or he mightn't like to take it. He thinks it was sent him in a burst of contrition, poor old dear."

"So Cousin Hallelujah and all the little Hallelujahs will be rich. That's splendid. How about the rest of the money? Will the Crown get it after all?"

"No. Unless she wills it to someone, it will go to the Whittaker next-of-kin—a first cousin, I believe, called Allcock. A very decent fellow, living in Birmingham. That is," he added, assailed by sudden doubt, "if first cousins do inherit under this confounded Act."

"Oh, I think first cousins are safe," said Wimsey, "though nothing seems safe nowadays. Still, dash it all, some relations must still be allowed a look-in, or what becomes of the sanctity of family life? If so, that's the most cheering thing about the beastly business. Do you know, when I rang up that man Carr and told him all about it, he wasn't a bit interested or grateful. Said he'd always suspected something like that, and he hoped we weren't going to rake it all up again, because he'd come into that money he told us about and was setting up for himself in Harley Street, so he didn't want any more scandals."

"I never did like that man. I'm sorry for Nurse Philliter."

"You needn't be. I put my foot in it again over that. Carr's too grand to marry a nurse now—at least, I fancy that's what it is. Anyway, the engagement's off. And I was so pleased at the idea of playing Providence to two deserving young people," added Wimsey, pathetically.

"Dear, dear! Well, the girl's well out of it. Hullo! there's the 'phone. Who on earth—? Some damned thing at the Yard, I suppose. At three ack emma! Who'd be a policeman?—Yes?—Oh!—right, I'll come round. The case has gone west, Peter."

"How?"

"Suicide. Strangled herself with a sheet. I'd better go round, I suppose."

"I'll come with you."

"An evil woman, if ever there was one," said Parker, softly, as they looked at the rigid body, with its swollen face and the deeper, red ring about the throat.

Wimsey said nothing. He felt cold and sick. While Parker and the Governor of the prison made the necessary arrangements and discussed the case, he sat hunched unhappily upon his chair. Their voices went on and on interminably. Six o'clock had struck some time before they rose to go. It reminded him of the eight strokes of the clock which announce the running-up of the black and hideous flag.

As the gate clanged open to let them out, they stepped into a wan and awful darkness. The June day had risen long ago, but only a pale and yellowish gleam lit the half-deserted streets. And it was bitterly cold and raining.

"What is the matter with the day?" said Wimsey. "Is the world coming to an end?"

"No," said Parker, "it is the eclipse."